BOOK 1
The Lost Legacy Series

THE OBSIDIAN STAFF

Jaz Azari

The Obsidian Staff
Book One, The Lost Legacy Series
Copyright ©2023 Jaz Azari

ISBN 978-1506-910-89-5 PBK
ISBN 978-1506-910-90-1 EBK

January 2023

Published and Distributed by
First Edition Design Publishing, Inc.
P.O. Box 17646, Sarasota, FL 34276-3217
www.firsteditiondesignpublishing.com

ALL RIGHTS RESERVED. No part of this book publication may be reproduced, stored in a retrieval system, or transmitted in any form or by any means — electronic, mechanical, photocopy, recording, or any other — except brief quotation in reviews, without the prior permission of the author or publisher.

Cover art designed by Deborah E Gordon
Illustration of the obsidian staff and map of Ilian created by Nathan Hansen.

To Tp and Carla,
*For reminding me to trust the questions of the
present to the clarity of the future*

ILIAN
NORTHERN TERRITORY
HARKIMER
SEVEN RINGS PASS
COTLASS
PEREGRINE
BIBI SEA
AURIELLE SEA
LYSTERN
HILLITH
CALONIA
SANGLIER
SERPENTS LAKE
DUNESTOR
HORNBEAM PASS
SILVER LAKE
EDOIN FOREST
WIZARDS HIGH COUNCIL
ANCIENT FOREST
HOGARTH
THANESGARD
FARCAREN
GRASSLAND
SILVIAS

Prologue

Will this be the sixth time they've tried to kill me or the seventh?

Kyra's heart pounded to the fierce cadence of the horse's hooves. She gripped the reins with white-knuckled hands as she struggled to stay balanced. It wasn't an easy task. Her roan galloped with urgent abandon through the open expanse of sunbaked earth. The land had once been a beautiful verdant valley, but the dark wizards had scorched the earth. No plant or blade of grass had existed since.

Kyra glanced up. Yellow and pink trailed like tailfeathers from the cheerful, bluebird-colored sky. It was paradoxically out of place with the black dread in her heart and the drab brown beneath her. Her jade-flecked eyes dropped to the horizon. Eventually, the barren ground ended in an unnaturally pinpoint-straight line, magically sheared off from the dense hills of scrub bush pines and firs. The forests formed the base for Kyra's destination—the towering slate gray mountains capped with white, their peaks piercing the high clouds above and disappearing beyond.

The Southern Mountains. Harkimer, the dark wizards' cursed kingdom, it was the home of her enemies.

Kyra leaned lower in the saddle. *Six times or seven?* she repeated. It was getting hard to keep track of the dark wizards' attacks. Only four months ago, the dark wizards had tried to ambush her and Talis in Edoin Forest. With the night sky obscured by charcoal-gray clouds, the wizards undoubtably believed they had the upper hand, slinking between the trees like liquid shadows. If Kyra had been alone, they might have succeeded. Her gaze couldn't discern them in the darkness. But she hadn't been alone. The dark wizards had underestimated Talis' eagle-eyed vision. The elf's quick draw of his bowstring had forced the figures' retreat.

A gust of crisp autumn wind sent dust swirling into the air, setting Kyra into a fit of coughing. She tried to cover her mouth with her sleeve. The leather from the reins dug into her skin. Gritting her teeth against the pain, Kyra gripped the reins more tightly. She shook her head, trying to brush aside the waves of honey-brown hair that whipped across her face. Her azure cloak, the same color as the cloudless blue sky above, flapped behind her as she hugged the roan's neck.

For Inishmore's sake, don't the dark wizards have any hobbies in Harkimer? Other than chasing a teenage wizard around Ilian? Kyra tried to laugh at her joke. Normally, humor helped Kyra quell her anxiety. Not today. It didn't seem like anything could unseat the terror that rode alongside her in the saddle.

Kyra's mind cycled through possible scenarios of what dangers lay ahead. What if the dark wizards finally managed to ensnare her? Truss her up, smuggle her into Harkimer? Or, this time, put an end to the cat-and-mouse game once and for all? *A dead Kyra would cause less trouble for them,* she thought dryly. Imprisonment in Harkimer wasn't any more pleasant than death.

Not helpful, Kyra, she scolded herself even as her chest felt as though it was on the point of bursting. *Positive thoughts. You're alive, even if the dark wizards have come after you . . .*

"Seven times," Kyra voiced the rest of the sentence aloud.

The roan turned his head slightly, his powerful legs continuing to pound the ground. "Seven times for what?"

"Seven times that the dark wizards . . . have come after me." The wind stole Kyra's words as soon as she spoke them.

"You are keeping count?"

"I wasn't. Just thought about it now."

Even riding at a breathless clip, Kyra heard the horse snort. "I think you are underestimating that number."

"Fine. At least seven." *And I'm giving them another opportunity,* she added without daring to speak the words aloud. Kyra's magic gravitated toward other sources of magic in the past. This time was different. She was shackled to the energy, commanded to follow it somewhere near the Southern Mountains. Even if Kyra had wanted to turn away, she couldn't.

Icy waves of dread roiled through Kyra as she stared at the awe-inspiring, and deeply foreboding, towers of stone. She had seen the Southern Mountains many times before. Every time safely within the borders of the Elven Realm. Now there was no protective barrier between her and the gate to Harkimer. As if in response to her thoughts, the magical chains yanked on her forcefully.

"Raven, hurry!" Kyra shouted over the wind. "The energy is growing stronger, and it's not coming from anything good. I can't tell how many of them are out there either."

"Them? I thought you said there was only one dark wizard?"

"I did . . ." Kyra again centered her concentration inward. She was positive the magic emanating around the Mountains didn't come from a single strand. Unfortunately, the multiple cords binding her own energy were themselves, chaotic and knotted. In her mind's eye, she saw them as a bundle of lights possessed by various magical beings. The lights flared as they tried to smother the others in their invisible combat.

Kyra was certain one thread came from a dark wizard. Solarus told Kyra once that all magical beings possessed an aura, and beings from the same race had the same distinguishing characteristics. It was like smelling a bouquet of flowers with a blindfold; Kyra could separate the roses by scent alone. It was the same with the dark wizards. Kyra had been exposed to enough of their magic that she could extract it from the jumble within her. The trick was disentangling the other strands. Those sources of magic were foreign to her. Foreign, and terrifyingly powerful.

"There's one wizard," Kyra confirmed, dragging her focus outward and back to Raven. "Who the others are, I don't know. It's confusing. The magic is a complete mess, like hair snarled together. It's impossible for me to tease out which magic belongs to what. And it's almost like there's a war going on among them."

"A war?" Raven repeated. His strong hooves dug into the ground, spraying bits of cracked earth into the air like pellets. "Something fighting against the dark wizard? Or the dark wizard and an ally fighting against something else?"

"It could be either."

"Either." The roan huffed impatiently. "Why in the Healer's name are we sprinting like ten packs of greeloks are behind us so that we can throw ourselves into a battle with a dark wizard? A battle that could quite logically be between the wizard and one of Harkimer's ancient and loathsome monsters. No villages lie this close to the mountains. That means there may not *be* an innocent party requiring our support. In fact, I would welcome the chance for one vile being to rid Ilian of another."

"Even if that's true, we have to confirm it," Kyra responded with a trace of frustration. "A duel between a dark wizard and whatever else affects Ilian as badly as a duel with an innocent creature. A gryphon maybe, or an Iona, or, I don't know, a unicorn . . ."

"Unicorns don't exist."

"You get my point."

"And what do you intend to do if we find these creatures you are so bent on seeking out?"

"I haven't gotten that far yet."

"That does not inspire confidence, Kyra."

Kyra admitted quietly it wasn't exactly rational to drive Raven and herself into assured danger. Then again, the intangible sensations that brushed against her heart had never given her an explanation for why she should do a certain task. It had started in the past year. The first time she felt the wordless whisper, Kyra thought she had been daydreaming. It stirred her emotions, which her mind interpreted into words. At the time, it had been guidance encouraging her to be patient during a disastrous archery lesson. Later, it also offered warnings. In all instances, the whispers had been subtle. But not the one a few hours earlier. The impression had struck her during the Council meeting with the force of a meteor: *Ride to the Southern Mountains. Ilian is imperiled. All will perish.*

That was what drove Kyra forward, despite her fear.

The magical jumble within Kyra suddenly unsnarled itself. "Three," she exclaimed. "There are three more creatures with the dark wizard. We have to hurry!"

Kyra's arms and thighs burned from the effort of riding, and it was all she could do to stay seated. The roan raced beyond the edge of the desolate earth and into the foothills of the mountains. The sure-footed Raven surged through the forest with all the fleetness his elven heritage could offer. Kyra ducked under tree boughs and branches as the roan's hooves tore through the pine needles and detritus. The earth sloped steeply upward. Kyra leaned closer to the saddle, clutching the reins to her chest.

The air grew steadily colder the higher Raven climbed. Kyra's breath crystallized into thick puffs. She looked down as they passed patches of snow coating the trees' roots. It may be autumn back in the valley and in Silvias, but winter had already invited itself into the mountains.

Abruptly, the forest leveled off. Kyra wrinkled her nose as the stench of a searing heat mingled with the crispness of the air. She raised her gaze, looking for flames or some source of the fire. The sky was free of the telltale smoke.

Raven slowed to a trot as the woods thinned. Kyra looked around cautiously. The magic squeezed her so tightly that, for a moment, she felt like she was suffocating. A rumbling in the ground shook her to the core, and the magic eased slightly. Kyra exhaled shortly. "Where are you?" she muttered. "More importantly, *what* are you?"

A short, few minutes later, Kyra spied splashes of color. The trees obstructed the full view of the creatures. She squinted. She saw an arm with red, sandpaper-like skin, a blue barbed tail, and an ink-black hand with curved claws.

Kyra's curiosity crowded out her apprehension. She reined in Raven so that they proceeded at a walk. The foothills stripped back and finally gave Kyra the complete picture of the scene before her. Against the backdrop of the mountain face, not a hundred meters in front of her, were three colossal beasts. Slabs of rock littered the ground around them. There was no vegetation, just hard-packed earth.

Kyra's eyes widened in astonishment.

"They're dragons!" she exclaimed. "In front of the mountains. Three of them. That's the magic I felt. It belongs to them, not the wizard or any other creature."

Raven's lustrous brown eyes, too, had lit upon the beasts. He stopped so suddenly, Kyra lurched forward. "Dragons? Inishmore delivered us to dragons?" The roan jerked his head against the reins. "No, we are not going further, absolutely not. It is madness to think you can survive five minutes around one. They do not discriminate when it comes to killing whatever has the misfortune of crossing their path. If they are battling each other, all the better, and if they attack the dark wizard you sensed . . ." Raven's gaze roved to a figure cloaked in black. His ears went flat against his head. "By the Healer, it's *Diamantas*! The wizard is Diamantas. Of all the situations you have dragged us into, this is the worst a hundred times over."

Kyra's blood went cold. The wizard's back was to her as he angled a staff toward the ground. Not *a* staff. The obsidian staff. The fabled weapon that Hayden and Solarus had spoken about in grave, cautious tones. Even from a distance, Kyra saw it was blacker than night and glossy, the sun's bright light reflecting from it as though it were glass. The obsidian was as straight as a rod except where it parted at the top. There, the stone twisted over itself like gnarled tree roots. A tendril of gray smoke wove its way upward from the base. An unnatural white flame blazed from the staff's tip brightly, as if a miniature sun were trapped within the curling stone.

Diamantas was channeling the white flame into the earth. The energy burned through the surface like lava, and tremors rippled under Kyra's feet.

"The staff has no equal," Solarus' warning rang in Kyra's mind. *"If Diamantas is able to bind enough magic to it, he will cut a swath of blood through the kingdoms that cannot be stanched."*

The roan jerked his head to the side, dragging Kyra from her thoughts. "We will return to the Council. Solarus is there. He can decide what action to take."

"Raven, listen to me!" Kyra slackened the reins and wiggled backward in the saddle until she was sitting upright. "There's no time to go to the Council. We need to stop whatever is happening *now*."

"Kyra, Solarus himself would not be so reckless as to fight Diamantas alone. What chance does a fifteen-year-old wizard have against the most powerful wizard in generations?"

Kyra had already swung her leg over the side of the saddle. "I don't have a choice, Raven," she said, dropping to the ground. "I don't really want to find out. Except this doesn't have anything to do with what I want . . ."

A bellow drowned out the rest of her argument. The red dragon's claws were raised, and his thin-membraned wings spread wide like two large palm fronds. A slender, black female dragon crouched opposite him, teeth bared. Bright green energy swathed her and trickled out of her hands.

A third dragon, blue with a sharply ridged back, positioned himself away from his kin. A strange fog clouded his eyes. The dragon watched listlessly as Diamantas' white magic penetrated the earth. After a moment, the creature opened his large jaws and blasted blue flame over the ground. It crystallized and formed an icy sheen over the wizard's magic. A loud crack resounded. The earth split open, creating a chasm at the edge of Diamantas' feet.

Raven neighed in panic. He marched backward as trees groaned and rattled. Trunks sundered by magic crashed to the ground around them. Kyra stumbled into Raven, clutching the straps of a saddlebag to steady herself. Consternation filled Kyra as she watched the ground splinter away from Diamantas. It rapidly ran parallel to the forest. Her expression slowly changed to one of puzzlement. The destruction wasn't targeting her or Raven. Nor was it moving toward the dragons. What was Diamantas trying to accomplish?

"He and the blue dragon are using their energy to trench the earth," Kyra said out loud. She cast a probing gaze around her. The fissures continued to stretch across the ground like spokes on a wheel. "The dragon is freezing the surface, which makes it more brittle and easier for Diamantas to cut underneath it. That's where the tremors are coming from. But why is Diamantas doing this?"

"The magic heads west," Raven replied, with a flick of his tail. "It will eventually reach the Aurielle Sea."

"The Sea?" *Ilian is imperiled.* The warning pressed against her heart. *All will perish.* Kyra suddenly gasped as comprehension struck her. She released the saddlebag. "That's the answer. Diamantas is trying to split the shores. The Sea's water would flood any land south of it. Dunestor and Thanesgard would be submerged . . ."

"And Silvias' river would swell to the peaks of the hills," Raven added in a somber voice. "The elves would suffer the same fate as the kingdoms of men."

Kyra suddenly knew what the impression wanted from her. Why she had been compelled to come to this place. She felt a humming in her hands from her wrists to her fingertips. She glanced down. They were bathed in a glittering, golden glow. Kyra strode to Raven's side. "I have to stop this. We can't risk going back for Solarus. If Diamantas continues pouring magic into the ground, the rift could reach the Sea before we ride back." Her imploring yet firm gaze searched the roan's large brown eyes. "If there were any other way, I would take it. I have enough doubts about how much I can do, especially since Solarus had me leave my staff at the palace. It really would have come in handy. I need you to have confidence in me, Raven. I need someone to trust me. I'm asking you as your rider and as your friend to give me courage. Will you do that, Raven?"

The roan let out a long breath. "Yes, Kyra. You already had my support. You have my trust. And it appears you don't need any more courage." He nodded at the magic around her hands.

Kyra let out a nervous laugh. "We'll see if it's enough. Wait for me here. There's nothing you can do against the dragons, and I can't get back to the Council without you."

Raven lowered his head. "I would not leave you. Promise me you will not leave me? We are a pair."

It was all Kyra could do to swallow back her fear. "I'll come back as soon as this is over." Turning away from Raven before her resolve faltered, Kyra sprinted out of the cover of the forest.

Diamantas had stopped sending flame into the earth. His eyes were on the black dragon, who advanced menacingly toward him. The red dragon struggled against a magical green net. The black dragon raised a claw, around which the bright green energy blossomed.

Diamantas gripped his staff tightly against his body. "Recker!" he screamed as the green intensified. "Stop Schirmeera!"

The red dragon roared in response. He grabbed the green net with both hands, sending red flame overtop. The magic ensnaring him dissolved. Recker bounded forward and made a circular motion with his claw, creating a ring of fire. In the same instant, the black dragon flung her hand forward and fired clusters of diamond-like magic at Diamantas. Recker's fire enveloped the crystals before they reached the wizard. The green evaporated, sending a pungent plume of magical smoke into the air. Schirmeera growled. She squared off against Recker, nostrils flaring.

Diamantas' lips drew back into a pleased expression. "Gyre, assist Recker," he calmly instructed the blue dragon. "Schirmeera is distracting us from our work."

Gyre snaked his head to the side, the magic-induced trance clouding his eyes. He obediently bounded beside Recker. Schirmeera's gaze flitted toward the blue dragon. He observed her with a strange, detached expression.

Gyre, you know not what you do, Schirmeera implored. *You are spelled by Diamantas. Break free!*

Recker grinned wickedly. *Come now, Schirmeera,* he said, taking a step forward and grinding his claws into the ground. The movement drew the black dragon's gaze back to him. *Your weak-minded friend cannot hear you. You are better served minding your own survival. I was promised a battle against the champion of our race, yet all I see before me is a toothless kit.*

You are a fool, Recker, Schirmeera growled, thin tail snapping through the air. *Diamantas will control you, too. He threatens us all if he seizes the . . .*

He does not threaten me, Recker cut in. He spread his wings and reared on his hind legs. Flame erupted from his hands. *Diamantas is true to his allies.*

"Diamantas, get away from them!" Kyra yelled. She had almost closed the distance between herself and the dark wizard. Diamantas glanced over his shoulder. His face was craggy, with slicked-back, grayish blond hair that fell above his shoulders. Sharply angled cheekbones complemented his short, hawk-like nose and square chin. Diamantas' blue eyes, pale and cold as glaciers, lit with surprise. His expression quickly settled into one of calm curiosity.

Recker roared and charged Schirmeera at the same time Kyra raised her hands and hurled a ball of golden magic at Diamantas. The wizard casually planted his staff in the ground. A white shield materialized in front of him. The golden blast pummeled it without any effect. Diamantas scrutinized Kyra as she came to a stop in front of the shield. Her hands were still at her chest, steeled for a fight. Diamantas made a quick gesture, and the shield separating them disappeared.

"This is unexpected," he remarked in a pleasant voice. His gaze roved the area around them. "Where are Hayden and Solarus? I do not see your guardian and mentor. I doubt very much they would have condoned your speaking with me without their presence." A thin smile came to Diamantas' lips. "Yet, if you are alone, it is an auspicious occasion. I have long hoped to speak with you plainly, Kyra. Your companions have made that quite unachievable."

A sizzling electrified the air. Kyra jumped. She glanced up as the sky lit as though by firecrackers, red sparks showering down. Kyra dropped into a crouch, instinctively raising her arm to protect herself. White light again blazed from Diamantas' staff. An oval, flat and smooth as glass, appeared over Kyra's head. The sparks dissolved as they beat against Diamantas' shield. Kyra stared at the dark wizard, heart thumping frantically in her chest.

"I would prefer a conversation without interruption," Diamantas continued as Kyra slowly rose. "This earsplitting skirmish does not lend itself well to that goal. Fortunately, that is easily remedied."

White energy jetted out from the staff and the shield above Kyra. Before she could move, the white oozed down so that it formed a sphere around her. The booms, cracks, and crashes of the dragons were suddenly muffled. Kyra looked around in alarm. Diamantas tightened his grip on the staff. The sphere extended outward, sliding up and around Diamantas, until he was also fully enclosed within it.

Kyra punched the white walls with her golden energy. As before, her magic fizzled out harmlessly. Kyra whirled around, pulse racing. Diamantas watched her with an indulgent smile.

"Let me out," she demanded.

"The shield is not designed to keep you in. It keeps the danger posed by our skirmishing dragons out. Our discussion will not take long." Diamantas rubbed his chin. "I have followed your progress these past years with great interest, Kyra. The reports I have received indicate you are intelligent, resourceful, and brave. All qualities I greatly admire and rarely find in individuals. Yet you are also impetuous and impressionable. This is neither an affront nor a failing," he added, as Kyra's eyes narrowed. "Maturity is gained through experience, of which you have very little due to your circumstances."

Keep talking, Kyra thought as she gauged the space between them. Kyra estimated she needed three quick steps before she could strike. *It would have been easier with my staff*, she thought ruefully. However, she *was* skilled in hand combat. One well-placed blow could knock out her opponent, obsidian staff or not. Kyra shifted her weight almost imperceptibly forward.

"I would not recommend that." Diamantas raised a brow and tilted his head. "While the elves have undoubtedly taught you to fight formidably, you cannot hope to contest a wizard without your staff. Unless you can strike faster than a spell."

Kyra tensed. Diamantas waited. She finally let out a short breath and straightened. Her eyes darted around the sphere, searching for weaknesses in the magic.

"It is a regrettable yet unalterable fact that you were not raised among your kin," she heard Diamantas say. "Our brethren would have welcomed you with open arms and hearts. You would have been part of a large family, one that fully accepted you as a wizard, not as an outcast as the elves are wont to do with those not of their kind."

The words snagged Kyra's attention. When she looked back at the wizard, she was bewildered to see the planes of his face lined with remorse. His gaze had moved from her to the dragons.

Gyre locked claws with Schirmeera and was forcing her against the mountain side. "I do not blame the elves," Diamantas continued, watching as ice streamed through Gyre's hands over Schirmeera's. "They did what they could. However, a falcon understands not what nourishes a dragon. What bonds unite them?

Both creatures have wings, and they can fly. They have nothing else in common. So, it was with you. The elves taught you many things, including to defend yourself, but they are not wizards. Now you face another problem." Diamantas' blue gaze shifted back to Kyra. "The dragon eventually outgrows the falcon. It becomes stronger, faster, and deadlier. The falcon must recognize the threat its adopted kit poses before that kit is too powerful. You, Kyra, are growing into that dragon. If I understand correctly, you will soon be sixteen and, as such, of age. Your magic will not be able to be restrained, not if you grow. Your life will be endangered by the individuals who profess to protect you."

"My life will be endangered by the elves?" Kyra balled her hands into fists, heart thrumming against her chest. "I've lived with them my whole life. Talis and *Raenalyn* Carina have protected me, not tried to hurt me. The only ones I've had to defend against are other wizards. *Your* wizards from Harkimer. If anyone should be worried about my being 'of age', it should be you and any other wizard who attacks me."

Diamantas shook his head. "I do not control the wizards' words any more than I direct their actions. Any wizard can claim he or she follows my command. That does not make it true. It is no different from you and Solarus. Did he sanction your decision to come here? I think not." Kyra's silence confirmed Diamantas' statement. The wizard ran his hand over the smooth obsidian. "You view the wizards of Harkimer as evil. I assure you, our intentions—at least those of most of us—are honorable. We desire the opportunity to live in Ilian." His pale blue eyes strayed to the looming gray rock around them. "Wizards are being punished for atrocities committed by their forefathers generations ago. Why? The wizards of Harkimer have done nothing wrong. Why should one pay for the crimes of another? I will not deny that some, like Adakis, desire revenge for their mistreatment. Those sentiments are spawned from frustration. Through Inishmore's grace, you were one of the privileged wizards born in Ilian." Diamantas gave Kyra a grim smile. "You cannot begrudge the wizards a chance to live freely as you do. You also cannot despise me for seeking a better life for our kin. Our children."

For a moment, Kyra's resolve faltered. She couldn't ignore Diamantas' sincerity or the truth of his words. What would life have been like had Kyra grown up in the Southern Mountains? How would she feel, banished from the rest of Ilian for no reason other than that her ancestors had fought for an evil cause? Could she blame Diamantas for trying to provide the wizards the same freedom she enjoyed?

Dread wormed in her stomach at a second thought. *What if Diamantas was telling the truth about Adakis and the other wizards? That the ambushes hadn't been ordered by him? Could the dark wizards have acted on their own?* The conviction Kyra had long held that Diamantas was sinister, a conviction buttressed by Hayden and Solarus, began to flake away like rusted metal.

Beware. Lies and truth are often coupled, both correct and yet neither.

The emotion brushed against her heart. Kyra rubbed her temple, her head aching. *What does that mean?* she responded silently to the feeling.

Seeing Kyra's hesitation, Diamantas pressed his advantage. "In many ways, Kyra, you are trapped. Being marked with a divine responsibility places a burden on you that no other must carry." His voice lowered a notch. "Do you not fear that, if the seers are correct, you may choose the wrong path? Does it not wake you at night, the thought that you will not be Ilian's savior but something else? That you will cause the annihilation of those you hold dear?"

An involuntary shudder ran through Kyra at the words. Annihilation? "I don't know what you're talking about."

Diamantas' brows furrowed. Then they arched with incredulity as comprehension slid across his face. "You *don't* know, do you?" He silently ran his hand along the obsidian. When Diamantas spoke again, his tone chilled Kyra to the bone. "Your lack of knowledge about what magic truly entails is not a happenstance. Solarus has forestalled your training with purpose. He has offered you glimpses into your abilities while cleverly keeping you ignorant of your full potential. You are like a caged bird, believing itself happy in captivity because it has never soared freely. Solarus himself erected the bars constraining you."

"He hasn't held me back," Kyra answered, but her voice wavered. "Solarus has been training me for years. He's the reason I've survived the attacks from the dark wizards, because of what I'm capable of. I couldn't have a more loyal mentor."

"More the pity you believe it. At your age, you should be well versed in basic spells and ones specific to your talents. Yet yours are lamentably infantile. You have not even learned how to bind magic to your staff." Diamantas took a step forward, causing Kyra to reactively step back. "I ask you. Join me. If not for the wizards of Harkimer's sake, then for your own. Your sixteenth birthday approaches. Your powers will fully manifest at that point, regardless of Solarus' attempts to restrict them. All pretenses of protecting you will disappear. You will be hunted." Diamantas' tone blackened. "The elves will not risk Silvias for one girl, and I doubt very much that Hayden or Solarus would sacrifice Ilian either."

Red flames sprang unbidden to Kyra's hands. They spooled around the gold, fueled by rage at his accusations and the horror that they might be true. "You're lying. They accept me despite my being a wizard. It doesn't matter to them now, and it won't when I am of age."

Diamantas raised a hand. "The concern lies not in the fact you are a wizard. It lies in who you are. Of *what* you are. They are right to fear you. Without guidance, you pose a risk to us all. I only ask for the chance to provide you with insight into yourself. You must recognize your role in the war that approaches. Let me show you what you are meant to be."

Kyra felt an unexpected giddiness as the red magic grew bolder, licking the edges of her fingertips. "No. I will never go to Harkimer. If Solarus has hidden anything from me, he will tell me. I'll *demand* it. There's nothing you can say to convince me to voluntarily go into these mountains. I know what you're doing,

Diamantas. I won't let you destroy the Sea." Kyra raised her right hand, palm facing outward. The red swirled brightly. "Fight me or leave."

Diamantas' gaze traveled to Kyra's hands. Alarm flickered in his pale blue eyes. Then his eyes narrowed, and his features hardened until they looked cut with the same jagged lines as the rocks around them. "We are at an impasse. You have made your choice, as reckless as it may be. It leaves me with one response. My responsibility is foremost to our brethren." He tilted his staff, the white light flaring. "The sacrifice of your life will save the lives of many. I regret it, but it is the sacrifice required for our kin."

Kyra took a defensive stance. The red flame blazed hotly around her hands. It jerked against her, like a pack of frenzied pit bulls, poised to attack. Diamantas pointed the staff at the wall behind her and intoned a spell. White magic jetted forward and chained her hands. Kyra let out a small cry. She struggled fiercely against the magic as Diamantas aimed the staff at Kyra's arms. The white magic girdled them quickly. Kyra continued to fight. The red flames sprang from her hands and raced up her arms. Strangely, the red twisted around the white, suffocating it. Feeling the white slacken, Kyra poured the red into her magical shackles. The more red magic that emerged, the more intoxicating the power.

Suddenly, blue and green energy gushed forth, unbidden, from her hands. Kyra stopped, eyes widening. Where was it coming from? The blue and green energy muzzled the red magic as it spread. Both the red and white magic vanished immediately. Kyra pitched forward, abruptly released from the white magic's grip. She gaped at the blue-green magic. It draped over Kyra like a mosquito net. Diamantas took an astonished step backward. The white sphere convulsed violently, the blue and green pulsing within. With the sound of a thousand mirrors shattering, the sphere exploded.

Kyra gasped. A rush of shrieks and bellows assaulted her ears as the blue-green magic faded away. With the sphere destroyed, her protection from the dragons' war was gone. Kyra covered her ears with her hands to block out the noise. Diamantas blinked, then spun toward the din. Schirmeera had Recker half-raised off the ground and hurled him into a boulder. The red dragon hit the stone and collapsed. The earth quaked under his bulk.

Kyra glanced up at Diamantas. He seemed to have forgotten about her in the shock of being returned to the fight.

Strike now.

Kyra didn't hesitate. She summoned the golden energy again to her hands and lunged forward. Diamantas turned as she fired a golden bolt toward his shoulder. The wizard swiftly raised his own hand and brought it down. The gold snapped in two. Vengeance highlighted every plane of his face. Diamantas propelled a stream of fire toward her using his left hand. Kyra had anticipated the attack. She leapt to the ground, tucking her head, and rolling. In one fluid motion, Kyra rose in a crouch and flung a second bolt at Diamantas' exposed chest. She heard a crack as the magic made solid contact with Diamantas' ribs. With a hiss of pain, the wizard crumpled. The back of his hand smacked the ground, and the obsidian staff slid from his fingers.

"Looks like I can strike faster than a spell after all," Kyra growled, breaths coming in short, frozen wisps. She tore her attention away from the wizard and back to the dragons.

Schirmeera loomed over Recker, who was scrabbling for a large chunk of shattered rock to pull himself upright. Yet Schirmeera's yellow-flecked brown eyes were not on her adversary. The sound of Diamantas' shattered magic had diverted her gaze. Noticing Kyra for the first time, Schirmeera's face fell in anguish. *No,* she whispered. *You cannot be here, Kyra. It is not time.*

Kyra took two steps back, eyes wide. A dragon was talking to her. A dragon who knew her name.

Diamantas was back on his feet, staff in hand. "Enough. You will die today, and the prophecy will die with you. As it should have years ago." White flame gushed from his staff with such intensity that even Gyre and Recker paused to stare at it. Diamantas began to chant.

Kyra couldn't stop her hands from trembling as she raised them. Gold sparkled around her wrists like clouds of glitter. Blue and green spritzed to life within the gold, but Kyra didn't notice. Tears wet her lashes. She knew her magic would be a futile defense against the full fury of Diamantas and his staff. Kyra squeezed her eyes shut.

Hayden. Solarus. Talis, she thought. *I'm sorry I couldn't say goodbye. I tried.*

Diamantas' chanting crescendoed... until his words were suddenly chopped apart by a rasping voice.

Schirmeera's voice.

Kyra's eyes flew open. The dragon's hand was raised. She made a sign in the air and whistled shrilly. Kyra watched as green lightning shot upward. Crackling and exploding, the lightning cleaved the air above her. Kyra's jaw dropped. Like the ends of parchment set on fire, the folds of the ether peeled back under the force of the green flame. A blinding brightness filled the hole that had formed.

Schirmeera's green energy continued to ripple from her open palm. *Please,* she beseeched the air. *Deliver her to safety. Please hide her from the evil of Harkimer.* The dragon looked one last time at the stunned Kyra. *Zephryn,* Schirmeera whispered.

A gust of wind lifted Kyra off her feet, her cloak billowing like wings behind her.

"No!" Diamantas' outraged scream came from below. Kyra glanced down to see him raise his obsidian staff toward the sky.

Schirmeera cast Kyra toward the light. With a shocked cry, Kyra hurtled toward the white emptiness. Her last sight as she plunged into the light was a deadly helix of red and blue flames chasing after her.

PART ONE

KATE SMITH

Chapter 1

The girl stood motionless in front of a warped metal fence at the end of a square plot. Her jade-flecked eyes were wide in consternation. The structure in the center was a mess of cracked stone and buckling metal, consumed by the fire's monstrous maw. The girl's face was flushed, exposed skin burning from heat so intense it evaporated sweat before it slid down her brow. The acrid smell of burnt plastic and wood stung her throat and eyes. An azure cloak hung lifelessly over her shoulders. Strangely, her body was cool underneath. The red and blue flames roared, assaulting the night sky with an unnatural light.

What happened? Where am I?

The girl had ordered herself to wake up, to escape the nightmare. Except the blaze was not imagined. Her eyes briefly flickered to the neighboring square plot. A white home squatted in the center, white siding and tan shingles scorched black. The girl's stomach sloshed with dread. The mutilated building before her had been a home.

The sirens of fire engines, ambulances, and police cars screamed. A convoy of vehicles soon tore down the street and screeched to a halt. Firefighters leapt from their vehicles, unrolling hoses and fixing ends to fire hydrants, shouting to one another, charging forward toward the inferno. One grabbed the girl around the waist with one arm. He started to drag her backward. Jolted out of her daze, the girl thrashed against him.

"It's okay, I'm not going to hurt you," the firefighter said, struggling to hold her.

"Let go of me!" she yelled. The girl planted her feet and jerked to the side. The firefighter, weighed down by the cumbersome uniform, couldn't keep his hold on her. The girl broke free.

"Wait!" he called as the girl sprinted away from the fire. She didn't get far. A police car parked on the side of the road obstructed her path. The girl looked around frantically. She was fenced in by the vehicles that created a perimeter around the house and nearby streets. Her throat was dry, lips cracked. Her gaze ranged the throng of first responders around her. White and blue emblems on their uniforms caught her eye, a strange serpent-entwined staff surrounded by a star. The girl stared. In the recesses of her mind, she recalled being taught the meanings behind such stitched emblems. They represented kingdoms and families, occupations and hierarchy, a wealth of information captured by seemingly simple designs. *What family does this belong to?* she wondered, momentarily forgetting her impulse to flee.

"Hey, hey, are you okay?"

The girl glanced over her shoulder. A female police officer rushed forward, her long black hair crinkled in the heat.

The police officer stopped in front of her. "I saw you run from the firefighter back there. I'm sorry if he scared you."

"He surprised me," the girl replied hoarsely. "It was just . . . an instinct. I'm fine."

The officer glanced at the fire, then back at the girl. "What's your name?"

"My name is . . ." The girl broke off. Her mind didn't have a name to draw from. She stared blankly at the officer. "I don't know," she answered, stunned. "I don't remember."

The officer's chocolate brown eyes were bright with concern. "You don't remember?" She glanced behind her. "Waters, where's Jocelyn? Can you find her? I need her. Right away."

"I'm on it, Officer Martinez," the man answered. He turned and wove through the responders.

The girl craned her neck around the officer. Her eyes passed over neighbors congregated across the street, hastily dressed in bathrobes and jackets, though the fire burned away the biting autumn air. Families clutched small children close to them. An elderly man squeezed his wife's hand tightly as she wept. A man in socks and sandals spoke to his neighbor, pointing in the girl's direction. The girl quickly averted her gaze.

She didn't recognize any of them.

"Come with me," Martinez told the girl in a soothing tone. She steered the girl toward the back of an ambulance. An older woman wearing a shirt with the same snake-staff emblem was waiting for them, an oxygen tank and mask ready next to a stretcher. "Jocelyn is our medic. She's going to do a quick examination to check your breathing and see if you have any injuries."

Jocelyn nodded, gesturing toward the stretcher. "Sit here, please. I also want you to cover your mouth with the mask and breathe normally. It's standard procedure for fires in case you've inhaled smoke or some other toxin." The medic handed the girl a mask.

"Even if there's no smoke," Martinez muttered in a perplexed tone.

The girl complied, climbing onto the hard plastic and putting the mask to her face. She sat rigidly as Martinez consulted with the medic in an undertone. The girl's temples pounded. She inhaled with shuddering breaths as her gaze fixed on the firefighters. They continued to grapple with the demonic blaze but without success. The fire seemed to toy with the responders, lashing out blistering limbs to keep them at bay. Close to the stretcher stood two men, a firefighter sergeant with a thick black hat and a grizzled-looking police captain with crew-cut hair.

"I've never seen a blaze like this, Sarge!" one of the firefighters shouted, arms quaking with effort. "No matter how many hoses we add, we can't stop it!"

"Then contain it!" the sergeant barked. He removed his black hat and rubbed his bald pate as another of the men hollered, "Get back, get back!"

"My dad always said, 'it's hotter than the blue blazes,' Captain," the firefighter sergeant commented in a dumbfounded tone to the police captain.

"I didn't reckon there'd actually *be* blue blazes. You see my men there? They're working harder than a three-legged cat in a sandbox to keep it in check, and it ain't working. Look." He wiped sweat from his head with his hat and nodded to the house. "The fire's got no smoke. Don't see any cinders either. No ash. What in the devil's drink could cause a fire like that?"

The captain chewed furiously on a piece of gum, his expression dark. "It might be a chemical fire. Arsonists are getting clever. We arrested a chemist last year. It would explain the blue flames, but you're right. Why isn't there smoke?"

"Might be a basement drug lab blown two ways to Sunday," the sergeant agreed. "Won't know until this thing's over, though."

The captain creaked his neck, grinding the gum between his teeth. "Our forensics teams have picked through buildings that weren't more than wastelands. They'll find something here." The captain's voice belied his belief that any evidence could be salvaged. He clapped the sergeant on the shoulder and strode off toward the police cars.

Still holding the mask to her mouth, the girl's eyes flitted from the two men back to Officer Martinez and Jocelyn. They had finished talking, and the medic smiled at her. Jocelyn promptly began her inspection as Officer Martinez climbed into the ambulance. It was only when she reemerged with a bottle of water that the girl remembered her rasping throat. She lowered the mask and guzzled the water. Martinez smiled as the girl handed her the empty bottle. She returned to her vehicle as Jocelyn finished her assessment. "No trauma to the head, and your lungs are clear. All good news. You can stop using the mask now. You don't need it. Wait here for me while I put this in my report." Jocelyn returned to the ambulance, leaving the girl alone. An overpowering impulse to run filled the girl's aching chest.

A slice of light reflecting off metal caught the girl's attention. A firefighter had accidentally kicked a flat silver coin as he backpedaled away from the blaze. The girl's eyes followed the object. The coin rolled down the road, hit a piece of uneven pavement, spun in circles, then fell. Red and blue glinted off its surface.

The girl darted a glance around her. Medics were tending to the firefighters, who wheezed and coughed. Some held oxygen masks to their face. The onlookers remained mesmerized by the flames. Officer Martinez was in her vehicle, occupied with her work.

The girl slid off the stretcher and dashed across the road to where the coin lay. Without pausing to think, the girl bent down and carefully lifted the piece. It was a heptagon, unblemished except for strange lines and figures etched across the surface. Surprisingly, the coin was cool to the touch. The girl stared at the markings. They weren't solely red and blue as she had thought earlier. Instead, they seemed to pulse with their own energy, changing from red to purple to orange to blue to green to white and then back to red. The girl ran her finger along the edge of the coin. It was cool to the touch. Puzzled, the girl slipped the coin into her pocket and sprinted back to the stretcher.

Her heart was thumping when a dour-looking officer strode toward her from behind the row of police cars. His pimpled face was pale and doused in sweat. The officer folded his arms and looked down at her.

"I have some questions for you," he said without pretense. "When did you arrive here tonight? Where were you before the fire?"

The officer's sharp tone provoked a flash of irritation in the girl. "I don't remember," she replied flatly.

The officer's surly expression deepened. "You don't remember where you were," he echoed. "What about this house? Who lives here?"

"I haven't a clue." The girl tried to hide her own anxiety at the answer. Her mind was a peculiarly empty space, as though someone had ransacked it of a lifetime of faces and images. The panic that coursed through her was second only to her anger at the officer.

"You haven't a clue." Each repetition of the girl's response brought on a more mistrustful tone. The officer reached behind the girl and tugged on the cloak covering her shoulders. The girl recoiled, but his grip tightened. Unconsciously, the girl's fingers slid over the silky surface, trying to smooth creases from the material. Inexplicably, there weren't any to smooth. The material cloak was flawless and featherlight.

"There isn't a single burn or tear on this . . . outfit of yours," the officer said, releasing his hold on the fabric. "I'm guessing you aren't from here, not with that accent, yet you somehow came to Chicago. There's a lot of crime in this city. I doubt a teenage girl would be walking around by herself at night, not even in Garfield Park. A suburb in Chicago is still a suburb in Chicago. Whatever you're hiding, you're going to tell me." The officer's eyes narrowed. He leaned forward, his face so close to the girl's she could count the pimples on his cheeks and chin. "Maybe you have a friend over here, is that it? Went to a party around town? Maybe had a drink or two. Maybe you're protecting your friend. You're pretending you don't remember how or when you came to this street, because you're aware alcohol at your or her age is illegal. What were you doing before you showed up here? Hanging at a party you shouldn't have been at?"

The girl's fists balled up as riotous emotions warred within her. "I. Can't. Remember. I told you that already. Stop asking me. My answers aren't going to change."

The officer's cheeks flushed. Before he could retort, Martinez's voice cut in sharply, "Armstrong, what is wrong with you? Get back from her. This is a terrifying enough situation for her without an added interrogation from you." The dark-haired officer strode forward beside the girl, placing a protective hand on her shoulder. "Have some sense. Halloween's next week. Obviously, the girl's wearing a costume. Even a rookie would put the two together." Martinez's scathing tone elicited a chastened expression from the pimple-faced officer. "Leave us alone. I can take it from here."

Armstrong didn't meet her eyes as he stalked off. The girl's hands relaxed as Martinez let go of her shoulder. The officer turned to the girl and gave her a strained smiled. "I'm sorry about Armstrong. He's new to the force and needs some mentoring. My name's Christin." She paused, seeming uncertain as how to continue. "I looked into our records about this house. There was a couple who lived here, Simon and Abigail Smith. Do you recognize those names? No?" Christin sighed lightly. "Simon and Abigail have a fifteen-year-old daughter named Kate Smith. Wavy brown hair, jade-flecked eyes, average height. We have reason to believe it might be you."

The girl averted her gaze as she absorbed the information. *Kate? Her name was Kate? Kate Smith.* Even though she didn't have a counter-explanation, the girl's gut stirred quietly. It didn't feel right. The name had to belong to someone else. Or was that merely a desperate hope?

Christin's lustrous brown eyes were full of compassion. "It's a lot to take in, Kate. We have to figure out if your parents were home when the fire started. We're going to look for them, ask friends and neighbors if they're normally out Friday nights, if anyone saw them drive away . . ."

"Martinez?"

Christin and Kate both glanced to the side. It was the grizzled police captain who had been speaking with the firefighter sergeant. He was gnashing gum as though to spare his teeth the brunt of his frustration.

"Yes, Captain?"

"What do you have so far?" he asked gruffly.

With a quick glance at Kate, Christin turned and dropped her voice under the bedlam of the blaze and firefighters. Kate leaned forward subtly, trying to hear the conversation. The captain's face was impassive as Christin reported what she had learned.

"We ran a basic background check on the family," Kate heard Christin say, a tense note entering her voice. "We found a notation on Simon Smith's younger brother, Eric. He's serving a ten-year sentence for drug trafficking. It's his second offense. The first was car theft. Eric may also have ties to the gang responsible for the murder of those teens in Roseland last month."

The captain stopped chewing as Christin broke off. When she didn't continue, he wagged a finger at her. "And? I know that look, Martinez. What else did you find?"

Christin pushed strands of frizzy hair from her face, expression somber. "Eric was living with Simon and Abigail at the time he was arrested on the trafficking charge. That was two weeks ago."

Silence ruled the air between them as the captain shook his head. He reached into his uniform pocket and removed a wrapper. He spit the gum into it. "Does Simon have a record?" he asked, wadding the wrapper, and pocketing it.

"No. The heroin epidemic has been growing worse over the past few years, though. If Eric already had jail time before this sentence and was dealing on the southeast side, he might have had problems with buyers who didn't get what they paid for or gang members who didn't get their cut . . ."

"I'm aware of the problem, Martinez. You're speculating."

Christin's jaw tightened, but she replied in a measured tone, "Yes, Captain. I only meant it's unlikely Kate had anything to do with the fire. There may be someone who had a motive to commit arson."

"The sergeant and I were talking about this." The captain's gaze roamed to the firefighters, whose goal seemed to have shifted from extinguishing the fire to preventing it from spreading beyond the boundary of the property. "It's too complicated to be a kid's prank gone wrong. Looks more like a criminal who understands his chemicals or has associates who do. We're going to have our work cut out for us getting evidence." He fished a new pack of gum from his pocket. "Find out what you can about surviving relatives," the captain instructed crisply. "We'll look into safe locations where we can keep the girl for now. Armstrong and Haddad will interview the neighbors."

"Yes, Captain."

The captain gave her a curt nod. He moved to the side, allowing a medic carrying bandages to pass, then strode back to the sergeant.

"Christin, can I see you for a moment?" Jocelyn had reemerged from the ambulance. Christin nodded. She looked at Kate, whose gaze was on her with a mixture of curiosity and dread. "We'll get out of here as soon as I finish with Jocelyn, I promise."

Kate nodded her understanding. Christin walked to Jocelyn, who guided her around the ambulance.

Alone again, Kate rubbed her aching temples. She tried to pull up images of her mother and father, Abigail and Simon Smith. Of herself, Kate Smith. Her mental photo album was filled with empty pages, no matter how many times she leafed through them. *Am I really Kate Smith?* the girl asked herself again.

Christin approached a moment later. "Jocelyn says she didn't find anything wrong. She's insisting on a full examination at the hospital though. The doctors will do some blood work and take a few x-rays."

"I'm fine," Kate answered immediately. She wasn't familiar with "x-rays," but her stomach twisted at the thought of intrusive prodding.

Observing the apprehension stamped on Kate's face, Christin added, "It's standard procedure, Kate, nothing to worry about. I'll drive you to the hospital. In the meantime, we will be looking for your parents and contacting your relatives. It will work out."

Kate cast a glance again at the strangers across the road. "What if I don't have any family?"

"You'll have someone," Christin replied firmly. "I have permission for you to stay with me until then." She smiled reassuringly and indicated with her head. "Come on, my vehicle's over there."

Christin started toward her car as Kate put a hand on the stretcher to steady herself. A wave of dizziness swept over her. She wasn't supposed to be here. She didn't know *where* she was supposed to be, but she didn't recognize this place, these people, or the name Kate.

Still, there was no place to go. Not yet. Behind her, Kate glimpsed vans coming to an abrupt stop. News crews scrambled out with large cameras. Reporters holding microphones climbed out behind them.

Limbs heavy, Kate climbed off the stretcher and trod behind Christin. She glanced over her shoulder one last time. The firefighters looked defeated. Along with the police, they watched the harrowing blaze swallow the wreckage that was once Simon and Abigail Smith's home.

For a fraction of a second, an intense fury drowned out Kate's fatigue. A raw, repressed fury. Her hands itched like badly dry skin. Kate scratched one fist as she silently promised to punish whoever was responsible for the devastation. She owed that much to the people trapped inside and to herself, with the personal history that had been erased, possibly forever. Kate was still scratching her hand as she turned to leave. She didn't notice the tiny red flames that flickered from her fingertips.

***

"Physical trauma can affect one's memory, but psychological and emotional stresses are equally impactful. Sometimes more so," Dr. Jordana told Kate the next day. The middle-aged African American woman pushed her glasses further up her nose as she skimmed through an open folder attached to a large clipboard. Kate tiredly sat on the papered table beside her. The previous night, Christin had taken Kate to the hospital as agreed. The tests and scans weren't nearly as hard for Kate to endure as the staff's stares and whispers of "the poor girl from the fire" when she was shuttled from room to room. Kate only managed to sleep a few hours at Christin's apartment. Then she was back in the car with Christin, this time to visit Dr. Jordana, the physician assigned by the hospital to discuss with Kate her test results.

Kate's eyes wandered the room. Three of the four walls were dotted with small, stenciled flowers. The fourth was painted with a mural of smiling farm animals. It was strangely incongruous with the strong, sterile scent that hung in the air. Kate coughed, then looked back at Dr. Jordana.

The physician ran a finger over her lips. "The x-rays came up negative for injuries to the lungs," she summarized without looking up from the folder. "Your bloodwork is normal, no signs of toxins. The CAT scan shows everything is functioning normally, no injuries to the brain. Physically, you're in perfect health."

"Except that I can't remember anything," Kate replied tonelessly. She didn't need to understand the medical terms to know she was in anything other than "perfect health." "I didn't know my name. My memories are completely gone. Something is wrong with me."

Closing the file, Dr. Jordana met Kate's distraught gaze. "I believe your psychological distress is causing an acute form of amnesia. Death is traumatic, particularly of loved ones as close as one's parents. My best estimation is that you have suppressed memories because of your grief and shock. However, one eventually heals by accepting what has occurred. It takes time."

Kate downturned her eyes, focusing on her legs as they dangled from the high table. The police had determined through interviews with the neighbors that the Smiths had driven home that evening, and no one saw the garage door open again before the fire. It was almost a certainty that her family had been home that night. Oddly, Kate's eyes were dry, as though her tear ducts had been taped over. She wanted to cry, hoping the tears could purge the detached poison in her heart. But she couldn't.

"None of the neighbors recognized me?" Kate asked, still looking down.

Dr. Jordana shook her head. "Officer Martinez mentioned that your neighbors never exchanged more than a greeting with your parents if they were entering or leaving the house. They all said they had seen Simon and Abigail's teenage daughter but had never met you personally. Your parents kept to themselves. Officer Martinez believes that had to do with your uncle. He committed serious crimes. The police said your parents probably avoided contact with your neighbors to prevent them from discovering his situation." Dr. Jordana gave Kate an inquisitive look. "Does that sound familiar? That your uncle lived with you?"

The paper under Kate crinkled as she shifted on the table. "No, it doesn't," she answered. Kate traced a line around one of the flowers as she added in a quieter voice, "It's like I don't exist."

"You certainly exist, Kate. There is another aspect that we should consider."

Kate lifted her gaze to Dr. Jordana, who was tapping a finger to her lips. "Sometimes informational gaps in your mind apply to a single area of your life. Everything you have mentioned thus far has a connection to relationships. Not factual knowledge. Tell me about your classes. What can you recall about science, for example?"

A book cover blinked into Kate's mind. *Serth a lin ae serth a playnara li Silvias.* The letters rearranged themselves to form a new title: *Identifying the Trees and Plants of Silvias.* "I learned about nature," Kate responded. "Trees and plants."

"What about literature?"

Specters of the Seven Rings Pass. "Novels, mostly fiction, and history."

"Foreign languages?"

Kate bit her lip. She could hear euphonious sounds in her mind, like music, except there were no words attached to the melodies. She shook her head. A hopeful thought suddenly popped into her mind. "Couldn't we ask my teachers what I'm studying? When do I get to see them?"

Dr. Jordana let out a compassionate sigh. "You won't, Kate. I'm sorry. Officer Martinez said the police are considering the fire a deliberate act of murder. For your safety, they don't want you speaking with anyone until they determine how it was started and who was behind it. Your teachers have already been notified of the situation. Your friends would have seen what happened on the news, I'm sure. Unfortunately, they aren't allowed to contact you either."

Kate's face fell. Another dead end.

"The good news is you can remember objective information," Dr. Jordana went on in a placating tone. "Facts aren't associated with emotion. People are. I am more convinced now that your subconscious is temporarily denying you memories that invoke feelings, good or bad."

Kate's heart skipped a beat as she clung to the word. "Temporarily?"

"Yes. You will regain your memories in due time. First, you need to allow yourself to grieve over the loss of your parents. I can recommend some counselors who could help you work through this." She smiled again. "Judging by what I've seen in you, Kate, I have complete confidence you will resume a normal, happy life."

Switching topics, Dr. Jordana pulled out a business card and pen from her coat pocket as said to Kate, "Here's my number if you need to call me or if other doctors want to speak with me." She flipped the card over and jotted down a number. "Please keep in mind the time difference if you do call," Dr. Jordana added, handing the card to Kate. "My husband can be a grouch if he's woken before six."

Kate stared at Dr. Jordana, picked up the clipboard, and held it against her chest. "Time difference? What do you mean?"

For the first time in their discussion, Dr. Jordana looked stunned. "Officer Martinez didn't mention anything to you?" She shook her head sympathetically. "The police located an aunt of yours in London. Her name is Millie. She is your mother's older sister, I believe. Officer Martinez called her and told her what happened with your parents and your memory. Millie has offered to be your guardian, Kate. Officer Martinez says you'll be flying out to London as soon as she can get you a new passport . . ."

Dr. Jordana continued to speak, but the words sounded distorted, as though coming to Kate from underwater. She hadn't considered the fact that she would have to find a permanent home. According to Dr. Jordana, that home was with a stranger in another place Kate couldn't remember, if she had ever been there at all. She felt as though she were standing on a frozen lake, its ice so thin that when she tried to move forward, cracks formed beneath her. There was a fragile uncertainty in every direction. Kate's sole option was to go forward to try and regain her memories. Kate wasn't convinced she ever could.

Chapter 2

The crush of people transiting the airport jostled Kate. She let herself be caught up in the crowd that wove through the area marked "Arrivals." Loudspeakers bellowed travel updates overhead. Gripping the handle of a suitcase almost as tall as she was, Kate moved toward a kiosk and stopped. She let the sea of people break past her, scanning the harried faces and people in monochrome coats as she searched for Millie.

Kate's luggage jerked to the side. She caught it before it fell over as a man in a striped suit shot Kate a nettled look. Without an apology, the man adjusted his jacket and hurried away. Kate tightened her grip on her luggage handle with a grimace.

Five days. That was how long it had taken for Kate to make it through the rest of her appointments before she left. There were interviews at the police station, visits to the psychologist, and a trip to the passport office. Christin gifted Kate an old cell phone and loaded minutes onto it. Kate turned over the phone in bewilderment. When she had raised it to Christin, Christin had laughed good-naturedly and showed her how to use it.

"You'll call me about the investigation?" Kate had asked Christin again when they were at the airport.

Christin nodded sadly as passengers gathered near the boarding gate. "I promised I would. Remember what I said yesterday, though. We won't get any immediate answers. The forensics team didn't have anything to salvage from the house. Normally there's evidence they can use, like metal from the car, scraps of furniture, cement from the foundation . . . something. That wasn't the case with this fire. There wasn't anything to recover. All the team has to work with are samples from the soil where the house stood. The investigation will take months, if not longer." Christin sighed. "Hang in there. I'm here if you need me." Christin hugged Kate tightly as an airline employee made the announcement to board.

Robotically, Kate disappeared down the plank into the airplane, leaving the only person she trusted. Eight hours later, Kate had touched down in London. It felt like a lifetime.

Kate fished a photograph out of her coat pocket and held it up. Millie was a paunchy woman in her early fifties, with sparkling blue eyes and tight, blond curls. In the picture, Millie sat on a chaise longue chair, hands poised over her knees. She wore an extravagant sequined blouse, red velvet skirt, and knee-high boots. Costume jewelry hung from her neck, and bracelets dangled on both wrists. Even in the photo, Millie's childlike grin was infectious.

Kate returned the picture to her coat and checked the giant clock overhead. Half past nine. Kate's plane had arrived punctually an hour earlier. Millie had instructed her to wait in the "Arrivals" section. Kate would have preferred to have met her aunt on a full night's sleep, but her nerves were too fritzed during the flight with questions about where she was going and if she would like this stranger to allow her any rest.

Kate again cast a scrolling look over the crowd for Millie. As if on cue, she heard a voice chirp, "Kate!"

A woman in a flamingo-pink peacoat, a yellow and blue polka-dot shirt, and a matching hat waved a handkerchief in the air. She squeezed through the crowd, her heels clicking and clacking on the hard floor. "Kate, sweetie, there you are!"

Before Kate could reply, Millie had made her way to her. She planted a fuchsia-lip sticked kiss on Kate's cheek and swept her up in a bear hug. Kate stood woodenly, unsure of how to respond to this stranger. Her head was close to Millie's shirt, which was doused in a potent, cherry and vanilla perfume. Kate gagged as she inhaled the scent. Mistaking Kate's cough as a heartfelt sob, Millie patted her head.

"Oh, my dear, dear, niece," Millie crooned. She released Kate from her embrace. Even in her stilettos, Millie stood only a hair above Kate. "I am *so* sorry I am late, sweetie. I thought you were coming on the *second* of November, not the first. I am dreadful with dates and times. Can't be expected to remember so many details."

Millie inspected Kate from head to toe, blue eyes sparkling. "You have grown into a beautiful young woman, Kate! My goodness, the last time I saw you you were a wee thing of three, and here you are, fifteen, and a stunning young woman."

Millie's delight was so genuine, Kate was coaxed into smiling. "I, um, I'm taller than I was."

"Your hair is lighter than I remember." Millie smoothed a few strands from Kate's forehead. "Your eyes too. You're quite a piece of art, my dear, that you are." She took Kate's free arm in hers. With a quick glance at Kate's suitcase, Millie went on without pause, "Let's go collect the rest of your luggage. Robert's got the car out front."

Kate's face burned in embarrassment. "I don't have other luggage."

Millie's appalled expression at the thought that someone would travel with anything less than four suitcases of clothing and accessories deepened Kate's humiliation. Kate uncomfortably tugged her peacoat straighter. *Even the clothes aren't mine,* she thought. Christin had given Kate a few of her sister's old outfits. They didn't quite fit, her sister being older and leggier than Kate. The sweater Kate wore was baggy, and the jeans reached past her shoes. The one item that was Kate's was the gray wool peacoat Christin bought for her before she left. It was slim and snug against Kate's petite figure. Kate had also refused to part with the cloak and boots she had worn the day of the fire. They were clues to her past, and she clung to the hope they would remind her of her life like a child to its blanket. After the forensics team had meticulously searched the cloak for evidence and found nothing, Christin had persuaded her chief to let Kate keep it. Now the cloak was neatly packed in the suitcase.

Kate looked up to see tears swelling in Millie's eyes like a blue lake. "I'm so clueless at times, I am," she said with a small sniff. Taking out a handkerchief from her shirt pocket, Millie dabbed her eyes. "Of course, you don't have anything else. We'll remedy that. My poor, dearest Abby . . ." Millie again pressed the handkerchief against her eyes before tucking it away in her pocket. She squeezed Kate's arm tightly and zipped through the crowd toward the airport exit, Kate double-stepping to keep up.

A biting wind smacked Kate in the face as she followed Millie outside. Shivering, Kate watched as people bundled up in hats and wool coats rushed past and hopped into cabs stationed near the exit doors. When Millie released her arm, Kate shoved her hands into her pockets for warmth. Her fingers brushed the surface of the heptagon coin. Strangely, the feel of the etchings comforted her. Like the cloak, the coin was a keepsake of her past.

"There he is." Millie pointed to one of the spacious black cabs in the row. A driver with a checked cap was waving at her. "Come on, dear."

The driver moved toward the car's open boot as Millie and Kate approached. He was flat-nosed and had white hair retreating from his forehead. A lopsided smile decorated his face as Millie and Kate approached. "All set, Millie?" he greeted in a gravelly voice.

"Quite, Robert, thank you," she replied, rubbing her hands together. Millie beamed at Kate, who set her luggage to the side. "Robert, this is my dear niece, Kate."

Robert doffed his cap politely. "Pleased to meet you, Miss Kate. I'll take that for you."

He returned the cap to his head and hefted Kate's suitcase into the open boot.

"Pleased to meet you, Mr. . . . um . . ."

"Robert, if you please," the driver chuckled. "Mister's a bit stodgy, eh?" He shut the boot and moved to open the cab door. With a small bow, he said, "After you, Miss Kate."

Kate smiled self-consciously and climbed inside.

"Thanks for being such a dear and waiting," Millie said to Robert.

"Anything for you, Miss Millie."

Millie pretended to blush and waved her hand. She settled in beside Kate. "I'm no spring chicken to be a 'miss,'" she said as Robert shut the door and scooted behind the wheel. "You make me feel young, Robert."

Robert winked into the rearview mirror. "You're like a newly-budded rose, Millie."

Kate stared out the window as Robert navigated the cab away from the airport. The clouds refused to provide a cheerful welcome. The cab puttered into the queue of cars politely taking turns to enter the highway. When it was their turn to leave, Robert shot off away from the airport.

Kate's eyes were glued to the window. Industrial buildings sprouted on both sides of the highway as they traveled. They were gray and unwelcoming. *Is this what London is like?* The buildings faded into sprawling fields, brown and barren in the late autumn months. Plots of farmland and houses were identical, as though stenciled into place. Sheep, distant puffballs, grazed peacefully, unaffected by the cold in their bushy coats. The landscape slowly shifted back to buildings as the highway wedged together into narrow lanes packed with cars. Kate sighed, resting her chin on her hand. She preferred the peace of the countryside to the congestion that now forced the cab to a crawl.

"I know, sweetie, traffic's abysmal," Millie said in a placating voice. "We're almost there though. A few more turns, and we're in Hampstead."

"Hampstead?"

"Our home, sweetie. It's grand, away from all this ruckus. You'll absolutely love it."

Kate nodded without answering. Dread bloated within her. *Home*.

They finally veered off the highway, wove through city roads, and turned onto a street that divided a large, hilly park and a neighborhood. Robert guided the car into a quiet neighborhood. Kate looked to her left and right. Orderly lines of houses with wooden doors were surrounded by hedgerows and gooseberry bushes. Skeletal trees bookended bare garden patches, flowers nestled cozily underground, protected from the chilly air. Kate's gaze roved to a statue of a nectarine-colored glass cat poised on the doorstep. Its light was muted under the sulking gray skies.

Robert parked the cab. He stepped out and grandly opened the door for Millie and Kate. Millie took out her purse as Robert lifted Kate's suitcase from the boot.

"Thank you again, Robert," Millie said, handing him the fare.

Robert glanced down at the money, grinned, and tipped his cap. "That's a generous tip, Miss Millie, thanks kindly. Pleasure to make your acquaintance, Miss Kate. We'll be seeing you around no doubt. Millie will take grand care of you, she will."

"Nice to meet you," Kate replied distantly, eyes scanning the house.

"Toodles!" Millie said with a small wave. Kate heard the cab putter away. The engine suddenly turned off. She glanced down the road. Robert had parked along the cul-de-sac a few houses away. Millie grinned, seeing Kate's puzzled expression. "Robert's our neighbor. So very convenient for trips, you know." She put a hand on Kate's back and steered her to the door. "Plenty of time to explore, Kate. Let's get you inside first, introduce you to your new home."

Kate cringed. That word again. *Home*. As Millie put the key in the door, humming to herself, Kate was again seized with the compulsion to run. She had been so occupied with her errands and travel that she couldn't think more than hour to hour. Now she had arrived at a place that wasn't just a layover: it was her final destination. A shiver that had nothing to do with the chilly air ran through her. Kate had to escape. But the same thought badgered her as it had at the fire: escape where? What would she do?

"Quick now, out of the cold, sweetie," Millie said, oblivious to Kate's consternation as she opened the door. "Be sure to clean your shoes on the mat."

Kate mustered up her courage and thrust it into a silent command. *Keep moving.* She stepped through the door's threshold, dragging her suitcase behind her. Kate's jaw dropped. The living room assaulted her with a cornucopia of color. Yellow-painted walls were graffitied with paintings and portraits in every size and shape. Chairs and a couch were set around a coffee table in the center of the room. Lamps took up every corner, and tall shelves chock-full of knickknacks were set against the wall.

Millie closed the door behind her. "Leave your things there for now, sweetie," she instructed, pointing to the side of the door. Millie unceremoniously kicked off her heels, shedding a few inches in the process. She tossed her purse onto a pile of purses on a rack and swept past Kate to the coffee table. Spinning around, Millie raised her hands in a grand gesture. "What do you think? Marvelous, isn't it?"

Words failed Kate. She wiped the bottoms of her shoes on the mat and removed them. Millie's smile broadened as Kate walked forward. Her gaze skipped from picture frame to picture frame. One held a black-and-white sketch of a curly-haired woman in a long coat. She clutched an umbrella close to her body as black clouds rained down onto her. Another piece of artwork depicted a scene with three cats frolicking through fields of violets. Then came pastel portraits, paintings of castles and landscapes, and still-life photographs of various fruits.

"It's . . . you have so many paintings," Kate finally answered, shocked to honesty.

"You can have a closer gander later," Millie said with a pleased look. "I don't imagine you've had breakfast yet. I'd fancy a cup of tea myself. Would you like one?" Millie breezed past a staircase on her left and disappeared into an adjacent room before Kate could answer, "Yes, please."

Kate's gaze continued to skim the paintings as she followed Millie. The kitchen was smaller and cozier than the living room, with large glass doors that opened to a patio and garden chairs. Kate stared as Millie placed a kettle on the stove. The kitchen was littered with cat paraphernalia. The countertops were cluttered with figurines of kittens and feline salt and pepper shakers. The tablecloth had a scene of cats chasing mice. Even the tiled floor was painted with tiny paw prints.

"Can I, um, help with something?" Kate asked, slowly dragging her gaze back to Millie.

"There are cups and saucers in the cupboard," Millie directed as she opened the refrigerator. "Silverware is in the second drawer from the right, sweetie. Serviettes are underneath."

Kate found the cups and saucers and set them on the counter beside the stove. She also found the silverware and serviettes.

Millie emerged from the refrigerator with a small plate of pastries. "Lovely, thank you, Kate," she said, bustling over to the table. She set the plate next to a sugar bowl and a pitcher of cream, its handle curled like a cat's tail.

Kate arranged a place for herself and Millie, placed the silverware on the serviettes. The tea kettle whistled shrilly.

"Go on, dear, sit," Millie said over her shoulder as she dropped tea bags in two of the cups. "There we are, almost done."

Kate sat as a sweet, floral fragrance wafted into the air. Millie brought the tea and saucers, putting a set in front of Kate. Kate gratefully cupped the drink between her hands. Steam tickled her nose as warmth spread from her palms to her fingers. Millie eased herself into a chair beside Kate.

A loud gonging suddenly sounded. Kate started. Turning, she saw a grandfather clock hanging on the wall. She heard Millie chuckle. "You'll get used to that. Your nana bought it at an auction years ago. It was given to me when she passed. It was a bit of a bother at first, what with it chiming every hour. Fortunately, our dear Robert discovered how to stop it ringing at night. Now it wakes at dawn and sleeps at dusk, like my own little rooster." Millie chortled again. She nudged the plate of pastries toward Kate. "Try one of the scones, dearie. I'm partial to the ones with raisins. They go well with tea."

Kate took the proffered pastry, stomach gurgling. Anxiety had robbed Kate of her appetite on the plane. Now her stomach vocally protested its hours-long neglect. She bit off an edge. Kate's eyes lit up as the soft, buttery scone flaked in her mouth. She noticed Millie was watching her intensely. Her aunt seemed anxious, fidgeting in her chair. Millie opened her mouth to speak, then closed it as if she had changed her mind. She poured cream into her tea. An awkward silence filled the room. Kate chewed slowly, unsure of what to say. Millie lifted the pitcher of cream a second time. Her tea was almost completely white when she set it down again.

Uncomfortable with the protracted silence, Kate pointed to the figurines on the counters. "Do you have cats?"

She instantly regretted the question. Millie's eyes welled with fresh tears. She removed her handkerchief from her pocket and dabbed the corners of her eyes.

"I used to have three. A friend was visiting one day, and it was absolutely brilliant outside, and I was so careless, leaving the patio doors open. The dears ran away. Probably were scared by all the company. My calico, Rosalind, had the most adorable purr. Prince Albert was a ginger tabby. He loved his meals, that one. Fifi was a petite thing, black with white stockings. Oh, I do miss them!"

Millie folded the handkerchief and laid it next to her saucer. Now that she had started speaking, Millie seemed eager to continue. "I'm terribly sorry so many years have passed since I last saw you. I truly missed you and Abby." Millie sniffed. "She was also my best friend, your mum was. You don't remember, but Abby brought you to England every summer and Christmas. Until you were five. Then she and your grandfather had that row and, well, your mum never came back. I don't blame her, not at all," Millie put in hastily. "Your grandfather was quite mulish and had a, well, narrow view of things. Your mum was just as stubborn. She lived her life her way, you see."

Kate saw Millie expected her to nod, so she did. Secretly, Kate didn't know what to feel. Without memories or emotions to associate with them, the Smith family history sounded like it belonged to someone else.

Millie's blue eyes were alight with hope as she leaned forward. "It's a silly thing to ask you, sweetie, what with your thoughts as scattered as feathers from a pillow fight. Except . . . did Abby ever mention me? I did miss her so. I always wondered if she ever, well, if she regretted like I did that we didn't talk afterward. You probably don't remember, though, what was I thinking to as you . . ."

"I do remember her talking about you," Kate fibbed. She hadn't a clue if it were true, but her heart panged seeing Millie's desperate expression. "My mum missed you a lot. She said . . . she said she wanted to visit you. This year. During the holidays."

"Oh, my poor Abby." Millie shook her head. She wiped her eyes again with the damp handkerchief, smearing her mascara across her face. "Your grandfather didn't look kindly on her marrying Simon. Simon was an American artist without a pound to his name. Both of which were unacceptable to your grandfather. Simon was 'A man completely unbefitting our family,' your grandfather had said. 'He's a swindler looking to filch our fortune.' He was a proud man, your grandfather, very concerned with social standing," Millie elaborated, bundling the handkerchief. "His many greats-grandfather was a baron and had several estates. After a couple generations, what with taxes and poor management, all but one of the estates were gone. Your grandfather inherited a modest home and a title. Much good it ever did him. My mum, your nana, said he strutted around with a puffed-out chest like he was a boy dressed up in his father's military uniform. He was so proud he was of being a 'noble.' I always thought the whole thing was poppycock.

"Simon was a dear lad, a real gentleman," Millie went on. She removed the tea bag and set it on the side of her saucer. "As I said, he wasn't a man of great means. He was a painter, not a collector. The money is in the acquiring and selling of the art, you see. It's not in the work itself. Most painters don't get a quid for their effort until they've finally bought the farm. Then overnight, the world declares the art a masterpiece and auctions it off for a pretty penny."

The more Kate tried to follow the conversation, the more muddled it became. "Why do painters buy farms? Is it a tradition?"

Millie started to laugh. Understanding suddenly passed through her eyes. Her expression turned to self-reproach. "'Bought the farm' means someone has passed," Millie explained, pain swimming in her tone. "I'm so woolly-headed sometimes, me going on like that. I'm sorry, sweetie. That was such an appallingly thoughtless thing for me to say."

She sipped from her cup, not raising her eyes to meet Kate's. For her part, Kate found the family's story intriguing, even if she felt detached from it as her personal history.

"How did Abby . . . I mean my mum . . . how did she meet my father?" Kate encouraged Millie to continue.

"In the portrait gallery." Millie set her cup down. "Abby didn't care two pence that Simon wasn't wealthy. She married him a few months after they met and moved to America. Our father was furious. He thought Abby was squandering the family fortune. The last time Abby came to visit, our father lost his temper. He said he wouldn't let her blemish the Paulett family name, and she had no reason to be in Britain. As I said, your mum was headstrong . . . and passionate. She never came back." Millie reached out and stroked Kate's long, wavy strands of hair with a sad smile. "That's why I didn't recognize you at the airport. I never had your mum's luck. I never found a Simon of my own, oh no. No love at first sight for this old bird." Millie dropped her hand. "Abby's story's very Shakespearean though, isn't it?"

Kate's mind fished for a card with the word 'Shakespearean' and drew another blank. "What does 'Shakespearean' mean?"

Millie's despondency dissolved into mortification. "You don't know Shakespeare? One of the greatest literary minds in English literature? The playwright who penned *Romeo and Juliet*. *Julius Caesar*. *As You Like It*. Nothing? Goodness, what do they *teach* in those American schools? Unless," Millie murmured aloud though the comment was directed to herself, "unless you did read one of the plays and simply can't recall it."

Kate didn't respond. She bit into the scone and chewed slowly. Her cheeks burned with shame and aggravation. Didn't Dr. Jordana say Kate could remember facts and what she learned in her classes? If Shakespeare was so famous, what was preventing her from pulling up his work? Kate let out a small, resigned sigh. It seemed that, at least in the short term, her conversations would be limited to asking basic questions that everyone knew the answer to or answering others' questions with the tediously repetitive, "I don't know who/what that is."

"No matter," Millie replied dismissively with a wave of her hand. "We'll remedy your lack of instruction. In fact," she added with a self-satisfied smile, "I've taken the liberty of working on the matter of your education."

The scone suddenly felt like a clump of clay in Kate's mouth. She swallowed with effort, then repeated, "My education?" School meant more strangers. More references she wouldn't understand. Fear of humiliation fluttered in Kate's stomach. To her dismay, the feeling was viscerally familiar. Had Kate been embarrassed in her classes before? Was she not as smart as her peers?

"You needn't be so worried, dear," Millie told her. She removed a blueberry muffin from the platter. Cutting it neatly with her fork, Millie commented, "I was told before you came you remembered your studies in America. That said, I wouldn't plop you into a British school. Not without ensuring you had the same educational foundation as the other students. It's clear the pedagogy in America is woefully deficient if Shakespeare was neglected." Millie's tone of disapproval was accompanied by an expression of disbelief. She popped a piece of muffin into her mouth. "Scrumptious! Anyhow, I've arranged for you to have private tutelage instead."

Kate felt a glimmer of hope. "I'm not going to be in school then?"

"Not at first. I have hand selected tutors to cover subjects you will need. Math, history, literature, science, logic, those sorts of things. We'll also take cultural excursions, you and I. The Globe Theater, museums, galleries, festivals, shows. Oh, the fun we'll have together!" She chortled, crumbs decorating her lips. "Makes me feel like a little girl on an Easter egg hunt."

Millie's words triggered relief and gratitude in Kate. If she had struggled in the past, it was better to do so away from the eyes of strangers. "Thank you, Millie," Kate replied sincerely. "I'd like that."

"Aunt Millie, sweetie. Call me Aunt Millie. I am your aunt after all."

Kate hesitated. Millie held her fork in the air, waiting with a shy yet expectant look. "Yes, Aunt Millie," Kate said. The words stuck to the roof of her mouth. Was Millie her aunt?

Millie beamed, seeming blissfully unaware of Kate's discomfort. She popped another chunk of muffin into her mouth. When she was finished eating, she said, "Tomorrow, we'll go shopping. Hand-me-downs won't do. You need some proper outfits. They'll be a bit dear, since you've a full wardrobe that needs replacing, but you're my niece. If the Queen can fuss over a few Corgis, I'm well allowed to spoil you." Millie stood, leaving her serviette on the table, and scooped up Kate's plate. "If you're finished, we'll head to your room."

As Millie brought the dishes to the sink, Kate retrieved her suitcase from the living room. She lugged the suitcase up the winding staircase. The air was laced with the pungent smell of wood polish. Kate sneezed. Millie's perfume soon eclipsed the scent of the polish as she joined Kate.

"Now, the water closet is there." Millie pointed to a closed door on the right. "That's my room back there." She indicated a door ajar before them. "And yours is over here." Millie stepped inside a room on her left. Flicking on the light switch, she remarked, "I tidied up today, hoovered and polished and such. Goodness knows the room needed it. I found a litter of dust bunnies under the bed. I never had many guests." Her eyes sparkled as she looked at Kate. "But I have *you* now, dearie, and that's all I need!"

Kate entered, dragging the suitcase behind her. The scent of polish was as potent inside. Wrinkling her nose, Kate's eyes circled the room. It was small enough that she wasn't drowning in space and large enough that she didn't feel stuffed in a cubby. The room was tastefully adorned with a closet, a bed with a downy patchwork quilt, a nightstand, and a small desk. Two casement windows adjacent to the bed had yellow curtains, which were drawn back to allow in subdued rays of sunshine escaping the gray sky. A plush chair was beneath them. A pair of paintings of rural scenes decked the walls.

Kate's gaze found a stone mantel situated above a fireplace. Picture frames and ceramic collectables competed for space. One blue and white glass figurine caught her eye. Leaving her suitcase at the door, Kate walked to it. The rodent-like animal's head was raised. The glass netted every ray of light in the room, creating the illusion that the animal's whiskers were twitching. Its beady eyes seemed to follow Kate as she stepped closer.

Kate turned to Millie in wonderment. "Where did you get this statue, Aunt Millie?"

"Which statue, sweetie?"

"The blue and white one."

"Oh, I've had that since I was a girl," Millie replied cheerfully. She walked to the mantel and fondly stroked the back of the glass. The light seemed to ripple like water under Millie's fingers. "It's from a family friend, Martin Viscarl. The Pauletts have been acquainted with the Viscarls for generations. Carvings are the Viscarls' business, you see, passed down father to son. It's been a tradition that a Viscarl gives a Paulett a glass figurine for his or her fifth birthday. Each one's unique. This one here is mine. They say the most peculiar thing though, the Viscarls. The one receiving the gift is the only one allowed to touch it. And they're strict about it. Made my grandfather promise when he got his statue, then Abby with hers, then me with mine." Millie tapped her lips thoughtfully. "It's probably an old man's superstition, but a promise is a promise. The statue's been on the mantel ever since. Not a flaw in it, so far as I can tell." Millie patted the creature's back. "It's my favorite piece. Wouldn't trade it for the Hope Diamond if someone offered."

Kate studied the figurine again. She was curiously drawn to the creature. Its ears were small and flat against its head, and it had a nub for a tail. Her repertoire of animal names failed as she tried to pull up one for the rodent. "What kind of animal is it? I'm sure I've seen one before."

Millie chuckled. "Only in your studies then, dear. It's called a pika. There are loads high up in the mountains like the Himalayas, not in the British hills. Mr. Dullwane—he's your history and geography tutor—he'll have maps to teach you about these places."

Kate nodded. *A pika.* She added the name to her mental log.

"Do you like it?" Millie asked earnestly.

"Yes, I just wish I could see one in real life. It looks so real."

"No, no, sweetie. Not the figurine, the room. How do you find your new home?"

"Oh. The room." Kate took a step back from the mantel, a pit forming in her stomach. No matter how hard she tried, Kate couldn't dispel the feeling that the room belonged to a stranger. Not her. As Kate turned to answer, she saw Millie's hands clasped together. Millie rocked up on her toes and back, eyes innocently questioning.

Kate arranged her features into as genuine a smile as she could muster. "Everything is wonderful, especially the quilt and the figurines. Thank you for letting me stay here. Aunt Millie," she inserted quickly.

Delight shone on Millie's face. "Of *course,* you would stay here, dearie! I would never let my niece be anywhere other than home with her family." Millie hastened through the room to double-check everything was in order. She unnecessarily plumped the pillows on the bed. "You can take a nap if you'd like. I'll be downstairs. Have to ring the tutors now that you're here." Completing her round, Millie pulled Kate into a bear hug. "Oh, sweetie," she said in a thick voice as Kate involuntarily inhaled an even thicker floral perfume. "We'll have a grand time. I promise."

Millie released Kate and swept out the door. The knob clicked quietly behind her.

Kate stared at the door for a moment. The aroma of wood polish smothered the air. Kate strode to the window and threw it open. Her lungs drank in the cold, fresh air. Kate walked back to her suitcase and rolled it into the closet. She unzipped the front pocket. The heptagon coin that she had found in Chicago was tucked away behind her cloak. A yawn escaped her. She crossed the room to her nightstand and put the coin inside the drawer. Then Kyra moved to the window. She turned the plush chair beneath it sideways. Kate knelt on the cushion, leaning with her elbows on the windowsill. Alder and maple trees snuggled together in the backyard. Clouds linked together in an endless, gray chain. Except for the cheeping of birds and an occasional chirping of squirrels, it was quiet. So, so quiet.

Kate rested her chin on her palm. A sob came to her lips. The levees Kate had built in her mind against her emotions burst open in a hurricane of suppressed anguish, anger, and fatigue. She moved from the chair to her bed and lay on top of the quilt. She was here, in her new life. Her identity was as much a mystery after meeting her aunt as it had been the day of the fire. Despite Dr. Jordana's reassurance, Kate wasn't sure that feeling, being lost to herself, would ever go away. Kate hugged one of the pillows closer. Her shoulders shook, tears silently streaming down her cheeks.

Chapter 3

Far beyond the small bed occupied by the distraught girl, beyond Hampstead and across the outskirts of London, flung outside the confines of the United Kingdom and into the world, there was a scar in the ether. It couldn't be seen. It could, possibly, be remembered by the few who had witnessed its existence.

The lack of certitude was problematic for Diamantas. It was not a feeling to which he was accustomed, and it had burrowed deeply into his conscious. Diamantas' anger burned as brightly as the white light flaring from his staff. He stood for a moment in the cool, stone passageway. He abruptly rammed the hard ground. The loud bang of the staff echoed off the bare, tight walls that surrounded him. The translucent white barrier that stretched from the floor to the cave's ceiling sucked in the sound.

Behind the magicked wall was the grainy outline of a rail-thin prisoner. He folded his arms. "I was of the impression that the point of a barrier was to prevent anything from passing through it," his hoarse yet amused voice remarked. "If you wish to hold a conversation under a charade of civility, it would be better to remove this obstruction, would it not?"

Diamantas' eyes narrowed waspishly. "I have no such wish."

"I expected as much. Your tongue is not so silver as to convince another of such pretense."

Diamantas willed himself to ignore the provocation. He had to focus on the issue at hand. Kyra. He blamed himself, at least in part, for the predicament. Diamantas hadn't foreseen what would happen to the rift after he had thrown a spell into it. He wanted to stop Kyra. How could he have predicted the girl would simply vanish? Diamantas rapped the staff on the ground. Kyra had caught him off guard with her display of red magic. Magic she did not understand, could not control, and that was potentially powerful enough to destroy them both.

If the prophecy were correct.

The white light from Diamantas' staff tossed shadows over his brooding expression. He hadn't even been able to accomplish what he had set out to do. Gyre was freed from Diamantas' influence. Recker was injured. Schirmeera had advanced on him. The spell to rip asunder the Aurielle Sea failed.

"Some mark should have remained in the sky," he muttered to himself. "How did Schirmeera so cleverly hide it?" Diamantas quelled the desire to revisit the site. If two days of searching had provided no clues, he had to pursue new avenues to obtain the vital information. Diamantas' thoughts went to his followers. They were assembled nearby in the great chamber awaiting his news. Some wizards would quickly lose faith if Diamantas revealed his own misgivings.

"I cannot believe that in all your studies you did not happen upon accounts of magical rifts," Diamantas now addressed the prisoner in a measured tone.

The thin figure shrugged. "If there are no accounts, I couldn't have happened upon them, could I?"

If only I could better see his face, Diamantas thought. *I would be more certain if he speaks with cunning falsities or is offering the truth.* The barrier was inconvenient. Necessary, but inconvenient, since Diamantas couldn't see any more clearly outside the makeshift cell as the person within it.

"You scribes are repositories of all knowledge pertaining to Ilian. I am sure this is not a unique situation in the thousand-year history of these lands." Diamantas automatically dropped his voice to a lower pitch even though he was alone with the prisoner. "You were also among the few elite scribes dedicated to studying magical affairs. That makes you singularly positioned to provide the information I need."

"You may have noticed I haven't been in Ilian for some time." The figure gestured vaguely to the cell. "Inishmore wishes for you to release me if you want me to attain this magical enlightenment."

Diamantas tilted the staff toward the barrier. "Or Inishmore wishes me to make life very unpleasant for you. That would provide you inspiration to speak."

The figure laughed dryly. "Life is sufficiently unpleasant, thank you. The stew is gamey and lacks flavor. I would advise you fire your cook lest you are poisoned by spoiled meat." The prisoner's chest was suddenly wracked by coughs. He doubled over, gasping. Diamantas watched emotionlessly.

When wizards were first exiled to the Southern Mountains, they discovered concave spaces like pockmarks that marred the otherwise smooth rock. They made ideal cells for individuals unwilling to abide by Harkimer's rules. Historically, Harkimer's wizards were rarely incarcerated. Punishment for crimes was always swift and routinely deadly. To be placed in a cell and not at the edge of a cliff was comparatively benign.

The contours of Diamantas' face were highlighted with cruelty born of one used to getting his way. "Your callousness toward Kyra's disappearance is mystifying. You speak of Inishmore. Yet you are either ignorant of or choose to ignore the warnings that affect us all. The number seven, Inishmore's celestial number, has indicated times of great importance." Diamantas turned and paced in front of the magical wall. "Inishmore bestowed seven blessings on the first seven founders of Ilian. Six kingdoms were founded in Ilian, were one to include the coastal villages. Harkimer became the seventh kingdom. And it was on the seventh day of the seventh month all those years ago that the seers made their prophecy." He paused and stared at the white shield. The prisoner's outline was rigid. "A girl would unwittingly alter the future of Ilian. Do you doubt she will bring the 'deliverance or destruction' they claim?"

Diamantas didn't seem to expect a response from the prisoner. He resumed pacing. "This year marks seven hundred and seventy-six years since the wizards were banished to these divinely accursed mountains. Kyra will be sixteen next year. She will be of age as a wizard in the seven hundred and seventy-seventh year of our imprisonment. Is this mere coincidence? Do you believe Inishmore leaves matters of such gravity as a people's survival to chance? No, you do not. That is why you should be equally motivated to find the girl before she achieves her full potential and threatens the fabric of our existence."

"The only threat I see is standing before me. That is, as well as one can see behind this wall," the scribe replied coldly. He dropped his arms to his sides and walked closer to the barrier. "At least speak plainly. Your vision is for the dark wizards to rule Ilian, not to create lasting peace. You have planned for war for years. It must be frustrating that despite your machinations, Kyra remains a variable you can't control. Shame. I will not help you find a girl who has done nothing wrong."

Diamantas slammed his staff on the ground. White magic exploded into the earth, cracking it down the center. Chips of stone flaked off the walls and fell around Diamantas like snow, but he didn't seem to notice. His gaze was as hard as quartz. "If three years in this cell has failed to loosen your tongue, I have other means at my disposal to do so. You will be more forthcoming in our next exchange."

"If the repast remains so unappetizing, my conversation will likely devolve to that of a child. How can I recall tales and legends when my energy is devoted to survival?"

Diamantas thrust his staff in the shield and twisted it. The scribe cried out as magical needles sprayed from the wall. Throwing himself reflexively against the corner of the cell, the scribe covered his face with his arms. The sharp projectiles laced his back, neck, and legs. Diamantas grinned maliciously.

Painfully, the scribe rose. "You lose control when you must justify your failure to the assembly."

The smile was wiped from Diamantas' face. He pivoted on his heel wordlessly. Diamantas' staff clacked against the ground as he stormed down the corridor. The light from the staff grew faint.

The scribe watched Diamantas turn the corner. As darkness descended on him, the scribe's face fell. His sunken cheeks revealed the strain of his imprisonment. A new fit of coughs drove him to his knees. Taking labored breaths, he raised a quivering hand. A green wisp of magic trailed upward from his palm. The scribe directed it unsteadily over his abrasions. He winced as the cuts began to close.

Secretly, the scribe was distressed by Diamantas' news. Where had Kyra been sent? Had she endured the journey through the rupture in the air? "Yes, you coward," the scribe murmured. "There are accounts of such events." *One account*, the scribe noted silently. A disheartening report of an elf disappearing, then returning to Ilian with no memory of the land or his history within it. The elf couldn't even recall his name.

The scribe felt his magic ebbing. He couldn't begin to guess at Kyra's fate. He had to trust Inishmore to watch over her. *May Inishmore guide you back to us, my young friend,* he thought as spots appeared in his vision. The scribe collapsed facedown, surrendering to blessed unconsciousness.

***

"Well? Did he have anything useful to say?" a young female wizard with spiked, red hair demanded. She leaned forward on the cold stone table. Her cloak sleeves were rolled back, revealing tanned skin. "Or did he speak in his usual meaningless circles?"

Twelve other pairs of eyes turned toward Diamantas, who stood impassively behind a chair on the opposite end of the rectangular table. Modeled after that of the Wizards' High Council, the table was the centerpiece of the large chamber. The room was an unadorned, hollowed-out space with a magicked ceiling that prevented water from dripping from the massive stalactites overhead. The air carried a damp scent from the two passages leading into the chamber. The wizards' staffs rested against the rounded walls. Magic from the staffs' tips created a kaleidoscope of light around them.

Diamantas kept his staff in hand as his eyes panned the room. He struck a more impressive figure standing at the head of the table. It compelled the others to look up at him, a reinforcement of his status as their undisputed leader. All assembly members were present: seven senior members, including himself, and seven junior members. They maintained the celestial number. It was a good omen.

Diamantas had left the prisoner's cell in aggravation. On his way to the chamber, however, he dressed his expression with composure and confidence. The assembly was not a place to show weakness of character.

"The scribe offered nothing of worth, Elanaras," Diamantas replied evenly. "His expertise on previous incidents is less than one would hope. However, scribes are artful fabricators of information or ignorance as it suits them. I am unconvinced the spell that removed Kyra is the first of its kind."

"Clearly, he was lying," another wizard sneered. Large ears protruded from his oval face as though there had not been enough room to fit them. "I can cast the spell of truth to coerce the scribe to speak. Let me go to him now, Diamantas. No one is more capable of getting answers for you than I am."

A female wizard with pencil-straight, onyx-colored hair and full ruby red lips threw a scathing look at the speaker. "Are you really so arrogant as to think that you can accomplish what Diamantas has not, Adakis?" she hissed. "Diamantas has considered other options to gain that information. Don't delude yourself into thinking any of us isn't more—*considerably* more—capable than you."

Adakis didn't look the least bit chagrined. "I'm experienced in prying open secrets from the tightest-lipped prisoners. See if I am wrong. Diamantas, allow me a few hours with the scribe."

"The effectiveness of such methods is questionable," Diamantas responded calmly, "and the information produced is therefore not always something on which we can rely. However, if I determine it is necessary to use more . . . direct methods, I will do so."

Adakis' affronted look didn't go unnoticed by Diamantas. Adakis remained silent, though. He ran a hand down his goatee, where the hair tapered to a perfect point.

"And for the moment you have determined other means are not necessary?" challenged a wizard, who pushed back his chair and stood awkwardly. His left shoulder sagged, as did his left eye, but the other expressed enough contempt for both. "Our greatest menace—or ally—is unaccounted for. You're the only one among us who beheld Kyra's final moments in Ilian. You claimed a dragon spelled her into some chasm in the sky, yet what evidence exists to support your assertion?"

Syndrominous, Diamantas thought as the wizard's single-eyed gaze ranged over the assembly members. *You are ever so predictable.* He had counted on his rival to attempt to discredit him in front of their peers. Lilias had spoken more truly than she knew; Diamantas had intentionally excluded information about his battle to draw Syndrominous into a confrontation. His rival would entrap himself with his proclamations.

Syndrominous raised his voice as though he were an actor making a dramatic entreaty to his audience. "Diamantas has a staff with powers beyond any of our own, and he had a dragon for an ally. Despite this, he couldn't trap a girl who is not yet of age. He couldn't begin our conquest of Ilian. Now," he said, directing his words to Diamantas, "instead of scouring the area in which this supposed disappearance occurred, you waste your time with the scribe. It is inexcusable."

"I agree, Syndrominous, it is a terrible situation," Diamantas replied, offering him a polite nod. "Like everyone here, I am flawed. Inishmore grants us the ability to make progress, not perfection. I am a humble servant of the wizards of Harkimer. I have taken the mantle of responsibility not for my own ambition but to see our shared goal through. To be liberated from these shadows."

Diamantas was silently pleased to see the wizards murmuring and nodding in agreement. His manipulation of Syndrominous' words was securing loyalty from the assembly members.

"I would gladly relinquish the responsibility to a worthier wizard," Diamantas resumed. He laid the obsidian staff lengthwise over the table. "The staff is yours if you choose to accept it."

Syndrominous' good eye focused on the obsidian. Then it turned upward to Diamantas. A cold expression hung from Syndrominous' long face like an icicle, from his pompadour hair down to the end of his voluminous beard. "You know I can't take it. None of us can touch the staff."

"No, you cannot. As your current condition has proven." Diamantas withdrew the staff and again held it at his side. "Your act to steal the staff has been long forgiven, Syndrominous. I only regret that I was not present when you tried to move it. I might have spared you this suffering."

Diamantas' reminder to the group that his rival had tried to thieve the staff achieved its purpose. Most of the assembly members didn't bother hiding their scorn for Syndrominous. Diamantas knocked his last verbal arrow and fired.

"You have correctly observed, however, that the site of Kyra's disappearance needs a thorough examination. I entrust this task to you, Syndrominous. I expect it will take some weeks to exhaust the spells that could reveal what magic cleaved the sky. With your skill and expertise, I have no doubt you will detect something I could not."

Diamantas paused. Syndrominous had stiffened. He knew, as clearly as Diamantas did, that he had been outmaneuvered. The wizards were united in their admiration for Diamantas and contempt for Syndrominous. Syndrominous was now sentenced to weeks of onerous work without the aid of any of the assembly members. Work that he had suggested.

Syndrominous tilted his head and took his seat. "Thank you for your confidence," he said tersely.

Diamantas centered his attention back on the room, waiting for other detractors. No one spoke against him. "Is there any other counsel from our members?" he asked the group graciously.

"Solarus brought Kyra to the Wizards' High Council," a female voice commented in a mild tone bordering on boredom. Her curly ink-black hair was combed to the side and hung down her cheek, narrowing at her lip. "I saw her at the last session. As much of a traitor as Solarus is, one of us should approach him about the matter. We have common interests."

Diamantas' brow furrowed. "Solarus may be amenable to working with us," he replied at length. "Reach out to him, Nymphrys. Tetris will accompany you." Diamantas cast a look at a wizard with light gray eyes.

Tetris inclined his head in acceptance. Diamantas felt a small sense of relief. Convincing Solarus of anything would require his best negotiators. Tetris comported himself with dignity and maintained a level-headed approach to the thorniest of issues. Nymphrys frequently displayed disinterest in the assembly's deliberations—as she did now, running her finger along a white earring that curved around her ear to her lobe. Beneath the moodiness, Diamantas knew Nymphrys to be as sensible as Tetris.

"What about the dragons?" a twiggy boy burst in. His ginger-colored hair was parted, and he had an angst-ridden expression on his round face. "The dragon helping you, would he share any dragon spells? Could he use them to reopen the tear? Could you pass through it and look for Kyra? Maybe . . ."

Lilias rolled her eyes. Syndrominous grumbled under his breath and crossed his right arm over his left. Tetris' expression was thoughtful.

"Astute questions, Janus," Diamantas praised, ignoring the other wizards. Secretly, he wished his nephew had kept silent. Janus had inherited neither the perceptive judgment of his father nor the strategic patience of his mother. Diamantas had secured a place for the boy as a junior assembly member. It was one of the few actions in which Diamantas openly ruffled the other members. "Unfortunately, Recker seemed as stunned by the spell as I did. I did not have time to confer with him. I was defending myself against the combined power of the other two dragons. Finding another dragon to be of assistance would be a difficult task. They are reclusive creatures and not inclined to aid wizards. It took several months for me to ascertain which dragons were willing to fight alongside us. Recker has sealed himself far within the Mountains. While your suggestion is a good one," Diamantas added, seeing Janus' crestfallen expression, "it would take more time to seek him out than we are afforded. We must look to other sources to aid our informants in Silvias."

"There aren't other sources," Elanaras interjected impatiently.

"There is one."

Diamantas turned toward the speaker. Tetris sat with his hands folded, gray eyes contemplative. "Kyra would not have reached the Mountains without a steed," Tetris continued. "One can assume she planned on departing the Mountains in the same fashion."

Diamantas unconsciously pressed his palm against the chair in front of him. How could he have missed such an obvious solution? "Tetris is right. The horse would have fled once Kyra disappeared. His trail is one we can easily find. Syndrominous, look for signs of the steed in your inspection," Diamantas instructed. Syndrominous replied with a brusque nod though his eyes housed disdain. "Hanorus, Nehas, and Elanaras. You will ride west. Search for the steed. Adakis, Galakis, and Pallinas. You will search the east with the same goal. Nymphrys, Tetris, seek out Solarus. Lilias, Omarus, Janus, and I will travel to the Ancient Forest through Edoin Forest. If anyone finds the horse, send a rider to me. Kyounas and Zeinas, you will remain in Harkimer. You are in charge in my absence. We will reconvene in three weeks." Diamantas' words were charged with confidence. "We *will* succeed."

The meeting was adjourned. The wizards rose and collected their staffs from the wall. As they filed out of the chamber, Diamantas beckoned subtly to Janus. The boy shot a questioning glance toward Tetris. A frown creased Tetris' lips, gray eyes troubled. He gave Janus a slight nod and followed Elanaras to the corridor.

Janus turned and shuffled toward Diamantas. "Ow!" the boy yelped suddenly.

Adakis had elbowed Janus as he passed. Adakis smirked as the boy rubbed his side. At a glower from Diamantas, Adakis marched out after the other assembly members.

"You did well, nephew," Diamantas told the boy, placing a firm hand on his shoulder. Janus' cognac-colored gaze was on the shiny stone floor. "It is not easy being the youngest in this assembly, particularly as you have just come of age. You have immense worth, both to me and our brethren. Do not waste your energy on those too small-minded to notice."

Janus nodded mutely. He scuffed the ground with his boot. Diamantas hoped the boy had the trappings of a leader buried beneath his insecurity.

"One day, nephew, you will have the power to dispose of those who disparage you."

Janus' head jerked up. "How, Uncle?"

Diamantas' blue eyes held a calculating look. "You will possess a weapon whose powers surpass those of the obsidian staff. I search for it even now. When you have it, you will answer to no one." His grip on Janus' shoulder tightened. "First allow us to see what opportunity presents itself in our mission. If nothing else, Adakis was correct about the scribe. We have ways to persuade him to be more forthcoming."

Janus blanched. Diamantas, however, was smiling as he steered his nephew out of the chamber. Another phase of his plan was complete.

Chapter 4

When Kate awoke, she was surprised to discover night had fallen. Her cheeks were caked with salt from her tears, and her throat was parched. Sitting upright, Kate saw a pair of plum-colored fleece pajamas and slippers folded at the end of her bed. Her window had been closed. A candle on her desk scented the air with a smell of fresh linen, its gentle flame illuminating the corner wall of the otherwise dark room.

When did Millie come in? Kate wondered. Rising quietly, she changed into the pajamas and slid on the warm slippers. She walked to her closet and placed her clothes atop her suitcase. Then Kate walked to her door, opened it, and looked around. The master bedroom door was shut. The tick-tock of the grandfather clock had gone silent.

Kate tiptoed to the bathroom. Her slippers muted her steps. She splashed cool water on her hands and washed her face clean of tears. Glancing in the mirror above the washbasin, Kate saw her eyelids were swollen. "I look almost as good as I feel," she joked dryly to herself. Kate filled one of the paper cups next to the basin and took it with her to her room.

Kate moved back to the window, cup in hand. Questions drifted untethered through her mind. She was starting a new life, in this place, with no memories and no plans other than to start her lessons. And discover the cause of the fire. Dread sank like a stone in Kate's stomach. She didn't know which task scared her more.

Kate gulped down the water and set the cup on the desk. With a sigh, she peered out the window. The day's gray gloom had become a beautiful white night. Snowflakes danced lightly from the sky. The trees and earth were dusted with sparkling white crystals. Kate's breath fogged the glass as she looked from side to side. The scene was beautiful, even as it evoked feelings of melancholy. Exactly like the pika figurine.

Kate turned unconsciously at the thought. The blue and white statue rested on the mantel, head cocked to the side. Kate left the window. The pika's eyes seemed bright, as though it were scrutinizing her. Goose bumps pricked Kate's skin. *Wasn't the pika facing the door earlier? How could its head have moved?*

It didn't, Kate answered her own question, though her pulse quickened. *It's a statue.* It looked even more lifelike. Kate wondered that if she touched its back, she would feel the rodent's soft pelt.

Feeling unsettled by the pika, Kate's gaze strayed to a picture frame. She hadn't paid the frame any attention earlier. Now she lifted it curiously from the mantel. The frame held a sepia photo of a handsome couple sitting together on a bench. The man sported a suit jacket with striped pants, while the woman wore a sundress. In her lap was a girl with a broad smile that revealed a missing front tooth. An older girl stood behind the man, long, blond ringlets of hair falling freely over her shoulders and down her back. Even then, Millie's features were unmistakable. Kate held the picture more closely to her face. Kate hadn't inherited the blond locks of her aunt, and the little girl she guessed was Abby hadn't a single wave in her short, dark hair. Kate's grandparents' eyes were round, not almond-shaped like her own. Her heart thudded in her chest as she returned the frame to its place on the mantel. She didn't bear any resemblance to her family.

My mum's family, Kate reminded herself. She needed to see pictures of her father. Or did she? A chill went through her. What if Kate didn't look like Simon either? Kate returned to her bed, rubbing an arm for warmth. She hadn't given up the core question of her identity. Was she Kate Smith? Or was another couple frantically looking for their missing daughter?

Kate lifted the rumpled quilt and fanned it over the bed. She plopped down on it. "I'm looking for excuses to be someone else," she muttered to herself. "I don't want to be Kate Smith. I want my parents to be alive." Dr. Jordana's words suddenly rang clearly in her mind. Kate had to accept what had happened in order to move on. She had hoped the police were mistaken. She wanted the pictures to confirm she wasn't a Smith. When Kate lay down again, she silently wished her memories would return and bridge her past to her uncertain future.

***

After a few hours of fitful sleep, Kate rose. Dawn's dim light sprinkled through her window. She changed into her outfit from the previous day. She quietly opened her door so as to not wake Millie. To her surprise, Kate heard the sound of water running and the chinking of cups. She walked to the top of the stairwell. The warm smell of toast and eggs mingled with an acrid and oddly familiar scent.

Kate's pulse quickened. She squeezed the banister as the pungent scent catapulted her into a conversation.

"You won't like it any more than the last time." It was a man's amused voice.

"I'm freezing, and we're out of tea. I just want a sip, Hayden, really. Maybe I'll like it better this time."

Kate covered her mouth with her free hand. It was *her* voice.

"I'll wager Talis ten gold florins that you won't."

"I'm not accepting that bet. I would make the same wager against you." Another man's voice, this one smoother and musical.

An image flashed through Kate's mind's eye. She watched a younger version of herself hold a steaming mug to her lips with gloved hands, face highlighted by the flames of a campfire and sip. The younger Kate swirled the drink in her mouth. And spat it out onto the grass. She handed the mug back to someone across from her.

"It's because it's hazelnut. You shouldn't put nuts in coffee."

The men's laughter followed Kate as she blinked. The image flashed away, leaving only the banister before her. Kate felt her fingers cramp. She eased her white-knuckled grip on the banister and flex her fingers. Kate strained to remember more, but the scene had flittered away as quickly as it had appeared. Her heart skipped a beat in its excitement. *A memory!* It was short, fleeting, and lacking anything of substance, yet it was a memory. Who were the men? When was she at a campfire?

The thoughts kept Kate company as she walked into the kitchen. A hearty breakfast had already been set on the table, along with silverware and serviettes. Millie bustled about, setting mugs steaming with the bitter fragrance in front of two place mats. Her hair was up in curlers, still damp from the shower. She glanced up as Kate approached.

"Good morning, dearie," Millie said merrily. "You're up early. I like being out and about in the morn, right when the birds begin to cheep and chirp. Get a jump on the day before it gets a jump on you, I like to say. Did you sleep well?"

Kate's reply was cut off by the grandfather clock's loud gonging. It stopped after announcing the seventh hour. Millie gestured for Kate to sit. "I called the tutors yesterday," Millie continued as though she had forgotten asking Kate a question. Tucking her skirt beneath her, Millie took a place beside Kate. She pushed a plate of the toast and scrambled eggs toward Kate. "Eat up, dearie. You can't fill an empty mind on an empty stomach."

Kate accepted a couple slices of toast and spooned eggs onto her plate.

"What was I saying?" Millie asked as Kate tucked into the meal. "Oh yes, the tutors. Lessons start next week. That gives us plenty of time to get you oriented with the city. I have a full itinerary for us, starting with the museums and ending with a visit to Buckingham Palace. Drop by and see the queen if she's in. Do you drink coffee, dearie?" she questioned, abruptly changing topics. Millie dolloped liberal amounts of sugar and cream into her mug. "I didn't make tea this morning. I thought you might like some coffee instead. The hazelnut is one of my favorite brews. It was your mum's too."

Hazelnut. Just like the conversation. Kate added sugar and cream to her cup as Millie had done, even more curious about who the men were in the memory. Kate lifted the mug experimentally, then took a tentative sip. Her eyes lit up. The drink was rich and creamy.

"It's delicious," Kate replied. She allowed the taste to linger on her tongue, unsure of how to pose the next question. "Aunt Millie, did my parents like being outdoors? Around a campfire, maybe in the winter?"

Millie laughed good-naturedly. "Oh goodness no, not at all. Abby wasn't fond of insects. Couldn't even touch a ladybird. The sole time she went outside was during our Sunday picnics. Abby liked to say there was no reason to bed down in dirt with creepy, crawly things and sweat in the heat or freeze in the cold. Not if you could rest in a soft bed." Millie wiped a smudge of jam from her lips. "As for Simon, well, gosh dearie, we never spent much time together. He might have camped overnight a time or two. Not sure he ever convinced Abby to join him."

Kate bit her lip. One of the men could have been her father then.

"Why do you ask anyhow, sweetie? Do you remember camping?"

"No, I was just wondering." Kate sealed a smile on her face and focused on her food. It was a strange question to ask, and Millie probably would want a more complete explanation. For some reason, Kate didn't want to share the spark of memory she had had. It was too personal and too vague.

Fortunately, Millie didn't press the issue. Instead, she recounted anecdotes from Abby's and her childhood, animatedly gesturing and chortling as she went. The tales didn't stir up any feelings of longing from Kate, but Millie's vivacious narrations made the hour pass quickly. They finished and cleared the table. Millie wrapped Kate up in a thick scarf, beret, and leather gloves. "Like I said yesterday, you are a stunning young woman," Millie remarked as Kate buttoned up her peacoat. "Let's be off. The train comes at quarter past the hour."

Millie briskly led the way to the Hampstead Tube station. She expertly wove her way down the stairs, squat heels clunking on the cement, with Kate in tow. Brandishing their fare cards, Millie ushered Kate through the gate and down to the platform. They arrived early. Millie used the time to show Kate a map of London's underground railway. Intrigued, Kate studied the layout of lines and routes as Millie pointed out the key stations. When they left the map, Kate found to her surprise—and pride—that the map's details were still sketched in her mind. She had retained at least one useful skill.

Millie looked through her purse as Kate stared down the dark tunnel. A feeling of unease swept through her as she heard a faint rumbling. It rose to a growl, then lifted to a monstrous roar. The ground beneath Kate's feet quaked. Light began to fill the dark space. Kate's eyes widened in consternation. Yellow flames suddenly burst into the narrow passage in which she and Millie stood. A man's voice boomed, his words indistinguishable, followed by a blazing white light that illuminated the entire station.

Kate wanted to run, but her legs wouldn't move. Panicked, she glanced at Millie. Her aunt was swinging her purse, looking in the opposite direction, exquisitely oblivious to Kate's fear. In fact, Kate observed as she glanced at the row of passengers waiting on the platform, no one seemed worried or frantic. They were calmly checking their watches, reading newspapers, and talking on cell phones.

Bewildered, Kate turned back to the tunnel. A train charged out of the darkness, its headlight blindingly bright. There were no flames, no roars, and no man's voice. The train slowed to a stop. Doors slid open. Kate's heart drummed against her chest. Had she imagined it?

"Hurry in then, dearie," Millie said with a wave as people streamed around her, "and mind the gap." Kate stood, stunned, as her aunt stepped into the compartment. Her eyes darted left and right. It was silent. Kate sprinted into the train just before the doors slammed shut. Millie smiled, holding onto a metal handrail. "Our adventure starts," she announced.

Kate stared out the train window. Her thoughts stayed with the sights and sounds in the tunnel as the train slowly sped away.

***

Kate leaned forward on the living room couch. She nervously rolled a pen back and forth on the coffee table. She glanced at her phone beside her. It wasn't yet nine. Kate bit her lip. Silence reigned in the house apart from the reliable ticking of the grandfather clock. Millie was upstairs, readying herself for a visit to an art auction. Still toying with the pen, Kate surveyed the coffee table. Notebooks and pencils were neatly organized to her left. To her right were a kettle, tea bags, a pot of coffee, sugar, cream, and teacups for the tutors. A bouquet of golden-ray lilies on a side table filled the room with a sweet fragrance.

Kate's gaze flitted to the coffee. For the last week, she and Millie had developed a routine of drinking a cup together in the morning. This morning, though, Kate had forgone the caffeine in favor of chamomile. She was already jittery with anticipation. The coffee could wait.

The pen clinked against Kate's glass of water as she again tugged at the sleeve of her new, white sweater. True to her word, Millie had taken Kate from store to store in a whirlwind of energy. They bought dozens of outfits for various occasions. Kate had objected to the small fortune the wardrobe would cost, but Millie dismissed her concern. "Tut, tut, take it all," Millie had said firmly. "You wouldn't put a million-quid painting in a cheap frame, would you? You, dearie, are a priceless work of art. Look at this dress. The emerald brings out those gorgeous green flecks in your eyes. And these leggings, all the young women are wearing them. No, sweetie, we're buying the lot. You won't have anything less than the best."

Which is how Kate ended up with the astonishing soft cashmere sweater she now wore. Kate let go of the sleeve and took up her pen. She flicked the pen up the table, then down the table, then back up again. Her mind cartwheeled from thought to thought in time to the pen's cadence. Kate knew intuitively that she had cared what her teachers and peers thought of her. She knew she had studied hard. She could have been one of the first-rate students. Kate brightened at the thought.

Until she landed on a second, equally likely explanation, one she had turned over when she spoke with Dr. Jordana. The intense need to be accepted by her tutors could be a result of her not meeting the accomplishments of her fellow classmates. A strange feeling of rebelliousness rose as Kate tried to pull up memories of her schools. Rebelling against what? What if Kate was a thick-headed, cheeky troublemaker who earned whatever punishments thick-headed, cheeky troublemakers were given by their teachers? Kate shook her head. Star pupil or misfit, it didn't matter. Whatever she was before, Kate was getting a fresh start. Kate didn't have a reputation, save what she created for herself.

Someone rapped sharply on the door at the exact moment the grandfather clock tolled nine. Kate jumped. The pen tumbled off the table as she rose to her feet, heart knocking against her chest.

"Here she is!" Kate heard Millie exclaim from upstairs. There was a hasty footfall overhead, followed by Millie running down the stairs. "Punctual as always, that Deirdre," she said over her shoulder as she hurried past Kate.

Kate stood, nervously brushing her wavy hair from her face.

Grinning ear to ear, Millie swung the door open. Icy air gusted into the living room. "Deirdre!" Millie welcomed sunnily. "So happy to see you. Come in, come in. It's a bit brisk, isn't it?" Millie ushered a petite woman with a stern expression into the room and pulled the door closed behind her.

"Thank you, Millie," the woman replied curtly. She stepped inside, casting a gaze around the room behind her square, frameless glasses.

"Let me take your coat for you," Millie went on breathlessly. "That's better. Here is my dear niece, Kate. Kate, this is Professor O'Leary."

"Pleased to meet you," Kate said politely.

Professor O'Leary nodded as Millie placed the coat on a peg on the wall. "Likewise." Professor O'Leary wore a crisp, navy-blue skirt-suit under a knee-length coat the same color. She cradled two bulky textbooks under one arm. Her blond hair had splashes of gray and was pinned up in a compact bun that dared a strand of hair to try and free itself.

"You'll have a grand time," Millie commented from the door. She had put on a pink coat with faux fur lining the neck. Millie bent over and rummaged through her rack of purses. "I'll be back this afternoon, Kate. Your math tutor will be here at quarter past ten, then your history tutor at half twelve. Or do you have your history lesson and then math? I'm dreadful with times." Millie scooped up a leopard print purse as Professor O'Leary continued to stand near the door. "Anyhoo, you'll be finished by three. I'll be back in time for afternoon tea."

Kate also remained on her feet, awkwardly unsure of what protocol was required. Professor O'Leary's strict expression seemed sculpted into her features. Millie was finished bundling herself in her winterwear. She turned the doorknob, the cold again wisping inside. "Thank you again, Deirdre. Don't be too hard on my niece. It's her first day, after all." Millie winked, which did nothing to assuage Kate's anxiety. "Toodles!"

The door clicked shut. Professor O'Leary walked to an armchair near the coffee table. She sat stiffly. Not a crease was to be seen in her blouse or skirt. Kate resumed her place on the couch as Professor O'Leary placed the textbooks beside Kate's litter of notebooks and pencils.

"Science is a complex discipline," Professor O'Leary stated without preamble. Her words were clipped, as though she believed words referring to anything outside of the lesson were an inefficient use of their hour. "We will cover as many topics as we can in the next year. Today, we will start with biology. Where did you leave off with your other teachers?"

Kate looked at her blankly.

Professor O'Leary let out a short sigh. "Very well. We will start by defining 'biology.' Biology is the study of living organisms. This can include physical characteristics, behavioral elements, and other—" Professor O'Leary interrupted herself, her gaze critical. "Where is your pen, Miss Smith? Why aren't you writing this down?"

Kate realized she was gaping at the prim professor. She grabbed her pen from the floor and took a notebook.

Professor O'Leary nodded curtly as Kate flipped it open to the first page. "I will repeat. Biology is the study of living organisms . . ."

Kate's pen flew across the paper as Professor O'Leary lectured. She filled six pages before the clock rang, bringing an end to the lesson.

"Chapter One," Professor O'Leary said brusquely. She rose, textbook in hand. "Review it for tomorrow." Before Kate knew it, Professor O'Leary was at the door, had buttoned her coat, then departed swiftly. The door clicked shut behind her.

Kate dropped her pen. She massaged her fingers, which had cramped from the effort. Kate fervently hoped Millie's choices for tutors were not all like the stern Professor O'Leary.

Her math teacher, Mrs. Lakshmi, had a gentler approach. She wore a soft bob-cut of dark hair, and her shimmering brown eyes were rich with kindness. Kate relaxed as Mrs. Lakshmi gracefully sat in the chair. She removed a burgundy-colored jacket and draped it over the arm. Mrs. Lakshmi gifted Kate a supportive smile.

"I want you to enjoy math," she told Kate in a melodic accent. "We'll see how you learn best first, and then go from there. There's no need to rush through the problems I give you. We need to establish a good understanding of the concepts behind the equations. Otherwise, everything else will be more difficult to puzzle out. If you find you remember any of this from your previous classes, we'll move on. How does that sound?"

Kate reclined back on the couch. She couldn't stop a relieved sigh from escaping.

Another hour passed. Mrs. Lakshmi left Kate with a sunny smile and a homework assignment. As the door closed behind the tutor, Kate rested her math textbook on top of her biology one.

Her third tutor, Mr. Dullwane, arrived early. A skeleton of a man with a mop of hair and a wispy beige beard that stretched to his belly, Mr. Dullwane seemed to be pushed inside by the wind rather than moving his feet. He carried a tote bulging with books. The history tutor dropped the tote unceremoniously on the floor and sat.

"History," Mr. Dullwane said in a monotonous voice. "It is everything we know and knew. It will inform everything we predict about the future. We will begin with ancient Greece. This is the first book we will use." He removed a tome from his bag. Kate took it from him and read the cover: *Western Civilizations*. "Page One," Mr. Dullwane began, speaking so slowly as though he were falling asleep. "Greek History. The Greek era is known to have begun during the Dark Ages, which lasted from the twelfth to the ninth century B.C., B.C. standing of course for 'before Christ,' to the end of Classic Antiquity around the sixth century A.D., A.D. standing of course for 'anno Domini' . . ."

He has the personality of a potato, Kate thought as she scribbled notes. Bland, colorless in his speech, and desperately in need of spices to make his teaching more palatable. The chiming of the clock didn't come soon enough for Kate.

Mr. Dullwane took his leave, plodding out the door. Kate closed her notebook with a sigh. She wandered to the kitchen, her brain pounding. How could someone cram so much information into it in one day? Kate took a sandwich from the fridge and munched on it half-heartedly. It looked like her theory about having been a substandard student was proving to be the more accurate of the two.

Kate's logic tutor, Mr. Stevens, was more engaging than Mr. Dullwane. He was a middle-aged man with large, circular glasses that sat slightly askew on the bridge of his nose. His ankle-length turquoise coat was a strikingly handsome complement to his umber-colored skin. Mr. Stevens walked not to the armchair but instead to the couch. Surprised, Kate scooted over to make room for him. Mr. Stevens sat beside her with a grin. He bestowed thin books on Kate. "For your collection," he commented wryly, eyes roaming over the floor.

Kate grimaced as she followed his gaze. The texts, loose pieces of paper, and work assignments from the morning created an unruly pile up to her knees.

"Don't trouble yourself too much," Mr. Stevens commented tranquilly. "We won't be starting with reading just yet."

Kate added the books to the stack.

"Unlike your other subjects," Mr. Stevens continued, adjusting his glasses, "ours relies not on whether you can memorize equations or recite historical facts; it instead tests your ability to assess situations and use logic to reason your way to a rational conclusion."

"That's it?"

"More or less."

Another hour chimed, and Mr. Stevens was off. Kate's temples pulsed fiercely as she emptied a glass of water. "More or less" had translated into decidedly "more." His hour had entailed taking a hypothetical situation and leading Kate through all potential ways of dealing with it. The "what ifs" and "how abouts" taxed her mind. She wearily returned the glass, wishing for a quick end to her final lesson of the day.

The knock that came was so faint, Kate thought she had imagined it. It was accompanied a moment later by a second, slightly louder knock. Rising, Kate answered the door. A man with a mailbag slung across his shoulder stood on the other side, uncomfortably shifting from one foot to the other. His sienna-colored hair fell in layers to his chin, with short bangs that ended just short of his brows. Earmuffs fit snugly on his head, and a checkered scarf puffed out around his neck. He was shivering, despite the tan wool coat that hugged his wiry frame. Kate guessed he was only a few years older than she was.

The man's green eyes met hers timidly. "Are you Ms. Smith?" he asked quietly.

The other tutors had been so self-assured, opinionated, commanding. Kate felt a swell of compassion for the man. "Yes, I'm Kate," she replied kindly. "Are you my literature tutor?"

"Yes." The man glanced over his shoulder as a car drove past. He looked back at Kate, clutching the mailbag tightly. "My name is James Adler."

Kate opened the door wider. "Please, come in."

James stepped through the threshold, carefully wiping the soles of his shoes on the mat. He removed his jacket, his expression as timid as that of a teenage boy at his first school dance. "May I hang my coat?"

"Of course," Kate said. "I can take that for you . . ."

"No, no, it's fine, thank you." James draped his coat, scarf, and earmuffs on a peg. As he turned, he inhaled deeply. An indecipherable look entered his green eyes. James' gaze wandered the room as Kate motioned for him to follow her.

Clutching his mailbag, James walked in as though entranced. "Those flowers," he said as he paused in front of the armchair. "Are those *Lilium auratum*? That is, are they golden-ray lilies?"

Kate glanced in the direction of the kitchen. *Lilium auratum*. "Yes," Kate was surprised to hear herself answering. "Robert, a neighbor who lives down the street, brought them over yesterday for Millie when she was at an art auction."

James' eyes held a preoccupied look, but excitement had sparked within Kate. Millie had gushed over the flowers when she found them on the kitchen countertop. Her cheeks flushed with the same bright pink as the roses in the bouquet. ("What a gentleman, that Robert!" she had exclaimed in delight.) Millie had never named the flowers in the bunch. That meant Kate had learned about the lilies somewhere else. It was another sign that her knowledge wasn't lost. It was locked away. All she needed was the key.

Grinning, Kate returned her attention to James. Her happiness dissolved. Grief was pressed along every plane of his face and in his green eyes. "My sister's favorite flowers were golden-ray lilies," he said softly.

Kate watched James as he turned away from the kitchen and unslung his mailbag in silence. Her heart ached with sympathy. His sister's favorite flowers "were" . . . It was clear from James' sorrowful expression that he had lost his sister. Millie's expression was identical when she spoke about Abby. What had happened? James was young, which meant his sister had been young as well? Had she been ill? Suffered some other tragedy? Kate felt the urge to ask about her. How James had coped with the pain. He might be able to help Kate with hers. But Kate held back. It was an intimate question. Kate wouldn't intrude on the private life of James any more than she wanted others to intrude on hers. Still, the insight opened Kate up to James in a way that she hadn't been able to with anyone else.

"Robert said the flowers livened up the house," Kate commented now, trying to inject cheerfulness into her tone. "He said the kitchen needed a bit of color if it wanted to keep up with the other rooms."

James' gaze moved to the profusion of paintings adorning the walls. The corner of his lips twitched into a smile at the joke. As Kate sat back on the couch, James extracted two sets of books from his bag. He stacked them neatly on the table. Then he took his place in the armchair. He fished out a water bottle from his mailbag and set both items beside his feet.

"Are you an instructor at one of the universities?" Kate asked.

James' cheeks reddened. "No, I'm a student in my third year. I attend University College London. My specialization is world literature." James reached out to the teacups and saucers, which after the day's lessons were in a disorderly group. Kate was puzzled as James began arranging the saucers in a straight line.

Kate waited for the silence to coax him to elaborate. When it was clear James wouldn't continue, she nudged, "Where did you meet Aunt Millie?"

"At the university. Mildred—Millie—had originally asked one of my professors to help you. He is far more qualified. Unfortunately, he is on sabbatical. My professor recommended that Millie interview me for the position. We spoke about three weeks back. She thought I would be a good fit for you. And, well, I'm here now."

The red in James' cheeks spread to his ears and neck. He was clearly embarrassed by the obviousness of the statement. His fingers moved over the saucers, which were now perfectly aligned. James began turning the teacups so their handles faced him. "Millie mentioned you had not read Shakespeare?"

Kate's neck grew hot. "If I did, I don't remember," she admitted. Kate absently rolled her pen back and forth on the table. "The other lessons I had today proved that I'm going to be pretty—what was the word Mrs. Lakshmi used?—obtuse when it comes to learning these subjects."

James looked up, a frown forming on his lips. "Mrs. Lakshmi? The math instructor? She's wonderful. I couldn't imagine her saying something so dispiriting."

"I was the one who said I wasn't as bright as her other students." Kate bit her lip, avoiding James' gaze. "Mrs. Lakshmi told me I wasn't obtuse. She said after a few weeks I would see I had an 'acute understanding' of the subject."

To Kate's surprise, James laughed lightly. "That's clever. I've always appreciated the English language's versatility when it comes to witty expressions."

Despite James' smile, humiliation spun within Kate. "I'll appreciate when the lessons don't make me feel like I'm a child doodling squiggly lines but can't draw a recognizable shape."

James' expression was contemplative. "Millie informed me—informed all your tutors actually—about your loss of memories. It can be vexing to not have the proficiency you once did."

"If vexing means annoying and makes me want to throw my books out the window, then yes, it's vexing." Kate stopped the pen with her thumb. Her gaze moved to the books and notebooks, which, with pages sticking out like tongues, seemed to mock her with the enormity of information she was expected to possess. "Everyone else my age has years of courses they remember. How am I supposed to catch up?"

"'The man who moves a mountain begins by carrying away small stones.' Or, in this case, the woman." James' lips quirked into a smile as Kate's brows furrowed. "A quote from Confucius. He was a Chinese philosopher who authored many such aphorisms. Right now, no, you cannot recall the depth of knowledge of your peers. What you *can* do is thin your pile page by page." James' hair swayed as he indicated the books and papers with his head. "By your thinning, learn piece by piece." As he spoke, James removed the careworn books he had brought from the stack. He handed Kate one pair of plays and kept a second for himself. "Millie was adamant that we begin with Shakespeare's *Romeo and Juliet*. She probably mentioned Shakespeare is one of England's—indeed, the Western world's—most renowned playwrights. I find his monologues to be long-winded at times, but every child in Britain will read some work of Shakespeare's before he or she has left school." James lifted his water bottle, unscrewed the lid, and took a drink. Kate peered at the faded picture on the cover of the first play. It depicted a man with a brightly colored tunic climbing up to a ledge where a maiden waited. Her hands were clasped together, her gaze longingly on the man.

"What is *Romeo and Juliet* about?" Kate asked, though she guessed she knew the answer.

"Star-crossed lovers," James said, setting the bottle back on the floor with the lid off. "Two teenagers from rival families fall in love. Romeo and Juliet try and keep their relationship secret from their families. As it often is with Shakespeare's plays, a series of events lead the protagonists to a tragic end."

"It's a love story?"

Kate's aversion registered on her face. James laughed. "I had a similar reaction when I first read the play. Might I suggest we try one of Shakespeare's comedies instead?"

James put down the first play and held up the second. Kate set hers aside also and read the second play's title: *Much Ado About Nothing*.

"The plot of *Much Ado About Nothing* is complex, and the banter is quick," he noted as Kate flipped to the first page with interest. "It can be challenging to understand the antiquated language, since no one today speaks the way in which the dialogue is written. I'm sure you and I can muddle through it together, though." James rested the play on his lap and opened the half-torn cover delicately. "I will begin by reading both Leonato and the messenger's lines. You will join me as Beatrice."

Kate nodded. James cleared his throat and began to read. His shoulders relaxed, his voice assuming an air of confidence as he adopted the role of Leonato. Kate hearkened intently to James' inflections. She discovered a melody in the dialogue. Something pulled faintly on her heart as though Kate were used to the smooth cadence. When Beatrice entered the scene, Kate's tongue sailed through the lines with ease. Kate stopped reading with the arrival of a new character, assuming James would pick up the oration. It took Kate a moment to realize James hadn't spoken.

"Oh, am I supposed to be Don Pedro?" Kate asked as she glanced up from the page. James stared at her, agape. The play sat forgotten on his lap. Kate bit her lip. "I didn't read it correctly, did I?" she said, chagrined. "I was trying to recite it like you did. Was the pace off? Did I skip a line? Or . . ."

"No, nothing was wrong. That was perfect." The confidence had been stripped from James' voice as he glanced away. "I didn't expect you to get it so quickly." James reached down for his water bottle. In his haste, James knocked it to the side. Water spilled over the carpet. "I'm sorry," James said with an abashed look. As he bent over lower to right the bottle, the play tumbled from his lap onto the wet carpet.

"It's okay." Kate hid her smile as she took a handful of serviettes from the table. She was secretly proud of James' praise. She knelt down and handing James the play. "It's just water," she added as she sponged the spot. James didn't speak as Kate left the serviettes pressed onto the carpet. She resumed her spot on the couch. "Should we keep reading?"

James screwed the top securely on the bottle. The damp book cover had fallen off. "Yes, um, we left off with Don Pedro. If you would start with his lines, please."

Kate and James finished the first scene just as the hour ended. Kate felt a stab of disappointment. She was thoroughly enjoying the play and, equally, James' company.

"I've never heard Shakespeare recited so eloquently," James told Kate after he was bundled in his coat, scarf, and earmuffs. Away from the safety of the books, James again seemed uncertain about what expression to wear. He dropped his green gaze to his mailbag, where he had stashed his water bottle and the plays. "You must have been an exceptional student, Ms. Smith."

Kate was glad that her skin was not as fair as James' or else he would have caught her blushing. "Kate," she answered, opening the door. "Not Ms. Smith."

A cold breeze ruffled James' hair. "Good day then, Kate."

Without waiting for Kate's response, James practically ran from the house, the mailbag bouncing at his side. Kate watched him for a moment. Then she quickly pulled the door shut before more cold air could leak into the living room. Kate walked to the couch and plopped down with a broad grin. "I *am* good at something," she commented aloud. Kyra picked up the serviettes and dropped them on the side of a saucer. She might catch up to her peers after all.

Kate's gaze trailed to the mountain of papers and texts at her feet. *The man who moves a mountain begins by carrying away small stones.* Kate tilted her head. *Or . . .* With her foot, Kate shoved the offending heap under the coffee table, sending the books flying and littering papers over the floor. "There. Mountain moved in one trip."

Kate snatched the play from the table and flipped to the page where she and James had left off. Leaning back, legs crossed, shoeless feet on the table, she resumed reading. Kate was so engrossed she forgot that her strong connection to James was built on shared experiences of sorrow.

Chapter 5

"Hayden, a wizard! To your left!"

Hayden pivoted mid-run at the sound of Talis' voice. The unnatural white fog pervading the pines and firs of the Ancient Forest distorted light and the forms of his enemies, and Hayden couldn't clearly see if the bandits or wizards were closing in.

But his elven friend could.

Hayden unhesitatingly slid, feet first, beneath a fallen tree trunk. He covered his head with his arm as orange magic exploded around him. Shards of wood pelted the ground on both sides of his makeshift cover. When the rainfall of splinters ended, Hayden dropped his arm. He rolled onto his stomach. Detritus and dry needles stuck to his cloak, unable to penetrate his leather jacket. Hayden's hair was matted, his forehead creased with feverish concentration. A shallow gash ran along his collarbone. Hayden waited. He didn't hear more warnings from Talis.

Hayden shoved himself out from beneath the trunk and sprang to his feet. Hayden sprinted to the closest fir. Like its kin in the hallowed woods, the fir's branches started growing several feet from the ground. Hayden pressed himself sideways against the trunk. The white mist slithered around wide spaces between the trees, continuing to obscure his vision. Hayden slid his sword carefully from its scabbard. He drew in deep, controlled breaths. His gray eyes browsed the area around him. The *Y'cartim Allegra*—as the elves named the forest—was rich with scents of pine and freshly fallen rain.

An arrow whistled past Hayden's ear. Someone grunted. Hayden craned his neck around the tree. He was able to make out a cloak and staff as a wizard crumpled to the ground. Glancing to his right, Hayden spotted Talis fifty meters away, standing beside a large pine. The elf's amber gaze was fixed on the fallen wizard as he tilted his bow downward.

"Expert shot," Hayden called to his friend. His words echoed as though carried by the mist. A smile worked its way onto Talis' face.

"We have three wizards yet to remove," the elf shouted back. Talis suddenly raised his bow against his cheek. "In addition to the bandits." As if on cue, shadows of men swarmed through the haze, weapons in hand. Talis fired a spray of arrows into the group. Thumps, screams, and curses resounded as the arrows found their mark.

Hayden launched himself from behind the tree as the bandits converged on him. Hayden parried a lunge from the first bandit, then spun to block a stab from a second. The second bandit recovered faster than the first and slashed at Hayden's side. Hayden's blade met the bandit's, the metal ringing shrilly as they connected. Using his momentum, Hayden kicked the bandit's knee with the heel of his boot. The man cried out. Hayden followed through with a strike from the hilt of his sword. The bandit dropped to the ground. The first bandit advanced again, but Hayden's sword was faster. The man fell as quickly as his companion.

Hayden glanced up as more bandits broke through the mist. His sword pulsed with an unnatural blue-silver glow. In a fraction of a second, Hayden recognized he was outnumbered. He raised his sword. Hayden blocked consecutive blows from the bandits in front of him and knocked down the outstretched blade from a third bandit to his right. Weaponless, the bandit threw himself to the side as Hayden charged forward. An opening formed between the bandits.

They didn't have time to react as Hayden ran through them and headed toward Talis.

The elf had slung his bow over his back and drawn a pair of short swords. Talis' silver-blond hair shone in the mist as he ghosted among his attackers. He felled one after another as rapidly as he had with his arrows. Hayden raced closer. Out of the corner of his eye, he spotted a bandit aiming a crossbow at the elf's back.

Hayden flicked a knife into his left hand. Sprinting faster, he hurled it with all his might. The knife cartwheeled through the air and punched the bandit in the chest. With a scream, the bandit's knees buckled. The crossbow angled upward and misfired, the arrow disappearing among the boughs of a pine.

"They have crossbows!" Hayden shouted, sheathing his sword. "We need an area with more cover."

Talis' head shifted almost imperceptibly. Swiftly returning his pair of swords to their scabbards, the elf leapt high and grabbed the lowest-hanging branch of a pine. Like a gymnast, Talis swung himself up as another bolt whizzed into the space where he had stood a half second earlier. "This way!" he yelled. Hayden turned sharply to the left. He sprinted parallel to Talis as the elf lithely hopped from branch to branch. Boots trampled the ground as the bandits gave pursuit.

Suddenly, brilliant magenta and ivory-colored magic lit up the forest, refracting in every direction off the fog. Hayden shielded his eyes and glanced behind him. The bandits had fallen further back. As the light faded, Hayden looked forward again. Two wizards came into focus, staffs flaring, as they sneaked through the trees. They hadn't noticed Hayden, who was angled toward them but out of their line of sight.

"Those are our wizards," Talis called down.

The female wizard whipped around at the elf's voice, her hood swaying. Her dark eyes narrowed as she spied Hayden. The younger male wizard stopped also. He stepped on the end of his cloak and tripped. The wizard managed to catch himself before he fell.

"You're here then," the female wizard hissed.

"We are." Talis rolled the bow from his back, drawing a pair of arrows from his quiver. He vaulted high from his branch, seeming suspended between the trees, nocked the arrows, and released them together. Talis touched down on a neighboring branch, which barely bent under his weight.

The younger wizard let out an undignified shriek and dropped to the ground. His staff clattered from his hands and was enclosed in the fog. The female wizard raised her own weapon. She sliced it through the air. Magenta magic cleaved both arrows in two. Her eyes followed the splinters of wood with an unimpressed look. Her gaze dipped to her companion. He continued to cower in fear, keeping his head low to the ground.

"Janus, for the love of Harkimer," the female wizard berated with a roll of her eyes. "Get up. That's a *staff* in your hand, not a stick. You have spells bound to it, don't you? Use them."

"Sorry, Lilias," the younger wizard mumbled. He groped along the ground for his weapon. Lilias let out an aggrieved breath as Janus' fingers finally grasped the staff.

Hayden used the distraction to disappear into the woods. He kept his distance from where he had last seen the bandits. Hayden pumped his arms furiously as he ran. Sweat streamed down his face despite the cool air. His trained eye found a small stand of trees. Hayden trotted toward it. When he was partially hidden behind the trees, Hayden allowed himself to rest. Fatigue had begun to set in from hours of battling the bandits and wizards.

Hayden's mind strayed to the reason he and Talis had entered the *Y'cartim Allegra* in the first place. Three weeks of combing Silvias and its neighboring kingdom of Hogarth hadn't produced any signs of Kyra. The elven scouts brought rumors of wizards on the Realm's border. It wasn't likely Kyra was in the Ancient Forest. He never would have thought Diamantas and his ilk would dare cross into the heart of elven magic, no matter how powerful the obsidian staff. And yet, here were the dark wizards. They had. The question was, was Kyra likely to be *anywhere* in Ilian? Grief at the thought ravaged Hayden anew.

Which was why he heard the sound of a click and snap of a string too late. Hayden glanced up in time to see black fletching. Blinding pain exploded in his shoulder. He was thrown against the ground, landing hard on his side. The sword bounced from his hand. Hayden's vision flashed black. He groaned and lay motionless.

"Hayden!" Talis cried out in alarm. The elf had caught up to Hayden and spied the bolt right before it slammed into his friend. The elf backflipped from the pine, landing noiselessly at the edge of the stand of trees.

"Bagged one of 'em!" a bandit shouted triumphantly. He stood several meters diagonally from Hayden, crossbow in hand.

Talis' expression hardened. He sent an arrow spiraling through the mist. The bandit collapsed wordlessly.

"So did I," Talis muttered. He ran to Hayden, who had pushed himself up and onto his knees. Blood streamed through his fingers as he clutched his right shoulder. The fletching of an arrow protruded from it. The head of the bolt extended out the back of Hayden's cloak. Hayden's face was ashen and contorted in pain.

"This is not one of our finer moments, *Estienen*," Talis remarked with a grimace.

"For the number of arrows they lost, I should be dead ten times over," Hayden responded dryly. "I'm surprised they had luck with even one."

"Even then their luck was limited. The arrow went through cleanly, but we must remove it. The sooner we get you to the Healer's Hall, the more likely you will regain full strength in your arm."

As Talis spoke, the sounds of swords and boots resounded from all sides of the woods. The elf tilted his head. "There are too many to battle. We must stall them." Talis held a hand over the mist. He let out a deep breath as the irises in his eyes flashed with an unnatural green glow. The white fog became infused with an identical green that poured from Talis' palm. The colors intertwined with each other until they formed a giant net. Talis arced his hand, dragging the magic across the stand of trees until it had encircled them completely. The bandits' yells became garbled behind the magical screen.

Talis dropped his hand with a shuddering sigh. His eyes continued to shine supernaturally green. "I can attend to your wound now, though it won't be pleasant."

Hayden nodded. "A gold florin if you make this quick."

Talis gripped the shaft of the arrow jutting from Hayden's back. The elf deftly snapped off the bolt. Hayden grunted as Talis tossed it to the side. The elf moved to Hayden's front, taking hold of the shaft just beneath the fletching. In a swift motion, he pulled out the remainder of the arrow. Hayden gasped as pain enveloped him. Talis caught Hayden at the waist as he fell forward. With the obstructions gone, blood flowed freely from Hayden's wound.

Talis removed Hayden's cloak. The elf drew his short sword and sheared several pieces of cloth from it, then dropped the sword to the ground. He packed strips of cloth into thick wads.

Sharp, crackling noises erupted around the magical net. They were followed by a cry and the smell of singed clothing. Hayden's eyes darted to the green. An outline of a man was pressed against the net like a stamp on a wax seal. The man fell back. The green crackled again as another silhouette struck it. He, too, shrank from the energy.

Talis, who hadn't looked up from his work, shook his head. He grabbed the remaining strip and bound the two bunched strips in place. "We are blessed by the ineptitude of our foes. If one cannot breach elven magic, how could another?"

"Inishmore must have a fondness for witless individuals," Hayden said with a strained smile.

"You say that because . . . ?"

"Because Ilian has so many of them."

Talis pressed the wads firmly against Hayden's shoulder. Hayden shook as a spasm of pain ran through him. "Hold this," Talis instructed. He picked up another piece of bundled cloth and slipped it under Hayden's cloak. Talis finished by wrapping the final strips of cloth over both sides of the wound and around Hayden's waist.

Hayden tested his right arm, moving it gently to the side. The cloth flexed and held. "I can fight. Thank you, Talis." Hayden's left hand scrabbled along the ground and found the cool hilt of his sword. He gripped it tightly.

Talis slipped an arm under his friend and helped lever Hayden to his feet.

A voice boomed an incantation. Talis and Hayden glanced at the green net. White-hot light struck the elven magic. The green quaked before disappearing. White mist seeped back into the space as Diamantas stepped forward. Lilias and Janus stood behind him.

The green light vanished from Talis' eyes. He unsheathed his short swords, his long braid swaying along the side of his face. Hayden flexed his fingers around his weapon's hilt.

Diamantas' cold gaze moved from Talis to Hayden. His eyes landed briefly upon the bloodstained bandages wrapped around Hayden's arm and waist. "You are not looking well, Hayden," he remarked coldly. Over his shoulder, Diamantas commanded, "Handle the elf. I would like a word with my dear friend in private."

Hayden's weariness was borne away in a torrent of fury. "Lead them as far away from us as you can," he told Talis in an undertone. "Then send for the *Sirenyle*. The bandits need to be cleared from the *Y'cartim Allegra*."

Talis' amber eyes were deeply troubled. He gave Hayden a sidelong glance as Lilias and Janus detached from Diamantas and moved forward. "I will return and expect to find you whole, *Estienen*. You owe me that gold florin yet."

Hayden nodded curtly. Talis turned and sprinted off, Lilias and Janus chasing after him. The mist shrouded them as their footsteps faded. The forest was eerily silent.

Hayden's gaze was as hard as flint as it locked squarely on Diamantas. Now that they were alone, Hayden could see the strain in the lines on the wizard's face. His breaths were labored, though he maintained calm.

"You aren't looking your best either, Diamantas," Hayden spoke. "You made a mistake by sending away the others."

"Elven magic," Diamantas replied simply. He kept his staff leveled before him. "It rejects that of the wizards, most forcefully the wizard possessing the greatest threat. I did not expect that kind of power from this forest. It is of little consequence, however. We share a common goal, Hayden. It is worth discussing."

"There isn't anything to discuss. I do have one question, though." Hayden took a step forward. "Where is she?"

"That question I have asked myself numerous times without success," Diamantas responded truthfully. "I was not responsible for Kyra's disappearance. I also have not chanced upon information as to where she may or may not be."

Hayden let out a hollow laugh. "You think I can be persuaded of your innocence and ignorance? You have tried for years to capture Kyra. Solarus, Talis, and I have for an equal length of time prevented you from doing so. Now we're in the Ancient Forest. You wouldn't be so bold unless you believed the prophecy to have ended." He advanced again. The blade in his hand shone blue-silver as it harnessed the forest's dissipated light.

Diamantas' gaze suddenly lit on the sword. His blue eyes betrayed a hint of uncertainty. The wizard murmured under his breath. Glittering white light bubbled around the tip of the obsidian staff. "It is true, you had no reason to trust me in the past," Diamantas responded. "You have reason to now. Think, Hayden. How would I benefit from losing the one wizard who could tip the scales of fortune in my favor? I could yet convince Kyra to join me. She does not have to be an adversary. Even if I failed to enlighten her to the plight of our kin in Harkimer, would it not behoove me to ensure Kyra were dead? Does it serve me to be unaware of her fate?" Diamantas' face regained color as the white magic gushed from the tip of the staff and ran down its sides. "Our enmity toward each other, Hayden, has been based on different interpretations of the prophecy. Should we not unite over it?"

"The dark wizards built a reputation for retaliation and conquest long before the prophecy. However, I agree with you, Diamantas. We share the responsibility for Kyra's disappearance. Possibly her death. It is fitting we should seek her together."

A relaxed smile appeared on Diamantas' lips. "I am happy you see the reason in this choice." He rapped the staff against the ground. "We must put aside our . . . aaaahh!"

Diamantas' instincts saved him from Hayden's unexpected attack. The wizard shot to the side as Hayden punched his blade toward Diamantas' neck. Diamantas counterattacked with a whirl of his staff. Blue and red fire twisted through the air. Hayden raised his sword to his chest. The flames collided with the metal, vanishing like steam as though doused with water. The sword pulsed as brightly as Diamantas' staff. New splotches of blood formed around Hayden's shoulder as he feverishly darted forward and slashed again. The blow wasn't directed at Diamantas; the blade chased the obsidian staff.

"Are you mad?" Diamantas shrieked as he backpedaled away from the blow. He stared at Hayden as though seeing him for the first time. "You cannot destroy the staff. Its release of its magic will kill us both!"

"As I said, we will seek Kyra together. I didn't specify if it is in this life or the next. You brought this sentence upon yourself, Diamantas. You removed the last person that tied me to this world. My single purpose is to deliver justice in her memory. This ends tonight."

Diamantas' eyes were wide with shock. "I swear by Inishmore, I did not send her away! You may yet get her back with my help." He raised a quick shield, but Hayden sliced through it with ease. Diamantas staggered backward as the magic dissolved around him. His eyes were riveted on Hayden's sword. For the first time, he seemed afraid.

The staff was tantalizingly close. It was over. Hayden took one, deep breath, sent a silent prayer of gratitude to Inishmore, and arced his sword for the final strike.

Hayden's muscles suddenly seized. His arms were frozen above his head, breath crushed in his chest. A turquoise light ringed Hayden's neck like a chain. His eyes rolled into his head. Hayden's arms fell as he dropped to his knees and slumped to the ground. His eyes were closed, but his sword remained firmly in his grasp.

Diamantas watched Hayden, breathing unsteadily. He was stunned by the turn of events. Diamantas' blue eyes trailed to the space where Hayden had once stood. A hooded stranger filled it, an azure cloak draped over his shoulders. The cowl of his cloak masked his face but revealed downturned lips and a dark, neatly trimmed beard. A brilliant turquoise flame bloomed around one hand, and he held a hornbeam wood staff in the other.

"I would advise you to leave," the stranger spoke in a cold tone.

Diamantas blinked at the voice. "*You?*" he whispered. "You have undertaken every effort to oppose the wizards of Harkimer. Why would you stop Hayden when victory over me was assured?" His eyes lidded with suspicion. "Or you are one of us after all."

The stranger snorted derisively. "I am assuredly not one of *you*. Men with noble hearts are a rarity in these lands. Hayden deserves better than to destroy himself for a morally decrepit individual like yourself." The stranger's staff flared, and he slanted it ominously at Diamantas. "Leave. Or Talis and I can finish what Hayden started. The elf approaches."

Diamantas lifted the black cowl over his head. He turned and began to walk away, then paused. "You are still welcome in the assembly, Solarus," he commented without looking back. "You have friends among us. Even if you do not care for me in particular."

"*Leave.*"

Diamantas shrugged. He coaxed more magic from his staff and sent it into the mist. The air glimmered. Diamantas was camouflaged by the white as though behind an ocean's spray. He stalked away, disappearing into the woods.

Solarus released a deep sigh. The turquoise magic vanished. Lowering his hood, Solarus knelt beside Hayden. He set his staff on the ground. Solarus placed two fingers on the side of Hayden's neck. His pulse was steady if not fainter than normal. Solarus rocked back on his heel. When Hayden awoke, he would have to face the anguish and anger from which he had so desperately tried to escape.

But they needed him.

"Forgive me," Solarus muttered. Taking up his staff, the wizard rose. Solarus tread silently over the carpet of needles and vanished into the forest, leaving an unconscious Hayden unaware of the exchange between Ilian's most powerful wizards.

Chapter 6

Dark clouds clumped together like armies warring against each other. Thunder pealed across the sky. Raindrops the size of marbles pelted the tree canopy. The foliage bent and broke under the barrage. The rain couldn't descend further; instead, it splattered harmlessly against the invisible magical shield that protected the glade in which the animals of the *Al-Ethran* were gathered. The shield's original purpose wasn't to protect against storms; the first Council of Elders spelled the glade so that none could intentionally or accidentally find the sacrosanct congress of animal kind. The secondary benefit was that the magic kept out less than favorable weather.

Raven's ears pricked at another round of booms. It wasn't unusual to have violent, short storms in the autumn months. It *was* unusual for all members of the *Al-Ethran* to be summoned. It was even more troubling that the Elders had called an emergency session just three weeks prior, when tremors uprooted trees and quaked the waters of the Aurielle Sea. Not since the time of Malus had the Council of Elders assembled twice in one season.

As the thunder ebbed, Raven's head again drooped, expression desolate. He stood at the fringe of the glade. Only the eight Council members were permitted within the glade's inner circle. However, as the sole individual present during Kyra's disappearance, he had been subjected to numerous rounds of questioning by the *Al-Ethran*. To his and the Council's dismay, Raven's memories started the evening before the fateful day, ended the following morning, and resumed later that evening. What happened between dawn and dusk was as much a mystery to Raven as to the *Al-Ethran*. Raven's shame drummed in his heart louder than the rain overhead.

Seven of the *Al-Ethran*'s members sat in silence. The eighth, a massive brown bear, plodded back and forth with agitated, uneven steps.

A stag with wide antlers regarded Raven with a haughty look. "You haven't *any* recollection, Raven? Or do you have something to regret that you wish to hide from us?"

The roan shook his head without looking up. "I have described all I know. Kyra and I rode out from Silvias accompanying Grayhaven and the wizard Solarus. Dawn's light had not yet risen. I cannot speak to our destination, whom we encountered, or what transpired afterward. That time has been sealed in my mind, like a stable door without a window. I am sorry, Harold."

The stag stamped the ground with a delicate but sharp hoof. "It is a result of the weakmindedness of your kind, cousin," Harold condescended. "Horses sacrificed the intelligence and instincts of the deer when they allowed men to shelter them. You are servants. Your senses have been dulled by your complacency." The stag puffed out his chest. "A stag would remember the events of that day. We have no fear. We withstand and adapt to whatever condition, including the storms that ravage both the body and the mind."

"You should be capable of adopting humility, Harold," a wolf put in dryly. "If you are not able, pretend you are." The wolf was nearly as large as the pacing bear, with fur that was so black it seemed to embody a starless night sky. She grinned, her skin stretching over sharp canines. Harold suddenly became interested in a flea on his leg, which he nipped at vigorously. The wolf's lavender-colored gaze shifted to the other members. "We are all concerned, but Raven of Silvias has repeated his account several times. The magic that wreathed our brother when he arrived here was wicked enough to consign him to eternal madness. Let us be grateful Raven was sound enough of mind to bring the *Al-Ethran* this news."

The bear paused long enough to huff. "Gratitude, Blackhunter? For what? The roan has nothing to offer except that he lost his rider. As far as you have explained, such a thing does not merely *happen*. For once, I agree with Harold. This horse is useless."

Raven's conspicuous misery produced a soft bark of sympathy from a blue merle collie. She rose from her haunches. "Calm down, Khron," she reproached, walking past him with a sideways glare. She rubbed her nose comfortingly against Raven's long snout.

Khron's piggish eyes followed the collie. "Why do we continue to waste time?" he demanded. "For four days, we have discussed. We have deliberated. We even raised the *ragnor prelim* around the horse, hoping that the shadows of our ancestors could bring the missing memory to light as they have done for centuries. The *ragnor prelim* produced *nothing*." The bear snapped off the last word as though crunching into a bone. "No echoes of memories. No images. No voices. After all this, the *Al-Ethran* continues to make a simple problem unnecessarily difficult. You walk through a berry patch, eating one piece of fruit from each branch. Why not rip out the bush and its berries in one motion?" Khron shook his head, folds of skin rolling as he moved. "We decide. Today. If not, then, Blackhunter, as the most senior member of this Council, dismiss us. I will not starve waiting for the outcomes of your ponderings."

Blackhunter's ears flattened against the back of her head. She growled.

"What would you recommend, Khron?" Two hawks perched on an oak branch. One had scarlet-colored plumage, the other tawny gold. It was the scarlet-colored hawk who had spoken, her eyes zeroed in on the bear as though he were a field mouse. "You have shared your many doubts these past days yet provided no solution yourself." She pecked at her feathers before adding, "My eyas are a noisy bunch of fledglings, yet they complain half as much as you do. You add nothing of value to this conversation."

"Zalia," Blackhunter warned.

The bear's snout wrinkled. He plodded to the tree and pushed himself up on two legs. Khron grabbed at a branch with his thick paw to steady himself. At his full height, the bear was almost eye-level with the hawks. "*Your* only value, Zalia, is in the meat you would provide as a meal, however meager."

The scarlet hawk's eyes glinted with amusement. "Not a meal for you, I hope." She calmly looked Khron up and down. "You've stored more than enough for the winter, and perhaps the better part of spring."

Khron snarled, exposing teeth as long and sharp as his claws. Zalia turned to the tawny gold hawk. "I never knew bears were such sensitive beasts, Zellion."

The hawks suddenly launched from the branch as Khron's paw swiped the air. Zellion folded his wings and swooped down. His sharp talons sliced the bear's ear. Khron roared with rage. He dropped on all fours, looking around as Zellion landed on the ground. Khron turned menacingly on him, but Harold quickly stepped in front of the bear. The stag bowed his head and trained his large antlers on the bear like a row of swords.

"Stop, all of you!" The collie bounded within the circle as Zalia landed gently beside Zellion. The collie's crystal blue eyes flashed with passion. "Kyra is gone. That's what we must focus on. That is what is important. Men, wizards, and elves will all be searching for her. Khron is right," she added, garnering a surprised chuff from the bear. "We must *do* something. We're bickering and posturing like pups in a litter."

"Hazel speaks truly." Blackhunter intervened. "We are the *Al-Ethran*. We are a Council of Elders." Her severe lavender gaze fixed on Khron. "Act like one."

The standoff between the bear and stag lasted a brief moment. Khron yielded, averting his eyes. He silently lumbered back to the circle and sat with a thud that sent leaves and brushwood scattering.

Blackhunter tilted her head. "We can all agree, at least, that we must choose a course of action."

"I propose we seek out Kyra ourselves. Our time runs short, and the consequences are too great for us to allow her to stay in whoever's hands she has been delivered."

A black panther had spoken with a slight inclination of her chin. He sat calmly across from her, arms crossed. His tail swept the ground. The panther spoke little during the meetings; when he did, he commanded everyone's attention. His golden orbs for eyes lingered on Blackhunter expectantly.

"Continue, Raff," she said.

"As I understand it," the panther said diplomatically, "we have considered this issue from the perspective that Kyra, herself, will wield the power to protect or destroy Ilian. I put forward that we consider Kyra's role differently. No individual is mightier than Inishmore or the Healer. A *group* of peoples, united, can resist Inishmore's will and bring terrible destruction to our lands. Yet not one. Kyra will influence the direction of Ilian's future, but not determine it as a single person. Her true power is that she is a *symbol* for both sides in this conflict. Diamantas undoubtedly carries hope that Kyra will be an ally in the extermination of the citizens of Ilian. Kyra's guardians have spent eleven years instilling in her Inishmore's principles. It is said that she who lives by integrity, loyalty, and faith cannot become an agent for immoral deeds. Kyra's guardians believe this. They hope she will save Ilian, not destroy it. To this I say, it is possible. The seers offer glimpses into possible futures. They provide conjecture as to which will come to pass. Neither they nor we will have the answer until that time. Whether Kyra becomes a force for Harkimer or a defender of Ilian, she will be the banner around which forces will rally. She will lend them the courage and conviction they need to triumph."

"If that is your argument," Harold put in, "then Diamantas is incapable of razing Ilian's lands."

"Again, as an individual, no. Not any more than Malus could. Malus was not alone, though; he had armies. Armies comprised of more than wizards. Indeed, wizards are among the weakest of the creatures that lurk in the darkest shadows and pits of the Southern Mountains. Wizards are not the only ones we must fear. They are not even the ones we should fear most." Raff's yellow-orbed gaze moved over each member of the *Al-Ethran*, who were enraptured by the panther's words. "What of the Reapers? The Okse? The Variavryk? Yes, the Variavryk," Raff repeated as every animal except Blackhunter shivered at the name. "The spirits of those too depraved to pass from our world to the next will be seen again in Ilian. I believe these evils are already stirring. They will quench their thirst for death and revenge by spilling blood." The panther's deep tone was laden with foreboding. "Kyra's disappearance has heralded the first flakes of snow from Harkimer's peaks. The cold fury of Harkimer will bring an early winter to our lands. Wizards and beasts will turn snow into stinging needles of ice with their attacks. If too much time passes without Kyra's return, Ilian will be buried under an avalanche of wickedness. Kyra herself will not create the avalanche any more than she would have the power to stop it. She would be a symbol, nothing more."

"Then is it not better if she is dead?"

Raff's golden orbs moved to Khron. The bear stared down at him menacingly. "It is not. The dark wizards are better unified in Harkimer than we are in Ilian. They have banded together in their suffering. Diamantas feeds their dismay as much as he nourishes their hope. Those are two powerful motivators. Who in Ilian has seen as much misery? We live in an era of relative peace, save occasional skirmishes among feuding families or bandit incursions. The men, wizards, and elves of Ilian do not understand the evil that threatens them. If and when they do realize, it will be too late. The seers are the ones who relate the prophecy and could persuade their kings and queens to act—if Kyra were present and on their side. She can unite the six kingdoms. I do not believe any other has that ability."

"Kyra has already united men, wizards, and elves, she has," a chipmunk chimed in shrilly. "Yes, more elves than men, and a single wizard, it's true. She was a child, a child. Imagine when she is of age and explores and meets others. Kyra can do more, she can, she will, she will."

"Yes, Chere, Kyra can." Raff stretched his shoulders, his long, black tail swishing across the grass. "Furthermore, if Kyra has been killed and Diamantas finds her, he can bring her to Harkimer and use her as a martyr. He can claim those in Ilian had slain her to prevent her from leading the wizards out of exile. He can ignite hatred and demands for retribution. If any wizard in Harkimer were hesitant to kill, the desire to avenge Kyra would eliminate that hesitation." The other animals murmured with looks of dread. "That is why it is critical we begin the search for her. I volunteer to lead it."

"I will join you," Hazel barked.

Blackhunter cocked her head in consideration. "We cannot spare more than two of the *Al-Ethran* for this quest," the wolf decided. "There is too much uncertainty in Ilian. I must be able to call upon this Council at short notice." Blackhunter rose. The rain had faded into a drizzle, and shafts of sunlight streamed into the glade, falling on her ink-black fur. "I entrust this task to you then, Raff and Hazel. Find Kyra's guardians. Alert them of your search, but remember your oaths. Our discussion about our concerns for the future of these lands may not be shared with anyone else." Blackhunter turned to Chere. The chipmunk rubbed a tiny paw over her ear, nose twitching excitedly. "Chere and I will confer separately with *Raenalyn* Carina. The elven and animal scouts will rely on each other more than ever in these times. Are there objections?" When no one responded, Blackhunter spoke the ritual blessing in a commanding tone. "May Inishmore guide you in your quest, Raff and Hazel. As in all things."

"As in all things," the *Al-Ethran* echoed solemnly like parishioners at a sermon.

"May Inishmore protect the *Al-Ethran*. Keep us strong in heart and mind, ready to serve and protect our kin with fang, claw, and hoof."

"Ready to serve."

"May we have the courage to make whatever sacrifices Inishmore demands of us. May Inishmore bring us to green meadows and clear skies should we be taken from this world forever. May we never falter in our commitment."

"Never falter."

"We make this oath, now and always."

"Now and always."

The meeting was concluded. Chere scampered onto Blackhunter's back, her tiny claws digging into the hair of the wolf's nape. The giant wolf loped into the woods and out of sight. The other members disbanded. Khron lingered. His bulky body swayed as he forcefully expelled air from his nostrils.

"If Kyra has been turned when you reach her," he growled, beady eyes on Raff and Hazel, "you will make the 'sacrifice Inishmore demands.' Kyra might be a butcher when you find her. *If* you find her. Remember that."

"If your concern were genuine, you would have elected to join us." Raff's tone was even, but he raked the ground with his claws, carving deep lines into the forest floor. "Never pretend to be something that you are not. You do your part as a member of the *Al-Ethran*, Khron. We will do ours."

Khron huffed. He turned slowly and trudged away from the grove. Raff and Hazel listened as the twigs and underbrush were crushed under his heavy paws.

When the sounds faded, Hazel beat her tail irately on the ground. "I have to agree with Zalia. There's no reason for Khron to be part of the *Al-Ethran*. He contests every suggestion and welcomes conflict. He is completely and utterly unbearable."

The muscles on Raff's face folded into a grin. "I am sure Khron would completely and utterly disagree with that statement," he replied. The panther's ears flapped. Raff glanced over his shoulder. Raven, who had stayed quietly in the glade's periphery, clomped toward them. His large, brown eyes shone with anger and self-reproach.

"I am coming with you," he said, stamping the ground for emphasis. "I am bound to Kyra as her steed as she is bound to me as her rider. It is my duty to find her at whatever cost."

Raff held up a paw in a mollifying gesture. "We welcome your company. Hazel and I are known by the elves, but we have not been introduced to Kyra's guardians. From what I understand, they consider you, as Kyra's steed, a friend. They will trust what you tell them."

Raven dipped his head in thanks. The trio took off, heading eastward from the glade. The magic encircling the glade ended abruptly. Leaves and plants dripped water onto the panther as he brushed against them, and the air was warm and scented like moist earth. Strangely, a chill ran through Raff's body as a sense of foreboding surrounded him. The panther glanced up.

Impossibly in the hot sunlight, a single snowflake floated down from the sky.

Chapter 7

It was one thing for Kate to know London was her home. It was an entirely other thing for Kate to *know* London. Hampstead was a beautiful suburb, and the Heath offered a pleasant hike and breathtaking view. Kate was fond of this place, but she had an irresistible craving—not craving, she realized, a need—to explore and understand London and all that was a part of it. Kate might never get back her memories of Chicago. She was determined to set roots in London. To build her identity. Any identity. That meant Kate needed to master its streets and its culture to be able to call this city her home.

Millie readily brought home a map of London's streets and landmarks. Kate committed the map to memory. On Saturday, her first day without lessons, Kate left for the Tube station alone. Millie was hosting a lunch for her fellow art collectors and was busy preparing for their arrival. Though Kate appreciated having the freedom to roam wherever she liked, she remained a bundle of nerves. Just stepping out of the house involved a mental tug-of-war; one side warned Kate she wouldn't be safe among strangers and strange places; the other demanded she overcome her fears and march on. Kate took a deep breath, held her courage close, and went to the underground.

Kate's anxiety of being in a cramped space among strangers and hearing the terrifying rumbling and roaring from the tunnel made her want to flee back to the comfort of her room. Kate suppressed the feelings and waited. When the train zipped into the station, Kate quickly filed in after the other passengers.

Kate's first solo outing went better than she expected. From her trip with Millie to Oxford Street, Kate had experienced the crush of businessmen, tourists, and students on the sidewalks. She had heard the discordant honking from buses and cars. She had smelled the tantalizing aroma of pub food and pasties. When she emerged at Westminster station, Kate expected her senses to again be overwhelmed by the sounds, sights, and scents. To her surprise, the scene wasn't jarring. Kate's head swiveled side to side as she took in the goings-on around her. Then Kate caught herself smiling. She wasn't afraid; she was *thrilled* being out in the vibrant environment. She was still grinning from ear to ear when she related her adventure to Millie that evening over dinner.

Millie's delight matched Kate's own. "I *knew* you'd love it, sweetie!" she exclaimed, clapping her hands together. "I just knew it."

From that day on, Kate devoted afternoons and weekends to rooting out every street, alley, and shop in the city. She grew accustomed to the city's pace. She sampled foods from kiosks and coffee from cafes. Kate learned to ignore most sounds and zero in on the treacherous ones, like the screeching of buses that careened unexpectedly around narrow corners and through lights that were fully red.

When she wanted a break from the helter-skelter streets, Kate took leisurely jogs around London's parks and monuments. She trotted past Buckingham Palace, loped around gardens, and raced beside the waters of the Thames. Kate reveled in the delight of being fully in the moment.

The runs also rejuvenated Kate as she doggedly worked through her lessons. Kate visualized her mind as a frog, finding facts hovering in the air and lashing out a sticky tongue to capture them. She rarely made a mistake. When she did, it was usually a result of carelessness rising from impatience to move to the next topic.

Mr. Dullwane tested Kate's resolve. He continued to give splendidly uninspiring lectures about what Kate thought should have been captivating topics.

"How could Millie hire someone whose name has the word 'dull' in it?" Kate griped to James after one such session. She scratched out a line she had written as though it had personally offended her. Stick figures with bows and swords were sketched on the edges of the page. "Today he was describing the Battle of Agincourt with as much enthusiasm as if he was reading the dictionary." Kate tossed the pen onto the table and plopped back against the couch cushion. "Ugh."

"'The two most powerful warriors are patience and time,'" James quoted astutely. Kate had come to recognize James' expectant smile when he cited a famous author or philosopher that she had either read or had yet to read. "Tolstoy. A nineteenth-century Russian author and, like Shakespeare, a literary genius. He endured hardships that led to many enlightened observations regarding the human condition."

"Clearly, Tolstoy never had to endure Mr. Dullwane's history lessons," Kate muttered.

James laughed.

That night, Kate lay on her bed, knees bent, elbows propping her up. Her nose was close to her textbook as she read. Her sheet that listed the day's homework was beside her notebook. "Chapter Seven: The Royal Court." For as tedious as the lecture had been, Kate was riveted by the subject of medieval monarchs and their strategic maneuvering. Kings, queens, and nobles siphoned off prestige from their rivals through well-placed gossip and annexed lands through well-planned skirmishes. Kate found it strange how often this happened; after all, the nobility were all relatives of some sort. But power was a pendulum. It was only a matter of time before the demeaned nobles turned the tables on the victors. They reconquered land that had been theirs at the start. Kings and queens came and went. That was how it went for generations.

Finishing the chapter, Kate's eyes landed on a two-page-long chart with names and titles. She glanced back at the sheet with her assignments listed. "Memorize the royal titles and the proper way to address each according to his station," she read Mr. Dullwane's notes aloud. Kate's lips downturned. She snapped the textbook shut and tossed it onto the bottom of her bed.

"No, thank you," she spoke to the paper as the book bounced. "It's useless information." Kate reached over to her nightstand and picked up her copy of *Henry V*. "It's not like I'm going to be dining with the queen."

Kate flipped over onto her back. She put one arm behind her head and dove into her latest Shakespearean play. She and James had finished *Macbeth* and *Much Ado About Nothing*. James had chosen *Henry V* as their next reading, as it complemented Kate's history lessons. Kate had to admit having the lively dialogue and treacherous plot helped her trudge through those lessons.

Kate's sessions with James remained her favorite. The habitually bashful and soft-spoken James had started to open up to her. Kate discovered he had a good sense of humor. He also maintained a perennially positive outlook on life. On occasion, James stayed past the hour to have tea with Kate and Millie before heading back to the university. Kate considered James her lone confidant—and in her opinion, James was worth a thousand friends her own age.

***

The hour with Mr. Stevens was the most thought-provoking. Kate quickly learned logic and reasoning was not limited to a set of clearly defined rules. Mr. Stevens taught Kate the fundamental categories of arguments. "These will form the bedrock upon which you will build your case for whatever you're defending," he explained placidly. "I'll add some golden nuggets of— I'm not bold enough to call them 'wisdom,' so, let's say personal insights from experience and reading. Not to mention countless hours debating with my daughter what outfits have enough material to them to be considered acceptable in civilized society."

Kate was given a hypothetical question to which she had to provide her reason-based conclusion. Kate thought she created solid justifications for her answers. Until Mr. Stevens promptly dissected the logic she had presented to make his counterpoint. The more days that passed, the deeper Kate's scowl became. It was hard to think she was making progress when Kate herself was persuaded that Mr. Stevens' conclusions were the right conclusions.

"I'm always wrong," Kate grumbled when she again yielded in a debate. As had become her habit when she was anxious or frustrated, she rolled her pen back and forth. "It doesn't matter what topic you give me or what side I'm on. You always win."

"Your logic isn't wrong, it just lacks sufficient information," Mr. Stevens pointed out calmly. He reclined in the armchair, rolling up the sleeves to his oversized knit sweater. "That's why you can't confidently state your conclusion was more reasonable than mine."

Kate flicked her pen a little too hard. It skidded into Mr. Stevens' teacup with a loud *tink*. "Sorry," Kate mumbled sheepishly as she retrieved it. "How do you get 'sufficient information?'"

"Here's a golden nugget. You don't always have to decide on the spot. More often, and more intelligently, you should spend time researching and analyzing the situation or challenge what has been proposed. When you collect a solid base of facts that can support a well-founded conclusion, that's when you act. You need to focus more on fact gathering."

"We're here for an hour," Kate replied sullenly. "I won't ever feel like I've got enough to be right. Not unless you want to debate whether cat lovers can ever collect enough feline-related accessories."

"Who says you only have an hour?"

Kate sighed. "If I didn't have another lesson after this one, I could stay later, but I can't."

"Again, who says you have to decide in one session?"

"Didn't you?"

"No. I said from the first day of our debates that I would give you a topic and a position. You would have to persuade me to accept your version of the argument. I never limited you to an hour. I also didn't say you couldn't ask for more time."

"Oh," was all Kate could think to reply. Here she was, learning about logic, reason, and using common sense, and for a basic problem, she had evicted all three. "For tomorrow's topic, may I have more time?"

Mr. Stevens chuckled. He leaned forward, the sleeves of his sweater consuming his arms and hands again. "You might not need it for tomorrow's topic, since you don't know what the topic is. It's a waste of energy to fret over something that hasn't happened yet. As Mark Twain said, 'I've had a lot of worries in my life, most of which never happened.' Mark Twain is an author, if you haven't read him yet."

"You sound like James," Kate replied, chewing over Mr. Stevens' words. "I still don't understand how you decide when you have enough pieces of a puzzle to create the full picture. I might think I do and miss the point completely."

"That's a matter of judgment you develop through experience, analysis, and intuition. Of the three, intuition often proves the most useful. Even in a hundred lifetimes, you'll never fill your pot with golden nuggets. You will always learn and experience new things. Your gut instinct won't fail you, though. Not if you listen to it. Alternately, if you have enough fact-driven information, you can always fall back on logic and reason." Mr. Stevens raised a brow, causing his glasses to slide forward. "Your expression suggests you don't believe me."

"I believe you." Kate bent over her notebook and made a pretense of jotting down notes. She didn't want Mr. Stevens to see the doubt splayed across her features. *I'm not sure I'll ever believe myself.*

***

"Not much progress since our last call, Kate," Christin's voice came from the other end of the phone. The patter of rain on Kate's window mirrored the thumping anxiety in her heart. She leaned against the windowsill, waiting for the police officer to continue.

"The forensics teams are working on finding evidence to analyze. The police have a few leads on suspects or former associates of your uncle, but they don't have any hard facts either."

Kate held back an aggravated sigh. In the few times she and Christin had spoken since Kate arrived in London, it was always the same. The inquest in Chicago continued. The perpetrator had been deadly efficient and thorough. It was a painstakingly slow process. Investigations usually were.

"It's only been two months, Kate," Christin said in a placating tone. "We'll get to the bottom of this, don't worry. Have patience, and hang in there. Okay?"

"Okay. Thanks, Christin."

Kate hung up. She tossed the phone on her bed harder than she intended. As Kyra did after every call, she tried to dredge up a fragment of memory about her home, her parents, and her friends. Anything. It didn't work. A storm of frustration blitzed her heart. She silently repeated her promise to find the murderer if the police couldn't. Which, Kate had to admit, wasn't likely. If the teams of experts couldn't track him down, what chance did she have?

Trust the questions of the present to the clarity of the future.

The sensation was so subtle, muted, that Kate almost missed it.

Trust the questions of the present to the clarity of the future.

Kate turned and watched rain assault the trees. She wondered if she had offloaded her roiling emotions to the world around her.

Chapter 8

"There was no one, *Estienen*. I saw Diamantas and those in the woods whom we battled."

"It doesn't add up, Talis. We had to have overlooked someone in the Forest. I don't have a bruise on my neck or a blow to the head. If it were a bandit or someone else who attacked, you would have found me in much worse shape than unconscious."

"Worse shape than with a gaping hole in your shoulder from a crossbow's bolt?"

Hayden smiled wanly. "'Point' taken."

He limped forward. His left arm was wrapped tautly over Talis' shoulders while the injured right arm hung at his side. Talis grasped Hayden's wrist and held him around the waist. In his free hand, the elf held his bow. Together, Hayden and Talis hobbled over the needle-carpeted forest in the direction of the elven palace. Though it was daytime, the colossal pines seemed clothed in perpetual twilight. Talis' amber gaze pierced the white fog around them, seeking wizards lying in wait for another ambush. The spaces between the trees were empty. Only the cawing of ravens overhead and Hayden's leaden and irregular footsteps revealed life in the woods.

The path from the *Y'Cartim Allegra* gradually began to merge with dirt trails framed by dense grass, clumps of ferns, and verdant bushes. Beeches and oaks swapped places with the pines and firs. Sunlight sprinkled through gaps in the tree canopy. Birds trilled cheerfully, and rodents forged through the tangled underbrush.

Talis visibly relaxed. They had safely cleared the Ancient Forest. He glanced sideways at Hayden. His friend's face was drained of color. Hayden had stopped more than once along their journey when dizziness threatened to send him sprawling. Hayden's leg suddenly buckled. Talis immediately gripped his friend tighter to prevent his fall.

"We can afford a short rest," Talis said quietly, helping Hayden stand upright. "No wizards or bandits will hide around the outer limits of the palace. Your wound is now the greatest danger. We must reach the Healer's Hall. In the woods, there is little more that can be done."

They carefully picked their way around a clump of branches to a fallen, lichen-covered oak trunk. Hayden clenched his teeth as Talis eased him onto the green bark and released his arm. Cold sweat beaded on Hayden's forehead. He tried to wipe the water from his brow. The movement sent waves of pain through his shoulder. Hayden's vision swam. Squeezing his eyes closed, Hayden put a hand on the trunk and waited for it to pass.

Talis set the bow against the tree. He crouched beside his friend. The bandages that the elf had fashioned from the strips of Hayden's cloak were still tight across Hayden's back, though the once earthen-brown fabric was stained black with blood. The elf inspected the bandages around Hayden's waist, which had begun to unravel. With a slight frown, Talis readjusted the strips and pulled them more securely. Hayden let out a small grunt, eyes crinkling in pain.

"I'm sorry, *Estienen*," Talis apologized as he checked the bandages once more. "I have stanched the blood for now. These must stay tightly packed or else you will be the worse for it."

"The Sadyran salve has numbed the worst of the injury," Hayden replied, opening his eyes. "It will be fine until we reach the palace. So long as we have no more company along the way."

Talis untied a waterskin on his belt. He uncorked it and offered it to Hayden. Hayden tipped the waterskin to his lips, sipped, and handed it back.

"I wish I had seen who did it," Hayden picked up the thread of conversation from earlier as Talis restrung the waterskin. "The last thing I remember was standing before Diamantas, threatening his life. He could have killed me, Talis. He *should* have killed me. I was defenseless. He had the opportunity to end the fight once and for all. Why didn't he? What's equally worrying is I heard nothing before being struck. Not a single crack of a twig or the crunching of leaf litter under a boot. The person was noiseless." Hayden's gray gaze looked dully at Talis. "We have to consider the attacker was an elf."

"An elf fighting against us?" Talis tilted his head, amber eyes contemplative, then shook his head. "In this case, it isn't likely. Diamantas may have elven allies of which we are unaware. However, there were no new marks when I found you. An elf would have had to harness the forest's magic to assault you without evidence of the fact. Had that happened, I would have sensed it. An elf can't use energy without other elves perceiving the shift in the environment."

Hayden ran his right hand over his face and then through his hair in frustration. His gaze dropped to a ring on his left hand. The silver glinted in the sun's bright rays. Hayden rubbed a thumb over it. Silence descended between the pair.

"I'm afraid, Talis," Hayden spoke quietly. "What if all this is for nothing? What if Inishmore has taken her? Kyra was my responsibility. *Is* my responsibility if she's . . ." Hayden broke off, eyes crinkled in pain. After a moment, he continued. "Diamantas seemed genuinely puzzled by Kyra's disappearance. He claimed he didn't know what happened to her. He said it was in his best interests to have insight into her fate. I almost believe he is searching as blindly as we are. Almost. I have as much faith in his words as a daggerfish promising a turtle it won't bite. My own doubts, though. I can't run from those, Talis. I feel so lost." When Hayden looked up, Talis saw the entreaty in his gray eyes. "I have to find her. I can't live with more guilt than I already have."

"Your fear grows, and your confidence weakens. I understand that. I have felt the same. But *Estienen*, these come from your mind." The elf paused, then asked softly, "What does your heart tell you?"

Hayden twisted his ring. "She lives."

"We agree."

Talis spun. In one fluid motion, he had snatched up his bow, fit an arrow to his string, and trained the weapon in the direction of the voice. Hayden's hand went to the hilt of his sword. He half-rose, then gasped and fell back.

A black panther stepped out of the forest. His yellow-orbed eyes calmly observed Talis and the bow. The panther dipped his head in a respectful gesture. "Greetings, Talis of Silvias."

Hayden's gray gaze was muddled in confusion. He gave Talis a sidelong glance. He was surprised to see recognition in the elf's amber eyes. Talis lowered the bow and dropped the arrow in its quiver. "Greetings, Raff of the *Al-Ethran*," he said, putting the bow aside. "It has been many years since a member of the Council visited the Realm."

"Indeed, yet our tidings may be welcome."

Raff looked back as a clopping of hoofbeats announced the arrival of Raven. The roan's auburn mane glimmered in the pockets of sunlight. Hazel was at his side, bits of leaves clinging to her thick coat. The roan exhaled deeply through his nostrils.

Hayden started in astonishment. "Raven!"

The roan walked forward and bent his head. Raven's luminous brown eyes were filled with concern as Hayden stroked his nose. "You are injured."

"Raven," Hayden repeated. "We've been looking for you and Kyra for weeks. Solarus said you both left wherever it was he had taken you. Yet you're here alone and without a saddle."

"The *Al-Ethran* removed the saddle when I sought their counsel," Raven replied without elaboration.

Hayden turned toward Raff. Tears streamed unabashedly down his face. "Where is Kyra? What happened? Is she alive?"

"We do not have that answer," Raff responded. "We believe, as you just mentioned, that she is. The *Al-Ethran* has agreed that you and we are best served by joining efforts in our search. Kyra's fate is as important to the future of animal kind as it is to that of men and elves." Raff's tail swished along the forest floor. He exchanged a meaningful look with Hazel. "We have theories as to where she may be found, if she can be found at all."

Hayden swiped back the tears with his good hand. "What theories? Please, tell us what you know."

"When we are in the Healer's Hall," Talis interrupted. "You are in no shape to help Kyra, nor will you be if you insist on weakening yourself."

"I will take you," Raven said. He carefully bent a knee so that his back was level with the tree trunk. "If you can ride without a saddle, that is."

Talis stooped low and helped lift Hayden by his waist. With effort, Hayden managed to slide onto Raven's back. Hayden gripped Raven's mane with his left hand, right arm hanging limply at his side. Talis grabbed his bow and swiftly mounted behind Hayden.

"Let us be off," Raff rumbled. "If the dark wizards' resolve is as great as our own, time is not our ally."

Chapter 9

James strode down the hallway of the literature department. His thick layers of hair swung in time to his mailbag. There was a lightness to his step. As he greeted a pair of his fellow teaching assistants, James suddenly caught himself humming. He laughed.

"I haven't done that since I was a boy," James murmured to himself. He readjusted his mailbag and headed down an adjacent corridor. Humming was a habit he had picked up from his sisters, who had adopted it from their father. He sang as he played his dylar every evening, entertaining his three children as their mother cooked supper. The middle sister's pitch was always off tune.

A nostalgic and sorrowful smile formed on James' lips. When their father was thrown from his horse during a bridge crossing, James' sisters filled the haunting silence by humming their father's melodies. It had gotten him and his mother through the worst months after the accident.

James approached a gaggle of students crowded around the professors' main office. They chattered with nervous anticipation as they peered at the grades posted on the department's bulletin board. James weaved his way in between them. He glanced back. A girl with a long, fiery red braid squealed in delight as she saw her score.

Fiery red. The color of his older sister's hair.

James proceeded forward as his mind spiraled back to his earlier ruminations. To his sisters. His mother took over the responsibility of hawking goods in Thanesgard. His sister, a child herself at the age of twelve, was in charge of the cleaning, cooking, teaching, and scolding. She was overbearing and bossy. At night when they were in their room, too small for one let alone three, she ordered her younger siblings to stop their brazen attempts to steal the air she was breathing while she studied.

Why did it take so long for us to become friends? James asked himself. He didn't have an answer to this question any more than he had had for the last thirteen years. He had taken for granted she would always be there. When James left for the Academy at fifteen, his oldest sister stayed behind to care for their ailing mother. His middle sister packed her belongings and moved. James never heard from her again.

He paused in front of a classroom door. Through the window he saw Mrs. Lakshmi at a whiteboard, pointing to a graph she had drawn. The scene lanced James' heart with sorrow. It reminded him of his own days as a student attentively focused on the scribe's explanations of numbers and figures.

"If my sister had gone to the Academy instead of me, she would have lived," James said to himself as he continued to stare through the window. "As would I."

Water pooled at the corners of his eyes. James turned away and strode down the hallway, his steps mired by his pain. He could hear his sister's laugh, as pure as temple chimes. James imagined her twirling and dancing under eternal sunlight in a garden filled with golden-ray lilies. Humming. He had to have faith that Inishmore had rewarded her devotion in Ilian by returning her to the Healer.

James, on the other hand, had become a Lyneera. He left Ilian swaddled in pain and had awoken not to serenity but to a hard desk, face pressed against it. A blue light pulsed in and through him. Inishmore didn't believe his duty was satisfied. Or else he should have passed on after his sister. James had one last service to Inishmore.

James glanced up at the clock at the end of the hallway. He had thirty minutes to get to Hampstead for his lesson with Kate. His pace quickened. "That is why I'm here," James reminded himself. The moment Millie had approached him, proposed he tutor her niece, a girl without a past and a victim of tragedy, a girl who needed a confidant, James felt it. The breeze that stirred his heart. Inishmore. It whispered this was his purpose. Kate was the reason he was a Lyneera, in this world.

James reached the entrance to the building. Students blocked the doors, straggling inside as the ringing of clocks signaled the start of lessons.

He was going to be late. James looked down, adjusting the mailbag that clapped against his side, and rushed toward the door. And collided with a muscly, taller boy. James began to apologize. The words vanished from his lips as his gaze met the boy's.

The boy shoved James forcefully. James stumbled backward. His blood went cold, though not on account of the boy's size. It was the malicious upturning of the boy's lips and sinister glint in his dark eyes that chilled James from the inside. "Reuben," he stated warily.

"I would watch where you're going, James," the tall boy sneered. "You might accidentally run into someone you didn't want to see."

James' jaw clenched. Instead of responding, he started to go around the boy.

Reuben roughly seized James by the shoulder. "What's the hurry?"

"Clear off, Reuben."

Reuben's grin formed pits at the corners of his mouth. His hand slid in and out of his jacket pocket so swiftly, James barely caught sight of the switchblade that snapped into his hand. An orange glow splashed over Reuben as he held the knife close to James' neck. "When I ask you a question, you should answer it. You might not feel the strike of a mortal, but you aren't immune to the sting of a Variavryk."

James gritted his teeth. He knew too well that Reuben's words were accurate. "The Variavryk are equally vulnerable to a Lyneera's blade. Whatever your purpose is here, it isn't to kill me, any more than my purpose in London is to kill you. Inishmore sent me here to do something greater than seek revenge."

Reuben laughed mirthlessly. "What if I'm in London to seek mine? You Lyneera are slaves to Inishmore. You believe you have a purpose here, yet you must wait for Inishmore to reveal what that mysterious purpose is. You have waited many years, Jamison. How many more will pass before you act? That is why the Lyneera are weak. The Variavryk answer to no one. We move as we like."

"The Variavryk commit unspeakable acts in life," James replied unflinchingly even as Reuben held the knife closer. "As such, you are rejected by Inishmore in death. You speak of freedom? You are imprisoned because of the evil you wrought. Lyneera serve Inishmore willingly. We protect those who cannot protect themselves."

"Rejected, James? Is that what the scribes teach?" Reuben's black eyes were empty chasms as he dropped his voice. "I am here because I choose to be. The scribes abhor us, because they fear us. Scribes don't care to admit we are similar. Scribes have also taken the lives of others, though they claim to abstain from violence. Your brother-in-law, for example. It was by his hand, the hand of a scribe, that I was erased from Ilian." The orange light flared. The outline of a long, black cloak formed over Reuben's shoulders. His hair was the same inky black of his cloak and fell to his shoulders. Jeweled rings appeared on his hands. "Who is more loathsome, Jamison?" he hissed. "My kind, who embrace the wickedness others proclaim us to possess? Or the scribes, who profess a false holiness? I cannot get my vengeance on your brother-in-law. Not yet. *You*, Lyneera. You are a different matter."

James' fist tightened around the mailbag. He saw a glint of light off the windows and realized he was wreathed in a blue glow. The outline of a leather jacket and pants tucked into boots appeared around his frame. "Leave, Reuben. This will not end well for you."

"I wonder if the girl would survive if you tried to carry out that threat. Yes, Jamison, I know about Kate," Reuben said with ominous pleasure as a look of alarm flew across James' face. "I have been patient. That is a gift with which Variavryk are blessed. I promised to inflict pain on you as your brother-in-law did to me. You might accept harm to yourself. I wonder if the girl feels the same way?"

"You want to take reprisal against me and my brother-in-law, then take it. Your vengeance and our history don't involve her."

"It does now. You should think on that."

Reuben glanced up at the sound of laughter down the hallway. He flicked the switchblade closed and returned it to his pocket as students walked toward the entrance. The orange around Reuben vanished, as did the image of the cloak and rings. In the same moment, James' blue light faded.

Reuben moved to the side and away from the entrance. The depraved grin returned to his lips. "Enjoy your lesson," he said in an undertone. "We'll see each other soon, James."

James stared, pulse racing, as Reuben sauntered toward the students. The boy paused. He added without looking back, "If you think we wreak havoc as mortals, imagine what we can do as Variavryk."

Reuben disappeared in the throng of students. It was then that James tasted blood in his mouth, having bitten tightly on his lip. James swallowed the terror that spiked within him. He turned and raced out the main entrance doors.

The Variavryk knew about Kate. And James couldn't think of any way to protect her.

***

"I'm coming!" Kate called over her shoulder. She rubbed her hair with the towel for another moment then touched it. Her hair was still damp. Fortunately, spring had bowed early to the warmth that normally accompanied summer. The May sunshine was hot enough to dry Kate's hair. She draped the towel over the shower rod and rushed out of the bathroom. Back in her room, Kate went to her dresser. She grabbed a comb and started impatiently teasing out a few stubborn knots.

I wonder what Millie's got planned, she thought. Her aunt had mentioned during breakfast that they had an event in the afternoon without offering further details. It was a surprise, Millie had insisted.

"And I don't like spoiling a good surprise," she chuckled as Kate put the dishes in the sink. "Why don't you wear one of those gorgeous blouses we bought the other day, sweetie? The pink with the gold fringe is absolutely dazzling, don't you think?"

Kate didn't, but Millie had picked out that particular blouse the previous weekend. Since their first excursion to Regent Square the previous autumn, Kate had sprouted four inches. When Kate's ankles began peeking out from her jeans, Millie declared it was time to replace her wardrobe. It was toward the end of the day's shopping that Millie had discovered the flashy blouse. Kate tried it on because Millie insisted. Unfortunately, it only confirmed in Millie's eyes that the blouse was a "spectacular fit." Millie was adamant Kate would have it. Kate was too tired to argue.

"In hindsight, I should have argued a bit," Kate muttered, putting down her comb. She agreed it was "spectacular" in that it made her a spectacle for anyone who laid eyes on it. Regardless, it made Millie happy, and it was the weekend. Her humiliation would be limited to whatever strangers they encountered at Millie's secret event.

"Kate, sweetie, chop-chop! We're going to be late!"

Kate sighed. She shook her hair, letting it fall in waves, and then strode into the hall. She was enveloped by a syrupy scent, which Kate guessed was one of Millie's newest perfumes. There was also a faint yet distinct smell of smoke. Kate's heart hammered. She frantically looked around for the source. The last time she had smelled something burning in the house was when Millie charred her toast. Except this wasn't the scent of food. Kate took the stairs two at a time, shouting worriedly, "Aunt Millie, do you smell smoke? I looked upstairs and didn't see anything . . ."

At the landing, Kate froze. There in the living room, Millie waited with a grin as eager as an auctioneer opening the day's bidding. Her hands were clasped together. She rocked on her neon-green stiletto heels, which matched her green-and-silver-spotted dress. Millie's hair was pinned in perfect curls atop her head.

She was flocked by a small group. Kate's insides squirmed. She hesitantly made her way toward Millie. Her gaze passed over men and women dressed in eccentric clothing. She vaguely recognized them from art exhibitions Millie had taken her to. Robert the cab driver was also there in one of his suits, as were her tutors. Professor O'Leary was dressed as sharply as ever in a tan suit. She stood next to Mr. Dullwane, who wore a plain shirt and an even plainer expression. Mr. Stevens donned a bowtie and was listening to Mrs. Lakshmi, who was smiling widely at Kate. Kate gave her an uncertain smile back.

Then she felt a flutter of relief when her eyes landed on James. He stood alone at the edge of the assembly. His hands gripped the mailbag he wore slung across his body. James had missed their lesson the day before. He had a fever, Millie informed Kate when she came home that afternoon. James looked unusually pale, and his gaze seemed strangely empty. When Kate caught his eye, though, James gave her an encouraging smile. *I really should have argued against the shirt*, Kate thought, feeling her cheeks grow hot.

Kate's gaze at last moved to a vanilla sheet cake that spanned the living room table. Candles dotted the top, too many to count, flames flickering merrily. That solved the mystery of the smoke's source.

"Happy birthday, sweetie!" Millie exclaimed, sweeping her into a giant hug.

The perfume swirled around Kate. She felt light-headed as she stared past Millie at the guests. *I'm not excited to have a room full of people I barely know watching me as though I'm about to perform some sort of trick.*

"Are you surprised?" Millie asked cheerfully when she finally released Kate.

"Very." Kate glanced back at the cake. *It's my birthday?* Kate wished fervently that she hadn't been ambushed with a crowd.

"It's not every day that a girl turns sixteen," Millie went on, taking Kate's arm and walking her to the cake. "This is an important year, sweetie. You're a proper young woman now, sweetie. Everyone's here to celebrate this wonderful occasion with you!"

I really rather they weren't, Kate thought, but Millie had already turned around and raised her hands. "Happy birthday to you . . ." she sang loudly. The group picked up the cheerful chorus. Even Mr. Dullwane joined in, though his voice was as monotone as it was during their lessons.

Kate wanted to hide. A birthday reminded her that she was a year older and with few memories of her past. How much time had to go by before she began to remember who she had been? Even after seven months, the police investigation hadn't turned up any clues. The gleeful singing was starkly at odds with the dismay filling her heart.

". . . tooooo yoooooooouuuu," the crowd concluded. Millie led a boisterous applause. "Make a wish." Millie nudged Kate forward so that she was almost leaning over the candles. "Quickly, though, dear, the wax is dripping."

Reluctantly, Kate closed her eyes to the candles. *I wish . . . I wish this year I can find out what my life was like before the fire. I want to find out what happened to my family.* She blew on the candles, tears hidden behind her lids. She smelled the scent of smoke curling up from the wicks as her guests clapped loudly. Kate waited for the water rimming her eyes to return to their reservoir before she opened her eyes again. Millie's face beamed with joy. Kate moved back as Millie took the knife beside the cake and began cutting slices.

What's the point of a wish? Kate wondered, listlessly watching Millie hand out plates to the guests. *Who am I asking to grant my request?*

Kate plastered a smile to her face as guests came forward. As she greeted them, Kate's eyes sought out James. He was the one person around with whom she was comfortable when she felt vulnerable and defeated. She spied James studying a painting of a Scottish castle near the stairwell. One hand was on his chin while his other arm supported his elbow. Kate was surprised to see pain lining his face.

Kate suddenly felt ashamed. She relied so heavily on James, as she did on Millie. Instead of appreciating what they had done for her, Kate was wallowing in self-pity. Her gaze flickered to her aunt. Millie was relating a story to Robert and a couple from the art gallery. Her aunt gestured animatedly, which gave way to laughter from her attentive audience. Kate smiled. Millie had organized the party to show Kate she was special and cared about. Kate crossed the room.

Millie had finished her story. Robert chatted with the couple as Millie noticed Kate approaching. "Hi, sweetie! Are you enjoying the party? I thought . . . oh!"

Kate embraced Millie and held her for a moment. When Kate let go, Millie's blue eyes looked at Kate with surprise. "What was that for, sweetie?"

"I wanted to say thank you," Kate replied, feeling a tug in her heart. "For everything."

Millie touched her curls self-consciously. Color came to her cheeks. "It's only a little get-together, dear. Really wasn't much to put together at all, called a few friends, and your tutors were delighted to attend. In fact, would you believe that Deirdre made this delectable cake herself? It's absolutely flawless. I never pictured Deirdre in an apron with her hands covered with flour, she's always so sharply dressed." Millie gave Kate a lip-sticked kiss on the cheek and went back to cut more portions of cake.

Thank you for giving me a home. Kate turned, excited to talk to James next.

When Kate's eyes landed on the painting of the castle, though, James wasn't there. Puzzled, Kate scanned the room. He wasn't tucked away in any conversation, nor was he off somewhere else by himself. Crestfallen, Kate realized James had left. He hadn't even come over to wish her a happy birthday.

"You haven't spoken with Priscilla yet, dear," Millie was saying now. She had a plate of cake in hand. Washing her disappointment from her expression, Kate fixed a smile to her face. She and Millie circuited around the room to finish greeting the guests. All the while, Kate turned over in her mind what could make James leave so abruptly.

***

June's long days of sunlight boosted Kate's spirits. Unlike Millie, Kate's skin craved sunlight and turned a golden copper hue as the weeks went on. She and her tutors spent their hours sitting on Millie's patio in iron-wrought chairs. They poured lemonade from the cat tail–handled pitcher into glass cups with paw prints and ate sandwiches from plates that had "Home is where my cat is" written on the bottom as they worked through new topics.

Kate wiped sweat from her brow. Her chair was positioned close to the alder trees that offered spotty shade, but the sun baked the paver stones under her feet. Despite the aberrant hot summer weather, Kate grinned. It was the end of her logic lesson. She had finally, finally won a personal victory over Mr. Stevens. Her tutor doffed a large-brimmed hat, which spared him from the brunt of the heat. His glasses slid down his nose.

"Well done," Mr. Stevens commended as he pushed his glasses back up. "I haven't had such a spirited debate since my son attempted to persuade me to purchase him a motorcycle. His argument wasn't as articulate as yours was today. Unfortunately for him, fortunately for the car dealer we visited instead."

Kate's grin widened. Her eyes followed a pair of finches who fluttered to the ground. Kate picked off the crust of her sandwich and tossed it toward the birds. They hopped forward, pecking merrily at the crumbs.

"We have a few minutes left," Mr. Stevens commented. "After that verbal checkmate, I need a break."

The sparrows hastily hopped to the side as Mr. Stevens pushed his chair back. He withdrew a long, thin pipe from his jacket pocket. "Do you mind if I have a quick puff? Unless the smoke bothers you."

"I don't mind," Kate replied. Tilting her head back against the chair, Kate watched as more finches dove from the alder branches toward the remaining crumbs. The heat filled her with a sleepy contentedness. Kate closed her eyes, listening to the tweets of the finches and the striking of a match.

"That's much better," she heard Mr. Stevens say. A heady aroma of apples, cloves, and unfamiliar scents fanned through the air. Kate's head began to reel as she breathed in the vapors. Her eyelids blinked open. The alder branches began to fade behind a screen of an intense white light. Kate squeezed her eyes shut as the light burned behind her lids.

"What is that?"

"Kolker leaf mixed with Calonian spices. It is quite soothing, particularly on days when your curiosity cannot be sated. Today you seem to have stored a manuscript of questions since our last session."

The voice was familiar. Except it wasn't Mr. Stevens.

After a moment, the light ebbed from behind her still-closed eyelids. The plastic back of the chair suddenly felt spongy against her neck. A cool breeze tickled her toes. Kate chanced opening her eyes. Her hand shot to her mouth in astonishment. Kate sat upright so quickly, she nearly tumbled sideways onto the lush rug of grass beneath her. The house, patio, and alders were gone, replaced by a panorama of forested hills. She sat barefoot above a long dirt bank. Beyond it, a vast lake glittered as though made from millions of white opals. Wisps of white clouds capped the blue sky like combed-over hair.

Kate goggled at the scene. It felt unfathomably and unsettlingly real. The breeze caressed her face, and the lake's waters rippled gently below her. *Was this all caused by Mr. Stevens' pipe?* she asked herself as the heady fragrance of apples and spices enveloped her. Had it made her delirious? Did she fall asleep? Kate's fingers grazed the top of the grass. It was soft and not a sensation she could create in a dream.

"I will humor you, however. Your query is pertinent to our practice."

Kate glanced sideways. A stranger in an azure cloak sat cross-legged next to her. He held a pipe in one hand from which white smoke curled into the air. He was pensively rubbing his cropped beard. His dark brown hair was sprinkled with silver. The stranger's ocean blue eyes brushed over the lake. A long walking stick lay parallel to him.

Kate scarcely breathed, transfixed by the cloak. It poured over his shoulders and streamed across the grass as fluidly as water. It was the first time Kate had seen anything resembling her own cloak. She drove back an impulse to reach out and touch the material.

The stranger regarded her with an expectant expression.

"I, um . . ." Kate tucked a lock of hair behind her ear, surprised to find herself replying. "What question was that?"

The stranger's brow raised, somehow managing to look both mildly irritated and moderately amused. "The most recent, Kyra. While I would not be surprised if you have already jumped through another three questions, it would behoove you to listen to my answer first."

Kate's bewilderment grew as she repeated to herself, *Kyra? Who's Kyra?*

The stranger didn't seem to notice Kate's openmouthed stare. "The question to which I am responding, Kyra, is why your magic reacts to others while mine does not. It is simple: I have years of practice and mastery over mine. You are not yet of age to have control over yours. Magic attracts magic. Thankfully, young wizards do not possess enough power for their magic to be accidentally summoned by the presence of another's. If they did, bundles of magic would be flinging themselves toward whatever spell is closest. On a wizard's sixteenth birthday, his or her magic can move unconstrained. It can be developed to its fullest extent. That is not to say that nascent magic cannot be a potent force before then. Do not ask me why," the stranger interjected brusquely, though Kate hadn't any intention of interrupting. She felt like a squirrel running through a cache of acorns, unable to focus on any single part of the stranger's words. *Wizards? Magic? What on earth is going on? Who the heck is Kyra?*

The stranger took another long draw on his pipe. He released the smoke slowly. "To tell you life will become more complicated is putting it charitably. You related yesterday that your magic already gravitates on its own accord and with the force to 'pull you with it.' This is an indication that your energy is more powerful than that of an average wizard. Do not ask me why," the stranger preempted again. "It simply is."

Kate's lips tugged into a puzzled frown. She gathered that whoever Kyra was, she was curious and, based on the stranger's brusque interruption of questions, persistent. Why did he believe Kate was this girl?

"What is most important is not whether your power moves toward another's as I have just explained, since this can be easily mastered once you are of age. The danger is that energy also responds to your emotions and thoughts." The stranger rubbed his chin again, and Kate saw a troubled look in his eyes. "One can easily lose control outwardly if one does not have control inwardly. You must have the capacity to experience fear without being overcome by it. Fear breeds anger. Anger blackens the heart. You must choose to respond to all situations in a calm and rational manner. Which, presently, is not an easy request of you."

The stranger smiled thinly. Kate met his gaze and suddenly felt a lump in her throat. She averted her eyes. She picked a blade of grass, trying to decipher the sudden stitch in her heart. Tears welled. Kate knew him. She *missed* him.

No. I'm definitely hallucinating. Kate thrust the feelings back. She glanced up at the stranger, who contentedly puffed on his pipe and gazed across the water. *Why am I acting like this is an actual conversation? He isn't real.*

What was real was the unbearable compulsion to unearth who he was. Where this place was. As Kate opened her mouth, she noticed the sun had begun to swell. She watched it continue to inflate like a giant balloon. Without warning, the sun burst. Kate closed her eyes and ducked her head. The cushioned earth became hard. The light disappeared, as did the breeze. A voice trickled into her ear.

". . . in the university, my daughter has the blissful freedom to make clothing decisions without her old-fashioned father. Apparently, financing her education doesn't give me a vote . . . Kate, is something wrong?"

Heart pounding, Kate lifted her gaze. She was back on the patio, seated on the iron-wrought chair beneath the alders. Mr. Stevens reclined comfortably, pipe in hand. His forehead was wrinkled in concern. Kate blinked slowly. Mr. Stevens was still there.

"I have a headache from the heat," Kate replied in a voice that sounded distant to her. The blood in her ears pumped furiously.

"Have some lemonade." Mr. Stevens refilled a glass on the table and pushed it toward her. "It may be the pipe, too. Apple tobacco is milder than other types, which is why I prefer it. Some people are sensitive to any kind of smoke, though. I'll put it out."

Kate's throat constricted. "Apple tobacco?"

"Yes," Mr. Stevens replied, turning the pipe over and rapping out the remaining leaves. "It's smooth and one of my few vices. That and a good Merlot. Two vices then."

"What about the kolker leaves? Do they affect people more than the apple?"

Mr. Stevens gave her a puzzled look. "What are kolker leaves?"

The clanging of the grandfather clock rescued Kate from answering. She exchanged goodbyes with Mr. Stevens, who recommended more lemonade and aspirin for her headache. When he had left the patio, Kate slumped back in her chair. She turned her gaze upward. The blue sky was cloudless behind the veil of the leaves. The finches had settled on tree branches, chirping noisily.

"None of this makes sense," Kate muttered out loud. Except when she visualized the lake, Kate could hear its gentle waters lapping the bank. She also had seen the stranger's azure cloak. Kate was convinced it was identical to the one in her closet, the one she had worn in Chicago. Her heart skipped a beat. It was a long shot, impossible, but was what she witnessed a memory? Had the conversation with the stranger taken place?

A strange pairing of excitement and dread coursed through Kate. Excitement to uncover any clue to her past, even one with a fantastical conversation about wizards and magic. Dread because the stranger had called her by another name. Kyra.

Kate's gut instinct didn't reject the idea that the identity could be hers.

Chapter 10

Kate stretched her arms over her head, closing her eyes with a sigh. Sweat matted the back of her hair and her T-shirt. Tall lime trees and weeping beeches protected her from another hot summer's day.

Kate had reached the halfway point in her run, a wide bridle path at the south end of the large, verdant Hyde Park. The park was one of her favorite places. Fellow joggers waved as they went by, and riders trotted finely groomed horses down the dirt path. The steeds contributed a musty scent to the pervasive fragrance of daffodils and bluebells that dotted the ground. Kate swung her arms gently from side to side. Her taut muscles loosened with each movement.

An older woman pushed a stroller down the path. Kate turned, stretching her back, and followed the stroller with her eyes. Her face broke into a grin. Two Pekingese lounged inside the stroller like canine royalty, tongues lolling with pure joy. Kate laughed as the woman cooed to them.

"*That* is exactly why we are superior to those pompous pooches, Rosalind," came a disdainful voice as the woman and dogs continued down the road. "They have four healthy legs and refuse to use them. Lazy, spoiled creatures."

That's an odd thing to say, Kate thought. She cast a glance around the park. The joggers were far ahead of her, and there was no one coming up behind or beside her. Birds trilled overhead. Shrugging, Kate widened her stance and leaned down near a weeping beech to touch her toes. Another smile came to her face. Kate had company. Three cats basked in a spot of sun that streamed through the beech's thick leaves.

"Humans have the nerve to say *we* loaf around all day," a small calico criticized, ears twitching. "What's wrong with taking a nap here or there? How else would our fur keep that purrrfect sheen? How, Fifi?"

"Exactly my point." A black female turned and leisurely licked her white stockinged leg.

Kate's eyes widened in astonishment. Were the cats *talking*? No, that was absurd. Kate looked left. A poodle strutted primly on its leash as his young owner bopped his head to music from his headphones. Kate's gaze flew to the right. The path was empty.

Kate heard a delicate sneeze. She dragged her attention to the cats. Fifi shook her head, nose twitching. Then she resumed her preening. The last of the trio, a ginger tabby, stretched out his paws with a yawn. He seemed wholly uninterested in the female cats' conversation. He flipped over, belly exposed, and closed his eyes.

Kate straightened, the astounded look spreading across her face. Three cats. Three cats unmistakably fitting Millie's description of her long-lost feline companions. Including their names, Kate suddenly remembered. Rosalind and

Fifi. The orange tabby would have to be Prince Albert. *If,* Kate disputed in her head, *I actually understood them.*

Fifi was now eyeing the ginger tabby, whose chest rose and fell peacefully. She gave the calico a mischievous look. The black cat flattened herself against the ground. With an exaggerated leap, Fifi buffeted the sleeping cat's nose. With a shocked yowl, the tabby's limbs shot out. He leapt on all fours and looked around wildly.

"What? Who's that? *Fifi!*"

Fifi made a show of looking for the perpetrator. "What, Albert? What happened?"

The ginger tabby looked affronted. "Did you see her attack me?" he asked Rosalind in an accusatory tone. "You saw her, didn't you, Rosalind?"

Rosalind gave Albert a noncommittal look, then scratched her ear with a claw. "How would I know? I was watching that girl watching us. Over there." She upturned her head, green eyes meeting Kate's. "It's rude to stare."

"Stare back," Fifi suggested.

"You're Millie's cats," Kate said, flabbergasted. "And you're talking. You're ... really ... talking."

Rosalind itched her ear as though Kate hadn't spoken and looked at Fifi. "Humans are so irritating. How many times do they say silly things like, 'Awww, you're so cute!' and pretend to meow? Then the children grab our tails."

"I *can* understand you," Kate found herself continuing. Her initial shock faded to fascination. Unlike the other strange experiences she had had, entering into the cats' conversation was *fun.* This time, Rosalind froze mid-scratch. Barely moving her lips, she mewed anxiously, "Fifi, did she hear me? I mean, really *hear* me say that?"

Albert's ginger fur stood on end. "Oh no, oh no, oh no, she recognizes us, she knows we escaped, we're done for, oh no, oh no ..."

"Shh, Albert!" Fifi hissed. The black cat started biting at her claw. "Stop having kittens and relax. It's not like she brought a box and is ready to scoop us into it. Be quiet and act *normal.*"

"What's normal?"

"Aloof, Albert. Act aloof."

"What's aloof?"

Fifi swiped at Albert with a peevish scowl. The ginger ducked as Fifi continued to glower at him. "Aloof, Albert. Like you don't care about anything. We're cats. That's what we *do.* What on earth did you do in your last five lives?"

"I've been aloof," Albert said unconvincingly. "I've been very aloof. I'm aloof right now. See?"

"You know what? Forget aloof. Just play dead. You're good at that."

Rosalind sat on her haunches and stared off into the distance. She reminded Kate of a sphinx, poised with a timeless gaze. Looking panicked, Albert began to swat at an imaginary foe. Fifi went back to biting a claw.

Kate watched silently. After a moment, Albert stopped batting the blades of grass. "Is she going to go away, Rosalind?" he mewed tentatively.

"I'm not a human, Albert," came the black and white cat's testy reply. "They're complicated. They don't do things that make sense, like sharing a house with a dog instead of a feline. Why don't you ask her if she's going to leave?"

"It's just..." Albert looked imploringly at Fifi. "Do you remember the pâtés that Millie served? The whitefish? Every day at half four on those silver platters and with a side of catnip."

Rosalind snorted disdainfully. "That wasn't worth being forced to wear those foo-foo outfits."

"They weren't too bad," Albert said with what Kate swore was a pout.

"*You* got to wear a crown," Fifi put in sulkily. She had given up her pretense of grooming. "I had to wear a *tutu*. It was embarrassing. The ducks still mock me. That's why we left, remember?"

"Disgraceful," Rosalind agreed. Her eyes became narrow slits as she glanced up at Kate. Quickly looking down, she resumed her imperious stare. "She. Is. Staring. At. Us."

"I can also hear you," Kate replied. To Albert, she said, "I'm sure if you went back to Millie, she would give you whitefish. She misses you a lot."

Albert's eyes widened. Rosalind's ears flattened, and Fifi's back and tail puffed out with raised fur.

"Run away!" Albert yowled. He didn't wait for a response from the females as he sprinted out of the beech. "She's after us! Run away!"

Fifi's expression soured again, but she needed no encouraging. She and Rosalind bounded after the tabby.

"Albert, I'm going to turn you into dog food for this!" Kate heard Fifi hiss. Kate's gaze trailed the cats as they zipped down the grass and darted into a line of trees. For a moment, she didn't move. Finally, Kate began to trot back onto the path. She imagined her bewildered expression wasn't so different from Rosalind's.

***

"I saw some cats at Hyde Park today, Aunt Millie."

"Oh?" Millie's blue eyes reflected a nostalgic melancholy. "I wish you had brought them here, sweetie. I would love to have some kittens gamboling in the house."

Kate attempted a half-smile. She hoped Millie didn't notice her hand trembling as she lifted a fork and took a bite of the cod Millie had cooked for dinner. "What did you, ah, what did you feed Rosalind and Fifi and Albert?"

Millie tapped her filet thoughtfully with her fork. "Whitefish. It was a pâté actually. I had small, silver dishes for each of them. Afterward, I gave them a nip of catnip. A nip of nip! On the side, their special treat." She laughed at her own joke. Unexpectedly, Millie released a deep sigh. "I do miss them, the dears. The house was never quiet, what with them chasing each other like children on a playground. They might have broken a lamp and a teacup,—a few teacups—but I would replace my whole dining set to have them back."

Kate's temple pounded forcefully. "May I be excused, Aunt Millie?"

Her aunt peered at Kate with concern. "What's the matter, dearie? Not feeling well?"

"I have homework to do," Kate said, which was true but not the reason she needed to go someplace else. "Mrs. Lakshmi assigned me more worksheets tonight. I really should get started."

"I wouldn't want you to disappoint Mrs. Lakshmi," Millie replied with a smile. She scooped up the plates. "Tell me if you need a cup of tea or anything else. I'll be up for a while yet."

As Millie scurried to the sink, hands full of dishes, Kate trod out of the kitchen. Thoughts churned in her mind, which intensified the pressure in her temple. Only days earlier, Kate had had her experience with Mr. Stevens and the stranger with the azure cloak. Now she was hearing conversations with indignant felines. The pleasure of being able to communicate with them had been driven out by the bizarreness of the event. Millie confirmed what the cats had mentioned. Kate couldn't dismiss this incident as a dream any more than she could the discussion with the stranger.

Does anyone else have the ability to speak with animals? Kate wondered as she ascended the staircase. *If not, what does that mean about me?*

***

August came. Her tutors, she discovered on her last day with them, would take the month off to go on holiday with their families. To Kate's dismay, James would be among those absent. Kate tried to press the disappointment from her expression as she watched James arrange the pens on the table in a perfect row. He explained he had an invitation from his professor to work in The Public Record Office in Northern Ireland. University students weren't often invited to delve into the ancient manuscripts. It was an honor. He would return at the end of August in time for her first lesson. James didn't lift his gaze once as he spoke.

Kate placed her best impression of a smile on her lips. "Congratulations, James. That's fantastic. I'm excited for you."

"Thank you, Kate," he muttered. James set the last pen in the row. "I hope it will be enlightening."

Kate's heart dropped to her stomach. She silently watched him pack up his belongings and step out the door. She wondered if it was her imagination that James seemed downcast or if she only hoped he would miss her as much as she would miss him.

***

The first morning of her summer break, Kate rose and began her usual preparation for the day's lessons. Until it struck her there were no lessons. Her tutors had dispersed to their vacation destinations. Including James.

Dread lanced the joy in her heart. Overnight, Kate's lone friend had abandoned her. Not abandoned, Kate reminded herself as she walked to her window. It was a temporary separation. A month wasn't that long. Still, Kate's rational self was crowded out by her emotional one. She threw open the shutters. The warm scent of summer drifted around her. Kate leaned forward, palms pressed against the sill, and stared outside at nothing in particular.

Kate had grown comfortable living with Millie. She took pride in her successes when she solved a complex equation or outdebated Mr. Stevens. Kate had established a reliable routine. The people in her life gave her a sense of permanence she so desperately needed. Overnight, that certainty had been snatched away.

How will I fill my time? Kate pushed herself off the sill and turned back to her room. *I'll figure it out,* she reassured herself silently. *I came to London without any friends, I can deal with a month.* As Kate went to her closet to change, she knew it would be a long month.

Gratefully, Millie was true to her word. She had a laundry list of excursions and short trips outside the city preplanned. Millie brought Kate to the Globe Theater to see a production of *Much Ado About Nothing*. Despite her excitement watching her favorite Shakespearean play, Kate's heart panged at James' absence. In her mind's eye, Kate could see James leaning forward over the balcony railing, green eyes lighting up as he watched the actors with rapt attention. He would turn to Kate during scenes they particularly enjoyed and smile broadly. But James wasn't beside her. He sat in a fusty room with no windows, scrawling notes from old manuscripts and tomes with faded covers. That was how Kate imagined it anyway. She didn't know the first thing about archives. James was also more comfortable with his books than he was with people. No, James was undoubtably enjoying his time. Without her.

Kate let out a light sigh. She pulled herself from her thoughts as she heard Millie laugh along with the audience at the witty banter onstage. For the rest of the play, Kate focused on the characters and tried to ignore the continued ache in her heart.

The theater was one part of Millie's cultural immersion. They visited London's museums, toured Windsor Castle, and attended high-end art shows and auctions, of which Millie was a part. Kate recognized a few of the eclectic art enthusiasts from her birthday party. Kate found herself grinning as she listened to them bubble with a giddiness that made Millie look calm by comparison. Kate also enjoyed long runs through the city and spent hours reading on Hampstead Heath's downy summer grasses.

Kate's favorite outings were beyond the city limits. When Millie went to tea with old colleagues in Oxford, Kate hiked through nearby pastoral pastures freckled with sheep and wildflowers. She and Millie explored the idyllic university grounds of Cambridge. The next week, they traveled to the steaming Roman baths in the eponymous town of Bath.

Of all their excursions, Kate found nothing compared to their trip to Scotland. The medieval architecture of Edinburgh's Old Town and the castle that towered over the skyline called to Kate in a way unlike anything she had experienced in London. Kate's smile was the brightest light under the otherwise somber gray skies. For the first time, she appreciated Mr. Dullwane's lessons, as tedious as they had seemed at the time. She and Millie also took a bus tour to the highlands. A soupy fog bathed the dark green hills and moors, and the cool air was scented with rich earth and wildlife. Kate barely heard the tour guide's overview of the hills as she stared into the fog. A haunting and mystical sense swelled within her. It was far too soon when the tour guide ended her presentation, and they drove back to Edinburgh.

On the train ride back to London the next morning, Kate's heart tugged with sadness. The longing to stay in the grand Scottish city and its majestic highlands confused her. When they had returned to London, Kate realized why. She *lived* in Hampstead, yet in Edinburgh, Kate felt she had returned *home*.

***

Kate knew something was wrong when she walked out of her room. The acrid scent of burnt toast congested the hallway, and she heard Millie's flustered "Oh dears!" below. The teakettle whistled shrilly. Troubled, Kate descended the staircase.

It was the first day of her new semester. Kate's excitement prevented her from having a restful night. As much as she had enjoyed her time with Millie, Kate was ready to resume a life with a dependable schedule. She had missed her tutors, including, to her surprise, Mr. Dullwane. Kate expected his lessons to be more tolerable now that she had applied her education to real life. Most of all, Kate wanted to see James. How painfully she had missed her best friend.

Kate's happiness waned as she entered the kitchen.

"Oh dear, come now," Millie was saying frantically to herself. She snatched the wailing teakettle from the stove and set it on the countertop. Millie's curlers, normally tight and tidy, hung haphazardly from her hair like a person gripping the edge of the cliff. Her lipstick was noticeably absent. Millie rushed to the pieces of charred toast, picked them up, and dropped them on a plate with an "Ouch!" She sucked on her sore fingers. Millie still hadn't noticed Kate at the entrance.

"Good morning, Aunt Millie," Kate greeted cautiously.

Millie jumped, her hand flying to her chest. "Goodness!" she exclaimed as a curler shook loose and fell. "Oh, good morning, Kate dear. Did you sleep well? I didn't wake you, did I?" Without waiting for an answer, she gestured to the table. "Sit, dearie, I've heated some water for our tea. Unless you want coffee, I can make some . . ."

Kate remained standing. Her brows knitted with worry. She had never seen her aunt so out of sorts. "Is everything all right?" she asked as Millie flung open the fridge door. The grandfather clock gonged, interrupting Millie's response.

"Quite all right, dearie, never better," she answered after the noise had stopped. Millie pulled out a small plate of scones. "You've your lessons today and all. The holidays passed so quickly, didn't they? I'm sure you are happy to get back to work and not spend all day, every day, with an old fuddy-duddy like me. I completely forgot to buy some flowers, wouldn't you know. I can be so forgetful sometimes. I've asked Robert to bring by a bouquet after lunch. The flowers will rid us of this awful smell." Millie's face turned a shade of pink as she glanced over at the blackened pieces of toast.

"Let me help you," Kate said as she went to the cupboard. She removed two mugs and placed them on the table.

Millie hastened beside her. She held the kettle in one hand and a plate of scones in the other. "No dearie, sit yourself down," she said, almost spilling the kettle as she put it on the table. "Have some tea and eat. You need your energy to sweep away those cobwebs in your mind from the long break."

She patted Kate on the back and hurried to the sink. Kate glanced over her shoulder. Millie picked up a dishrag and began to wipe the countertop. Kate frowned. The surface didn't have a smudge on it.

"It's always a shame when summer ends though, isn't it?" Millie said. Her voice was a higher pitch than normal. "We had a grand time. A quite grand time." Millie's chipper veneer couldn't mask her sadness. She dragged the cloth repeatedly over the same spot on the counter.

Kate's ballooning excitement was suddenly popped by a needle of guilt. Her aunt was lonely. Kate hadn't realized how important their month together had been until now. Millie continued to chatter and clean as Kate miserably nibbled on a scone. If only her aunt had someone to keep her company.

After breakfast, Kate walked to the living room with a heavy step and heavier heart. Her gaze flickered to the paintings on the wall. Her eyes found the sketch of two young girls. Not for the first time, Kate thought Millie would have been a wonderful mother if she had had children of her own. Kate's gaze floated up to the pastel painting of three cats frolicking in a meadow. Her heart skipped a beat.

The cats.

Plans began to reel through Kate's head. Maybe she could help Millie after all. The idea for how was a little crazy, a lot bizarre, and completely unnerving. Kate had to try.

Chapter 11

Despite her impatience to see James, Kate's day had sped by. Professor O'Leary started the morning with an unexpected exam about topics they had studied before the break. As Kate recited the functions of cell parts, she silently chastised herself for not having opened a single book during her summer vacation. Her other tutors provided her with new textbooks and assignments. Kate's head spun as they, too, tested her memory from the previous months.

When the last session came, Kate couldn't contain her excitement. She tapped her notebook, glancing up at the door, looked down at her new stack of books, and glanced up again. As promised, Robert had brought a bouquet of flowers earlier that morning and had left them on the kitchen's countertop. The stink of charred toast had been traded for a light, floral scent. Including, Kate was able to pick out, traces of golden-ray lilies. Finally, the clock chimed, and James arrived.

Kate's first impression of her friend was unlike her other tutors. He appeared anything but refreshed from the monthlong break. His face was wan, and gray bags sagged under his eyes. His movements were sluggish as though he were sleepwalking. When James sat on the couch, his green gaze went to the kitchen. He smiled wearily.

"There is nothing like the scent of golden-ray lilies," he said to Kate. James set his mailbag on the ground but made no move to open it. "Tell me about your holidays," James asked before Kate could pose the first question.

Kate hesitated. James leaned over and took a teabag from the table. Seeing that he wouldn't offer anything from his own experiences, Kate launched into her adventures with Millie. James' eyes were fixed on his teacup, swirling the hot water with a spoon as he listened. A grin spread over James' lips at the mention of Kate's trip to see *Much Ado About Nothing*, but he didn't interrupt. Kate ended with her trip to Scotland. She was surprised to find herself unwilling to talk about how Edinburgh had made her feel. That sense that it was more home than London had ever been. Instead, she described what she saw in the same manner as her tour guide. When her story ended, Kate waited for James to respond. Or ask her another question. Or comment or say *something* to her. James mutely continued to stir the tea without taking a drink. Kate couldn't hide the crestfallen look on her face. James didn't seem as enthusiastic about seeing her as she had been about seeing him.

"How did it go with the archives?" Kate ventured finally, desperate to punch a hole in the silence. "Did you get a lot of research done?"

"The trip was productive, even if it wasn't as successful as I had hoped," James answered softly. "The archives are enormous. I—my professor, that is— had a question that I was supposed to research. We took the fragment of information we had and searched the archive's oldest texts and manuscripts for the next clue. We assumed the answers would be found in those texts; we found references in those texts to the questions but not much more. I spent the last week reading through more recent accounts. I didn't find anything. A month is admittedly too short a time for a meticulous study of the texts."

James' vague description didn't give Kate any idea of what he was researching. "You must have spent a lot of time in the archives," she remarked, hoping James would elaborate. "You look a lot paler than you did when you left."

Kate's cheeks burned as the offending words slipped off her tongue. To her surprise, James laughed lightly. "Indeed. I didn't enjoy the summer sun as much as you did." His green gaze indicated the golden tone of Kate's skin. He left off his stirring and sat back. "The break has passed for both of us. We have the arduous task of refreshing and expanding your mind with new literature." James reached into his mail carrier bag and withdrew a large hardcover book.

Kate took the book inquisitively from James and skimmed the title. "*Beasts of Myth and Lore*," she read in a curious tone. "Is this fiction?"

James' green gaze held a peculiar look. "Yes and no. Fantastical animals play key roles in ancient tales, from the Minotaurs in Greek mythology to dragons in Chinese legends. Before we read stories from those eras, I want you to have a familiarity with these creatures' origins. You should understand what they represent to different peoples and cultures. Besides," he added in a lighter tone, "no need to plunge into complex philosophical texts on our first day back. We'll start with Chapter One: the history of gryphons."

Kate grinned and began to read.

***

Gray clouds met Kate as she loped to Hyde Park that afternoon. It was oppressively humid. Sweat stuck to Kate's back and hair. Kate ran hard, carrying a small bag, heart pounding with anticipation. It had been three days since the start of her lessons. Now it was the weekend. Kate had a chance to carry out the scheme she had devised to get Millie the company she deserved.

When Kate reached the park, her eyes swept the crowded grounds. *Where are you?* Kate thought, biting her lip. *I need to find you.*

She discovered that the spot near the weeping beeches and lime trees was deserted. Kate trotted down the main road, then veered off onto the grass. She looped around the winding lake in the center of the park. *Come on, you have to be here somewhere.* As though in answer to her pleas, Kate finally spotted the three cats on the far end of the lake. Fifi was dipping a paw in the water. Rosalind and Albert were grooming.

Thank you, Kate said silently to no one in particular. She darted a glance around the area. The parkgoers were mostly clustered at the restaurant on the other side of the lake. With luck, no one would chance upon her. Kate slid the bag onto her shoulder. She walked toward the cats with slow, deliberate steps so as not to scare them off.

"Fifi? Rosalind? Prince Albert?"

All three jumped in surprise. Fifi and Rosalind's hair stood on end, tails puffed out. Albert flattened himself on the ground, poised to run.

"Please, wait, don't leave yet," Kate said hastily as she crouched in front of them. "Here, I brought you something."

She reached into the bag and extracted a can. Kate pulled open the can's metal lid.

Albert sniffed the air. His mouth widened into a grin. "Whitefish! That's whitefish!"

Kate set the can down and backed away. The cats bounded forward eagerly. Fifi and Rosalind shoved against each other, but Albert pushed past both felines and smashed his nose into the pâté.

Fifi swiped at the orange tabby. "Stop hogging it, Albert!" she hissed.

Albert munched away happily.

Kate watched, then cleared her throat. "I was hoping I could talk to you. Millie, she misses you. Very much. I was wondering if you would consider living with her again."

Fifi's head jerked up, eyes narrowing in suspicion. Juice dripped from the end of her nose. "That's why you're here? You want to snatch us up and stuff us in those silly outfits?"

"No, that's not it at all," Kate replied. She chose her next words carefully. "I was hoping you would consider moving back. You don't have to do anything you don't want to do. Millie's lonely, and you meant so much to her. She kept the silver platters. I'm sure if you came back, she would serve you pâté every day."

Albert looked up too, licking his lips. "Wet food on platters?" He gazed longingly at Fifi. "All we've gotten since we left are scraps here and there from the restaurant. And we've been rained on. And we've chased by dogs. And I can't get rid of that itch behind my ear. It would be nice to be indoors."

Fifi shook her head. "Absolutely not. I refuse to be put in that ridiculous fancy dress. It's an offense to my dignity, not to mention my natural beauty."

"I would go back," Rosalind said. She cocked her head at Kate. "Albert's right. I haven't felt properly clean since we left. We might like living there better now."

"I could ask Millie to not use costumes," Kate proposed. "I could also suggest she give you time outdoors so you can enjoy the sun and, well, whatever you do outdoors. I can't promise Millie will listen, but I'll do my best."

"That sounds divine," Albert said. He had a sated grin on his face. The can was empty, and his tail flicked enthusiastically.

Rosalind nodded her agreement as she licked a paw clean.

Fifi's whiskers twitched. "We'll give it a go," she meowed. "But one tutu . . ."

***

Millie was waiting at the door when Kate returned from her run the next day. A wide smile spanned her pink-lip sticked lips. "My babies came home!" she exclaimed ecstatically. "Prince Albert, Fifi, and Rosalind! It was after you left. I was going to tend to the garden, what with the day as clear as it is, and there they were, my sweet muffins, sunning right by my peonies. I almost dropped my watering can, you can imagine the shock of it!"

Millie's words were strung together like beads on a necklace as she ushered Kate inside. "They've all lost a bit of weight, poor dears, I mean, goodness knows what they have had to live on, and Albert had a nettle in his fur that I had to cut out, but I'm going to pamper them." Millie patted Kate on the cheek and hurried across the room. The thick aroma of roasted chicken wafted through the living room. Kate removed her shoes and followed the scent. "To think of how miserable they must have been out there in the rain and snow and all sorts of conditions . . . oh, makes my heart ache!" Millie's voice carried from the kitchen. "I'm going out straight away to buy them the finest pâtés in the city, and catnip of course. Their silver dishes are in the cupboard, oh they'll love it so . . ."

"Aunt Millie," Kate interrupted as she joined Millie in the kitchen. She spied a half-carved chicken breast in a pan on the stovetop. A plate was piled high with shredded chicken meat. "I saw something on the telly the other day," Kate went on as Millie filled a bowl with water. "It was a report about cats and cat, ah, behavior. A veterinarian explained it was common for cats to run away after being put in clothing. Like fancy dress. The veterinarian said the experience was traumatic for cats. Especially females."

"Really?" Millie turned off the faucet and set the bowl on the table. Kate silently hoped that Millie would believe her fib. "I used to put them in fancy dress. Not always of course. It was for special occasions like birthdays and holidays and on occasion for teatime visits with friends. Would they have minded the outfits? I don't think so. Do you think so?"

Kate shrugged. She looked out the patio door. Albert stretched his arms and legs out as far as he could. Rosalind licked her mottled paw, and Fifi chewed on one of Millie's plants. "It's possible. It wouldn't be too much to not have them wear clothing anymore, would it? Just in case."

Millie looked contemplative, though her lips were pursed in a frown. "But they're so cute in the knitted sweaters. Fifi had an adorable tutu that she absolutely loved. I could tell when she had it on. She seemed so proud of it . . ."

Kate held back a groan. It wasn't going to work.

"Maybe, well, maybe I won't do that anymore."

"That's a safe decision, Aunt Millie," Kate said sagely. "I was thinking too, if they're happy in the garden, you could keep the door open so they can roam outdoors. They won't leave. They came back to you already, right?"

Millie lifted the plate of chicken and glanced out to the patio. "They *do* look happy. Although Fifi shouldn't be trying to eat the mint leaves. That's exactly what I'll do then. Robert can help me make a cat door. You're wonderful, Kate, all these good ideas!"

Kate opened the patio door for Millie. As her aunt breezed outside, Kate saw the cats glance up. Albert sprang to his feet, tail wagging like a dog.

"Have some pride!" Kate heard Fifi hiss. Still, all three felines huddled around the plate that Millie placed on the paver stones with a tickled, "Eat up, dears!"

Kate let out a relieved sigh and sank into her chair. She had done it. She had convinced the trio to return to Millie, and Millie wouldn't feel alone. Yet Kate couldn't stop the chill that ran down her spine. The conversation with the stranger about wizards and magic wasn't as improbable now. "No, wizards and magic are fantasy, something you read about," Kate said aloud. "They're not real."

A whisper in Kate's mind countered, *Or are they?*

***

The leaves turned a myriad of colors to celebrate the change of seasons. Gray clouds muscled their way back into the sky, forcing off the brilliant blue of summer. Millie's flowers and mint plants retreated underground. Jackets and scarves were brought out of closets. Kate and her tutors migrated from the patio back into the warmth of the living room.

The beauty of the season was marred by a sudden barrage of nightmares. More accurately, a single, recurring nightmare. Kate was at the edge of a forest. The night sky had swallowed its stars and moon and left faint outlines of ghoulish figures in cloaks. She heard otherworldly screeches of pain. People yelled in an unrecognizable language. Kate sensed danger everywhere as she tried to track the liquid shadows with her gaze. Her legs seized, crippled by fear.

Run, Kyra! a woman's voice screamed behind her. *Run as far as you can from here. We won't let them get you. You must run, now! Go, Kyra, go and don't come back!*

Kate's dream-self was shoved forward. The action thrust aside Kate's paralysis, and she sprinted into the darkness. Blue and red flames exploded around her. Kate sensed one of the cloaked figures chasing after her, getting closer . . .

Kate shot upright in her bed. Sweat drenched her shirt. Her chest heaved and her pulse raced as though she had run for hours. Kate didn't move until the images of the fire and the yells and screams faded from her mind.

Running a hand shakily through her hair, Kate rolled over toward her nightstand. She pulled open the top drawer. She removed a small velvet pouch she had bought months before. Untying the strings, Kate dropped the heptagon coin into her hand. For a moment, all she did was hold it. The coin had become a cherished source of comfort to Kate during nights like these, when her thoughts were so fractured, she felt she would never be normal. Her fingers ran over the surface. Kate had touched the etchings on it enough that she knew them as intimately as her own hand. Her thumb traced the carat symbol, then an "e," the hooked line, the small arc, and finally a squiggly line.

Releasing a shuddering sigh, Kate reverently set the coin on top of the nightstand. She rose and swapped her wet nightshirt for a clean one. Kate tried to keep the dream from resurfacing as she stripped the bedsheet and pillowcase, pulled out new linens, and remade her bed. Kate couldn't help looking left and right in the hallway when she stepped out. Was something lurking in the house? Kate quickly washed her face in the sink. It was a nightmare. Like the night before. And the night before that. Kate wearily returned to her bed and sank on the fresh sheets. She laid her head on the pillow. Kate had never told anyone about the coin, not even James. It was the one secret that was completely hers. As sleep cradled her, Kate took the coin from the nightstand and pressed it firmly in her palm. Her eyes closed. Kate drifted off without noticing the metal begin to pulse orange and red.

***

Kate and James leaned against the low, rectangular stone wall that formed the border to the courtyard of Somerset House. Cold seeped through Kate's jeans. She shivered, stretched her legs, then pulled her knees close. Her breath crystallized into small clouds. They were easy to see in the night air. Wrapping her scarf tighter around her neck, Kate glanced sideways at James. His cheeks were rosy, as was his exposed nose. James rubbed his gloves together for warmth. He didn't seem nearly as frozen as Kate. His emerald eyes sparkled as he watched the dancing fountains in the center of the courtyard. His face had relaxed into a contented smile.

Kate's gaze orbited the gray building that ringed the cobblestoned ground. For a person like James who liked items to be orderly, Somerset House was the perfect location. James mentioned he loved the symmetry of the three sides, with columned entrances and two levels of windows. Tonight, the columns and windows were back lit, as was the dome directly before them. Streetlights illuminated walkways outside Somerset House.

Kate's eyes brushed over the two large bronze statues to her left before returning her attention to the fountains.

The synchronized jets leapt joyfully. Colorful lights changed beneath them as they fell. The water slapped the stone, shot into the air, and slapped the stone again. The sound was hypnotically peaceful. Kate let out a deep sigh.

James glanced over at her, his gaze soft. "This is the last week we can view the fountains," he told Kate. He picked up his ever-present water bottle, took a quick drink, and set it beside him. "The square will be converted into an ice-skating rink for winter. It's smaller than the one in Hyde Park we visited last year, but this is better for a beginner. You would like skating here."

Kate rewarded him with a wry smile. "I don't think skating is supposed to involve inelegantly slamming into the rails. Or colliding with other people on the ice. I swear I still have a bruise on my elbow from the one fall when I tried to avoid that grandmother. But I will happily observe your elegant gliding from outside the rink."

James' grin widened, accentuating his rosy cheeks. "You did better than you realize. I had my fair share of mishaps when I started. Skating isn't any different from your lessons. Anything worth mastering requires hours of practice and patience with the mistakes you will make along the way. I am far from perfect myself. As Sandra Scofield said, 'We are not beginners forever, but we never stop learning.'"

"Sandra Scofield. Another philosopher?"

"An American author actually. Will you now allow me your presence on the ice?"

Kate stared at the courtyard, soon-to-be-skating rink. "I'm as graceful as a rhino performing ballet, so no, thank you."

James grinned. "You may change your mind. I'll keep asking until then." His brow suddenly creased. Over the smacks of water came raucous shouts and drunken laughter. James cast a glance over his shoulder toward the arched entrances to the courtyard. "Who is that?"

Puzzled, Kate followed his gaze. "Who's what?" Her question was answered as a huddle of young men swaggered through the middle arch. Kate guessed they were James' age. Were they university students? The first of the boys was thick-chested and broad-shouldered. His legs seemed to have trouble coordinating their movements, with one waggling to the left and the other tottering to the right. Beside him, a boy with a black cap teetered rather than walked forward. He tripped over an uneven part of the courtyard and knocked into the third boy in the group. The boy lurched forward, spilling beer from an open can. He rounded on the boy in the cap.

"Oi, watch where you're walking, Billy!" he barked. He cuffed Billy with the back of his hand, sending the boy reeling.

Billy fell onto the cobblestones with a yelp. He looked up from the ground. "What'dyoudothatfor, Preet?" he asked, slurring his words.

The thick-chested boy glanced back and sniggered. "Shows you not to mess a man's drink, eh, Preet?"

Preet shook the can. "Aye, Jude." He tilted his head back, drinking the can dry.

The fourth and final member of the group sauntered up to Billy. Kate's hair pricked on the back of her head. His coat was as dark as the sky and flowed from his neck down to his ankles. Unlike the others, the boy was sober, his stride even. But what set Kate on edge was the casual ruthlessness that radiated from him. His black chasms for eyes were filled with cold contempt as he regarded Billy.

"Get up," he ordered in an icy tone. "Jude, give him a hand."

"It's not my fault he can't hold his alcohol, Reuben," Jude grumbled. He walked back to Billy and heaved him onto his feet.

Kate glanced sideways at James. Dread flooded through her. James' previous cheerfulness was eclipsed by a dark expression she had never seen in him before. James grabbed his water bottle and thrust himself off the wall. Kate rose too.

Reuben's gaze traveled around the courtyard and fell on James. His lips formed a warped grin. Kate looked from Reuben to James and back. It was clear the two knew each other. Equally clear was that Reuben despised James as much as James seemed to loathe him. Kate's body was taut as tension clotted the air.

"James," Reuben said in a falsely conversational tone. He beelined toward James and Kate, hands tucked in his coat pockets. "How lucky for us that you're here. I haven't seen you at the university recently. I was getting worried that something might have happened to you. Now I see I had no reason for concern. You've been spending your time with more pleasant company." Reuben tilted his head in Kate's direction. His grin widened, though it couldn't penetrate his eerily unnatural gaze. "Aren't you going to introduce us?"

"I'm not," James growled. He gripped his water bottle firmly in his glove. "Unless you want to witness the full force of a Lyneera, you will leave the courtyard."

Reuben made no sign of leaving. The other three boys had also noticed James and Kate. They fanned out behind Reuben. Billy's expression was dazed. Preet crumpled the can in his fist and threw it on the cobblestones.

Jude leered at Kate. "Who's that, Jimmy? You got yourself a girlfriend? Looks like you had to find a young one—can't get a university girl to look at you twice, can you?"

Anger and fear smoldered within Kate, but not on account of her own safety. They were threatening James. Kate met Jude's gaze with a steely one of her own. "I'm sure you don't have any luck with girls," she said coolly. "Your head looks like a rotten pineapple, except for your nose. That's more like someone smashed peas on your face and left them there. Not very attractive."

Jude touched his stubby nose, face splotched red. Billy giggled. Jude spun toward him, fists raised.

Before Kate could shoot off another verbal barb, James grabbed her arm. He pulled her with him behind the bronze statues and out of sight of the boys. James' emerald eyes held an intense urgency. "We can't fight them," he said. The fountain's water concealed James' words as he continued, "I'm going to distract them. When I draw them further into the courtyard, you will have a few moments to escape. Go directly to Millie's. I'll contact you as soon as I can."

Kate tugged her arm free. "I'm not leaving you to face four of them," she replied sharply. "If you don't think we can beat them together, how do you expect to beat them alone?"

"It isn't the four I'm worried about." James craned his neck around the statue. Preet, Jude, and Billy had circled around the right side toward Kate. Reuben strolled to the left. He was fiddling with something in his pocket.

James took Kate by the shoulder and ran her back further from the statue. "This isn't a discussion or a debate. I'm telling you, you can't stay here. I need you to trust me."

The boys had arced around the statues. Reuben drew his hands from his pockets. He held the handle of a switchblade in his black leather glove. Reuben flicked the handle. A serrated blade snapped into place.

"Who is he?" Kate asked James in an undertone. Her eyes fixed on the blade that Reuben twirled in his hand.

"Trouble and dangerously capable. I can't fight him if you aren't safe."

"The girl's a cheeky one, eh, Jamison?" Reuben sneered as he stepped closer. He rubbed the handle of the switchblade. "She should show some respect for the dead. Looks like her tutors failed to teach her manners. Fortunately, I'm skilled in that area."

Kate gaped, wondering if she had heard Reuben correctly. *Respect for the dead?*

James moved in front of Kate. "I've spoken plainly, Reuben. Try your hand with me, but only with me. Or are the Variavryk so cowardly as to skirmish with unarmed teenage girls and not more equal opponents. Like a Lyneera."

"I wouldn't taint the reputation of the Variavryk by attacking this girl," Reuben scoffed. "Even a Lyneera is hardly worthy of my time. Still, I promised I would get my revenge." Reuben motioned to his companions. "James and I need to have a chat, lads. Keep the girl here. He needs motivation not to run like a dog with his tail between his legs once he feels the sting of this blade."

Kate was completely baffled by James and Reuben's exchange. She saw Reuben's companions also wore befuddled expressions though, Kate reasoned, that was as much a result of the alcohol as the conversation. Surprisingly, the boys obeyed. Jude removed a knife from his coat pocket, as did Preet. Billy seemed preoccupied with staying on his feet. Jude advanced on Kate.

James moved sideways to intercept him. At the same moment, Reuben charged. James pushed Kate back as Reuben slashed at his chest. Kate stumbled and watched in horror. To her amazement, James dodged to the side and blocked the blade with his bottle. The shrill ringing of metal scraping metal cut through the sound of the fountains. Kate and the other boys temporarily forgot about each other, captivated by the duel. Reuben immediately brought the blade toward James' head. James stepped inside the swing and slammed the bottle down on Reuben's wrist. There was a crack as the bottle connected with bone. Reuben tossed the knife to his right hand. Kate's eyes widened. He wasn't fazed by his broken wrist. A malevolent expression spanned Reuben's features. He lunged forward, forcing James to spin and run into the fountains themselves. Water splashed over James as he turned and planted his feet in a defensive stance. His face was highlighted by the blue lights.

"Is that the power of the Variavryk?" James goaded. "It's weaker than I imagined."

"It is but a taste, Lyneera." Reuben unhesitatingly pursued James, ignoring the water that shot up on both sides of him.

Kate started to run to James, but Reuben's companions suddenly blocked her path. Blood pounded in her ears. She had to get past them and quickly. Kate's eyes raked the attackers. Unthinkingly, she discerned their weaknesses. Jude favored his right leg. His eyes weren't completely focused, but he wasn't as woozy as Billy, who seemed to be losing a battle against his legs to stand straight. Preet stood in the center of the arc. Kate determined he was the most clearheaded of the three. Preet's warped lips formed a nasty line as he patted the flat of his blade against his palm.

"Where're you going, girlie?" Jude sneered, moving closer with his lopsided gait. "Reuben said you're going to stay, so staying is all you'll be doing."

Kate balled her hands into fists. The skin under her gloves pricked as though bitten by the cold. "Try keeping me here, you miserable louse."

Jude sprang forward. His movements were sluggish, and Kate easily evaded his knife. She was close enough to smell the stench of alcohol on his breath. Nose wrinkling in disgust, Kate spun around Jude and landed a hard kick to the back of Jude's knee. Jude let out an "Oi!" as his leg buckled. He fell onto the cobblestoned ground.

Billy's glossy eyes moved to Jude. He pointed with an unsteady finger and laughed. "Look, Preet, Jude's on the ground now." He made no attempt to stop Kate as she tried to dart by.

Preet grabbed her wrist. Kate's arm wrenched painfully as Preet jerked her backward. Instinctively, Kate pivoted on her foot so she was facing him. She opened her hand and torqued it around Preet's wrist. In one fluid motion, Kate broke his grip and grasped his wrist instead. She drove her hips toward the ground. Preet's arm was forced to follow his wrist. He lost his balance but started to bring his knife around in his other hand. Kate struck him in the neck with the side of her palm. Preet sputtered as he collapsed. The knife clattered at Kate's feet. She kicked it aside.

"I warned you, you sleazy, puffed-up scumbags," Kate said in a low, dangerous tone that didn't sound like her own. The pricking sensation had grown more intense, as though burrs were sticking to her hands.

"She got you good, Preet, she got you good!" Billy guffawed, oblivious to the seriousness of the situation.

A shout rose above the noise of the fountains. Kate glanced behind her. James and Reuben's battle had taken them to the opposite end of the courtyard. Water streamed down their faces as they maneuvered, parried, and counterstruck, Reuben with his knife, James with the bottle. The fountain lights shone on the two, the colors enveloping their entire persons. Reuben was encompassed in orange, James in blue. Kate gasped. Reuben was holding his knife in his left hand. The one that, moments before, had been broken. Reuben closed in on James and made a daring attack. This time, Reuben's blade sliced through James' jacket. Blood flowed down James' arm and onto the cobblestones, where the splashing water washed it away.

"James!" Kate cried out. Before she could move, an arm snaked around her neck. Kate raised her wrist to stop the arm from squeezing her. Kate froze. Golden flames pranced around her glove. Her gaze darted to her other hand. It was also lit with a golden glow. Fury and confidence flared up in Kate as she resisted her attacker. She didn't fear the flames. She sensed—knew—they were somehow a part of her.

Which meant she could control them.

Burn his sleeve, Kate silently directed the energy. The flame leapt in response and crawled up the arm that restrained her. She heard a shriek. The grip around her neck slackened. Kate turned to see Jude stumbling backward, cradling his arm with a whimper. Steam rose from his coat sleeve.

Kate glanced at Preet. He was again on his feet, eyes riveted on her flaming hands. Preet recoiled in fright as she took a step toward him. Kate glanced at Billy. The laughter was wiped from his face.

"She's on fire," Billy stuttered as he swayed. "Preet, how's she on fire?"

"She's crazy!" Jude said, holding his singed arm. "She tried to set me on fire! I'm getting out of here, don't care what Reuben says. Preet, Billy, leg it." He turned and half-ran, half-limped toward the arches.

Preet sprinted after Jude, shooting Billy a fleeting, "Move, you dolt!"

Billy continued to stare dumbfounded at Kate. "I'm coming, wait, I'm coming," he finally slurred, running crookedly after his mates.

Kate shook her head derisively. She had dealt with three attackers. Now it was Reuben's turn. Out of the corner of her eye, Kate saw Reuben tackle James. James hit the ground back first, his head striking the hard stone. He lay prone, eyes closed. The fountains sprang up in unison around him. His fingers wrapped around his water bottle. For an agonizing moment, Kate watched as Reuben knelt over him. The knife was poised in his hand.

Kate's emotions whirled like dervishes. Her fear fed her rage. Power surged unbidden through her hands. If James weren't dead yet, Reuben was going to make sure he was. Kate wasn't close enough to fight Reuben. But she didn't need to be. Her eyes flashed with fury as she started jogging. Red light trickled from her wrists over the gold energy. She thrust out her arms.

Attack Reuben, Kate ordered the flames as Reuben grinned. *Pin him down. Keep him down.* The red energy bolted through the fountains in two streams, one from her right hand, one from her left. As they passed each sprout, water stuck to the red like flypaper. Kate braided the energy and water together. Like a dancer with streamers, Kate twirled the magic around Reuben's waist. Reuben glanced down. His brow creased in puzzlement as the magic bound to itself. Kate jerked her hands down. With a startled cry, Reuben was thrown against the stone.

Kate pulled the watery lasso more tightly. She felt giddy, strong, ready to squelch the life from Reuben the same way he had been prepared to take James'. A haunting stillness filled the courtyard. All the water had been sucked from the fountains and bound to the red magic. Kate didn't notice the lights had also been snuffed out or realize the significance that Reuben was clothed in an orange glow, James in a lighter blue.

Reuben futilely fought against the red rope. "How is this possible?" he growled, lashing left and right. "I'm a Variavryk!"

Kate stopped a few paces in front of him. Her eyes blazed. "Your companions left you behind, Reuben. They knew better than to fight against me. Now you'll pay for hurting James." The intoxicating power flowed faster through Kate. She channeled more energy into the ropes. The water pulsed red, popped, and then cracked as it started to freeze.

"Kate, stop . . ." a voice said distantly.

Reuben's black eyes widened as the ice crept up his chest. He hacked at it frantically with his knife. The blade shaved small pieces from the ice but didn't stop it from spreading. "I'm a Variavryk!" he yelled again. "How are you doing this? You aren't a Lyneera. Answer me!"

Kate ignored Reuben's shrieks. *Pin him down. Keep him down.* The two sentences were Kate's mantra, playing themselves over and over as she watched Reuben's arms stiffen. He writhed in pain, the orange ebbing. Kate's manic delight grew.

"Kate, stop," the voice repeated. It was clearer and more forceful.

The ice passed over Reuben's shoulders. The Variavryk strained his neck above the ice, eyes bulging in panic. "You've rescued Jamison; you have what you want. Killing me will accomplish nothing except bring every Variavryk in Ilian to this world. They will never allow someone to live who has the power to eliminate our kind. When they arrive here, they will seek out any who helped you, which means your precious James. In return, Lyneera will flock to James' side. You will ignite a war among the Lyneera and Variavryk that will devour London. Would you risk the devastation of your home to take revenge on a single individual?"

Kate smiled darkly. "I've saved James from you tonight. Let war come. My priority is to stop you from threatening him again." The icy noose worked around Reuben's neck. He gasped, eyes growing wide in shock.

"Kate, *stop!* Release him, Kate. It isn't worth it. Stop, now!"

James' voice broke her trance. Kate turned her head as she continued to feed the ice. James was crouched, his face pasty white. The blue light ringing him had grown in intensity while Reuben's orange faded like dying embers in a fire. Kate's heart skipped a beat. James was okay.

James crawled to Reuben. The Variavryk's black eyes silently pleaded to him for help. James lifted his green gaze to Kate. "Let go of your anger, Kate," he instructed quietly. "Let go of your fear. I'm not hurt. You aren't hurt. See the energy as a cloud on a breezy day. Let it disperse. Release Reuben."

Kate felt a strange heaving within her. She sensed the gold resurfacing, wrestling with the red energy. Abruptly, something snapped. Kate's arms dropped to her sides as her connection to the red magic was severed. The ice ensnaring Reuben exploded without warning. James shielded his face as fragments sprayed over the courtyard.

Reuben scrabbled to his feet. His arms quaked, and he spat blood on the ground. Chips of ice stuck to Reuben's coat and hair. Kate kept her hands raised even though the energy was gone. Reuben regarded her with an inscrutable look. Comprehension dawned in his eyes. "I know who you are," Reuben said, backing away slowly. "It all makes sense now. I *know* who you are."

Kate glanced at James. She stared, stunned. She expected a gash or blood on the back of James' head where he had hit the courtyard. His skin was whole.

Color was returning to James' face, which didn't register any pain. In fact, Kate noticed, other than his arm, which through his torn sleeve seemed to have stopped bleeding, James didn't have any sign of being attacked. Or of having been in the fountains, Kate realized with bewilderment. His hair and coat, which the fountain's waters had drenched, were completely dry. The strange blue light was gone.

"You are no Lyneera." Reuben's voice drew Kate's attention to him. The malignant smile returned to the Variavryk's face. "You are *her*. Jamison has sheltered and protected you all this time. No one believed the girl was anything more than a myth devised by the seers. A myth to instill fear in the wizards of Harkimer and bring hope to the kingdoms of Ilian. Yet here you are." Reuben pointed an accusatory finger at James. "You claimed to serve Inishmore. Does Inishmore tell you to bring destruction to our lands? Because this—" he gestured to the courtyard, "—this is a small demonstration of what is to come if you protect her."

Kate glanced at James. His face was grave, graver than she had ever seen him. "I have faith in Inishmore's plans, even if I do not yet understand them. That is the difference between us." He raised his bottle. "Let us finish this, Variavryk."

Reuben hesitated. He let out an uncertain laugh. "Another time, Lyneera."

Orange light burst into the black night like a star exploding. Kate winced and shut her eyes.

"By the Healer," she heard James say, followed by a sharp breath. "I should have seen this months ago."

Kate opened her eyes. James was raking a hand through his wavy hair. His gaze strayed over the deathly silent fountains and the ice debris strewn along the ground. "This is why I was brought here," he uttered to himself, seeming to forget Kate's presence. "Not because she needs to forge a new life but to be reminded of her past."

Kate's legs trembled beneath her, like a wind-up doll whose gears had jammed.

James turned suddenly and took her by the hand. "We need to leave. Come on, this way." He pulled her under the arch and out of the courtyard. Kate had to double-step to keep up with James' long-legged stride. James led her across the street to a two-story pub on the other side. "In here," he told Kate. Kate obeyed and stepped inside. James cast one last furtive glance around. Reuben hadn't followed them. Kate heard James mutter something about 'by Inishmore' before he, too, darted inside the pub.

Chapter 12

The Wellington was a lively establishment, especially on a chilly Saturday night. It was normally one of Kate and James' favorite pubs. Tonight, Kate would have preferred to be somewhere else. The chatter and music hammered against Kate's already pounding head. The stench of alcohol mixed with the smell of meat pies made her stomach churn. She absently followed James upstairs, where it was quieter and the scents fainter. James steered Kate to a secluded table adjacent to a window. Kate plopped into the chair as James caught the eye of a waitress in lime green heels.

"Two cups of Earl Grey, please," he said. "And a couple glasses of water."

"Anything to eat for you?"

"No, thank you, we're grand."

Kate unbuttoned her coat as though in a haze. The timid, gentle tutor Kate knew had been replaced with this confident and assertive one sitting across from her. A confident, assertive James who apparently glowed blue on occasion. As the waitress clacked away to another table, Kate rubbed her temples. Nothing made any sense. She removed her coat, tucked her gloves into her pocket, and slung the coat around her chair.

James set his bottle on the floor and unwrapped the scarf from his neck. "I don't believe we will have any more disturbances tonight," he remarked. "Still, I feel more comfortable discussing what happened without prying ears or eyes. I owe you an explanation for what happened in the courtyard. I will share information that affects you most immediately and will shed light on recent events. That's all, though. Too much knowledge about what you have witnessed will be overwhelming." James undid the buttons to his coat and shrugged the coat off his shoulders. He put the coat and scarf on the back of his chair. Then he rested his arms on the table, hands folded.

Kate's gaze trailed to his shirt. Dark red stained his sleeve from above his elbow to below his wrist, and the fabric was ripped open from Reuben's serrated blade. Kate was jolted out of her trance at the sight. "We need to get you to a hospital," she said in alarm. "Your arm, we shouldn't be sitting here, we have to . . ."

"My arm is in much better condition than my clothing," James replied with a half-smile. He rolled back his sleeve. Kate stifled a shocked cry. The skin was whole, the blood rinsed in the fountain's waters. Kate gently touched his arm, eyes wide.

"I saw Reuben cut you," she said, running her fingers along where the wound had been. "You were bleeding. The coat and your shirt, they're torn, but you're . . . fine."

"Yes, so there is no need to worry." The sound of heels clacking announced the waitress' return. She carried cups of tea, a bowl of sugar and cream, and glasses of water. James thanked the waitress as she placed them on the table. He nudged a teacup toward Kate and kept one for himself. "Here, you need something hot to drink."

The sweet scent of Earl Grey wafted from the cups. Kate inhaled deeply, feeling the tension in her muscles loosen.

"Why aren't you injured?" Kate asked as James blew on his tea to cool it. "No one heals that fast."

"Let me answer that question by providing you with the context. You heard Reuben talk about Lyneera and Variavryk? Neither a Lyneera nor a Variavryk can be injured by the blade of a mortal. Only one of our kind can brandish the weapon. We can inflict wounds, but the wounds heal quickly. For a Lyneera or Variavryk to cease to exist, however, the strike must be fatal. I am a Lyneera, as you might have gathered through our conversation. Reuben is a Variavryk."

A swarm of questions buzzed loudly in Kate's ears. She didn't touch her cup as she leaned forward.

"What are Lyneera? And Variav . . . Variav-what? You aren't mortal? You aren't human?" Kate recalled Reuben's statement in Somerset House. It was almost impossible to wrap her mind around the conclusion she was nearing. "Reuben said I didn't have 'respect for the dead.' He was referring to himself, wasn't he? That would make him, and you . . . ghosts?"

James smiled patiently. "We aren't ghosts, and we are not immortal. We are spirits that have not yet passed from one world to the next. Again, let me answer one question at a time or else this will become complicated very quickly."

"You don't consider *this* complicated?"

Laughing lightly, James shook his head. He reached over and spooned sugar into his cup. "When someone dies, two things can happen. A person who has served Inishmore faithfully has the promise of living in the Healer's land. It's a place of eternal spring and peace. Not everyone passes directly to the Healer. Some are called by Inishmore to remain behind and to fulfill another obligation. The Lyneera are these spirits. We are not alive, yet we exist. We are committed to serving others until Inishmore decides the task to which we were given is complete. The Variavryk are also spirits, but they don't serve Inishmore; they serve themselves. They are the vilest of beings in life, and they are rejected by Inishmore in death. As I mentioned earlier, Variavryk can only be killed by a Lyneera or another Variavryk. Beyond that, I'm afraid my understanding is limited."

"That's why Reuben's wrist healed," Kate said, working through the logic of James' words. "Because he's a Variavryk."

"Exactly."

"And that strange blue light that surrounded you. That's also because you're a spirit?"

"A Lyneera specifically. It's a manifestation of our energy. The Variavryk's energy is orange." James gestured toward Kate's cup. "You should drink that before it gets cold."

Reluctantly, Kate put the cup to her lips and took a long sip. Warmth streamed through her, from her frozen fingers to her toes. Kate sighed. Putting the cup down, she asked, "Where did you learn how to fight?"

To her surprise, the corners of James' eyes tightened in pain. He picked up his linen serviette, gaze turned inward. When he didn't respond, Kate glanced out the window. Snow fell lightly under the streetlights. Pedestrians hurried along the sidewalks. A bus flew down the street.

"My brother-in-law trained me when I was eighteen," James answered unexpectedly. Kate turned back to him. He had unfolded the serviette and was refolding it. "I wasn't raised to be a warrior. My family had a small farm and sold goods at a marketplace. My two older sisters helped my mother with the house and animals. When my father died, my oldest sister raised me and my middle sister. I went to the Academy when I was fifteen to become a scribe. My oldest sister took care of my mother until she passed and then got married. My middle sister moved to a large city called Thanesgard."

Kate stared at James, stupefied, as he made a long, even crease in the serviette. He had rarely mentioned his sisters or his family before. His story produced a host of new questions. Kate forced herself to stay quiet and listen.

Water rimmed James' eyes. "You asked where I learned to fight, not why. I was in the third year at the Academy when my oldest sister's village was attacked. My brother-in-law had been away at the time. No one survived. I never got to see her again." James' voice cracked. He took the ends of the serviette and folded them robotically. A tear dropped onto the linen.

A lump formed in Kate's throat. "Is your oldest sister the one who liked the golden-ray lilies?" she asked quietly.

James nodded. "My brother-in-law and I blamed ourselves for her death," he said softly. "My brother-in-law swore to find those responsible and bring them to justice. I made the same oath. If I were to join his crusade, I needed the ability to attack and defend myself. My brother-in-law was well-versed in weapons. I left the Academy without finishing my studies and trained with him for a year. I hope he hunted down the murderers, since I couldn't keep my promise to my sister."

Kate noticed James left out the cause of his own death. She didn't press the issue. It was his personal story, and she wasn't sure she could stomach hearing the reason.

James set the serviette aside and took his bottle from the booth. He placed it next to his teacup. The bottle had scars from where Reuben's blade had skimmed off it. "A metal bottle is an improvisation of a weapon. The principles of combat are the same as if I were to use a sword or a tartar." James ran a finger over one of the knife marks. "It's effective."

More questions competed for Kate's attention, but James intervened. "You understand the Lyneera and Variavryk. You've learned about my background. Now I need information from you." James' emerald eyes were intense as he pushed the bottle aside and again laced his fingers. "How did you summon the red energy?"

"How?" Kate echoed. "I . . . I don't know. It wasn't red at first. I saw gold flames on my hands when Jude grabbed me around the neck. The flames didn't hurt. I knew somehow that they were a part of me. I knew I could use them. I turned them against Jude, and they burned his arm. It was later when the color turned to red. Wait a minute." Kate eyed James suspiciously. His expression was enigmatic. "You called it red 'energy.' You've seen it before then? What formed around my hands? Can you explain what I did?"

"Possibly. When you said 'later' the color changed. Was 'later' while you were defending against Jude?"

Kate glanced away as she reran the sequence of events at Somerset and matched them to the colors on her hands. "Jude, Preet, and Billy ran away after they saw the golden . . . energy? The golden flames. Then I saw you and Reuben at the fountains. Reuben had cut your arm, and you fell and hit your head. I couldn't see if you were alive. That was the moment the red came out."

Kate returned her gaze to James. Her stomach twisted more sharply than Preet's wrist had. James' expression was uneasy and somber.

"The red trickled into the gold when you saw I was in danger," he repeated. "What were you feeling?"

"Afraid. Angry. Desperate, I guess."

"What were you feeling when you drew on the red magic? When you pulled Reuben away from me and bound him in ice?"

Kate hesitated. She slid a finger around the rim of the saucer. "Relieved. Determined not to give up until I knew you were safe." *And strong, in control,* her mind added silently. *You wanted to cause Reuben pain to the point that you almost killed him.* A shiver went down Kate's spine as guilt flooded through her. What kind of person was she to have those emotions, even against an enemy? Kate wanted to deny the ecstasy—yes, her gut confirmed, that was the word—of trapping her opponent. She couldn't.

"Relief and determination are natural responses," James replied carefully. He rested his chin contemplatively on his hands. "They are also initial responses. You said when the gold energy surfaced, you turned it against Jude. Presumably, you would have been able to control it if you used it against Reuben as well. You didn't. Red energy replaced the gold. I assume you had other emotions when you regarded Reuben apart from the desire to help me. Did you feel exhilaration when you realized you weren't defenseless? Or powerful when you inflicted harm on the Variavryk?"

Kate's dismay was as readable on her face as though she had signed a confession of her thoughts. She made a pretense of adding cream to her tea and stirred slowly. "Maybe those, too. I don't remember exactly."

"Against Jude, you didn't feel those emotions. What was the difference?"

"He was attacking me, but I wasn't worried about myself. It was a reflex. When I saw you, I was, well, like I said, I was terrified Reuben had killed you. Or he was going to. I was horrified. Angry. I was focused on stopping him." Kate tucked a honey-brown strand of hair behind her ears, cheeks burning in shame at her admission.

James studied her carefully. "It's okay, Kate. It appears your desire to help others outweighs your concern for your own safety. That is a noble and selfless quality." A look of relief escaped Kate as James continued, "Is this the first time you have ever noticed either the gold or red energy? No? Have there been other experiences in London that seemed unusual? Unexplainable?"

Kate didn't answer. If she nudged open the door where she had stashed her secrets—Millie's cats, the azure-cloaked stranger, all of them—what would James think of her? Kate would risk alienating her only friend.

Tell him everything.

Kate almost started in her surprise. The sensation pressed upon her heart forcefully. It had been months since she felt the whisper. It had consoled Kate back then, when she was losing hope the investigation in Chicago would never give her an answer. This time, the impression bid her to speak.

Tell him everything.

"Yes. I've had strange things happen to me besides the gold flames. I've heard things, seen things, *done* things, that aren't normal. At least, I haven't met anyone who could do what I've done. I never mentioned it to anyone, not even Millie. If you think it will help, though, I'll share what's happened."

James' emerald gaze met Kate's. He smiled, and Kate knew beyond a doubt that she could confide in him. She should have confided in him a long time ago.

"It will," James said. He leaned forward again. "Tell me everything."

***

It was like removing bricks from her heart. Kate summarized her experiences that, until that night, had seemed like hallucinations rather than events with plausible explanations behind them. She described her first day in the Tube station when she heard the inhuman roars and saw flashes of light. She relayed her conversations in Hyde Park with Millie's cats. James' brows raised when Kate discussed her vision of the man wearing an azure cloak, but he listened without interruption. Kate even disclosed her nightmares of ghoulish creatures, fires, and the woman's screams to run. Kate felt these were the most intimate parts of her life and her fears. She plunged forward with abandon.

Kate struggled to explain the intangible sensations in her heart. "I'm having a hard time putting this into words," she apologized. "It's like hearing music and seeing an image or words because of it. No. Not hearing. It's *feeling* music in my heart or breathing it in. The sensation fills every part of me at once."

When Kate finally finished, she slumped back in her chair. The retelling was exhausting, but her heart was lighter. She didn't have to shoulder the burden of the occurrences alone. Kate waited for James to offer his opinion. He hadn't spoken at any point of Kate's account, and he remained silent after. Kate's heart submerged in apprehension. Was her fear about pushing away James coming true?

"I wish you had mentioned this to me sooner," James said at length.

"I . . . I couldn't."

"Why not?"

"I assumed you would think I was—what does Millie always say? A few slices short of a loaf? If the situation were reversed, and you told me you spoke with a man who didn't exist and eavesdropped on cats, my reaction would have been confused and probably scared. I was afraid you would think I was crazy. I thought I would push you away. And I wouldn't see you again," she added in a small voice.

James offered Kate a half-smile. "You see that was an unfounded fear. I heard your story, and look. I haven't fled the pub."

Kate tried to return the smile. "It all seemed real. I could even smell the kolker leaves from the man's pipe. I asked Millie's cats to come back, and they did. There's no proof anyone else can speak with animals."

"Because no one *here* can. At least, not in recent memory or written history." James reclined in his chair contemplatively. "I may be able to explain your experiences, in part. First, there is nothing 'wrong' with you. What you've seen and done is unique to this land; it isn't in another. In fact, those abilities— communicating with animals, raising energy—they are common and expected."

Whatever Kate expected James to say, it wasn't that her abilities were "unique to this land" and "common" in another. "Common in another land? Do you mean in another country?"

"Not another country, another land," James answered cryptically. "Let me finish answering your first question about what this means before we move to the next."

Kate couldn't help but compare James' comment to that of the azure-cloaked stranger. He told her she should listen to his response before jumping into the next thought.

"I have a theory," James continued. "I believe the energy you manipulated at Somerset House was magic. You didn't have full control over it. You couldn't have, not without a mentor teaching you how to feel and direct that energy."

Kate's jaw dropped. "Magic? Not like illusionists-on-television-doing-card tricks magic. Like wizards with wands and staffs magic?"

"Wizards and staffs magic. It would explain specific abilities, with one exception. A wizard doesn't have the power to affect a Variavryk or a Lyneera in any way. You were able to physically constrain Reuben. That indicates you have capabilities that reach beyond the boundaries of a wizard. It may be that you are more than a wizard."

Kate applied all Mr. Stevens' logic and laws to James' words but found nothing that made them more fathomable. "I'm a wizard, and I'm not a wizard?"

"Reuben was a wizard before he was a Variavryk," James replied, his brows creased. "He wouldn't have been able to attack me if he had not become a Variavryk."

"Does that make me a Lyneera? Or a half-Lyneera?"

"No. You are neither a Lyneera, nor a Variavryk. You are a wizard of some sort."

Kate pressed her palms against her eyes. Her temples throbbed again. "What does that mean, a wizard of some sort?"

James released a light sigh. "That is where my schooling falls short. Fortunately, there are others more expert in this area than I am. We just need to get you to them."

"Where are these experts?"

"In Ilian."

Kate pulled back her hair as she lowered her hands. "In Ilian? Is that a city or something in England? I don't remember seeing it on any of the maps."

For the first time that night, James gave her a genuine smile. "It wouldn't be on the maps, Kate. Ilian is not part of this world. I told you there was 'another land' where magic is common. Ilian is that land. It's the land from which Reuben and I come. It is the land to which you must return."

"To meet other wizards?"

"Because it's your home."

James glanced to the side at the sound of the waitress' footsteps. She carried a check in hand. As James paid the bill, Kate stared out the window with a faraway look. Had it really been only a couple of hours earlier that Kate and James' biggest concern had been her gracefulness on a skating rink? If someone had asked her that morning if magic existed, she would have answered no. Magic was as farfetched as a Yeti riding the Tube to avoid the cold. Now magic had turned her world on its head. James wasn't human. He wasn't even alive. He and Reuben were spirits who radiated blue and orange energy and healed from knife wounds and broken bones in minutes. Kate had braided red energy to stop the unstoppable Variavryk. A chill went down Kate's spine. *What happens next?*

When the waitress left, Kate and James prepared to leave. Kate stared at James' torn and bloodied sleeve as he slipped on his coat and wrapped his scarf tightly around his neck. James' eyes met hers. She cleared her throat in embarrassment and put on her own coat. James motioned for her to follow him as he wound his way down the banister. The waitress called 'Good night!' as Kate and James exited the pub.

Frosty air bit into Kate's cheeks as she stepped outside. Snow sprinkled onto her honey-brown hair. Kate raised her hood and jammed her gloved hands in her pockets. Her thoughts moved two steps behind her legs. She was mired in the collective fatigue from the fight, the revelation of a year's worth of secrets, and the effort of trying to understand what James had told her. As tired as she was, Kate anxiously turned her head left and right. What if Reuben was lying in wait? If he had gathered his courage and renewed his strength and was ready to continue the battle? Kate gave James a sideways glance. His green eyes probed the distance. Like Kate, he seemed lost in his own thoughts.

As they started to cross the bridge, James abruptly broke the silence. "I won't make our lessons next week. I must travel somewhere. It will take some time before I can return."

Kate stopped midstride. "You didn't mention that earlier," she said, hoping she didn't sound as nervous as she felt.

James paused beside her. He placed a gloved hand on the bridge's rail. "I wasn't aware that I had to until now. You described earlier the sensations you feel in your heart, the ones like music? I also have those impressions. Everyone does, though most are too hurried to heed them or choose to ignore what is communicated. Those sensations we have come from Inishmore. What is Inishmore?" James preempted the question that Kate had opened her mouth to ask. "Inishmore is that which surrounds us. It is what leads us on our noblest paths. Inishmore guides us in times of uncertainty, helps us decide what action to take, and warns us of hardships to come.

"Inishmore spoke to me months ago, at your birthday party," James continued. "Millie has a painting of a castle in northern Scotland. It is called Dunvegan. I was drawn to it."

Kate remembered seeing James standing apart from the crowd and studying the painting. She nodded.

"As hard as I tried, I couldn't discern any reason for the castle's importance. Why had Inishmore shown me this particular image? What was I to learn or do? At the time, the sensation offered no insight. For months after, I felt murmurs, like water in a brook. Tonight, the meaning crashed down like a waterfall. I must go to Dunvegan."

Kate's blood ran colder than the river beneath them. "Why? What do you have to do?"

"That much hasn't been revealed to me." James sighed. He brushed snow from his waves of hair. "Inishmore requires faith to do what is asked of us. We often don't understand why something happens until long after it has come to pass. The path we must follow may bring suffering and loss, but we cannot shy away from it. It troubles me that Inishmore summons me elsewhere when Reuben is a threat. The Variavryk are clever. They don't like defeat. Reuben will strike when he thinks you are vulnerable and unsuspecting. He won't chance you taking him from this world forever. I must trust Inishmore has a reason." James paused as a couple holding hands walked by them. "I need you to make me a promise," he continued when they were out of hearing range. "About using your magic."

Kate looked at him, puzzled.

"You must promise me you won't summon the magic. If it begins to arise regardless, you will resist every temptation to use it. You can't fight. If you see Reuben, run from him. If Reuben threatens Millie or any of your tutors, get them to safety, and get help."

"Run?" Kate repeated in disbelief. "How can you ask me to run if I see someone I care about being threatened by what you said was an invincible spirit? What good is calling the police?"

"It isn't about the police, Kate. It is about preventing you from being consumed by the red magic. I saw the look in your eyes at Somerset. The magic had hold over you, not you over it. That is more dangerous than anything Reuben can do. The police won't be able catch him, you're right, but Reuben won't risk revealing that he is not human."

Kate pulled her hood as far as she could over her head. Anger rushed through her. She had saved James' life, and he was reprimanding her for it? Kate couldn't deny that the red had spiraled within her, then from her. She couldn't have reined it in any more than a hundred wild horses. It took James' pleading for her to release it. What James was asking, to not protect the people she loved, was impossible. "I'm sorry, James," Kate replied. "I can't promise not to use it, not if I thought Reuben would hurt Millie. Any more than I would ignore Reuben coming after you again."

James raked a hand through his hair. "The loss of two individuals to prevent a catastrophic event is a reasonable trade."

Kate shivered. What could she do that would be "catastrophic"? "I promise I'll try to control the energy if I'm in a situation where it appears. I can't promise I won't use it."

This time, James sighed in resignation. "All right, Kate. I can't persuade you to do something that you're unwilling to do. Be vigilant while I'm gone, especially when you are alone. Avoiding an encounter with Reuben will be our best, maybe only, way of ensuring the red stays dormant within you."

That night, after James had escorted her home, Kate lay on her back, staring up at the ceiling. One hand was behind her head. The other held the heptagon coin. As Kate turned it over, her mind replayed James' sentence: *The loss of two individuals to prevent a catastrophic event is a reasonable trade.* James was conspicuously more afraid of her power than that of a Variavryk. One of the most pitiless and brutal creatures in that land, Ilian. And now in London.

Kate didn't dare voice it to James, but she had withheld one, immensely important, and atrocious secret. The fire in Chicago. Its blue and red flames were unquenchable. It had razed the house and taken a family. The forensics teams were empty-handed, the police baffled. If James thought Kate's magic could be so barbaric, maybe she had already done something unforgivable.

She closed her eyes, feeling scared, guilty, and worst of all, alone.

Chapter 13

Diamantas pressed his left hand against the slick stone pillar. In his right was the obsidian staff, which threw light against all corners of the cave. Water dripped lazily from stalactites onto Diamantas' head. He paid it no notice.

Unlike the corridors near the chamber room, this section of the Mountains was littered with naturally formed stone columns. The vast latticework allowed Diamantas to hide from the mysterious intruder slinking through the passage. Unfortunately, it also obstructed Diamantas' view every time his blue gaze combed the light and shadows between the columns.

Then he saw it. The tail end of a black cloak. Its owner was so quiet he seemed to be gliding rather than running between the pillars. Diamantas slid to the right, arcing his staff. "*Prea lin raxin!*" he boomed, aiming the staff where he had seen the cloak. White energy materialized in the air and enclosed the columns like a giant lion cage. Diamantas crept around the shimmering white bars, looking for his prisoner. His brows slanted sharply. The cage was empty.

Diamantas imposed a placid expression on his face as he tread slowly around the magic. "I know you are here," he called into the cave. "We have played this game of cat and mouse for months. It is needless. As I have said before, we are not enemies. You do not wish to be revealed. I understand your hesitation. You are searching for a weapon buried somewhere in the Southern Mountains. I have searched for it also. You can trust me. If you wear a black cloak and belong to Harkimer, you are aware I am a sworn servant of the wizards of Harkimer. I have dedicated my life to ending the imprisonment of our kin by those who covet their wealth, their lands, and their status in Ilian. We may share that goal, you and I . . . if that goal is to use this weapon to free our kind."

Diamantas had now woven around the entirety of the cage. The intruder was nowhere to be seen. Diamantas rapped the gnarled stone at the staff's tip against one of the white bars. The energy dispersed.

Undeterred, Diamantas prowled through the caves. The pillars became thicker and increasingly sparse. The cave soon opened to a large room with arched ceilings and small pools of water. The air was cooler, and the black stone walls seemed to glimmer of their own accord. Water trickled faintly along the ground. Diamantas heard a whisper of footfall. It came from behind the largest column. Diamantas spied a passage behind it and knew the stranger was about to escape.

"You should accept my offer," Diamantas said, turning almost imperceptibly toward the column. He spoke in a normal tone, but the cave magnified his voice as though he were shouting. "I will extend it this one last time. Someone who wishes to keep his presence secret is not someone who has the interests of Harkimer at heart but his own."

Silence was the stranger's response.

Suddenly, there was a tinkling of pebbles being dislodged at the passage. Diamantas whirled around and sprayed white magic as though from a hose. The blinding white light tore off chunks of the column. He heard a squeal of terror from the opposite side. Diamantas raced forward as the light faded back to his staff. His boots crunched on rock that had been part of the now pitted column.

Diamantas halted before the passage and readied his staff for a killing blow. Until the white light fell upon the face of a wizard. Janus' hands were raised, his face drained of color. His cognac-colored gaze was riveted on the obsidian staff.

Diamantas' lips pressed together. "What are you doing here, Janus?"

"I . . ." Janus stammered. "I . . . um . . . we . . . we were . . ."

"Calm down, and lower your hands," Diamantas ordered. "Did you see anyone else on your way here? Did you pass anyone?"

Janus shook his head anxiously. His hands remained raised. "No, Uncle, I . . . I'm alone."

Diamantas let out a short, aggrieved breath. The intruder escaped. Again. The staff's tip dimmed until only a small ring of light encompassed the two wizards. Diamantas motioned to Janus. "*Lower your hands*, nephew," he repeated with forced calm. "Explain why you are here."

Janus dropped his hands and responded uncertainly, "We found her, Uncle."

Diamantas instantly forgot the intruder. His pale blue gaze was hard as quartz as he stepped closer to Janus. "What did you say?"

"We found Kyra. She isn't in Ilian, she's somewhere else, I didn't understand what the wizard meant, or he used to be a wizard but he's not anymore—" Janus gulped in a breath as though trying to squeeze his entire account into a single sentence, "—and he, the wizard, said a girl had magic more powerful than his and that he recalled the prophecy about a girl who would destroy Ilian. This wizard contacted us in Ilian, though he isn't in Ilian, because Variavryk can pass between worlds . . ."

"The wizard is a Variavryk?"

Janus stopped. Diamantas' tone was sharper than steel. Janus averted his eyes to the ground as though the rest of the sentence lay somewhere near his feet. "That's what he said," he mumbled. "He was glowing orange, and we could see he wore a black cloak."

"Anyone can acquire a black cloak, Janus. It does not make him a wizard. Did he have a staff?"

"Um, no."

Diamantas rubbed his eyebrow. "Did he tell you his name?"

"No. Adakis might have some insight. He questioned the wizard, because he wanted to prove the wizard was a Variavryk . . ."

"Adakis questioned him?"

"To prove the wizard was a Variavryk," Janus repeated uncertainly. "Adakis said he had more experience negotiating with the Variavryk than any other wizard in Harkimer and that he could tell if the wizard was lying."

"Of course, he did." *It is ever my misfortune that Adakis would be the one to find her,* Diamantas thought with a grimace. "I am leery when it comes to dealings with the Variavryk. This is the first time you have met one, is it not?"

Janus glanced up, puzzled. He nodded. Diamantas tapped the staff on the ground as he continued disdainfully, "Variavryk are not like us, Janus. In life, they have no scruples, no loyalty to anyone or anything save what serves their own ends. They will sacrifice their children if they believe it brings them one rank closer to power. Also, Variavryk are not always wizards. They can be men and elves. It is only when one is dead that he becomes this cursed ghost we call a Variavryk. He can continue his barbarism. Importantly, a Variavryk cannot be hurt save by the hand of another Variavryk or a Lyneera. That is the being with which you were speaking. However, the Variavryk can be useful allies if they are approached in the right manner." *Which is likely opposite of whatever Adakis has done.* Diamantas paused. "What was the result of Adakis' exchange with the Variavryk?"

"The Variavryk said he would lead us to the rift so we could travel from Ilian to this other world where Kyra lives, and he would also help us catch her and bring her through the rift or kill her there, depending on what we decided, except that—" Janus came up for air before plunging back into his answer. "We would have to do something for him as part of the trade, and Adakis agreed to it."

"He made an unwise bargain," Diamantas replied, mulling over the implications. "As I told you, nephew, the Variavryk do nothing that will not further their personal ambitions. If Adakis has made a deal, he has unknowingly bound himself to commit whatever act the Variavryk demands. It may cause us trouble. Unfortunately, we cannot concern ourselves with Adakis' error. Kyra was discovered alive. That is what is important. Adakis sent you to report this news to me?"

"Nymphrys did. Adakis was busy with the Variavryk, and Nymphrys was going to ride to Galakis and Orkanis, since she said they were the closest to us and could help. That's why I came back. Will it work, Uncle? Will we find Kyra?"

"I would have preferred more than four wizards accompanying the Variavryk." Diamantas rapped his staff again on the ground, which sent waves of sound rippling through the passage. "Without fulfilling the divine number of seven, we are not blessed with the same good fortune." *Particularly when Orkanis and Adakis are counted among the four,* Diamantas noted scornfully. Orkanis was too sycophantic and nervous to be a capable wizard. Adakis, with his narcissistic arrogance, was equally inept. Diamantas tilted his head thoughtfully. He did have devilishly clever allies in Nymphrys and Galakis. They would prevent Adakis and Orkanis from sabotaging a year's worth of work. "Where is this rift?" Diamantas asked aloud.

"In Edoin Forest, on the north side of the river. They said it was a day's ride from the Mountains."

Diamantas stroked his beard. "We have another chance to turn the prophecy to our favor, Janus. Be proud. These days will be recorded as pivotal moments in our history, ones in which we redeemed our oppressed brethren. *You*, Janus, have proven your importance to this cause."

Janus' cognac-colored gaze was filled more with relief than happiness. "Thank you, Uncle."

"When I last saw Kyra, she refused our company and my guidance," Diamantas mused. "A year exiled to another world, using her magic ungoverned and undisciplined, may make Kyra more willing to hear what I have to say. She would be an asset to us."

"What if Kyra doesn't listen, Uncle?"

"Then she dies. We cannot have her in the custody of Hayden and the elves. They will use her as a weapon against us." His eyebrows angled sharply as Janus balked. "What is it?"

"She . . . Kyra . . . she's my age," Janus replied timidly. "Do we have to kill her? There's no other way?"

"If Kyra does not accept, then no, that is our recourse." Diamantas stepped closer to Janus, a surge of fury flaring within him. In response, the obsidian staff's tip shot white energy into the air. Janus cringed. "She is of age now, not some mere child. Do not presume Solarus would not kill *you* if it served his ends, Janus. He and Hayden would show no mercy if it would save Kyra. That is why we must find her first." Diamantas put his hand on Janus' shoulder. "You are my nephew. As I have always told you, there is nothing more important than family."

Diamantas released Janus and stared down the passage. "Come, I want to share the news with our brethren. It has turned out to be a splendid day after all."

***

The first week after James left, Kate's nerves felt like live wires. For half an hour before her morning lesson, Kate paced the living room. She glanced at the door as twitchily as a squirrel. Millie left early for an art auction. Kate walked Millie to the door under the pretense of wanting to see what the weather was like. When Kate poked her head outside, she almost wilted in relief. She half-expected Reuben to be outside, waiting to pounce. Millie gave Kate a kiss on the cheek and left. Kate started her pacing.

When she finally did sit, Kate chose the chair at the end of the coffee table rather than the couch. She needed to keep the door in sight and not behind her. Kate rolled her pen along the table as was her habit. Uncertainty invaded her thoughts. *Does Reuben know I live in Hampstead? Would he attack again so soon?* Kate jumped at the sound of someone rapping on the door. The grandfather clock hadn't yet rung in the hour. *Was* Reuben on the other side? Kate turned her head wildly, looking for something to defend herself with and finding nothing more useful than a floor lamp. She glanced at her hands. Her skin didn't prick or itch, and she couldn't see the faintest trace of golden energy. Kate's heart thrummed for a few more anxiety-filled seconds as she stepped cautiously to the entrance. Professor O'Leary stood tapping her foot impatiently. Turning a shade of pink as Professor O'Leary strode past, Kate chided herself for her fear. James had said to be vigilant. He didn't tell her to evict her common sense. A Variavryk wouldn't politely announce himself by knocking. Kate let out a short breath and closed the door.

A month passed without incident—or any word from James. Kate's apprehension grew daily. As much as she fought against the thought, Kate wondered if Reuben's absence was because he had journeyed north to follow James. After all, hadn't James also made Reuben look foolish? There was nothing Kate could do but stay on guard.

In mid-December, Kate's tutors departed for the winter break. Fortunately, like the previous year, Millie had lists of activities to fill their time. Kate deliberately steered Millie away from Somerset House, always finding a reason to take another route to wherever they were visiting. Kate dutifully smiled at the appropriate times and laughed on cue as Millie burbled over Christmas decorations and ice-skating rinks and winter markets. When they returned home, Kate allowed her worry to flow from her and into her dreams.

The weekend before Christmas, Millie invited Kate to a holiday party. "Joseph is an art curator, hosts a feast every year," Millie had explained. She wore a festive green sweater with the words "Santa Claws Says You're Purrfect!" written beneath a cat in a red hat. "Delectable food, Joseph has. The lad has a talent in the kitchen. He makes his own eggnog, bakes his own cookies, prepares the whole kit-and-kaboodle! It's good old merriment. Robert will be there, too." Millie took a knitted red hat and fit it over her tightly coiled curls. "Doesn't that sound delightful, dearie?"

Kate demurred. She had woken that morning to a headache pulsing as steadily as a metronome. After a strong cup of coffee, Kate's headache abated, but she wasn't in any mood to have to socialize. Millie was immediately sympathetic. She prescribed tea and rest and left with a cheerful wave.

Kate milled around the house listlessly. Her eyes drifted to the living room walls. The painting of the Scottish castle was sandwiched between two portraits. Since James left, Kate had spent hours examining the picture. The gray stone parapets and open drawbridge were beautifully rendered. The hill upon which the castle sat was a green the color of James' eyes. *I wonder if he's there now,* she thought, peering intently at the drawbridge as though James would pop up in the picture. Her chest tightened with sadness.

The house was suddenly earsplittingly quiet and claustrophobically small. Kate needed someplace that could distract her restless mind. She swiftly crossed the room to the entranceway, threw on her boots, grabbed her coat and scarf from a peg, and was out the door.

Clouds sagged moodily overhead as Kate traipsed in the direction of the Tube station. A film of white covered the ground, and snow sprinkled down. The air was thick with the scent of a heavier storm yet to come. Kate lifted her hood over her head as flakes stuck to her hair. She didn't have a specific destination as she boarded the train. She absently climbed out at Waterloo station. Kate paused on the steps, gazing out. The city was bedecked with white, and a sharp wind swept the snow around her. Goose bumps pricked Kate's arm. She had the unnerving feeling that she was being watched.

Pulling her hood over her head again, Kate tromped down the steps and headed to the Strand. The streets were eerily empty for a Friday night during the holidays. The sense that someone was near dogged her steps. Doubling her pace, Kate turned her head left and right. Two buses passed her as she cut across the street. Her hands began to itch with the intensity of a thousand mosquito bites.

No, not now, not now, she thought desperately. Kate looked down, though she knew what was happening. A gold luminescence had formed around her hands. *Go away!* she silently commanded the energy. The gold flared more brightly in response.

Kate sprinted toward the closest pub, darting a glance over her shoulder. No telltale orange glow was visible in the white around her. Heart pounding, Kate flung open the door to the Lyceum Tavern and dashed inside.

"It's snowing that bad out, lass?" a voice called.

Kate immediately shoved her hands in her pockets and glanced at the bar. A bald-headed patron grinned at her from his stool, a pint of beer in hand. The bartender had also looked up as he filled a glass from the tap. She nodded mutely, stamping snow from her boots at the door. The bald-headed man continued to smile as Kate hurried past him.

Kate didn't stop until she was at the back of the tavern. She spied a table near a cozy fire in a large hearth. Its warmth reached out in a wide embrace. Keeping her hands inside her coat pockets, Kate gratefully sat. She saw the room was empty, save for two teenagers playing darts. Their friends sat nearby and cheered them on.

Kate welcomed the luxurious heat that unfroze her nose and cheeks. When a waiter came over, Kate ordered a mug of cocoa. The tingling had vanished from her hands. Kate carefully removed her hands from her pockets under the table. The glow was gone. Kate stripped her coat and scarf and laid them on a chair next to her.

The waiter soon returned. Kate sighed. The delicious cocoa, the lulling crackle of the fire, and the laughter from the pub's patrons eased some of her tension. Kate sipped on her drink, watching the dart players.

A lanky boy with dirty blond hair stood behind a red piece of tape on the floor. He was poised with a dart.

"Watch now, Inga," he was telling a girl with braided hair sitting among the other teenagers. He bit his tongue in concentration. "You have to hold the dart with a steady hand, like so, and then you release it, and it goes right in the . . . oh bloody hell."

The dart made a loud *thwack!* as it hit the outer ring.

The girl unsuccessfully tried to smother a giggle. Reddening, the boy rubbed the back of his neck sheepishly. "Something's wrong with this one," he muttered. "Feathers are bent. Kautik, let me use one of yours."

"Nope, mate, you had your chance," a swarthy boy with a toothy grin replied. He shooed the boy with the dirty blond hair away from the line. "It's done like this, George . . ."

Kautik held the dart eye level before snapping it forward. The dart embedded itself in the second ring from the bull's-eye.

"That was luck," George said. Kautik gave him a triumphant grin. The girl with the braid laughed.

Kate felt a pang of loneliness as George stepped up to the line. *What would it be like to be one of those teenagers? What would a life with friends my age be like? A life without strange abilities and spirits? A life with a past, with parents? A life that was normal?* Kate shook her head. Dwelling on who she could have been didn't change who she was or what she had experienced. Even if, in that moment, watching the teenagers' easy interaction, Kate wanted nothing more than the chance to forget about magic and Lyneera and Variavryk, and start over.

The lights in the room sputtered off and on. Kate started, torn from her thoughts. The wind crashed against the pub's old wooden door. The frame groaned in protest. Ice-covered tree branches clinked against the windows.

For a fraction of a second, Kate thought she heard a distant rumble. Her hands buzzed intensely as golden energy blossomed around them. Kate almost dropped her mug in her haste to hide her hands under the table. Her eyes skimmed over the patrons. No one seemed to have noticed.

"I get to take that shot over," she heard George grumble.

Kate snatched her coat from the chair and slipped it on. She had to see what was outside. She threw the scarf over her neck and shoved on her gloves. The lights guttered again. Keeping her hands stowed in her pockets, Kate rose and strode away from the dart players.

"Weather's picked up now, hasn't it?" the bartender commented as Kate walked toward the entrance. He was leaning forward on the bar and squinted across the room. "I'll be, it looks like we've a blizzard. Imagine that. A blizzard in London." He shook his head as the waitstaff started distributing candles.

Kate slid into a booth and stared out the window. Cold air had materialized on the pane. It spread across the glass like a virus and hardened into ice. Kate's stomach flipped. The ice she cocooned Reuben with had stretched over him the same way. Was she unintentionally causing this too?

The glass began to crack. Patrons shrieked and leapt out of their booths. Kate also sprang from her seat and crouched on the ground, covering her head with her arm. The glass shattered. More people screamed as wind blasted snow through the newly formed hole.

Kate stood shakily. The wind whipped the glass from her hair. Kate's jaw clenched as she glanced down at the gold flames around her hand. Reuben had come for her after all. The initial terror Kate felt was smothered by fierce determination. She was fed up with her fear. It was time to act.

"Fine. You wanted to find me, you've found me," Kate growled. She removed her other hand from her coat, fists balled tightly. "I'm not going to run from you." Kate tromped toward the door.

"Oi, what's . . . what's that on your hands?" the bartender's shocked voice came.

Kate was reaching for the door handle when it banged open. Snow swirled violently into the room. Kate shielded her face against the fury of the raging storm. She heard soft footsteps. Keeping a hand over her eyes, Kate looked out. A large black form stood before her, obscured by the whiteness. It tilted its head and roared so loudly, the air itself seemed to quake. Kate's pulse quickened as the figure stepped forward. His figure became clear.

It was a panther. His black fur was partially blanketed with snow as were his large paws. The panther's tail swished as his yellow-orbed eyes met Kate's. Kate gaped at him speechlessly. She had been prepared to fight the Variavryk. She hadn't anticipated a creature with claws, teeth, and two hundred pounds of muscle. Strangely, the panther radiated calm. Kate's curiosity subdued her fear.

"Close the door!" she heard the bartender's panicked yell. "Bloody hell, girl, close the door!"

Unthinkingly, Kate pulled the tavern door shut behind her. She could have sworn the big cat grinned.

"The good man intended for you to close the door with you on the *inside*," the panther said. "Not for you to stand on the *outside*." He raised his paw and let out a low noise from the back of his throat. The doorknob clicked, locking the patrons inside. He set his paw on the snow, yellow eyes bright. "We do not need interruption."

Kate stared at him. She tugged her hood over her head as a gust of wind smacked snow against her cheeks. "I don't mean to sound rude, but who are you?"

"My name is Raff," the panther replied. "I am a member of the *Al-Ethran*. My companions and I have roamed the lands this past year in search of you, Kyra. Hayden, Solarus, and Talis joined us in this endeavor. They feared Diamantas would happen upon you first. Through Inishmore's hand, you have been delivered to us instead."

Kate's heart thudded. The sentences were jumbled with names she didn't recognize. All except one. Kyra. What the man with the azure cloak had used at the lake. "My name is Kate, not Kyra," she replied without conviction. "You have the wrong person."

Raff's gaze shifted from Kate to the white haze around them. Ice had begun to form on his whiskers. "You are Kyra," he answered, "though you may have been called by another name. You do not belong to these lands. It is our good fortune you are hale. But your life is imperiled. It is not safe for you here. We must get you back quickly. They may have discovered us."

A chill ran down Kate's spine. *You do not belong to these lands*. That was what James had told her over a month earlier. "Who is we?" she asked. "And who are they?"

"We are friends. They are dark wizards." The panther's gaze pierced the snow. "We did not know where you were, specifically. We divided when we arrived and used our magic to bring forth yours." Raff's ears twitched. "They are coming."

Kate heard the sound of hooves clopping on the snow-covered stone. A horse emerged from the white curtain before her. Like the panther, the roan's handsome reddish-brown coat was mottled with snow, and his regal auburn mane had clumps of ice. The roan slowed to a walk, his large hooves parting the snow. "Kyra," he breathed. "I never gave up hope."

A merle border collie bounded past the horse. Her thick coat was patched blue and white, and her long tan snout sniffed the air. The collie's face was lined with distress.

"Hazel," Raff greeted. "Have we been followed?"

The collie nodded. "He says they're almost here, Raff. We must get to the rift."

Raff let out a huff, tail flicking in the snow. His eyes went back to the astonished Kate. "Kyra, the wizards are near. You must come with us."

The tips of Kate's hair had frozen, and the storm battered her with greater fervor. In her shock, Kate didn't feel the cold. Her gaze traveled from Raff to Hazel and finally to the roan. "I don't know you," she replied warily. "How can I trust that you want to help me? How do I know Reuben didn't send you?"

The panther's brow furrowed. "Reuben?"

"They aren't with the Variavryk, Kate," came an unseen but familiar voice. "They are here to help."

Kate's heart skipped a beat. A figure bundled in a black wool coat and checkered scarf gradually became visible as he stepped through the white veil. His emerald green eyes were bright yet troubled.

"*James!*" Kate exclaimed, flabbergasted. "You're back!" She ran forward and hugged him tightly. James stood woodenly, surprised, then returned the embrace.

"Hello, Kate," he greeted as Kate pulled away. "I'm sorry I was so long delayed."

"Where have you been?" Kate demanded in a tone more accusatory than she meant. "How did you know I was here? Why didn't you tell me you could understand animals like I could? How do you know they—"she gestured to Raff, Hazel, and Raven, "are here to help me? And why did . . ."

"Kate, Kate," James interrupted, raising his hand to stall Kate's questions. "I don't have much time to explain. I told you Reuben and I are from the same place you are, the land of Ilian. You know about the Variavryk and Lyneera. You also know you possess magic. What you aren't aware of is that Reuben threatened you a long time before Somerset House. Reuben approached me in the university and said he knew about you. It was right before your birthday."

"The day you canceled my lesson," Kate remembered. "That was the reason?"

"I was worried. In all my years in London, Reuben never referenced an attack on any of my other friends or colleagues. Only you. Though I am a Lyneera, my knowledge about the Variavryk was deficient. To protect you, I had to research accounts of their strengths, their vulnerabilities, their desires and motivations, and any deeper information on what prevented them from joining Inishmore. Then could I protect you from Reuben. That was why I was away this summer." James glanced over his shoulder as he spoke, as though expecting Reuben to appear. "It was not at the behest of my professor that I traveled to Northern Ireland, nor was my search limited to that country. I spent hours in archives and libraries across Great Britain. I hoped to find any example of someone in this world defending against the Variavryk. Unfortunately, I found but two references to Variavryk. Neither offered insights into how a non-Lyneera defeats one. The whole time, I believed I had to better understand the Variavryk. I was wrong. I had to better understand *you*."

James turned back to Kate. His expression was grave. "It didn't occur to me to learn more about you, Kate. I never considered that you might have magic. I never imagined you could come from my land. However, you had no memory of your past. That fact should have opened my eyes to new possibilities. When I studied in the Academy, I read about individuals who crossed between worlds. Actually, let me clarify that statement. Individuals who are not Lyneera or Variavryk. Spirits exist anywhere and everywhere. We are not limited by body or time. We travel to where Inishmore needs us to serve. In the case of non-spirit beings like you, memories are affected. Few travelers such as yourself exist in our history. Those who did uniformly claimed to have forgotten their previous lives. Until you trapped Reuben with the red energy, I didn't make the connection. Once I realized you were from Ilian, I knew I had to return you to your home. How to achieve that goal was, again, beyond my knowledge. Then Inishmore called me to Dunvegan." James nodded toward Raff. The panther's yellow-orbed eyes were fixed on James as he listened. "It was there that I learned of your friends' quest to find you. I was able to call to them, and now they are here. You can trust these noble creatures, Kate. I do."

"I can't . . . I can't up and leave," Kate protested. Her thoughts swirled and collided with the passion of the storm. "My home is here in London, with Millie. I don't want to be taken anywhere."

James' expression was sympathetic, but he shook his head. "It is not a choice, Kate. I asked you to resist using your magic. Whether you desire it or not, your powers will grow stronger. You need a teacher. You need to learn how to govern the energy within you. Magic is like a child. It must be nurtured and then matured before you can call on it reliably. You need training. That means you must travel to Ilian."

Deep inside, Kyra yearned to do exactly as he said, to uncover the secrets to the golden energy. "Millie will be worried sick if I don't come back," she said, though the fight had gone out of her voice. "I can't do that to her."

"Millie will be cared for as she had been before you moved to London," James said softly. "She will be safe. You won't. Not anymore."

As if in response, Kate's skin began to tingle. Her heart thudded in her chest. She glanced at her gloves. The golden energy had returned, pulsing around her wrists like a beacon in the storm.

James followed her gaze. "It is time to go," he said in an urgent tone. James directed his attention to Raff. "From my count, four wizards and three Variavryk pursue you."

"*Three* Variavryk?" Kate echoed.

"Reuben has friends."

"Seven attackers then." Raff gave Hazel and Raven a meaningful look.

James nodded. "Seven exactly."

Kate looked from James to the panther and back, bewildered. She knew something had passed between them, but she couldn't parse out the significance of the statement.

"I will do what I can to stall the Variavryk," James continued as Raven let out a low nicker. "The wizards will be up to you."

"You're going to fight Reuben and two other Variavryk alone?" Kate stared at James in consternation. "You can't do that. You said they can kill you."

"They can try," James responded with a peaceful look. He was haloed in a soft blue light, and his outline began to shimmer. "Reuben didn't succeed in his first attempt. I doubt he will have any more luck in a second."

Kate saw his coat and scarf disappear, replaced by a leather jacket, tunic, and knee-high boots. The wind tussled James' wavy hair, which had grown so that it fell just above his shoulders. If Kate hadn't witnessed the transformation, she wouldn't have recognized her friend.

"That's because I was with you," Kate argued. "Let me help you, and then we can escape. Raff knows the way . . ."

"Inishmore doesn't call for me to join you," James interrupted gently. "Our paths diverge. We must both embrace the change. As the writer Rosalia de Castro said, 'Not knowing where I am going is what inspires me to travel that path.' I have faith in Inishmore's will. I ask that your faith in me and yourself is as unwavering."

Water swam in Kate's eyes. Her heart was saturated with grief. She wanted to scream at him, convince him that she needed him with her, but she couldn't get out the words. "How am I supposed to do this without you?" Kate finally asked in a small voice.

A smile creased James' sorrowful expression. "You are strong. Have faith."

Kate threw her arms around James, tears sliding down her cheeks. "I'll miss you, James."

"As will I, Kate . . . Kyra." His emerald-green eyes were like the sea, pools of water and light. "Go. I will handle the Variavryk."

Raven stepped forward. Kyra noticed for the first time he was fitted with a saddle and bridle. "Do you remember how to ride?"

Before she could change her mind, Kate placed her foot carefully in one stirrup, held the saddle, and swung her other leg over the side. The saddle's smooth curves felt comfortable beneath her. Strangely, Kate's upright posture came as naturally as though she had ridden countless hours before. With a spurt of confidence, Kate took up the reins. The leather was slick from frozen snow. Kate clenched them as tightly as she could in her gloved hands. She cast one last glance down to James.

"Take care of Millie for me?" she asked.

James nodded. He smiled, his form wreathed in the blue light. "Until we meet again, Kyra." Raising a hand in farewell, he turned into the storm and strode off.

Raven didn't wait another moment. He pivoted sharply. Kate lurched forward, her ribs hitting the curve of the saddle, as the horse cantered down the street at breakneck speed. Kate's heart drummed in her chest. She barely kept her grip on the slippery reins. Her hood flew back. Wind smacked her exposed face with snow and ice. Kate bent her head to the side. Hearing Hazel's bark, she guessed the panther and collie weren't far behind.

Raven thundered through the storm. The snow obscured Kate's vision, leaving her without her bearings as to where she was being taken. Raff sprinted ahead of Raven and took a bend in the road.

"This way!" he roared, tail streaming behind him.

A succession of cracks and booms pierced through the wind. Kate's ears rang as the sky lit up with purple sparks like giant firecrackers. Instinctively, Kate lowered herself in the saddle. She heard the snow around her sizzle as green showered down. The roan deftly pivoted away from the magic without breaking his gait.

Kate looked over her shoulder for a heartbeat. She glimpsed a purple orb bobbing in the air, with more colored lights near it. The snow couldn't completely disguise the forms of horses and their riders. Kate saw black sheets flapping behind them.

"Keep your head forward, Kyra!" Hazel barked.

Kate obeyed. She didn't have to ask if those were the wizards James had mentioned.

Raff ducked into an alleyway. The narrow passage was devoid of its usual, heavy pedestrian traffic. The panther zigzagged through it, turned the corner, and zipped through an opening. Kate was again struck by snow and wind as they emerged at a wharf. Raff sprinted down the riverbank, with Raven and Hazel closely in tow.

The storm whipped over the Thames. The river's waters crashed over themselves, forming white waves. Kate focused on what was ahead of her, though it was difficult to make out anything in the screen of snow. Two tall forms began to appear. Towers, she realized. They were nearing Tower Bridge. Lights accentuated the large stone structures and lined the length of the bridge. The glass walkway that connected the towers at their peaks was also illuminated.

There was something else. Midway across the bridge, suspended in the air between the towers, the sky was . . . torn. As they neared, Kate saw it looked like a roughly hewn piece of cloth that flapped downward. Not so different from James' slashed shirtsleeve. In the space between the sky and the flap was a line of white so bright it hurt to look at it. Kate blinked, her eyes tearing up from the arctic air. Was it a figment of her imagination? As Raven brought her closer, the blinding white grew as though the night's stars had been captured and crammed together in the space.

Raff was far in front of them now. He loped down the riverbank. At the steps to Tower Bridge, he waited, paw raised, his yellow-orbed gaze looking beyond the roan and collie.

"Hurry!" he bellowed into the storm. "They are almost upon you!"

Kate heard her pursuers' horses, snorting and huffing, hooves clomping on the paved ground. She clutched the reins. Cold nipped at her skin through the gloves, and her hands were growing numb despite the gold flames eddying around them. Kate's pulse galloped as furiously as Raven.

They finally reached Raff. Hazel panted, staying close to the roan. The panther turned and sprinted up the steps. A crackling sound alerted Kate to her enemies' attack. She looked back in time to see cardinal red magic rocket toward her. Raven clambered up the stairs. The red smashed into the stone below them. Rocks burst and sprayed into the air, but the roan and the collie had already cleared the steps. The sharp white tear remained ominously suspended in the air between the towers.

Kate chanced another glance over her shoulder. She could see the wizards clearly. There were four as James had said, their black cloaks like soot against the purity of the snow. They carried staffs, each flaring with a different color.

Raven was almost under the first arch on the bridge when a bolt of orange lightning whizzed past. It grazed the side of Kate's hood before it sliced the side of the arch. Large chunks of stone split off and splashed into the river. More pieces dropped onto the arch, partially blocking their escape. Raven didn't slow down. Kate held her breath as the roan jumped over the debris. She almost fell from the saddle as he landed heavily.

Raff had again stopped. He waited directly before the white gash. *What is he doing?* Kate wondered. Orange energy spiraled above her and struck the walkway. The glass overhead shattered. Instinctively, Kate ducked and threw up a hand as shards cascaded down. Gold flew from her hands over her head. The energy created a ceiling that stretched from Raff back to Hazel. The glass ricocheted off the gold energy. Amazingly, the glass didn't penetrate the ceiling. Kate again gripped the reins, hands quaking.

"Go, Raff!" Hazel shouted.

The panther nodded. He turned and leapt into the void.

"What are you doing?" Kate wanted to yell, but her consternation glued the words to her throat.

She heard chanting. A volley of red, orange, and purple energy shot into the air and over her head like mortar shells. Each landed on the bridge and exploded. Gaping holes began to form in the bridge as stone after stone collapsed into the waters below. Time seemed to slow. The entire structure began to give way. Kate's heart leapt to her throat. There was no way out.

The roan surged forward in desperation. Without warning, Raven sprang. The blinding light seemed to snatch the roan, pulling him and Kate into the white abyss. Kate bent over the saddle and squeezed her eyes shut. Her mind's eye locked onto images of Millie and James.

I don't want to die was Kate's final thought as light exploded in her vision. Then there was darkness.

PART TWO

ILIAN

Chapter 1

The impact never came.

Kyra lay on the ground, head turned to the side, cheek pressed against something soft. She didn't move. She wasn't certain she could. She recalled her frozen hands. Clinging in terror to the saddle of a horse. A bridge in front of her blowing apart. Kyra kept her eyes tightly closed, afraid of what she would find if she opened them.

Where was the pain? Kyra wondered. Her hands were warm, as was her nose. Had death been so immediate that she hadn't felt herself crashing into the river, devoured by its brutally cold waters?

Kyra sucked in a panicked breath. A sharp pain filled her chest. It was a blessed breath of air, not water.

Gradually, Kyra became aware of the merry warbling of birds. A warm breeze kissed her cheek, carrying the sweet perfume of honeysuckle and budding trees. Insects buzzed close to her ear. She didn't hear yells or explosions. Just the tranquility and quiet of a perfect spring's day.

Kyra's heart slowed. *If this is life after death, it isn't so bad,* she thought.

Kyra cautiously opened her eyes and immediately flinched. She shielded her face with her hand. The cloudless, robin's-egg blue sky was piercingly bright after months of London's drearily ashen days.

As Kyra's sight adjusted, she lowered her hand. The sun's rays bathed her face. Lush grass and a rainbow of flowers stretched before her. Exhaling deeply, Kyra pushed herself upright. She put a hand to her cheek and felt imprints from the blades of grass.

Kyra's peacoat was stifling hot, as were her gloves. Kyra pulled off her gloves and set them aside. As she began to unbutton her coat, her fingers grazed bits of ice stuck to the wool. Kyra paused, fingers on a half-unfastened button. She looked down. Remnants of snow and ice clumped in patches, though most had melted.

Kyra's brow furrowed. *Why is there snow on my coat? Why am I even wearing a coat? Is that what happened when you died? Did James wake up in London wearing the same clothes he had had on when he became a spirit? The clothing I saw before he left to fight the three Variavryk?*

Kyra swallowed hard as she removed the coat. James. He had said he would delay the Variavryk. Had James been successful? She rose on unsteady legs. Her thighs ached from where the saddle had jostled her, and her muscles burned from the exertion of gripping the reins. Rubbing her arm, Kyra's gaze scrolled across her surroundings. She stood in the lush grasses of a meadow the size of two football fields. Buttercups and daisies dotted the ground, and a handful of wych elms sprouted like weeds. Tiny, ruby-throated birds flitted overhead.

Kyra turned slowly clockwise. The meadow was bordered on all sides by forest, its tiny pink-and-white-flowered trees scattered among leafy, verdant neighbors. Kyra had almost completed her circle when her eyes widened in awe.

Far along the horizon were imposing gray mountains. She had never observed anything so colossal. The mountains reached upward and broke through the clouds, which hung like a necklace around the gray masses. Pointed, white peaks that looked like gnomes' hats extended further into the sky. The majestic crags made Britain's rolling hills and the Scottish Highlands look like bumps in comparison.

Kyra jumped as she heard a protracted yawn. Her gaze whipped to her right. Raff was stretching his paws, raking the grass as he dragged his claws back. Raven grazed contentedly nearby. Strands of his auburn mane were frozen. Hazel sniffed the ground experimentally. She lifted her nose and looked at the panther.

"The wizards' stench is recent," she reported with a grimace. "It's possible that passing through the rift affects time and that the wizards reached Ilian before us."

The panther's whiskers twitched. "Let us hope not. We agreed that Hayden would meet us here. Between him and Talis, I do not imagine they would have difficulty picking up our trail." Raff's yellow-orbed gaze shifted to Kyra as she stepped toward him.

"I'm sorry, but where are we?" she asked Raff. The question came out as a croak, her voice hoarse from gulping down the icy wind.

"This is Ilian, Kyra," Raff replied. "You are of this land, even if you do not remember it. The Lyneera ensured that the gap through which we traveled would deliver us safely. I am relieved we arrived in full health."

"Ah." Kyra hesitated. Her gaze went from Raff to Hazel to Raven, who had raised his head at her voice. "So, we aren't dead?" she asked.

Raff let out a low chuckle and shook his head. "No, Kyra, we are very much alive. Death is a realm to which none of us has, gratefully, yet journeyed. Nor do we plan to, despite the dark wizards' attempts to send us there." Raff motioned to the trees with a nod. "This is the border of Edoin Forest, on the north side of the river near the Southern Mountains. We are awaiting friends. But I have been remiss in not making introductions." He offered a sweeping bow with his paw. "My name is Raff. My companions are Hazel of the *Al-Ethran* and Raven of Silvias."

The collie wagged her tail in greeting. The roan regarded Kyra with his lustrous brown eyes.

Raven's an odd name for a horse, Kyra thought as the horse strode forward.

Raven bent his head and nudged Kyra's face affectionately. "I have missed you, Kyra."

Kyra rubbed the roan's muzzle. The softness of Raven's hair, the warmth of the sun, and the cheerful birdsong assuaged some of Kyra's apprehension. Her mind was chock-full of questions. "James mentioned Ilian, but there's a lot I don't understand. I remember the bridge was destroyed. We . . . what you're saying is we didn't fall into the river with it? Why not? Then there was that light in the sky. Where did it come from? Did the wizards create it? And why were they after us in the first place?"

The animals shared amused smiles. "Your curiosity has not abated," Raff replied. His long tail swished through the grass. "I will answer with what I know while we wait. The wizards that pursued us, who are also called the 'dark wizards,' come from the kingdom of Harkimer. It is located within the Southern Mountains, the same that you see there." Raff pointed with a paw to the formidable mountains in the distance. "Not all wizards live in Harkimer. These wizards' ancestors waged war on the kingdoms of men and elves eight centuries ago in what is called the War of Calonia. The original dark wizards killed hundreds of thousands. Animals and the free wizards of Ilian fought alongside men and elves and suffered heavily. When the dark wizards' leader was killed, the wizards were defeated and banished to the Southern Mountains. Now the wizards of Harkimer have a new leader. His name is Diamantas. He has united the dark wizards for the first time since the war. He seeks another bloody battle for our lands."

"Diamantas is a detestable man," Hazel added, a cloud shadowing her crystal blue gaze. "Detestable, cunning, and notoriously persistent in pursuit of his enemies. He considers you one of his foremost, Kyra. That's why, since your disappearance one year past, he has used every resource to find you. We, your friends and allies, have been equally fervent in our search."

"As for the light," Raff took up the thread again, "the wizards did not create it. It is a rift, a portal between your world and this one. Our knowledge of these events is limited. The annals of the animals and scribes allude to a handful of such portals throughout Ilian's history. Unfortunately, the language of the accounts is so archaic, it is mostly incomprehensible. Without your Lyneera, we would never have looked for such a rift. We had no record of one being created in Ilian nor of anyone voyaging through one. We took a chance. As you see, it worked. We made it to that other world."

Kyra nodded, though the answers were adding to her confusion.

"Your Lyneera said Inishmore would deliver us to wherever we chose if we beseeched it to do so," Raff continued. "We asked for Edoin Forest. This place."

Kyra's lashes were wet with tears. She was even more indebted to James than she had realized. She could have died. *Would* have died, more accurately. Kyra's stomach flopped. Where was James at that moment? Had he found Reuben and the other Variavryk? The image of James lying on the cold stone courtyard was burned into her conscious and made her blood run cold. What if he was hurt, or worse? What if he needed her? Whatever state James was in, Kyra couldn't do anything to help. James was firm in his instructions. Kyra was to find a mentor to help her gain control over the gold and red flames.

"We arranged to meet Hayden and the others here," Raff finished. His gaze rooted to the tree line. "As soon as they arrive, we will depart for safer grounds."

Kyra's lips creased into a small frown. "You haven't explained why the wizards were after me. That seems like a lot of effort, traveling from Ilian to another world to find one teenage girl. Or am I the only wizard who doesn't—didn't?—live in Harkimer?"

The panther exchanged a furtive look with Hazel. The collie's gaze was troubled.

"Many wizards still live outside of Harkimer," Raff answered, looking back at Kyra. "These are the free wizards about whom I spoke, the wizards who fought against the dark wizards in the War of Calonia. They remained in Ilian. You belong to them."

It was clear Raff had intentionally skirted the question. Kyra bit her lip. The shards of information she was getting lay in front of her like glass from a shattered window. If she were able to fit the pieces together, Kyra could look through the pane. She wanted to see what her life was before and what it meant for her now.

"Who is Hayden?" she asked.

"Hayden was your guardian and protector, as were Talis and Solarus."

"I already know them?"

"You used to." Raff sighed. "The Lyneera informed us of your affected memory. You can relearn what skills have been lost. Will memories of your friends be so easily restored? Can they be retrieved at all? I do not know." The panther's ears abruptly perked upward. Hazel sprang to her feet. Raven craned his neck so that his eye was on the woods. "That would be Hayden now."

Kyra heard a drumming on the ground and the crash of branches. A fleet of birds burst out of the tree canopy, squawking loudly. Her hands were pricked by a familiar sensation. Kyra raised them. The golden energy had ignited around her fingers. Kyra's heart pounded in response. Was Hayden a wizard too?

When she looked to Raff for confirmation, she saw the panther had lowered himself to the ground. His ears were flattened against his head.

"That is not Willow." Raven stamped the ground uneasily. "We should flee to the river. We can cross more quickly than they. Kyra, you must remount."

Kyra grabbed the saddle unhesitatingly and swung astride. It wasn't the time to second-guess the animals offering to help her. Raff and Hazel took up defensive positions in front of the roan. Grabbing the reins, Kyra watched as four horses stampeded out of the woods, their sharp hooves gouging the earth. Their riders wore black cloaks and carried staffs pulsating with magic. Kyra breathed in sharply. The dark wizards. They steered their steeds into a semicircle around Kyra and her companions.

"How in the name of the Healer did they follow us?" Raff growled.

Kyra quickly assessed her situation. Two wizards barred her entrance into the woods. The first wizard had shoulder-length hair, cedar-brown with gray stripes, with a matching goatee that narrowed to a point. Large ears protruded from his oval face as though there had not been enough room to fit them. Under different circumstances, his appearance would have been comical. His companion was a woman with dark skin and full lips. Her black curly hair was combed over her head and reminded Kyra of a fox's tail. Unlike her companion, the woman had an indifferent, even bored, expression.

Kyra cast a glance to her left. A swarthy wizard with scraggly, coal-black hair glowered at her through slitted eyes. He projected power and confidence. Dread mushrooming inside her, Kyra's gaze moved to the right. The last wizard was the least imposing, with a swivel-eyed gaze, sallow face, and hair hanging like wet noodles.

Together, the wizards blocked an escape from every direction except the one directly behind her. Kate discounted it as an option. She had no intention of turning her back and making herself an easy target. Kate also would not abandon the panther and collie to the dark wizards.

Kyra kept a tight grip on Raven's reins. She didn't remember the years she and the roan had practiced working together as a team, but Kyra's instincts plugged the hole in her conscious knowledge. She pressed her thighs against Raven's flank and subtly steered him to the side.

"Kyra, what are you doing?" Raven protested. He flicked his head against the reins. "We are leaving. You cannot fight them."

"We're staying," Kyra murmured under her breath. "I trusted you. Now you have to trust me."

The wizard with protruding ears raised a pencil-straight mahogany staff. His lips were downturned in what was a battle between a child's pout and a bully's sneer. He gestured dramatically to Kyra. "At long last. Kyra, the miserable upstart of a girl, has been returned to Ilian. She hid. She fled. And in the end, I found her, as you all knew I would." The wizard gave Kyra a superior look. "It was foolish of you to think you could escape. I'm Harkimer's most accomplished tracker. It was only a matter of time before this hunt ended."

"The Variavryk found the girl, actually," the female wizard put in flatly. She rubbed a helix-shaped earring.

Adakis either didn't hear or ignored the comment. The sneer won out over his pout.

Kyra's hands burned as gold spit from her fingertips. "Am I supposed to be impressed?" she retorted, her anger mingling with her fear.

Adakis waved his hand dismissively. "I don't expect a child to recognize greatness. Nymphrys," he addressed the female wizard, "You and I will deliver the girl to Diamantas." Adakis pointed to a scraggly-haired wizard on his left. "Galakis, kill the animals."

The wizard beside Galakis cleared his throat. His gaze waggled between Adakis and Kyra. "Adakis, I can assist you . . ."

"I don't need your assistance, Orkanis," Adakis cut him off scornfully. "I could handle the mouthy wastrel myself if I wanted to, and the animals to boot. I just choose to not waste all my energy on them. Sometimes I forget how exceptional my powers are and . . ."

Kyra kicked her heels into Raven's flanks before Adakis finished his sentence. The roan barreled toward the trees, head low and nostrils flaring. Adakis' mouth formed a stupefied line. Clutching the reins with one hand, Kyra raised the other and willed the golden energy to strike. It burst from her hand like a cannon. Adakis raised his staff almost too late as the magic crashed against it.

Kyra jerked the reins sharply to the right. Nymphrys was quicker to act. Purple magic gathered at the tip of her staff and sprayed slivers of hot energy at Raven. Kyra ducked and reflexively cast a hand before her. She waited for blistered skin and the smell of singed hair. Nothing happened. Kyra raised her eyes and gasped. Blue-green magic shimmered in front of Raven like a bowman's shield. Her golden light was tucked protectively within it.

Nymphrys' dark eyes betrayed a moment of surprise. Her expression dissolved into disdain. "You're inconveniencing me. I have no patience for being inconvenienced."

"I'll keep 'inconveniencing you' if it keeps me alive," Kyra replied warily.

Nymphrys loosed another bolt of lightning against Kyra's shield. The blue-green magic absorbed the purple bolt, though Kyra reeled from the impact. Nymphrys glared sullenly at the blue and green. She muttered something indecipherable before throwing waves of fire at Kyra.

Sweat matted Kyra's hair as she struggled to hold the shield. The blue-green and gold magic flickered like candles in the wind. Right as the shield was on the verge of collapse, Kyra glimpsed a black blur. With a roar, Raff swiped at Nymphrys' horse. Nymphrys jerked her steed to the side to keep from being unseated. Panting, Kyra pivoted Raven away from Nymphrys.

To Kyra's left, Hazel loped toward Orkanis. The steed crow-hopped as the collie nipped at the horse's legs. Orkanis yelled, and cardinal red magic streamed toward Hazel. The collie nimbly zigzagged around the wizard and attacked again.

Adakis had regrouped. Rather than seeming embarrassed or shocked, he looked splendidly affronted by Kyra's sneak attack. Kyra steered Raven away from him. She realized too late that she drove the roan directly into Galakis' path. Galakis grinned maliciously and thrust his staff toward her. A spiral of orange scorched the air. Kyra's heart skipped a beat. The magic passed inches from her arm and instead struck Orkanis squarely in the chest. The swivel-eyed wizard was thrown from his mount. Orkanis hit the ground with a grunt. His staff bounced from his hand. Orkanis' horse bucked in fright and streaked off into the woods.

"Blast you!" Galakis cursed as his companion lay gasping. "For Malus' sake, Orkanis, stop moaning and get up!"

Kyra was on the verge of a smile when a purple explosion caught her eye. Her triumph plummeted to horror. Raff was thrown into the air. He hit the ground with a louder thud than Orkanis. His chest rose and fell, but the panther didn't move.

Aghast, Kyra inserted Raven between Nymphrys and Raff. Desperate to prevent another attack, Kyra grabbed Nymphrys' staff. Searing pain shot through her arm. Kyra cried out. Nymphrys shrieked. They released the weapon at the same time, and the staff fell to the ground. Kyra glanced at her throbbing palms. The skin was red and raw under the shimmering golden light.

"Good effort, Nymphrys, but there's no need to continue with Kyra," Adakis said from behind her. "I have it under control." Kyra glanced over her shoulder. Adakis aimed his mahogany staff at her chest while Galakis angled his toward Kyra's head.

Nymphrys brought her steed forward. Her foxtail-like hair was disheveled as she glared daggers at Adakis. "How nice of you to join the fight now that we've trapped the girl. Clearly, you have the most gifted timing in all Harkimer."

"Naturally so," Adakis agreed, missing the sarcasm in Nymphrys' tone. "There are two staffs pointed at you, Kyra, and I never miss a target. If you don't surrender to me—"

"Us," Galakis spat.

"—then I will . . . I will . . ." Adakis pulled on his earlobe, seemingly at a loss for how to end his sentence. "Well, I think you can figure out what I'm capable of," he finished instead in a satisfied tone. "The battle will end unpleasantly for you."

Goose bumps sprouted on Kyra's skin. Adakis didn't strike her as exceptionally bright. Unfortunately, she was convinced that with the help of the other wizards, he could deliver on his threat.

Orkanis was sitting upright, face pallid. He stretched out to grab his staff. Using it for support, Orkanis rose woozily to his feet. Adakis kept his staff trained on Kyra. Galakis moved his horse forward and used his free hand to haul Orkanis into the saddle behind him.

Hazel had rejoined Kyra and Raven. The collie's breath was ragged, but a quick glance told Kyra she wasn't injured.

Heart racing, Kyra cast lines in her mind for a way to defeat the wizards. Every hook came back empty.

"Galakis, bind her so we can leave," Adakis commanded with a small wave of his hand.

Galakis gave him a sour look. "I wouldn't entertain the thought of casting a spell of such importance, Adakis. Not when I have the mightiest of wizards present to do so himself."

Adakis puffed up with pride, again missing the sarcasm in the comment. "I appreciate your reluctance. It isn't the first time a wizard has been intimidated by my magical prowess."

Nymphrys snorted.

"One might feel ashamed of his abilities in my presence," Adakis continued condescendingly. "However, I can assure you . . ."

His sentence was interrupted by two sharp *thwack*s. Adakis' staff jerked upward as two arrows struck it from behind in quick succession. Kyra's gaze shot to the woods.

Adakis' face was beet red. His dark eyes also flew to the tree line. "That is the second time someone has interrupted me!" he shouted petulantly. "Who dares to attack?"

In response, a man burst through the forest, holding a knife between his forefinger and thumb. He hurled it at Orkanis. The knife cartwheeled through the air and grazed Orkanis' arm. Orkanis yelped and cowered in the saddle behind Galakis. Galakis countered the attack with a ball of orange flame. The man ducked as it soared overhead.

Nymphrys spurred her horse away from the trees. She wheeled her steed behind Kyra. Adakis hastily steered his own horse beside Nymphrys. He kept his staff pointed at Kyra as his eyes scanned the trees for the unseen attackers.

Three more horses surged through the opening. A man in an earthen brown cloak brandished a sword that glinted in the sunlight. Beside him rode a figure clad in a forest green cloak. His bow was raised, an arrow drawn across his cheek. An azure-cloaked rider on a large, dappled gray flanked them. Kate's jaw dropped. It was the cloak from her vision. *Her* cloak. Wielding a staff in his hand, the man was unmistakably a wizard.

"Ride forward, Kyra!" he commanded. Kyra immediately clapped her heels into Raven. The newcomers parted around Kyra and the roan and streamed past. Kyra spun Raven around so her back was to the tree line and watched the turn of events in astonishment.

The man in the brown cloak charged Adakis, blade raised. Hastily, Adakis flipped his mahogany staff so it was horizontal across his body. A crimson shield spread from his head to his torso as the man's blade came down. The shield shuddered as the metal bit into it. Adakis counterattacked with a fiery crescent of magic. The man's horse agilely leapt to the side. The magic continued to the forest, slicing off branches and leaves.

Kyra's attention flew to the man with the knives. He had slowed before the unarmed Nymphrys. When the green-cloaked figure had caught up to him, he hurled the knife. Nymphrys unconcernedly raised her palm. Purple magic flared and met the knife midair, disintegrating it.

At the same time, the figure fired another arrow at Galakis. Galakis deflected the arrow with a twirl of his staff.

Out of the corner of her eye, Kyra saw crimson light. She glanced back to Adakis. The magic bloomed around the tip of his staff. The man in the brown cloak held his sword with two hands, slanting it in front of his chest as he braced himself for the blast.

What are you doing? Kyra screamed in her head. What good was a sword against magic?

Adakis fired a ball of crimson magic. Even as the magic left Adakis' staff, a turquoise wall materialized in front of the man. The ball splattered against it and dissipated like dust. The azure-cloaked wizard guided his steed beside the man. His staff rippled with an intense turquoise magic. The man inclined his head in thanks.

The fighting came to a standstill. The figure with the bow kept a pair of arrows trained on Galakis and Orkanis. The other man held a knife between his forefinger and index finger, poised to throw.

"Adakis, really?" the azure-cloaked wizard said with a disparaging arch of his brow. "You have not tired of these misbegotten ventures to kidnap Kyra? I am surprised. You have added another failure to your list, which is impressively long already."

"Failure, Solarus?" Adakis snorted derisively. "You call this is a failure? It's an undeniable victory. Kyra is here in Ilian, and *I* found her. Me, Adakis. Not you."

Nymphrys rolled her eyes and muttered "Variavryk" under her breath.

"Without me, this annoying girl would still be stuck in the other world," Adakis crowed. "Diamantas will reward me with a drink from the cup of glory."

"I'll take bets on whether the cup is poisoned," the man with the knives remarked casually. "If Diamantas is as smart as everyone says, he'll kill you off. I'll go ask him myself, do us all a favor. That means I won't have to listen to the yapping of Harkimer's most mediocre wizard."

"You rode on the Variavryk's coattails to cross from Ilian," the man in the brown cloak added. "There isn't any way to claim that as your success."

"Hayden is right," Solarus said calmly. "You have not demonstrated any talent. You can now, however. You have the opportunity to test your mettle. Let us duel, you and I. Defeating me singly in a battle would give you the right to boast."

Adakis' confidence slipped from his face. His eyes darted back and forth between the newcomers. He tried to infuse boldness into his words as he spat, "What a *kind* offer, Solarus, but I have no need to 'test my mettle.' Diamantas is aware of my unparalleled worth. In fact, I am one of an exalted few entrusted with Diamantas' plans. He has promised to procure me my own obsidian staff. Then I could crush you all in a single blow. You're jealous, Solarus. I will achieve greatness while you languish among men and elves."

Solarus' irked expression showed Adakis were a pesky midge to be slapped away. "As always, Adakis, your delusions run rampant. A staff is only as effective as its bearer. It cannot gift an amateur wizard with abilities. I also doubt Diamantas would allow the fashioning of another obsidian staff. Now," Solarus finished, turquoise flame running up and down his staff as he spoke, "prepare yourself."

Someone suddenly bellowed a string of words Kyra didn't understand. She looked for the voice. Galakis twirled his staff. Orange fluttered from the top like thousands of monarch butterflies. In the exchange between Adakis and Solarus, Kyra had neglected the other wizards. Galakis swept the staff down in a straight line. Kyra watched in consternation as the orange tore through the air like bullets.

Solarus held his staff above his head. A rich turquoise light flowed through it. The magic spread out like a bird, soaring high into the air before pirouetting and diving backward toward the earth. Kyra shivered as the blue swathed her with a feeling of icy rain. The turquoise also covered the rest of the wizard's companions. The orange magic parted around the blue shield and peppered the wych elms and forest. Kyra turned in awe. Large trunks cracked and shuddered.

Some toppled down like twigs while others exploded into the air. Scarcely breathing, Kyra looked up. Chunks of tree trunks and massive branches collided against Solarus' magical bubble. The turquoise held firm. The trees crashed to the ground on all sides of the shield, the sound deafening even within the bubble.

Kyra glanced to the side, anticipating Galakis' next attack.

The dark wizards were gone.

Chapter 2

"I'd call that a hasty retreat." The man with the knives cocked his head. His midnight blue eyes stared at a point along the tree line. Kyra followed his gaze. She caught a glimpse of black cloaks flapping with the same frenzy as their riders. A final trunk crashed on Solarus' shield as the dark wizards ducked into the woods.

Solarus' expression was sour. "When you are utterly incompetent, a retreat is the wisest course of action." He touched the turquoise bubble with the tip of his staff. The magic flowed back inside until there was nothing left.

Glancing down at her hands, Kyra saw the golden glow disappear.

"Leave them for now, Talis," Hayden told his companion in the forest green cloak, who had pulled his reins in the direction of the wizards. Hayden sheathed his weapon. "Let's establish what threats could come from the west or south."

Talis nodded. He returned the arrow to his quiver and slung the bow over his back. Wheeling his golden-colored steed around, he set off to the west.

The man with the midnight blue gaze twirled a knife in his hand. "That wasn't a very satisfying skirmish. Jaren and Garen, I was looking forward to having a repartee with our clueless Adakis. I feel robbed of the opportunity."

"Interesting choice of words," Hayden replied. His arched brow elicited a grin from the man. "You'll have your chance, Jyls. I doubt Diamantas is forgiving of repeated debacles that end in our favor. He'll send Adakis out again. At least until he does something useful."

Jyls fluidly returned the knife to his belt. "Diamantas is going to be six feet under before Adakis does something useful."

"Raff's hurt," Kyra announced suddenly, drawing the group's attention to her. "The panther over there. The wizards attacked him."

Hayden's gray gaze went to the forest. "Ash?" he called. "Are you there?"

A young man with a shock of red hair rode out of the woods. His face was sheet-white, shavings of bark and leaves in his short locks. Ash's filly halted near Raff. The young man half-slid, half-fell out of his saddle. Kneeling, Ash placed a hand on the panther's chest, then probed the panther's back and legs. Kyra watched as he stood and rooted through his saddlebags. Ash withdrew a pouch and a liquid-filled vial. Then he again crouched beside Raff. "*Ruska rankala,*" Ash chanted in a soft, monotone voice. "*Nezorov alikani, dochuva ex terkuska...*"

Hazel padded over to the young man and sat. Her crystal blue eyes conveyed her worry as Ash began to remove bandages and a small pestle from the pouch.

Kyra shakily crawled down from Raven. The adrenaline that had coursed through her during the fight seeped out. Like at Somerset House, Kyra's use of magic left her body as depleted as if she had run three marathons.

The rest of the group also dismounted. Hayden approached Kyra, gray eyes sparkling. He wore an open-collared, charcoal-gray leather jacket over a white tunic. His vest, the color of a wolf's fur, cinched below his waist. Hayden absently brushed away strands of wavy, sandy hair plastered to his forehead from sweat. Kyra was surprised when he embraced her.

"It's been a long time, Kyra," he said. "You have no idea how relieved we are that you're whole and safe."

Kyra stiffened. As it had been with Millie the first time they met in the airport, Kyra wasn't sure how to interact with someone from her past. Without her memories, Kyra couldn't reciprocate Millie's happiness then. She couldn't reciprocate Hayden's happiness now. Except . . . there was a subtle difference with Hayden. His presence was oddly comforting. Familiar.

Hayden released her. A worried line had formed on his brow. "Is everything all right, Kyra?"

"Um . . ." Kyra's response was caged by the myriad questions and emotions battling for supremacy. She had been attacked by a group of wizards. She had called upon the golden energy and used it to defend herself. She had been saved by Hayden and this group of strangers. Strangers who treated her as a long-lost friend. Kyra was flummoxed, apprehensive, and intrigued by the events.

Hayden's gray eyes combed Kyra's face with concern. Feeling uncomfortable under his gaze, Kate looked to the red-haired man and the panther. Ash had created a poultice in the pestle. He gently blotted the mixture along the panther's ribs, continuing his staccato chant. Raff's leg was wrapped with a white bandage. Hazel's eyes were trained on the panther, anxiously looking for signs of recovery.

Kyra glanced back at Hayden. "I'm grateful for your help. I wouldn't have been able to stop the wizards without you. Did I . . . have we met before?"

Hayden frowned. "Of course we have, Kyra. We've known each other since you were a child."

Kyra bit her lip. "I'm sorry but I don't remember. I'm also not . . . Well, Raff called me this name too—Kyra. My name isn't Kyra. It's Kate. I think you might have the wrong person."

Hayden's expression darkened. "There aren't many things I'm sure of, but I am certain your name is Kyra." Hayden turned to Solarus, who stood behind him. "Solarus, what happened to her? Is there a spell that the dark wizards used to erase Kyra's memories?"

Solarus folded his arms. The wizard was tall in stature and carried himself with a naturally commanding presence. Solarus' wheat-colored hair was crewcut and sprinkled liberally with silver, and his fastidiously trimmed beard exhibited traces of gray. A line cut across one side of his hair, forming a cursive Z. His ocean blue eyes were deeply contemplative.

Kyra suppressed a gasp. Solarus *was* part of her mental photo album from London. When Mr. Stevens had pulled out his pipe, Kyra had slipped into a—vision? memory?—of the lake. With the wizard sitting next to her. Solarus' cloak shimmered in the sunlight as though it possessed its own vitality. What hadn't appeared so clearly in her vision was his white tunic, with its laced collar and open, blue-stitched cuffs. The tunic was complemented by a navy leather vest, tan trousers, and brown knee-high boots. The boots looked chic and stiff.

"It would be powerful magic to conquer an individual's mind so fully," Solarus mused. "No wizard has that ability. As far as I can understand, the obsidian staff also cannot endow a wizard with the strength to cast such a spell. It is possible this lapse in memory is a temporary one. Kyra may have retained knowledge about her magic and us. What is now a dried streambed could be flooded with memories. But we need a trigger." For the first time, the wizard seemed to notice Kyra's astonished expression. He raised a brow. "Or Kyra already recognizes someone."

Kyra's face grew hot. "I've seen you before," she mumbled. "Not in person. I was with my professor, and he started smoking a pipe. The sun started to, I'm not sure how to describe it, expand in the sky. Then it flared, and I couldn't see anything. Like if you looked at a camera's flash, where you're blinded for a second. I'm sorry, a camera isn't the best analogy," Kyra said as she saw the puzzled expressions around her. Based on their medieval clothing, Kyra guessed cameras didn't exist in Ilian. "When the light faded, I wasn't sitting at a table with my professor anymore. I was with you."

"Hmm. Where were we precisely?"

"On a hill in front of a lake," Kyra answered, the image springing to mind. "It was hot, and you were wearing that blue cloak. You also had a staff and a pipe with . . . you called them kolker leaves?"

"What did we discuss?"

Kyra bit her lip. Months had passed since that experience, and it was much more difficult to extract the conversation than it was to visualize the scene. "You mentioned my sixteenth birthday. Coming of age," she added abruptly as Solarus' words popped to mind. "You also talked about emotions and how they influenced magic." Kyra paused as the wizard's brow furrowed. "Was that real? Have we ever been to a lake?"

"We spent many an hour at the lake of which you speak if it is the same one as what I believe. You have spent as many hours tolerating the scent of kolker leaves." Solarus' lips turned slightly upward. "I also have tried to impress upon you the need to control your emotions. How gratifying that I succeeded in that endeavor."

"What else can you remember?" Hayden asked.

Kyra's gut clenched as she heard the dismay in his tone. She *did* know Hayden. Her mind might not remember, but her heart anchored her to a certainty: Hayden had been telling the truth. He was a part of her past. Kyra burrowed into her thoughts, digging for a revelation with Hayden in it. The strain fueled an increasingly intense ache in her temple; it didn't give her more answers. "Nothing. I'm sorry. All I know about Ilian is what my friend in London told me. That Ilian existed, and I'm from here."

"Kyra, Kate, Queen of the Land," Jyls heralded from behind Solarus. He stepped forward and gave her an exaggerated bow. "We've never been acquainted, so we don't have any catching up to do. We instead have the pleasure of an introduction."

Jyls had a shaggy head of straw-colored hair, and freckles dotted his fair complexion. His earth-brown jacket and cloak were identical to Hayden's. A tunic draped loosely on Jyls' frame. His trouser legs sported four pockets that Kyra could count. A silver chain with a pendant of a lanky bird dangled around Jyls' neck. Kyra couldn't help smiling as the man gave her a crooked grin.

Hayden's gaze strayed to the horses. They had nuzzled Raven in greeting and now listened attentively to the conversation. "Raven, was Kyra injured during her rescue? Was she caught in any of the wizards' spells?"

The roan's ears drooped miserably. "The wizards had no part in this. Kyra was without her memories when we first found her. Kyra did not trust us, nor did she remember Ilian. It was the Lyneera who persuaded Kyra to accompany us."

Hayden's expression was unreadable. He twisted a ring absently on his finger, exchanging a look with Solarus. "We'll have to work through this," Hayden said finally. "For now, our priority is to get Kyra to safety. I'm leery of remaining so close to the mountains, even if Talis returns without having spotted any enemies." Hayden dropped his hand and looked at Kyra. "It might be helpful to make quick introductions. You must have reservations about heading off into a strange land with a group of individuals you can't remember. Learning about us might give you more confidence."

Kyra tried to hide her surprise. Hayden had hit exactly upon her doubts.

"I'm Hayden. As I said, we've known each other for many years."

"My name is Solarus," the wizard identified himself next. There was a note of self-importance in his tone. "I am a wizard, a free wizard of Ilian, with no relation to the dark wizards of Harkimer or their leader, Diamantas." His tongue lingered on the word as though he had bit into a sour grape. "The kingdom of Harkimer was founded by traitorous and scheming wizards. The dark wizards are their descendants. They are no better."

Kyra began to mentally catalogue what she was learning. Adakis. A dark wizard. Solarus. Not a dark wizard. Harkimer. Home of the dark wizards.

Solarus' gaze moved to the freckled man. "Jyls of Lystern has already presented himself," he said waspishly.

Jyls waved his hand with a flourish. "I come from the kingdom of Peregrine which, while not the oldest, is the most reputedly respectable kingdom in Ilian."

Solarus glared at Jyls, whose shameless grin broadened. "Jyls has a peculiar sense of humor. As he mentioned, you are not acquainted. He joined our company mere weeks after you disappeared. Much to your good fortune," the wizard inserted wryly. "*My* role in your development has been in instructing you in the use and control of your magical abilities. It comes as no surprise that you would remember me, even if the names of our companions fail you." His inflection on the final sentence indicated to Kyra that Solarus believed he was the most influential in her upbringing.

"Talis, the elf who is scouting, is from Silvias," Hayden came again. "Silvias is the Elven Realm and the oldest of the kingdoms in Ilian."

Elves exist, Kyra repeated to herself. She had seen elven ears curved neatly into points. *They live in Silvias. Silvias is the Elven Realm.* She craved a map in her mind to join the names of these unfamiliar places.

Hayden's gaze turned to the young man tending to Raff. "And that is Akheeran of Hillith."

The young man had stopped chanting and sat back on his heels. Raff's eyes fluttered open. Akheeran smiled as the panther shook his head groggily. The young man began stuffing extra bandages back in the pouch he had brought, looking up at Hayden while he worked. "The panther's wounds are minor," Akheeran reported. "He's bruised from the fall and has a mild sprain in his ankle. It's lucky there are no broken bones. If the bandage holds, he'll have full range of motion even before the ligament heals."

"Perhaps no bones, but my head pounds," Raff groaned. He rolled onto his paws. Akheeran started as the panther pushed himself upright. Raff shook like a wet dog, dislodging clumps of dirt and grass stuck to his fur. "I have yet to meet a wizard who fights claw to claw. They will not dare entangle themselves with magic older than their own." He let out a gruff breath. "Cowards."

Kyra suspected Akheeran hadn't understood Raff's words. His face paled at the sound of the panther's low growl. Of all the companions, Akheeran looked to be the youngest—although, admittedly, it was hard to estimate the elf's age. The young man's pale skin was offset by fiery red hair cropped above his ears, wavy and curling up at his forehead into a short brush. Akheeran wore a loose brown cotton jacket that bloomed at the sleeves. A black tattoo with indecipherable symbols was inked on the back of his neck.

"Akheeran is a healer," Hayden told Kyra, beckoning to the young man. Akheeran picked his way over clusters of leaves to join them.

"Come on, Akheeran, it's your turn to present your credentials to the Lady of Ilian," Jyls said. He slapped the healer jauntily on the back. "We don't call him, Akheeran, by the by. Just 'Akkkkhhhhh.'" Jyls drew out the guttural sound with deliberate exaggeration.

Akheeran's face reddened a shade closer to his hair. He rubbed the back of his neck self-consciously and mumbled, "I'm usually called 'Ash.' Akheeran isn't a common name in Calonia. That's where I come from, the kingdom of Calonia. Calonians have trouble pronouncing Akheeran." Seeing Kyra's puzzled expression, he elaborated, "Akheeran was my father's best friend. He came from a different kingdom. I was named after him."

"I prefer 'Akh,'" Jyls said with a grin that stretched the freckles on his face. Solarus rolled his eyes.

"Pleased to meet you, Ash," Kyra replied with a smile. "Or to meet you again. If we've met before."

The healer continued to rub the tattoo on his neck uncomfortably. "We haven't. Hayden came to Calonia last summer. I wanted to see other kingdoms and learn about their medicines. That's how I got here."

"It's a tremendous honor to be a healer," Hayden supplied, putting a hand encouragingly on the healer's shoulder. Kyra noticed Hayden's silver ring was framed by white gold and was engraved in an elegant script. "Unlike with other occupations, where anyone can study or train to become whatever he chooses, you can't decide to become a healer. Healers are identified and selected by other healers. Healers possess exceptional discernment, intelligence, and fidelity. Most individuals are hard-pressed to demonstrate one of these qualities, let alone all three. Hence, why there are few practitioners of the profession."

Hayden's praise brought a bashful smile to Akheeran's face.

"More lives have been saved because of healers than warriors or wizards," Hayden added.

"That is debatable," Solarus put in archly. "I agree that Ash is unquestionably more valuable than *others* in our company." The wizard looked pointedly at Jyls.

Jyls shrugged. "I'm here for the delightful conversation and delectable cuisine. I never claimed to be useful. And, by the way, you haven't objected to my presence."

"I have," Solarus' dapple-gray horse grumbled. "Many times."

The steed's words coaxed a grin from Kyra.

Hayden's gray gaze shifted to the south at the sound of hoofbeats. Talis' steed cantered back from the flat lands. The elf reined in beside Hayden. Talis had a smooth face with high cheekbones and long, silver-blond hair. A single braid draped over his brow. His tunic was the same amber color as his eyes. Talis met Hayden's gaze calmly. "You were right. Something—some things— move toward us. They aren't the wizards. What creatures they are, I can't say from such a distance. We are in no immediate danger, but I recommend we depart all the same."

This time, Kyra looked more closely at Talis' ears. They curved neatly into points. Kyra openly marveled at him.

The sun was still bright in the sky, but a dark look clouded Hayden's eyes. "Then it's time we left. It may be that Diamantas sent others. Or whatever you glimpsed could be among the host of undesirable creatures in Harkimer and Ilian. Either way, I want Thanesgard's walls between us and everything else out here."

The group readied themselves to leave. Kyra carefully stepped around the leaf and tree litter to reach her peacoat, which amazingly hadn't been trampled during the fight. She lifted it and dug into her pocket. Her fingers found the cool surface of her heptagon coin. Kyra released a small sigh of relief. She hadn't lost it then. Kyra fished the coin out of her coat and placed it in a pants pocket. Then she walked back to Raven, carrying her coat under the crook of her arm.

Kyra didn't mount. Her gaze again toured the group. Despite the familiarity of the individuals, Kyra had misgivings about blindly following them. She remembered Mr. Stevens' advice when she asked how she could know she was making a decision that was "right." He had told her to rely on her gut instinct; it wouldn't fail her if she listened to it. Kyra bit her lip. Her instincts were normally her steady compass. Right now, their spindles spun madly out of control. She didn't have a clear intuition. Kyra recalled Mr. Stevens' second piece of advice: if she had enough facts, she could work her way to an answer through logic and reason.

Kyra placed a hand on Raven's side and stroked his hair absently. She had unearthed several facts already: that this group had rescued her from the dark wizards; that Solarus had been the wizard in her vision of the lake; that Hayden and Solarus had stores of information on her; and that, other than their names, she had no facts on them. *Still,* Kyra pointed out to herself, *I'm in Ilian because James asked me to go.* He insisted she needed a mentor to control her energy. Of the five wizards she had encountered so far, Solarus was the first interested in her well-being. He wore the azure cloak. Kyra's innate wariness about trusting strangers succumbed to her need to learn about her past and her abilities.

Kyra flung the coat over the front of the saddle and pulled herself up behind it. "What's Thanesgard?" she asked Hayden, gathering up the reins.

"The capital of the kingdom of Farcaren," he answered from atop his mare. "Their king, Arkin, is a stalwart ally against Diamantas. The castle is a fortress whose walls haven't been breached since the War of Calonia centuries ago. It would be a costly miscalculation were Diamantas to test its defenses. We need a safe location while we assess how much you've forgotten. And what you remember, of course."

Safe, Kyra echoed silently as Talis walked his steed toward Hayden. The assault by the four wizards didn't foreshadow a quiet life in Ilian.

There was a soft rumble beside her. Kyra glanced down. Raff had padded up beside Raven. The panther's yellow-orbed gaze was contemplative as he stared into the forest.

"I'm safer but I'm not safe, am I, Raff?" Kyra asked quietly so only Raff could hear.

The panther tilted his head as he looked up at her. "Whether you are in London or in Ilian, the dark wizards will be unremitting in their pursuit," he rumbled. "The members of this company are devoted to protecting you. There is no safer place for you then among them." Before Kyra could ask another question, Raff posed his own. "You are going to Thanesgard, are you not?"

Kyra nodded. "I will. But if I want to go back to London eventually, will you help me?"

A sorrowful expression filled the panther's eyes. "I think it unwise. However, if that time comes where you desire to return, I will try and help you. If it is possible to return."

If it's possible? Kyra had assumed she had a choice whether she wanted to stay in Ilian or leave. Raff was telling her that assumption could be wrong. Kyra's stomach wormed with apprehension.

"What do we do with the staff?" came Ash. He pointed to the walnut-colored staff on the ground. Kyra recognized it as the one she had grabbed from Nymphrys during the skirmish. Her hands still throbbed, her palms and fingers bright red. Jyls, who was standing next to Ash, wound his leg back to kick it.

"Do not touch it!" Solarus commanded severely. Jyls stopped mid-swing, boot in the air. Solarus gave him a reprimanding look like a parent finding a child about to poke a cobra. "In what kingdom do you believe it wise to disturb a magical object? Particularly one about which you know nothing? This is a wizard's staff, Jyls. It is not some flimsy blade. A staff can only be reclaimed by its bearer or one of the bearer's blood relations."

Jyls eyed the staff. "Out of curiosity, what happens if I do give it a good punt?"

Solarus' eyes narrowed. "For a non-wizard, physical contact causes significant injury. Scarring, for example, or blisters or illness. For wizards, contact is not as serious unless the bearer has poured years' worth of spells into the staff. If it is potent enough, the weapon will cause the death of he who lays a hand upon it."

"If that's all then," Jyls replied, stepping back.

Kyra's gaze ran over the staff for the first time. The walnut-colored wood was glossy, and hints of purple gleamed in the sunlight. Solarus cautiously tapped his own staff against Nymphrys'. Purple sparks sprayed the air as the two touched.

"There is considerable power stored within this one," Solarus muttered with interest. He rapped the ground directly behind the staff. There was a loud pop. The ground split and peeled back, like someone pulling open a zipper open, until it formed a giant cleft. The staff teetered on the edge. Then it fell in noiselessly, along with splintered tree trunks and branches. Solarus knocked the tip of his staff on the grass a second time. The earth slid together with a grinding noise.

Kyra gaped. There was no visible seal or sign of a giant hole.

"This will delay Nymphrys from retrieving her weapon," Solarus said smugly.

Jyls, Ash, and Solarus mounted. Hayden directed his mare toward the opening in the woods.

"Hayden, you're forgetting something," Talis remarked as he walked his steed forward. The horse had a stunning white mane and tail and seemed to grin as Talis raised a brow expectantly. "I believe I won the bet."

Hayden turned halfway in his saddle. His gray eyes sparkled good naturedly. He pulled a silver coin from a pouch on his belt and flicked it toward the elf. Talis snatched it with a smile. Hayden shook his head in feigned disappointment as the elf placed the coin in a similar pouch tied to the saddle.

"It seemed a reasonable gamble that you would strike Adakis' staff once, not twice," Hayden commented.

Talis tilted his head. "How often have I told you not to bet florins against an elf with a bow?"

"Apparently not often enough." Hayden resumed his position facing forward and gently clapped his heels into Willow. The mare clopped into the woods.

Without Kyra's guiding, Raven took up a position after Talis, with Raff and Hazel in tow. Kyra's heart thumped heavily. She was about to discover if the decision she had made was the right one . . . or if she had unknowingly taken a path that would separate her from James and Millie forever. The only family she had ever known.

Chapter 3

Hayden led the group along a well-worn earthen path that was divided by a stretch of grass. He paced the horses at a brisk walk.

As they traveled deeper into the woods, Kyra's apprehension was supplanted by her wonder. She breathed in the earthy scent of the forest, fresh from recent rains, and drank in the sights of wych elms and whitebeams. Young birds cheeped loudly, and ravens cawed. Bright sunlight streamed through the latticed tree canopy. Kyra rolled back her sleeves, absorbing the warmth. Her sole discomfort was her extreme thirst. Kyra didn't know how long it had been since she left London, having escaped through the white void at night and arrived in Ilian during the day.

Talis reined in his steed to allow Raven to come alongside him. The elf held out a leather canister. "You must be thirsty," he remarked as though having read Kyra's thoughts. "Use this waterskin. I have another in the saddlebags."

Kyra accepted it gratefully. Uncorking the top, she drank eagerly. The water was sweeter than any she had ever tasted. Kyra couldn't tell if it was because she craved it so desperately or if the water in Ilian was purer than London's. When her thirst was slaked, Kyra looked back at Talis. He smiled and spurred his steed back in line behind Hayden.

The woods ceded to a wide clearing. Hayden spurred his mare into a trot. Hazel and Raff had no trouble jogging alongside the horses, even with the panther's bandaged ankle. Kyra found herself enjoying the ride. She let her body follow the motion of Raven's clopping, her hips and thighs bumping up and down rhythmically.

Hayden glanced back at Kyra every now and then, keeping one hand on the reins. She was sure he was evaluating her ability to ride. Kyra pretended not to notice, continuing to flow with Raven's movements. A ghost of a smile appeared on Hayden's lips. He faced forward again. Kyra guessed she had passed Hayden's test.

"Raven," Kyra said as they twined around the trees, "can you tell me about the other horses?"

"Certainly." The roan tossed his mane. "We are descendants of two breeds: the elven horses from Silvias, and the horses of the Southern Mountains. Centuries ago, the latter group traveled into the forest, crossed the river, and settled in the fields and hills of Ilian. I am an elven horse. We are light and fleet footed." Raven nodded toward Talis' steed. The palomino was slenderer than the other horses and seemed to barely touch the ground as he skipped along. "Windchaser is another elven horse. He is the youngest among us and has the spirit of a colt. Unfortunately, he is also the fastest. It encourages his antics because he can outrun anyone trying to discipline him. He listens to Talis. No one else.

"Willow comes from the Hidden Lands," Raven went on. His gaze was on the mare paired with Hayden. Willow was a beautiful copper-colored horse, with a braided, dark brown mane that ran down the length of her cheek. "Her instincts are keen, and she is calm in the most distressing of situations." Kyra nodded and pointed to Solarus' steed. His hair was decorated with light rings of gray that resembled a snow leopard. "What about him?"

"That is Grayhaven. He has been Solarus' companion for seventeen years, which means he is a veteran of seventeen years' worth of battles. Add together the number of times they have encountered dark wizards, not to mention bandits and other dangers. In the last year alone, we have skirmished with one of these foes a dozen times. I would guess, then, that Grayhaven has survived over sixty battles in his life. As a low estimate." Raven's expression was one of great reverence. "Anyone would do well to heed his advice. Jyls rides Odin, who has retained many of the characteristics of the original mountain horses. He is steady and bold."

Kyra had to spin in her saddle to see Odin. He towered above the other horses and had shiny, black hair and white stockings.

"Odin was born mute," Raven added, "though he communicates through his gestures and has hearing more acute than us all."

Kyra's eye lit upon the last horse in their group, the filly Ash rode. This time Raven also turned his head. The filly high-stepped along the trail, her light brown eyes twinkling. "That is Autumnstar. She can adapt her gait to any rider, be he amateur or expert. Most horses require the skill of the rider to guide them. She does not as much."

Kyra swore Raven sounded shy as he spoke. Autumnstar was a dazzling coral-colored horse with a lighter mane of the same color.

"Windchaser pursues Autumnstar relentlessly," Raven said with a horsey laugh. "She is too strong-willed to accept his overtures."

As the sun began its descent, the path widened, and the trees thinned. Soon dusk disguised the forest floor, though the sure-footed horses continued with ease.

"*Ascera*," Solarus said. A turquoise light formed like a globe atop his staff, illuminating the area around them.

Hayden reined in Willow when they reached a flat clearing within a ring of ferns. Kyra glanced around. Patches of bare earth and clumps of small bushes were sprinkled over the thick grass. "We will camp here tonight," Hayden announced. "If we go further, we will enter a large meadow. It's far too exposed for my comfort. This clearing conceals us from any danger that approaches while we sleep." Hayden gestured to his right, where the land dipped and sloped downward. "We should refill the waterskins in the stream."

"I will go," Talis offered. Even though Kyra ached to lie down and massage her sore muscles, she volunteered to help. She wanted to be useful. If Kyra were honest with herself, she was also apprehensive about being around the full group, who might ask her questions she wasn't ready to answer. She had chosen to go with them, but they were strangers after all.

She and Talis collected the waterskins before riding off. Instead of heading down the hill in the direction of the stream, Talis steered Windchaser back toward the woods. Puzzled, Kyra urged Raven to follow.

Talis guided Windchaser to the open meadow Hayden had referenced. There he paused. Talis' hawklike gaze fastened on the horizon. Kyra blinked. The night sky was ink-black, dotted with pinpricks of starlight and the glow of the moon. Even during her excursions to the countryside with Millie, Kyra always had man-made incandescent lighting. In comparison, the valley seemed laden with an all-consuming darkness.

Kyra walked Raven behind Windchaser. She was able to see moonlight glimmering on Talis' silver-blond hair. His braid swayed lightly as his gaze swept over the meadow.

"What are you looking for?" Kyra asked.

"Enemies," he answered briefly.

Kyra strained to make out something around her. "More wizards?"

"Among others."

Not wanting to distract Talis further from his search, Kyra stared out with him. Her hearing compensated for her lack of vision. The night's silence filled her ears as loudly as the honking of cars. A beetle crawling over a blade of grass was like a soldier stamping on dried corn husks. The chirping of crickets was as shrill as fire alarms. Kyra half-smiled. A raccoon wouldn't be able to sneak up on them, let alone a wizard. Or "any danger," as Hayden mentioned. She shuddered, wondering what monsters existed in Ilian.

"Silvias lies to the east," Talis said softly. "We are a three-day ride from it. The kingdom of Farcaren is directly south of us, but it's twice the distance."

"Shouldn't we go to Silvias then?" Kyra asked, remembering from earlier that Talis was referring to the home of the elves. "If Silvias is closer, I mean."

Talis turned Windchaser and walked him beside Raven. "Diamantas expects us to return to the Elven Realm. He will have learned by now that you have no memories and are vulnerable. The dark wizards would try to intercept us at the river before we crossed into the Realm. That's why Hayden predicts, rightly I believe, that Diamantas will dispatch wizards along Silvias' border. To confront us before we have the elves' protection. It's less likely Diamantas would foresee us taking this lengthier route and thus less likely wizards will await us in Thanesgard."

"You said Diamantas knows about me already? Does that mean the kingdom of..." Kyra rummaged through her mental bag of names. "Harkimer. Does that mean Harkimer is close to this forest? Adakis has already reached Diamantas?"

"No, Diamantas gleans information from many sources. Like us, he has allies outside of the dark wizards. Don't worry," Talis added. He stroked Windchaser's neck as the palomino stamped the ground impatiently. "We will return to Silvias as soon as we establish the path is clear. Solarus and Hayden agree Silvias is where you can restore your memories, given that it was where you spent the most time." Talis guided Windchaser back toward the campsite.

"It is?" Kyra asked as they set off at a trot.

"Yes. You used to know the trees and flowers as intimately as the fingers on your hand. There's no better place to start than the place in which you were raised."

Kyra's stomach folded on itself like a crepe. She instinctively tightened the reins in her hands. Raven slowed in response to her accidental command. He peered at Kyra from the corner of his eye. "Is something wrong?"

Kyra cleared her throat and slackened her grip. "Oh, sorry, no."

As Talis' gaze spanned the darkness again, questions percolated in Kyra's mind. Why would she be raised with elves rather than other wizards? Solarus said wizards lived in Ilian and not only Harkimer. Why didn't she grow up with one of the 'free wizards?' And yet . . . James said wizards didn't have the power to trap a Variavryk. Kyra did. James believed she was a wizard and more. Did Kyra had some relation to the elves? *Pretty unlikely*, Kyra thought as she unconsciously rubbed the upper part of her ear. She didn't look like an elf. As before, Kyra kept her reflections to herself. She wouldn't express any thoughts until she was sure the group was trustworthy.

Talis led Kyra in an arc around the campsite and down to the stream. Water burbled over pebbles and fallen leaves. The other horses already lined the bank and drank in large gulps. Hazel and Raff were further upstream, lapping the water sparingly.

Talis and Kyra dismounted. Windchaser immediately pranced next to Autumnstar and dunked his head in the stream. The filly gave him an irritated look. Windchaser greedily glugged the clear water.

"*Lox teranas, gil teranas*," Talis warned, giving the palomino a stern look. Windchaser ignored him. The elf shook his head.

"*Lox teranas, gil teranas*," Kyra repeated with a quizzical expression. "I've heard that before."

"It's a common elven saying," Talis explained. "It means 'take some, save some.' It emphasizes the value of patience over haste. You would have heard it in your lessons in swordplay. In that context, the saying means a student should be prudent when fighting in battle and not exhaust reserves they may need later. We use the saying to caution *Hydranyle*—that is to say, our guards and warriors—against the impulse to consume their rations without saving any for the rest of the journey. We also use it to teach children etiquette. If they are a guest in one's home, they should accept part of what the host offers and decline the rest. The host may be sharing the last of his meal, and if you take it all, he will have none." Talis hunkered on the ground. He uncorked the first waterskin. "In this case," he said as he placed the skin in the stream, "I'm attempting to remind Windchaser that if he chooses to inhale water as he does air, his stomach will be the worse off for it."

Kyra laughed. She took the full waterskin from Talis and gave him another empty one. Laying the remainder on the bank, Kyra knelt on a dry patch of earth. Grime and sweat from the day's ride were caked on her neck and itched under her clothing. Kyra placed her hands in the stream. She felt the cool water run beneath her fingers. Kyra splashed her face, rubbed her neck, and washed her hands and arms up to her elbows. Refreshed, Kyra shook the water from her arms and wiped her face with the back of her sleeve. Hazel and Raff padded up the hill to the campsite. When Talis had finished filling the skins, Kyra and Talis walked the horses back to the campsite.

When they reached the clearing, Kyra saw blue light dancing from the center. It created elongated shadows on the trees. The air was redolent with the aroma of herbs and meat. Hazel and Raff bounded into the clearing. Kyra and Talis left the horses grazing on the lush grasses as they also entered. Kyra's mouth watered. She surveyed the campsite.

Ash knelt next to a small cauldron that squatted on a cheerful fire, stirring its contents with a metal ladle. His face was highlighted with a flickering, teal light. For a moment, Kyra's thoughts flitted to James and his blue glow. *Is Ash a Lyneera?* Kyra rubbed her eyes. Then she noticed the campfire's blue flames. Kyra's jaw dropped. *Blue flames?* Kyra walked closer. She didn't hear the usual pops and cracks from burning wood, nor were there any signs of smoke. Mystified, Kyra looked beneath the flames. The fire rested directly on the ground, without twigs or forest litter providing it sustenance.

Kyra's skin crawled with apprehension. Blue flames. In her mind's eye, she vividly pictured the fire in Chicago. The blue and red fire had appeared so violently alive and untamed. These flames also behaved as a sentient being, except in stark contrast to Chicago, these were bright and merry.

When Kyra's gaze returned to Ash, she saw he wasn't bothered by the unnatural light or its eerie silence. He added a pinch of herbs to the pot and continued stirring. Jyls also seemed unsurprised by the blue fire. He reclined against a tree at the edge of the clearing, hands behind his head. Hayden and Solarus stood together on the other side of the fire. At their feet was a neat row of blankets, tack, and saddlebags. Solarus was speaking quietly as he leaned on his staff. Hayden listened intently, one hand on his chin. His gray gaze swiveled at the sound of Kyra and Talis approaching. Hayden interrupted Solarus with a covert raise of his hand. The pair turned in unison. Kyra felt uncomfortable under their gaze and looked away. She had a suspicion she was the topic of their conversation.

As Talis went to Hayden and Solarus, Kyra joined Hazel and Raff. The animals had plopped down away from the fire. Hazel sniffed the air. A grin stretched across her long snout as Ash ladled stew into bowls. Kyra wearily leaned back on her palms. Her muscles were flooded with fatigue from the ride and fight, and she felt the crushing weight of so many changes. She thanked Ash when he delivered her and the animals their dinner. Kyra was famished, but her stomach cramped as she ate. It took all her effort to hold the bowl, which felt like it was made from lead. As she chewed, Kyra stared into the blue flames. Their flickering was gentle, hypnotic. Kyra's head drooped. The spoon clinked against the side of Kyra's bowl as it slipped from her fingers.

Kyra's head snapped up at the sound. She fumbled with her bowl before it dropped and set it carefully to the side. She looked around. Hazel and Raff had taken up spots closer to the fire. The collie rested on her side, eyes closed contentedly. The panther was awake, leisurely licking a paw.

"Kyra. *Kyra.*"

"What? Oh," Kyra replied dumbly. It was going to take time to get used to the new—or rather, old—name.

Talis stood over her. He held a thick bundle. "We've just entered the spring months," he told her as she rose groggily. The elf held out a forest green cloak, along with a woolen bedroll. "The nights can be cold. This will serve you until we buy you supplies in Farcaren."

"Thank you," Kyra said, touched by his kindness. She accepted the cloak and glanced around the campfire. There didn't seem to be any spare bedrolls. "What will you sleep on?"

Talis' amber eyes held an amused smile. "Elves don't require as much sleep as humans or wizards. I'm taking the watch tonight. I won't need for it. My strength will last through the morrow." He gently set the bedroll in Kyra's arms.

Talis stood at the edge of the clearing as the group bedded down for the night. Solarus waved a hand over the fire. The flames dimmed until there remained a cozy twinkling of light.

Kyra unfurled the bedroll and spread it along the ground, then walked to the pile of equipment. Her peacoat was neatly folded beside the saddles. Kyra brought it back to her spot and lay down. The peacoat's soft wool made for the perfect makeshift pillow.

Kyra let out a deep sigh. She missed James. He could have helped her bring her recalcitrant thoughts to heel, which like children on a playground fought for her attention. The dark wizards' attack. The strangers' rescue. The feelings of familiarity coupled with a degree of mistrustfulness. Leaving London. Abandoning James. Abandoning Millie.

Guilt keened in Kyra's heart. She never said goodbye to her aunt. Kyra pictured Millie eating a lonely, disheartened meal. Millie mopping up tears with her handkerchief. Millie wondering what happened to her dear niece. Kyra desperately hoped James had checked in on her, had consoled her with whatever excuse he had invented about Kyra's disappearance. If James had escaped the Variavryk unhurt. Kyra's lashes were wet. She hastily swiped away the tears before anyone could notice. Pushing herself up on one arm, Kyra called softly, "Raff?"

The panther, who had curled up near the fire, raised his head. Rising, he padded noiselessly over to her. "Yes, Kyra?"

"Can you . . ." she paused, embarrassed. "Can you lie near me tonight?"

"Of course." Raff sat. He stretched his paws out before him, his hindquarters sinking down onto the earth. His tail swished rhythmically.

Kyra laid down again. She settled a hand on his back. The velvety fur rippled in response to her touch. The tension in Kyra's neck eased as she felt the rumbling purrs beneath her fingers.

"You have nothing to fear from them, Kyra," Raff said, his voice sounding distant as her breathing slowed. "They are your family. They will take care of you."

Kyra didn't remember answering. She trusted Raff. She could let her guard down. He would protect her. With that thought, Kyra surrendered to sleep.

Chapter 4

The heady aroma of coffee tickled Kyra's nostrils. Her head hammered as though she had been awake the full night. Her dreams had been confused and harrowing, with wizards and elves and swirling snow. She needed a strong jolt of caffeine to get rid of a headache this persistent. Millie's brew would do the trick. Kyra smiled groggily at the thought, eyes still closed.

"Kyra," she heard a man's voice call. "Oh, Your Magical Royal Highness. Time to wake up."

Who is that? Kyra thought drowsily. The voice was strange and somehow familiar. It had to be a dream. She tried to tuck her head under the pillow and sink back into sleep.

"Sorry, Highness, we've got a long day ahead of us," said the voice. "Rise and shine. Or just rise. Don't shine. Whatever your Royalness prefers."

A horse snorted in irritation.

What on earth . . . ? Rubbing an eye with her knuckle, Kyra opened her eyes. She started in shock. Jyls was perched over her. His bird's-nest of hair was mussed up, but his midnight blue gaze was bright. His silver pendant swung from his neck and dangled above her face. Kyra's arm was wrapped around a giant stuffed animal.

Jyls sat back, a lopsided grin accentuating his freckled cheeks. "Well, how about that. You're awake."

"Let her sleep, Jyls," a deep voice reprimanded. "There is no reason to rouse her yet."

Kyra jumped as the fur moved away from her hand. Head smarting in protest of the sudden motion, her gaze darted to the sleek black animal who rose beside her. Raff shot Jyls a nettled look.

"It's okay, Raff," Kyra answered, slowly remembering where she was. "I'm up."

The panther rose and moved to the side. His golden eyes narrowed at Jyls. Jyls shrugged unapologetically. "She would have missed breakfast," he said, straightening the cuff of his sleeve. "You know what they say, 'An empty stomach leads to an empty mind.' If Kyra's got no memories, her mind needs filling."

Kyra stared at him. *'An empty stomach leads to an empty mind.'* Millie said the exact same sentence when Kyra started her lessons. What else was similar between London and Ilian?

She heard an aggrieved sigh to her left. Solarus was sitting cross-legged, a small, black leather-bound book in his hands. He was wearing thin-framed, square glasses, which balanced on the bridge of his nose. "That is not a real saying. You have inordinately empty space between your ears. That has nothing to do with lost memories but your obdurate refusal to pack it with useful knowledge."

"I'm reserving that empty space," Jyls replied, working on his other cuff. "Your 'useful knowledge' might crowd out information more suited to my profession." Jyls winked at Kyra. His cryptic answer left her puzzled about what he meant.

Kyra sat up stiffly. Painful knots had formed in her back. The side of her body ached from being pressed against the rocky ground. Her thighs were bruised from where they hit the saddle.

Kyra kneaded her neck as Raff padded over to where dried strips of meat were laid out. She ached for a hot bath. *Or at least a comb*, Kyra thought as she ran her fingers through her rumpled hair. She stole a glance around the campsite.

Like the night before, Ash tended to a small cauldron that rested atop teal flames. Kyra regarded the healer thoughtfully as he picked up a large spoon and ladled dark, hot liquid into a mug beside him. She had never had a friend her age. She wondered if the healer harbored insecurities and doubts like she did. He was, after all, as the youngest in a group with the likes of Hayden and Solarus.

As if feeling her gaze on him, Ash looked up and met Kyra's eyes. Ash smiled shyly. He took the mug in one hand, scooped up a jar and a lumpy handkerchief in the other, and rose.

"Good morning," Ash greeted as he walked to Kyra. Steam carrying the delicious smell of coffee wafted to her. "I made coffee. Do you drink coffee?" When Kyra nodded, Ash handed her the mug. He smiled uncertainly. "You might not like it, though. Calonians prefer a stronger flavor than most of the other kingdoms. Solarus says it's too bitter for him. I added anise. It makes the taste smoother. In my opinion, maybe not yours . . ." His tone was apologetic.

"Strong and bitter are exactly what I need right now, Ash, thank you." Kyra gave him a heartening smile. The healer's ears flared the same red as his hair. "Have you had anything to—?"

"The jar has honey, if you'd like some," Ash interrupted as though anxious to get away. He hastily put the jar and handkerchief on the ground. "There's also bread, cheese, and nuts in the handkerchief."

"Did you eat already?"

"I did, thank you." Ash hurried back to the cauldron without saying anything further. Disappointed, Kyra half-heartedly spread honey on a piece of bread.

Solarus had returned to his book. He flipped through the pages impatiently. Solarus lingered on one, using his finger to scan the lines as his lips moved silently. His brow creased. Solarus dog-eared the page and continued thumbing through the book.

Kyra's gaze toured the campsite for Hayden and Talis. She found them standing near a flattened fern bed at the edge of the woods. Hayden's arms were folded, body taut. He listened as Talis spoke. The elf made a motion toward the trees. Hayden nodded. Kyra was too far away to hear the conversation, but her curiosity was piqued. Even as Kyra wondered how to get closer, Talis turned and spotted her. Hayden's gray eyes also fell on Kyra. Kyra felt heat flush her cheeks as though she had been caught spying. Uncrossing his arms, Hayden said something to Talis before walking away from the fern bed.

Hayden's smile belied the concern in his gray gaze as he joined Kyra. "Good morning, Kyra. Did you sleep well?"

Relieved that Hayden's tone was free of accusation, Kyra replied, "Very well. I'm grateful Talis gave me his bedroll. It was comfortable." Comfortable was the exact opposite of Kyra's first experience camping outdoors. But she refused to complain. If she expected to fit in, she had to be prepared to follow the actions of her companions.

"It's likely not as soft as what you're used to, unless your home in the other world was a hut and a hard bed." There was a friendly jesting in Hayden's voice. His gaze went to Kyra's mug. "You've changed. As a child, you found coffee repugnant. Now you've developed a taste for it?"

"My aunt and I drank coffee every morning with breakfast. It was our routine." Sadness washed over Kyra. She again visualized Millie with her curls pinned on her head, her coffee cup sitting neglected on the table, tears on her cheeks. Kyra's own eyes filled with tears. Hayden didn't prod her. He respectfully looked away until Kyra had willed the tears back. Then another thought entered her mind.

"I tried coffee as a child," she repeated. Kyra gave Hayden a questioning look. "Was it hazelnut?"

Hayden seemed surprised. "Yes, it was. Why?"

"I remember sitting with you and Talis at a campfire. It was cold, and I wanted something to warm me up. You wanted to bet Talis I wouldn't like it, but he didn't take the bet. He said he would make the same wager against you."

Kyra was happy to see delight in Hayden's eyes at this simple recollection. "I remember that night. You said nuts don't belong in coffee."

Kyra grinned at Hayden. They finished their breakfast in silence, each lost in his and her personal memories.

The group packed up their bedding and prepared for the day's ride. As many questions as she had, Kyra remained resolved to observe the group before she divulged more details about herself. Kyra also hoped the group's conversations might trigger more memories.

They set off into the trees, following a winding path with dense ferns and a mélange of leaves. Hayden set the pace at a brisk trot. Talis rode ahead, eyes raking the spaces between the trees. Around midday, the group left the sanctuary of the forest and entered a valley. Kyra spied a blue, lacelike ribbon in the distance. As they rode closer, she saw the ribbon was actually a river, its waters driving forward swiftly. The air was thick with the odor of fish and of plants growing on the bank. Kyra frowned. There were no bridges, man-made or natural, to allow the group to cross.

Talis reined in several meters before the bank. Hayden rode up beside him. His sidelong glance carried an unspoken question. The elf answered by gesturing toward the water.

"This is a shallow section of the river," Talis explained. "The horses will be able to ford the river here. The current isn't strong."

Kyra eyed the rushing waters skeptically. If this was a tamer part of the river, she didn't want to know what a rougher patch looked like.

"Keep a tight grip on the reins," Hayden instructed as he took up the slack in his own. "Don't shift your weight in the saddle while the horses are swimming. It makes it more difficult for them to move forward."

Hazel sat back on her haunches. "I prefer not to swim," the collie stated, sticking her chin in the air. "I will find another way across." Hazel's feigned haughtiness didn't mask her anxiety.

"That won't be necessary." Hayden calmly turned to Jyls, who looked askance at the water. "Jyls, would you be kind enough to relinquish your saddle for the trip? Hazel needs a mount. Odin is the largest and most able to take her across."

Jyls arched a brow. He cast a glance at Solarus, who was observing him with a wry smile. "I don't relish the idea of a swim," he remarked, pulling his jacket tight around his body. "Jaren and Garen, if you're trying to get rid of me, I'd prefer a means that wasn't drowning. Though I do appreciate that a corpse would be impossible to recover underwater."

"I wouldn't dream of parting with your company," Hayden replied with a slim grin. "You'll ride with one of us."

Jyls' eyes reflected doubt. He glanced at Solarus' steed. "I take it 'us' doesn't include a horse who will 'accidentally' pitch me overboard."

Grayhaven snorted. "I make no promises."

Kyra chuckled, catching Ash's eye. For the first time, he met her gaze and grinned back.

"You will join Kyra on Raven." Hayden dismounted and moved toward Odin. "Kyra is lighter than the rest of us, and Raven should be able to manage an extra rider."

"Kyra also has endured your presence for the least amount of time," Solarus put in dryly.

"Why didn't you say that in the first place?" Jyls swung a leg over Odin and hopped lithely to the ground. He patted the draft horse on the side. With a flourish, Jyls said to Hazel, "He comes with my compliments."

Hazel's tail wagged as Hayden lifted her atop Odin. "Much better," the collie sighed.

Hayden turned to Raff. The panther vehemently shook his head. "Absolutely not. It is below a panther's dignity to ride a horse. I will swim."

Hayden gave him a short nod. Kyra smiled. Millie once said that cats avoided water as a matter of pride. It seemed Raff was willing to brave the wetness to preserve his.

Jyls grabbed the back of Kyra's saddle and deftly pulled himself onto Raven's back. Reaching around Kyra, Jyls took the reins in his hand. He lifted them so they passed over Kyra's head and enclosed her within them. "It's either me holding the reins or me holding on to you," Jyls told her as Kyra glanced back at him questioningly. "No offense, but it's safer with the reins. You're new at this. Don't worry. I'll make sure you don't fall."

"How thoughtful," Kyra said. She rolled her eyes even though Jyls couldn't see her.

Talis led the horses down the bank and into the rushing waters. Raven swayed gently. His hooves sank into the soft silt of the riverbed. Cold water seeped into Kyra's shoes and jeans as Raven plunged in up to his chest. Kyra gripped the sides of the reins. Having herself enclosed inside of them helped her stay upright as the roan paddled parallel to the current.

Kyra glanced over her shoulder. Hayden and Solarus looked perfectly relaxed while Willow and Grayhaven plowed through the water with powerful strokes.

Kyra's gaze traveled to Ash. The healer leaned forward, and his arms wrapped around Autumnstar's neck. His tunic was soaked. His green eyes screamed his silent panic. *Why isn't Ash holding the reins?* Kyra wondered. *And why isn't he in the saddle?* Autumnstar strained against Ash's grip as she fought to keep her head above water.

"Ash," Kyra heard Jyls call out. The healer barely turned his head. His cheek was pressed against Autumnstar's mane. "You're choking her. Sit up. Like this."

Whatever it was Jyls showed Ash seemed to work. The healer slowly eased his grip. As he began worming back into his saddle, the healer rocked unsteadily to the side. Kyra held a tense breath, wondering if he would be swept up in the river. Ash grasped Autumnstar's mane with his left hand to stay balanced. He used his right hand to fish through the water. He pulled out the filly's reins. Ash released Autumnstar's mane, grabbed the reins in both hands, and held himself upright. Kyra exhaled in relief. Ash's face was chalk white, but he was okay.

"You, Queen of Other Lands," Jyls' voice came. "It'd make Raven's life easier if you didn't fidget so much."

Kyra was about to shoot Jyls a dirty look except she realized he was right. She had unconsciously been trying to rebalance herself with Raven's every stroke. Kyra centered her attention on staying still.

Partly through skill, partly by luck, the entire group made it safely to the other side. Raven climbed up the bank. He breathed easily despite the hard swim. Windchaser also skipped out of the water playfully. The non-elven horses clomped up the bank with more effort, sides heaving.

Raff stalked out of the water with a sour look. "It will take a week to clean off this muck," the panther grumbled. He shook his fur, spraying Talis as he dismounted. "No more rivers."

Hazel cheerfully bounded from Odin's saddle. Her paws were wet, but the rest of her thick fur was dry. Her grin widened as Raff glowered at her.

"We need to move further inland before we can rest," Hayden stated. His eyes trailed up the incline and into the forest. "If we can cross the river, so can the wizards. We have a few hours of daylight. I'd like to put as much distance as possible between them, whatever Talis saw, and us before sundown."

Jyls dropped the reins to Raven, allowing Kyra to untangle herself. Her arms felt like two overstretched rubber bands from the strain of holding on so tightly. Her jeans clung uncomfortably to her skin. Despite this, Kyra felt a rush of pride. She hadn't capsized herself and Jyls, despite her worry of doing exactly that. As Jyls swung a leg over Raven and hopped to the ground, Kyra admitted Jyls deserved the credit for them making it to the bank intact.

"That was delightful," Jyls commented. He rubbed his inner thigh with a grimace. "Next time, though, I get the saddle. Riding bareback isn't my preferred means of travel."

"When we ride Odin, you can sit wherever you'd like," Kyra replied with a grin. "If Raven is carrying us, I stay in the saddle. Or Raven might accidentally 'pitch you overboard,' as you were saying."

The roan let out a horsey laugh in agreement. Jyls moved to Odin and swiftly mounted. Meanwhile, Solarus guided Grayhaven beside Kyra. He put his hand on her arm and uttered, "*Is-ter-AH-ha.*" Warmth flowed from Kyra's shoes to her chest. It traced lines down her hair, which was damp from water that sprayed up during Raven's swim. Kyra's jaw dropped. Steam rose from her clothing. Kyra touched her jeans, then a lock of hair. All traces of water had disappeared. Solarus removed his hand with a smug look.

"It is a drying spell," he explained as Kyra stared, agape. "You will learn it."

Kyra reached down and felt her shoes as Solarus repeated the spell on Ash. A thrill of excitement raced through her. Magic had its benefits.

"Do you think the wizards are still following us?" Kyra heard Ash ask. "We haven't seen any since we found Kyra."

Kyra glanced over to Hayden. He rubbed his ring contemplatively, gray eyes panning the water. "I know. That's what worries me."

***

The next three days passed in a blur. Kyra compulsively squirmed in the saddle as they rode, searching for signs of black cloaks and staffs flaring with magic. Luckily, the wizards seemed to have lost their trail.

Kyra's behavior evoked more than one troubled frown from Hayden. Kyra guessed he wasn't yet middle-aged, his hair lacking the silver streaks Solarus had already acquired. When they took short breaks to rest the horses, Hayden huddled together with Solarus and Talis, reviewing routes, assessing possible dangers, and making adjustments. The trio's unfinished sentences and subtle gestures made Kyra believe they had a long history together.

Sometimes, though, Kyra spied Hayden standing alone, staring at nothing in particular. His expression varied between being vacant, forlorn, or laden with such a profound sadness Kyra couldn't find the words to describe it. She wondered what thoughts tormented Hayden that made him seem so vulnerable.

Kyra continued to seek opportunities to talk to Ash. He was as dexterous at avoiding conversation as he had been at bandaging Raff's ankle. In fact, Ash rarely spoke at all, and then only if his opinion was solicited. His answers were always tremulous as though unsure whether what he said was correct. Ash's behavior surprised Kyra. Hayden had said healers were uniquely hand-selected and therefore admired. Kyra, on the other hand, didn't have anything to offer. Her magic was fickle. She was in a foreign land and in a group of older, skilled, and mostly confident individuals. Kyra felt adrift, struggling to understand her usefulness to her company.

Of all the companions, Jyls was the most easygoing. And the most mysterious. He always carried his slanted smile and was armed with an endless arsenal of jokes. Jyls could coax Ash out of his timidity. He also had opinions about everything, from the city with the choicest meat pies (Sanglier) to the most melodious instrument (a dylar) to the most affluent and amiable man in Peregrine's history (King Laetus). The more Kyra observed Jyls, the more she noticed he staved off questions about himself. As with fenced-off land, trespassers into Jyls' personal history weren't welcome. Kyra understood too well protecting secrets. She respected his privacy and stuck to topics he raised.

On the fourth night, the group made camp early. Clouds had marched in, and thickets had sprung up between the trees. Talis found a small glade near a stream. Solarus used a spell to remove the few brambles littering the ground and made himself comfortable in the center of the cleared space. When the elf dismounted, his bow was in hand. His amber eyes swept the forest. He suggested using their extra hours to hunt and replenish their supplies. After days of dried meat and fruit, Kyra was happy for a fresh meal. Raff immediately volunteered to go with Talis.

"I appreciate the healer's stews," Raff told Kyra as she lowered herself from Raven. "However, a panther does not normally receive his meals from others. I prefer to catch that which I eat."

Hazel stretched her front paws with a yawn before sitting back. Her tail thumped on the ground. "I will happily let myself be fed," she said with a grin. "Hunting is laborious work."

Kyra laughed. Talis and Raff stalked off together through the woods. The rest of the group removed the equipment from their horses and settled in for the night. Solarus conjured up the blue campfire and sat in front of it. Ash brought packets of herbs to the fire, along with several metal skewers. He left for the stream with waterskins and the cauldron. Jyls reclined against a tree, methodically running a knife blade over a sharpening rod. The blade screeched with every stroke. Kyra winced at the shrill sound. Hayden, who took up a spot beside him and polished his sword, didn't seem to mind.

Kyra was halfway through unsaddling Raven. The first day Hayden had taught her how to remove the equipment, Kyra hadn't anticipated the weight or bulk of the saddle. She had fumbled with it for a moment before it slipped from her grip and fell inches from Hayden's boot. She sheepishly dragged the saddle to the side. Hayden patiently watched as Kyra wrangled the tack from the roan, which, to her relief, went more smoothly. It was a long process, but Kyra eventually had managed to remove all Raven's equipment. She had practiced the next two nights under Hayden's watchful eye. Tonight, though, Hayden trusted Kyra with the task alone. Kyra took Raven's saddle in her arms and laid it gently beside Solarus'. Then she removed the rest of Raven's gear with similar ease. Kyra grinned. She had managed to finish without help. It was slow-going but a step forward.

Kyra's fingers caught in a tangle of hair as she brushed strands from her brow. Her smile slid into a frown. Kyra tugged on the knot. She tried to rake her hand through the snarls in her waves, but it was a hopeless endeavor.

"I hope Thanesgard has a comb," she muttered grumpily. "And a bath." Kyra took out a hair tie, which she had gratefully found in her peacoat's pocket, and pulled her hair back in a ponytail. Then she turned to join her companions.

Kyra's time with Raven had taken longer than she thought. Talis and Raff had already returned. The panther sat behind the fire, licking his large paws. Kyra didn't want to ask what Raff had caught and, it seemed, already devoured. Ash plucked feathers from Talis' gift of a pheasant. Kyra walked toward them.

Hayden was no longer near Jyls. He had moved to the edge of the campsite. He raised one leg on a moss-covered rock while resting his elbow on his knee. Talis was saying something, gesturing to the forest. Kyra's brow creased. The elf leaned on his bow, hair shimmering in the reflection of the campfire. Talis' posture was stiff. *Why is he still holding the bow?* she wondered. He hadn't used it before during his night watches. Hayden's expression was also unusually grim. Kyra slowed her stride, hoping to overhear their conversation.

"No matter which direction we choose, we'll face some risk," Hayden was replying in a dark tone. "I would keep us on the course through the woods until we reach the flatlands. Any cover is better than none. It doesn't look like you agree."

"I agree circumnavigating the forest attracts other adversaries," the elf said almost too softly for Kyra to hear. "Which foe is most dangerous given the abilities of our company? If it were just you and I, I would decide on the first route. With Ash and Kyra, I would choose the latter. They aren't ready to fight."

Hayden let out a tense breath. "I know," he said, eyes roving the camp, "and I'm not saying your reasons aren't valid . . ."

Hayden cut off abruptly. His gray gaze fell on Kyra, and his mouth pursed into a suspicious frown.

Kyra turned away, cheeks hot with guilt. She hastened over to Solarus. She didn't look back to see if Hayden and Talis were watching her.

Solarus had withdrawn a long pipe from within his tunic. He tapped the opening with his finger. A teal flame sparked to life. Solarus puffed on the pipe, then released a line of white smoke. Kyra caught the tang of apples and spices. She stared slack-jawed at the pipe. Solarus gave her a questioning look.

"Those are kolker leaves," Kyra blurted out. "The pipe you had when I was imagining—remembering—us near the lake had that same smell. They're kolker leaves."

"They are indeed." Solarus tamped the leaves in his pipe with his forefinger. "It has a variety of uses, the kolker plant. As a tea, it can speed recovery from an illness. As a poultice, it can heal abrasions. As a vapor . . ." Solarus turned the pipe lengthwise, considering it thoughtfully. "It clears the mind when the mind needs clearing."

Kyra nodded. Her eyes strayed to the blue flames. Tonight, Ash was minding the skewers, which now were packed with meat and vegetables.

Solarus observed Kyra, then gestured with his pipe toward a spot beside him. "Sit."

Kyra obeyed. Solarus let out another curl of smoke. His invitation tipped the scales to put Kyra's curiosity over her reservations. "How did you light the fire?" she asked. "There's no wood."

Solarus let out an amused hmph. "After four days, you finally ask the question. I have seen it in your eyes. You have developed enough patience to resist an immediate inquiry." Solarus set his pipe on the ground. "Wizards do not need wood to bring about flame. We harness energy from the natural world. I will show you. Ash, please remove the skewers for now."

The healer, who was turning the skewers over, looked at the wizard, puzzled. But he didn't ask any questions. Kyra only then realized as Ash took the four skewers from the fire that nothing had been holding them in place. More magic, she assumed.

Solarus made a circular motion with his hand above the fire. The flames flared with such intensity Kyra half-turned away. "Watch," she heard Solarus instruct. Kyra hesitantly glanced back as Solarus waved his hand again. The fire dwindled into a fainthearted flame. "Now we return it to its original state." Solarus cast his hand over the fire a third time. The blue flames capered happily.

"To create the fire, you say '*Ithansil.*'" Solarus held his palm before the fire. It seemed to disintegrate as it vanished. Hand raised over the empty space, Solarus intoned, "*Ithansil.*" The fire popped back into existence. "Ash, you may resume your preparations."

"That's amazing," Kyra whispered, mesmerized. Ash lifted the skewers and placed them on top of the flame. She noticed the healer didn't share her awe.

Of course not, Kyra thought as Ash sat back and picked up his seasonings. *Magic isn't anything new to him.*

"When we came upon you and the dark wizards, I noticed a golden energy swirling around your hands. Golden flames to be exact." Solarus' tone was even, but a grave look belied the calm words. "Have you seen that energy elsewhere?"

Kyra's heart beat faster. She noticed Talis and Hayden had stopped conversing and observed her with inscrutable expressions. She nodded mutely.

"When?"

Kyra carefully summarized her experience at Somerset House. How she escaped from Jude. Then she described how the gold had appeared when she was fleeing the dark wizards in London. Kyra omitted how red flames had sprung to her hands in her rage. How she had bound a Variavryk in ice. And how she had seen blue flames the night she found herself in Chicago. Kyra also described the golden shield that protected her during her battle against Nymphrys. As with the red, Kyra didn't mention the peculiar blue and green energy that had bolstered her shield. Solarus' face had increasingly become a study of mistrust during Kyra's retelling. She didn't want to add to his suspicions by including other sources of magic. Especially ones that were out of her control.

When Kyra finished, Solarus was silent. It was clear from his slanted brows that he knew she was hiding something. Kyra tried to banish any trace of guilt from her features.

"James the Lyneera thought I might be a wizard," she ventured. "You said I used magic before in Ilian. I'm guessing I'm a wizard?"

From the corner of her eye, Kyra saw Hayden and Talis exchange an enigmatic look. Solarus' wary frown lifted slightly. "Yes, you are a wizard. Normally, a wizard's magic matures when they are of age, after their sixteenth birthday. However, you have not been trained this past year—or I assume you have not been trained? No? Then it stands to reason that your magic has largely remained dormant. Magic manifests more strongly after sixteen. Even if you have not seen it often, you have a well of magic inside you. It merely requires drawing out."

Sixteen. Solarus was right. Kyra's first glimpses of magic were after her sixteenth birthday. She wondered if the nightmares she had had in the autumn were also influenced by the appearance of the golden energy. "How does magic work?" she asked.

Solarus arched a brow. "That is a question that would take several lifetimes to answer. Magic is not limited to wizards. Elves, dragons, gryphons, and animals each have unique bonds to Inishmore. They therefore call upon energy in their own ways. I can provide you a basic explanation of wizards' magic. There are two kinds: intrinsic magic and learned magic. Intrinsic magic is magic with which a wizard is already born. It underpins a wizard's ability to summon energy by hand rather than rely on spells. Learned magic is that which a wizard is taught. Learned magic is derived from Inishmore. It is everywhere."

Solarus took a long draw from his pipe. Kyra leaned forward, eager to hear more. The wizard's body relaxed as he exhaled. "Just as no two snowflakes are alike," Solarus continued, "so are wizards distinct because of their intrinsic magic. I was unable to thoroughly test and train you before you disappeared at the age of fifteen. However, the golden magic you witnessed indicates a strong presence of intrinsic magic. I myself was unable to use magic in such a fashion until I was older. Now that you are sixteen, we can examine your aptitude.

"More common to wizards is learned magic," Solarus continued in a pedantic tone. "This consists of spells and incantations that are accessible to all wizards. Through rigorous study, even a wizard deficient in innate abilities can become formidable. Summoning *Ithansil* is one example."

He stopped as Ash removed the skewers from the blue fire. "Dinner is ready."

Solarus left off as Hayden and Talis joined them. Jyls set his knife and sharpening rod aside with a "Finally. I'm starving."

Kyra ate silently as she chewed over Solarus' information. She had demonstrated powerful magic already. What else could she do? Had she been taught spells before? What were they? Would she remember them? The thoughts were as elusive as dandelion fluff, blown to all corners of her mind.

When the group had finished, Jyls and Ash collected the skewers to clean and waterskins to fill. Hazel bounded after them, playfully circling Ash's legs as they trekked into the woods.

Kyra stretched as Hayden, Talis, and Solarus retrieved their bedrolls. Her body was ready to sleep; her mind continued to churn up questions. Did intrinsic magic have properties that made a wizard inherently "good" or "bad?" Were all "bad" wizards from Harkimer? As far as Kyra understood it, Solarus belonged to a category of "good" wizards; he wasn't from Harkimer. But just because the dark wizards were from Harkimer, not all dark wizards were necessarily evil. There could be "good" wizards trapped in the Southern Mountains. Couldn't there? There could also be scheming wizards living in Ilian. Were there more dark wizards than free wizards? *And*, Kyra wondered with a pit in her stomach, *which one am I?* Raff had told her the dark wizards were hunting her. He never specified why. Kyra's mind turned over theory after theory and landed on the possibility that she might be a dark wizard herself. She could have escaped Harkimer, and Diamantas wanted her back. It was feeble, but it was more reasonable than her other conjecture.

When she lay down that night, Kyra draped an arm around Raff. The panther hadn't left her side since their first day. Raff's presence comforted her, even as she grappled with Solarus' disclosures. One insight astounded her. Dark wizard or not, the group she was with accepted her. And Kyra's goals of discovering what her magic was and learning how to control it were coming true.

Chapter 5

"Already?" Kyra looked at Raff, aghast. "You've only been here a few days."

The panther's yellow gaze reflected the soft pink and yellow rays of dawn. He had risen early. Kyra, feeling him shift beneath her hand, had woken. Talis was again on watch at the edge of the campsite. He stood straight backed, one leg bent with his foot on a large rock. The elf held his un-spanned bow as though it were a staff. Talis' other hand rested near his belt, his gaze scanning the woods and following the flight of merry birds zipping in and out of the tree canopy. Kyra was certain the elf's keen ears could pick up her conversation, but his expression hadn't betrayed any sign he was eavesdropping.

"Yes," Raff agreed softly, drawing Kyra's attention away from the elf and back onto the panther. "Our time with you has been too short. There is much yet to be done. Hazel and I were charged with your safe return to Ilian. Now we have other duties to which we must attend."

"But . . ." Kyra scrambled to find the right words. "I thought we could find out more about that tear in the sky. You said you hadn't learned anything from the old accounts, but someone must have information, someone who wasn't a—you called them scribes?—a scribe. I need to know how to re-open the rift." She met Raff's eyes with a silent plea. "It's the one way I can go back to James and Millie."

Raff's expression was heartbreakingly pitying. He opened his mouth then, as if considering something, closed it again. A sigh breezed from his lips. "My promise to you today is the same as when I made it the first night you asked: should you desire to return to the other world, I will do everything in my power to help you. You should not return soon though, regardless of your desires. Diamantas can pursue you in any land. You are among friends here. You have a mentor for your magic. That is your priority."

There was movement to Kyra's left. She glanced over to see Hayden propped up on one arm, watching them intently.

Kyra turned back to Raff. Tears welled in the corners of her eyes. "I don't want you to leave."

"Nor do I wish to leave you. It is what it must be, Kyra. Do not be sad. We will see each other again. It may even be soon, depending on Inishmore's will and the Council's determinations. You are embarking on a dangerous but also fascinating journey of rediscovery. You must learn who is Kyra. Who you were, who you are now, and who you want to be."

Hazel was up now as well. Her crystal blue eyes regarded Kyra with the same regret as Raff. It touched Kyra that they were as sad to part ways as she was.

Hayden had risen quietly to his feet. He and Talis walked over to Raff and Kyra. Hazel stepped forward noiselessly.

The panther bowed to Talis and Hayden with a gracious sweep of his paw. "My friends, we will take our leave," he said, yellow eyes shining. "You are near enough to Farcaren that you do not require us further. We must return to the *Al-Ethran* and confer with our scouts about what they have learned about Harkimer. Diamantas will strike quickly. His seers will have advised him to take the most certain course, lest his plans for Harkimer be foiled before he can see them through."

Kyra's lips pressed together in puzzlement at Raff's words.

Hayden, on the other hand, nodded as though understanding the tacit meaning behind them. "We will feel your absence," he replied.

Talis knelt beside Raff and Hazel, touching their paws. "May you be as shadows on your journey, hidden to any who seek you," he said, reciting the elven blessing. "By the light of the moon and stars, you will be returned to us."

"Raff, Hazel, thank you," Kyra said huskily. "You saved my life." She hugged the collie first and then the panther. Hot tears dropped on Raff's fur as Kyra closed her eyes. The collie and panther had not only been her guardians; they and Raven were her connection to London.

The roan clopped forward and bent his head close to Raff. "I also owe you my full gratitude. Kyra is dear to me. You did not have to volunteer to find her, but you did. You lent me hope when I had none. Thank you."

"Debts are always repaid in some form." The panther's lips parted in a melancholy smile as Kyra released him. "It is the way of the world. Keep her safe."

With a final nod to the group, Raff and Hazel loped out to the meadow. Kyra saw their silhouettes against the morning light as their tails swished behind them. Then they passed beyond a copse and out of sight.

More tears swam in Kyra's eyes. She swiped them away with the back of her hand. Hayden and Talis strode across the clearing together. The elf said something that elicited a nod from Hayden. Talis slipped away into the forest. Kyra looked to the side. Ash scooped liquid from the cauldron, whose steam carried the bitter aroma of coffee. Solarus again skimmed his small book, square-framed glasses on his nose. His hornbeam staff lay on the ground next to him. Jyls furled his bedroll into a tight bundle.

Kyra began rolling her own bedding, trying to ignore the pain in her heart. She glanced at Raven. The roan had clomped back to the other horses to graze. Kyra had him at least.

Ash rose and walked toward her. He held a mug in his hand, green eyes deeply sympathetic. Kyra plastered a grin to her face as Ash extended the mug toward her.

"I'm sorry," he said quietly. "Solarus said Raff and Hazel went back to their home. I know they were your friends. It's not easy to have someone you care about leave. We're here, though." Without waiting for a response, Ash gave her an awkward half-smile and walked back to the cauldron.

Kyra observed the healer as he laid out a spread of rolls and honey. Ash seemed to genuinely understand her feelings. She wondered if he might be more willing to talk to her now. Ash could be her first friend her own age. Heart lighter, Kyra tied the bedroll, set it aside, and joined her companions around the fire.

Jyls tore into a roll glazed with honey. "Our clawed companions are gone?" he asked Solarus as he stuffed a large chunk into his mouth. "Shame. I wanted to ask what wonderful things the panther and collie were saying about Ash and me, as the two nonanimal-language speakers. Compliments about our wit, I imagine."

Solarus had set aside his book and glasses and sat with one knee raised. "Observations about the odiousness of Peregrinians," he replied dryly.

Jyls grinned. He swallowed and wiped his mouth on a handkerchief he produced from one of his many trouser pockets. "Astute creatures."

Solarus glowered at Jyls. Laying a hand on his knee, the wizard cast a gaze at Kyra. "Before we depart for Farcaren, there is a matter we should discuss. You have heard about Diamantas and the dark wizards. You do not have a foundation in who they are and why they are here, however."

"We will have time in Thanesgard to discuss the dark wizards," Hayden interrupted. He shot a furtive look of warning at Solarus.

Solarus countered Hayden's disapproval with a testy tap of his finger against his staff. "I am sure you agree, Hayden, that it is wise to understand our adversaries. I am sure you also agree Kyra should learn about Harkimer and its history from those who have her best interests at heart."

Hayden's jaw clenched. A charged silence saturated the campsite. Kyra looked from Hayden to Solarus. She had never seen Hayden angry with the wizard, and she couldn't puzzle out the reason. Jyls seemed unaffected by the tension, eating his roll with gusto.

Kyra cleared her throat. "Actually, Raff told me about the War of Calonia and the dark wizards."

Solarus gave Hayden a superior look. "Then we can elaborate.:

Hayden folded his arms. "You've made up your mind."

"It is sensible to offer Kyra insight into that which is relevant." Turning to Kyra, Solarus asked, "What do you know?"

"Raff mentioned the wizards in Harkimer are descendants of wizards who were exiled," Kyra replied. "He also said their leader is someone named . . . Diamantas? And Diamantas wants to invade Ilian."

Solarus nodded his approval. "Good. That simplifies things somewhat. I will expound upon the brief introduction you have been given. Diamantas was once part of the Wizards' High Council. The Council is a body comprised of the most sagacious and preeminent wizards. I, of course, am among them," Solarus added primly. "It predates the War of Calonia. The members represent and advocate for the interests of the wizard diaspora. At least they claim that is their intention. I have my doubts. Wizards on the Council come from both Ilian and Harkimer. It is the forum in which the two families of wizards can meet safely. Members swear an oath to do no harm to other members, no matter what wars they wage against each other outside the Council. We shall discuss this later.

"Returning to the War of Calonia. It is important for you to understand the origins. Then you will understand the dark wizards. The story begins with a young, calculating wizard named Malus. Malus manipulated wizards into believing that men and elves feared magic. He claimed because of this fear, they were systematically exterminating the wizards in Ilian."

"Why would the wizards listen to him?" Kyra questioned.

"It is believed that Malus orchestrated the disappearances and assassinations of several wizards. He pointed to the attacks as evidence that he spoke the truth. Those wizards who vanished from Ilian were never found. The killings were so thorough, none could prove Malus was responsible. Malus gained the popularity he needed to mobilize many wizards against the kingdoms of elves and men. Although Malus had allies from those kingdoms as well."

"It doesn't seem like a good idea to join someone whose goal is to wipe out your people."

Solarus arched his brow. "There are always those who are seduced by greed, wealth, and power. Malus promised these to any willing to fight with him. That included men and elves. Conversely, Malus failed to account for the many wizards who did *not* support his ambitions. These wizards adhered to the doctrine that decisions were to be devolved among wizards. Power was not to be given to a single individual. Thus, a coalition of men, elves, and wizards rose up against him. This started the War of Calonia."

Kyra looked to Ash, who was sorting through packets of herbs. His head was half-raised as he listened with the same rapt attention as Kyra. "Was the Calonia the same Calonia Ash is from? Raff made it sound like the war wasn't limited to one kingdom but was all over Ilian."

"Raff is correct. Borders at that time were not the same as now. Calonia spanned the lands of Hogarth and Farcaren. These are kingdoms that were founded after the war. At that time, the kings and queens of Calonia had little authority. Like the wizards, the citizens demanded freedoms and the right to solve their problems independently. Like the wizards who didn't follow Malus, the citizens abhorred the idea that judgment could be rendered by one person. That said, when conflicts among noble families threatened the greater good of the kingdom, monarchs presided over negotiations for peace. Then came Malus and the War of Calonia. The Calonian king, King Regnum, assumed a greater role than his predecessors. Only through a unified army were Ilian's citizens strong enough to face Malus. After the war, Calonia was divided into three kingdoms: Calonia, Hogarth, and Farcaren."

"You left out Peregrine," Jyls put in. An enigmatic grin had hijacked his expression. He picked up a knife from the ground and began twirling it. "My kingdom has a proud tradition of independence and zero interference from the outside."

Solarus' eyes narrowed. Kyra couldn't decipher the look that passed between him and Jyls. Whatever it meant cemented Jyls' grin. "There is enough interference from the inside to dissuade others from getting involved. To finish the story," Solarus continued, "Regnum was aided by the most powerful wizard of the time, Peretikus, and the elven king, Clasil. Malus and his acolytes battled against this coalition. Blood was shed on both sides, the casualties too numerous to count. Ultimately, Malus was defeated. His followers fled to the Southern Mountains. They have been in exile ever since.

"Which returns us to the Wizards' High Council. Diamantas demanded the resettlement of Harkimer's wizards to the lands of Ilian. His arguments were no different than Malus'. Men and elves fear wizards' magic. They will never agree to allowing the dark wizards to return to their ancestral lands. Diamantas maintained that the injustice to our kin had to end. He wanted the Council to support actions to bring wizards out of the shadows of the Mountains and live as we, the free wizards of Ilian, do. That is to say, wherever we choose."

Solarus' words settled uncomfortably in Kyra's heart. "Letting the dark wizards return to Ilian doesn't seem unreasonable," she commented, tucking strands of hair behind her ear. "They haven't done anything wrong, have they?"

"Other than attack you groundlessly?" Solarus responded dryly. "Yes, they have. For the past two decades, Harkimer's wizards have conducted brazen attacks on wizards and non-wizards alike. Diamantas' impassioned speech to the Council failed to address these odious actions. He portrayed the dark wizards as victims. It is hauntingly reminiscent of Malus' early days of power. Malus, too, was an eloquent orator who understood what motivated his followers.

"The Council voted against Diamantas' request by a narrow margin." Solarus had a black look in eyes, as though a storm was roiling the ocean blue. "Several Council members sympathized with his views. Diamantas quit the Council immediately thereafter. Now he espouses his vision of Ilian to Harkimer's wizards and hunts those who oppose him."

"But we oppose him so nicely," Jyls commented. He stopped twirling the knife and examined it.

"Diamantas does have one advantage that his predecessors lacked. It is the one that troubled the Council the most. He possesses an obsidian staff. I have never seen its equal." Solarus glanced down ruefully at his own hornbeam staff. "There are qualities inherent to the rock that one cannot find in wood. Beyond that, the obsidian has become a compelling symbol within Harkimer. Those wizards who before said Diamantas couldn't fulfill his promise of their return now rally around the obsidian staff. Diamantas told them Inishmore bestowed it upon him. That it was a sign of the dark wizards' deliverance."

A chill raced down Kyra's spine. Her limited understanding of magic prevented her from fully appreciating what the obsidian staff was capable of, but she caught the hint of awe in Solarus' tone. "How can you say the staff motivates the wizards?" she asked before she could stop herself. "Have you been to Harkimer?"

Solarus' brows angled so sharply they almost touched. Kyra immediately regretted the question. He replied stiffly, "I do not need to enter Harkimer to understand their motivations. They have stated it outright in our encounters."

Kyra cleared her throat uncomfortably. Her eyes trained on the hornbeam staff, looking to tack back to safer waters. "If obsidian is more effective than wood, why don't other wizards use it?"

"The source of the obsidian is a secret. Diamantas, its sole bearer, hoards the knowledge so he can lead unchallenged. My postulation is he found the obsidian within the Southern Mountains."

Kyra was quiet as Solarus took up his glasses, folded them, and returned them to his pocket. Her head felt uncomfortably full, as though she had eaten three breakfasts and was trying to digest them all. The War of Calonia. Malus, the first dark wizard. Diamantas and the obsidian staff, their greatest threat. Despite the information Solarus had given her, Kyra was missing the crucial part of the discussion: where she fit in. It was the same question Kyra had posed to Raff. If Diamantas had command of an entire kingdom of wizards, why would he spend so much effort looking for a sixteen-year-old girl? Unless . . . Unless she had some value to him. If Kyra were a dark wizard herself.

Kyra rubbed her temple. She unconsciously glanced over at Hayden. His jaw was clenched as he regarded Solarus. His gray eyes blazed with anger.

"You've heard enough for one day, Kyra," Hayden intervened brusquely. "You have a lot to think on. It won't help if—"

"Hayden."

Talis strode toward them, bow in hand. Sunlight sprinkled on his silver-blond hair. His visage was serious. For a moment, Kyra wondered if the elf's disquiet had to do with the discussion.

"The Reapers are crossing the valley," Talis told Hayden somberly. "They are headed for the forest."

Chapter 6

Kyra didn't know what "Reapers" were, but the word sent a ripple of alarm through her companions. Ash's face drained of color. He immediately shuffled together the herb packets, hands shaking. Beside him, Jyls' midnight blue eyes darkened with revulsion. He coiled, snatched the knife from the ground, and sprang to his feet. Solarus swept his hand once over the blue flames. They blinked out of existence.

Hayden seemed unsurprised by the news. He rubbed his silver ring and faced the group. "Jyls, Ash, pack the saddlebags and tack up the horses," he instructed. "Solarus, hide the signs of our campsite."

Without missing a beat, Jyls grabbed his and Ash's bedrolls. He hefted one over his shoulder and brought them to the horses.

Hayden's severe gaze shifted to Kyra. "Kyra, come with us. We need an idea of how much time we have before the Reapers enter the forest."

Kyra's stomach plummeted. Hayden wanted to go *toward* the creatures that had given her companions this frenzied energy? Still, Kyra needed to prove she was a worthy member of the group. She nodded wordlessly. Keeping his bow at his side, Talis took off through the woods. Hayden sprinted after him. Without allowing herself another second of doubt, Kyra plunged into the trees.

The sunlight retreated behind the tree canopy, leaving the woods mantled in twilight. Kyra's jade-flecked eyes tried to lock onto Hayden as she ran. His brown cloak seemed to camouflage him within the dim light. Fortunately, Hayden glanced over his shoulder often, checking to make sure she was still with him, and slowed at points so Kyra could catch up.

As the trees thinned, Kyra noticed the whirs and clicks of the insects were gone. An oppressive silence pervaded the woods, as though the trees themselves were fearful of being discovered by the Reapers.

Talis signaled for them to stop. He hunkered behind a large cluster of ferns squeezed between a pair of oaks. Hayden dropped beside the elf's shoulder. Kyra knelt too, holding her breath.

"There," Hayden muttered softly as he pushed aside a fern in front of them. He pointed through the leaves toward the valley. "Those are Reapers."

Kyra's hand flew to her mouth. Sunlight streamed down on four enormous, broad-shouldered creatures in black cloaks. They tramped through the grass with long, birdlike steps. Peculiar shapes bulged out from beneath the cloaks. Even hunched over, Kyra guessed they were an arm's length taller than she was. The largest stood a head above the rest.

The sight of the hulking figures made Kyra's throat go dry. What hideousness was concealed beneath? She watched agog as they cut a diagonal path toward the forest. Her eyes darted to Hayden. Neither he nor Talis moved.

"Reapers are among Harkimer's most savage and formidable creatures," Hayden said in an undertone, eyes tracking the monsters. "Their skin is as impenetrable as stone, and their wings can carry them aloft as swiftly as falcons. They also travel in even numbers. It's hard enough to fight a single Reaper. It's almost impossible to survive a battle with two if you're alone." Hayden ran his hand over the hilt of his sword. "The Reapers took the lives of many brave warriors in the War of Calonia. I have no desire to confront one myself." Hayden released the fern. His gaze shifted to Kyra, his face grim. "I wanted you to see these creatures so you would understand the gravity of our situation. In the past, you took a fair number of risks when you should have exercised caution. I'm hoping that has changed." Hayden arched a brow as though to indicate he doubted it. "However, I will warn you anyway not to engage them. Your options are to hide from them or run. That's it."

Given the raw fear that washed over her just looking at the cloaked beings, Kyra had no intention of getting any closer.

"I must have seen them the first day in Edoin when we found Kyra," Talis said, eyes narrowed. "There was too much distance for them to reach us by foot. My guess is they flew at intervals and held to the fringe of the trees. This morning their course changed." Kyra's mortified expression didn't escape the elf. "Reapers aren't invincible. Their vision is their greatest weakness. They can see only a few meters in any direction."

Hayden dismissed Talis' words of comfort with a wave of his hand. "That isn't a reason to be lax. Their sense of smell more than makes up for their lack of sight. Our scent would draw them as bees to honey."

Kyra's heart skipped a beat. "Wouldn't they have already noticed the coffee?"

"The wind is blowing south of us. There wouldn't be anything to detect. I don't believe they are aware of our presence." Hayden turned on his heel. "Let's get back to the others. We've seen enough."

He and Talis set off in the direction of the campsite. Kyra wasted no time in scurrying after them.

"The bedrolls and bags are packed, and the horses are saddled," Ash told Hayden when they returned. The campsite had been cleared.

As Hayden and Talis quickly briefed Solarus and Jyls on what they had observed, Kyra detoured to the horses. They formed a protective cluster, pressing against each other uneasily.

Raven pawed at the earth as Kyra rubbed his muzzle. "Not five days since your return, and Reapers are already upon us," he neighed. "Take heart, Kyra. Our parting will be short."

Kyra had stopped mid-stroke. "What do you mean 'parting?' You're coming with us, right?"

Raven's brown eyes reflected torment eddying within. He silently looked over Kyra's shoulder. She turned to see Hayden, Talis, and Solarus observing her with grave expressions. The elf's bow was draped across his body along with a quiver of arrows. A second quiver was strapped to his leg. Hanging from Talis' belt was a slender scabbard and a square leather pouch. Hayden carried waterskins and a similar square pouch attached to a long strap.

"You and Talis will go ahead," Hayden explained. "With the Reapers so close, they may yet discover us. If we were facing only two creatures, I would have confidence that we could defeat them. With four, on the other hand, we aren't equally matched."

Solarus gripped his staff with a raised brow. "You have a wizard among you. That makes the situation less dire than you predict."

"If you're fighting the Reapers, I'm staying too," Kyra argued even as her stomach roiled with apprehension. She was grateful she hadn't eaten anything that morning. "I can help. I've got magic, right?"

"Volatile magic is often more an enemy than an ally," Solarus said sternly. "You have not learned to harness your gifts. You may have the best of intentions, but you could do more harm than good if you accidentally strike one of us."

Kyra averted her eyes to hide her dismay. She again questioned why the group was so determined to help someone who was a burden, not an asset. "Talis should stay," she said in a small voice. "Then you'll at least have five versus four."

"Talis is your guide and protection," Hayden replied firmly. "We aren't planning to combat the Reapers. We'll delay them long enough for Talis to get you safely to Farcaren." His calm tone carried an almost imperceptible shade of worry. Kyra realized as she studied Hayden that he wasn't worried about his welfare; he was worried about hers.

She cast a look at Jyls and Ash. Jyls calmly twirled a knife in his hand. Ash's face retained its sickly pallor, and he rubbed the tattoo on the back of his neck.

Kyra turned back to Hayden. "Where are Talis and I riding to?"

"You aren't. I'm sorry, Kyra. Raven and Windchaser have to stay with us. Reapers can pick up a horse's scent over great distances. It's too much of a risk having them with you. You'll proceed through the forest on foot."

Raven gave a slight flick of his head in agreement. Kyra's heart sank to her stomach. She let Hayden take her hands and place the waterskin and pouch in them. "The food in the pouch can be rationed over several days, though you shouldn't need to. We don't intend to spend more time with the Reapers than necessary."

Kyra's hands quaked as she slid the waterskin through a loop in her jeans. She slung the strap of the pouch across her body. The pouch fit snugly against her back.

"Take this, too." Jyls slid his knife back in his belt and unclasped his cloak. He walked forward and draped it over Kyra's shoulders. "This mud-colored clothing is drab compared to your Royalness' dazzling scarlet shirt, but the Reapers would spot you in that like a fox in the winter. Not what you want. Better if we make you as interesting as the fungus on that tree. Keep the cloak on."

Kyra nodded. She clipped the metal fasteners together. Thanks to Jyls' wiry frame, the cloak fit loosely and comfortably around her. It was a bit long, the hem falling over Kyra's shoes. She secretly hoped she wouldn't trip and give the Reapers an easy catch.

Talis clasped hands with Hayden. "By the light of the moon and stars, you will be returned to us, Caleril. And I will say for a florin, that the moon will be this night's."

"I'll wager a florin that we reach you by dusk." He released Talis' hand. "Go, and be careful."

Talis grabbed Kyra's arm and pulled her after him. She cast a last look at Raven. His head drooped, brown eyes full of misery. Swallowing her fear, Kyra turned and loped after Talis.

***

The moment Talis and Kyra disappeared from sight, Hayden regarded the group with a steely gaze. "Jyls, I need you to track the Reapers. Report back how long it will take them to reach this point. We want the Reapers to be close enough to see us but far enough away that we can escape. That will give us a couple minutes in between, at best."

Jyls stealthily slid into the forest before Hayden finished his sentence. Hayden nodded. He turned to the healer, whose face was white-sheeted. "Ash, you're responsible for the horses. They don't usually shirk from danger, but Reapers affect them as no other being can. As I told Kyra, Reapers hunt horses by scent alone. A horse has no protection against those monsters."

Ash glanced at Autumnstar. The filly's ears were pinned against her head. Windchaser hopped on his back hooves while Odin looked out beyond the circle. Grayhaven stood stoically and stomped his front hoof on the ground as if delivering a challenge to the approaching Reapers.

"Ash." Hayden placed a firm hand on Ash's shoulder. The healer met Hayden's confident gaze. "Inishmore has finally seen fit to bring Kyra back to Ilian. She isn't meant to be taken away from this land. Neither are we. The Reapers aren't aware of our presence. That buys us the time we need to get ourselves and the horses to safety."

Ash blinked. The healer's face slowly filled with shame. "I'm sorry. You're right. My father told me once that a healer's calling is sacrosanct, that our abilities are given to us to be used for good. We pledge to be loyal to Inishmore. We serve, regardless of our personal safety and in spite of our fears." Ash touched the black tattoo on the back of his neck. "My father, if he saw me now, would have regretted choosing me as his apprentice."

A smile lightened the grave planes of Hayden's face. "He did well to train you. The best of us can lose our way when confronted with our demons. We need to keep faith in our strength. I've told you many times, Ash, we need you. Right now I need you to take care of the horses." Hayden glanced back at the group. "If they're spooked, you must lead them to safety within the forest. Ride Willow, not Autumnstar. She and Grayhaven know where to go."

"I will," Ash replied. His tone carried a new note of confidence. The healer walked over to Autumnstar and put a hand on her neck. "It's all right," Ash cooed, stroking her neck. "Everything will be all right."

Hayden and Solarus remained together.

Solarus rubbed a thumb against his staff. "You erred in your words," he remarked tartly. "We do not *all* lose our way, nor do we all shirk from evil when it approaches."

The composed demeanor melted as Hayden rounded on the wizard. "What in Inishmore's name possessed you to scare Kyra like that?" he demanded. "She's suspicious of us already, and you launch into the history of Harkimer and the dark wizards. I thought we were trying to shield her from that for now."

Solarus gave Hayden a condescending look. "I prefer Kyra to fear her current situation. Or would you like her to be persuaded by the dark wizards that their cause is just? Without memories, Kyra's mind is a blank piece of parchment. What is written on it is what is told to her and what she experiences. Dark wizards have attacked her, which does not endear them to her. Kyra does not understand why they pursue her. Diamantas has not had the opportunity to inscribe his version of events on that empty page. The more we write, the more likely it is she will be our deliverance." Solarus' eyes narrowed. "Is that not the purpose of all this?"

Hayden's fists balled together. "It isn't," he replied frostily. "I care about Kyra because she's Kyra, not because she's a line in a prophecy. We need to save Ilian, and we need to save her. I shouldn't have to remind you that Kyra was *your* protégé. Her foundation about Ilian needs to be built, yes. I don't agree with your timing. You said she shouldn't be convinced of the righteousness of Diamantas' cause. Didn't *you* explain Diamantas' actions were magnanimous in their own way? A means to free the wizards? You didn't consider that one statement that provided some reasonable explanation of Diamantas' cause could be enough to spark her curiosity? What does that accomplish?"

"I did not paint Diamantas as a generous leader," Solarus snapped. His staff buzzed as turquoise energy sparked from the top. "I spoke the truth. I also clarified that the dark wizards have committed significant crimes in Ilian. Perhaps, you should pay more attention to my words rather than reach half-formed conclusions."

"If you want to help the Reapers find us, raise your voice a bit louder." Jyls had returned, his knife in hand. Hayden and Solarus' argument was forgotten as their heads swiveled in unison. "They're in Edoin, heading north. Reapers are impressively ugly close up, by the way. I'd put them on par with greeloks, minus the slobbering and biting and pungent odor."

"We have to draw them east on a course toward Silvias," Hayden responded without hesitation. "How much time do we have until they're within range?"

"Fifteen minutes, maybe twenty."

Solarus' hand shimmered with the same turquoise as his staff, which flowed with energy from top to bottom. "I will create a chasm that spans the length of the forest edge along which we ride. If it is five horse-lengths' in width, it should be a sufficient defense."

Hayden turned and called, "Ash! Are the horses ready to travel?"

Ash looked up. He was scratching Autumnstar behind the ears. "I think so," he called back.

Hayden nodded. "We won't ride until we are further within the forest. Harkimer's creatures are not limited to Reapers. Without knowing who or what could be before us, I would rather proceed slowly. We might first hear a danger before we see it."

"Why did we agree to let go of our elf?" Jyls questioned. He strolled over to the horses. "C'mon, Odin," he said as the large draft horse's ears turned forward. "Time to go."

"Speaking of Talis, I need you to keep Windchaser close as well," Hayden told Jyls. "Ash, you will take Raven with you."

"I make one joke, and you give me his overly eager elven horse," Jyls grumbled. Windchaser continued to prance. Jyls took Odin's reins loosely in his hand. Then Jyls stretched out a hand and caught Windchaser's reins. "Calm down, or you're on your own."

Raven straightened as Ash approached, as though looking to demonstrate the proper behavior of an elven horse.

With the horses ready, Solarus told Hayden curtly, "I will join you as soon as my preparations are finished."

"I appreciate the value of having a wizard among us," Hayden said in a tone of reconciliation.

Solarus accepted the verbal peace offering with a thin grin. He turned and marched through the trees, staff rhythmically stamping the ground like a hiking stick. Turquoise flame zoomed up the wood as the wizard disappeared.

Chapter 7

Kyra's blood pounded in her ears as she sprinted to keep up with Talis. The elf forged a path over flattened ferns and mossy undergrowth. It was an easier—if not more detectable—route than that through the underbrush. Kyra guessed Talis chose the way for her sake. Compared to the elf, Kyra felt as nimble as an elephant, crashing through dead bark and leaves loudly enough for any pursuer to hear.

Still, Kyra was grateful for her countless runs in London. She didn't have Talis' speed, but she had endurance. Kyra had also developed a trained eye to avoid obstacles, particularly unpredictable ones, like children, bikes, and dogs off leashes. Kyra was laser focused as she followed Talis' trail. She hurdled fallen branches, swerved around large stones, and splashed through a creek. Her heart skipped a beat as her shoes slipped on the mossy pebbles. Arms flailing, Kyra caught herself, then sprinted after Talis with terror-inspired purpose.

Deeper in the forest, the soft underground gave way to prickly shrubs and brambles that snatched at Kyra's borrowed cloak. Talis slowed to a jog as Kyra picked her way through the thick underbrush. Kyra also noticed the land had begun to slope upward. Gritting her teeth, Kyra focused her effort on keeping close to Talis. She was a few steps behind the elf when he stopped abruptly. He put out his arm. Kyra smacked into him full force. The breath was knocked out of her as Talis caught her reflexively. The elf nodded toward the edge of the trees. Kyra's gaze followed his gesture downward. Her eyes widened. The flat earth dropped off precipitously, with nothing but rocks and tree trunks to break her fall.

"The elves have a saying—*'Lonix tha sari, sari tha lonix.'* 'Slow is fast, fast is slow.'" Talis' eyes ran down the decline. "Moving quickly and without thought can lead to injury. A sprained ankle will cost you time you gained. Likely add to that time tenfold. Proceed here with care." Kyra noted with some envy that there wasn't a trace of tiredness in Talis' voice. "The soil is drier than it was before and may be brittle. Don't place your weight on the earth before testing that it will hold." Talis pointed his bow to the side of the decline. "You can use the roots to keep your balance. Go slowly. I'll be below you in case you fall."

Comforting words, Kyra thought. She watched as Talis skipped down the hill as spryly as a mountain goat. Expelling a terse breath, Kyra turned so she faced the hill. She made her way down, grasping saplings and roots. Following Talis' advice, Kyra kicked the earth beneath her foot. At times, the soil crumbled, and Kyra was forced to hug the mountain. When the earth settled, she dragged herself horizontally across the incline and tried again.

Soon Kyra's arms and back burned from the effort. Her legs quaked with each step. Exhausted, Kyra carelessly stepped down without checking the firmness of the earth. The ground broke apart. Heart leaping to her throat, Kyra frantically scrabbled to regain her purchase on the slope.

It was too late. The weight of her body pulled her downward, prying her fingers from their tenuous grip on the roots. Branches and rocks jutting from the slope grabbed at her tunic as she plummeted down the hill. She didn't even have time to scream.

Hands suddenly caught her shoulders. Kyra jerked to a stop, a root scraping her cheek. She didn't dare move, her breath ragged. Finally, Kyra turned her head. Talis stood perfectly balanced on the slope as he held her steady. A latent smile creased his lips.

"We've arrived," Talis said. "Well done." The elf lowered Kyra gently until her feet planted themselves on firm ground.

Kyra doubled over, gulping in air. Sunlight poured from the sky, no longer constricted by tree cover. Sweat from Kyra's scalp trickled down her face. She pushed matted strands of hair from her forehead as she stared down at the sheet of rocks beneath her feet. Kyra lifted her head slightly. The rocks were round and uneven and led to a bank abutting a creek. The sound of the water dribbling over and around the rocks complemented the soft rustling of leaves overhead.

With a sigh, Kyra straightened. She crossed her hands over her head and paced back and forth as she had done so often after her runs. Her eyes went to Talis. The elf was scanning the ridgeline.

"Are we safe here?" Kyra asked after a moment. She dropped her hands to her sides.

"For now, yes." The elf looked back at Kyra. His eyes ran over her arms. Jyls' cloak, as large as it was for Kyra's lean frame, had taken the brunt of the abuse from the brambles in the forest and rocks jutting along the hill. When Kyra tenderly rolled back her ripped shirt sleeves, she saw red cuts lining her arms.

Talis walked lithely over the rocks to the creek. Kyra stepped more deliberately. The rocks, slick with water, shifted under her weight. Kyra reached the narrow stretch of the stone-free bank without incident. She collapsed onto it gratefully. Lifting the long strap over her head, Kyra removed the square pouch and set it behind her. Then she untied the waterskin from her belt loop, uncorked it, and tipped it back. Cool water slid down her parched throat. When the skin was empty, Kyra dunked the waterskin in the creek to refill it. The cuts along her palms and on the back of her hands burned, but she ignored them. From the corner of her eye, Kyra caught Talis grinning at her.

"You forgot my counsel to Windchaser?" he asked jokingly. "'*Lox teranas, gil teranas.*' 'Take some, save some.' You should drink more slowly."

"I'm sympathetic to Windchaser," she said, pausing to take another gulp from the waterskin. "After running for so long, I feel like there's much more water *on* me than in me."

The elf chuckled. He indicated Kyra's square pouch with a tilt of his head. "May I see that, please?"

Kyra reached back and handed him the pouch. With her thirst slaked, Kyra was becoming aware of the sharp pain from her cuts. Kyra gingerly moved the sides of the cloak away from her arms, wincing where the dried blood stuck to the fabric.

Talis removed a white cloth from Kyra's pouch. He also took out a jar of a Vaseline-like salve. "It's too early in the season for the leaves' poisons to have matured. Still, your wounds can become infected if not treated. Remove your cloak. We want to avoid it touching your arms."

Kyra complied, unfastening the clasp and letting the cloak slide from her shoulders. Talis dipped an edge of the white cloth in the creek's clear waters. Kyra extended her right arm. The elf tenderly cleaned the angry red nicks. Kyra flinched as the water stung her skin. The elf gave her an apologetic smile. Kyra caught the fragrance of mint as Talis administered the jar of goo on her cuts. A cooling sensation assuaged her pain.

Kyra released a deep sigh. "What is that?" she asked.

"A salve to quicken healing. It comes from the Sadyran tree in Silvias. Let me see your palm." Talis' hands moved deftly over her skin. One arm finished, Talis turned to treat her other arm. "These cuts are shallow. They should heal overnight so long as you don't rub away the balm from the surface."

Talis' eyes went to the thin red line on Kyra's cheek. He cleaned it and smeared salve on it as well.

"Thank you," Kyra said. She appreciated the elf's foresight in bringing the medicine. "It already feels much better."

The sun beat down hotly on them. Kyra was comfortable with her sleeves rolled up. She folded Jyls' cloak into a neat square and placed it beside her. Even with the tatters along the back, Kyra had promised to return the cloak.

Talis strolled along the bank. The uneven rocks merged into a path of larger, flatter stones. They reminded Kyra of Millie's patio pavers. Water streamed in mini waterfalls over rocks in the middle of the creek. Talis lifted the quiver from his back, then removed the second quiver at his side. He placed them and his bow gently on the ground. He spread his cloak out like a picnic blanket. Taking up a position next to his weapons, the elf motioned for Kyra to join him.

Kyra walked to him and eased herself down tenderly. Her legs groaned as she stretched them out before her. The mini waterfall provided a soothing background noise.

Talis read Kyra's weary expression. "We can rest until Hayden and the others come to us. I don't expect it will take them long." He lifted his own leather pouch and removed bread, cheese, and berries. Kyra's stomach growled in approval. It took all her willpower to eat sparingly. Silence reigned over Talis and Kyra as they ate.

"What litter of questions has been birthed about Ilian?" Talis asked suddenly.

Kyra looked up, having been absorbed in her thoughts. Talis sat with both knees bent. His hands were draped loosely over them.

"I've known you a long time, Kyra. You curl your hair like that when something troubles you."

Kyra released the strand she hadn't realized she had been twisting. Resting her back against the hill, Kyra thought for a moment. "You said I grew up in the Elven Realm," she started. "Is that when you and I met?"

"Yes. Hayden brought you to us when you were very young."

Kyra's brow scrunched. "Why would Hayden bring me to the elves? Where were my parents?"

She was surprised to see worry decorate Talis' features. His gaze went to the creek as though deciding how to respond. "Hayden can answer those questions better than I," Talis said at length.

Kyra ran her hand through her ever-more tangled hair. *Why were the important questions the ones that no one ever answered?* "It can't be normal for a wizard to grow up among the elves," Kyra pressed. "It makes more sense to have a wizard raise a wizard." *Unless the only choices for a wizard mentor were in Harkimer.*

"It's a reasonable assumption. It isn't normal. *Raenalyn* Carina made an exception in this case."

The ambiguity of Talis' answer magnified Kyra's curiosity and suspicion. *What is he keeping from me? More importantly, why?* Kyra shelved the two questions and instead asked, "Who is *Raenalyn* Carina?"

"Our queen. She had my word that I would teach you to behave according to the standards of the Realm." There was a hint of amusement in Talis' voice as he added, "I hadn't anticipated the task would prove so trying. You had a penchant for following rules that you believed fair and contravening those with which you didn't agree. Having to learn subjects that you believed had no practical use, for example."

Kyra's neck grew hot. That did sound like her. How many times had she skipped over homework assignments from her tutors in favor of reading topics she found more interesting?

"I have great respect for *Finna* Fiora. She was your teacher. *Finna* Fiora had the impossible mission of keeping you to your studies."

Kyra felt a flutter of recognition. She couldn't draw up the image of *Finna* Fiora, but a female voice accompanied the name, one with a stern tone and carefully enunciated words. Someone like Professor O'Leary. "I must have caused her a lot of trouble," Kyra replied. "Especially if they didn't have to let me stay there as a wizard."

"*Raenalyn* Carina and *Finna* Fiona's forbearance enable them to handle challenging individuals," Talis said good-naturedly. "Besides, your punishments benefited the Realm. You swept the kitchen floors and mucked the stables, among other things. Without your misbehavior, many chores would have gone uncompleted."

"If I was graciously volunteering for tedious jobs, I couldn't have spent a lot of time in my classes."

"That you did not," Talis agreed, "not compared to your course mates." He tilted his head upward as the tree canopy rustled. A pair of hawks burst through the leaves and soared into the open sky. Kyra watched the birds grow small in the distance. She dropped her gaze back to Talis.

His amber eyes sparkled. "You spent more time under the castle staff's eye than you ever did *Finna* Fiora's."

"I must have been a terrible student."

"You learned as much as the elven children, if not more," Talis replied without a trace of mocking in his tone. "Which perhaps explains why you had the irrepressible inclination to explore instead of study. The fact that you excelled despite your continual absences was another source of exasperation for *Finna* Fiora."

Kyra saw the poignant sentiment behind Talis' gaze. She wished fervently she could share in his nostalgia. If only she had her memories. Kyra looked down, plucking blades of grass, disheartened.

Patience.

The mysterious sensation embraced Kyra. She dropped the blade of grass and looked up. She hadn't felt the subtle whisper since she had spoken with Christin. A lifetime ago.

Patience, it repeated, nudging her gently like a doe with a fawn. *Trust the questions of the present to the clarity of the future.*

"Kyra?"

She glanced at Talis, bewildered.

His gaze was on her, eyes full of concern. "What's wrong?"

Kyra waited, hoping for another message. The feelings had passed. "Nothing," she fibbed. "I was just thinking about . . . about magic. Solarus mentioned elves had their own form. Did I learn this too?"

Talis shook his head. "Wizards' magic is separate from the elves' in its nature and manifestations. However, you did learn the common tongue of animals. You can also speak elvish."

"That's why Jyls and Ash didn't understand Raff," Kyra replied, "and I could."

"There were many advantages to spending your childhood among us. Hayden and I were responsible for your training in traditional, nonmagical weaponry and self-defense. Despite Solarus' opinion to the contrary, we believe that if magic fails you, you should have other skills upon which to rely."

"Other skills." Her eyes traveled to Talis' bow. Excitement thrilled through her. "Can I shoot like you do?"

Talis gave her a droll smile. "You have had practice on the bow, staff, sword, and bolas. Like any student, you preferred the weapon you found most enjoyable: the staff. But, here. See if you remember anything." The elf lifted the bow and handed it to her. Kyra reverently ran her fingers over the flawless wood. She expected the smooth texture to bring her some reminder of happiness. As Kyra's hand went to the rough leather wrapped around the center serving as a handhold, she wasn't filled with empowerment; she was filled with embarrassment.

Puzzled, Kyra looked at Talis. His amber eyes were on the bow as well, but his gaze was focused inward. *What is he thinking about?* Kyra wondered. Her longing to sink into the elf's private recollection was so strong, her head throbbed from the effort. The land began to blur around her. Kyra shook her head. Disembodied voices echoed around her. The louder the chatter grew, the more her vision swam. Until everything snapped into focus.

> *"Aim higher, Kyra," Talis instructed. He demonstrated with his own bow, raising it and drawing the string back until his forefinger reached the corner of his mouth. "When you release, release gently. It should be like fresh snow falling from a leaf." His fingers barely moved as the arrow sailed toward the bale of hay. The arrow sank into a silver circle so small it could have been mistaken for a speck on an otherwise perfect target. The silver was dead center. A perfect shot.*

Kyra gasped. She stood beside Talis as she watched the scene. He didn't seem to notice her. She was present but not a part of what was happening. Kyra turned her head. Her jaw dropped. A younger Kyra was mimicking Talis, drawing the bowstring back.

> *Twenty-five meters away, a row of circular haystacks painted with silver bull's-eyes mocked Kyra. She hadn't hit one yet.*
> *Kyra released. The arrow twanged. The string snapped against her arm. "Ow!" she yelped. She shook her arm as a red welt began to form.*
> *Talis laughed good-naturedly. "Where is your bracer?"*
> *Kyra looked dumbly at her arm. Rooting through her bag, she withdrew a leather bracer. She eyed the targets again. Her arrow had smacked a mud-colored ring on the lower left end of a haystack. Not the haystack she had been aiming for but its neighbor. Cheeks burning in embarrassment, Kyra strapped on the bracer. "Better?"*
> *"It's okay, try again," Talis told her patiently. He pulled a second arrow from his quiver and again displayed the proper technique. "Remember, snow falling from a leaf. The more delicate the motion, the more accurate your shot. Now, loose."*
> *Kyra breathed in deeply. Then she exhaled and released.*
> *Thwump!*
> *Kyra's face fell. She trudged forward and yanked the arrow from the side of the hay bale. She looked morosely at its bent feathers. She also retrieved the errant arrow embedded in the neighboring target. Kyra returned to the shooting line.*
> *"I don't have any talent for this," she told him in a deflated tone. "Can we try something else?"*
> *"All the more reason to practice."*
> *Kyra sighed. "Okay, I'll do a few more rounds . . ."*

Kyra was wrenched free from the scene as Talis raised his eyes. She stared at him. Had she *seen* Talis' memory? No, that was impossible. Yet, Talis wore an identical smile now to the one in his "private" memory. What was more, Kyra had vividly and unmistakably witnessed a younger version of herself. Her gut confirmed her suspicion. It was a memory, one she had unwittingly pulled from Talis. The revelation sent a bolt of delight through her. In her year in London, Kyra had never once had an experience like that with Millie.

Kyra's delight flowed out as shame trickled in. She doubted Talis was aware of what had happened. If Kyra knew someone had intruded on her thoughts, she would be furious and probably fearful. As Talis glanced at her, Kyra quickly arranged her features to look less guilty than inquisitive.

"You're smiling," Kyra remarked, hoping her curious tone complemented her expression. She handed him the bow. "That means I was either a fantastic archer or a miserable one."

"Neither," he replied, eyes perusing the weapon. "Archery lessons weren't among your favorites, but you did passably well as a beginner."

That's putting it nicely. "I'm sure I was better at other things."

"You were. You have many talents others would envy."

"Let's talk about those." Kyra rubbed her right hand against her jeans unconsciously. Her skin itched as though insects were scuttling over her skin.

Talis noticed Kyra's movements. His gaze dropped to her hands. Wordlessly, Talis grabbed his quiver and slung it over his back. He threw a look toward the ridgeline.

"What is it?" Kyra asked, head swiveling.

Talis snatched up the second quiver and fastened it to his leg. "Do your hands always glow?"

Kyra abruptly stopped scratching her hands. Horror-struck, she looked down. The golden energy pulsated from her wrists to her fingertips. Kyra grabbed Jyls' cloak. She hastily dragged it over her shoulders, smearing the moist salve on her arms in the process. Her fingers trembled as she snapped the clasp closed.

"The Reapers may have found us. We'll have to go up the hill." Talis took Kyra's hand and hauled her to her feet. He bent down, grabbed his cloak, and swung it over his shoulders. "Follow me but not too closely," Talis ordered. He flipped the bow in his hand. "I'll draw them away from you." Talis sprinted across the creek with long strides and ran up the opposite side of the forest.

Kyra commanded her tired legs to run. She hopped across the stones, slipping on the slick surface of one stone and letting her momentum propel her to the next. As soon as Kyra's feet touched the other side of the bank, she charged up the hill. Talis had outpaced her and was out of sight.

There were more trees this time. Kyra grasped thick branches and pushed herself off tree trunks. Her muscles protested having to work again; her breath came in fits and starts. She heard something thundering behind her.

Keep going! Kyra's mind screamed, even as her limbs shook. *Come on Kyra, run, don't stop!* She felt the spine-chilling futility of her dreams in London, of a hidden monster approaching, of her feet cemented to the ground, paralyzed by her fear . . .

Kyra looked around wildly for Talis. He was gone. Panicked, she launched herself toward a wide tree. Sidestepping behind the trunk, she turned and pressed her back against it. The square pouch dug into her skin, but she didn't dare move.

Soon Kyra caught the sound of heavy clomping below her. Her heart leapt to her throat. The Reapers had found them. Chest heaving, Kyra tried to still her breathing. Grunts were followed by clopping and splashing. Metal scraped against rocks. A horse nickered.

Kyra's brows knitted in confusion. The Reapers weren't riding horses.

"They have to be nearby, Galakis," a voice rasped. Kyra's eyes widened in recognition. It was Orkanis, one of the dark wizards who had attacked her in Edoin. "We saw the elf run. Kyra was with him, I'm sure of it. Frankly, I can't see how Diamantas considers them clever adversaries. They weren't even on horseback." Orkanis laughed derisively. "How incompetent do you have to be to lose a horse?"

"As incompetent as a wizard who puts himself exactly between my spell and the girl," replied Galakis sardonically. "I would have caught her if not for your stupidity. You're lucky the blow wasn't intended to be lethal."

Kyra could hear Orkanis' discomfort as he said, "That could have happened to any of us."

"It didn't. It happened to *you*. That's why we're searching this godforsaken forest for Kyra while Adakis spins some tale about why we failed to bring her back."

Orkanis' reply was muffled as though he had turned his head. Kyra held her breath. *Are they coming closer?*

Whatever Orkanis had said provoked a scornful snort from Galakis. "*You* should be leading this expedition? Your conceit rivals Adakis' at times, Orkanis. This isn't a feat to be proud of." The tension in the silence was as thick as the forest's underbrush. "Let me remind you of our situation. *You* were unhorsed by a girl who can barely raise a shield. *I* was the one who rescued you, though I'm questioning the wisdom of that action. *I* noticed the Reapers during our retreat. *I* suggested we shake the Reapers from our trail by turning back to the creek and using the water to mask the horses' scent."

Smart. Kyra thought with a silent groan. If she and Talis had come up with the idea, she wouldn't be cowering behind a tree with dark wizards standing meters away.

"If you prefer being torn limb from useless limb by a Reaper," Galakis hissed, "I will enthusiastically leave you behind the next time you drop from the saddle."

Kyra dared a glance around the tree.

Orkanis and Galakis sat atop their horses in the middle of the creek. Galakis' black steed snorted and shook his head while Orkanis' mare was straining to drink from the cool waters. Orkanis' face was pallid. He was avoiding Galakis' glare. Orkanis hastily released the reins as though fearful Galakis' reminder of his previous fall could jinx him to have a second. "I didn't mean I don't trust Adakis will lead us to her," Orkanis retracted. "And I trust you, out here. And I trust Nymphrys, and . . ."

"I get the point."

Orkanis ran a finger nervously over his lips. "To be frank, I deserve the opportunity to help in her capture. Upcoming capture. Very soon."

"Don't fool yourself, Orkanis. Your performance thus far has been profoundly inept." Galakis shook back his thick hair, dark eyes perusing the forest. "*Frankly*, you haven't been helpful in anything."

The edge of the leather pouch continued to press painfully into Kyra's back. She moved slightly to readjust it. Her heel skidded against the side of the trunk. She gasped, panicked, as a pair of rocks tumbled down the hill and clattered into the water. Galakis glanced up sharply as Kyra spun around again. She pushed as hard as she could against the tree, ignoring the pain in her back.

"What was that?" Kyra heard Orkanis ask nervously.

"Quiet."

Kyra scarcely breathed. She heard the running water, the snorts from Galakis' horse, and the birds warbling high above them.

"It was nothing," she heard Galakis say. "A squirrel perhaps."

Orkanis cleared his throat. "Shouldn't we cast a locating spell? That is, if Diamantas knew we didn't at least use one to determine if she were here, he wouldn't be pleased."

"By all means, Orkanis. Demonstrate your talent."

Kyra heard water sloshing and the clopping of hooves on rocks. She stood rigidly against the tree. Orkanis intoned an unintelligible set of syllables. At first, nothing seemed to happen. *Maybe he didn't do it right*, Kyra thought. She sent up a silent prayer that the duo would give up and leave. To her dismay, Kyra glimpsed a cardinal red plume out of the corner of her eye.

The spell hadn't failed then.

She turned her head inches to the left. The red rose as an ominous cloud like smoke from a fire. Kyra's eyes widened as the red began to stretch in all directions like a bloodhound sniffing out her trail.

In response, a golden glow sparked to life around Kyra's hands. A pit of dread sank in her stomach. *Not now*.

The gold strained against Kyra and drifted upward toward the red. Kyra wasn't sure what would happen if the two energies touched. It seemed rational that a locating spell was meant to lead to her discovery. *Stop it*, Kyra mentally ordered the magic. *Stay. Stay here. Stop floating.*

Orkanis' red plume drew Kyra's golden energy with the strength of a magnet pulling iron shavings.

Stop, Kyra repeated desperately. The gold hovered at the edge of the red cloud. *For Pete's sake*, stop.

Blue and green light suddenly coursed from her hands. It swelled like a balloon, encircling the gold magic and trapping it inside. The gold magic was suspended harmlessly in the air.

"It seems your locating spell has only confirmed that we're wasting our time," Galakis said caustically. "I suggest we do what Kyra and the elf did. Leave the horses and go on foot. If they were in this part of the forest, our crashing about has given them ample warning to escape."

"Give me more time," Orkanis pleaded. "The spell works, Galakis. If you joined your spell with mine, we could find them."

Kyra took in a deep breath. The gold energy was yoked in place by the strange blue-green magic. She could steel herself for a fight, or she could run. Neither option was appealing.

The squawking of birds whipped Kyra's attention down the creek. A murder of magpies shot out from the tree canopy. At the same time, rabbits, squirrels, and other rodents fled in a frenzy from the same direction. Over the chaotic sounds of the animals rose a haunting, drawn-out tone, like a single note played on a cello.

Kyra stared in astonishment. A neon green comet streaked through the sky. A second streak rocketed close behind.

"It's Kyra!" Galakis shouted triumphantly. "There, in the trees! Orkanis, stop gaping like a hooked fish, it's just magic. Follow me. When we find her, stay far from my staff, or I swear by Malus I will aim for you instead of her. Then you can spend the next few months with more than a sore rear end."

Heavy clacking of hooves against the creek's floor signaled the wizards' departure. The red cloud evaporated. Kyra wilted in relief. She let the back of her head rest on the trunk and glanced at the blue-green energy. It eased away, releasing the gold from its confinement. Like a flame suddenly exposed to the wind, the golden energy guttered out. The blue-green energy disappeared.

Kyra waited, partially concealed by the tree. Orkanis and Galakis were gone, but the threat wasn't. *Something* had scared the animals. *The Reapers.* They had found her after all. But the thought that two of her enemies might end up battling each other gave Kyra the tiniest bit of hope.

A figure darted through the trees. Kyra tensed and stepped to the side.

"Kyra!"

Talis came into focus. His bow was slung over his back. Suddenly dizzy, Kyra put her hand against the tree to support herself. Talis held out his hand and steadied her elbow.

"Are you all right?" he asked. She noticed his normally amber eyes were ablaze with an unearthly green color. The green ebbed as Talis watched her.

Kyra couldn't speak. Fear and relief had cycled through her so many times she wasn't sure which emotion to trust. She nodded several times before finally responding, "I'm fine. Orkanis and Galakis were here, but they rode off." Kyra unconsciously glanced up at the sky. Faint green wisps faded like the contrails of an airplane. "Was that you? Did you use elven magic?"

Talis' gaze traveled to the green wisps as well. "Elven magic and two arrows. It was enough to create an effect resembling a wizard's spell, a ruse to make them believe you had released the magic. Often, wizards can detect the difference between our energies and theirs. Fortunately, elven magic is strongest in the woods. By the grace of Inishmore, the trick seems to have worked." Guilt pained Talis' features. "I had been so preoccupied with thoughts of the Reapers that I neglected the dark wizards. I should have anticipated they might be in the forest. I'm sorry for leaving you."

Kyra couldn't bear to hear Talis' self-reproach. "There's nothing to be sorry about, Talis. You rescued me."

Talis nodded, but the somber look stayed with him. "With luck, Galakis and Orkanis will follow the magical trace. That said, elves don't put much stock in luck. We will follow the ridgeline lest they return."

Kyra wasn't keen on more climbing but didn't argue. "You came back just in time," Kyra commented. She kept a firm grasp on Talis' hand as she put a foot on a sturdy shelf of earth. "Orkanis summoned that red cloud. He called it a locating spell. The moment the red smoke or cloud or whatever it was started drifting toward my tree, my own magic appeared. By itself. It was fighting against me to get to Orkanis' magic."

Talis paused mid-step. Kyra stopped in unison with the elf. She was so absorbed in recounting the events, she didn't notice the elf's body had tensed.

"Maybe the locating spell is supposed to locate magic and not a person," Kyra continued thoughtfully. "If that's true, the golden energy should have acted as the spell wanted. If the spell is meant to find *anything*, though . . . and isn't limited to magic . . . why did the gold react the way it did?" Kyra sighed. "Anyway, if you hadn't created a barrier around my energy, Talis, they would have found me."

"What barrier?"

Kyra's tumbling thoughts on the potential effects of magic smashed against Talis' terse question.

"What barrier?" Talis repeated. His eyes showed alarm.

"The blue and green magic you sent. When the gold yanked itself away from me. The elven magic you said you used, it trapped my gold so it wouldn't reach the red cloud. Then my magic and yours vanished when Orkanis left. You saw it . . . didn't you?"

Kyra's blood turned to ice as she saw Talis' suspicious expression. He brushed his braid from his face. A line of sweat formed along his brow.

"I used no such magic," Talis answered at length. "What you witnessed in the sky was my own, yes. I had spied Galakis and Orkanis and the red spell of which you speak. But I didn't notice you until after they had left the creek. I wasn't the originator of any blue-green magic. Have you seen it before?"

The wariness in Talis' tone made Kyra uneasy. She hesitated. "Once, against Nymphrys. I accidentally brought out a shield to stop her spells, but I wasn't strong enough to hold it. Right when the gold was about to fail, the blue-green appeared and . . . I don't know, layered my magic. It was like armor. No matter what Nymphrys sent, the blue-green was able to block or absorb it. At least, it looked like the blue-green was doing that."

Kyra's frustration built the more she tried to verbalize what she felt. She didn't have enough of a grasp on magic to say more. In recapping the events, Kyra realized Talis hadn't entered the fray until several minutes after the blue-green had materialized. He wouldn't have seen her or known of her dilemma.

When Talis didn't respond, Kyra latched on to another explanation. "Raff and Solarus mentioned animals harness their own types of energy. Raff or Hazel could have rallied the animals in the forest before they found me. They could have warned them about the dark wizards. Then I would have had support I couldn't see. What if animals are shadowing us? It's possible, isn't it?"

"It's possible," Talis answered skeptically. "Have you shared this information with anyone else?"

Kyra shook her head.

"We'll have to determine who is sending this magic. Until then, we keep this information between us. Don't discuss what you've seen with the others."

Kyra's expression clouded in confusion. "Wouldn't Solarus have the answer?"

"Don't mention this to him either." Talis didn't offer an explanation. He extended his hand again to Kyra. "Come, we have yet to reach the ridgeline."

Talis' vague answer sprouted more questions, but Kyra let them go. She grasped Talis' hand. The two made their way up the hill in silence. Kyra wearily concentrated on the placement of her feet and gripped branches to pull herself up. When they reached the top, Kyra leaned against a tree to rest. Fortunately, the ground here was mostly clear of leaf litter. It had a mossy rug that covered loose stones and dirt. Kyra let Talis lead her to a small opening in the trees and decided it a safe place to stay. He instructed Kyra to wait while he surveyed the area. Talis had a peculiar expression as he spoke. Kyra was too exhausted to ask why. Seizing his bow in his hand, the elf loped silently through the trees.

Kyra unfastened her cloak, spread it on the spongy ground, and plopped down. *Someone rescued me,* she thought. Kyra lifted the strap to the leather pouch over her head. An involuntary shiver went down her spine. *Someone rescued me, because someone is watching me. Well, at least whoever it is wants me alive.* Kyra tossed the pouch to the side and laid on her back. Her protector hadn't revealed himself. What secret was he was keeping?

***

The sun was trading places with the shiny white orb of the night sky when Kyra woke. She found herself curled up comfortably on her side. Kyra rubbed her eyes sleepily, forgetting where she was. Pushing herself up, she spotted Talis sitting across from her. The elf's face was half-visible where the moonlight sprinkled though holes in the tree canopy. His gaze was peaceful as he wove together tall grasses.

Kyra cast a glance around the opening. Anxiety squeezed her heart together like a clamp as the reality of the Reapers and the dark wizards came rushing back. Where was Hayden? They should have been back by now.

Talis' hands stopped their work as he noticed Kyra's worried expression. "They haven't arrived," he confirmed. The elf set down the grasses. "That doesn't mean they are in trouble. Hayden wouldn't have left until he was certain that neither Reapers nor any others might follow us."

"Like Adakis and Nymphrys?" Kyra asked, wondering why they had separated from Orkanis and Galakis.

"Assuredly," Talis replied. "You and I also didn't take a direct path through the woods specifically so that we wouldn't leave conspicuous clues to follow. This makes the task of tracing our course as complicated for our friends as our enemies. Even for a skilled tracker like Hayden."

The elf took Kyra's square pouch and rooted through it. He withdrew dried fruit and meat. "You haven't eaten since last night," Talis commented, handing her the food. "You need to keep up your strength."

Kyra's stomach gurgled its approval. As she took the food, Talis nodded to her right arm. "It looks like we'll have to apply more salve, too. You've rubbed most of it off."

Even though the rations were cold and stringy, Kyra wolfed down every bite. Talis used his waterskin to wash away dirt and fibers from Jyls' cloak that clung to Kyra's wounds. The scratches on Kyra's left side, which she could make out in the starlight, already looked better. Talis reapplied the balm as Kyra finished her meal. She gazed longingly at the pouch. Her body craved more food, but she was reminded of Hayden's words. The provisions might have to last them days.

Kyra wrapped her arms around her knees, resting her head to the side. Her thoughts anxiously tumbled across every possible disaster that could have befallen her companions. Talis returned to braiding the grasses. Time crept by.

Suddenly, the elf lifted his head. He rose to a crouch, bow in hand. Kyra's heart thudded in her chest. Talis' lips spread into a grin.

"Hayden!" he called into the trees. "We're here!"

Kyra leapt to her feet as Talis put his bow down. Kyra saw a light bobbing, then heard Raven's nicker. A moment later, four individuals emerged from the trees, with six horses in tow.

The tip of Solarus' staff flared with a brilliant yellow light that illuminated the small area. His azure cloak gleamed brightly. Relief filled Kyra as she surveyed the group. They were all there, unharmed. Jyls gave her a lopsided smile as he led Raven and Odin by the reins.

"Your champions remain victorious," he announced, releasing the roan. Raven trotted to Kyra and butted against her happily.

Grinning, Kyra rubbed Raven's nose. "You *did* fight the Reapers?" she asked.

"We did not," Solarus replied. He planted the staff in the ground. It cast a circle of light as Solarus folded his arms. "I created a hindrance to dissuade the

Reapers from entering the forest. That was an accomplishment. Jyls was 'victorious' in remaining concealed within the safety of the trees and evading discovery."

Jyls didn't seem bothered by Solarus' clarification. "Gallantly slaying a monster or cleverly camouflaging oneself in leaves and mushrooms, it's the same. Survival is victory."

"We won't be followed," Hayden said as Ash reunited Windchaser with Talis. The palomino whickered and pranced around the elf. "We drew the Reapers south along the woods' edge—toward Silvias," Hayden added with a quick look at Talis. The elf, who had grabbed Windchaser's reins before he accidentally trampled Ash, gave Hayden a brief nod. "They shouldn't cross into the Realm."

"The scouts would spy the Reapers far before they reached the river," Talis replied. "*Relith*, Windchaser. Stop." The palomino ignored Talis and continued to tug friskily on the reins. The elf sighed and looked back at Hayden. "Did you happen upon Adakis?"

Solarus answered for him. "No, but you were happened upon by Orkanis, were you not? I detected traces of a spell he used when we rode along the creek. A locating spell, if I am not mistaken, which I never am. It was fortunate. We may have not found you otherwise. Hayden pieced together your trail after we left the creek."

"Orkanis was accompanied by Galakis," Talis said. "We were lucky. I was able to distract them with magic. Where they went after, I don't know."

Solarus frowned. "I am certain there is more to the story."

"I love a good story," Jyls interrupted. His gaze dropped to the ground where Kyra had been sleeping. "Hey, is that my cloak?"

"Oh. Um, yes." Grateful for the distraction, Kyra hurried over to the spot where Jyls was staring. She lifted the cloak she had used as a blanket. Shaking off dirt and more than a few insects, Kyra smoothed out the material as best she could. Then she held it out. Jyls took the cloak with a raised brow. "Here. Thanks for lending it to me, Jyls and, um, sorry it's a bit dirty."

Jyls turned the cloak front to back and then front again. "We left you and Talis for a few hours," he said in disbelief as he poked a finger through one of the many holes. "What in the name of Jaren and Garen did you do to it?" He tried to fit the cloak over his shoulders. With a yelp, Jyls smacked the cowl and shook the cloak back off. A pair of beetles scuttled out of the hood. Jyls grumbled as he tossed the cloak on the ground.

Solarus raised a hand and intoned, "*Ithansil.*" Blue flames sprang up on the ground. The wizard freed his staff and extinguished its light as Hayden set a silver florin in Talis' open palm.

As they settled down for the night, Kyra couldn't remember feeling so happy in Ilian. Her companions were uninjured. It surprised Kyra how worried she had been. When had Hayden and the others become so important to her?

When she glanced at Talis, Kyra saw his eyes on her with an expression of warning. The elf couldn't have spoken the message more clearly. Friends or not, Kyra, like her mystery rescuer, still had secrets to keep.

Chapter 8

Protecting those secrets was harder than Kyra expected. As they rode out the next morning, Solarus demanded a full description of what had transpired with Orkanis and Galakis and the locating spell. Kyra found recounting the events was like hopscotching through a verbal minefield. She avoided certain words and phrases—like her magic moving "without her control"—and leapt over details like the blue-green energy. It was even more challenging to keep her expression neutral. Kyra's face could betray her even if her words didn't. When Kyra reached the end of the tale unscathed, she almost sighed.

Until Solarus peppered her with questions.

"Your magic surfaced after the release of Orkanis' spell," came the first round. "Did you deliberately call forth the gold? Were you attempting to defend yourself?"

The accusation in Solarus' tone told Kyra a "yes" would bring as much rebuke as a "no."

"No," she responded truthfully.

"You summoned it to test his spell? You brought it to examine what was approaching?"

"I didn't do that either."

"Then the golden magic came forth without your active choosing."

Kyra's stomach clenched. "Yes."

"You failed to mention this." Solarus' tone grew colder. "To revise your account of the gold and how it behaved—which you said rose from your hands—we should say that your magic was, of its own accord, reaching out to Orkanis' magic?"

"It seemed to be."

Solarus' lips pursed into a frown. "Did it concern you that your magic was acting in such a manner? You did not stop it before it connected with the red cloud?"

"I tried."

"Trying and achieving your goal are not the same."

Kyra fought back a groan. She had stumbled into one of the mines.

"Fortunately, what occurred is not unusual."

"Ah, what?"

"Magic attracts magic. Wizards are trained to harness their energy. Untrained wizards cannot control when their magic is drawn to another wizard's. That was what happened in this instance. Your magic was drawn to Orkanis'. What *is* unusual is that the magics didn't meet." Solarus' tone was suspicious. "Talis, you stated, was not with you at the time of the locating spell. Why did the gold not reach the red?"

"The golden energy . . . stopped."

"It stopped."

"Yes, it, um, stopped." Kyra knew how inadequate the answer was. As did Solarus. He scratched his beard, ocean blue eyes never leaving Kyra's face. She didn't blink, forcing an innocent expression to replace the neutral one. *It's not lying*, Kyra thought. *It did stop. Just not because of something* I *did.*

"I see." The wizard cast a look at Talis as though looking for more information. The elf's face was impassive. "Then fortune is on your side."

"Can you tell me more about 'magic attracting magic?'" Kyra jumped in. "Why does that happen?"

Solarus gave her a thoughtful look. "Magic always seeks to unite with other magic. As I told you, all magic stems from Inishmore. However, because it is possessed and utilized by so many, magic is fragmented. It always wants to be whole again, as Inishmore is whole."

"Why isn't it pulling me to you? You use magic to create fire. I've never felt the gold drag me toward it."

"That is because I am aware of your presence. I am able to calm it." Solarus rubbed his forehead, looking tired. "We will need to address this problem as soon as we reach Thanesgard. We cannot count on luck to rescue you a second time."

The conversation had ended there. Solarus' mistrust, Kyra believed, had not. As they now rode through the woods, she felt Solarus' eyes studying her.

Sunlight filtered through gaps in the woods. The grassy tracks were wide enough for the horses to trot beside each other in pairs. The trees grew sparse as they neared the forest's boundary. The group emerged on the green shore of a sea of tall grasses and reeds. Hills undulated in waves, speckled with purple and pink foxgloves.

Kyra reined in Raven as she took in the tranquil sight. Solarus walked Grayhaven past her. The heels of the wizard's boots brushed the tops of the reeds. Talis trotted Windchaser next to him.

"Come on, wizard Highness," Jyls said as he and Ash also went by. "I hear if we make it by supper, we'll get a decent meal at the castle's expense. Maybe a glass of claret to go with it."

Kyra watched the grass part before Odin and Autumnstar as they plodded forward.

"I'm envious of you."

Kyra glanced sideways. Hayden had brought Willow beside her. A light spring breeze ruffled his hair as his gray eyes scrolled over the land. "I know what it feels like to gaze upon the simple beauty of the hills. They are never so full of wonder and peace as when you see them for the first time."

Kyra smiled, feeling a rush of gratitude. Hayden made it sound like her loss of memories was something to be cherished, at times.

Hayden and Kyra urged their horses after their friends. They followed a hard-packed dirt lane around a bending brook flanked by reeds and grasses. Colossal copses stood beyond the brook. Near them, new paths splayed in all directions. Some led north, some south, but all gradually headed west. Talis, who rode point, steered the group onto a careworn road. Deep ruts were carved into it from wide wheels and hooved animals carrying heavy loads.

Solarus slowed Grayhaven, changing places with Hayden. The wizard unfastened the clasp to his cloak, removed it, and bundled the material together neatly. Then Solarus opened a saddlebag and tucked the cloak inside. Kyra watched quizzically. In their days of travel together, she hadn't seen him take the cloak off except for when he slept. Seeing Kyra's eyes on the saddlebag, Solarus explained, "Wizards are neither common nor welcome visitors in Farcaren. The dark wizards raided the homes of its citizens for years. It has left a bitter taste in people's mouths."

"But you aren't a dark wizard," Kyra pointed out. "They were wearing black cloaks."

Solarus gave Kyra an approving nod. "A good observation. Yes, dark wizards wear black. The free wizards of Ilian wear azure. The complication lies in the fact that many travelers wear black. Therefore, one would not readily assume the individual is a wizard. The blue cloak, however, is unique to our kind. Free wizard or dark, we cannot conceal our staffs so easily." Solarus glanced at the staff, which fit in a loop between the saddlebags. He shrugged. "It is the way of things."

Kyra nodded, though she bit her lip. The fight against the dark wizards made sense. They threatened harm to those in Ilian. To be a target of scorn, mistrust, and violence simply because she was born a wizard in a world where most others were not, even if she had a good heart and noble intentions, was wrong. It was easier, Kyra knew, to both sets of wizards in one category. Bad. Evil. Wizards had power. It was natural to fear someone who could misuse that power. It was also simpler to fear something a person didn't understand rather than attempt *to* understand. Understanding required dialogue. In this case, dialogue between wizards and men. Kyra wondered how Mr. Stevens would square the philosophical circle of thoughts about creating trust in Ilian when trust was the essential component to move forward. Troubled, Kyra forced herself to redirect her focus to Raven's steady clopping as they continued onward.

Hayden steered Willow down the main thoroughfare toward the castle. Passersby trickled down the road, traveling to and coming from Thanesgard. As Raven trod up the sloped land, Kyra wondered how far they were from the city. Her question was answered as they crested the hill. Thanesgard opened up before them. Its sprawling buildings were stacked tightly together and looked as small as a doll's furniture. The castle, a circular gray structure with points rising from its sides, sat atop another hill overlooking the city.

The traffic became a steady stream as Kyra followed Hayden. Stone houses sprang up along the road like mushrooms. In the outskirts of the city, the abodes were situated on wide, shaved plots of land. They had uniformly plain white faces, gray chimneys, and wooden doors with elaborate iron knockers. The homes were also hemmed in by wooden fences whose function was far less to thwart would-be robbers and more to separate neighbors from each other. Glass statues marked the entrances to the homes. From her vantage point astride Raven, Kyra couldn't make out what the statues resembled. Most plots hosted a second, larger stone building, over which a wooden sign was posted.

Kyra glimpsed the goings-on with interest. One woman with a wicker basket on her hip walked inside the nearest building. Women with hair tucked under scarves knelt beside heaps of clothing, vigorously scrubbing shirts and skirts on flat washboards. The soap's eucalyptus-like fragrance drifted into the road. Kyra's gaze traveled to the wooden sign. In black, calligraphic letters was the word "Laundress."

They were shops, Kyra realized. Her head swiveled toward the next building. Mouthwatering aromas of melted sugar and warm dough leaked through windows thrown open to the warm weather. Kyra paused longingly before the door. A pair of girls skipped outside. The girls wore large smiles as they licked sticky sweet glaze from their fingers. Solarus cleared his throat impatiently. Kyra reluctantly walked Raven forward.

Soon the thoroughfare became too congested to see anything beyond the travelers. Wide lanes for caravans, narrow alleys for horses, and footpaths split from the main road like veins on a leaf. Shops disappeared as homes smooshed together so closely inhabitants of one house could see out their window and into their neighbor's.

Kyra grasped the reins as Raven halted abruptly. Glancing down, she saw a pack of dogs bounding in front of and around the roan. The animals yipped and nipped at each other. Kyra grinned. How many times had she had to veer around free-wheeling pups during her runs in London?

Kyra twisted in her saddle to watch the dogs lope down the road and cut in front of a rickety wagon. The driver jerked his horses to the side. Wares chinked as they knocked against each other. His long, dark hair was tied back in a ponytail. A thick, orange-embroidered sash draped around his shoulder and waist like that of a beauty pageant contestant. He eyed the dogs darkly as they skipped away.

"That man there is a trader," Hayden told Kyra. His eyes were on the driver, who snapped the horses' reins. "They're rare in Ilian, as rare as healers. They have the ability to find anything you need, no matter how obscure."

"They're as prized as truffle-snuffling pigs," Jyls added. "It's a compliment!" he defended as Hayden shot him an acerbic look. "Truffles cost more than claret, which is why those particular farm animals are in demand."

"Why do traders wear those sashes?" Kyra asked as the wagon rumbled down the road.

"The sashes have meaning to other traders," Hayden replied thoughtfully. "That meaning is a coveted secret among the group and not shared with outsiders. Even if a trader isn't wearing a sash, you can identify him in other ways. Men wear a single stud piercing in their left ear. Female traders wear bracelets with charms they've collected. It's a way of advertising their degree of travel and experience to individuals seeking certain services." Hayden let Willow's reins lie on his lap as he gazed up at the castle. "Before the War of Calonia, Thanesgard wasn't a city; it was a fortress. There was an outpost much smaller than the castle that stands there today. A former king of Calonia built that outpost for soldiers to observe, report, and defend against threats."

"You said Harkimer wasn't founded until after the war," Kyra replied thoughtfully. "What threats could there have been?"

"Ancient beasts lived in the Southern Mountains," Hayden replied. "They still do. You've already seen one example, the Reapers. Other evils reside in the Mountains that make Reapers look as threatening as eaglets. The creatures often hunted in Ilian, which created the need for towers and fortresses. Watchmen alerted citizens about creatures' incursions. Threats also came from bandits and marauders. The watchmen offered protection for farmers and craftsmen living in the exposed meadows and hills beyond. Thanesgard's importance over time wasn't for its defenses but for its diplomacy. The thane in charge of the fortress—hence the name 'Thanesgard'—had the foresight to offer an olive branch to Silvias. He wanted the elves as allies."

"They weren't already?"

"Elven interests didn't always align with those of men," came Talis, who hearkened to the conversation. "Disagreements between our peoples made the elves wary of their western neighbors. The War of Calonia led to our long-lasting peace. Our king, *Veralyn* Clasil, respected King Regnum for his leadership and courage."

"And King Regnum admired *Veralyn* Clasil for his wisdom and sought his counsel," Hayden said with a nod to Talis. "The kings' mutual respect was the bedrock of their trust and of their success in the War of Calonia.

"After the war, King Regnum appointed a duke named Erling to rebuild the markets and homes that had been ravaged," Hayden went on. "It took years to plant seeds for grasses and flowers to grow as they once did. Erling was a sage man. He predicted that Farcaren wouldn't be successful as a farming community. It would take a generation of rain and snow to bring the soil back to its natural cycle. He also recognized that the families that settled on the land bordering the Aurielle Sea would be content with their new home as long as there was food, water, and shelter. Once those were assured, Regnum believed the historical and cultural ties of the Farcarens to their homeland would lead them to return to their ancestral lands in the south."

Not for the first time, Kyra mentally reminded herself to buy a map as soon as she could.

"Erling took advantage of the kingdom's location and made Farcaren Ilian's center of commerce. He was ambitious. Erling wanted to trade with the other kingdoms of men, naturally. What was unusual was he sought to attract specialized goods from Silvias. He also wanted the expertise from wizards who had, at that time, settled in the north of Farcaren and in Hogarth. Farcaren was also close enough to the coastal villages to draw them to the market he established." Hayden gestured to the sunbaked lane beneath them. "Erling was the architect of the roads. He personally and meticulously planned out routes that would be easily accessible by men, wizards, and elves. At the same time, Erling drafted a plan for the city. He wanted to build homes and permanent shops for Farcaren's citizens. However, he lacked the revenue to pay for the construction of the buildings. The treasury had been depleted by the war. He also lacked many of the resources required for the construction, like brick and steel. Erling's solution was a clever one. He would entice merchants and craftsmen to set up shops in Thanesgard by renting them land for a fraction of the cost required by other kingdoms, and with negligible taxes." Hayden glanced at Ash. He leaned forward in Autumnstar's saddle, listening to the story with rapt attention. "Erling sent emissaries to Silvias, Hogarth, the coastal villages, and Calonia. He invited merchants and craftsmen to Thanesgard. His plan was successful. Many came, and their businesses thrived in the growing city. Word spread quickly, bringing in more vendors from across Ilian. Over time, Erling created the most lucrative marketplace in Ilian. Taxes since Erling's time have been raised, and space is more expensive, but merchants converge here daily, in all seasons. Erling's vision has lasted more than seven hundred years."

The sun started its languid descent as the stream of travelers coming from Thanesgard became a congested river. Merchants wearing fine tunics rode by on horseback, saddlebags bulging. Others drove flat-backed wagons brimming with everything from tapestries to furniture. Men carried arms full of wares while children chased after fireflies. Kyra and her companions were forced to dismount and walk the horses.

"Master Hayden!" a female voice called over the crowd. A rider wearing gold and midnight blue livery maneuvered a dun-colored horse through the thong of travelers. Her long, blond tresses flowed down her back. She smiled at Hayden. "I'm Larisa of His Majesty's Royal Guards," she introduced. "King Arkin bids you welcome. His scout spotted you on the road. The king wished to greet you himself, but he is occupied with visiting dignitaries. King Arkin has arranged for you to sleep in his royal quarters tonight and will give you an audience in the morning. I'm here to escort you to the castle."

"Thank you, Larisa," Hayden replied, raising his voice over the din. "We are grateful to King Arkin."

Larisa inclined her head. She pivoted her horse and pushed through the crowd. "Make way for the His Majesty's Royal Guards!" she hollered in a commanding voice. "Make way!" Travelers on foot parted to allow the group through, though the wagons and horses pressed on unheeding.

Kyra's heart beat faster as they approached the castle. The sight of the mammoth stone citadel, with its round outer wall, was unlike anything she had ever seen. Including in Edinburgh. The gray stone castle towered over them with forests of crenellations. The largest structure stood in the center of the castle. It reminded Kyra of a rook on a chessboard. Banners flew proudly from the parapets.

As they neared the castle, Kyra realized Thanesgard was comprised of several walls. The parapets were staggered on every other wall, starting with the outermost and working inward. Archers and guards paced the tops. Several cast down wary looks on the travelers.

Larisa navigated her horse off the thoroughfare and onto an inclining cobblestoned road. The crowd thinned. Larisa paused while Kyra and her companions remounted. Larisa's cinnamon gaze ran over Kyra. Kyra reddened. She guessed her clothing seemed outlandish in Ilian. Larisa's eyes passed on to Talis, Solarus, and then Jyls and Ash. If Larissa had any questions about the group, she kept them to herself. Kyra was relieved. Clicking her tongue, Larisa nudged her horse forward. She led the ascent up the road, nodding to guards and passersby.

The wall's stone was well-polished and painted with murals depicting coronations, battle scenes, and life at court. The road progressively tapered to a bridge, which arced over a moat ringing the castle. On the other end was the castle's portcullis. It was raised for stragglers leaving for the evening. With Larisa in the lead, the horses marched single file across the bridge.

"Don't fall over," Kyra heard Jyls remark from behind. "I've heard daggerfish find women particularly sweet."

Kyra lobbed a vexed look over her shoulder. She didn't know what a daggerfish was, but the name seemed self-explanatory. "How would they find *you* if you ended up in their waters?"

"Bad for digestion. Peregrinians are a disagreeable sort, even for daggerfish. One sniff, and they'd toss me back on dry land."

Kyra laughed. She looked down. The tales Kyra had read claimed that moats had alligators, barracuda, or other repulsive creatures lurking in their waters. Lurking and waiting for a meal to splash in. Kyra couldn't tell in the low light whether it was true. Goose bumps prickled on her skin at the thought.

Larisa piloted her horse through the portcullis and turned left. The others passed through the gate behind her. The guards nodded briefly. Talis, who rode in front of Kyra, looked to both sides of the entrance. His amber eyes were troubled. He glanced at Hayden. His gray eyes reflected his puzzlement.

"Where are the *Sirenyle*?" Hayden asked Talis in an undertone.

The elf shook his head. His brow wrinkled.

What are Sirenyle? Kyra asked herself. Her gaze roamed from the bridge to the castle entrance, not sure what she was looking for. Whatever—or whoever they were,—their absence seemed to unsettle Talis and Hayden.

"How high are the walls?" Kyra heard Ash ask.

"Ten meters each," Larisa called back. "The king's tower in the center is about fifteen meters. The width of the rings between the outer wall and the fourth wall and the fourth and third wall are five meters. The other rings are narrower, except for the innermost ring. There is where you find the main palace. It's comprised of the king's rooms, guesthouses, the courtyard, gardens, and all the principal stations required to run a court and its daily life. Many of the servants' quarters are also located near the tower so that the king can call upon help at any time."

They approached a pair of thick oak doors, which, while broad, only reached Raven's neck. "The most direct route to the king's court is through there," Larisa continued. "The doors aren't tall enough for the horses though. This path brings us to the stables, which are within the third ring. If you want to visit Thanesgard's marketplace tomorrow, you will turn right here instead. The merchants' bridge faces the south and is the main entryway into the castle. You would cross it to access the city. There are also merchants and craftsmen that serve the king and are separate from the market proper. Returning to your earlier question," Larisa added, turning her head to the side toward Ash, "the reason for such a broad space between the outer wall and the fourth wall is to allow merchants to hold their business. Even with the shops abutting the wall, four wagons or six horses can easily travel side by side." Larisa turned her head forward again and laid her reins across her lap. Her steed continued on his own, clearly familiar with the route. "To visit the shops, you would continue past the main bridge and the portcullis. Follow the flow of merchants until you see the stalls and buildings. There is another bridge on the western side of the castle where vendors with large merchandise can pack their wagons."

"Which craftsmen have shops within the wall?" Hayden asked.

"The blacksmith, the cartographer, and the bookseller, for example. A chandler named Aleesa, from Calonia, is the newest addition. She set up her shop this past winter. None of the food vendors are allowed within the inner wall." Larisa gave Hayden a sunny smile. "The cook had a small tantrum when a baker petitioned to have a space within the wall. He said he could make a leg of lamb as well as he could an apple tart, so why bother with a baker? The king denied the petition. Callum told me later that the king didn't want to jeopardize his favorite dishes for the sake of another pastry."

Though the sun hadn't fully set, torches were lit in sconces. The torches were spread out at regular intervals along the castle's walls. Larisa followed the circle and turned right at a gate manned by two guards. The gate was tall enough for the horses to pass through.

Larisa dismounted within the third ring. Hayden and the group followed suit as groomsmen in crisp brown shirts and pants rushed forward.

"The Royal Guards have two sets of stables," she explained. Larisa handed her reins to a young groomsman. "I pointed out the first. The second lies beyond the castle at the front of the woods. If we're sent on an errand that requires speed, it's too cumbersome to navigate the walls. The horses stabled near the woods are always saddled. If we need them, we don't have the time to equip them."

Ash's brow creased as he let a grooms woman guide Autumnstar away. "Wearing a saddle and bridle without a rest must be a burden on the horse though, isn't it? Wouldn't it tire them before you rode?"

Larisa offered him a white-toothed smile. "Yes, it would. We rotate the horses every few nights, so they get more than enough rest. Besides, Farcaren has more groomsmen and women than any of the other kingdoms. The fear isn't that the horses aren't well cared for; it's that they're spoiled from groomsmen and women sneaking them treats." She winked.

A beanstalk-thin groomsman waited beside Grayhaven. He paled as Solarus removed his staff from its sling. However, the groomsman's poise never left him as he took Grayhaven's reins. He bowed deeply to Solarus and turned to depart. Kyra hesitated when another grooms woman held her hand out expectantly. How could she trust Raven to people she didn't know?

"The stables will be preferable to the outdoors for a time," the roan reassured Kyra. "You heard what they said about treats. I could use an apple myself. Preferably one with smooth, green skin. They're sweet and crunchy."

"I'll find some for you," Kyra promised. She released him to the grooms woman.

With the last of the horses gone, Larisa said, "If we return to the pedestrian gates, we can reach the hall more quickly." She set off in the direction of the main palace with a confident gait. Now at eye level with Larisa, Kyra noticed a brown leather scabbard at the guard's side. A beautiful silver hilt decorated with a sapphire in the center shone in the torchlight. Larisa's livery had an insignia embroidered over the heart. A dragon raised its left claw in a threatening pose, its tail wrapped around an arrow and a sword.

"The captain says you met years ago," Larisa told Hayden as they strode briskly. "He was anxious to know when you arrived."

"The captain?"

"Captain Callum. He said you trained him in sword fighting when he was younger."

Hayden's eyes lit up at the name. "Callum is the captain?"

"He was promoted a year ago next month," Larisa replied. She brushed her long blond hair over her shoulder. Kyra raked a hand through her own hair, suddenly very aware how disheveled she looked. "Callum deserves the title," Larisa continued as Kyra tried to surreptitiously free a knot. "He's outstanding. Callum speaks highly of you. He said he wouldn't have made the rank if not for your lessons."

"Callum gives me too much credit," Hayden replied as they passed through the door to the second ring. "I offered him tips. He worked harder and longer than any of the guards, even the more experienced ones."

"He's a bit of a perfectionist." Larisa and Hayden exchanged knowing grins. They walked through the last door to the inner courtyard.

"Wow," Ash breathed in awe. They had entered a stunning expanse of emerald green grass with flagstone footpaths. Large flames danced from iron sculptures that reminded Kyra of elongated coat hangers. The sculptures lined the paths in perfect symmetry. At the center of the yard was a large fountain, atop which was a statue of a man holding a jug to the sky.

"Have you been here before?" Kyra asked Ash as castle staff and guards walked with purpose down the footpaths.

"Hayden took me through the south of Farcaren when we first traveled to Silvias," Ash replied. "I had never left Calonia before then. Hayden and I stayed in the smaller towns but never came to Thanesgard. My father visited the city before though."

More questions flew to Kyra's tongue as Solarus walked up beside her. She was surprised by the disdainful expression Solarus wore. Kyra followed his gaze to servants who had stopped to stare at the group. Not the group, Kyra amended. Their eyes were fixed with suspicion and trepidation on Solarus' staff. A smaller crowd pointed at Talis, who had been silently inspecting the courtyard. Solarus' eyes narrowed. He angled his staff marginally. The servants hurried away, whispering to each other.

"How delightful," Solarus remarked in a piqued tone. He placed the staff on the ground. "Already they begin to gape and gawk." Seeing Kyra's questioning look, Solarus elaborated, "News of an elf and wizard in the castle will spread among the staff more quickly than a Peregrinian plague. Neither of our kind is often seen in the kingdoms of men. Certainly not both at once. We will be the source of gossip until we leave."

Meanwhile, Larisa had proceeded to a tower with a set of arched double doors and large iron handles. It was the largest of four towers within the courtyard. Two guards armed with spears stood at attention on either side. Hayden waited behind Larisa.

"Edyn, inform Reston that Master Hayden and his companions have arrived," Larisa instructed one of the guards. Edyn nodded. She pulled the iron handle to open the door and disappeared inside. Larisa turned back to Hayden.

"Thanesgard's steward, Reston—you may already be acquainted—will see to your supper and accommodations."

An amused expression lit Hayden's face. "We've met."

The doors opened again. Edyn stepped to the side, allowing a dumpy man to stomp out behind her. Bowl-shaped hair capped the steward's head. His outfit had enough lace and stitching to make Millie's art friends jealous. Around Reston's neck was a large key.

"I'll leave you with Reston." Larisa bowed elegantly to the group. "It was a pleasure meeting you."

Reston didn't acknowledge the guard as she departed. His eyes appraised the group with an expression of distaste. "Hayden," he stated.

Hayden smiled. "Greetings, Reston. You look well."

Reston scowled. "It was a miserable, damp, cold winter. I spent the season suffering from bouts of fever, earaches, and daily stomach pains. Aside from those trifling matters, yes, I'm '*well.*'"

Kyra heard Jyls snort as though trying to cover a laugh.

"You will sup in the guest dining room," Reston continued imperiously. "I hope the guard explained to you clearly and unequivocally that His Majesty is not to be bothered tonight. He has guests of great import." Reston's tart tone conveyed his belief that Kyra's group belonged to a category of 'not of great import.' "You should have sent word to His Majesty about your visit to Thanesgard before you arrived. It's a colossal inconvenience for my staff to scramble to accommodate you."

"For which we have the deepest gratitude and appreciation," Hayden responded diplomatically.

Reston hmphed. "This way." The steward stumped down a footpath to the left of the main doors.

Despite his short stature, Reston maintained a quick pace. He seemed eager to be rid of the king's guests, who were stealing precious time from the steward to return to whatever else he had planned to return to. Kyra double-stepped to keep up with her companions. They followed the path toward the next tower, passing a man dressed in a fancy doublet and stockings. The man greeted Reston. Reston grunted without looking in his direction. The man was unruffled and continued on his way. Kyra decided the citizens within Thanesgard were familiar with Reston's temperament.

The walkway led to the second tower. It had similarly arched doors, which a guard opened respectfully. Reston barged inside.

Kyra had expected the interior to be as spartan as the castle's pragmatic gray exterior. She couldn't have been more wrong. Kyra was barraged by a slew of discordant colors and textures. Like a car splattered with bumper stickers, it was hard to focus on any single picture or painting. Chandeliers sequined with diamonds hung from the ceiling and lined each side of the hallway. The floors were mosaics of blue, white, and yellow tiles.

Jyls, who strode in front of her, nudged Ash. He pointed to a large, unoccupied space on the wall. "They missed a spot."

Smothered by frames, it was as though the palace's interior needed at least one free square to breathe. Ash half-grinned as his eyes toured the palace in amazement.

Reston didn't slow his pace as he guided the group from hallway to room to hallway. Kyra's eyes seemed to travel a greater distance than her legs. Parlors overflowed with herds of furniture. The furniture looked more like extra items dumped haphazardly into an attic than décor for a king's home. Gaudy cushioned chairs and sofas shoved up against tables adorned with gemmed lamps and statues.

The crammed space was tricky to navigate. Despite his paunchy frame, Reston knew where to turn to squeeze between the objects. Jyls followed nimbly. Ash bumped into a candelabrum but clumsily managed to catch the piece as it fell. Kyra herself had to turn sideways to move between the furniture. She heard Solarus mumble crossly after several *thwacks* of wood against wood.

Reston trod into another hallway. When they reached an open arch opposite another parlor, the steward stopped. Kyra smelled a piquant aroma of spiced fowl and vegetables beyond the opening. Her mouth watered at the scent.

"Your meal is prepared," Reston said brusquely. His face was beet red, and his forehead was dotted with sweat. The steward removed a handkerchief from within his vest pocket, dabbed his forehead, and then gestured with the handkerchief to the arch. "There are servants in the dining hall should you require something. The kitchen was given scant time to prepare for an additional six guests." Reston stuffed the handkerchief back into his vest. "I will return in an hour to show you to your chambers. I expect you to be ready."

"Master Steward, we have need of items from our saddlebags," Solarus said calmly. "Might your attendants bring them to our rooms?"

Reston's lips pursed. He looked as put upon as a peacock among roosters. "I will look into it."

Jyls patted the steward jovially on the back, causing the key around Reston's neck to jangle. "Good man." Jyls sauntered into the dining room. Reston scowled.

Not owning anything that needed retrieving, Kyra followed Jyls. She winced as she entered the room. The extravagant chandeliers illuminated a room filled from gold. Geometric patterns were etched in golden walls and across the golden ceiling. Golden drapes hid windows. Two circular tables were garbed with golden cloths and place settings with golden cutlery. The brick fireplace was the blandest piece in the room.

"This is literally an eyesore," Kyra muttered.

Jyls took a seat with his back to the fireplace. He grinned, looking perfectly at home. Servants descended on the table with golden platters carrying meats and vegetables. Kyra's craving for a meal after hours of travel won out over her aching head. She and the rest of her companions took up places at the table and dug into the meal with relish.

When Kyra's initial hunger was sated, she turned to Hayden. "Are all palaces this . . ." Kyra searched for a tactful word and failed to find one.

Jyls swallowed a chunk of potato. "Garish?" he supplied. "Tasteless? A waste of citizens' taxes for a pathetic display of wealth? No. They aren't."

"It's impolite to insult your host, Jyls," Hayden said, cutting into a turnip.

"Servants aren't here to tell our good host," Jyls observed. He leaned back against his chair with his fork in hand. He pointed it at Hayden with a crooked grin. "Do you disagree? C'mon Hayden, you know I'm right."

Hayden's gaze never lifted from his plate. "I said it wasn't polite. I don't remember offering an opinion about the ornamentation."

As she finished her meal, Kyra's delight faded into remorse. It was the first time since leaving London that she was eating at a table, not around a campfire. Up until then, Kyra's time in Ilian had felt transitory. She thought that once she was armed with knowledge about her magic, Raff could take her back to James and Millie. Now sharing the meal at a table, with the prospect of sleeping in a bed, Kyra's sense of a short-term stay was turning into one of permanence.

As it had throughout the trip, guilt nettled Kyra. How could she feel happy believing Millie wasn't? Was Millie heartbroken? Did she feel abandoned? She remembered the joyful expression on Millie's face when she met her at the airport. How happy Millie was to have Kyra in her life. Then Kyra had been wrenched away without any explanation or goodbye. The cats would be some comfort, but they weren't exceptional conversationalists.

James said he would take care of her, Kyra reminded herself, choking back a sob. *He promised. And James told me to come here. I did the right thing.*

When Kyra lifted her gaze, she saw Hayden scrutinizing her with concern.

Jyls flagged down a servant. "I've heard His Most Magnanimous Majesty has the finest stores of claret in Ilian," he said. "Would you be so kind as to bring me half a shot, with another glass of coffee beans?"

The servant's brow wrinkled in confusion. "A shot of coffee beans?"

"Yes. In a separate glass from the claret."

Like the groomsman, the servant was too well mannered to show more surprise. "Certainly, sir. I will bring them." He bowed and left through the arch.

"The king has the finest stores, does he?" Solarus drawled with a disapproving look at Jyls. "The one you denounced for his tawdry furnishings?"

Jyls shrugged. "His décor is tasteless, not his claret."

The servant returned with the promised glasses, one filled with coffee beans, the other half-full of a viscous white liquid. He set both on the table. Kyra's nose wrinkled as the stench of alcohol wafted into the air. Jyls picked out three coffee beans and dropped them into the claret.

"What is it?" Kyra asked, trying to keep her thoughts from Millie.

"Claret, an expensive spirit and the elixir of royalty," Jyls answered. He swirled the liquid in the glass. "You won't catch me dead with a tavern's stale ale, but I'll not pass up a swig of claret with coffee beans." Jyls raised the glass with mock sincerity. "A toast. To light hands, heavy purses, and feet quick enough to enjoy them." He took a leisurely sip of the drink and sighed. "Jaren and Garen, how I've missed you."

Reston arrived punctually an hour later. The inconvenienced expression was buttoned on his lips. The steward wordlessly led the group up a winding set of stairs to the third floor. Candles in sconces ornamented the walls. They cast ambient light upon the four corridors that split off from the staircase. At the entrance to each hallway, shelves lined with small animal figurines protruded from the walls. They were too high for Kyra to distinguish whether the animals were dogs or wolves. They were crouched, teeth bared, as though to ward off unwelcome visitors. Kya felt a shiver go down her spine.

Reston veered to the left. The candle at the front of the hallway illuminated the first two doors on either side. The rest of the corridor faded to darkness. The steward cracked the nearest door ajar.

"These are the men's chambers," Reston said flatly. "The king has provided the first five for your comfort, which in my opinion is three more than necessary."

Jyls waltzed past Reston and flung the door wide open. He dropped onto a canopied, four-poster bed, sheets pulled tightly over the edges. His mud-caked boots hung over the edge.

Reston's eyes narrowed. "Your boots are to be left at the *door*. You are not to track in whatever sludge you have brought with you. Your moth-bitten cloaks are to be hung on the wall pegs. Whatever state in which you leave the room is what determines how much time your attendants will spend cleaning it in the morrow." The steward turned stiffly to Kyra as Jyls let out an exaggerated yawn. "The women's chambers are in the hallway around the corner. Yours is the third on the left. I assume you can find it without my assistance."

"Third room on the left," she repeated. "Thank you."

"Fine." The steward waddled toward the stairs without a farewell. His chain clicked against his neck.

Hayden and Talis took the second two rooms near Jyls while Solarus and Ash went across the hall.

"If you need anything," Hayden told Kyra, "don't hesitate to wake us."

Kyra left her companions and followed Reston's instructions. When she opened the third door in the hallway, Kyra was met with the sweet fragrance of flowers. Candles brightened an immaculate room with walls painted with star-shaped pink flowers. A bag of potpourri lay on a four-poster bed. There were nightstands, a tall wooden screen, a mirror, and a table with a washbasin. To Kyra's relief, a set of combs and powders was beside the basin. The rug covering the wooden floor didn't have a speck of dirt on it.

Kyra carefully removed her shoes and set them near the door. She walked to the screen and peeked curiously around it. A large tub roosted on golden legs. It was disappointingly empty. Kyra sighed. It had been too long since she had felt decently clean. Kyra settled for washing her hands, face, and neck with a bar of soap beside the basin.

After blowing out the candles around the room, Kyra flopped down on the bed. She rested her head on the fluffy pillows wearily. She extinguished the last candle on her nightstand. As the room plunged into darkness, Kyra's eyes closed. She felt loose feathers from the pillows scratch her hands, but the sensation wasn't enough to keep her from falling into a troubled sleep. Not at first.

Chapter 9

The itching finally woke Kyra. Eyes closed, she yawned and rubbed her hand absently. Her skin felt covered with a million mosquito bites. *I must be allergic to goose feathers*, Kyra thought grumpily. Millie's pillows never oozed their down.

The room was inky black as Kyra unwillingly opened her eyes. Almost inky black. A bright glow drew Kyra's gaze. She started, almost falling off the bed, as she registered what was happening. Golden energy swirled intensely around her hands.

Slipping off the bed, Kyra's eyes darted around the room. The golden energy jerked on her like a lasso. The glow illuminated shapes in the room as it pulled her forward. Heart pounding, Kyra tried to resist. Her efforts were futile. As it was with Orkanis' spell, the gold was in control. It directed Kyra toward the wooden screen. She looked left and right. The one time the gold had behaved with such authority was in the presence of other magic. Kyra silently reprimanded herself. Why hadn't she insisted Solarus teach her that night how to bring her magic to heel?

After a moment, Kyra stopped struggling. Instead, she gently slackened her grip on the gold. It was better to move on her own than be coerced. Kyra held out her hands to see more clearly. The gold steered past the tables, floated to the wooden screen, then coasted behind it. Kyra stepped around the screen to the bath. Her brow furrowed. She was facing the wall.

Boots scuffed the ground somewhere in front of her. Kyra tensed. They were accompanied by muffled voices. A man spoke in a high pitch. He was promptly silenced by someone else. Kyra stared at the spot.

The gold energy threw itself at the wall. Kyra guessed it sought to unite with whoever was on the other side. Kyra opposed her magic with all her might. Her rational mind screamed at her to run. If she felt the intruders' magic, they might feel hers in return. Still, Kyra's curiosity about the identity of the strangers rooted her to the spot. *Are there wizards in the castle? Could it be someone else, like an elf? What if it's Diamantas?* The thought of coming face-to-face with the nefarious wizard spiked Kyra's interest and stalled her decision of what to do.

Suddenly, Kyra's magic snapped like a rubber band stretched too tightly. She was flung backward. Kyra's elbow slammed against the ground as the gold vanished. The room instantly descended into darkness.

Kyra's head reeled as she lay on her back, elbow smarting. The sounds behind the wall were gone. Kyra slowly righted herself and leaned forward on her knees. Her fingers groped for the edge of the tub and found smooth porcelain. She pushed herself up gingerly. Then Kyra reached out her hand and brushed against the candle. That was good, but it needed a light. Kyra vaguely remembered seeing something that looked like large matches. Sliding her hand over the table, Kyra felt long, wooden pieces and something like sandpaper. *Ah ha.* Kyra snatched up the matches and struck them against the sandpaper block. A small flame sprouted to life. Kyra lit the candle and blew out the match.

Candle in hand, Kyra moved back to the wall. The flickering light illuminated the wooden slats. The upper portion was painted pink, though the color was faded. Flecks of paint chipped off at spots. The lower coat of paint was fresher and had no similar signs of wear. Kyra set the candle on the ground. She slid her fingers against the line where the two pinks met. One slat protruded outward. Heart drumming with anticipation, Kyra grabbed the uneven wood with her thumb and forefinger and pulled. A crack formed, large enough for Kyra to fit her hand in. She heaved again. The wall groaned open. Eyes wide, Kyra raised the candle. Behind the wall was a tunnel.

You should get Hayden, Kyra thought to herself even as the temptation to explore thrilled through her. *There could be dark wizards or someone else. You should really get Hayden.*

Kyra threw caution to the wind. She ducked into the opening. Cool air surrounded her. Her feet were uncomfortably cold as she stood in her socks on compacted earth. Shivering, Kyra lowered the candle to her knees. Boot prints covered the ground, slapdash and overlapping. She looked around. Who had been skulking in the hidden passage? Why? Had they accidentally happened upon her room or . . . The thought chilled her more than the ground. *Was someone spying on me?* Whoever it was had magic. That was reason enough for Kyra to hand the matter to someone more experienced.

***

Kyra sat in a stiff-backed chair beside a curtained window. Hayden paced, twisting his silver ring. His gray eyes were pensive. Kyra had double-checked the intruders hadn't entered the women's hallway before she skirted off to Hayden's room. She had hardly rapped on his door when he answered. To Kyra's surprise, Hayden was dressed in his travel clothes except for his leather jacket, which he had hung together with his cloak on a peg. Two candles lit his room. After listening to Kyra's breathless account, Hayden straightaway searched the walls of his room for similar passages. He discovered one on the other side of his bed. Unlike Kyra's, this tunnel was empty.

"I didn't expect whomever you overheard to loiter," Hayden said as he closed the slot between the wooden panels. "I should have anticipated spies. An elf, wizard, and woman in unusual attire would draw interest from more than a few individuals." His gaze remained on the wall as he walked back and forth.

"The king wouldn't be spying on us, would he?" Kyra asked. She shifted uncomfortably in the hard chair. "Larisa said he greeted us as guests."

Hayden's expression was grim. "All monarchs have networks of individuals tasked with learning the names and histories of their citizens. They also must be aware of everything that happens in their kingdoms and in those of their neighbors. Spies are the currency of the nobility. Today's ally could become tomorrow's enemy. Today's ally might even *be* the enemy but pretend otherwise. Trust is not easily gained or kept in the realm of royal politics. What worries me is the appearance of your magic again. We never found Adakis and Nymphrys. As far as I understood from your exchange with Solarus, your magic gravitates toward its kind." Hayden stopped abruptly. His face was half-hidden in the dim light, yet Kyra discerned a peculiar look in his eyes. "Did any of the blue-green magic manifest this time? Did it capture your magic as it did in Edoin?"

Kyra's shock paralyzed her words. After a moment, she managed to get out, "I never mentioned that to you."

The candlelight lit Hayden's half-smile. "Talis informed me after your briefing with Solarus. Don't worry. I haven't shared Talis' observation with anyone else."

"You didn't tell Solarus?"

"Not yet."

Kyra was taken aback by Hayden's wary expression. Logically, Solarus should, as the sole wizard in their group, be consulted about what happened. He might have an explanation for the strange appearance. Solarus might be able to divine who was controlling it. Yet Talis and Hayden chose to keep it secret. Did that mean they didn't trust Kyra? Or that they didn't trust Solarus?

"I'll speak with Arkin in the morning," Hayden went on, continuing to twist his ring. "Thanesgard may be infiltrated by spies, possibly dark wizards. I hoped we could rest here for awhile. Now we must avoid exposure to whomever was in the tunnels. We'll visit the marketplace in the morning and leave the city in the afternoon." Hayden stopped pacing. "You can't be alone tonight. I'll have Talis keep watch until the chambermaid arrives in the morning.

"One other note. No one knows you're a wizard. It benefits us to keep others ignorant of the fact. Which means when we have our audience with King Arkin tomorrow, you can't speak a word of your identity. The curtains behind the king's throne lead to two hallways not unlike the ones behind these walls. Assume someone is bending an ear to our conversation. Anything of consequence I will share with the king in private." Hayden glanced at the door. "Stay here. I'll get Talis."

Hayden silently slipped into the hallway. Kyra stifled a yawn. Sleep crowded her mind. She rested her elbow on the armrest. Kyra winced, forgetting it was sore, then leaned against her good elbow and rested her chin on her palm.

Hayden soon returned with Talis in tow. A knife was buckled to the elf's side. Kyra stood wearily. Together with Talis, she sneaked back to the opposite corridor, taking a candle borrowed from Hayden. Before she opened the door to her room, Kyra paused and glanced at her hands. No glow.

"Do you want my quilt?" Kyra whispered as Talis closed the door behind her.

"I wouldn't be a dutiful guard were I to sleep on my watch," the elf replied lightly. He strode toward the curtains. His hand ran over the dagger's hilt. "You can rest, Kyra. You won't come to harm."

Kyra set Hayden's candle on her nightstand. She pulled back her rumpled quilt and slid under it. Bleary-eyed, Kyra blew out the light. Suddenly, she smiled. As she had with Raff, Kyra wrapped herself up in Talis' protection more closely than the sheets drawn over her. "Thank you, Talis," she murmured. Kyra didn't hear his response as she faded into sleep.

***

A cord being pulled tight woke Kyra. Pale light pattered on her face. Another zipping sound accompanied by more light coaxed Kyra's lids open. *Morning already?* Hadn't she just fallen asleep? Kyra sat upright, eyes scrolling the room. Talis was gone. A young woman was finishing tying back the curtains to the large casement window. Outside, the morning sky was muted by moping gray clouds. Kyra stifled a yawn.

The woman glanced over her shoulder at Kyra. A sullen pout formed on her lips. She had a bulbous nose and dirty-blond hair secured into a bun by two long pins. The woman looked older than Kyra, though not by much. *She's the chambermaid,* Kyra recalled Hayden mentioning the night before.

"Good morning, milady," the chambermaid said blandly.

"Good morning," Kyra replied, rubbing an eye. "Could you tell me what time it is?"

The maid's expression was stony. She turned back to the curtains. "Eight, milady." She secured the curtains deftly with a knot. "You will find your companions in the courtyard at half past." The maid swept up a stack of large cloths she had placed on the nightstand and walked toward the washbasin. "The bath has warm water should you desire it."

Kyra grinned happily. "Thank you, that sounds grand."

The maid answered Kyra's cheerfulness with a sour look that could have curdled milk.

Kyra slid off the bed. She bent over to pick up her quilt, which had fallen off during the night. The maid paused mid-step. Her disparaging gaze went to the rug as Kyra placed the quilt over the sheets. Perplexed, Kyra looked down. To her embarrassment, Kyra saw the pristine fabric was spotted with dirt she had trekked in from the tunnel. Kyra's heart skipped a beat. Did the maid notice the tracks leading to the wall? Had she also discovered the tunnel?

If the maid had, or if she spied the faint footprints leading beyond the bath, she didn't mention it. The maid's gaze skipped from the rug to the bed. Kyra cringed inwardly. The previously unspoiled sheets had been sullied from the grime on Kyra's jeans and shirt from her days in the woods. Someone knocked on the door. The maid briskly strode to the door and opened it. Two girls tottered inside, swaying under the weight of the large buckets they carried. Steam rose from inside.

"Hurry up!" the maid snapped. The girls staggered toward the tub. Kyra stripped the socks from her feet as the maid folded her arms. "As I was saying," she resumed curtly, "you may use the bath as you wish."

Kyra read the maid's scowl as, "Use the bath and stay off of my once-clean, now grubby furniture. You look and smell like a farm animal."

It's not like I was rolling in mud, Kyra thought with a spike of irritation. *You try sleeping outside for a week. See what happens.* But Kyra smiled politely and said, "I'd love that, thank you."

Behind the screen came a loud splashing, followed by an "Oops!" from one of the girls. The maid's eyes narrowed. She stomped to the wooden screen. "Enough, you useless midges!" she scolded the unseen girls. "You have eyes, can't you see it's full? Get out before you flood the room!"

The girls dashed out from behind the screen and through the door. Huffing, the maid went to the basin and snatched up the large cloths. One she threw over the wooden screen. The other she dropped unceremoniously on the wet floor.

"I can take care of it," Kyra said. "Thank you for your help." She wondered what protocol was required to dismiss the woman.

The maid ignored her and mopped up the water. "Your new vestments are over on the chair. Leave your other . . . attire—" she glanced up disdainfully at Kyra's jeans, "—with the sheets. I will collect them later."

New vestments? Kyra thought back to the women she had seen on the road to Thanesgard. Some had worn dresses with lace and trimmings. Others were plain and rough-hewn. All seemed cumbersome and impractical for travel astride a horse. "I'd like to keep my jeans—my trousers," Kyra said. "They're very comfortable."

The maid snorted derisively and tucked the wet cloth under her arm. "The king has gifted you with garments of the finest quality. You would insult him if you didn't accept what he's given you."

"I'm grateful to the king for the, um, vestments. I just wanted to keep these in case . . ."

"You will not need those clothes," the chambermaid cut in coldly. She pivoted on her heel, the pins in her hair shaking. "If you require anything else, ring the bell beside the door." She bustled out of the room before Kyra could respond.

"Service with a smile," Kyra murmured as the door clicked shut behind her. She went to the chair, expecting the worst. Then she grinned. A velvety midnight blue cloak sat atop the pile of clothing. Kyra lifted the cloak and discovered it had two long pockets. It wasn't her wizard's cloak, but it was perfect for fitting in in Thanesgard. Kyra set the cloak aside. Underneath it was a soft, cream-colored shirt with long, flowing sleeves and a V-neck. A black belt was tied at the waist. A ribbed, formfitting lavender vest fit over the shirt. Black leather breeches completed the ensemble.

Kyra let out a relieved sigh. No unwieldy dresses. It was pragmatic attire not dissimilar to what she was already wearing. Untarnished leather boots were placed beside the chair. Kyra would have preferred a secondhand pair, already broken in. Still, she was grateful. Kyra's final accessories were three empty pouches, each the size of her hand. She made a note to ask Talis what they were for.

Steam infused with a subtle aroma of jasmine filled Kyra's nostrils. Kyra set aside the clothing. She had a much more important chore first.

"I've never been so happy to see hot water," Kyra said to the bath. Before shedding her clothing, Kyra carefully fished out the heptagon coin from her pocket. She placed it in one of the empty pouches. Then she undressed and slid into the tub.

The bathwater and flowers instantly soothed Kyra's weary muscles. To her wonder, Kyra saw the scrapes and cuts on her arms were healed. Kyra scrubbed herself free of grime and lathered her hair. When the water grew cold, Kyra considered ringing the girls to refill the tub. Then she remembered it was getting close to the time to meet Hayden. Kyra picked up the large cloth and toweled off. Kyra impatiently ran a comb through her damp tangled waves of hair. The knots unraveled. Kyra's smile broadened as she touched her smooth layers. She left the comb on the basin and went to get changed.

Fitting on her new clothing proved challenging. Kyra slipped the white shirt over her head, tying the laces in the back. She had more trouble with the vest and its petite buttons. After a fruitless attempt to get those near her neck, Kyra left them open. *Breathing takes priority over fashion anyway*, Kyra thought as she tugged on her collar. The trousers were comfortable.

Kyra sat on the chair and wriggled her foot into the right boot. Instead of a stiff heel, her foot touched a soft fur lining. Kyra quickly put on the left boot and clipped the buckles on each side. Standing, Kyra threw the cloak over her shoulders. The material fell loosely, the hem ending a few inches above her boots.

Thus outfitted, Kyra stepped in front of her mirror. A stranger looked back at her—someone who appeared confident and ready for the world.

Grabbing the three pouches, Kyra skipped out of the room and descended the winding staircase. At the bottom, Kyra paused. The hallway formed a T-intersection. She looked left, then right. Reston's demanding pace hadn't left Kyra time to orient herself as she walked. She would have to guess the way to the courtyard. Kyra settled on the hallway to her left. As luck had it, Kyra came upon a large door almost immediately. It was ajar, and Kyra smelled dewy air. Her hand was poised over the handle when she heard a voice trickle through the crack in the door.

". . . was furious, Catt," a young man was saying. "Bee told me that Dominique said that she heard Ollie was gossiping about her. Something about Bee having the personality of a cross-eyed pig with a stomachache. I think she's going to leave this time."

A crisp, crunching sound followed the man's words. "I'll be a priestess before Bee skips out of the royal life, Linden," a woman's deep voice replied with a short laugh. "Yes, that girl declares daily how awful court is. She says the ladies bicker and gossip like schoolgirls and the men posture like peacocks." There was a smile in Catt's voice as she chomped on something. "And you know what? Bee *loves* the drama. She's an earl's daughter. She's one of those nobles who shoves her way to join in the blather the way a pup in a litter vies for its mother's milk."

"Catt, you can't say that!" Linden said in a horror-stricken tone. "What if someone hears you?"

"They'd agree." Another crunch and chewing. "Bee's got a flair for groaning and griping. She's as tight with the court as a corset and as suffocating to those of us who have to listen to her. You heard her gabbing about that girl who came last night."

"I didn't hear it from Bee, but Dev mentioned the girl—he heard from Reston that her name's Kyra?—Dev mentioned she rode in with the company of men. *Without an escort*, Catt." Linden underscored the last sentence. "It isn't appropriate."

Kyra frowned. Cautiously, she eased the door open enough to peer outside. A woman leaned against one of the iron statues Kyra had seen the night before. Catt wore a blue blouse that ended at her elbows, a matching vest, and a white skirt. Catt's clever blue-green eyes made her otherwise unremarkable outfit striking. Golden hair was braided and pinned in a circle atop her head. Her cheeks were the same color as the peach that she bit into leisurely. Beside her was a guard in the livery of Farcaren. He was trying to assume a properly aloof expression but couldn't work the incredulity from his face.

"Oh? That's familiar muck men say about women. About *appropriateness*." Catt pushed off the iron statue. Walking in an arc around Linden, she continued, "I spend my day haggling and peddling and pushing wares to men. I don't care if they're from the gutters or the mansions. There's no one checking over my shoulder to see if the customers have their mind set on something other than the fruit and greens. What does that make me?"

A flustered Linden shuffled his feet. "I wasn't implying . . . Everyone knows you, Catt, they wouldn't . . ."

"My clients wouldn't be happy if anything happened to their supplier," Catt cut in. She dropped her gaze to the peach in her hand. "Who else in the market has peaches? They're not supposed to be ripe this time of year, but mine are. That's why I don't need an escort. And it's perfectly *appropriate*." She tossed the fruit into the air and caught it. "Funny, isn't it? Almost magical even."

Kyra held her breath. It sounded as though Catt used the word intentionally. Linden's face flashed with a look of terror. He cast a nervous glance around the footpaths. The palace grounds were starting to come to life with guards and servants hurrying down the paths.

"We weren't talking about my peaches and clients," Catt said nonchalantly. "We're talking about His Majesty's *scandalous* mystery guest. Bee says this girl—Kyra, is it?—said she's as hideous as a dust mite, rude as a cardjack, and fit for a who—I mean, a 'place of ill-repute,'" she amended, rolling her eyes. "Have to use proper terms. That means the girl's pretty as a sunset and polite as a *real* lady-in-waiting. I'll drop you a hundred florins if Bee didn't get that description from a friend who was as drunk as a Calonian sailor on a two-day pass at port."

Kyra covered her mouth, but a laugh slipped through. She noticed Catt's gaze flit to the door. Their eyes met for a fraction of a second before Kyra leaned away from the crack.

"Speaking of peddling, the morning sales have already started." Kyra heard Catt say more quietly. "Tell Jocelyn she'd better send a runner for the apples and peaches soonish. They sell out fast."

"I'll tell her."

There was a long pause. Kyra chanced another look outside, wondering if they had left. Catt's round face held an impish expression. She lobbed her half-eaten peach to Linden. The guard reflexively reached out his hands to catch the fruit. Catt removed a handkerchief from her vest and dabbed the fruit's juice from her mouth.

"Excuse me, my most noble guard." Catt deposited the handkerchief on Linden's shoulder. "I have to see if one of Braydon's Nine got an itch to nick a plum from my stall."

Catt sallied off. Her cheerful whistling faded as she rounded the corner. With a sigh, Linden took the handkerchief from his shoulder. He wrapped the peach within it and wiped the peach's nectar from his hands.

Kyra heard footsteps behind her as servants got to their tasks. She pushed open the door and walked out under the moody skies. Linden was stuffing the remains of the peach and handkerchief in a trouser pocket.

Kyra cleared her throat. "Excuse me. Hi."

The guard leapt. The peach tumbled from his hand as Linden regarded Kyra.

Kyra smiled widely. "My name is Kyra. Can you help me?" She was pleased to see the guilt that splashed over Linden's face. *Serves him right for accusing me of behaving 'inappropriately.'* "I'm supposed to meet my friends near the fountain, but I'm a bit lost. Could you show me where it is?"

The guard's face reddened. "Of course, Lady . . . my lady. It's this way."

Linden led Kyra down one of the paths. The iron statues disappeared and opened up to a large, green courtyard. Kyra heard the gentle spattering of the fountain's water. The many intersections of the paths here were busy with servants. Kyra spotted Jyls loitering by himself beside the fountain. So, Kyra wasn't late.

Jyls ran a thumb absently over the bird pendant around his neck. When he noticed Kyra, Jyls straightened. He offered her an exaggerated bow.

"Ah, there's the princess now," Jyls announced. His eyes trailed to Linden. "Has the princess acquired her own guard?"

Linden hurried away without a parting farewell.

"He showed me how to get here, that's all," Kyra replied to Jyls' raised brow.

Jyls shrugged. "I had a bet with Ash you would be late."

"That I'd be late?"

"Of course. What with powdering your nose and freshening up with perfume and drowning your hair in seed oil for that wonderful sheen. I didn't bet you'd be wearing trousers and boots, though." Jyls considered her. "You look like you're off to hunt us some breakfast, not to regale a king."

"Really." Kyra ran a hand through her wavy layers, enjoying their softness. "I didn't powder my nose or spritz myself with perfume. I *did* wash my hair and made myself presentable." She pretended to inspect Jyls as she tapped her lips. "I'm guessing someone forgot to leave you a comb. And a bar of soap. Should I lend you mine?"

Jyls had a giant grin slapped on his face. He patted his nest of straw-colored hair. "Kind of you to offer, Milady. Sadly, I must decline. I can't preserve my manly presence fragranced like flowers."

The rest of their companions soon arrived at the fountain. She guessed Hayden had shared news about the spies with Solarus and Ash. The wizard's countenance was wary as his gaze followed others on the footpath. He gripped his staff firmly. Ash also glanced uneasily around the courtyard.

Hayden smiled at Kyra. "They fit you well," he said, indicating the clothing with a nod. "I asked Reston to provide you with garments that were appropriate for travel. You look more like you come from Calonia or Peregrine with that outfit. I prefer you to wear something practical at the expense of enduring questioning looks."

"Jaren and Garen help you if the king thinks you're from Peregrine," Jyls said with a sly smile. He turned as someone coughed loudly.

Reston stood behind them. His garb was showier than the previous day's, with a gold cap, green and gold doublet, striped green leggings, and white shoes. Reston's neck was adorned with several golden necklaces in addition to his giant golden key. Kyra wondered how his neck and shoulders didn't bend like willow branches under the weight.

"His Majesty is ready to receive you in the throne room," Reston told the group waspishly. He turned and double-stepped down the footpath toward the center tower. The companions followed.

The double doors to the palace were flung open when they arrived. Reston stomped inside. Hayden and Solarus stood together as the steward's voice rang out, "Presenting Lord Hayden and his company, Your Majesty!"

"Have them enter," replied a silky voice.

Hayden glanced over his shoulder. "Be careful what you say," he told Kyra out of the corner of his mouth.

Talis came beside Kyra as Hayden and Solarus proceeded through the doors. His posture was relaxed, but his eyes were serious. "We're next," he said to Kyra. A golden carpet rolled out like a tongue from the entrance. Kyra expected the room to be as hideous as the others in the palace. Strangely, excepting the carpet, the throne room was conspicuously devoid of decoration. There were no windows, no furniture, and no paintings or tapestries. Candelabra fixed in the wall provided the only light into the windowless chamber. As Kyra automatically walked in sync with Talis, she noticed the carpet was like a runway designed to draw the attention of the audience to a single point: a raised dais atop which sat two midnight blue thrones.

The king waited in one of the regal chairs. He sat straight-backed, square chin tilted slightly upward. The king's elbow rested on the gold-braided arm of his throne. His fingers drummed on the edge. Reston stood at attention near an open archway at the far end of the room. Behind the thrones, curtains were drawn closed. Goose bumps pricked Kyra's skin as she recalled Hayden's words. Were spies watching them at that very moment, concealed behind the curtains' folds?

As they approached, Kyra spied a midnight blue statue of a wolf. It hunkered at the foot of the king's throne. The translucent glass seemed to absorb and refract the light from a candelabrum. The wolf's hackles were raised, body coiled and set to spring. Kyra remembered the statues in the hallways near the guest rooms. She knew now they were smaller versions of what stood before her.

The wolf's most realistic feature were its eyes—dangerous, calculating, and energized by the promise of prey. The lifelike appearance of the statue struck Kyra as oddly familiar. She couldn't place why.

Hayden and Solarus stopped at the steps to the dais. The throne sat high above the carpet, allowing Arkin to look down at his visitors. Kyra guessed the throne was designed to make the king seem superior to anyone else in the room.

"King Arkin," Hayden said, keeping his head low. "It is an honor to see you again, Your Majesty. Thank you for this audience. We appreciate the value of and demands on your time."

"Welcome, Hayden," Arkin greeted in a smooth tone. His head was angled as Hayden and Solarus straightened. "I was surprised to learn from my scouts that you and your companions were within Farcaren's borders." The king's lips pulled back into a shallow smile. "It is a welcome and timely surprise."

Kyra studied Arkin. A circular, golden crown nested on his sheared gray hair. His accoutrements were of the Farcaren midnight blue. A golden belt girdled the king's waist, and a cape pooled at his feet. Not a hair or thread was out of place. The king's bearing struck Kyra as stiff, reserved, and formal. His pale brown gaze hadn't an ounce of warmth as he scrutinized Hayden.

Hayden and Solarus straightened. The throne sat high enough above the carpet that Hayden had to tilt his head upward to meet the king's gaze. "I also offer my sincerest condolences, Your Majesty." Hayden's tone was stricken. "The news of the queen's illness came to me but recently. I would have done whatever was in my power to help her and the child. I am truly sorry. Genevieve was one of the kindest and most compassionate individuals ever to grace Ilian."

Arkin's expression blackened. His fingertips turned white as he gripped the armrest. "She was. A man's loss of a virtuous wife and his innocent child should be but a tale sung by troubadours to bring their audiences to weeping. It should not be real. Yet I have experienced this tragedy. And I tell you, there are no songs that relate the agony one feels when such a horror comes to pass. Had I known Genevieve's time in this land was so short, I would have made many different decisions." Arkin's eyes flickered to the wolf statue at his feet. An indecipherable expression formed on his lips. "Genevieve was fond of you, Hayden. She admired your loyalty. Genevieve told me she hoped our child would display such fidelity. He never had the chance."

Hayden's gray gaze seemed swallowed in a thick haze, as though he were trapped within himself. He pressed a thumb against his silver ring. "I have faith that Inishmore has delivered her and your child to the Healer, Your Majesty."

Arkin rested a bejeweled hand on the head of the wolf. He resumed his tapping on the chair with his other. "Faith should be placed in those who deserve it," he replied coolly. "And those who deserve that faith today may not merit it tomorrow. However—" the king turned his head, his gaze ranging to the others, "—to mourn the past is unproductive for those living in the present. Let us not neglect your companions."

Kyra copied her friends' action of bowing. Her heart pounded anxiously. She reproached herself for not paying more attention to Mr. Dullwane's lessons on court etiquette. *Or memorizing lines from Shakespeare's plays*, Kyra thought as she rose. It would have been something to go on.

Arkin leaned forward. The crown didn't budge as though glued to his hair. "Solarus," he stated. "You are still a friend of Farcaren."

Kyra wasn't the only one to notice the question in the king's flat tone.

Solarus' jaw tightened. He shifted the staff slightly in his hand. "Should I not be?"

"Unlike others, you will find that I do not consider a wizard a threat. On the contrary, I find a wizard a worthy asset. I am honored that you came, Solarus."

"I thank you for your hospitality." Solarus bowed, though more rigidly than before.

Anger welled inside Kyra. The distaste in Arkin's pale eyes belied his friendly words. But as the king turned to Talis with a smile, Kyra wondered if she was wrong in judging him. Maybe all monarchs came across as unsympathetic or aloof.

"Talis of the Elven Realm," Arkin continued. "Is Queen Carina well?"

"She is, Your Majesty. *Raenalyn* Carina sends her blessings to you and the people of Farcaren."

Arkin nodded, not seeming to expect or require elaboration. His eyes browsed Ash, Jyls, and finally Kyra. His gaze lingered on Kyra with an interested expression. "Hayden, I am not yet acquainted with the rest of your company."

"This is Ash of Hillith." Hayden stepped to the side and beckoned for the healer. "Ash joined us a year past. He is an accomplished healer."

"Ash of Hillith," the king repeated. "Your father was Parthan, the healer of great renown, was he not?"

Ash shifted uncomfortably. "Parthan was my father, Your Majesty."

Arkin rubbed his beard appraisingly. "You bear a strong resemblance. Parthan was a guest in Thanesgard on several occasions. There is no shortage of tales about his courage, yet your father was always humble. He refused accolades. It is said Parthan saved King Isman's life during the Battle of Borath. Your father said merely that the king lived. Parthan claimed he played a small part. King Isman made it known that your father's role was anything but marginal."

Ash's neck reddened. He started to rub his black tattoo self-consciously, then quickly dropped his hand. "My father told me Inishmore bestowed skill and luck during the battle, Your Majesty. King Isman had suffered shallow injuries when my father tended him. The king had neither punctured organs nor broken bones. As my father explained it, the blood that stained the king's clothing made it seem as though he was mortally wounded. Really, the king could have been treated by any medic in his court. My father believed soldiers embellished his deed to bring themselves comfort, Your Majesty. That even if they were grievously injured, a healer could restore them to life."

Arkin nodded. "We all mourned Parthan's premature death. However, I, like many, see great aspirations for his son. It is not every day providence brings a true healer to Thanesgard." Arkin's tenuous hold on his smile slipped. "Had you been at court for Genevieve, I am certain she would have lived. If you ever grow weary of travel and seek a place of comfort, you are most welcome in my court."

"Thank you, Your Majesty," Ash said quietly.

"To our lady in the company." Arkin's pale eyes raked Kyra's appearance. The corner of his lips upturned in an expression that bordered on a smirk. "Reston mentioned Hayden's request for special attire. I admit I was surprised. Farcaren women are envied throughout Ilian for their fashions and fineries of dress. However, Hayden does nothing without consideration. Why, then, this outfit?"

Kyra did her best to mimic Talis' neutral expression. "These clothes are the finest I've ever worn, Your Majesty. I'm grateful for your gifts, especially the cloak."

She saw Hayden give her a tacit nod of approval.

"Then this is clothing to which you are accustomed." Arkin's eyes bore into hers. "Reston also informed me of the distinctive garments in which you arrived. Trousers made of a material that has never been traded in Farcaren's marketplace. As well as the shoes. I assume these were fashions from another kingdom." His eyes glinted. "What is your name?"

"Kyra, Your Majesty."

"Of?"

"Of?" Kyra repeated, confused, then belatedly inserted, "Your Majesty?" From the corner of her eye, Kyra noticed concern crease Hayden's brow.

"From which kingdom do you hail? Peregrine? Calonia? Or do you hail from nowhere?"

Arkin didn't hide the scorn in his voice. The anger that simmered in Kyra's heart rose to a boil. Nobility didn't give the king a pass to act however he chose.

"Your Majesty," Hayden interjected. "Kyra's background is unique. To ask her from where she hails is . . ."

"Silvias." Kyra unflinchingly met Arkin's piercing stare. "I'm Kyra of the kingdom of Silvias."

The king drummed his fingers on the armrest as though looking to drill a hole in the material. "Silvias, as I understand it, is the *Elven* Realm, Lady Kyra. Do you have elven blood?"

Before Kyra could retort, Talis put a hand on her arm. "*Raenalyn* Carina requested she be raised in the Elven Realm," he answered for her. "The circumstances under which she was brought to us were unique. *Raenalyn* Carina declared it was Inishmore's will that brought Kyra to Silvias. She allowed Kyra to remain in the Elven Realm."

Kyra felt an outpouring of warmth for Talis for intervening, though she was certain the nebulous answer wouldn't sate Arkin's curiosity. The king's arched brows confirmed her theory.

"How unusual. However, Kyra of Silvias, if the queen believes you were foreordained to live among the oldest of races in Ilian, I would be foolish to question her wisdom." Arkin's slick smile made Kyra's skin crawl. "Your destiny must lie in building the great future of our kingdoms."

Kyra wasn't sure, but she thought she saw Hayden and Talis exchange an enigmatic glance.

"And *I,* Your Majesty, am Jyls." Jyls gave the king a perfected bow. Arkin's attention strayed to him, his brows knitting. "I hail from everywhere. Or nowhere, as Your Majesty prefers."

Arkin's lips screwed together with mild displeasure. "You are the company's jester then."

"Of a sort," Jyls answered without missing a beat. "I am replete with wit and raillery. I am able to upend the condescending and steady the unstable."

"Interesting." The king's gaze combed Jyls. He gestured with his bejeweled hand. "What need would a jester have for such an outfit? There are other professions to which such a profusion of pockets is suited. Particularly for one from Peregrine. From where you may come if you come from everywhere."

"A jester has need for many props, Your Majesty." Jyls pulled at the sides of his trousers. "Jesters must estimate a man's character before choosing the words with which to entertain him."

To Kyra's surprise, Arkin seemed amused by Jyls' answer, as though facing a respected adversary. "Well put, Jyls of Everywhere." Arkin turned his head toward the archway. "Reston."

The pudgy steward waddled forward. His hands were at his sides. In the exchange with Arkin, Kyra had completely forgotten Reston was present. Even his key had been obediently silent, though it now clinked against his many necklaces.

"You will see to their accommodations for the remainder of their time in Thanesgard," the king instructed. He looked at Hayden. "Which is . . . ?"

"That is a matter about which I hoped to speak with you in private," Hayden answered.

"Reston will schedule a time for us to converse. The delegation requires my attention. The politics within our kingdoms are as fickle as ever."

"At your leisure, Your Majesty."

Arkin rose. His cloak swept the sides of the floor. He stood as straight as a column, as though he and his gold crown were a statue carved from a single piece of marble. "Would you visit the marketplace?"

"Our provisions are low," Hayden said. "I will use our time this morning."

The king nodded. "If you lack funds, tell the vendors they can settle your debts with the royal treasury."

"That is a great kindness," Hayden replied with a bow.

"It is a modest one. Reston, see to it that Hayden and his companions have a decent meal before they leave for the market."

Arkin departed neatly through the open arch and disappeared into an adjoining room. Reston cleared his throat loudly. He lumbered down the dais and onto the golden carpet. Hayden, Talis, and Ash parted as the steward bowled through. Reston's chin was tilted so high it looked like he was inspecting the ceiling for imperfections. Kyra grinned.

Reston took them outside to the courtyard. As they walked, Kyra mentally mapped their path using landmarks they passed. The steward led them to another door and zipped inside.

Hayden dropped back next to Kyra and Jyls, who took up the rear of the group. "You two shouldn't antagonize the king," he admonished in an undertone. "Namely because it isn't proper decorum. It is also because Arkin is one of our staunchest allies against Diamantas."

Kyra bit her lip to suppress an affronted response. Jyls had intentionally provoked the king, not her. Kyra had defended herself against Arkin's abrasive questions. How could Hayden blame her for that?

Jyls, on the other hand, displayed no signs of shame. "King or no king, ally or no ally, he's obnoxious."

"I have heard the same said about you," Solarus deadpanned. He walked beside Ash, though his head was turned so that he saw Jyls from the corner of his eye.

"I embrace my vexing qualities. I'm also not the ruler of a kingdom. Your expectations should be much lower."

Solarus' eyes narrowed. Reston suddenly stopped. Kyra saw they had arrived at the dining hall where they had eaten the previous night. Servants were scuttling into the room like cockroaches, carrying pitchers of water, cups, mugs of coffee, and plates with fruit and pastries.

"Wait here," Reston ordered.

"Hayden," Solarus said nonchalantly as Reston marched into the dining room. "It occurred to me that the mice that pattered behind your wall last evening may well be an infestation. In fact, I would not be surprised if they seek a morsel of our morning meal."

Kyra's brow furrowed. *What mice?* She glanced from Solarus to Hayden.

Hayden rubbed his ring thoughtfully. "That may well be. Where you find one rodent, many more remain hidden." He watched Reston gesture furiously at a servant who had dropped silverware on the ground. "Talis," Hayden asked as the servant hastily bent down to scoop up the cutlery, "do you have such problems in Silvias?"

The elf's eyes were on the activity in the dining room. His head was angled to the side. Talis wasn't looking at anything in particular; instead, he hearkened to the noise around them. "We do. Mice are cautious when they perceive others are nearby. They appreciate the need for silence. If there's a wall between us and them, it would be even more difficult to hear them. Even if some are present while we dine, I'm not sure we would notice."

Hayden nodded. "Kyra, do you remember our conversation from last night? When we discussed what topics were appropriate to raise in front of the king? Those same guidelines apply here. It's considered ill-mannered to discuss one's personal life in public."

"Oh." Kyra finally caught on to Hayden's meaning. The "mice" behind the walls translated into the spies. She nodded. "Sure, I remember."

"Good."

"You may go in." Reston had reappeared. He tapped his foot impatiently.

Hayden inclined his head and went in first. Kyra followed, heart racing. *Talis may not have heard anyone behind the walls in the dining room,* she thought as she took a seat by one of the gold place settings, *but the spies could be anywhere.* Kyra folded her hands under the table. She wouldn't talk about magic openly. Any golden energy, however, would give her away. Kyra smiled wryly. Seeing as how the dining room was clothed in gold itself, someone might think a glint of golden magic was simply a reflection of the chandelier's light. Still, it was better not to take that chance. Her companions' chatter turned to white noise as Kyra spent the meal silently warding off the gold.

***

After a while, the strain of concentration scrubbed away Kyra's appetite. Halfway through the meal, she rose from her chair. "I'm going to walk around the courtyard," she told Hayden. "It's beautiful outside."

Hayden's brow knitted. "We'll join you shortly."

Kyra was grateful. She needed time alone. Besides, Kyra thought, she couldn't be in any more danger in an open space than she was with spies snooping around the castle. After taking a couple of wrong turns, Kyra found the palace's main entrance. The doors were open. Sunlight bathed Kyra as she stepped outside. The clear blue sky complemented the brilliant emerald green courtyard and marble white fountain. She breathed in the smell of pre-summer warmth. People promenaded, quickstepped, and dallied down the intersecting paths. Tilting her head back toward the rays, Kyra closed her eyes. The fountain water splashed tranquilly.

Until a sharp bellow cut into the peaceful sounds. Kyra's eyes flew open in alarm. In the distance, she heard steel clanging against steel. Kyra wildly cast a gaze around the footpaths. Strangely, no one had slowed their pace or looked for the source of the clamor. Kyra's head swiveled left and right. She pivoted toward the path to her left and sprinted down it.

She followed the sound of screeching metal. It grew louder as she made a sharp turn that took her around the palace to a smaller, circular courtyard. It was empty, save for a man encircled by three individuals in black cloaks. One of the cloaked individuals held a sword. Another twirled a pair of daggers. The last wielded a staff. Kyra took in a sharp breath. She had found the spies.

Chapter 10

The man wore a grim expression as he faced off against the attackers. He wielded a sword in his left hand and a shield in his right. His face glistened with sweat. Platinum blond hair swayed across his brow. The man's blue and silver uniform stuck to his skin as he spun on his heel. His lustrous brown eyes kept the spies in sight.

Finally, Kyra thought as she ran. *Magic is going to be useful for once.* She raised her hands in anticipation, ready for the golden energy to spring to her fingertips. Yet there was no tingling, no prickling. Kyra glanced down. Her eyes widened in disbelief. Her hands were conspicuously absent of the golden glow.

"You've got to be kidding me!" Kyra exclaimed. "Come on. Now's the time to show up."

The golden energy obdurately refused her angry command.

Kyra dropped her hands. "Fine." She didn't have time to think about it. The spy with the dagger had lunged forward, his blade aimed high. The man deflected the blow with his shield while spinning away from the spy's immediate second jab.

Kyra raced toward the spy with the staff. Her boots clacked loudly against the stone. Hearing her steps, the spy glanced over his shoulder. His surprise slowed his defense. Remembering the pain of gripping Nymphrys' staff in Edoin, Kyra slipped close to the spy and grabbed a fistful of his thick cloak. Kyra planted her leg behind the spy's leg and shifted her hip. The spy gave a startled yelp as Kyra yanked him off-balance. He countered by seizing Kyra's wrist. He pulled Kyra down with him as he fell. Kyra flew forward and instinctively turned her shoulder toward the ground. As they hit the earth, Kyra and the spy simultaneously released their hold on each other. Kyra rolled harmlessly to her feet. The spy crouched, staff horizontal at his side.

Kyra's gaze dipped to her hands. No glow. *What if the spies aren't wizards?* She chanced a look at the embattled man. He had trapped the spy's sword under his boot and kicked sideways. The man's heel struck the spy's chest, sending him flying backward. A sly grin replaced the man's grave expression. He shifted his boot off the spy's blade.

"How's the view from down there, Dev?" he asked. The spy groaned in response.

Baffled, Kyra stared at the man. He used the back of his hand to wipe his hair from his brow. His tone was bantering, not angry or nervous. And he knew the spy's name . . . ?

The man suddenly lifted his brown eyes from the spy on the ground to Kyra. His grin morphed into bewilderment. "Who are you?" he demanded. The spy with the daggers paused and turned to regard Kyra as well. When Kyra didn't respond, the man looked back at the spy on the ground. "Dev, did you bring a recruit? I wasn't expecting anyone else."

Dev levered himself onto his elbow, breathing hard. "Wasn't me, Captain. I've never seen her before."

Kyra's heart dove into her stomach as the individual with the daggers lowered them. It wasn't an ambush by spies. It was a training exercise.

The man lowered his shield and sword. His gaze trailed from the man with daggers to the man with the staff. "Larisa? Nikolas?"

One of the attackers set his staff on the ground. He pulled back the cowl to his cloak. He was as thin as an asparagus spear, his hazel eyes set in an aged, unshaven face. He shook his head. "I've never seen her before either, Captain."

Could this get any more embarrassing? Kyra thought with growing mortification.

"Oh! You were with Hayden yesterday, weren't you?"

Apparently, it could get more embarrassing. A woman sheathed her daggers and shook off her cowl. It was Larisa, the guard who had escorted Kyra and her companions the day before. Her blonde, glossy hair was tightly braided and pinned up on her head. Kyra rubbed the back of her neck. She looked everywhere but at the beautiful female guard.

Larisa smiled reassuringly at Kyra. "I hope we didn't scare you. Captain Callum rotates training sessions with members of the Royal Guard during the week. I should have mentioned you might see us." The female guard turned to the captain. "It's all right, Captain, she—your name is Kyra, isn't it?—Kyra is one of Hayden's companions who arrived yesterday."

Hearing Hayden's name, Callum's eyes lit with surprise and delight. He returned his sword to its scabbard. As he came forward, the captain's jaunty grin spread across his youthful face. Kyra guessed Callum was Jyls' age, yet he carried himself with the confidence of someone experienced beyond his years. Callum's uniform matched that of his companions except for the collar. It bore three gold stripes on one side, as did both shoulders. Kyra's neck grew hot. Callum was undeniably handsome.

"I wasn't expecting assistance," Callum commented, happiness flowing from his words. "I'm charmed to have received it from a friend of Hayden's." He gave her a gentlemanly bow. "Thank you, Lady Kyra."

The heat spread to Kyra's cheeks. Callum seemed to expect a response, but Kyra felt her tongue tied in a thousand knots. Gratefully, she was spared from answering.

"Callum! Kyra!" she heard Hayden shout. "Are you alright?"

Kyra and the captain turned as one to see Hayden marching over. Callum's grin widened. As Nikolas grasped Dev's hand and helped him to his feet, the captain set the shield on the ground.

"Hayden!" Callum exclaimed. He stepped forward to meet Hayden. They clasped hands. "Larisa told me last night you were in the castle. I was going to look for you after this morning's bout. You saved me the effort." Callum turned to his three guards. "We're finished for today. Well done. Larisa, you were exceptional with your footwork. I can tell you've been practicing."

Jealousy pricked at Kyra as Larisa beamed. Kyra felt the intense urge to point out she had disarmed one of Callum's highly trained guards without the protection of a weapon. That was more impressive than Larisa's use of her daggers.

"Thank you, Captain, but Dev and Nikolas were equally skilled," Larisa replied humbly.

Callum again wiped sweat from his brow with the back of his hand. He glanced down at the guard rubbing his sore chest. "Apologies about that last one, Dev. I'm surprised the hit landed so squarely. My form left a lot to be desired."

"No harm done, Captain," Dev replied. He retrieved his sword from the ground. Larisa and Nikolas bowed deeply.

"That was humiliating," Kyra heard Dev mutter as they started down the footpath.

Larisa laughed a golden laugh. "Don't worry," she replied. She took Dev's hand in hers and gave him an affectionate peck on the cheek. "I still love you. Looks like I'll be the knight coming to your rescue. Until the end of your days."

Dev squeezed her hand tenderly. "You are my beautiful and valiant heroine," he said.

Larisa laughed again. Nikolas strode silently beside them, hands folded behind his back. Larisa and Dev's voices faded as they traced their way around the corner and out of sight.

Kyra's attention returned to Callum. He rubbed his chin and was appraising her in a way that she found strikingly reminiscent of Arkin. "I don't believe they were prepared for such an uneven pairing," Callum said. "It's good for them to encounter an unanticipated situation. I'm sure they thought I had orchestrated your arrival." He laughed. "Of the four of us, I was the one most taken off guard by your appearance."

"I'm sorry," Kyra apologized, finally unraveling her tongue. "It didn't occur to me there was training. I heard a shout when I came outside and thought someone was in trouble. Then I saw you being attacked by what I thought were the . . ." Kyra caught the word *spies* and swallowed it back. "Well, I wasn't sure who. Honestly, I was focused on the fact that you were outnumbered and needed help. It looked like you needed help," Kyra tried to amend too late. She realized the last sentence made it sound like she viewed the captain as a poor defender. Kyra unconsciously tucked a lock of hair over her ear and cast a glance at Hayden. His expression was caught between reprimand and praise.

Kyra now noticed the rest of her companions on the footpath. A pit formed in her stomach when she saw Solarus. Unlike Hayden, his eyes screamed his rebuke.

"It was brave of you to intervene," Callum interrupted, waving off her apology. "Three against one aren't good odds for anyone. I do ask that you excuse me for meeting you in such an unkempt and filthy condition. I'm normally graced with only Hayden's presence, which doesn't require me to be well-groomed."

Self-conscious that her companions were within earshot, Kyra smiled awkwardly. "I don't mind. It was impressive, the way you avoided Larisa's attack. I was watching you. Your form. I mean, your technique," Kyra inserted hastily. She heard Jyls snicker behind her. "You made it look easy. I've never used a sword before, or I can't remember using one, but I'd like to learn how." She groaned inwardly. *Can this get any worse?* It was embarrassing enough that Callum's smile made her as tongue-tied as a child with her first crush. She was mortified her statements came across as though she were asking Callum, the captain of the Royal Guards, to personally tutor her in tediously basic moves. And yet . . . Kyra couldn't deny that that was *exactly* what she was asking. She had genuinely been mesmerized by Callum's lithe swordsmanship. But not as much as Kyra had been mesmerized by the handsome captain himself.

Jyls attempted to smother his laugh as a cough, which fooled no one.

"If you believe my technique adequate, I will happily give you instruction," Callum responded in a teasing tone. "Though it seems you can defend yourself without it."

Kyra felt an excited flutter in her stomach. He *had* noticed after all.

Callum turned back to the group. "Solarus, Talis, good to see you also. Who are your other companions?"

Hayden introduced them as he had with Arkin. Unlike the king, though, Callum graciously said, "I give you my welcome in addition to the king's."

"I hear congratulations are in order," Hayden told Callum. "A promotion to captain of the Royal Guards is no small feat."

Hayden's smile was one of pride, a mentor sharing the joy of his mentee's success. Callum straightened his collar, which was splotched with sweat. "It's owing to you that I received my new rank. There were only so many times I could land on my rear before my dignity objected. After that, I trained. And trained. And trained some more. I trained until the soreness I felt was in my feet from standing too long. Padric ensured my hands were well callused by ordering me to have double-sessions every day for a month before he retired. It was Padric's recommendation that the king choose me to succeed him as captain." Callum ran a hand along the elaborately stitched scabbard at his side. "I wonder how I would fare against you now, Hayden. Poorly, I imagine."

"Perhaps, perhaps not," Hayden replied good-naturedly. His gray eyes grew serious as he dropped his voice. "Since I saw you last, there have been incidences throughout Ilian involving the dark wizards. I will speak with the king this afternoon, but it would bring me peace of mind if you were apprised of recent events. Farcaren may already be affected."

Callum's fingers moved to the hilt of his sword. His fingers wrapped around the steel tightly as he briefly surveyed the courtyard. "We've also received reports from our scouts," he replied quietly. "A few months back, they observed greeloks on our northwestern border with Hogarth. I sent communications to my counterpart in Dunestor. King Theon dispatched a contingent of soldiers to the area. He also sent a second company south to root out other greelok packs. From last we heard, the soldiers found no trails of greeloks in that part of Hogarth. I think the greeloks have either remained in Farcaren or moved into Edoin. That's why I am holding more sessions with the Royal Guards," he added in a somber tone. "They're not exercises of luxury but of necessity."

Hayden exchanged a look with Solarus. The wizard listened attentively. His eyes reflected the gravity in Hayden's expression. "We came from Edoin," Hayden told Callum. "There were Reapers. No greeloks."

Callum's eyes flashed with alarm. "Reapers?"

"Yes. There are other threats we might face beyond the dark wizards. These are closer to, or already within, Thanesgard. It's best we discuss this outside the castle walls, away from prying eyes and ears."

"That seems prudent." The captain looked thoughtful. "Your audience with the king is in the afternoon?" When Hayden nodded, Callum said, "I would prefer for us to speak now, but I ordered a weapons inspection this morning. It wouldn't do for a captain to break his own rules on punctuality. We could meet under the clock tower in Thanesgard's marketplace. Three o'clock? Unless you get word the king wishes to see you sooner, of course."

"That's plenty of time for us to buy what we need."

Callum clapped Hayden on the shoulder. He picked up his shield from the ground and slung it over his back. Then he bowed as low as the shield would allow. "My good gentlemen." His brown eyes strayed to Kyra. "My good lady."

Kyra's stomach did another somersault. She nodded, averting her eyes.

Callum turned on his heel and strode down the footpath, the shield bumping against his back. Kyra followed Callum with her eyes with more than a little disappointment. It was so unlike her, words twisted and jammed in her throat. Even so, a grin slinked across Kyra's face. Callum hadn't minded her bumbling responses.

Kyra's smile instantly melted as Solarus stepped toward her. His lips were pursed. "Kyra, did you use any magic during your gallant interruption of the guards?"

Solarus' sardonic emphasis of "gallant" made Kyra bristle. "I didn't. I didn't need to. I was able to stop one of Callum's guards by myself, without magic. I handled a lot in the other world by myself. I'm more capable than you think I am." Her impertinent tone surprised her as much as it did Solarus, but she held his gaze firmly. She was sixteen. She wasn't going to be scolded like a child.

Kyra's irritation wasn't lost on Solarus or the others. Ash rubbed his neck uncomfortably.

The wizard recovered his look of reprimand. "Capable or not, your actions were reckless. You should have better judgment than to throw yourself into a situation that did not concern you, particularly after the occurrences of last night. What would you have done had they been dark wizards?"

"I wasn't thinking about that." Kyra clenched her teeth. "I heard yelling, I thought someone was in trouble, and that was it."

"Did it not occur to you to warn us? I hoped you had matured this past year. Yet you are running around like a child chasing a butterfly into a briar patch."

"You did well, considering the circumstances," Hayden cut in as Kyra opened her mouth to respond. Solarus glared daggers at Hayden, clearly vexed at having been overridden. "However, I agree with Solarus. Your good intentions to help would have exacerbated the situation had those been dark wizards. Whether you used magic or not would have been irrelevant. If these were the wizards we fought in Edoin, they would have identified you. They would have also deduced you wouldn't be traveling alone and sought out the rest of us."

Kyra bit her lip and studied her boots. Hayden was right. She could have endangered the entire group. She had blindly followed an impulse to go toward the fighting.

"Next time, come to us first. We'll assess what actions need to be taken then. Anyway, it's time we make our way to the marketplace," Hayden switched topics. "Like I told Callum, Arkin is expecting a conversation this afternoon."

"How many days' worth of supplies do we need to plan for?" Ash asked.

"Silvias is a three-day ride from Thanesgard. I would advise you buy a week's worth of provisions. We should plan for potential delays in our journey," Hayden clarified, seeing the healer's puzzled expression. "I would rather that we were overprepared than found wanting. Particularly if what we lack will heal or bandage a wound."

"It might take me time to find what I need," Ash said contemplatively. He adjusted a square satchel he had brought so that it was slung over his right arm. "The herbs and leaves come from across Ilian. I'm not sure one apothecary or vendor would have everything."

"*You* could use more leaves," Jyls said to Solarus with a foxlike grin. "The kolker would help ease the frazzle out of your nerves."

"I have a more efficient and lasting remedy for my 'nerves,'" Solarus said waspishly. His staff flared with turquoise magic so quickly and brightly it could have been mistaken for a trick of sunlight.

Jyls hopped back a step. "You give Kyra a fine lecture on the perils of displaying magic, but you're excluded from that rule?"

Solarus let out a huff. Striking his staff on the ground, the wizard stomped down the footpath toward the city. Hayden gave Jyls a disapproving look. "You already forgot what I said about provoking people."

"Provoking *Arkin*. Solarus is different."

Hayden raised his gaze to the sky as if looking for patience. Then he motioned to the rest of the companions with a flick of his head. They started off after Solarus. Kyra lingered with the pretense of fixing her boot. Her blood simmered with anger and shame from Solarus and Hayden's comments. Jyls sidled back down the path to her.

"Waiting for you, Your Ladyness," he said.

Kyra raked a hand through her hair before trekking down the footpath.

Jyls strolled beside her. "Don't worry about Solarus," he added after a moment. "He can be touchy, you know that. Doesn't mean you're the cause.

Maybe his bed was too fluffy or one of the attendants didn't heat the bath to an agreeable temperature. Those could get anyone into a foul mood."

Kyra was grateful for Jyls' arch comments. "Thanks, Jyls. It feels like whatever I do, he's not going to be happy about it."

"Yeah, pretty much. That's Solarus."

The late morning sun scorched the castle grounds. Sweat trickled down Kyra's neck and beaded on her chest. Kyra wished she had left the cloak behind. Though the material wasn't thick, it was uncomfortably warm. Sighing, Kyra forced the edges of the cloak over her shoulders. She noticed a small lump in her left pocket. Reaching inside, Kyra withdrew the three pouches she had brought from her room.

"Jyls, what are these for?" she asked, raising them up for him to see.

"For whatever you need to carry," Jyls answered. "Food, coins, that sort of thing. Women usually hoard hairpins and combs and Jaren and Garen know whatever other accessories women stuff in there."

"Where do I put them? The pouches, not hairpins and combs."

Jyls pointed to Kyra's trousers. She looked down, confused. There were three loops at the top that she hadn't noticed earlier, two on the right and one on the left. They were too small to fit a belt. Jyls took the pouches and deftly tied each through the rings. Kyra tucked a strand of hair behind her ear, feeling foolish.

"There." Jyls tugged gently on one to test his knot. "Now you can fill them. Except don't bother with carrying florins. Hayden's got enough to buy whatever you need. And if he doesn't, I have ways to supplement our funds."

Kyra's brow knitted. "How?"

Jyls spread his arms in the air like a circus showman. "Magic."

Kyra's confused expression widened his grin.

Kyra and her companions passed through a wide oaken door from the royal courtyard into the second circle. The previous day, Kyra had been too busy following Larisa to examine the walls. Now her pace slowed as she marveled at the castle's layers of stone-based protection. The space between the walls was large enough for three horses to walk alongside each other. Ornamental bushes taller than Kyra lined the edges of the walls. Two men were at work pruning the bushes as the group walked by.

Kyra's gaze fell upon the men-at-arms patrolling the grounds. Unlike the Royal Guards, who wore midnight blue livery, these sentries donned blue jackets and brown leather trousers. They lacked the Royal Guards' discipline. The men nattered idly and ambled along the wall as though leisurely strolling in a garden rather than watching for intruders. A small group sent cursory glances in Kyra's direction as she walked past, then returned to their conversations. Kyra's eyes trailed up the castle walls. Archers were tucked deep within the parapets. Their gazes were as hard and cool as those of the sentries were lackadaisical.

As they passed through the door separating the second wall from the third, Kyra's head turned left, then right. She couldn't see the next door until they had walked almost halfway along the wall. The doors were staggered, she realized. If an intruder managed to force his way through one door, he would have to run to the opposite side of the wall to reach the second.

Talis dropped back to walk with Kyra. "There are five walls separating the outermost wall and the king's keep," he explained. "An invading force might breach the outer wall. Perhaps even the fourth. But it would require the hand of Inishmore to penetrate all five."

"Aren't five walls a bit . . . excessive?" Kyra remarked, staring in openmouthed fascination. The wall itself had to be at least five meters thick. "You could probably stop an army with three."

"In these times, yes. During the war, however, the fortress Hayden described to you had two walls. Neither wall was designed to withstand the ravaging of Malus' wicked beings. Dragons rained fire and ice on the outer wall of the fortress. Those who survived the attack were brought down by the Mountain's other monsters. Malus' wizards bored holes into the inner wall and reduced it to rubble and dust. The thane was killed during the fight for the keep. If not for the elves riding to his aid, no man would have survived."

The bare inner walls finally gave way to a groomed courtyard. Every blade of grass seemed to have been shaved as though with a razor. The courtyard ended at a bridge. It wasn't the same bridge Kyra had passed over the day before, she noticed. This bridge was longer and wider. The portcullis was fully raised, and flocks of traders and buyers entered and left the grounds unimpeded. Two guards stood near a crank with a thick, tightly coiled rope. They donned emotionless expressions, but Kyra saw their gaze follow each visitor who came and left the bridge. She guessed the guards could lower the gate in a hurry. Kyra stepped onto the bridge.

***

Hayden was troubled. He took Talis by the elbow as Kyra passed them. The elf slowed his pace.

"The *Sirenyle* are absent from this entrance as well," Hayden said softly.

Concern was stenciled across Talis' features. He inclined his head. "I know. I looked for them shortly after dawn this morning. No elven horses are in the castle's main stables. It's possible they are saddled in the forest with the Royal Guard's reserves. It's unusual for both *Sirenyle* to leave. I can think of two reasons why that might happen: either *Raenalyn* Carina had an urgent need of which I am unaware, or they departed because an unforeseen circumstance required their combined strength." Talis brushed the braid from his face. "There are too many secrets within these walls. If I can't find the *Sirenyle,* I must at least warn *Raenalyn* Carina that something may have befallen them. I must also inform her of the events that have transpired since Edoin. The *Raenalyn* may send other *Sirenyle* to our aid."

"Agreed," Hayden replied. He glanced at the clear blue sky overhead. "We can meet at the clock tower in three hours' time, if that's enough to find the *Al-Ethran*'s scouts?"

Talis' eyes were dark and troubled. "If one of them is here. Inishmore help us if we are left with none." The elf turned and strode back through the portcullis.

***

Kyra lobbed a look over her shoulder. Talis turned right and disappeared along the wall. She frowned as Hayden came forward. "Where's he going?" she asked.

"To the stables, to see how the horses are faring," Hayden answered in a normal volume. "Talis will meet us in the city when he's finished checking on them."

"The stables outside the castle? Is he checking for the elven horses or these *Sirenyle*?"

Hayden's eyes betrayed a look of surprise. Then he swiftly glanced in the direction of the guards near the crankshaft. The unspoken warning immediately silenced Kyra.

Solarus had begun to descend the bridge, with Jyls and Ash close behind. Kyra and Hayden came next, picking their way through customers moving in the opposite direction. Kyra kept her head raised. She resisted the temptation to look into the moat in the daylight. Her ears were filled with a clamor of voices netted together with squawking, neighing, clinking, and chinking. The smell of smoke and cured meats drifted through the air.

"You understood the conversation?" Hayden murmured abruptly. If he hadn't been standing close enough so their shoulders almost touched, Kyra wouldn't have heard.

Kyra turned her attention away from the increasing flurry of activity. She shook her head. "Should I remember *Sirenyle*?" she whispered back.

"That's not what I meant. You understood what we said about the *Sirenyle*?"

Kyra forgot about the marketplace as her brow furrowed. "Well, yes, why wouldn't I?"

"It was in elvish."

"Elvish?" Kyra had thought of the language like a Rubik's Cube, with its smooth sounds like combinations of colors that she couldn't fit together. Apparently, the blocks had locked into place. She felt a spike of happiness even as it was accompanied by puzzlement. "Why were you speaking in elvish?"

"The threat of spies, magic, and possibly dark wizards bids us to be cautious with our words. It's unlikely any around us will understand elvish. Except the traders," Hayden amended as a woman with a purple sash and long black braids walked serenely in the opposite direction. Hayden waited until they had passed each other before continuing. "Traders are masters of languages. Assume they will understand you no matter what tongue you use. Then you won't accidentally reveal something of importance in front of them. That's all you and I can discuss about the *Sirenyle*," Hayden returned to the original conversation. "If we are overheard now, there would have been no point in using elvish in the first place."

Kyra wanted to speak in elvish. Frustratingly, she couldn't figure out how. Passively understanding the language was easier than remembering how to put together the words. Sighing, Kyra asked, "Why did you learn elvish? Was it because you met Talis?"

"My father thought it useful."

They had reached the end of the bridge. Kyra was bombarded by the noisy hustle and bustle she had only half noticed during her discussion with Hayden. She stared, slack jawed. "This is the city?"

Hayden's gray eyes sparkled. "This is the city of Thanesgard."

Chapter 11

It was dizzying trying to follow the scene in front of her. Kiosks, wagons, and people bartered for space in a spaghetti mess of streets. Hot food sizzled in large pans. Metalworks jangled from carts and wheelbarrows. Vendors shouted over each other to attract customers. A large tower with four clock faces towered over the kiosks, its bells chiming quarter past the hour.

"We'll go this way," Hayden instructed, beckoning with a nod of his head. He started down onto the main thoroughfare. "You don't have to watch your pouches in Thanesgard as much as in other markets. King Arkin's laws regarding the marketplace are strict. If throwing an apple core in the street is a crime, you can imagine what punishment stealing a purse would bring."

"You have to keep an eye on the street urchins," Jyls put in. His midnight blue gaze followed a boy with a moth-eaten cap slinking through the crowd. "Don't be fooled by their young age. They'll try and lift something from whoever they see as any easy target."

"Children?" Kyra asked, distracted by the activity around her. "Where do they come from?"

"Some are orphans, some are runaways," Hayden answered as Solarus, in the lead, steered them along the first row of stalls. Ash was beside him. He seemed as fascinated by the busy streets as Kyra was. "Some come from families too poor to provide for themselves and have no other options."

"They look for a squad to join," Jyls said. "Brennan's Nines and Henna's Sevens are the more infamous squads. Kids who want to join have to loose a pouch from a noble. They succeed, they're allowed to stay with the squad. They don't, they have to find another. Sneaky link lizards, those kids," he added with a grin in his voice. "Henna's Sevens can steal your boots right from your feet."

"How do you know?" Ash asked.

"'Cause they tried once when I was sleeping. It didn't go well for the boys, but I appreciated their gusto. Gave them a few coins for the effort."

Solarus beelined to an alley with a gutter running down the middle. The space was so narrow he had to hug his staff tightly against his body to fit. Kyra stepped in line behind Hayden, carefully placing her feet on the ground on either side of the gutter. Looking down, she saw the water was clear. Kyra thought back to Mr. Dullwane's lectures on the unsanitary conditions of medieval cities. The gutter should have been clogged with sewage and trash. Astonishingly, it was clean.

Arkin's punishments must be harsh, Kyra thought as she picked her way to the end of the alley.

They emerged into another line of stalls. Kyra mindlessly followed her guides as her gaze brushed over the crowd. The diversity of women's clothing put London's cosmopolitan shops to shame. As on the road into Thanesgard, the women here wore stiff, lacy bodices, poufy dresses, and frilled skirts. Some, like Catt, were dressed in plain, sensible frocks. Others donned attire like Kyra's—trousers, long shirts, and some even with leather gauntlets. The men's clothing was an equally interesting assortment. They swaggered through the market in leather boots, fancy tunics and vests, and capes and cloaks. A few men wore hats with wide feathers, adding dashes of flair to already flashy outfits.

Millie would love this, Kyra thought sadly. She imagined her aunt spending hours questioning the women about their favorite fashions.

The stalls receded at an oblong green space. An island among a sea of stalls, the area was bare except for the lone stone clock tower that rose from its center. An ornately designed clockface was set in each of its four walls. Kyra saw that the tower was positioned to be seen from anywhere in the marketplace.

Jyls' hands were on his hips as he flung a gaze around the stalls. One seemed to catch his eye. His lips curved into a mischievous smile.

Ash's gaze also drifted along the kiosks. He scratched his cheek. "I have to visit the apothecaries and spice sellers," he told Hayden. "And I'd like to buy fresh cloth for bandages. Do you know where they are? Thanesgard's market is a lot bigger than Hillith's."

"I'll help you," Jyls interjected. His eyes lingered on a pair of guards marching down the stalls. "Can't be too hard to find a spice seller. We'll follow the scent."

"Solarus and I are outfitting Kyra," Hayden replied. "Talis will meet us here in three hours' time. Be here by then. And Jyls," Hayden added with a pointed look, "kindly try not to provide the guards with a reason to speak with us. Unless it's about something as insignificant as the weather."

Jyls pulled an expression of mock hurt over his face. "I would never do so something like that."

Hayden raised a brow. Jyls let out an exaggerated sigh. "Come on, Ash," he said. Jyls stalked off from the green island and back into the bustling market. Ash hurried to follow. "You'd have more fun if you were like me, Hayden," Jyls called over his shoulder before disappearing into the tightly packed throng.

"You realize giving Jyls free rein in a market is like putting a hawk in a mouse's cage," Solarus commented dryly. His head was tilted, and he scraped the ground with the bottom of his staff. "You can't expect it to resist the temptation to eat its prey. I would have kept him on a tighter leash."

"If Jyls finds his way into trouble, he's capable of finding his way out." Hayden clapped a hand on Kyra's shoulder. He steered her under the eaves of the stalls. "So long as we aren't implicated in whatever he attempts, it may do Jyls good to be caught."

Kyra wasn't sure what Hayden was referencing. When she glanced at Solarus, she saw his mouth formed the widest smile she had seen yet.

***

Working their way through the crowd proved time-consuming. Kyra instinctively put a hand on the pouch with the heptagon coin as she was jostled from all sides. Once, Kyra glimpsed a pair of girls with scarves dart through the masses. She lost sight of them. Then she heard giggling as the girls ran back out. Sunlight flashed off pieces of silver in their small hands. Kyra grinned as they raced past her and disappeared into the crowd.

Then her smile collapsed. As it had been with the servants upon their arrival, marketgoers stole glances in Solarus' direction. Distrust was stamped on their faces. The women glowered at him, keeping their children behind them.

One boy's wide-eyed gaze locked on Solarus' staff. He slipped away from his mother and curiously reached out to touch it. His mother stifled a shriek. She snatched the boy's hand roughly.

"Don't touch and don't stare," the mother hissed. She glared daggers at Solarus as though he had goaded the boy into taking the staff. The mother yanked her son away from the wizard.

"I want to see the wizard's stick!" the boy protested. He continued to wail as his mother dragged him back into the crowd.

Solarus didn't acknowledge the woman's outcry or the boy's action. Kyra would have thought Solarus hadn't noticed at all, except that his brow arched at the boy's wailing. The wizard stopped at a kiosk with plants and flowers. As Kyra waited, questions tumbled through her mind. Was the people's wariness due to wizards' power? Did they know the dark wizards were in Ilian? Kyra chewed on her lip as Solarus purchased a packet of kolker leaves from the vendor. Maybe their reaction was part of the horrific legacy of the War of Calonia. That seemed less likely, Kyra reasoned. Almost eight hundred years had passed since the war. How many of Ilian's citizens even knew the full history? Solarus stuffed the leaves into his vest pocket, and they continued on.

Kyra's eye caught a wave of shimmering light. She glanced in its direction, then did a stunned double-take. Hundreds of glass statues were on crowded shelves and lined the counter of one of the larger kiosks. A wooden bowl occupied a free space at the end of the counter. Kyra's gaze perused the figurines. They were small enough to fit in the palm of her hand and were a mélange of animals, elves, dragons, and fantastical creatures Kyra didn't recognize. A trader with a long forest green sash over his shoulder leaned on the counter. He conversed in a foreign language with a dark-skinned customer wearing patterned clothing. The customer had a brass cane, which he was using to point toward the shelves.

Kyra nudged Hayden. "Hayden, look," she whispered. "Those figurines there. On the third shelf from the top. They look like the wolf the king had in the throne room."

Hayden turned and regarded the glass figurines. "They're replicas of Lyneera, but they aren't kaemins," he replied.

The trader had his back to them as he reached up to the highest shelf. Kyra looked at Hayden, flummoxed. "They're replicas of Lyneera? Lyneera, like my friend James?" Her voice caught saying his name.

"James was the Lyneera from the other world? The one who contacted Raff?" Kyra confirmed his questions with a nod. "Yes, they're Lyneera." Hayden watched the trader set the statue on the counter in front of the man. It was a green dragon with wings spread.

"The Lyneera Arkin had in the throne room was a—what did you call it?—a kaemin? Is that like a wolf?"

"A kaemin isn't a creature," Hayden explained. "It's a statue crafted from an element of the same name. The element kaemin resembles glass or crystal, though it isn't either. Like obsidian, kaemins possess unique magical properties. Elves and wizards believe kaemins have a strong connection to Inishmore." His gaze traveled to the dragon figurine on the counter. The customer was inspecting it. He ran his fingers over the statue's lifelike scales.

Kyra peered at the shelves. "If a kaemin looks like glass and crystal, how do you know these *aren't* kaemins?"

"Kaemin is a rare element. Its location is carefully guarded by the traders and the makers. That's why the element can't be commonly harvested. The gold in Arkin's palace pales in comparison to the worth of a kaemin. You would never find a kaemin for sale in a marketplace."

"How does anyone afford a kaemin then? If Arkin doesn't have enough gold to buy one . . . I mean, he's got a lot of gold."

"He does, but that which is treasured most in life can't be bought. Kaemins aren't sold," Hayden elucidated. "One can only acquire a kaemin as a gift given by a kaemin mage."

"A kaemin mage?"

"Someone who makes kaemins. They are normally wizards and elves, since they have innate magic and a better understanding of the element. I've heard that some men have crafted kaemins, though I imagine they were few."

Kyra pondered this. "How do you find a mage?"

"You don't really." Hayden watched the customer set the dragon back on the counter with a satisfied look. He pulled two gold florins from his pouch and dropped them in the wooden bowl. They clinked against the sides. The trader grinned and scooped up the coins.

"Kaemin mages are an elite group," Hayden continued as the customer delicately placed the dragon in a bag at his side. "They act in much the same way as traders, in fact. Their exact number is a secret preserved by the mages. Two groups alone know their identities: traders, who act as intermediaries, and seers, who divine matters relating to the mages."

The customer raised his cane in farewell. Kyra and Hayden moved to the side as the customer limped past, patting the bag at this side. The trader returned to his shelves, murmuring as he counted the figurines.

"Why would the mages prefer to be anonymous?" Kyra asked. "Wouldn't they want credit for their work?"

"They take pride in their work, of course." Hayden's expression turned serious. "Protecting their identity is a question of safety. Thieves, bandits, and even nobles have taken extreme measures to obtain a kaemin or to extract information about the element. The few occasions a mage's identity was leaked led to that mage's kidnapping. Sometimes torture."

Kyra shuddered. "That's terrible," she whispered. A thought struck her. "If the identity of the mages is secret, how do they give the kaemins to their recipients? Do they wear disguises?"

"As I said, traders serve as intermediaries between the kaemin mages and the recipients. Traders take an oath before being entrusted with the mage's identity."

"And if they break their oath?"

"There are consequences."

Hayden didn't elaborate. His gray eyes tracked one of the pieces in an upper shelf. The trader had taken a figurine of a woman with a long gown and was polishing it with a cloth. He glanced up and grinned at Hayden.

"Can I help you find something?" he asked jovially.

"Just looking," Hayden replied. He turned away from the kiosk and the vendor and motioned to Kyra. "Let's get Solarus and go to the shops. We have errands to run."

Kyra double-stepped to keep pace with Hayden as he set off away from the trader. "You didn't explain about the wolf kaemin," she said. "If you can't buy one, then Arkin got it as a present? And he doesn't know who sent it?"

"Arkin received a kaemin as a coronation present when he became king," Hayden answered. "My father was there for the ceremony. It's tradition for a mage to bestow a kaemin on a new monarch to bless him or her with wisdom, fortune, and virtue. Nobles aren't the sole recipients of kaemins, but it's rare for commoners to be gifted a kaemin." He slowed his steps. Solarus was on the other side of the path at a leather stall. He gestured as though haggling with the vendor.

"Why choose a wolf?"

Hayden's eyes were clouded. "It wasn't a wolf. The kaemin my father saw and what I remember from my last trip to Thanesgard was a woman with golden hair. She reminded me of Genevieve. When and from whom he got the wolf kaemin, I can't say."

Kyra bit her lip. "Is it normal for someone to get rid of a kaemin? If they're so valuable, then couldn't they sell it?"

"No." Hayden watched Solarus take out a coin from his purse. "You can't sell a kaemin that is given to you. Only the recipient can touch it."

Kyra's brow knitted. *Only the recipient can touch it*, she repeated to herself. *I've heard that before. But where?*

***

"They're in the marketplace?"

Nymphrys brushed her foxtail of hair from her face. Her expression housed boredom and irritation as she reclined on a gold-trimmed sofa in the parlor room. Her staff rested against a table with a fat blue lamp. "That is what I said,

Adakis. I also said now is the time to attack. They're preoccupied. They won't notice us until we are pointing a staff at their throats."

Adakis rubbed his protruding ear with an eager expression. He stood opposite Nymphrys beside a love seat. The only light in the room came from the lamp and a candelabrum on the table squished between the seat and another table. "If we move on them," Adakis mused, "everyone will see us."

Nymphrys rolled her eyes. "They'll see us. So what? Our job is to capture Kyra. That's it. Diamantas said nothing about these miserable marketgoers getting in our way. We have an advantage here. We should take it. Hayden won't draw his sword in a crowd. Solarus can't use his staff, because he fears harming someone. We don't share those limitations. Janus, are you paying attention?"

Janus had been turning in a slow circle as he looked up to the diamond-sequined chandelier overhead. He held his staff close. Janus tore his focus from the piece to Nymphrys. Seeing her narrowed eyes, Janus rubbed the back of his neck and stammered, "Um, sorry, I was, um . . . you were talking about Kyra?"

Nymphrys let out a long-suffering breath. "Obviously. Get over here."

Adakis' eyes glinted as Janus shuffled over. "Then that's it. I've beaten her!"

"You haven't 'beaten her' until you actually do something," Nymphrys countered. "When she is locked away, you can claim whatever you'd like. Idiot." Nymphrys muttered the last word under her breath. She regarded the large rings garnishing her fingers. "*Before* we go forward, send for Galakis and Orkanis. They were in the market proper."

Adakis waved off Nymphrys' suggestion. "I can handle this situation unassisted. We're fighting in close quarters. I have the most refined and controlled magic you've ever seen. Besides Diamantas," he amended as though through rote memorization of the phrase.

"I don't care. Send for them anyway."

Adakis' expression soured. "Fine. Janus, go retrieve Galakis and Orkanis in the market proper. Then meet us here."

"Where in the market?" Janus asked in a timorous voice.

"I don't know, just go look for them!"

"Usually, I would recommend a locating spell. With your feeble abilities, I doubt you would detect anything more than a fly." Nymphrys' voice leaked ridicule as she continued to examine her rings.

Color suffused Janus' pale face. He scampered to a painting of a still life depicting fruit on a table. Janus tapped the wall with his staff. A column of stones behind the painting groaned as it swung inward, revealing a dark opening. Cool air breezed into the parlor.

"*Ascera*," Janus intoned in a quivering voice. An ivory-colored light shimmered at the tip of his staff and cast streams of light into a long passage. He hesitated and glanced at Adakis. Adakis glowered back. Janus ducked into the opening and disappeared. His footsteps echoed in the hollow space.

Nymphrys rose from her seat. Snatching up her staff, she rapped it against the column. The stones slid back into place and sealed themselves into the wall.

"Diamantas will reward us greatly," Adakis remarked in the same triumphant tone. "This time we have her."

Nymphrys shot him a nettled look. "You had better hope so. Diamantas won't give us a third chance."

***

"A pretty tale for a pretty lady?" a voice asked.

Kyra paused. After leaving the kiosk with the glass figurines, Hayden and Solarus led Kyra back through the marketplace and up to the castle. The throng squeezed together like the teeth of a comb as they crossed the bridge. Kyra straggled behind the pair. She used Solarus' staff as a marker, its tip visible above the heads of the marketgoers. Kyra threaded her way around the outer ring where Larisa had mentioned the shops.

Kyra's hands started to itch. She looked down, stomach twisting with apprehension. Kyra expected to see the golden energy. But no, it was merely an itch. Kyra laughed quietly to herself. *A non-magical itch. Yes, I've got those too.*

Kyra crossed over the bridge and through the portcullis. Sweat trickled down the nape of her neck. The air muggy and stifling. That was when she heard the question. She glanced in the direction of the voice.

A swarthy man with thin-framed glasses and greasy hair peered over his counter. His stall was chock-full of books precariously balanced in tottering stacks and messy piles of yellowed manuscripts. Kyra was reminded, with a pang of heartache, of the mounds of homework she had always left in Millie's living room. The vendor slid a book from the top of the pile.

"Perhaps one with Ilian's legends," he said in a tone as oily as his hair. He flipped through pages with pictures in faded colors. "This is an easy book to read. You look Calonian from your garb, so I assume you may have learned that skill. This magnificent piece contains the adventures of the mischievous imp Leon. The transgressions of the seductive chambermaid Bessia. The escapades of the fetching Malino Malorin. A pretty lady like you would enjoy the illustrations of *that* ravishing young man."

"How appealing," Kyra answered flatly. "I'm not interested in buying anything today." Her eyes coasted over the crowd until she spotted Solarus' staff. He and Hayden were near rows of kiosks selling vegetables and cured meats.

"Don't listen to that cheat!" interceded a chubby man in a high-pitched voice. He waddled out from an adjacent stall and waved his hand in Kyra's face. She was tempted to swat it away. The pair of vendors reminded Kyra of used car salesmen trying to cajole her onto their lots.

"Nabil swindles customers with these silly stories. They're a lot of nonsense, better for boys with wooden swords than a sophisticated young woman." The vendor gave Kyra an obsequious smile that revealed several golden molars on his lower jaw. "My maps, on the other hand, are perfect renditions of Ilian's great cities and kingdoms. Come, come, I'll find you something you like."

Kyra's curiosity was piqued, though she disliked the pushy vendor. She *did* need a map. Except she didn't have any money—or florins, she remembered the coins were called—to buy one.

"Leave off, Arlo, you cheat," Nabil the bookseller snapped indignantly. Oil oozed from his hair and down the sides of his forehead. "Those tatty pieces of paper are children's scratches and scribbles. They're as authentic as those golden gnashers you've got in your oversized mouth."

Arlo's face turned red. He ran his tongue over his back teeth. "My maps are meticulously drawn. They are the most factually accurate maps in the four kingdoms. Not that you can appreciate their quality, Nabil." Arlo made a show of peering over Nabil's collection of papers and books. "I see your standard for a decent volume to sell is that it has a cover and words inside. The *condition* of the cover and what *words* are contained within it, well, that isn't so important to a novice like you. No buyer will be duped by such a pathetic offering." Arlo turned toward Kyra as Nabil made a rude gesture. "Come over here with me and have a look. Come, come."

Arlo grabbed for Kyra's wrist as he started toward his stall. This time, Kyra slapped his hand back. "No. Thank. You. I don't have any florins. Unless you want to give me one for free and show off how exceptionally amazing your map is, there's nothing else to say."

Nabil gave him a superior smile. "The lady has already exposed you as a fake. She feigns she hasn't a florin on her simply to free herself of your conversation." Nabil looked at Kyra. "Your coins are best spent on my wares, my dear. As the *top* scribe in my cohort, I can vouch for the validity of my tomes and scriptures."

"Odd that a scribe would be a vendor." Hayden had silently appeared at Kyra's side. He had a leather bag slung over his shoulder. His other hand rested on his sword hilt. Hayden sized up Nabil coolly. "I was under the impression a scribe's duty was to analyze the past and record events of the present. How does one fulfill those obligations selling the manuscripts he should be studying? Maybe you can enlighten me?"

Nabil's face flared scarlet. Arlo scampered back behind the safety of his own stall.

"What would you know about the Academy?" Nabil snapped. He looked condescendingly at Hayden's garb, his glasses slipping down his nose. "You certainly aren't from any *learned* profession. A lowly hunter or woodsman has no business giving his erroneous opinions on a scholar's work. Go preach to others about animals' scat or poisonous mushrooms."

Anger spilled out of Kyra. How dare he talk to Hayden like that? Her hands tingled as she balled them into fists. The retort on her lips was stopped like a cork in a bottle as Solarus came up on her other side. He placed his staff before him and clasped his hands around the center.

"Show me your forearm," Solarus requested calmly. "If you would be so kind."

Nabil quailed before the wizard. His eyes darted to the staff. "I . . . I . . . what?"

"Show me your forearm. It is a simple request."

Drops of sweat dribbled down Nabil's face alongside the streaks of oil. His glasses slid further down his nose. Nabil pushed them up only for sweat to loosen them again. "I don't have the mark," he confessed nervously. "I'm sorry, honestly. I didn't mean anything by it." He looked imploringly at Hayden, seeking an ally. "I did take the exam to enter the Academy. I, well, my score fell short of what was required for entrance. Scribes are so well respected. It's good for business when I claim I am . . ."

"Lying about what one does makes one question what other lies have been spoken." Hayden shrugged the leather bag further up his shoulder. Then he rested his hand on a dust-covered book propped up against the stall's wall. "To impersonate a scribe is a grave offense in Ilian. I personally find it more morally reprehensible than a violation of law." Hayden lifted the book and gently rubbed dust from its cover. "A man would be wise to present himself as he is. Failing that, he should present himself with qualities he aspires to achieve, without jealousy or pride."

Nabil's forehead scrunched in bewilderment. "You are quoting Lord Regnum. I memorized his treatises for the exam, but few others are conversant in his writings. How would you . . ."

"'It is best to judge not. If you must determine a man's intent, listen much, and speak little,'" Hayden quipped.

Nabil glanced nervously at Arlo. The cartographer buried himself in his maps, an action that stated he was steering clear of the conversation.

"You may want to reexamine Lady Imineral's texts," Hayden recommended casually. He turned the book so Nabil could see the cover. It read, "*Glanis*: The Teachings of Lady Imineral, Protector of Silvias. Translated."

"I would listen to him if I were you," a chipper voice chimed in. Kyra's eyes widened. She recognized the voice. Catt sauntered toward them, a scarf swathing her head. She held a plum. "The man's got a sword and enough nicks in the scabbard to tell you he's used it once or twice, yeah? Isn't it better to keep your jaw shut?"

Hayden's eyes flickered. He slowly turned to see Catt take a bite from the fruit. She had an expectant expression in her blue-green eyes. Hayden's face muscles went taut, but he compelled a smile to his lips. "I didn't realize you were here, Catt."

"Here in the marketplace, or here to say hello, Hayden?"

"Both."

Kyra looked at Solarus, confused by the exchange. *Hayden knows her?* The wizard's brows were knitted. He seemed as perplexed as she was.

Nabil seemed relieved that someone else was receiving Hayden and Solarus' scrutiny. He busied himself with reordering the slapdash papers on the counter.

"The marketplace has been home for some time," Catt replied neutrally. "I've got my fruit, my friends, and my clients. The pay's good, especially when my ear catches conversations and secrets that people would bankrupt themselves to be privy to. Anyhow, I thought it would be rude to have you come all this way without a how-do-you-do. And to meet your companions." Her blue-green gaze shifted to Kyra.

"As we are not staying long, introductions are unnecessary," Solarus intervened curtly. His mouth was a thin line of suspicion. "Catt, is it?"

"Depends on who's asking. The full name's Cattleya Gaskilliana." She curtsied. "Also called Ivy. Also called Pearls. Also called other names, depending on what business you've got." Catt rose and addressed Kyra. "You're the girl Bee was in a tizzy about this morning. Something about sheets and odd clothing and baths. Don't give any thought to it. That royal sulks like a child without a helping of pie."

Comprehension dawned on Kyra. "Bee was my attendant this morning?"

Catt grinned. "Yep."

"She wasn't too bad," Kyra said, feeling sudden sympathy for the maid. "I can understand if she was upset. No one wants to clean someone else's room."

Solarus' gaze fixed on the fruit in Catt's hands. "Interesting that you have a plum," he commented in a strange tone. "I have not seen one ripen so early in the season."

"Me neither. Lucky I got one." Catt took an emphatic bite. Rubbing juice from the corner of her mouth, Catt said to Hayden, "I'll be heading back to Terrance Lane. Already caught one of the Sevens snooping around my kiosk for some nosh. Be a gentleman and walk a ways with me? Have a quick chat?"

"Terrance Lane is not in the direction we're traveling, and our time is short," Hayden replied in a guarded tone. "So, thank you, but no."

Catt shrugged. "I've got some snippets and snatches from the tradesmen. I thought you'd find them interesting. Always tales to share. Or maybe Kyra'd like to stroll with me instead? Have a local show her who the fraudsters are in this place. You've already found one." Catt jerked her thumb toward Nabil.

An unsettled look hijacked Hayden's expression. He released a terse breath. "A short chat then." To Solarus and Kyra, he said, "I'll meet you at the blacksmith's."

Solarus tapped the side of his staff. His inquisitive look was answered by Hayden with a tacit shake of his head.

"G'day, Nabil, Arlo," Catt said sweetly. She set the half-eaten plum on the edge of Nabil's table. "Word of advice to you—I'd do whatever these two say."

The flustered bookseller bobbed his head as though it had a broken hinge. "Lady Imineral's works, I will read them, of course," Nabil bleated. He clearly sought to end the unwanted attention.

With a wink at Kyra and a general parting wave, Catt swept into the crowd and slipped out of view. Hayden shook his head once with an enigmatic expression, then followed. He was enveloped by the bustling mill of bodies.

"Who was that woman?" Kyra asked Solarus as soon as they had gone.

Solarus ran a finger along the Z line in his hair. "I have never seen her before. Hayden's speech implies he has. He was not keen on making introductions. That lends itself to one of two conclusions: either he does not believe her trustworthy to divulge our identities, or there is a reason to guard the secrecy of their affiliation. Still, she reminds me of someone."

Solarus abruptly glanced at Arlo. The cartographer shrank against the back of his stall which, judging by the anxious apprehension in his eyes, wasn't far enough away from the wizard. Smiling like a bear eyeing its meal, Solarus walked forward and set a hand on the counter. "I believe you were offering the lady a map."

Chapter 12

"How did you know?" Hayden asked without preamble. Almost at a trot, Catt and Hayden crossed the bridge back into the marketplace and wove their way through the crowd. Catt led Hayden through a series of shortcuts heading south. As they traveled further away from the rich upper and middle quarters of Thanesgard, the gutters became clotted with mud and muck. An occasional guard made rounds but turned a blind eye to the litter. Hayden wasn't surprised. Enforcement of Arkin's regulations on sanitation lapsed in Terrance Lane. It was an undesirable quarter. The stalls were as clean as the grubby hands of orphan thieves and vagabonds allowed.

Catt's destination was a kiosk capped with a triangular green awning. Hayden knew from previous trips to Thanesgard that Catt manned two stalls. The first was the one she and Hayden neared. Wooden boxes filled with fruits and pastries were spread across the counter. Hanging at the back of the kiosk was an assortment of regal-looking clothing. Even though Hayden couldn't see the shirts and vests up close, he guessed the material was coarser than the fine silks the nobility wore; residents of Terrance Lane couldn't afford anything more than imitations.

The other stall Catt owned was in the upper market. That was where Catt attracted higher-paying customers with her best products. During those transactions, Catt coaxed buyers into revealing information worth ten times the price of her goods. Hayden wondered which kiosk had fed Catt the secrets she wanted to share with him.

"We're here," Catt announced. Hayden followed her around the side of the kiosk, carefully stepping over a basket of workmen's tools. A pair of girls wearing brightly colored scarves like Catt's sat on cushions laid flat on the dirt. They were counting a small pile of silver coins. At the sound of Catt's approach, the girls' heads snapped up in unison. Catt's blue-green gaze took in the silver. She smiled kindly at the girls.

"You've earned some sweets today," she told them. "The best a gold florin can buy. Go fetch some cinnamon spice rolls from Chef. The ones with the melted glaze." Catt pulled out a gold florin from her skirt pocket as the girls jumped to their feet. She handed the older of the two girls the coin. "Take some of my peaches and apples to him too," she said as the girls grinned delightedly at each other. "He may be the king's cook, but even the king doesn't have fruit like mine. Tell Chef he also owes me that pecan tart he promised."

The girls loped off, grabbing a handful of apples and peaches on the way. When their giggling had faded, Catt crouched next to the workman's basket. She sifted through the tools. Hayden crossed his arms.

"Your question, Hayden," Catt commented as though there had been no interruption, "was how did I know about Kyra? Easy. Intuition." Catt selected a pair of rusted scissors and placed it outside the basket.

"Whose? Yours? Beatrice's? Or was 'intuition' purchased within your network?"

Catt let out a short laugh. "Mine." She removed a twisted metal chain. "I would've preferred a few florins accompanying it. I might still."

"Then you haven't told anyone about Kyra."

"No reason to, is there?"

"And no one else has found out?"

Catt glanced up, brow raised. "If someone has, the news hasn't made it to the streets yet. I caught word through Bee's rant, of which there're plenty—don't give me that look, it's not that bad. Bee's head is as empty as a cracked eggshell. I guessed who Kyra was. The guards were in a tizzy over a wizard and an elf strolling along the castle grounds." Catt's round face turned serious. "You realize your wizard friend is attracting more than the eye of the guard. Strutting around with a staff like he is isn't going to make you friends in Thanesgard. He stands out like a pup in a litter of pigs." She wagged a finger at Hayden. "You'd best tell him to stow it."

Hayden didn't answer as Catt returned her attention to the basket. His eyes followed a man with a tattered burlap sack. The man shuffled by Catt's kiosk. When the man was out of hearing range, Hayden replied, "Solarus does what he wants, whatever I tell him."

"As wizards are wont to do."

"As you're also wont to do."

"It's worked for me so far."

Hayden uncrossed his arms. "If you've gotten word, others will soon too."

"Not necessarily." Catt paused as her hand slid over a rectangular wooden tool. She lifted it by its handle. The wood was hollow except for an irregular cylinder at one end. Catt spun the object experimentally. It clacked with the sound of hooves on stone. "Useful tool, this is," she remarked. "Scares away birds, rats, and sometimes the Nines. Won't get rid of Bee though. That'd be worth a pouch of florins."

"Catt. Will Beatrice tell others about Kyra?"

Catt glanced up and saw the storm brewing in Hayden's gray eyes. She tossed the object back in the pile and stood. "Yes, but it won't matter. She's no queen. Bee can buzz with gossip to every hive in the city. Who's going to listen? She's attracted to the prettiest flowers at court, who are repulsed by her, and the court's weeds are attracted to Bee, who is repulsed by them." Catt's blue-green eyes widened with a sudden thought. "I take that back. The girls working under her'll be whispering to their friends, especially if Kyra's so . . . unique." When Hayden sighed, Catt shrugged. "They're kids. What'd you expect?"

Hayden rubbed the side of his temple. "Is that a problem?"

"Not if I set a few Sevens and Nines to chatting with them. We can have them change the story, put out a yarn that says Kyra's one of the Duchess of

Adea's cousins. A fifth cousin, someone you'd never have heard of before. We'll say Kyra's here to bring the king a gift of condolence." Catt's tone changed. Her smooth features roughened with a hint of pain. "The kids have a better imagination than I do. Let 'em color this up a bit. Then we'll get the story out there."

Hayden watched Catt smooth her hair beneath the scarf. "How much will it cost?"

Catt tucked loose strands under the fabric. She reached back and tightened the knot holding the scarf in place. "Nothing. Consider it a favor to a friend."

Silence spread over them before Hayden replied cautiously, "Your favors are usually more expensive than a price given in florins."

"Not this time. I'm doing it for you. Free of charge. *Just this once.*" Catt rocked back on her heels and stood. "If you need something else, we're back to haggling. It'd kill my reputation if I were thought to be tagging favorites and giving privileges. Particularly if one of my *clients* hears we've been chatting."

Hayden glanced down pointedly at the half-eaten plum Catt had left on a cushion. "The clients who can ripen fruit unnaturally early in the season?"

"My business is my business. Not yours." Catt's words ended with an edge as sharp as glass. Her blue-green gaze tracked the nervous movements of a skeletal boy prowling the stalls. His eyes were as large as his cheeks were hollow. The boy glanced around furtively. "You know my rules." Catt turned to look at Hayden directly. She wrapped herself in a cold demeanor that had none of its previous informality. "I don't care about your politics or prophesies. You and the wizards have your tiffs. I have my trade. And I've got my responsibilities." She turned her head meaningfully toward the boy. He craned his neck around a stall and eyed Catt's stand. "I don't get a pass to deal exclusively with the honorable members of society. The morally abject pay me a pretty price, too. Haven't you sacrificed for people you loved, Hayden?" she added in a bitter tone. "Can you look me in the eye and tell me you wouldn't be doing the same, if you could?"

Hayden winced as though physically struck. He opened his mouth to reply, then closed it again.

"Didn't think you could."

"Catt, it wouldn't have worked for us."

"Obviously," Catt cut him off. "You made a choice. Look at the fate of the woman you swore to love and defend. I pity her. But I've left the past in the past."

Hayden twisted his ring, a tortured look in his eyes. "If you get word about Kyra before we leave . . ."

"I'll send a runner. Price'll depend on how quick you need to know and what danger I'm putting my lads in."

"And if anyone asks you about her . . ."

"I hold my secrets close." Without waiting for a response, Catt strolled out from between the stalls. The boy froze, eyes wide. She scooped up an apple pastry from her counter and gave him a disarming smile. Catt extended the pastry. "Hungry?" she asked. The boy stared mutely. "Here, this one's free. If Brennen's Nine needs food, you don't have to nick it, see? Can't speak for the others 'round here, but my stall's got enough to sneak you a snack here or there."

The boy inched forward suspiciously. In a flash, he swiped the pastry from her and sprinted off.

Hayden stepped over the basket with the workman's tools. The boy had slipped into a nearby alley. He plopped himself on the ground, tearing ravenously into the food.

"Thank you for your kind escort," Catt said, her back to Hayden. Her words had a finality to them.

"Thank you also, Catt," Hayden said quietly. He stepped past her. "For telling me about Kyra. I'm just trying to keep her safe."

It was Catt's turn to sigh. For the first time that day, her expression was shadowed with fatigue. "It isn't that poor girl's fault. She's marked, and she shouldn't be. Prophecies, superstitions, revenge, it's all tied up to something that happened hundreds of years ago. Kyra deserves a normal life. A normal, *long* life, and she's not likely going to get it. We are cursed to lose the ones we love, aren't we?"

Wordlessly, Hayden turned down the street and left.

***

"Solarus, the map's wrong." Kyra flipped the large sepia parchment upside down. She unconsciously slowed her pace as she pored over the map. Where the compass had been in the lower right hand of the map, it was now in the upper left. Its arrow marked "N" was now pointing south. She tilted her head with a perplexed look. "The Southern Mountains aren't drawn in the south on here. They're in the north. When we were in Edoin Forest, Hayden said we had to go south to reach Thanesgard." Kyra turned the parchment back over. "Which is accurate if the map's right-sided."

Kyra ran a finger over the area where "Edoin Forest" was penned. Like the other names on the map, it was in a neat cursive. All the knowledge Kyra craved about Ilian was before her. She recognized the names of four of the kingdoms—Silvias, Farcaren, Peregrine, and Calonia. She also found natural features like the Aurielle Sea and the Hornbeam Pass. Dotted lines demarcated major roads. The forests had small triangles sketched for trees.

Arlo had claimed that it was the most detailed and current traveler's map he owned. "Sketched six years past," he had promised. "You won't find anything better, honest."

Solarus had scrutinized the map. To Arlo's conspicuous relief, the wizard agreed. After which the cartographer gifted them with the map. "No charge, happy to be of help," he had said hastily as he practically shooed them from the stall.

Kyra hastened to catch up to Solarus. Fortunately, the marketgoers left the wizard a wide berth, making it easy for Kyra to again fall in step beside him.

Solarus' lips were upturned at the corners. "The map is accurate," he affirmed. "The Southern Mountains lie to the north. They are called the Southern Mountains, because the original cartographers were Calonian, who, as you see, are in the south here." Solarus pointed to the kingdom with his index finger. "The Calonian cartographers believed themselves to be Ilian's elite denizens. Naturally, they felt Calonia should appear above all other kingdoms and territories. Hence, the mountains to the north were named the 'Southern' Mountains." Solarus snorted. "Pure nonsense."

Kyra considered this. She glimpsed a vendor pushing a wheelbarrow full of pots and pans. He noticed Solarus when he had almost rolled the wheelbarrow on top of them. The vendor stopped abruptly at the sight of the wizard's staff. Pots clanged and clattered as they spilled over the sides. The vendor hurriedly bent down and picked up the wares. Solarus raised his eyes as if in annoyance and continued past him. As the vendor glanced up, Kyra gave him an apologetic smile. The man was more fearful than wary.

"Why did the Calonians think they were better than the other kingdoms?" Kyra resumed their conversation about the map.

"I said the Calonian *cartographers* of that era considered themselves to be superior, not Calonians generally," Solarus corrected. "As for why, one can assume vanity and self-importance is equally shared across peoples. I have not given it any thought, nor do I need to. Wizards have more pressing matters than the nomenclature of the mountains."

Kyra grinned at Solarus' prim expression, which left no doubt that he considered wizards Ilian's true "elite." Her eyes again browsed the map. Over the Southern Mountains, the cartographer had written "Harkimer, Kingdom of the Dark Wizards."

"Solarus, where are the free wizards? I never asked you what your equivalent kingdom is for Harkimer. I mean, you must have an idea about what other wizards are doing or where you can find them, right? Do free wizards have a kingdom they don't discuss with non-wizards? Which means it wouldn't be sketched on a map, at least not one purchased at Thanesgard."

Solarus hmphed. "Wizards are as leery of men and their intentions as men are of us. We cling to the knowledge of our world as closely as a mother with a babe. You are correct. Had we a kingdom, the free wizards would have prevented it from appearing on a map, through magic or some other means. The fact is free wizards do not *have* a kingdom. Neither do we inhabit ancestral lands as other species in Ilian. We are and have always been a nomadic race. We are villages of one, rather than a kingdom of many."

"Why? The dark wizards created Harkimer. Why not the free wizards?"

Solarus' eyes surveyed the stalls as they walked. The wooden structures' carvings became increasingly ornate, as did the flourishes of color along their sides. Customers dallied around the stalls and chatted with each other.

"We are powerful," Solarus answered. "Power is not equally distributed or inherited. Some wizards have greater command over energy than others. As you might suspect, this means they can subject others to their will. A terrifying and very real threat. This was true before the time of Malus, when there was no distinction between the dark and free wizards. We were simply wizards. However, if we had any hope of uniting prior to Malus, we had none after. Malus' success illustrated the extent to which a wizard could do harm to his brethren. Whatever faith we may have held in one another was shattered. Eight centuries later, the free wizards' relationships remain tenuous. The bond between mentor and pupil excepting, a wizard is loath to form allegiances with another lest that individual betray him as Malus did our kin. This mistrust cemented the free wizards' decision to roam Ilian in secret. Gathering in one place makes us easy targets."

Kyra nodded. She folded the map and placed it in her cloak pocket.

"It is a miracle that the Wizards' High Council was founded at all, let alone that it has survived for so long," Solarus went on in a sardonic tone. "As I told you when you first asked about wizards, the Council has been a forum for the highest-ranking wizards to share news and debate issues affecting our kind. It has had moments of effectiveness. In recent decades, the egos and competing interests of the members have led to deadlock and subsequent inaction. The Council has become a forum in which wizards proselytize to persuade one side to aid the other. They come to speak, not to listen." Solarus interrupted himself. "I digress. Ironically, as you noted, Harkimer is the first and only kingdom of wizard kind. The banished wizards band together while the free wizards do not. Centuries of imprisonment encourage cooperation if one hopes for escape or revenge. Diamantas has used the dark wizards' grievances to strengthen his command over them. It would be better if there were a means of association between free and dark wizards. Beyond those limited to the Council," he said as an afterthought.

Kyra nodded. Her eyes followed the stalls' exquisite wooden frames. A spice seller's roof was painted in pastel hues and authentic depictions of beans, plants, and seeds.

"How are the vendors selected to be in the castle and not in the city?" Kyra tacked the conversation away from the topic of wizarding kingdoms.

"It depends," Solarus responded dryly. "One hopes based on the quality of products sold. However, hope is often a farce in the politics of royalty. Many of the vendors have curried favor with the king. Nobles plump up the king's coffers and are bestowed a stall in return. Wealthy entrepreneurs bring gifts, like the golden monstrosities in the king's parlor rooms, to obtain their spots. The luckiest are young nobles with no inheritance to their parents' estates. They need a trade; the king provides one."

Kyra considered this as they passed a stall whose wood was painted to look like ivy trickling down the sides. "Why would someone who has enough money to buy a stall need one to begin with? Wouldn't they want to do something else with their time and not sell, well, whatever they're selling?"

"Is there no end to your questions?" Solarus asked crossly. He ran his finger along the line in his hair. "Think, Kyra. Neither the nobility nor the wealthy require more money. Yet their manors and estates lie outside the castle's walls. To have unrestricted access to Thanesgard and the king, one must have a reason to be situated here. The stall provides this reason. Which begs the larger question—why would one desire admission?"

It was clear from Solarus' piercing gaze that this was a test Kyra had to pass. The image of Catt and the guard popped to mind. "Information," Kyra responded. "If something is happening within the castle, the vendors would learn about it sooner than if they lived outside of Thanesgard."

Solarus gave her a slim smile of approval. "Correct. Remember, though: one who has the grace of the king today may lose the king's goodwill tomorrow. The politics of nobles is as capricious as a wig on a windy day."

The wooden stalls ended. Shops made of whitish-gray stone and brown shingled rooves took their place in a perfect line along the wall. Brightly colored banners swung from poles outside the doors. Kyra caught one on which a golden harp was set against the background of a blue sky.

"Is that why there are banners?" she asked, gesturing to the harp. "Because there could be a new owner? Which would explain why the buildings look similar," Kyra added as the thought dawned on her. "In case the next person wasn't in the same trade."

Solarus indicated his approval with a subtle nod. "You are learning."

Kyra felt pride and relief that she had finally given the right answer. Her mind skipped to a question that had sparked earlier, a question that had been forgotten after Hayden's abrupt departure with Catt. "Solarus, back at the bookseller's—you asked to see his forearm. Why?"

"Scribes receive a mark after the completion of their studies at the Academy. It is a magical imprint on their forearm. Because scribes are the keepers of Ilian's secrets, others will impersonate them to gain scribes' information. The mark allows scribes to distinguish between a fake and a peer. The mark does not appear unless the scribe chooses to reveal it."

"What does it look like?"

"A quill with a sharp tip."

It was a short distance to the blacksmith's shop. A banner with a silver anvil and sword fluttered above a squat, square building. Heat poured out of high, rounded windows as though desperate to escape. The shop had two steps leading to a heavy door whose frame was reinforced with iron strips. Kyra heard a rhythmic pounding of metal on metal coming from within.

Kyra's head swiveled left and right. Hayden was supposed to meet them there. Unless he was inside, he hadn't arrived. She heard hammering, no voices or conversation. Kyra's heart thudded with dread. The threat of the spies loomed around her. Solarus unconcernedly reached into his pocket and removed his pipe.

"The lower quarter is no small distance from the outer wall," Solarus commented, noticing Kyra's concern. He sat on the taller of the two steps and placed his staff on the ground. Then he fished out the newly purchased kolker leaves from his satchel. "If Hayden is not here by the time I am finished, we will go inside. He can find us there." Solarus sent a teal flame into the pipe's opening. He inhaled deeply and exhaled with a sigh.

Kyra impatiently continued to look for Hayden. Fortunately, she didn't have to wait long. Hayden tramped down the path moments later. His heels dug into the ground with aggressive steps. His gaze was brooding.

Kyra wasn't the only one who noticed Hayden's edgy bearing. Solarus raised a brow and lowered his pipe. "I take it that was not a simple meeting between two acquaintances."

Hayden's face muscles tightened. "It was enlightening, but no, not simple. That's how it is with Catt." He glanced at Kyra and switched topics. "Did you buy a map?"

"We acquired a map," Solarus replied casually.

Hayden frowned. "Acquired?"

"The cartographer expressed his great desire to make Kyra feel welcome in Thanesgard, so he sent it with her as a gift." Solarus put the pipe to his lips and puffed. "It was a very considerate gesture."

Hayden let out an amused laugh. "I'm sure." He tilted his head upward. Gray clouds blotted the previously clear blue canvas of sky. "We should have started back to the clock tower by now. We'll be late."

Solarus waved his pipe in a circle toward the door. "I see no harm in reinforcing the value of patience for Jyls. He and Ash can tolerate our absence for a while. Take your time. I will wait here." He contentedly puffed on the pipe.

Hayden walked up the steps, turned the doorknob, and walked inside. Solarus let out a long breath as Kyra stepped past him.

The moment she entered, searing heat hit Kyra like a blow drier in the face. An acrid scent of melted metal hung heavy in the air. Trying not to breathe deeply, Kyra looked around the spacious room. It was filled with workbenches, stools, strips of leather, and tools. An enormous furnace dominated the center. A bald man stood with his back to its flames. Beads of sweat crowned his scalp. His sleeves were rolled back over heavily veined arms. The smith banged a hammer repeatedly on a steel blade set on an anvil.

Kyra's eyes flitted to the walls. They were festooned with weapons. Her eyes skimmed over ornamented daggers, finely curved bows, and—Kyra's pulse quickened with excitement,—swords. The assortment ranged from unadorned, functional blades to swords whose hilts were studded with precious stones. The largest blades were the width of Kyra's leg, the thinnest no thicker than a flower stem. An intense longing awoke within Kyra. She couldn't wait to hold a sword in her hand again.

Again. The word echoed in her mind.

"Greetings, Master Smith," Hayden said loudly over the clanging.

The blacksmith, glanced up, hammer raised. Seeing Hayden, he set the hammer atop the anvil and wiped his hands on a soot-speckled smock. "The same to you, sir," he replied in a gravelly voice. The smith's gaze fell on Kyra. "And you, miss." The smith used the bottom of his apron to dab his forehead. "What service are you needing today?"

"I would like to find the lady a weapon." Hayden's gaze slid along the walls, then dipped to the tables in the room, most of which were covered with piles of blades. He rubbed a hand over his chin. "A sword befitting one of her size."

The smith grinned, exposing a mouth missing alternating teeth. It reminded Kyra of a piano, its white keys set against black spaces. "I have swords for all sizes," he replied good-naturedly. "Name's Makral by the way. I do all the work this side of Farcaren, plus special orders for Hogarth and Calonia." Makral reached into his apron pocket and pulled out a thick piece of string marked with lines. "Pardon my reaching around, miss, but I'll be needing your measurements." He wrapped the string around Kyra's wrist. He noted the mark on her wrist and nodded to himself. Then Makral held the string up to Kyra's head, letting the tail drop to the floor. "Are you sure it's a sword you're after?" Makral asked Hayden. "She's a bit delicate for a sword. Daggers'd be lighter and easier to hide. A bow'd be even better. It'd let her keep a respectable distance against some eager brute, if you know what I mean."

Hayden shook his head as Makral rolled up the string. "All worth examining in the future, Makral. At the moment, I'd like her to be equipped with a sword. She's not as delicate as you think." Hayden winked at Kyra. She beamed.

Makral chewed on his lower lip with his remaining teeth. Kyra looked on hopefully. "Might take some doing to get you a good fit," he decided finally. "I've an idea or two. A few years back, I forged plenty of blades for the king's new batch of pages and errand boys. 'Course, they came in as hungry as bears in springtime for blades twice their size and three times as heavy. Then one of the pages comes close to losing a few toes trying to lift one. That convinced the others to take my special-made swords. I may have some left."

Makral moved to a workbench near the furnace. Shiny steel blades gleamed brightly in the flames. Kyra felt sweat matting her shirt now that she was closer to the flames.

Makral ran his fingers over the pommel of a short sword. He glanced over his shoulder. "I should've asked at the start. What're you willing to put forward for this? Everyone knows Makral's craftmanship's the best in Ilian. The simplest blade in my shop's better than whatever work you'll see elsewhere. That's why Hogarthians and Calonians, they come to me if they're serious about a purchase. 'Course, if a blade's got a gem in the hilt, that's a few more florins from the purse . . ."

"I'm sure we can agree on a fair price," Hayden replied evenly. He raised a fat leather pouch in his hand and shook it. Coins jangled inside.

Makral's toothy smile widened. "Then, miss, you've a buffet of blades to sample."

Kyra watched Makral select swords from hooks on the walls. He placed them on an open space on the workbench. The smith also chose swords from a nearby table and added them to the collection.

When there was no more space on the bench, Makral motioned to a sword at the top of the pile. Its hilt resembled a raptor's closed claws. "Try this," he instructed.

Kyra lifted it with a dubious look. It was worn, and there were nicks in the steel. Even before she turned it over, Kyra knew instinctively it wasn't right. Her palm remembered something lighter, more flexible, more . . . hers.

"Not that one," Hayden rejected before Kyra spoke. His discerning eyes were on the blade.

Makral took the sword from Kyra and swapped it with one with a thick, curved blade. The hilt looked more suited to the smith's large, meaty hand than that of a teenage girl's. "This here sword was crafted for a Calonian duke, but the stingy ba—ah, the bugger never bothered collecting it. Top-notch work, left to rust."

Kyra had difficulty grasping the giant hilt. It wasn't the one either. "The duke might want to buy it later," she said tactfully, handing the sword back to Makral. "I'd feel terrible if he went through the trouble of commissioning one and then found out you sold it. What about that one?"

Kyra tested more swords on the workbench. The glitzy swords were the least manageable; the epees and foils too narrow; and the others too long, too cumbersome, or too flimsy. Sighing, Kyra set the last of the batch on the bench. Hayden watched, arms folded.

"I've a few more," Makral muttered in a frustrated tone. He seemed to take his inability to locate a suitable sword as a personal affront. "It's like I was saying, though. Everyone comes to Makral's smithy for a blade. Except . . ." He used his apron to wipe his forehead again, leaving a black smear of soot. "The smiths making women's blades specifically, they're in Peregrine. You don't need to be poking around Peregrine unless you have to, if you know what I mean."

Kyra didn't. Hayden, on the other hand, caught the smith's reference. He nodded.

"What about the female Royal Guards, like Larisa?" Kyra asked, trying to hide her disappointment. "Who makes their swords?"

Makral reddened. "Ah, yes, well, the female guard'd be an exception." He scratched his arm. "A smith by the name of Preeya forges them. Been her family's tradition going back to her great-great-many-greats' grandmother to make 'em for the king. Before the War of Calonia. Started with one of the daughters of a noble who didn't fancy playing hostess to soldiers. She wanted to be out fighting with 'em instead. She sneaked off to a smith, fashioned her own blade, then went and had a bloody good time of beating wizards." He chuckled. "Regnum finds out after the war and declares her the new smith for his guard. The family's been the royal outfitters ever since."

"Preeya's family didn't teach other smiths how to make swords like the Guards'?"

"Can't, not allowed," Makral answered with a shrug. "It's 'gainst the laws in Farcaren to make a sham blade. Preeya's swords are reserved for the Royal Guards."

Kyra's disappointment turned to a sense of futility. Her eyes traveled over the pile of swords one more time. A smooth, nondescript silver hilt poked out near the top. Curious, Kyra grasped the hilt. It rested comfortably in her palm. She carefully slid it free from the pile. Kyra's heart fluttered. The blade was lightweight, tapered neatly at the point, and had thin grooves lining the steel. Kyra glanced at Hayden. His eyes were transfixed on strange symbols etched into the bottom of the sword.

"That might be the one," he said softly.

"It feels . . . right." Kyra left off the desire to swing it. She reckoned Makral wouldn't appreciate being impaled with his own weapon.

"If it fits your hand, it was likely meant for it," Hayden replied. "The weapon chooses its master."

Like pets choosing their owner, Kyra thought as she pictured the fastidious Fifi. *Except you don't brandish a cat at your enemies.*

As Kyra looked to Makral, she saw a puzzled expression on his face. "Odd you chose that one, miss. That's the sole blade that *wasn't* made in this smithy. A traveler brought it to me, said he'd found it outside the grounds, assumed it was mine. I should've corrected him, sure, told him he could've kept it, but I was interested. It's a beauty. My conscience plagued me to return it. By the time I'd bumped around looking for the man, he'd already left Thanesgard."

Makral found a chestnut scabbard and handed it to Kyra. She slid the sword into it reverently.

"We would also like to purchase three bolas," Hayden said.

Makral took three golf-ball-sized iron balls from an opposite table. The balls were each attached to a piece of rope the length of Kyra's forearm and were knotted together at the end. Hayden kept one and handed her the other two. Kyra dropped the bolas into a pouch. Her belt loop sagged slightly under the weight.

Hayden's eyes revealed their satisfaction. "Now, Makral, I have to settle a debt with the best smith in Ilian."

The negotiation was quick. Makral's grin showed every tooth still lining his gums as he took a handful of coins from Hayden. "Come back anytime!" he said gleefully. "'Specially if you get an itch for a dagger or the likes. Makral's shop'll have what you need!"

Kyra skipped out the door and down the steps into the fresh, cool air. The gray clouds had scattered. Solarus stood, pipe stowed, staff in hand. She grinned widely at the wizard and proudly held out the scabbard. Solarus returned Kyra's elated expression with a look of displeasure.

"What basic instruction you had before you disappeared was not enough to defeat veteran swordsmen like Hayden," he cautioned sternly. Hayden took the scabbard from Kyra and fit it to her belt. "Leave the sword sheathed until you learn to use it. I am sure Hayden agrees with me." Solarus' tone implied he expected support for his statement.

"Until we can practice, yes, I would prefer you not draw it," Hayden supplied, though not without flinging an unmistakable look of annoyance at Solarus.

Kyra's shoulders slumped, crestfallen. Her pep gone, she traipsed after Hayden and Solarus. The scabbard clapped against her thigh. Kyra tried to hold it as she walked. It didn't help that her skin felt as cracked as fields in a drought from the shop's oppressive heat. She resisted the urge to scratch her hands.

"King Arkin hasn't sent word yet," Hayden told Solarus. "My suggestion is we meet the others at the clock, and then I go . . ."

Kyra gave up and started digging into her skin. The pricking was unbearable. She wondered if she could use more of Talis' balm to soothe the angry, red skin . . . Except when Kyra glanced down, the skin hadn't turned red. Yet. Her hands were haloed in the sparkling golden energy. Almost instantly, the itching disappeared. The golden magic had been prodding her to pay attention, to alert her that something was out there. Now that Kyra knew, the need for the relentless pain vanished.

"Hayden?" Kyra asked, trying to keep the panic from her voice. "Solarus?"

They immediately stopped and turned. Kyra held up her hands.

The contours of Hayden's jaw hardened. His gaze circled the crowd.

Solarus gripped his staff firmly. "It appears we will meet your spies after all."

Chapter 13

Hayden didn't hesitate. Snatching Kyra's glowing hand in his, he pulled her back toward the smith's shop. Marketgoers crammed together in the ring. Hayden and Kyra expertly dodged between them. It was like running through the packed streets of London, she thought. Minus the golden energy. Kyra tripped over the heel of a man's boot, but Hayden held her upright. When the crowd thinned, Hayden released her hand and dropped his hand to his scabbard. Kyra pumped her arms to keep up. All the while, her eyes ran over the masses of faces. Where was the energy coming from? She didn't feel the usual tug in one direction or the other. The magic seemed strangely ubiquitous. Was it the dark wizards or something more powerful?

Kyra knew Solarus was close by. Every so often, he bellowed, "Clear the way!" She saw passersby leap aside. Some cursed and shouted only to be silenced by Solarus' sharp, "Move or be moved!"

"Where are we going?" Kyra gasped to Hayden as they sprinted by more shops.

"The merchants' egress," he shouted over his shoulder. "It's a large clearing reserved for vendors. They load and unload their wagons there. There's a separate gate and bridge they use to leave the castle. We want to take that exit into the forest. I'm betting the spies are coming from the marketplace proper. They won't think we would take the egress. No one except the vendors uses it."

To Kyra's relief, the egress soon came into view. Hayden stopped running, eagle-eyed gaze moving in every direction. As Hayden described, it was wide and had flattened grass and depressions where boots and wheels moved over it. Merchants oversaw apprentices who placed wares into tall, stiff burlap sacks and packed saddlebags. Other vendors loaded small wagons with bushel baskets and barrels. A trio of women knelt on the ground counting their days' wages. They dropped coins into purses as their lips moved silently. The outer wall curved, making it impossible for Kyra to see the gate Hayden had mentioned.

Hayden strode forward. Solarus moved at an angle past Kyra. Kyra's hands ached with power. The golden energy unexpectedly flared as though doused with lighter fluid. She took in a sharp breath.

Four wizards appeared like shadows in wraithlike black cloaks. A vendor screamed and clutched her husband's arm. Merchants and apprentices ceased loading their wagons. One of the women counting the coins dropped the silver from her hands.

Hayden's sword snaked its way out of its scabbard. Solarus raised his staff. Keeping her hands in front of her, Kyra silently pleaded for her magic to work with her, not drag her toward the danger. The dark wizards fanned out, their cowls back. Kyra saw Galakis, Orkanis, and Nymphrys. She didn't recognize the fourth and youngest wizard. His ginger hair formed sharp, uneven bangs that looked like icicles hanging along his forehead. His cognac-colored eyes darted uncertainly to his companions as though looking for cues on how to act.

Kyra noted Nymphrys had recovered her staff from the forest. The wizard's ringed hand held it loosely at her side. Her lips were creased with a look of bored hostility.

Kyra started toward Hayden. A knob of smooth wood suddenly pressed into the side of her neck. Kyra cried out as magic burned her skin like a branding iron. She struggled to free herself. A hand wrenched Kyra's arm behind her back. The heat flowed from her neck down to her shoulder. Kyra blinked back tears of pain.

Hayden and Solarus spun around at Kyra's shout.

"Fight, and I will kill the girl," Kyra heard Adakis sneer from behind her.

A steely glint flashed in Hayden's eyes. He rotated his body enough that he faced Adakis while keeping the other four wizards in his line of sight.

"You would be dead before you could, Adakis," Solarus growled. His hornbeam staff glittered with turquoise magic.

Adakis laughed derisively. "You would challenge me? Even an elf isn't quick enough to stop my magic if I chose to blast her right now. Go ahead, Solarus, try me if you think I'm lying. Gamble her life."

From the corner of her eye, Kyra saw men and women wearing the uniforms of the Royal Guards. They filtered into the merchants' egress with weapons raised. Many of the stunned onlookers shirked from the armed force. The women tallying the coins jumped to their feet and fled, leaving their bounty scattered on the ground. The remaining bystanders seemed to hold a collective breath. Their attention was riveted to the standoff with the dark wizards.

Kyra felt budding hope as the guards crept forward. Arkin or Callum had gotten word about the wizards. They sent the guards to protect them. Callum might be there himself. A twitter of anticipation filled Kyra. Her eyes scanned the guards as best she could without moving her head. Her happiness faded. Kyra didn't recognize any of them. Strangely, Kyra also saw that the guards' faces weren't saddled with the grim resolve and readiness for a fight; they were wholly unsurprised and unconcerned by the events. Even more bizarrely, none of the guards moved to arrest the wizards. They were content to watch.

Hayden's expression hardened as he, too, spotted the soldiers. "This isn't a battle we can win," he said flatly. "The guards aren't here to assist us. They're here to help the wizards, not hinder them." Hayden's flinty gaze shifted to Adakis. "Considering how you courageously took flight after our last battle, I'm not surprised you added guards to your ranks."

Kyra stared at the guards in disbelief. *The guards are helping the dark wizards?* Callum *is helping the dark wizards?*

"Your insults are an acknowledgment of your defeat," Adakis gloated. "You cannot compare a man's pathetic steel to the might of a wizard. I can destroy a stampede of maddened boars with a breath of a word. I can demolish Thanesgard's walls as easily as conjuring up a fire. No, the guards' worth is in escorting you until Diamantas decides what punishment he chooses to exact."

Kyra could hear the smirk in Adakis' tone. She noticed the guards shift and exchange angry looks.

Solarus stepped forward. His eyes radiated such intensity that Kyra wouldn't have been surprised if he had vaporized Adakis through his glare alone. She took in a sharp breath as energy blazed from the knob of wood down her back.

"Don't test me!" Adakis snapped.

Solarus' jaw clenched. The scintillating turquoise energy on his staff vanished.

"Very good," Adakis said. "Let the witnesses here attest to Diamantas that you submitted without a fight."

"Where are the elf and the other two men?" Galakis questioned.

Hayden met Galakis' stare. "On their way to Hogarth. We came to the marketplace to replenish our supplies. They went ahead to warn King Theon about Diamantas."

"They will not get far," Adakis jeered. "The Reapers and greeloks will make short work of a company of three." The staff was removed from Kyra's neck as Adakis used it to wave at Hayden. "Surrender your weapons."

"Certainly." Hayden flipped the sword in his hand. He extended it, hilt first, toward Orkanis. The sallow-faced wizard jumped forward. His fingers wrapped around the hilt. Orkanis instantly howled and dropped the weapon. His hand hung limply at his side, the skin swollen and blistered. Stunned, Kyra's eyes dropped to Hayden's sword. The blade burned bright red as though it had been in Makral's furnace. Hayden's lips curved into a wry smile.

Orkanis rounded on the nearest merchant. "Take me to an apothecary!" he yelled. The merchant trotted away, eyes wide with fear. Orkanis ran after him.

"How completely brainless," Nymphrys derided as the two disappeared. Her large dark eyes reflected the same, put-upon expression as her lips. "Was I the only one minding Diamantas' warning? He told us to leave Hayden's sword. His exact words were that you will be 'hideously scarred' if you want to seize it." She ran a finger over one earring and added blandly, "Orkanis can show us when he gets back."

"I knew that," Adakis retorted angrily. "It was obviously a test to see if Orkanis was following the instructions we were given. Orkanis failed. Diamantas will hear of this. As the leader on this expedition, it's my duty to weed out unreliable and ungifted wizards. Diamantas already knows I'm among the most faithful and most ingenious wizards Harkimer has to offer. But you, Hayden." Adakis paused. "You think you are so clever. Ha. Now drop the blade."

Hayden sheathed the sword and unbuckled the scabbard. He tossed it to the ground.

"And your dagger."

Hayden reached beneath his leather jacket and pulled out a short blade. The dagger landed next to the sword.

"Solarus, your staff. On the ground. Over here." Kyra saw the tip of Adakis' boot as he gestured with it.

Solarus stabbed his staff firmly into the ground. The hornbeam shimmered once as though daring anyone to approach it. "A pity, Adakis," Solarus said without a trace of pity in his voice. "You can confiscate neither the sword nor the staff. How embarrassing it will be for you to explain to Diamantas that you yet again botched a simple task."

Kyra imagined Adakis' protruding ears burning crimson. She heard him snap to the Royal Guards, "Take them to the dungeons."

The guards directly in front of Kyra were apparently the ones Adakis had addressed. They hesitated, glancing from Solarus to Adakis as if unsure who was the greater threat.

Adakis jerked his staff from Kyra's neck and aimed it at them. "You're trying my patience," he barked, "and I'm the least impatient wizard you will ever meet. Do it!"

Impelled to action by Adakis' threat, a pair of guards rushed Solarus. The wizard didn't react as they roughly pinned his arms behind his back. Hayden shot forward. The first guard was knocked off his feet and hit the earth back-first. Hayden stood over him, rubbing his knuckles with a dark look. He turned to the second guard.

Kyra's anger finally exploded. She broke away from Adakis and hurled a helix of red energy at the second guard. The guard cried out, clutching his chest. He fell at another guard's feet. Red energy swirled hungrily around Kyra's hands. She whirled around. The craving to attack Adakis consumed her.

Adakis stared at her, stupefied. He was too astounded to cast a spell to defend himself as Kyra again raised her hands.

"Stay away from Solarus," Kyra commanded. She felt a hand on her uninjured shoulder. It was Hayden.

"Our 'escorts' should reconsider manhandling a pair of wizards," Hayden said darkly to the group. "I would keep your distance if I were you. We'll come on our own accord." Hayden turned Kyra slightly to face him. "It's all right, Kyra. You don't need your magic anymore. Solarus is fine."

Kyra didn't respond, blood coursing hotly in her ears. Hayden squeezed her shoulder lightly. The feeling broke Kyra from her trance. Shaking her head, Kyra silently ordered the energy to disappear. To her relief, the red and gold dissipated instantly. Without magic to distract her, Kyra felt the pain from Adakis' staff rush across her neck and down her back. She winced, envisioning blisters like the ones on Orkanis' hands dotting her tender skin.

"Um, Adakis." The wizard with the ginger hair wrung his hands. "Kyra has her sword. Should we take that, too? I mean, Nymphrys said not to touch it—" he glanced at the female wizard, "—but you wanted them to give us the weapons, and she has one, and I thought—"

Adakis glowered at the young wizard. "There is nothing special about *that* sword, Janus. Take the bloody thing, and stop asking imbecilic questions!"

Kyra repressed a frustrated breath. She had hoped they would forget her weapon. Kyra removed the scabbard and shoved it into Janus' hand. She heard onlookers muttering and whispering. Kyra's gaze lit upon two tiny girls with colorful scarves. One held an apple, the other an overstuffed bag. Kyra recognized them as the girls with the silver coins she had seen earlier. They peered out from behind a woman's skirt before dashing back into the crowd.

"Nymphrys and Galakis, go with the guards to the dungeon," Adakis directed. "Diamantas will want to be informed of this victory, which I will relay." He turned on his heel. Nymphrys and Galakis exchanged annoyed looks. "Oh. And take Janus with you."

Adakis flounced off. The assemblage of marketgoers hastily retreated to let him through.

Hayden inspected Kyra's neck. "The skin won't scar," he said in a low growl. "It will ache for a while. When we're free of this place, I'll find you a poultice to ease the pain. The burn is on your neck and shoulder?"

Kyra creaked her neck. A bolt of fire streaked through her muscles. "My neck, shoulder, and down part of my back."

Hayden's lips pressed together. His gaze was so vengeful, it took the guards a moment to summon the courage to approach him. "Move," a guard told Hayden. He indicated the way with a quavering wave of his sword.

The posse of dark wizards and guards forced Kyra, Hayden, and Solarus through the egress. Two guards led the way, followed by Nymphrys behind them. Galakis and Janus flanked the group along with the rest of the guards.

Word of the confrontation had spread through the castle. Servants, attendants, and maids had come outside. They joined the merchants and gaped at the entourage. One dark look from Nymphrys convinced the onlookers to scurry off.

The procession passed through a door leading from the outer ring into the fourth ring. They walked the circumference of the fourth wall until they reached the door to the third. Wall by wall, door by door, Kyra, Hayden, and Solarus were paraded toward the castle's center.

When they stepped into the inner ring, Kyra tried to get her bearings. They were facing the back of the square of four towers. Kyra guessed they were on the side of the castle opposite the courtyard with the fountain. Small houses occupied modest plots, with shrubs and trees offering shade from the hot sun. Servants who hadn't gone to the marketplace hurried in and out of the houses along a wide dirt footpath. The guards proceeded forward, businesslike, down the path. Kyra glanced at the houses, then caught Hayden's eye.

"Servants' quarters," he mouthed in response to her questioning expression.

They finally passed the last house. The guards halted. Kyra turned her head in confusion. There was nothing in front of them except grassy earth.

Not nothing, she realized as the guards looked down. A heavy circular door with two iron rings was inconspicuously dug into the ground.

Two guards started toward the door, but Nymphrys raised a hand. She tapped the iron rings and said, "*Takkara.*" The door flew open. It smacked the grass so hard the ground shook. Nymphrys gestured for the guards to continue.

"I don't understand," Kyra whispered to Hayden as they were herded down a steep flight of stairs. "They're the king's Royal Guards. Why would the guards be in league with Adakis? Some of them anyway," she inserted quickly. Kyra clung to the hope that Callum wasn't involved, that he would be the first to notice something was wrong, that he would seek them out. . . . "Aren't they worried the king will arrest them?"

"Arrest would be kind. The Royal Guards know Arkin's justice would fall swiftly on their heads if they acted on their own volition. They didn't. The guard with the dark hair was positioned outside the throne room when we had our audience this morning." Kyra couldn't make out Hayden's expression, since he stood before her, but she heard the contempt wedged into his words. "It would have been reported to Arkin that the guard had deserted his post. Arkin hasn't merely sanctioned the guards' actions; he commanded them to detain us. The king is colluding with Diamantas."

Kyra's heart plummeted sharper than the stairs that dropped off into the darkness. Callum was part of Arkin's plot.

The lead guard removed a torch from a sconce on the wall and lit it. The flame cast feeble light into the corridor.

Nymphrys released a vexed sigh. "I can't see my feet much less this passage." She gripped the guard's shoulder with her bejeweled hand and pushed him back. "Put that away. *Ascera.*" Bright purple energy flared at the tip of her staff. Galakis repeated the spell. An orb of orange light budded onto his staff. Janus, darting looks at Nymphrys and Galakis, added his ivory magic. The three colors illuminated the dark walls of the underground as brightly as daylight. The guard sheepishly extinguished the torch and set it back in the sconce.

Kyra's hair was raised on the back of her neck as they trod down the earthy corridor. Unlike the dry and dusty hidden passages in the castle, the air carried a mildewed dankness. Kyra's eyes flitted to cells as they walked by. They were ten feet wide and looked barely tall enough for a man to stand. They were also eerily vacant and stank of rancid meat. Kyra's stomach flopped.

Nymphrys led the group through several turns. Kyra tried to keep track of the directions, hoping it could help if they escaped. After too many rights and lefts, she gave up. Kyra was confident that Hayden and Solarus could find their way back to the surface. Janus' head swiveled nervously as though expecting a monster to spring on them. He tripped on the hem of his cloak and fell. The staff's ivory energy evaporated as it clattered on the ground. Cheeks reddened, Janus muttered an apology. He struggled to his feet with the help of Galakis and reignited his staff. Kyra wondered how the hapless wizard was in the company of intimidating figures like Nymphrys and Galakis.

Nymphrys halted before a larger cell. It had enough space to hold three prisoners. "In there," she ordered brusquely.

Hayden stepped inside. His gaze panned the walls and then the ground. Kyra made to follow, but Solarus raised a hand for her to wait.

"There are no traps or demons hiding in the corners, Solarus," Galakis said blandly. He brushed his scraggly hair from his face. "If we wanted to kill you, we wouldn't have gone through the effort to bring you here. Get inside."

Solarus shot Galakis a look as hard as iron but motioned to Kyra. As she passed through the door, Kyra shivered. It felt as though she were wading into ice water. Kyra heard a screech, followed by the sight of something long, thin, and wormlike. It disappeared in the cell's shadows. She blanched. It was a rat's tail. *At least we have something to eat if Adakis tries starving us to death*, Kyra joked to hide her disgust. *Maybe they do taste like chicken.* Unfortunately, the thought made Kyra queasier. She tore her attention back to Solarus, who had entered behind her. He touched the cell's iron bars experimentally. A guard pulled the door shut with a bang.

"I would stand back," Nymphrys told Solarus. Solarus removed his hand. Nymphrys muttered a sequence of undecipherable words. Then she touched the iron with her staff. The bars squeezed together like elevator doors, halting halfway.

Galakis brought his staff next to Nymphrys and also murmured. The metal crammed closer until the bars were a hair's-breadth apart. He glanced at an older guard. "Put it on."

The guard came forward, lifting a large silver padlock from his pocket. He hooked it through a hole in the door and slammed the lock shut. The guard tugged on it. The lock was firmly set.

"We didn't want to leave your escape to chance," Galakis said to Solarus. "In the event you devised a magical means of freeing yourself."

"When will Diamantas join these underground festivities?" Solarus asked coldly.

"When he chooses to do so," Nymphrys responded. She rubbed a ruby-encrusted ring on her middle finger. "Why, do you have another engagement, Solarus?"

"I was hoping to impart some advice. Diamantas would be wise not to relegate important tasks to menial wizards. It will not advance his campaign."

Nymphrys stepped so close to the cell doors that her foxlike tail of hair brushed the iron. "Open your eyes, Solarus," she spat. "Diamantas isn't stupid. He calculates every action he takes for the good of Harkimer. Adakis is here, because Diamantas believes his presence will benefit our cause."

"You make it sound as though you are pieces on a hunkana board, and Diamantas is controlling each move. You have surrendered your free will to him. How does that make you feel?"

"We have freely chosen Diamantas as our leader," Nymphrys hissed. "Isn't a war simply a game of strategy between two monarchs? Doesn't that make us, in some sense, his assets? Your view is skewed, Solarus. I feel that Diamantas prioritizes rescuing wizard kind above all else. That is why Galakis and I tolerate Adakis. It isn't because we care for his company—in fact, I would be much happier if Diamantas named Adakis the permanent envoy to the furthest coastal village in Calonia. We put up with Adakis, because Diamantas prizes loyalty, both in giving it and receiving it in kind. Without loyalty, he can't save us. Which, while we're on the topic, is something *you* haven't done or attempted. You're a traitor to your lineage. I hate traitors."

"Is it treason to protect the innocent?" Solarus replied, though the edge on his words had lessened. "Nymphrys, you are sensible. You have a good heart. Is the price of jailing us and potentially condemning a young woman to an execution worth the supposed rescue of the dark wizards? Wizards on both sides will be killed if the sands of time spill over. That battle has not yet begun. You can still do the right thing. Release us. Allow us to leave Thanesgard."

"What is right is saving my family. You 'free' wizards have turned your back on us in Harkimer. Don't dare assume I would do the same." Nymphrys stepped back from the bars. Her dark eyes flashed with more emotion than Kyra had seen since she met the wizard. "Let's go," Nymphrys said curtly to Galakis and Janus. The purple light shone brightly from her staff as she strode away. Galakis followed with a last, contemptuous glance at the prisoners. A fretful Janus skittered after him. The guards left last and without ceremony. They trailed a cautious distance behind the wizards. The corridor plunged into an inky darkness as they disappeared.

"Solarus?" came Hayden's strained voice through the black.

"*Ithansil.*" A small blue fire whooshed into existence in the middle of the cell. Solarus whispered something else and waved a hand over the ground.

"Thank you," Hayden said. His face was unusually pale.

Solarus inclined his head. "The guards have sided with the dark wizards," he said, rubbing his chin. "Arkin permits the actions of wizards he has long purported to despise. What could Diamantas have offered him to change his view, I wonder." The wizard sat on the cell's floor. It was coated with what looked like green slime. Solarus didn't seem to mind as he crossed his legs and leaned against the wall. Hayden began to pace the short distance between the walls.

Kyra remained standing. Her blood simmered, and it was all she could do to hold back her magic. Within twenty-four hours, Kyra had been spied on, taken hostage by the dark wizards, and thrown into a dungeon to wait for Diamantas—and whatever happened after that. Kyra ripped the midnight blue cloak from its clasp and threw it on the ground. The insignia of the dragon landed face down. "I hope the dratted thing molds and rats chew it to shreds," Kyra growled. She stomped on the cloak for good measure. Pain shot through her back and neck from the motion, making her even angrier.

"I cannot speak for the rats, but the cloak will not succumb to the elements." Solarus looked at her calmly. "The cell is quite dry."

Kyra's gaze coasted along the ground. The floor's lime green veneer wasn't slime. She bent over, this time trying not to stretch her burned skin. The floor was cushioned with foamy, very dry moss. Astonished, Kyra's eyes returned to Solarus. He had the smug look of a cat after a good hunt.

Kyra settled beside him. Running her hand over the plush surface, she asked, "Can we escape?"

Solarus' gaze traveled the length of the bars. "Perhaps. The magic used to bind the cell was rudimentary; the unbinding requires significantly more energy." He gestured to the bottom of the bars. A faint purplish-orange glow hovered around the iron. "Nymphrys and Galakis' charms are overlaid upon each other, doubling the magic's properties. However, there is another source of power imbued in the metal. If I am correct, which I often am in these cases, it is not a wizard's magic but another's. I sense it in the walls as well."

Hayden, who had been listening to the explanation, paused, mid-step. His gaze scoured the walls. Unlike the bars, there were no visible signs that magic was present.

"Interestingly," Solarus continued, "the magic was intended to *escape* this place. Not to trap one within it. When we harness that which is already present, we will create the necessary counterharm to Nymphrys and Galakis' spells."

"You can use energy that's here, even if it isn't yours?" Kyra asked.

Her fascinated tone garnered a wide smile from Solarus. "That is correct."

"I'm concerned with what we don't know," Hayden put in. He resumed his restless pacing. "Dark wizards are present. Who else might Arkin have situated within the castle? He wouldn't endanger his citizens by allowing Reapers into his territory. However, Arkin's willingness to deal with the wizards makes me question who else he might have dealings with."

"He let that train wreck of a wizard Adakis come here," Kyra replied crossly. She stretched her legs out, trying to ease the ache in her back. "Are most of the dark wizards like him, or are they like Nymphrys? If most aren't exceptionally bright, we have a good chance of beating them."

Solarus scratched his beard. "Based on my interactions with Harkimer's wizards, I have found many like Nymphrys. She is the person to whom Diamantas entrusts a task of import. Adakis is a simple-minded braggart. I would venture to guess that his participation in this situation is a matter of luck, not intention. Diamantas is a complex individual. He is cunning, and, as I told you when we first discussed him, full of conviction that he is wizard kind's savior. He would not have chosen a regrettable individual like Adakis to handle a crucial responsibility. Nymphrys and Galakis are ensuring Adakis does not destroy Diamantas' plans. They are as hazardously competent as Adakis is narcissistically inept."

Solarus placidly produced his pipe and the bag of kolker leaves from his vest pocket. He tapped the leaves into the pipe's opening. With a snap of his fingers, Solarus lit them with his teal flame. Kyra couldn't hide a grin. Their captors could confiscate Solarus' staff, but his pipe was off limits.

"I look forward to Arkin's explanation as to what he gains through this alliance," Solarus commented as he took a puff.

Kyra's brow furrowed. "Arkin wants to talk to us?"

Hayden ceased his pacing. He stood in the light cast by the fire. With a sigh, Hayden raked a hand through his hair. "Arkin is the king. We have been friends for years. What Diamantas did to earn the king's patronage must be something exceptional. Arkin considered the wizards of Harkimer—"

Solarus coughed, but it wasn't from the kolker smoke. "Arkin considers wizards *writ large* to be contemptible and untrustworthy individuals. Myself included. No doubt his opinions arise from the inferiority he feels compared to our kind." Solarus' haughty look mirrored the arrogance in his tone. "One hopes when a new monarch assumes the throne of Farcaren, he or she will have self-confidence. Self-confidence and intelligence are the cure for narrow-mindedness."

Hayden folded his arms. "As I was saying," Hayden said with a look of reproach at Solarus, "Arkin considers the wizards of Harkimer to be his foes. I've never known him to loathe the free wizards. But Arkin would never consider a person like Adakis a respectable envoy. That makes the king's betrayal even more puzzling."

Solarus looked unperturbed. "Our current circumstance will delay our departure but not by much. Arkin's farewell will be as brief as his welcome."

"You said the bars are magicked," Kyra said, glancing at the hazy glow on the cell's bars.

"I did. However, I said it was possible to free ourselves from this impoundment." Solarus tilted his pipe. "Galakis asked earlier where our companions had gone to. We can make a reasonable assumption the dark wizards have not found them. Which means . . ."

Hayden smiled grimly. "We have help."

Chapter 14

"Jaren and Garen, how many herbs do you need?" Jyls groused. His elbow was on the herb-seller's counter, and he tapped his foot impatiently. Ash's concentration was on the echinacea he carefully poured onto one side of a scale. When the balancing bowl lowered to a mark on the scale, Ash stopped. He handed the herb-seller the remainder of the packet.

"It depends on what we expect to treat," Ash replied. He stowed the herb in one of the many labeled bags he had bought. Ash sealed the top. "We're traveling across Ilian. I need more samples than were we staying in Farcaren. The climate here is mild. Farcaren doesn't really have insects or diseases. Calonia is hotter and has plenty of both. Back in Hillith, I keep more varieties of medicine. You never know when you'll need to stop a snake's venom or cure a fever caused by the bite of the seeomyzid fly."

Jyls repeated "seeomyzid" as though testing if his tongue was working.

"I have enough florins to buy medicines for the most common infections and injuries," Ash continued. "I can purchase other items along the way." Ash's green eyes were on the shelves behind the herb-seller. He pointed to a jar near the top. "Might I see the jewel weed?" he asked. The herb-seller nodded. She took a small stool from behind her and climbed to the shelf.

Jyls gave up on the pronunciation of the fly's name. "'The most common infections and injuries?' Such as?"

"A paste to treat hives from onyx nettles," Ash replied, taking the jar from the vendor's outstretched hand. "Onyx nettles grow in every kingdom. That's why we're buying jewel weed." Ash gently tapped the crushed plant onto the bowl on the scale. "We can find jewel weed in the wild, but it's better to buy it from an apothecary or herb-seller."

Jyls' boyish freckles wrinkled in disbelief. "We're wasting coins here on *weeds* when we can pluck them *for free?*"

"We could try and pluck them. The jewel weed looks identical to a destrum plant except for its leaves. The jewel weed's leaves are shaped like lances and have small teeth on the edges. The destrum's are completely smooth."

"So what?"

"If you treat someone with destrum, he could lose the limb or appendage to which you apply the paste."

"I like the number of limbs and appendages I have currently, thanks much." Jyls picked up a vial Ash had bought. "What's this?" he asked, tilting it to look at the translucent liquid inside.

"Be careful!" Ash intervened quickly. He took the vial from his friend, handling it as delicately as a rose. "That's tungbell. It's a very expensive antidote for Karoline poison."

Jyls raised his hands in defeat. "You're the expert." His eyes trailed up to the clock tower. Having rooted through the kiosks of five apothecaries, one nurseryman, and the herb-seller, Jyls and Ash had almost come full circle to the green space. Jyls dropped his gaze from the tower. "I'm going to meander over to our island, see if our friends are dithering about."

Ash placed the vial in his satchel. "Are we late?"

"No, it's quarter till three. You know how tyrannical Solarus is about punctuality. 'On time' for him means we have to meet ten minutes early; 'late' is meeting him promptly at the hour. You'll be able to find the clock without me, right?"

Red suffused Ash's neck. "I can see it from here," he muttered. "I'm not that lost."

"Wonderful." Jyls smacked Ash on the back. The crushed jewel weed leaves spilled from the jar and onto the counter. The herb-seller looked askance at Jyls as the healer hastily scooped up the leaves with an apology. Jyls put his hands in his pockets and strolled through the crowd. The savory aroma of meat and spices wafted through the air. His ears picked up sounds of fat spitting in a pan. Jyls glanced toward a grouping of kiosks. They were mobbed with activity. His gaze homed in on four vendors wearing thick aprons. They handed out steaming, flaky meat pies to their customers. Men laughed and toasted with small shot glasses. Then they tilted their heads back and tossed the clear liquid into their mouths, emptying the glasses in a single gulp.

As they cheered, Jyls grinned. Claret. "I'll be coming back to you, dear friend," Jyls promised. He picked up his pace as his stomach argued with him to switch course. The sooner Jyls collected Hayden and the others, the sooner he could enjoy the delectably smooth drink.

Jyls walked toward the clock tower. Marketgoers had laid blankets on the island of grass. Families ate midday meals on the large blankets. Women in thick dresses fanned themselves, complaining about the abnormally hot spring day. Men gabbed closer to the tower itself.

Jyls stepped between the picnickers and searched the faces around him. Hayden wasn't among the men. Nor, Jyls noticed as he passed a couple kissing each other under the tower, were Solarus or Kyra. He double-checked the clock. There were a few minutes until their planned meeting time.

A sense of unease wriggled into Jyls' heart. He grasped the silver bird pendant around his neck. Outwardly, there didn't seem to be anything out of the ordinary. The sunlight invited a relaxed drowsiness. But Jyls' years in a profession of mistrust and awareness overrode the false calm.

Then he saw them. Two black-cloaked individuals swept along a row of kiosks. The cloaks made their bearers conspicuously out of place among the festive garments of the marketgoers, like funeral ushers in a princess' birthday ball. Jyls' eyes tracked them. The Royal Guards wore black cloaks, as did Peregrinians. It was too hot a day for the guards to wear the cloaks. Peregrinians wouldn't risk attracting attention by wearing different attire from the crowd. And bandits didn't possess the liquid stealth of the duo Jyls watched. The individuals flowed through the marketplace as easily as gutter water in the alleys. Even without staffs, Jyls pegged them as dark wizards.

The pair slid away from the kiosks and turned in the direction of the clock tower. Jyls sidled closer to the groups of men jabbering away, camouflaging himself from the wizards' prying looks. The wizards' cowls were lowered. Galakis, with his scraggly black hair, moved with intense purpose. Orkanis, with his noodle-yellow strands, followed with an air of obedience.

"Hello, Kyra's spies," Jyls murmured to himself. The wizards didn't glance at the clock tower, so focused was Galakis on his route. As soon as they had moved down another row of kiosks, Jyls whizzed away from the tower. He wove through a gaggle of noblewomen oohing and aahing over woven silk rugs. Jyls slipped in between more merchants and customers and ducked under a tall man carrying a crate of glass figurines. Jyls straightened and paused. His head turned left and right. Jyls spied Galakis and Orkanis moving toward an alleyway. Galakis' glanced around suspiciously. He pivoted on his heel and stalked down the alleyway with Orkanis in tow.

Jyls trotted to keep up. He followed the wizards west of the marketplace, then north before they looped back southeast. Brow knitted, Jyls stayed several paces behind them. He suddenly heard marketgoers shout indignantly, "Watch where you're going!" Jyls glanced over his shoulder.

A twitchy younger wizard with ginger hair ran through the throng. The wizard bumped clumsily into the crowd, which garnered him dirty looks in addition to the reproachful responses. Jyls' brows arched. The wizard was coming directly toward him.

Jyls slid behind a nearby broken-down cart laden with apples and dates. Had the wizard seen him? Jyls craned his neck around the cart's back wheel. The ginger-haired wizard shot past the cart without a second glance.

"Galakis!" he wheezed. "Galakis! Gal—oops!"

Jyls carefully moved so that he had a clear view of the wizards. Galakis and Orkanis weren't close enough to hear the wizard's calls.

The wizard ran headlong into a plump woman carrying a basket of assorted clothing. The basket flew into the air and flipped over. The laundress, as weighty as a statue, stumbled but remained standing. The ginger-haired wizard landed on his back. Clothing rained into his lap. A girdle landed on his head. Had the situation not been so serious, Jyls would have laughed at the sight.

Galakis and Orkanis heard the commotion. They turned around in unison. Galakis rolled his eyes while Orkanis' lip twisted scornfully. The ginger-haired wizard removed the girdle from his scarlet-red face. The laundress collected her basket and stomped forward.

"You. Clumsy. Boy!" she berated, smacking the young wizard over the head with the basket. "Do. You. Know. How. Many. Hours. I. Spent. Scrubbing. This. Laundry? Do. You?"

"Ow!" Janus said. He scrambled backward to escape the laundress. "Ma'am, I'm sorry—ow!—I didn't—ow!—see you—ow!—there!"

Brushing his shaggy black hair to the side, Galakis strode toward the young wizard. Galakis held the edge of the laundress' basket as she raised it again.

"He is, much to our displeasure, with us," Galakis informed the woman as she tried to yank back her basket. He released it gently. "We apologize for the inconvenience."

The laundress glared daggers at him. "Apologizing doesn't fix me having to do the work again."

The ginger-haired wizard, who had managed to rise, rubbed the top of his head. "Couldn't we, um, help her, Galakis? You know, maybe we spell the dirt away . . ."

"Be quiet, Janus!" Orkanis broke in. His sallow skin paled as he glanced around at the amused onlookers.

"He's not right of mind," Galakis explained to the laundress in a long-suffering tone. He picked up the clothing scattered on the ground and handed it to her. "He was hit on the head when he was training to be a squire. Hasn't been the same since. He imagines he's a wizard or a king or a troubadour. The latter is particularly vexing if you've had the misfortune to hear his song."

"Make sure he stays *your* problem, not mine." The laundress jammed the clothing back into her basket. "What are you all looking at?" she barked at the crowd. She stormed off, still grumbling.

Galakis grabbed Janus by the elbow and jerked him toward the cart. Jyls again slipped behind the wheel. When he heard Galakis' heavy boots stop, he craned his neck around as much as he gambled. Galakis released Janus' arm with a venomous look. "I expect you have a *very* good reason for being *our* problem."

"I do," Janus said. "I mean, I don't, I'm not a problem. I came from the castle. Adakis and Nymphrys and I were waiting for Adakis' contact. We were in the parlor room, the one that has an entrance to the passage, with the lamp that looks like . . ."

"Spit it out, Janus!" Orkanis hissed.

"Adakis told me to tell you to come back to the castle," Janus concluded hastily. He scuffed his boots uncomfortably on the ground. "He said someone saw Kyra in the marketplace. Adakis was going to find them. He's got some guards too."

Galakis cuffed Janus on the back of the head. Orkanis' eyes again swiveled from left to right. "Don't say another word until we're away from here," Galakis growled. "It isn't hard pretending you're thick, but we can't explain secret passages and guards if we're overheard."

Janus' lips sealed with embarrassment. Orkanis gave him a sour look.

Galakis motioned with his head. "Follow me, and do not say a word."

Jyls watched the trio stride away from the cart. Janus was elbowed and pushed forward with the flow of the crowd. Galakis and Orkanis didn't bother waiting for him. Jyls let out a dry laugh. With such an encumbered pace, it would be easy to shadow them. Jyls stood and moved around the cart, as tightly wound as a spring.

Right before Jyls prepared to sprint after the trio, a realization jumped into his mind. Janus hadn't been with Adakis in the woods. Galakis and Orkanis had. As had the wizard Nymphrys, who wasn't accounted for in this group. Jyls touched the silver pendent on his neck, his expression pensive. Jyls was more concerned about the dark wizards he hadn't seen in the marketplace than the ones he had just spotted. There was already one new face in the mix. How many others might be lurking nearby? He and Ash needed to . . .

"Jaren and Garen!" Jyls smacked his head with his palm.

Ash.

In his intrigue about the wizards, Jyls had completely forgotten about the healer. Ash would be defenseless against one wizard, let alone three. Jyls pushed off from the wagon. For all he knew, Ash had been seen by the other wizards. Maybe even captured. Guilt and fear lent Jyls greater speed as he threaded his way through and around customers. He veered east to where he had left his friend. Jyls hoped it wasn't too late.

***

Hayden and Solarus insisted Kyra remain seated on the moss-covered ground while they searched the cell. She was happy to comply. Kyra's muscles ached less as she reclined on the foamy carpet. Her mouth was dry. Her stomach grumbled. Was it really only hours earlier that she, Hayden, and Solarus had been at breakfast in the castle? Kyra watched as Hayden ran his fingers along the damp walls. The light from Solarus' blue fire cast shadows over the dark space, forcing Hayden to feel his way for a slit to a passage. Solarus extended his hand toward the ceiling. Turquoise sparks flew up. Solarus repeated the action with the bars. When Hayden determined the walls had no hidden outlet, Solarus sent another wave of magic at the cell door. The bars glittered, but the turquoise wisped away without effect.

"What's the source of the magic?" Kyra asked. Hayden took a seat against the wall abutting hers, knees raised. "Can you free it from the bars?"

Solarus regarded the door with a peevish look. "I don't know, and not yet. I must think on it." He returned to the fire and sat across from Kyra. His pipe lay on the ground, half lit. Solarus picked it up and drew in a long breath. The apple-spiced kolker leaves provided a pleasant scent to cover the dank-smelling air.

Kyra's gaze drifted from Solarus to Hayden. It would take time for them to break out from the cell. With nothing else to distract her, a spigot of questions opened in her mind. Kyra had them earlier; in fact, she had often posed them to Hayden and Solarus during their travels. They had deftly deflected the questions or found reasons to be elsewhere. Having to flee from Reapers and fight dark wizards didn't give Kyra the opportunity to raise the topics again. Until now. Kyra cleared her throat. "If we're going to be here for a while," she said as casually as she could, "I have some questions."

"How unusual," Solarus responded sardonically.

"We haven't talked about my past. About my history in Ilian before I disappeared. Who I was, who my family is, how we all met . . . any of it."

Uncharacteristically, Solarus didn't reply. Pipe in mouth, he suddenly became interested in his cloak, unnecessarily smoothing the creaseless material. Kyra's eyes moved to Hayden. He twisted his silver ring uncomfortably.

"You haven't told me about where I'm from," Kyra pressed. "Where are my parents? When did I go to Silvias, and why did I go? Talis told me when we were in Edoin that I was raised with the elves and that you—" she cast a glance at Hayden, who didn't meet her eyes, "—brought me there. He also said I sneaked out of class and did a lot of chores as a punishment. That doesn't give me much to go on for fifteen years I can't remember."

Kyra waited for an answer. The light from the blue fire accentuated the contours of Hayden's face as he stared absently into the flames. Solarus puffed quietly on his pipe. Kyra's expression dropped, crestfallen. Even in the cell, they refused to give her any insights.

After a while, Kyra's disappointment transformed to apprehension. Kyra assumed Solarus would launch into a diatribe about what Kyra, as a wizard, had once been taught, had likely now forgotten and, inevitably, had to be relearned. He should have scolded Kyra about letting her magic jerk her from place to place like a kite caught in a tornado.

Solarus didn't. Kyra tried to catch his eye, but he deftly avoided her.

A creeping suspicion entered Kyra's thoughts. She unconsciously rubbed a thumb over her palm. *It's the red magic. They must have witnessed it in the courtyard.* Kyra had caught Solarus' perplexed—or was it alarmed?—expression. She had never divulged information about the red magic before. Certainly not about her experience with the Variavryk at Somerset House. The manic pleasure she had taken in watching Reuben suffer. What if . . . Kyra's stomach sank. What if Kyra had faced a similar situation in Ilian that she couldn't remember? Had she hurt someone in a fit of anger? Had she destroyed something out of fear? As it had countless times before, Kyra wondered if *she* had started the fire in Chicago. She knew now that blue fire was real. The red magic was wild and savage. Combining the two could result in a blaze that consumed everything it touched. Christin had told Kyra repeatedly the forensics had found no evidence, no remains of the house or its inhabitants. How unusual it was. A shiver ran down Kyra's spine. She *couldn't* be a killer.

"You are not incorrect." Solarus said abruptly.

Kyra stared at him in consternation. Had he read her thoughts?

Shadows danced on the walls as Solarus raised a hand toward the blue flame. "You cannot hope to be a part of this world without understanding from where you have come."

Kyra released a nervous breath. He hadn't read her thoughts then.

"You are free to ask any question you would like. However, there are stipulations. We will answer some questions, but we will not answer all."

Kyra opened her mouth to object, but Solarus interrupted sternly, "Knowledge is to the mind as rain is to a forest. The trees require water for nourishment, yet their soil cannot absorb the deluge of a storm. The forest requires a modest, steady rain. It is no different with the mind. You can retain but so much at one sitting."

Kyra threw her fears about Chicago into a crevice in her mind. It would have to wait. "You don't think telling me the entire history of the War of Calonia *and* Diamantas *and* the Wizards' High Council was too much information?" she asked dryly.

"That was necessary context for you, without which we would not have gained your trust. Nor would you have taken the dangers in Ilian as seriously, I would venture."

"You're making up rules when it's convenient," Kyra grumbled.

Solarus glanced sideways at Hayden.

Hayden continued to twist his ring, staring into the fire. Finally, he raised his head. The light of the flame couldn't chase off the troubled shadows in his gray gaze. "All right," Hayden acquiesced reluctantly. "I agree with Solarus. What do you want to know?"

"Where did I come from? Where was—or is—my family?"

Hayden folded his hands. "I don't know who or where your parents are, Kyra. I never met them. By chance, I found you near a forest at the foothills of the Southern Mountains. More accurately, you found me."

Kyra's eyes flickered with confusion. "What do you mean, you 'found' me? Or I 'found' you? Why would I have been near the Southern Mountains?"

"I had ridden to the foothills of the Southern Mountains," Hayden explained. "The forest is thick with firs and pines. I was ... preoccupied. I didn't notice that you were among them, not until you walked out. You were about four years old at the time, and you were alone. I had no idea how you came to the forest. Your parents weren't with you. I searched for them, but there was no one in that desolate place save you and me. I decided to take you with me. You wouldn't have survived in the forest."

Kyra bit back a hint of frustration. Hayden's answers dribbled out, and they weren't even real answers. "A desolate place?" she repeated. "Then why was I there? How could I have gotten there?"

Hayden's expression was laden with a tumult of emotions. Sorrow. Torment. Guilt. "That's a mystery to which I have no answer. I returned to the spot several times, but I never found even a fragment of a clue as to your origins. All I can tell you is there was no one within leagues of the forest."

The vague answer fanned Kyra's frustration. "My parents abandoned me."

"I didn't say that."

"You aren't saying much." Kyra regretted her petulant retort as soon as she saw remorse added to Hayden's expression. "I'm sorry, Hayden. I didn't mean that. It's just that I've wondered about my parents and where I came from for a long time. I hoped you could tell me more." A thought popped into Kyra's mind. She reached over to her discarded cloak with the crest of Farcaren. Lifting it, Kyra rummaged through a pocket and pulled out her map. She was grateful Solarus had dried the ground. When Kyra peeled back the folds of the parchment, she saw the map was perfectly intact. "Can you show me where you found me?"

Hayden hesitated. Then he moved closer to Kyra. She turned the map to the side so he could see it more clearly. Kyra wondered if she imagined the fearful shadow that spread over his face as his eyes scanned the base of the Southern Mountains. He traced a spot with his finger along a tree line to the north of Edoin Forest. "Those are the foothills of the Mountains," he said in a strange voice. "That's where I found you."

Hayden's head snapped up at the sound of scraping. He stared into the darkness beyond the cell. Solarus raised a hand.

Kyra turned the map so it faced her again and consulted it. Her brows knitted. As far as she could see, no towns existed near the forest. If Hayden were telling the truth, it was almost impossible for Kyra to have come from Hogarth or Farcaren without a way across the river. How did she get to the foothills? Nothing added up. Her eyes wandered up the map. Her stomach plummeted as she reached a new conclusion. There *was* one way she could have made it to the forest. With her parents, then alone, for a time. It was the logical explanation. Kyra touched the image of the snowcapped Southern Mountains.

Kyra was from Harkimer. She was a dark wizard.

Chapter 15

Kyra's mouth was dry. She glanced discreetly at Hayden and Solarus. Their attention was focused on the sound that had distracted them from the conversation. She quickly looked away. The avoidance of a discussion of her past. The woolly answers. The meaningful looks they exchanged with each other. They didn't want her to discover the truth.

Maybe, having found her so young, Hayden and Solarus thought they could leach the disease of being a dark wizard out of her.

Kyra's pulse quickened. What if her parents had fled and taken her with them? Solarus had told Kyra that not all the wizards in Harkimer had malicious intentions. They had simply been born in a kingdom with a nefarious history. Her parents might have been desperate to escape the bonds of Harkimer. Were there others like her and her parents? Wizards who fled Harkimer? Kyra's instincts told her no. If there were others, Diamantas wouldn't expend so much energy on her. Those wizards would be older, more experienced, and far more important. If she *were* the only one though . . . It wasn't the first time Kyra wondered why Diamantas was so intent on the capture of a teenage girl. Kyra's escape provided an explanation. Had Diamantas sent Adakis and Galakis to hunt her down because he feared Kyra could spill secrets about the dark wizards? Or was Diamantas concerned the dark wizards would learn they could return to Ilian without his help? That they wouldn't be persecuted like he alleged. It would weaken Diamantas' claim to be the uncontested leader restoring his kin to their rightful place in Ilian.

Kyra was flung back to her contemplation about the red energy. Its wild nature had to be an evil manifestation of magic. She remembered the thrill of power as she used it. That was why Hayden and Solarus so urgently wanted to bring her to Silvias. To deter any temptation to return to Harkimer.

You choose who you are through your thoughts. You decide what you become through your actions. Have faith, not doubt.

The sensation, normally a soft breeze, swept like a gale inside Kyra's heart. The weight of the emotion took her by surprise. Her gut instincts felt muddled. Was this an affirmation that Kyra was a dark wizard but didn't *have* to be? Was it telling her she wasn't from Harkimer at all?

You choose who you are, you decide what you become.

Bewildered, Kyra silently answered. *I've decided I'm bewildered. What does that mean, 'you choose who you are?'* Kyra suddenly shrieked and scooted back toward Hayden. Two somethings skittered along the ground. Solarus turned from the bars. He raised a hand and pushed the blue flames nearer to where she had been sitting. The blue illuminated a pair of rats huddled in the corner near Kyra. Solarus held his hand steady. A turquoise bubble appeared around the rodents, trapping them inside.

"They share our misfortune, it seems," he commented as the rats futilely threw themselves against the shield. He tapped out the remaining kolker leaves, pocketed his pipe, and stood. Solarus' back was to Hayden and Kyra as he again inspected the cell's bars.

Kyra let out a sigh and turned. Hayden studied her, his countenance troubled. For a fraction of a second, Kyra wanted to confront him. Did he or did he not think she was a dark wizard? Her fear of his response held her back. Hoping her expression wasn't splattered with anxiety, Kyra asked, "Where do I say I'm from then? When I introduce myself? Like when King Arkin pressed me to answer as Kyra 'of' somewhere. Do I say 'of Silvias,' like Talis did? Because I'm not *from* Silvias."

"You are from Silvias, in a way. You are also from the foothills of the Southern Mountains. We might not be able to name a specific village or town yet. That doesn't mean we won't uncover the answers in time. Be patient." A genuine smile spread across Hayden's face. "We could always call you 'Kyra of the bridge to another world.' The point is the place doesn't matter right now. Take pride in who you are. You're Kyra."

Kyra. What did a name mean without a history attached to it? It was a just a word. Not an identity. Kyra sighed. "Why was I safest in Silvias? Because I was a wizard? Did you know I was a wizard when you found me?"

"I mentioned this already, but it apparently requires repeating." Solarus looked down from the bars and regarded Kyra with a severe look. "You are beginning to flood the soil with your inquiries. You have swallowed a draft of information. Allow it to nourish your mind before you drink further."

Solarus' tone left no room for argument. Kyra unwillingly turned off her faucet of questions, though lingering thoughts trickled out. "Can I ask you about Jyls?" Without waiting for a response, she went on, "Ash already mentioned he met Hayden in Calonia. Where did you meet Jyls?"

To Kyra's surprise, Hayden grinned.

Solarus rubbed the Z line in his hair. "Our friend from Lystern was employed by a wizard named Syndrominous. He was, at least at that time, Diamantas' fiercest rival in Harkimer."

Kyra's jaw dropped. "That can't be true. Jyls would never, I mean, I don't see him taking orders from anyone. Jyls strikes me as very . . . independent."

Hayden laughed for the first time since their imprisonment. "That's a tactful way of putting it. Jyls was not a friend of the dark wizards. He told us later that his employment was temporary and to execute one task."

"Jyls despises the dark wizards. What could Syndrom . . . What was his name again?"

"Syndrominous."

"What could Syndrominous give Jyls that would convince him to help?"

"Jyls' thinking at the time was opportunistic," Hayden explained. "When you don't have a steady means to secure your next meal, your scruples are somewhat flexible. Syndrominous offered him a small fortune for the job."

Kyra's brows arched. "Jyls never told me his profession. If the work wasn't reliable, then he probably wasn't a shop owner." She glanced meditatively to the side, where the rats scratched at the turquoise bubble. "I also doubt Jyls is a scholar. Not because he isn't smart enough; he would have to sit for extended periods of time. It doesn't fit his personality." *Which I can say, since he reminds me of me,* Kyra added to herself as Hayden's grin widened.

"Jyls is neither a shop owner nor a scholar nor a practitioner of a profession involving prolonged periods of sedentary work," Hayden confirmed. "His occupation is common in Peregrine." Hayden eyed the fire, placing his hands near the flame. His gaze turned inward, and he smiled at something only he could see. An idea wormed its way into Kyra's mind. She had accessed Talis' memory of their archery lesson. With enough concentration, Kyra might be able to do the same with Hayden.

That's his private memory, not yours, Kyra's conscience objected. *You wouldn't want someone peeking into your world.* But was different, Kyra argued against herself. Her past had been stolen from her. Hayden, like Talis and Solarus, had an intimate knowledge of Kyra. She barely had any information in return. This was a way of understanding her companions better. *Perfectly justifiable.*

Before her conscience could provide a rebuttal, Kyra stared at Hayden and channeled her thoughts into a forceful desire: to witness the scene unfolding in his mind. For a moment, nothing happened. Then Kyra was wrenched forward internally. Instead of hooking Hayden's thoughts, Kyra was tangled in the lines that led to the memory. As she was reeled in closer to him, the blue flame, Solarus, and the cell shimmered and fell away. Her new surroundings rushed in. The stink of ale and heat assaulted her. Raucous hoots and drunken laughter barraged her ears. A large room filled with tables, benches, and mugs came into focus.

> *Tavern benches were crammed full of travelers taking refuge from the winter's cold. Barmaids carrying trays deftly navigated the tables. They occasionally batted away a wandering hand as they delivered mugs and plates of food. The offenders grinned with mock innocence.*

Kyra stood beside one of the tables. Her eyes widened. Talis sat on a bench at the end, his elbows on the table as he leaned forward.

> *"There is little time left," Talis said in a hushed tone.*
> *Hayden sat across the table from the elf. In his hands was a mug. His gaze surveyed the crowd, lingering on a man who had spilled his drink onto his lap.*
> *"The Sirenyle have seen Reapers straying through the borderlands of Hogarth and Peregrine," Talis continued, amber eyes intently focused on Hayden. "We haven't seen the creatures in Ilian for . . ."*
> *"Centuries." Hayden's attention shifted to Talis. His eyes were steely as he turned the mug in his hand.*

"It's not only the scouts' reports that trouble me. I sense a darker presence. It suffocates Ilian like smoke trapped within a house. The Al-Ethran have sent messengers throughout Ilian. Normally, they interact only with the elven scouts at the castles."

"Lynerithan said Kyra wouldn't return by the moon or the stars," Hayden replied darkly. "He's been right thus far. It's been three months—three months, Talis—since she disappeared. What have we accomplished? What signs have we found? Nothing and none."

Hayden released the mug and unconsciously felt his right shoulder. He winced in pain and dropped his hand. With a sharp exhale, Hayden took out bronze florins from a pouch and tossed them on the table. They spun, clinking as they landed. Hayden stood. The man beside him eyed the bronze coins until Hayden's hand dropped conspicuously to his sword hilt. After the barmaid collected the florins, Hayden stepped over the bench.

"I've had enough of this company," he said as Talis moved beside him. "We've got a long way to Calonia. The sooner we find him, the sooner we can return to Silvias."

Talis nodded.

Do I follow them? Kyra thought as she watched the elf and Hayden weave their way through the crowded room. In the memory with Talis, they had been in one location. Would the memory continue if she stayed in the tavern? Hesitating for a heartbeat, Kyra darted to the door. She completely neglected the barmaid striding across the room with bowls of hot soup. Kyra couldn't stop fast enough. Wincing, Kyra turned away with her arm raised to keep the barmaid from running into her. The woman walked straight to Kyra—and walked through her as though she were as insubstantial as air. Kyra blinked and lowered her arm in amazement. She turned and stared at the barmaid, who placed the soup on a table in front of two ravenous patrons. *What just happened?* Kyra shook her head. She didn't have time to think on it further. She needed to follow Hayden and Talis. Fortunately, they had paused at the entrance. Kyra sprinted toward them.

Hayden was about to open the door when a man bundled tightly in a gray wool cloak stumbled into him. Hayden's jaw tightened as the man grabbed his wrist to steady himself.

"'Pologies, mate, so many 'pologies," the stranger slurred. His face was half-covered by a scarf, and he stank of alcohol. "Good strong ale, this, yeah? Good eve, good eve." The stranger flung open the heavy tavern door. Cool air whooshed inside. Courtesy of the ale, the man seemed impervious to the cold. He hurried away, boots barely making tracks in the snowy ground.

Hayden caught the door before it swung shut. He stepped out, with Talis behind him. Hayden's hawkish gaze followed the stranger. Instead of heading down the main road, the man veered sharply right. He was surprisingly quick and balanced for an intoxicated patron. Hayden started after him.

"Talis?" Hayden called over his shoulder as he trotted forward. *"Would you mind staying our friend for a moment? I'll give you a silver florin if you catch his cloak."*

Talis unslung his bow and notched an arrow to the string. Aiming low, he fired. The point pinned the tip of the man's cloak to the ground. The man lurched backward but managed to keep his balance. The cowl fell back. The man's pale, freckled cheeks had turned red from the cold, and his hair sprung out in a disordered mess. He frowned and tugged at the cloak. The arrow held fast.

Hayden untied three iron balls attached to thick rope from his belt. Wheeling the rope over his head, Hayden flung the iron. It whipped in circles and wrapped around the stranger's legs. This time, the stranger fell into the snow.

"Jaren and Garen . . ." Hayden and Talis heard him mutter as he sat up. He shook snow from his hair. Tilting his head, the man immediately set to unknotting the rope that secured his legs.

Hayden removed a silver florin from his pocket and flipped it at Talis. The elf caught it with a grin.

Kyra trailed Hayden and Talis, unaware she was holding her breath. It was Jyls.

The stranger left off with his work. "I'd appreciate it if you took these off." His tone was imbued with studied annoyance and had no trace of his former insobriety. "You don't want to hold me up from my journey."

Hayden arched a brow. "Why is that?"

"Because." The stranger straightened as best as he could, cultivating an indignant look. "I am King Trisanton's advisor. His personal *advisor. Do you want me to tell him that some vagabond and his ragtag elf delayed me from attending a council meeting?"*

Hayden glanced at the clear dusk sky. "Odd to have a meeting so late."

"The king prefers to work under the light of moonbeams and twinkling stars."

"If he's like other Peregrinian kings, I'm sure he's more comfortable hidden in darkness. As are bandits and thieves looking to make a quick and ignoble escape."

"I wouldn't know." The stranger looked at Talis. "Did you really need to shoot an arrow at me?"

"Yes," the elf replied evenly. "I don't want the cloak to suffer another indignity, but if you move, it will."

Hayden knelt next to the stranger and reached inside the man's cloak. On his belt was a leather pouch. Hayden removed it from the man and dumped the contents into his palm. A leather cloth fell out. Inside of it was an engraved silver ring rimmed by white gold.

"Hey, that's mine," the stranger protested as Hayden fit the ring on his finger. "Hasn't anyone told you stealing is against the law?"

"I know." Hayden's gray eyes locked on the man's midnight blue ones. "Obviously, you don't. Interesting that you used a cloth to lift the ring from my hand. What made you believe you couldn't touch it?"

The stranger seemed genuinely confused. "Why I couldn't touch it? I have no idea what you're talking about. The leather keeps valuable pieces from getting scratches or blemishes. I've never known silver or gold to bite."

"This silver does if anyone but me handles it." Hayden abruptly snatched a small dagger from his boot. He held the point at the stranger's neck. "If you dare to purloin my ring or any other of my belongings ever again, you won't live long enough to enjoy the spoils." Hayden glanced up at Talis. "What do you recommend we do with our thief?"

"He seems comfortable in the snow," the elf replied thoughtfully. "I see no reason to disturb his peace."

"What?" The thief looked resentfully from Talis to Hayden and back. "You can't leave me here. I'll freeze, and then you'll have to explain to Trisanton why his advisor . . ." The thief broke off. His eyes shone with alarm as he stared at a point beyond Hayden. "I take that back. I won't freeze. We're about to be that thing's supper."

Hayden and Talis pivoted.

Standing behind them was a four-legged beast. It resembled a large dog with fangs that hung below its lower lips like two swords. The creature's tongue hung lazily from its mouth. Its lips curled back to reveal rows of jagged-edged teeth. It stared at the group with clouded eyes.

Kyra gasped, forgetting in her terror that the greelok couldn't hurt her. It leapt into the air with an inhuman screech.

The beast was punched in the side, mid-flight, by an arrow. It crashed into the snow. Talis fit another arrow to his bow.

Hayden quickly stooped beside the thief. With a swift motion, he cut the ropes free from the thief's legs. Hayden set the dagger, hilt first, in the thief's hands and ripped the arrow free from the cloak.

"Keep that," Hayden told the thief. Hayden shot to his feet, sword drawn.

The thief jumped up nimbly beside him. "Much obliged," he said, flipping the dagger expertly with his wrist.

"Greeloks." Talis' eyes narrowed, searching the distance. "More will be upon us soon."

"Make for the stables," Hayden instructed. With a glance at the thief, he ordered, "You, too. You wanted to steal this specific ring, and I want to know why."

"No sense in waiting then." The thief immediately took off at a sprint. Hayden and Talis matched his pace.

Kyra ran after them.

"To answer your question," the thief said, his cloak flapping behind him, "My sponsor for this outing was a wizard. Name of Syndrominous. Left side's as limp as a rotten banana peel."

Hayden kept his sword drawn as Talis looked in all directions. "Syndrominous?"

"Friend of yours?"

"Enemy, actually."

"The greeloks are gaining distance," Talis interrupted. He halted, spun on his heel, raised his bow, and fired a pair of arrows. They were answered by yelps. The elf continued to turn until he completed a full circle. It took a fraction of a second for Talis to fire the action, barely losing his stride.

"This Syndrominous," the thief continued, showing no signs of tiring, "he dropped me a chunk of gold florins to filch that ring. Said I'd get double the price when I successfully delivered it to him."

"There are thieves by the dozens in Peregrine. Why did he choose you?"

"Thieves that make names for themselves inevitably get caught. I'm a humble man lacking any fame, fortune, and most importantly, a reputation. It makes me the best thief to have sneaking around."

"Fair point," Hayden replied, though he saw a missing link in the story. As expendable as wizards viewed thieves, Syndrominous had a reason to find this one for such a risky mission. Stealing from Hayden—and living—was an almost impossible task.

Kyra reached the open stable doors behind Talis. She had expected to be winded. Instead, Kyra felt completely normal. She glanced around in apprehensive anticipation of the greeloks.

The trio dashed inside. Talis leapt from the closest stall door onto the saddled back of Windchaser. Hayden unlatched the stall beside Talis where Willow whickered anxiously. The thief darted to the back of the stables and mounted a black-and-white draft horse. Like Hayden and Talis' steeds, the thief's horse had been left saddled in case of a sudden departure. Like this one.

The group piloted their horses toward the stable entrance. Greeloks blocked their escape, gnarring and gnashing their jagged teeth.

Hayden spurred Willow forward with a battle cry. As one of the creatures snapped at Willow's legs, Hayden swung down mightily with his sword. It skewered the greelok's side. The greelok sank to the ground as Windchaser shot out from behind Hayden with lightning speed. Talis' arrows found more greeloks, who shrieked and fell back. He had created an opening between the greeloks, allowing Hayden to ride through. The elf came next, with the thief covering the rear.

A greelok leapt toward Willow's back as they burst into the snow. Hayden twisted in his saddle and sliced through the air over the mare. The blade ran through the greelok's belly but not before the creature slashed at Hayden. The claws dug into Hayden's right shoulder, tearing into his recently healed wound. Hayden gritted his teeth. Blood stained his clothing.

"Watch out!" Kyra screamed, forgetting Hayden couldn't hear her. Her hand went to her mouth as Hayden turned hazily toward a greelok crouched to spring.

Before Hayden could react, the creature crumpled deep into the snow. Red spilled out around him. The hilt of Hayden's dagger was buried deep in the greelok's neck.

The thief rode next to Hayden. The elf had wheeled Windchaser around and rode back to them. The greeloks lay scattered on the ground as more baying resounded in the distance.

The thief vaulted from the horse, yanked Hayden's dagger out of the greelok, and remounted. "Thanks for the loan," he said, holding out the dagger.

Hayden held his sword and Willow's reins both in his left hand. His injured right shoulder continued to bleed. "Keep it for now. What's your name?"

The freckle-faced man gave a flourish from his saddle, a flourish Kyra had seen many times.

"Jyls of Lystern, thief extraordinaire, evidently now at your service. A hasty and respectable service."

Kyra was abruptly catapulted out of the memory. She closed her eyes to stop an onset of dizziness. When she opened them, the blue-lit cell had returned. Hayden raised his eyes, a grin on his lips.

Pulse racing, Kyra glanced to the cell's door. Solarus held both hands toward the bars, murmuring strings of words under his breath.

Her mind was fastened on the horrific creatures she had seen and her friends' narrow escape.

"What's wrong?" Hayden asked. "You're pale."

Kyra shook her head as though to dispatch the remnants of the memory. "Greeloks are terrifying," she responded unthinkingly. "I never would have guessed Jyls was a thief. Except he knew what the Nines and Sevens were," Kyra remarked, suddenly recalling his words in the marketplace. "I wonder if there are groups of orphans in Peregrine, too."

Hayden stared at her, thunderstruck. Solarus' head jerked in her direction as well. His gaze was as hard as ice.

Belatedly, Kyra realized her comments were unrelated to anything they had discussed.

"Where have these statements come from?" Solarus asked sharply. "We never mentioned greeloks. We also never revealed Jyls is a thief."

"I . . . well, I . . ." Kyra scrambled for an explanation, uncomfortably aware of Solarus' gaze boring into her. She tucked a lock of hair behind her ear and decided on the truth. "I saw . . . something. With Hayden. From Hayden. About Jyls."

Kyra shriveled inwardly as she saw Hayden and Solarus swap wary expressions. She knew it was her own fault. Even though her conscience warned her against it, Kyra had invaded Hayden's privacy with a voyeuristic selfishness. Just because she wanted to know what he was thinking didn't mean she had a *right* to know. *How would I feel if someone sneaked into my mind?* Kyra had her secrets, her fears, her doubts, all locked away in her mind. If someone found a key to those thoughts and exposed them . . .

Red-faced, Kyra avoided making eye contact with her companions and instead rubbed the leather on her boots. It was even worse that her self-reproach was accompanied by a sense of triumph. Kyra had again entwined herself in a memory. Kyra could collect scenes from others and create a montage of her past. Except that this memory had nothing to do with *her* past.

"Kyra." Solarus' tone was measured. "Please elaborate. You 'saw something' from Hayden?"

Kyra cleared her throat and glanced at Hayden. His face was drained of color despite the light of the blue flames.

"I wasn't trying to pry," Kyra prefaced. She stared at her boots, certain her stomach had dropped somewhere inside them. "After Hayden described Jyls, he looked like he was remembering how they first met. I imagined what it might have looked like, that moment. Then everything in the cell disappeared. Suddenly, I saw Hayden and Talis. Not Hayden here, but a younger Hayden and, well, I assume a younger Talis. He looked the same. It was like . . ." Kyra fished around for the words. "It was like I was watching a play. I could see and hear everyone in the room, but it wasn't reciprocated. In fact, a waitress walked *through* me as if I didn't exist."

"You did not exist if it was a memory." Solarus eyed her with a frown. "You are curious about many things. That has never led to you plunder another's thoughts. Or has it?"

Solarus' accusatory tone sent splinters of hot guilt through her. "Once," Kyra replied in a small voice. "It was an accident too. When Talis and I were in Edoin Forest and fled the Reapers. He was describing my weapons' lessons." Kyra quickly described witnessing herself in the archery fields. "And that was it," Kyra said at the conclusion. She kept her gaze on her boots, wiping a streak of dirt from the side. "It's frustrating sometimes. You all remember my life and the experiences I had or that we shared, and I feel like I'm listening to a story about someone else."

"Your longing for an insight was so intense you tunneled into Talis' memory," Solarus supplied. Kyra glanced up to see he was somewhat mollified by her explanation. "The same with Hayden. I correct that; it is not merely a longing. For you, it is a need. You believe you *needed* to participate in that moment. With an emotion so powerful and unchecked, you would have forced yourself into Talis' mind."

"Is it unusual?" Kyra asked hesitantly. "To share a memory?"

"Exceedingly." The severity in Solarus' expression was so stark it seemed to be chiseled in every plane of his face. "I am not sure in Hayden's case it was even a matter of 'sharing' but 'extracting.' You were present in Talis' memory; you were not in the one of Jyls." Solarus gazed out the iron bars with a far-flung look. "Let me summarize what you have told me so that I am perfectly clear on the events. You have had two incidences in which you have witnessed memories, as we assume them to be. No others."

Kyra's neck tensed. She kneaded the muscle, then stopped as a stabbing pain ran through her burnt skin. "There have been only those two," she said. When Solarus was silent, Kyra asked carefully, "Have you ever entered someone's thoughts?"

Solarus stiffened. "I have not tried. Even were I able, I would not be so callous as to share in another's private memories, regardless of whether I were a participant in that memory or not. It is not your right to do as you wish."

"I'm sorry," Kyra apologized directly to Hayden, her words tumbling from her tongue. "I didn't mean anything by it."

Hayden rubbed the side of his temple. The haunted look in his gray eyes was enough for Kyra to secretly vow never to try again. "I won't begrudge you a memory if it's relevant to you," he finally said. Kyra's eyes lit in surprise. "You're right. You're at a disadvantage when we have a history you can't remember. You shouldn't be punished because something took away your past. You need the opportunity to live, or relive, those conversations and moments. It could be useful in her magical training as well," Hayden added, this time to Solarus.

The wizard's eyes rained disapproval. "If they are your memories and you are willing to risk them, I will not stop you. If they are Kyra's and can aid her progression, I support that also. *No one*, however, will attempt to invade my thoughts. Not unless one wishes to face very unpleasant consequences."

"Agreed." Hayden folded his arms. "You're allowed to access a memory with our explicit permission," he told Kyra. "Further, since it doesn't seem that you can control this skill yet, Solarus and I will have you practice with trivial recollections at first. To test what you can do."

Kyra knew this was more than fair and nodded. "What about using this against the dark wizards? This might work on them. We could get more information about . . ."

"No."

Hayden and Solarus spoke the word simultaneously. Kyra bit her lip.

"What you witnessed from Talis and me was benign. What anger and hate are buried in the dark wizards would horrify you if you delved into their memories. There's no reason for it." Hayden sighed. "You're young, Kyra. One day, you will have burdens pressing down on your shoulders like an avalanche of rocks onto a valley. You haven't and shouldn't bear them right now.

Remember: what you see you can't 'un'-see, no matter how repentant you are afterward. Solarus and I want to spare you those nightmares. That's why it's in our interest and yours that you leave the dark wizards alone. We can talk about . . ."

Hayden cut off. His gaze darted to the end of the corridor. In an instant, Hayden had risen to his feet and stepped toward Solarus. The wizard's mouth formed an angry line. Kyra's confusion faded as she began to hear voices and the clinking of metal. Red, purple, ivory, and orange light danced along the walls. Shadowy figures rounded the bend and proceeded down the ever-brighter corridor.

Hayden's steely gaze centered on the lead individual, whose golden crown glinted in the multi-colored glow surrounding him. He glanced sidelong at Solarus. "It looks like you get to question the king."

Chapter 16

Talis' amber eyes skimmed over the parchment in his hands. The elf was hunkered low in the grass across from the moat and outside the castle. Though clouds clotted the sky, providing some cover, Talis stayed well away from the bridge. He didn't want prying eyes to notice him or the whippet sitting at his side. Tail beating the ground, the dog had patiently watched as Talis had penned a message. A pliable leather pouch was tied around the whippet's waist and over her back.

"'Snow melts from the Mountains and has reached Edoin,'" Talis read aloud. "'My charge was met by cold winds from the four directions when she arrived. Our company brought blue warmth and banished the cold. We have made our way to where the silver dragons fight in evening skies. Our kin are not to be found on these grounds. I hope this news comes as no surprise and that you had arranged for their absence. Whispers within the walls bid us to leave. We will depart when the sun sets. I also send a warning. The gargoyles have awoken, and they head toward the crossing. I ask you to be vigilant. These times bode great ill. May Inishmore bring this letter to you safely and find you well.'"

Satisfied, Talis folded the parchment. Even though the missive was written in elvish, there was danger someone would intercept the message and have the resources to decipher the words. This message was opaque enough that a wizard wouldn't easily make sense of it.

Raenalyn Carina would understand. The queen and Talis had known each other long enough that she would pick up on his words and take whatever action was needed. Talis placed the parchment in an envelope and sealed it. Chloe would deliver the message. Like all animal scouts, the whippet was fleet-footed, astute, and more than capable of avoiding bandits, thieves, and even dark wizards on her route.

"Thank you, Chloe," the elf said. He slipped the envelope into the pouch on the whippet's back. "Please extend my gratitude to the *Al-Ethran* when you see them next." Talis stood. "The missive must be delivered to *Raenalyn* Carina and Carina alone. My heart is uneasy. I thought the *Sirenyle* would at least mention to you their departure."

The whippet rose on all fours. "I will get your missive in the hands of the queen," Chloe replied, a solemn look in her deep brown eyes. "The animal and elven scouts have long supported one another in times of need. The *Sirenyle* have never hesitated to put themselves at risk when an animal scout has been threatened. It is an honor for us to humbly return the favor. I regret not having information about Emmeth and Muireann, particularly if there is foul magic afoot in Farcaren."

"There is certainly that." Talis placed his hand over his heart. "By the moon and the stars, you will be returned to us."

Chloe bowed her head respectfully. Then she bounded away across the fields, heading westward across Farcaren.

Talis watched until the dog was a speck in the distance. He ran a finger along his long braid. He had compassed the outer wall once more, seeking the *Sirenyle*, then crossed the royals' bridge to find the animal scout. It gave Talis some comfort that *Raenalyn* Carina would receive word of the recent events. He fervently hoped his fears over the *Sirenyle* would prove unfounded. That Carina would send word that Emmeth and Muireann had been sent on another mission. Talis felt the icy hand of dread grip his heart.

Pulling at his braid, Talis gazed over the grounds near the bridge. Men and women in fine attire or uniforms rode over the royals' bridge, but the traffic was sparse. Still, dark wizards or spies were loose in Thanesgard. Talis had to be a stealthy shadow under the veil of clouds. He looked to the west. Small fenced-off estates with smatterings of wildflowers governed a long stretch of trimmed grass. Talis knew that beyond the estates was grassland and, further on, the border with Hogarth. It was to the east that Talis had to travel to enter the marketplace. The clock tower where he planned to meet Hayden lay in the center.

Talis put a hand over the grass. The air glimmered as the elf bridled the natural energy from the earth. A dark, soupy green fog shrouded him. He could see as clearly through the magic as before; others would feel a breeze as he passed, with no figure behind it.

Thus cloaked, Talis sprinted across the grass toward the royal road. He was invisible to the cluster of Royal Guards who cantered out over the bridge toward the marketplace.

***

Arkin was flanked by Royal Guards and the dark wizards. The king's heels dug into the ground with wrathful authority as he strode down the corridor. Adakis walked to the king's left. The cardinal red light from his staff arced across the ceiling. Nymphrys, Galakis, and Janus followed, each casting their own light. A pair of guards carried torches that glowed faintly in comparison with the wizards' magic.

Kyra tried to rise and discovered her muscles had seized from sitting. Solarus reached down and helped her to her feet.

"... had the network of passages at your disposal so you would operate with discretion within my city," Arkin's cold, reproving words sailed up the passage, reaching Kyra's ears as she half-leaned on the cell's wall. "In your lavish incompetence, you neglected the secrecy I provided and arrested Hayden in full view of my citizens and guests. You also threatened a girl who onlookers believe was the innocent victim of wizardly aggression."

"It was necessary to use Kyra," Adakis replied in a tone devoid of contrition. "Hayden and Solarus would not have consented to forfeiting their weapons without persuasion. Trust me, Your Majesty, I am one of the greatest strategists in Harkimer. I would have avoided the confrontation had there been another means to do so . . ."

"You created a spectacle to flaunt your power," Arkin bulldozed through Adakis' rationalization. The king was close enough now that Kyra could see his disdainful expression. "As I told you, I sent my guard to accompany you to draw Hayden to the passages. Now I must reassure my people of their safety. Remember, wizard, neither you nor any of your kin has the cachet of the king of Farcaren. You do not have the prestige of *any* monarch for that matter. That includes those of Peregrine, and you cannot find any fouler individuals in Ilian."

Adakis' ears burned the same red as his staff. "My cachet is one of Ilian's best," he bristled. "Not better than the cachet of Your Majesty's. Its equal."

"He doesn't know what 'cachet' means," Nymphrys said with a blasé expression that matched her uninterested tone. She raised her hand and rubbed a nail. "Your Majesty needs to use simpler words with Adakis."

"What's a cachet?" Janus whispered to Galakis. "Is it a weapon? Is it treasure? Do we have a good cachet?"

Galakis closed his eyes as though hoping when he opened them Janus would be gone. "No, no, and not in Farcaren. It means having a standing or a status."

Arkin's lips formed a tight line. The light around the king sank into the chasm of his dark gaze. "You and your wizards are dismissed. Remain in the castle until I am finished. Inishmore help you if I have a report from a single servant that you were seen."

Adakis wasn't ready to concede. "I wouldn't recommend you speak with them alone, Your Majesty," he said in an oily tone. "Hayden and Kyra are toothless without weapons. Only a *wizard* can handle another wizard. Solarus has no staff, but he is powerful. It is wiser that I remain to protect you."

"It is *wiser* to obey my order." Arkin angled his head enough to see Adakis from the corner of his eye. "You are in my kingdom, not Harkimer. You will do as I say."

Adakis' mouth fell open in shock. Unable to develop an appropriately affronted response, he assumed his best impression of indifference. "Yes, Your Majesty. We are available to assist if you decide you need us."

"That is unlikely."

Adakis motioned to his fellow wizards with a violent nod of his head. With a swish of his robe, Adakis stomped off. Nymphrys unconcernedly followed. Janus was shoved forward by an impatient Galakis. The wizards' lights bobbed in sync with their long strides.

The guards carrying torches stepped closer to the king, replacing the magical energy with a soft, flickering light. The flames highlighted the contempt on Arkin's face as he watched the wizards turn the corner.

"Bestar, Goral, follow them," the king ordered. "Instruct the other guards that it is forbidden for anyone to be in the western courtyard until I say otherwise. Clear the servants' quarters. They are not to leave the castle. Then you will protect the entrance to these dungeons."

"Yes, Your Majesty," the guards answered in unison. Bestar took a torch from one of his companions.

Arkin regarded Hayden coolly as the guards rushed off. "I want to make it clear," he said in a hard tone, "that I did not intend for your journey to end behind these bars, Hayden. I have leaned on you for many years. I have been grateful for your counsel and friendship. Yet here we are." Arkin's gaze trailed from the bottom of the door to the top. "Never did I foresee you occupying a cell in Thanesgard like a common thief."

Hayden moved in front of Solarus and Kyra. His breath was on the iron bars, so close was he to the door. "Never did I foresee a king of Farcaren becoming a supplicant to paltry wizards like Adakis," he replied fiercely. "The man who stands before me deserves neither my friendship nor my counsel."

A crack formed in Arkin's composed veneer. His eyes flickered with a hint of shame, then burned with anger. "I do not serve any wizards. My arrangement with Diamantas derives from mutual respect. Diamantas' ambition is no more reprehensible than my own: to offer his subjects the chance at the best life Ilian has to offer. His is loyal to his cause, his people, and his allies." Arkin spat out the last word as though it were a piece of spoiled meat.

"The virtue of one's ambition is not in the ambition itself. It is in the actions that lead one to it." Solarus' scorn shone clearly in his gaze. "What is deplorable is the means with which Diamantas chooses to offer wizards a 'better life.' He seeks bloodshed, not peace. Diamantas does not see you as an ally, King of Farcaren. He sees you as a weapon in his arsenal. You forfeited your duty to your citizens when you made a pact with the dark wizards."

The king's face contorted with anger. The guards not bearing torches drew their swords. "Mind your tongue, Solarus," Arkin seethed. "I would expect nothing less from a wizard than to deride the wisdom of man. You would patronize me? You deride Diamantas' desire, and mine, to uplift our people? How is your imprisonment benefiting the children in Harkimer? Who are you aiding here, in this cell? No one. You consort with a few men, a waif of a girl, and an elf. Do not talk to me about duty when you are loyal to no one but yourself."

Kyra saw Solarus' mouth move ever so slightly. Flame trickled from his fingers. Hayden put a hand firmly on his shoulder. "Don't," he said quietly.

Solarus shook off Hayden's hand. The wizard's expression was so deadly, Kyra was afraid he would attack Hayden in his fury to get Arkin. To Kyra's relief, Solarus simply folded his arms.

Arkin indicated for the guards to lower their weapons. "What I hope for is a world where the wars among the kingdoms of men have ended. We bloody our noses in meaningless skirmishes. Duke against duke, baron against baron, earl against earl, down to the lowest thief. For what purpose? A title? An acre of land? An iota of power? The estates here change hands as often as a farmer tills his fields. I have tried through my office to mediate my people's claims of transgressions. It has not been enough." Arkin gestured to the walls, his rings glimmering in the torchlight. "I want to see these cells rot from lack of use.

Diamantas is not a better negotiator than the kings or queens of Ilian. Unlike the monarchs of these lands, however, he and only he can end the feuds and wars in our time."

"The answer to peace does not lie in the cowardly use of Diamantas as your most powerful guard," Hayden replied, gray eyes stormy. "You could have called for a conference with the other monarchs. You chose not to. You don't possess the leadership to bring the kingdoms together."

Arkin's brows furrowed so sharply they almost touched. "You believe I am unwilling?" he repeated, voice shaking with fury. "You believe *I* do not have leadership? Do you believe the other monarchs are amenable to discourse? They are too preoccupied with their petty internal squabbles to think of our greater future."

Hayden considered Arkin. His expression was sorrowful. "What changed, Arkin? What happened to the king I knew?"

"That man watched Genevieve waste away, powerless to do anything except hold her hand and deceive her with hope." Arkin turned from Hayden, a faraway look in his eyes. "Can you imagine what it is like to hear a voice every morning?" he whispered. "A voice that makes your waking sweet and joyful? The voice that takes the trials and frustrations of the day and washes them away with a word? The voice you believe Inishmore will protect until death? For seventeen years, I heard that voice, Hayden. I will never hear it again.

"I prayed for Inishmore to bring a healer," the king continued bitterly. "I sent word through the kingdoms, including Silvias through the elven scouts. Even you ignored my plea for aid. Diamantas, though, he heard of my plight. And he sent a wizard to heal Genevieve. Diamantas, our avowed foe." Arkin's lips screwed together into an ironic smile. "His wizard knelt by Genevieve's bedside, ministering what remedies and spells were available to her. She stayed for weeks. My wife and child succumbed to their illnesses." Unrestrained anguish and anger mingled in Arkin's voice. He removed his crown and regarded Hayden with contempt. "This—" Arkin shook the crown "—is what I have left. My throne, my people, and the loyalty Diamantas showed me when I needed it most. When my friends abandoned me."

Hayden rubbed a hand across his forehead. "Is that why you replaced the Lyneera?" he asked quietly.

The king's face drained of color. "The kaemin mage who forged the statue was gifted. The kaemin bore Genevieve's likeness as though she herself was frozen within the glass. It was a constant reminder of what I had lost. It was a reminder that Inishmore forsook me. I was a faithful servant. Inishmore rewarded my compassion and mercy by prematurely casting the one dearest to me beyond my reach. Inishmore is a heartless force." Arkin strangled the hilt of his sword with his bejeweled hand. "The new kaemin represents strength and power. Wolves do not tolerate weakness. They survive, no matter the cost."

"Nestor Arkin." Hayden shook his head with an imploring look. "Don't surrender the goodness and beauty Genevieve brought to your life. You are condemning Farcaren to enslavement."

Arkin released his grip on his sword. His mordant green gaze fell on Kyra. She locked eyes with him defiantly. "I ask Inishmore to grant me one wish, Hayden: that your grief will one day be equal to my own." The king turned away from the bars without another word. He continued to hold the crown in his hand as he strode away. The guards followed in lockstep. The company's torch-lit profiles disappeared down the corridor.

Only when the echo of footsteps faded did Kyra hear Hayden murmur, "How do you know it's not?"

***

"Where were you?" Ash was standing at the clock tower, holding his overstuffed satchel firmly over his shoulder. His green eyes inspected Jyls questioningly.

Sweat ran down the sides of Jyls' face, and Jyls squeezed a stitch in his side. Relief filled him as he looked at his friend. The wizards hadn't reached Ash. "I thought I'd have a look-see around the market, see if I'd be blessed by Inishmore with a claret seller. Except—" Jyls breathed in sharply, "—you haven't noticed anyone in black cloaks recently, have you?"

Ash responded with a puzzled frown. "Black cloaks? No. Why?"

Jyls released his side. His eyes roved the marketgoers. He didn't spy a single dark spot amid the collage of colors. "Dark wizards decided to go for a little shopping excursion. Adakis is up in the castle. He knows Kyra's here. The bigger problem is more wizards could be slinking around the streets, and we haven't run into them yet. I already saw at least one new, pretty face with Galakis and Orkanis."

Ash's eyes grew wide. He spun around, as though the wizards would pop out of the air before them. "Dark wizards? We have to tell the king."

"Not necessary. It turns out Arkin's a devious degenerate of a man. I overheard Galakis saying they have support from the Royal Guards." Jyls ran a finger over the silver chain around his neck. "I didn't like Arkin anyway. It's gracious of him to give me a justification to insult him properly. He's a . . ." Jyls went on to wield unflattering language that was uniquely Peregrinian.

Ash ran his hand nervously over the satchel. "Did Adakis find only Kyra, or do you think he captured Hayden, Solarus, and Talis too?"

"I'll assume, since Hayden and Solarus were with her, Adakis managed to snag all three. Talis—well, it depends. He isn't here, and I didn't see him. So maybe, maybe not. I'm hoping the 'maybe not.' The odds of you and I stopping Adakis and the cockroaches he has scuttling around Thanesgard are as good as them being scared by a couple of Calonian kittens. As for 'us,' I doubt Arkin sent his men or the dark wizards to hunt us. A healer and a nobody aren't worth the trouble."

Ash glanced up as the last bits of sun were veiled behind a sea of churning clouds. "Why would the king help the wizards? Hayden said he was one of our allies against Diamantas."

Jyls shrugged. "Diamantas must have dangled something valuable to 'encourage' him to switch sides. It has to be good for Arkin to go after two wizards and one Hayden. Maybe Diamantas promised him a new castle of gold, or perhaps to pave the streets with gold. Or paint the *king* with gold. The reason doesn't matter right now. We might be able to find Kyra before they do. If not, we'll be performing a gallant rescue of our friends."

"How?"

"Not sure yet. We'll improvise." Out of the corner of his eye, Jyls spied a line of midnight blue and silver. He hauled his attention to the troupe. They wore the uniforms of the Royal Guards. Jyls pushed Ash back against the clock tower and out of sight of the guards. Jyls cautiously poked his head around the other side of the structure. The way was clear.

"We're leaving," Jyls said in a low tone to Ash. "Remember my motto. Move as quietly as a corpse." Without a further warning, Jyls bolted from around the tower like a rabbit from a warren. After a moment's hesitation, Ash ran after him.

Jyls snaked and slithered through the throng with ease. When he checked over his shoulder, though, Ash lagged behind. Jyls suppressed a groan. Ash had the same grace navigating the crowd as Janus.

"Excuse me, pardon me, if you could . . . might I get through, please?" Jyls heard him saying.

"Ash." Jyls grasped the healer's arm when he caught up. "This isn't the king's court. Less apologizing, more moving."

The healer looked chagrined. He followed Jyls' instruction, though he bit his lip more than once to stop the automatic "Excuse me" that surfaced. Ash became trapped in the throng. He craned his neck, looking for his friend. Frustrated, Ash paused by a kiosk with wind chimes. His green eyes tried to breach the mass of marketgoers for a sign of Jyls.

A hand suddenly grasped his shoulder. Ash jumped. He whirled around to see a slender, green-cloaked individual with a raised cowl. Talis' amber eyes peered out, and a grim smile spanned his lips.

"Talis!" Ash exclaimed as the elf's gaze darted to either side. The vendor of the wind chimes wasn't in his kiosk.

"Jyls saw Galakis and Orkanis near the clock tower," Ash said in a too-loud whisper as they hid alongside the kiosk and out of the view of passersby. "He said Adakis knows Kyra is here." Unconsciously, Ash glanced behind Talis as though expecting to see her. "Did you go to the clock tower?"

"No, I haven't yet been to the tower," Talis answered. He sounded fatigued. Ash noticed as Talis' hood slid back that the elf's face was white-sheeted.

The healer frowned. Talis was never tired. What had happened?

"Where is Jyls?" Talis asked.

"Here." Jyls ambled around the kiosk, hands in his pockets. The thief cast a glance at Ash with a partially vexed, partially amused expression. "You and I are going to practice the art of moving less like a three-legged Calonian tortoise and more like a starving street urchin filching a meal. It's a good thing I noticed you'd gone missing when I did. Not a chance I would have spotted Talis if I didn't. The cloak's a good touch."

"Elven magic can disguise us from inquisitive eyes and ears," Talis replied. Sweat pearled on his forehead, and silver-blond strands of hair were frizzled beside his long braid.

Jyls raised a brow. "You look exhausted. By elven standards."

"It's not easy to summon magic around Thanesgard. Elven magic is connected to Inishmore through the earth and that which stems from it. Silvias was founded around the Ancient Forest for a specific purpose. Our magical bonds are strongest with the energy from the tree and plant roots in the earth. We can couple our energy with something more basic when the situation requires. In this case, the roots from the tall grasses on the other side of the castle. I prefer not to. It demands immense effort." Talis massaged his temple. "Where did you observe the wizards?"

"They were near the clock tower first, then beelined for the main gate. I haven't seen Kyra, Hayden, or Solarus since we split up."

"Where do you think they are?" Ash asked anxiously.

"In the outer ring of the castle." Talis looked down at a point on the ground. His gaze was contemplative, as though he were watching a scene playing out in the dirt. "Hayden intended to buy Kyra a sword. The smith's shop is among those permitted within the castle walls. If the wizards haven't happened upon them yet, we will find our companions there."

Jyls thumbed the hilt of one of the knives in his belt. "Them and Arkin's royal thugs. Yeah, the guards are part of this whole scheme." He pushed himself off the side of the kiosk. "And if our friends *have* been put in chains and fetters?"

Talis gave him a grave smile. "Then we go to the dungeons instead."

"Take the main bridge," Jyls told the elf as he again tugged the cowl over his head. "Straightest way to the shops."

The elf nodded under his hood. He drifted into the crush of bodies like a leaf carried by a river's current. Jyls and Ash glided into the crowd after him. Jyls kept a firm hold on Ash's arm to prevent him from being swept off in the wrong direction.

They reached the main bridge without incident. To the guards, Talis, Jyls, and Ash were three more droplets flowing among the tide of travelers. When they had passed into the outer ring, the marketgoers dispersed. Jyls set a pace he considered to be the brisk walk of a customer seeking a deal, not a suspiciously urgent trot. Talis led them from the stalls to the shops. They passed a bookseller and cartographer in a heated debate, continued by the candlemaker, then arrived at a thickset building. A banner of an anvil fluttered outside, and a hammer banged metal within. Talis paused. He walked under the open windows and hearkened to the sounds.

"They aren't inside," he stated after a moment.

Jyls crouched next to the steps. He scooped up a handful of brittle leaves and sifted them through his fingers. "They were definitely here. This is kolker." The thief's gaze dipped to the ground. "Look at the tracks."

Talis' gaze stepped from boot print to boot print, then slowly glided to the main road. "The impressions are deep, and they're many," he assessed. "They were chased. The wizards found them after all."

"A rescue it is then," Jyls replied nonchalantly. He reached into his jacket and pulled a small dagger from his belt. "Here," he said, handing it to Ash. "Talis and I should be able to handle a couple of lousy guards and inept wizards. This is insurance if one gets by us. Don't use it unless you have no other choice."

Ash's face was pallid as he tucked the knife in the side of his belt.

The trio worked their way around the outer ring until they reached the door to the fourth wall. Guards patrolled the grounds. They didn't amble in the manner of men used to tediously repetitious days. Instead, their eyes were alert, hands gripping their weapons a little too tightly. Merchants, customers, and members of the court and staff strode with jittery and anxious steps. Tension hung in the air. Jyls and Ash walked by as casually as they could, hoping not to raise the guards' suspicion. Talis surreptitiously darted behind the trimmed bushes that lined the wall.

The trio arrived at the door to the center circle. When they walked through the door, Jyls saw they landed near a row of servants' quarters. The group slinked behind the houses. At the end of the quarters, two guards stood on either side of a circular door in the ground.

"Puffed-up, self-righteous milksops," one guard said irascibly to the other. "They're like bandits, Goral, obedient to their king right up until they slip a knife under his ribs."

The other guard grunted in agreement. "They won't be here long, Bestar. The king will chuck them into the moat when we're done. With luck they'll drown."

Jyls and Ash lined up beside Talis. The elf kept his attention trained on the guards. "The guards are protecting a door. It's the entrance to the dungeon."

Jyls stretched his fingers before him and creaked his neck from side to side. "I'm ready. Ash, stay here. Remember, use the dagger if you don't have any other choice. Alternately, you could throw that fragile vial of poison you bought, and then run."

Concern was written on Ash's face as Jyls drew a straight-edged throwing knife. He twirled it once in his hand. Talis unsheathed his dagger. The duo left the concealment of the house and noiselessly jogged forward. The guards, caught up in spewing their derision for wizards, failed to see them. Talis sprung forward and struck Bestar on the temple. The guard groaned and fell. Jyls kicked Goral hard in the kneecap. With a scream of pain, the guard's leg buckled. As he clutched his knee, the thief brought the knife's hilt down on the back of the guard's skull. Goral slumped beside Bestar.

Jyls waved to Ash. The healer edged toward his companions, darting a glance around the courtyard. It was disconcertingly empty of castle staff and visitors.

Talis and Jyls each took hold of one of the iron handles. Together, they heaved open the thick circular door and eased it against the ground.

"Should we shut it behind us?" Ash asked as Talis hopped down the stairs. The clouds rumbled and roiled overhead, making the courtyard almost as dark as the hole into which the elf had disappeared.

"Leave it open," Jyls responded. "We might need to courageously flee the peril that awaits." The thief nimbly descended into the underground. "Watch out for the stairs," his voice carried up to Ash. "They're a bit steep. Long drop if you fall."

Swallowing hard, Ash proceeded after his friend.

The healer sighed in relief when his foot left the last step and touched the earth. His nose wrinkled. The air was dank and marinated with stenches of rot. Ash heard the scraping of wood against the wall, then the sound of a stone striking metal. A spark sprung onto bark strips and oil. Then a torch flared to life. Jyls held it outward, the light illuminating his freckles. With his free hand, the thief returned his flintstone to a trouser pocket.

Talis raced down the corridor without waiting for the light. "This way."

"Rotten, perfect elven eyes," Jyls said to Ash as they took off after him.

The dungeon was a honeycomb of corridors. Passages split off in different directions while others dead-ended. Talis' eyes narrowed at the stone wall that blocked the rest of the corridor.

"Arkin filled in the passage," the elf growled. "Hayden and I once delivered many of the dark wizards' allies to the king. He sent them to the cells beyond this wall. Let's hope Arkin hasn't blocked other tunnels."

Fortunately, the rest of the passages were unobstructed. Talis stopped at intervals to study the ground, then set off again. They didn't speak, using every ounce of energy to run and, in the case of Ash, stay close to the torch, the only source of light in the tunnels. Several zigs and zags later, Talis halted abruptly. Ash bent over, winded. Even Jyls sucked in short breaths.

"What?" he asked, wiping sweat from his face with the back of his sleeve. "Wrong turn again?"

Talis inclined his head. "Look down."

Jyls tilted the torch toward the ground. Imprints of boots speckled the dirt. Golf-ball-sized impressions were stabbed alongside them.

"Where are they?" Ash gasped.

Talis didn't answer. He again shot down a corridor and turned right.

Shaking his head, Jyls trotted after him. Ash stumbled along. As they rounded the corner, they saw a flickering blue glow cascading into the passage.

Talis was already halfway down the hall. "Hayden!" he called.

***

Solarus whirled around. Kyra started, gazing in the direction of the voice. A glow of torchlight came from the opposite end of the corridor. The figure who called out was swiftly approaching. Hayden unfolded his arms, his chary countenance replaced by a wide grin.

"Talis!" he exclaimed as the elf entered the blue luminescence. "Thank Inishmore. Arkin and Adakis didn't find you."

"Or Jyls and Ash," Talis answered as the pair caught up to him.

Ash's face was beet red. Jyls held the torch steady even as his chest heaved with effort.

"You're all right!" Kyra said, beaming at them.

Hayden glanced down the hall. "I imagine the guards outside are otherwise indisposed?"

"Otherwise . . . unconscious," Jyls answered in between breaths. He placed the torch in a sconce against the wall and rubbed more sweat from his eyes. "Arkin's dungeon? Kind of . . . plain. No gold?"

"Arkin has an accord with Diamantas," Hayden informed Talis as Jyls' gaze uncovered the padlock on the cell door. Hayden summarized their encounter with the dark wizards in the merchants' egress. When he related how Adakis held Kyra, Ash immediately looked at the red streaks on her neck. His expression hardened.

As Jyls knelt to see the padlock better, Hayden also recapped the conversation with Arkin.

"It answers many of our questions," Talis said when Hayden finished, "and raises as many new ones. Is there no way out of the cell?"

"If a room has an entrance, it has an exit," Jyls responded. "I assume you haven't found it, or you wouldn't be here." The thief moved his fingers along the ground just before the bars. "The bars are too narrow to be natural," Jyls muttered. "Have our underhanded wizards tampered with them?" Jyls reached out to touch the iron.

"Do you *choose* to ignore my warnings, Jyls of Lystern?" Solarus snapped. His irritation intersected with exasperation. "Or did you lose your wits somewhere in one of your many pockets? I said it with the staff in Edoin Forest. If you are dealing with a magical object—or magic generally—*do not act before learning about its properties*. This metal—" Solarus gestured at the iron "—carries a potent magic within it. I cannot predict the exact consequence of touching it, though I was tempted to let you provide me with a revelation. Suffice it to say, the magic is certain to cause injury. Possibly death."

"In that case, I will observe from afar." Jyls withdrew his hand. "Even magical armor has a chink."

"It does," Solarus agreed wryly. "You cannot get to it. Neither can I, individually. *Collectively*, Kyra and I might produce a countercharm."

Kyra stared, stunned, as Solarus turned to her. This was the first time he had voiced the suggestion. Solarus calmly rolled back his sleeves in perfect folds. "Kyra, how confident are you that you can use your magic in a small, concerted manner?"

Kyra coughed and tucked a lock of hair self-consciously behind her ear. "Not very," she admitted. "I don't even know if I can summon magic on my own. It's only shown itself when someone's in danger or if there's other magic around."

"'Not very' is not 'not at all.' We can make use of that sliver of confidence." Solarus waved his hand. The blue flames disappeared for the space of a breath as Solarus pointed to a spot on Kyra's left. "*Ithansil*," he intoned. The fire capered back to life on the cell's floor.

As Kyra looked down, Solarus extended his wrists toward the iron bars. "Jyls, if you would like to continue to observe from afar, I recommend you take more steps back."

Jyls unquestioningly joined Talis and Ash away from the cell.

The wizard's gaze settled on Kyra. "From this moment on, there is no one and nothing inside this cell besides the blue flames. You will be harnessing their energy. Turn toward them."

Nerves quickened Kyra's pulse. She did as she was told, facing the flames that leapt freely. *There's nothing here but the flames*, she repeated. A pit of dread dropped like a stone in her stomach. If Kyra failed, they would be trapped. *There's nothing here but the flames. There's nothing here but the flames.* Closing her eyes, Kyra took a deep breath and shoved aside her reservations.

"Visualize the flames," Solarus' voice blended with her thoughts. "They are like seeds in need of nourishment to grow. Feed them with your golden energy. Let the flames stretch their stems to the ceiling. Each flame is a plant, its stalk straight and stable."

Kyra's hands tingled intensely. In her mind's eye, Kyra visualized the gold that she knew was gushing over her wrists and through her fingers. Eyes still shut, Kyra sent the gold toward the blue flames. Her energy enthusiastically capered to the fire. The two magics danced together, gold through blue, blue through gold, then came together like partners touching hands. Kyra heard the first pop, then a crack. Her heart pounded. What was happening? There was another pop, another crack, then a gradual burgeoning of the noises like a hail of firecrackers.

Startled, Kyra's lids flew open. The intertwined blue-gold flames were stretching toward the ceiling in columns parallel in width and height. Bits of fire spritzed in all directions. Hayden had backed into the furthest corner of the cell. His gray eyes swam with blue light, looking almost fearful of the flames. Kyra's magic faltered as panic gripped her. Was she losing control? What if she obliterated the cell and her friends? Larger bits of flame sprayed from the columns.

A turquoise force suddenly buoyed her energy. The golden magic steadied. Kyra glanced over her shoulder. Solarus was mirroring her gestures. He flashed her a tense smile of encouragement. Kyra turned back toward the fire with a surge of determination. The light formed a boundary around the blue-gold energy. Kyra fed the columns with more gold, sending the bars sprouting to the ceiling. Soon all had touched the ceiling. Kyra's jaw dropped. The gold blue bars were identical to the cell's iron ones, as though looking at a reflection in the water.

"Move the energy," Solarus instructed. His voice sounded distant like an echo in her mind. "Plant it over the bars. Root the magic to the earth where the iron digs into the ground."

Keeping her grip on the blue-gold stalks of energy, Kyra thrust the energy forward. The moment the blue-gold magic met the iron, wrathful purple and orange magic exploded. The force punched Kyra like a blast of wind.

"Resist," Solarus ordered. "The dark wizards' magic seeks to dominate yours. Fight it. Use your will to overcome theirs."

Kyra marshaled her energy and pushed back. The magical skirmish created a kaleidoscope of light. Her upper body quaked, but she didn't let go.

Suddenly, the purple-orange magic clothing the bars shuddered. It fractured like ice crystals. In a blink of an eye, it shattered. Kyra gasped as the remnants of magic glittered like dust. It dissipated and vanished. No longer restrained, the iron bars sprang apart to their original width. Solarus' blue flames rained back onto the ground and collected themselves merrily into a small fire. The golden energy wisped out of sight.

Kyra dropped her arms to her sides. Her shirt was matted with sweat, and her muscles were as fatigued as though she had lugged fifty-pound weights for hours. Still, if her body didn't feel like a lump of clay, Kyra would have leapt into the air. Her heart pounded with exhilaration. She had directed the golden magic. Intentionally. Kyra turned breathlessly to Solarus. "Did it work? Did we break through the spells?"

Solarus gave Kyra a rare smile of praise. "We did. Well done, Kyra. That was no small feat." The wizard turned down his sleeves, looking across the corridor to Jyls. "You may touch the bars now."

Jyls arched a brow dubiously. He gave Talis a sidelong look. "You should try first. Elves are pretty indestructible. If you touch a not-quite-dead-and-buried-spell, it probably would be as painful as being tickled by a feather. Peregrinians, on the other hand, are delicate beings. I'd prefer avoiding being scarred or dead if Solarus is wrong."

"I'm never wrong," Solarus said acerbically.

Talis calmly returned Jyls' gaze with a smile. "No, thank you. Escape is your professional expertise, not mine. I also disagree that Peregrinians are a 'delicate' people.'"

Jyls' scowl only broadened the elf's grin.

During the exchange, Ash's green gaze had been glued to the padlock. He walked past Jyls, bending to see the lock more closely. Ash unsheathed the dagger. Jyls turned away from Talis. His mouth was forming a question when, without warning, the healer swung the blade down on the padlock with all his might.

Kyra flinched as a shrill ringing of metal against metal pierced the air. Talis' lips pressed together as he also winced. Solarus sighed and shook his head. Hayden's expression was sympathetic. Ash himself was more rattled than the lock, which had suffered a long scratch but was otherwise unscathed.

"My young Ash," Jyls said. He gently scooted the healer to the side. "We don't hack away at things because we have daggers and such. A lock requires a subtle and gentle approach."

Ash's shoulders sagged. "I was trying to help," he muttered, shuffling away from the cell.

"You have. I now have a guarantee that the iron is un-magicked." Jyls reached into his jacket pocket and withdrew a thin, hooked bar. He took another bar with bent ends from his trouser leg. Jyls scooped a third with tiny spikes on all sides from a slit on the bottom of his trousers.

Hayden's face was a study in accusation. "When did you get those?" he asked severely.

Jyls tutted, juggling the tools in his right hand. He put three back in his upper pocket. "You sound as disapproving as my mother." Jyls took the lock in his left hand. "Same condemning expression as my father. I didn't appropriate these in Thanesgard's marketplace. I promised I would be on my best behavior, didn't I?"

"You didn't appropriate them in *Thanesgard's* marketplace. You mean, you stole them from a different one."

"See, there's that tone again." Jyls finagled the hooked instrument inside the keyhole. "My parents didn't appreciate my skills either. Look how handy they can be."

After several moments of Jyls' artful adjusting and readjusting and twisting and jangling, the padlock clicked open. The thief grinned. He slid the bolt up and out and pulled the door open. "Lovely. I invite you to leave your accommodations, good lady and sirs."

Kyra went first. Her steps were stilted as her arms and legs refused to coordinate their movements. Talis caught Kyra under her arm and helped her out of the cell. "You're going to run out of salve if you travel with me," Kyra told him with what she hoped was a joking smile rather than a grimace of pain.

Hayden walked out next. Jyls gave him a smug look and dropped his tools back into their various pockets. "You've again repaid the debt of being saved from Syndrominous and the greeloks," Hayden commented.

Jyls acknowledged the respect in Hayden's tone with a nod. He snatched the torch from its sconce on the wall.

Talis looked at Hayden. "Footsteps echo down the passage from which we came. We need another exit out of the dungeons."

Kyra noticed Solarus had remained in the cell. His eyes were on the rats in the bubble in the corner. The two creatures lay on top of each other, having exhausted themselves from their early frantic racing. Muttering, Solarus raised his palm and evaporated the magic. The rats started in shock. They scrambled to their feet with noisy squeaks. Ash stifled a horrified cry as they skittered over his boot and dashed pell-mell out of the cell. Solarus sent a wave of magic rippling through the hallway and continued to intone a spell. Kyra heard what sounded like hundreds of pattering steps. Her eyes widened as rats began to pour into the corridor from cells on both sides. Large shadows formed on the walls as the rodents took up every inch of space. To Kyra's relief, the rats scampered after the original pair rather than in their direction.

Jyls' freckles scrunched as a look of disgust crossed his face. "That's creepy."

"It would have been rude of us to leave our jailers without a welcome upon their return," Solarus remarked as rats disappeared around the corner. The turquoise magic faded. Solarus waved a hand toward the ground and extinguished the blue fire. Jyls' torch offered the only light in the otherwise pitch-black hallway. Solarus held out his palm. "*Ithansil,*" he said. A tiny blue fire kindled in his hand.

From somewhere around the corner, Kyra heard a scream followed by a succession of blasts.

"We have to go," Talis said. "This way." He sprinted off, with the rest of the group at his heels. The ceiling dripped moisture on their heads as they negotiated the network of tunnels. Kyra felt like she was slogging through a bog. Her muscles from her neck to her back ached and protested every step. *It's just another run in London,* Kyra motivated herself. *You've pushed past this. It's just another run. In an underground that reeks like mold and rotten cabbage.* She kept close to Solarus. His magical flame was large enough to help her avoid smashing into a wall.

Kyra was so focused on her feet that she didn't notice Talis had stopped. She collided with him, bouncing back a step. Talis barely moved. He threw a look over his shoulder.

"Sor—" Kyra began to apologize as she was hit from behind. Kyra lurched forward with an "oomph." It was her turn to glance behind her.

Ash took in deep breaths, cheeks suffused with red. "Sorry."

Kyra gave him a half-smile and drew her focus back to Talis, wondering why he had halted. Before them, a thick stone wall obstructed their way. She glanced to her left, then right. There were no other corridors.

"Another wall," Jyls said dryly. "Fantastic."

Jyls and Talis parted to allow Solarus to move closer to the wall. His expression was contemplative. He pressed his palm with the blue flames firmly against the stone. The stone began to vibrate. Turquoise magic seeped into the wall. To Kyra's amazement, the stone slowly disintegrated. Solarus wore a smug look as a giant hole formed, large enough to let a man pass through. Warm air wafted through the opening, bringing with it a musky scent. The flames again danced in Solarus' hand. He held it closer to the hole, revealing a staircase.

Solarus took the steps two at a time. Jyls found a sconce nearby and left the torch in it. Catching her breath, Kyra climbed up after Talis as dry straw and hay crackled under her boots. When she reached the top, the grunting and snuffing of horses greeted her. Kyra's jaw dropped. They were in the king's stables.

Lanterns, not torches, provided an ambient light along the side of the stalls. Which made sense, Kyra thought briefly as her eyes browsed the stables for Raven. Unlike the rest of the castle, the stables were made of wood. Hay was scattered on the ground and stuck in the windows. The air was dry. In those conditions, the open flame of a torch was a hazard.

"We are here," Kyra heard Raven's deep voice. The roan hung his head over one of the stall's high doors. His brown eyes stared angst-ridden at her. The other horses also poked their heads over the stalls. Kyra's eyes brushed over them. Willow, Windchaser, Odin, Autumnstar, and Grayhaven, all accounted for.

Kyra ran forward and flung open the latch to Raven's door.

"A groomsman entered the stables earlier," Raven said as Kyra hugged his neck. "He was agitated. He said there had been a fight in the courtyard with wizards. Then he said they were marching the prisoners to the king's dungeons. The other groomsmen ran out of the stables to see for themselves."

"Too bad there's nothing left to see," Hayden replied, grabbing a saddle pad from an open closet door and heaving it onto Willow's back. "Adakis and his companions have made themselves welcome in Thanesgard. That makes us very unwelcome."

Talis helped Kyra as the group opened the rest of the stall doors. They hastily snatched up their riding equipment and began to secure saddles and fit reins. Kyra was grateful for the elf's aid. Her weary muscles were barely able to support her weight, let alone lift a heavy saddle or saddlebag. Ash also fumbled inexpertly with the bindings. Hayden, having finished with Willow, helped the healer prepare his mount. Ash thanked him quietly and lifted himself onto Autumnstar's back.

Out of habit, Hayden felt for the hilt of his sword. His thumb brushed over the empty belt. Eyes narrowing, Hayden clenched and unclenched his fist. He ran to a windowsill, grabbed a lantern, and blew out the flame. "Whoever was in the corridor will have discovered that we've absconded," Hayden told the group. He went to the next windowsill and collected a second lantern. "We need to get by the dark wizards, the soldiers patrolling the grounds, and any of Arkin's Royal Guards who are nearby. The greatest threat is from the archers. They have the advantage of seeing us before we see them." Hayden extinguished the second lantern. "Talis, the eastern bridge beyond the merchants' egress is the closest exit. I recommend taking that route. And here." He handed the elf the two lanterns. "You should have these for the journey."

Talis nodded.

Kyra looked suspiciously at Hayden. "What do you mean, 'You should have these for the journey?'" she demanded. "You're coming with us, aren't you?"

Hayden glanced at Solarus, who was seated atop Grayhaven. "There's the matter of our confiscated belongings. It would be a shame to leave such magnificent weapons in the hands of the dark wizards."

Solarus pulled his azure cloak from the saddlebags. "It *is* a galling thought," he agreed, throwing the cloak over his shoulders. The material shimmered as it draped down Grayhaven's sides. "The dark wizards have a shallow appreciation for the worth of my staff and your blades. We should liberate them."

Kyra stared in disbelief. Five wizards and Arkin's guards were on the hunt for them, and her friends were volunteering to go back toward the danger. "I'm coming with you," she told Hayden. "It's my sword they have too."

"You will do nothing of the sort," Solarus replied sternly. "We must return with stealth and leave in the same fashion. Having an inexperienced wizard with us will not aid our cause."

Kyra restrained her temper. "A few minutes ago, you needed an 'inexperienced wizard' to help break the magic of that cell," she argued. "Obviously, I'm not going to be a burden."

"Solarus is right," Hayden interjected. He swung astride Willow. "It isn't about your abilities. We can move in and out of the castle more easily as two."

"Where did Adakis take them?" Ash asked as Kyra looked away, crestfallen.

"I can locate my staff using magic similar to how Nymphrys presumably did when we left Edoin Forest," Solarus said without concern. Grayhaven stomped the ground as though for emphasis. "The swords should be with the staff. It stands to reason that the guards would keep all three weapons under the same lock and chain."

Talis gave Hayden a half-smile, though hints of worry lingered in his amber gaze. "Your presence will be incentive enough for the guards to return your property. Two gold florins if you deceive Adakis into touching either your sword or the staff."

A smile dropped to Hayden's lips. "Challenge accepted."

Solarus snorted. "Adakis is unconstrained by common sense and judgment. A taunt should be enough to have him grab after both." He clapped his heels into Grayhaven. The dapple gray surged forward out of the stables and turned left. Hayden spurred Willow after him.

Talis held his bow, which he had stashed among the saddlebags, firmly in hand. He impelled Windchaser out of the stables. Heart racing, Kyra clapped her heels into Raven. She held the reins in a white-knuckled grip as the roan barreled out of the stables and into the ring.

A small contingent of soldiers loitered on the grounds as the horses thundered down the grass. Taken by surprise, the guards leapt back as the horses' sharp hooves clipped dangerously close to them. One guard collected himself quickly and shouted to the parapets. Bells rang an alarm over the castle grounds. Archers immediately spread across the crenellations, bows raised. Talis swiveled in his seat and fired an arrow upward. An archer cried out and fell back. Another archer instantly filled the space. He was knocked off his feet as Jyls' knife whipped through the air and rammed him in the chest.

Talis veered sharply at the gate to the fourth ring and ducked through it. Kyra steered Raven to follow. An arrow whizzed by Kyra's ear. She ducked to the side as the roan shot through the gate.

The sounds of more hoofbeats followed her. Kyra began to look over her shoulder to check on Jyls and Ash when the wall before her exploded. Kyra's vision blurred, and her ears plugged with a shrill ringing sound. Shattered rocks sprayed like projectiles into the air. Raven reared in panic. Reflexively, Kyra thrust out her palm. A golden shield glittered over her and spread to Talis. The shards of the wall splattered harmlessly against it. Kyra maintained the shield, moving her head slowly, in a daze. Fuzzy images again took form. Kyra saw archers' mouths moving as they stared down at the rubble. A giant hole had formed where part of the wall had stood. Archers and soldiers were trapped underneath.

Kyra cast a glance behind her. Autumnstar and Odin had skidded to a stop. Too late, Kyra realized her shield hadn't extended back to Ash and Jyls. The pair was covered in dust, their skin marred by red cuts. Jyls' lips moved, but his eyes were unfocused. Blood from a gash on his forehead trickled down to his eyebrow and along the side of his face. Jyls' knife fell from his hand.

Ash drove Autumnstar next to Odin. The healer grabbed a fistful of Jyls' cloak, holding the thief sturdily in the saddle before he toppled over. The healer's face bore bloody flecks from the errant bits of stone.

The whine in Kyra's ears ebbed. In its place rushed a tumult of shouts and groans. Seconds later, Nymphrys and Galakis dashed through the cavity in the wall. Nymphrys raised her ringed hand as she ran, purple flame shooting upward from the center. She gathered it and flung it as though pitching a ball. Kyra's shield held, though a wave of heat crashed over her.

"Kyra, your magic, pull it back!" Talis called. He nocked an arrow. Kyra instantly obeyed, allowing the shield to disintegrate between her and the elf. Talis ducked to avoid a blow from Nymphrys, then swiveled and exchanged fire with new archers who appeared where the wall remained intact. Nymphrys raised her staff anew.

Galakis' black gaze was on Kyra. Bright orange magic streamed out of the staff's tip, converging into a spearhead-shaped point. Aware that Ash and Jyls were defenseless behind her, Kyra ignored her own safety. She cast the golden energy over her head as though it were a rainbow. The gold arced and cascaded over Ash and Jyls. At the same time, Kyra heard a loud whistling. Galakis' magical missile pierced the air and smashed against her shield. The impact jarred Kyra's hand and arm. The corners of Galakis' mouth formed angry pits as the gold held firm.

The ping of arrows tore Galakis and Kyra's attention abruptly to the crenellations. The archers were targeting all the combatants, either not caring or unable to distinguish their Harkimer allies from Kyra and her friends. Galakis fired orange magic at the nearest archers. They were knocked off their feet. He sent another volley of magic to a mass of archers, who bellowed at each other to retreat.

Kyra's brow was lined with sweat. Her arms began to droop. Maintaining the golden shield was sapping her energy. She frantically tried to grasp the fragments of gold as the shield waned. Then the gold petered out completely. Galakis had finished with the archers and returned his attention to Kyra. A wicked grin played on his lips.

Kyra's eyes flashed in anger. If she couldn't defend, she could attack. Kyra clapped her heels into Raven and charged Galakis at full speed. The dark wizard's eyes widened in surprise. He threw himself against the wall as Raven sprang over a heap of stone. Kyra heard Odin and Autumnstar galloping behind her. Talis fired one more shot at Nymphrys before spurring Windchaser forward again.

The gate leading to the outermost ring was only a few meters away. Talis impelled Windchaser and the group through it. Talis kept his bow raised, forcing back the soldiers. Most were smart enough to press against the wall instead of risk being run down by the four horses. As they rounded the final part of the arc, Kyra knew they had reached the bridge.

Windchaser crow-hopped as Talis reined in sharply. Kyra was forced to pull Raven back too. Her face fell, aghast.

The portcullis was closed. Ringed by torchlight from the sides of the wall, a full complement of soldiers formed an impregnable barrier in front of the exit. Half held spears at their waist and pointed the tips toward the horses. The other half stood poised with swords drawn. The night sky was ominously black as the clouds kidnapped the moon and stars.

Kyra glanced despairingly over her shoulder. Ash clutched the arm of the still unconscious Jyls. Facing forward, Kyra reached out and concentrated on conjuring up the golden energy. She felt a tug on her hands, once, twice. Then, nothing. Kyra looked down, aghast. Her magic seemed as drained as she was.

Talis made quick work of two spear-carrying guards as the soldiers bearing swords barreled forward. Kyra suddenly spotted three iron balls tied to one of the soldier's belts.

The bolas!

Kyra hurriedly opened the heaviest pouch on her belt and removed two weighted ropes. Her mind's eye invoked the memory of Hayden's technique while apprehending Jyls. Kyra felt the weight of the iron as she whipped the first of the bolas over her head. She released it with a snap. The bola lashed the legs of the first guard, bringing him crashing to the ground. Kyra immediately swung and threw the second at a guard closing in on Windchaser. The bola also found its mark. The guard tripped and fell face-first. Kyra glanced at Talis. Her heart sank to her stomach.

The elf had thrown his bow over his shoulder and unsheathed his sword. His quiver was empty. With nothing to close the distance, the group was at the mercy of the archers.

As if that wasn't enough, a second batch of guards filed in around the horses. They wore Farcaren's crest of the dragon over their hearts. *The Royal Guards.* They shored up the first group, standing in two perfect lines. The front line carried crossbows. Face taut, Talis lowered his sword. The guards edged forward. Talis suddenly turned in his saddle. His amber eyes stared at something in the distance, an uncertain expression lining the planes of his face.

Kyra wondered if more guards surrounded them. Then she heard someone shouting. Talis' eyes reflected surprise. The guards' gaze also fixed on the newcomer. They tightened their formation and stood at attention. When Kyra followed their gaze, her stomach clenched painfully.

It was Callum. He sprinted, sword in hand. "Stand down!" he was yelling. Perspiration plastered the platinum blond locks to his forehead. "Lower your weapons!"

Confused, Kyra watched as the captain slowed, ribs expanding and contracting as he caught his breath. "I ordered you to stand down," he growled. Callum stepped past Raven. He moved in front of Windchaser, putting himself between his guards and Talis. His sword glinted in the torchlight. "I will personally take the life of the man or woman who lets fly an arrow or swings a blade."

The guards traded indecisive looks with each other.

"Never would I expect insubordination from the Royal Guards. You are sworn to the king's service, yet here you stand with weapons raised to his allies. What possessed you to take such actions?" Callum cast a wide-ranging glare over the group. Some of the guards shifted uncomfortably.

Finally, a young guard dared to speak. "Captain," he squeaked. Kyra recognized the young man as Linden, the guard who spoke with Catt in the courtyard. Linden cleared his throat with an embarrassed look and continued in a lower pitch, "We were ordered to seize the prisoners who escaped."

"Ordered by whom?"

"By Reston, Captain." Linden refused to meet Callum's furious gaze. "He said he relayed it on behalf of the king. We weren't to delay."

Callum squeezed the hilt of his sword. "Since when did the Royal Guards take orders from a steward?"

Linden looked to his companions for help. No one volunteered, seeming to prefer their captain's wrath be focused on someone other than themselves. "It was a breach of protocol, Captain, but . . ."

"This isn't a 'breach of protocol,' Linden. This is breaking the chain of command. The Royal Guards report to the king, the captain or, if the captain is unavailable, the captain's second."

"But Reston . . ."

"The *reason* for this chain of command, Linden—" Callum torpedoed his sentence, "—is to prevent subterfuge from others to depose the king. Did you forget the history of the steward of Cheslynn? The conspirator and traitor who ousted the king with the help of the Royal Guards? The steward who then publicly executed the guards for their betrayal while proclaiming his innocence?"

Linden's cheeks turned beet-red. "Yes, Captain."

"Remember that the next time anyone other than myself or Larisa gives an order!" Callum barked. He pointed at Talis. "*He* isn't even one of the king's enemies! None of these four are. They—" he made a sweeping gesture, "—baited Hayden and Solarus to come to Thanesgard. They are the king's *allies*. Hayden and Solarus committed the crimes against Thanesgard for which they were jailed. Even if you could take orders from Reston, the orders were *not* to detain these individuals."

Kyra fought the urge to sink into the saddle in relief. Callum wasn't part of the plot with the wizards. He was *rescuing* Kyra and her friends.

"Captain, if I may," a female guard spoke up. Her gaze was fixed straight in front of her. "The girl was one of the escapees. If the king had demanded their return—if we hadn't received the directive from the steward, Captain—then the girl would also be under arrest."

"That is incorrect, Esteri. The 'girl' rides with, as I will repeat, the individuals responsible for our success in trapping Hayden and Solarus. If she were an accomplice, do you believe she would have left them behind? Or these others? I think not. She was part of the ploy. A convincing enough part to make my guards question my authority."

Esteri's face reddened. "I apologize, Captain," she replied in a low tone.

Callum shot the guards a murderous look, his face red with anger. He gestured with his sword to the line of men and women standing behind the Royal Guards. "And when was a score of soldiers and archers required to apprehend four alleged criminals? If your training has been sufficient, you shouldn't have to match two men to every one prisoner. I know Sergeant Marid. He isn't the type to allow such poor performance. I will have a thorough discussion with him regarding your behavior tonight. I'm sure he can rectify your lapse in judgment."

The mention of the sergeant's name sent a ripple of nervousness through the soldiers. The swordsmen sheathed their weapons. The archers unbolted the crossbows. The soldiers held their spears at their sides, faces stamped with trepidation. Callum watched them coolly, using the silence to draw out their discomfort. The Royal Guards exchanged uncertain glances, holding their weapons ready.

"What are your orders, Captain?" Esteri asked.

"Stop hindering their progress. Raise the portcullis, and lower your weapons, or Inishmore help me I will make sure at least the Royal Guards are reassigned. You will keep watch in the fields for the next six months."

The Royal Guards hastily obeyed. Two of the Royal Guards ran to the portcullis. The pair of soldiers that had been ensnared by Kyra's bolas had disentangled themselves with the help of their companions. They sheepishly handed the weapons back to Kyra. She returned the bolas to her pouch, heart racing. She heard the grinding of chains.

"Report to the castle," Callum commanded the troop. "Inform King Arkin that, as per his orders, we are in pursuit of Hayden and Solarus. I will bring news to him personally of the departure of these four. Go quickly, and I might be more lenient with your disciplinary action."

The company of soldiers, archers, and guards disbanded and marched at a quick-step down the outer ring.

Callum's eyes followed the group until they disappeared around the arc. He raised his gaze to the upper walls. The parapets were empty. Expelling a tense breath, Callum sheathed his sword. He faced Kyra, his lustrous eyes distressed. "I ask for your forgiveness," he said. "I can't tell you how deeply disgraced and ashamed I am. I had no idea the king was allowing Harkimer's wizards a free hand in Farcaren. I never would have believed he could make a deal with Adakis and his ilk if I hadn't seen the wizards for myself. The dark wizards have no right meddling in our affairs. By his own laws, King Arkin's actions border on treason."

As Callum spoke, Talis dismounted and strode to Odin. Ash kept a viselike grip on Jyls' shoulder. The healer watched with a perplexed expression as Talis slid the thief's boots from the stirrups.

Callum picked up on Talis' intent. He rushed to Odin's other side. "What happened to him?" Callum asked as he removed the opposite stirrup.

"Jyls was struck during the attack," Talis replied quickly. He lengthened the stirrup's strap as far as it could reach. "Ash has tended to him as best he can. If we intend to ride hard, we must guarantee Jyls is secure in the saddle or else he won't make the journey."

"I agree. Here." Callum threw the opposite stirrup over Odin's neck. Talis reached up and caught it. He quickly took the stirrup in his hand and set the pair next to each other. Pulling out his sword, Talis deftly cut the leather straps to one of Odin's saddlebags.

As Talis tied the two stirrups together in front of Jyls, Kyra asked Callum, "How did you know we were here?"

"A peddler named Catt found Larisa and told her two orphan girls saw your capture," Callum replied. He took Odin's reins and looped them around Jyls' back. "I wasn't in the castle at the time. The king had just sent me to investigate an incident in a town to the south of Thanesgard. I was under way when Dev overtook me on the road. He relayed what Larisa had been told. Thank Inishmore it was Larisa with whom Catt spoke and not another of the Royal Guards. I fear many of them are part of this conspiracy with the wizards." The captain released the reins to Talis, who immediately knotted them to the leather piece securing the stirrups. "Dev and I rode back at once. I had no information on your fate at the time save that you had been threatened and imprisoned."

Callum's voice was laden with concern as he looked at Kyra. Feeling her neck grow hot, Kyra averted her eyes. She tried to look gravely interested in Talis' actions and not affected by the intensity of the captain's gaze. "Larisa retrieved your weapons from Adakis. She knew something wasn't right. She claimed it was the king's command for the Royal Guards to keep watch over them."

Kyra's attention snapped back to Callum. "Orkanis was burned by Hayden's sword when he tried to touch it, and Solarus said only the wizard who owns the staff can move it . . ." Her eyes brushed over the captain, looking for signs of injury.

Callum gave her a bittersweet smile. "I was trained by Hayden if you remember. I can't count how many times he warned me about that sword when we sparred. We used a baldric to lift the sword and staff." He raised his hands, showing Kyra first his palms, then the back of his hands. "See, no harm done."

Kyra tried to smile in return. Inside, her stomach was weak with worry about the captain and her friends.

Talis stepped back to examine his work. Odin's stirrups were lashed around Jyls' stomach. The reins braced the thief's back. The elf tugged experimentally on the makeshift harness. Jyls didn't budge. Talis turned his head upward toward Ash. "You can release him, Ash. He's well bound."

The healer's shoulders sagged in relief. He relaxed his fingers and let go of his friend.

"Your weapons are being safeguarded by Larisa and Nikolas in the guards' common area," Callum continued as Talis returned to Windchaser and remounted. "It's a small building that lies within the fourth ring. I sent Edyn to intercept Hayden and Solarus and have a guard show them the way. With luck, they're already there. I would have gone myself," Callum added in an apologetic tone, "but then I learned you had fled, and the wizards were on the hunt. I was worried."

Now Kyra didn't know where to stare. Her stomach fluttered with happiness.

"My biggest concern now is who I can trust," Callum said in a strained voice. "I understand why King Arkin accepted Diamantas' envoy when she came to heal the queen and save the baby. I also justified the king's entertaining two more of Diamantas' wizards after the queen passed. He was fulfilling an obligation to Diamantas for his aid. The king hasn't been the same since Queen Genevieve's death. He convened meetings to which I was not privy. At the time, I didn't have a reason to suspect foul play. I see I was blind to what was happening. Harkimer's wizards were despoiling the king's honor, which means they were ruining the honor of Farcaren." Callum pulled at his collar. The three stripes of his rank were a dark mustard color from sweat. "If I had realized we entered into this disgraceful alliance, I would have resigned my charge as captain. Now I'm bound to it. It gives me leverage to battle the wizards from the inside."

"If King Arkin learns you helped us," Ash came, face pallid, "won't he arrest you? Or do something . . . worse?"

"I have nothing to fear. Adakis did us one favor. By parading Kyra, Hayden, and Solarus through the courtyard by force, Adakis marred the reputation of the king. The onlookers were given no explanation as to the charges against the three, innocent individuals. They *did* see wizards were in the castle. They discovered Farcaren's king was unwilling or unable to prevent the arrest. That will breed angst and suspicion among our people. The merchants will also be fearful. Some might leave. The royal treasury will lose revenue from the taxes on the merchants. I'm sure the king is aware of this. He'll need my support and that of the Royal Guards to regain the trust of Farcaren's citizens and the vendors. Besides," Callum said offhandedly, pulling on his sleeve cuffs with the captain's stripes, "the people of Farcaren wouldn't take kindly to the king imprisoning his own nephew."

Kyra gasped. *Callum is Arkin's nephew?*

Callum didn't notice Kyra's astonishment. He cast a scrolling look at the outer wall. "I've won you a few minutes more," he said. "You need to leave before the guards return. I will stall the king if Hayden and Solarus are still in the castle."

"Thank you," Talis said. He reached down and grasped hands with Callum. "I wish you the blessings and fortunes of Inishmore."

Kyra made a show of fussing with Raven's reins as Callum walked beside the roan. He took Kyra's right hand into his own. Kyra was so surprised by his touch that she could only stare speechlessly at their hands, resting together.

Leaning in, Callum said quietly, "I'm sorry you were here for such a short time. I hope to see you again. I did promise you instruction in swordplay, after all." Callum brought her hand to his lips and kissed her knuckles. Kyra wanted to say something witty or happy or even a "thank you," but the words were stuck in her throat.

Callum released her hand. "Until we meet again." He stepped to the side.

Talis leaned forward, his hand on the palomino's side. "*Teklin eros,* Windchaser," he murmured into the steed's ear. "Make haste."

Windchaser sprang forward, hooves grinding into the earth, and cantered through the portcullis. Odin followed Windchaser without needing Jyls' command. Ash spurred Autumnstar close to the draft horse.

Kyra held Raven's reins. A craving to stay wrestled with her duty to leave. A craving made worse as she met Callum's sad smile. "You should come with us," Kyra blurted out. "You have the dark wizards to deal with, even if Arkin won't punish you. Sure, Adakis is a mess, and Janus is as skittish as a cat in a thunderstorm. Diamantas is different though. Everyone is afraid of him. And he's on his way." Her eyes silently pleaded with Callum. "Hayden and Solarus can protect you if you come to Silvias. You'll be safe there."

The grin on Callum's face was wan and burdened by helplessness. "I agree, Adakis and Janus are both a few slices short of a loaf. There is nothing more I'd like to do than ride across Farcaren at your side. But my responsibility is to the people of Farcaren. I can't indulge my personal desires. Not yet. You have my word, though, that this is a temporary goodbye. I'll see you again, I promise."

"I hope so," Kyra answered. A lump lodged in her throat, preventing her from saying more. Raven galloped through the portcullis and onto the bridge. Kyra looked one last time over her shoulder. Callum began raising his hand in farewell, until a sizzling crack split the air. The captain spun toward the sound. From within the castle, a bolt of turquoise lightning streaked over the parapets. Thunderous booms and bangs ricocheted off the stone walls. Unsheathing his sword, Callum ran across the ring and out of sight.

Kyra fought the urge to drive Raven straight back to Thanesgard. She hugged close to the roan, leaving the fight behind.

Chapter 17

Kyra and her companions rode east. Wind whistled through the tall grasses and wildflowers of a long, wide valley as the storm clouds opened up. The air became thick with the scent of fresh earth as the ground drank in the rain. Kyra miserably gripped the wet reins. Without the protection of a cloak, cold rain streamed down her hair and matted the waves against her forehead. She brushed the strands of honey-brown hair to the side with one hand. Kyra's clothes were soaked through, and she shivered uncontrollably. Kyra hoped they would find shelter soon.

Finally, Talis pulled Windchaser to a halt and clicked his tongue. In response, Odin stopped too. He stomped his large hoof on the ground. Talis leaned forward in his saddle and checked Jyls' bindings and straps. Kyra glanced at Ash. The healer's face was pale, his red hair sagging like a wet mop. Talis nodded to himself, satisfied that the bindings held. Kicking his heels into Windchaser, Talis and the elven horse took off again, leaving Kyra and Ash to follow despite their equally wretched expressions.

The grass and flowers disappeared into a dense forest of soaring elms and oaks. When they reached a small glen, Talis decided it was safe to rest. Kyra slid ungracefully from the saddle. Her back and neck cramped from the feverish ride. The rain had eased, pattering lightly on the leaves. Birds chirped and trilled. Sunlight streamed through gaps in the leaves, warming Kyra despite the water that clung to her shirt and trousers. Her feet had stayed dry, snugly tucked inside her leather boots. Kyra rummaged through her saddlebags, found the waterskin, and drank it dry. Raven and Windchaser grazed contentedly on the sweet grass. They didn't seem to mind their wet flanks and manes.

Talis freed Jyls from the leather straps as Ash untied a bedroll from Odin's saddlebags. It was drenched and twice as heavy as normal. With considerable effort, the healer heaved the bedroll from Odin's back and laid it on the ground. Ash stood and helped Talis lower Jyls from the saddle. Together, they eased Jyls onto the bedroll. The healer hastened back to Autumnstar and rifled through his saddlebags. The urgency to help Jyls had washed away Ash's misery about the rain.

Dread sloshed in Kyra's stomach as she sat beside Jyls. Blood mixed with rain painted his forehead and streaked down his cheeks. The thief's face was ashen. Even his freckles had a sickly pallor. Hours after the explosion, Jyls still hadn't awoken. Bile rose in the back of Kyra's mouth. Was he dying?

Kyra glanced up at Ash as he rushed toward them. His hands were filled with cloth, vials, and herb packets not spoiled by the rain. He knelt next to Jyls across from Kyra. Setting the items on the ground, Ash placed a hand on Jyls' forehead. "*Preeyatna portentia*," he chanted softly. Ash pressed two fingers against the thief's neck. "*Preeyatna roskana*." Ash held a hand above Jyls' lips. "*Preeyatna kak vasla okuda.*" The healer rocked back on his heels. To Kyra's surprise, Ash's green eyes didn't reflect fear; they were filled with calm contemplation.

Talis hunkered next to Ash. Kyra recognized the jar of salve in his hand. It was the same ointment he had used to treat her cuts in Edoin Forest. "This salve is derived from the sap of the Sadyran tree," Talis explained, unscrewing the top and extending the jar. "It will heal Jyls' wound faster than any medicine in Ilian."

Ash took the proffered balm with his thanks. The elf nodded, rose, and moved to the glen's perimeter. The healer resumed his meticulous examination of Jyls. "Kyra," he said without looking up, "could you bring me two more pieces of cloth from my saddlebags? I'll also need the cauldron filled with water. The herbs need to be steeped. If the salve doesn't stanch Jyls' wound, I can apply a poultice."

Kyra lifted the cauldron and stood. "If the sap comes from the elves, I'm guessing it'll work," she replied, more to reassure herself than Ash. "Talis used it on the cuts I had in Edoin. They were almost completely healed overnight."

Of course, Kyra added silently as Ash again took up his chant, *those were oversized paper cuts. Not possibly fatal gashes across my head.* Kyra looked around. Was there a stream nearby? She noticed a dip in the ground and raced toward it. In the darkness brought by the storm and with her fatigued limbs, Kyra slipped on patches of slick mud and grass. She wanted to stop where she was and drop to the ground, mud or no mud. Her legs were leaden. Her arms dangled like wet ropes at her sides. Then Kyra's thoughts returned to Jyls. Her resolve to do her part strengthened. Soon she heard a gushing of water. Guided by the sound, Kyra discovered a stream bloated from the rain. She filled the cauldron and sprinted back the way she came.

"*Sooya vakhto piryani,*" Ash was intoning when Kyra returned. He glanced up, smiling gratefully, as she set the cauldron down. Barely breaking his cadence, the healer gave Kyra more instructions. Kyra spent the next hour as Ash's assistant. She retrieved items from his saddlebags, filled the cauldron with more water, and did whatever task he put her to. Finally, Ash had everything he needed.

Exhausted, cold, and legs aching, Kyra was getting ready to sink onto the soft ground as Talis walked beside her. "We should get a fire going. Jyls needs to stay warm, and you and Ash should be dry yourselves so you don't catch a chill. Unfortunately, the wood and branches are wet and, therefore, unusable. We need another way to build a fire." The elf's tone, combined with the tilt of his head in Kyra's direction and crossing of his arms, conveyed an unmistakable expectation. Talis himself seemed unbothered by the rain. Droplets fell from the leaves onto his head.

"I can help with that," Kyra answered his unspoken question. She put a hand to her lips and skimmed the ground with her eyes. "I think."

Ash, hearing her words, broke off in his chanting. He rested his hand on Jyls' forehead and lifted his gaze to Kyra. "You'll create a magical fire?"

"I should be able to," Kyra said, trying to inject confidence into her voice that she didn't feel. "The way Solarus does it . . . He normally picks a spot on the ground . . ." Kyra's gaze landed on a spot where the grass was thinly combed over bald patches of dirt. It was close enough to Jyls to provide him warmth. She knelt beside Ash, ignoring the mud, and faced the almost empty spot. "Then he waves his hand like this—" she made a vague gesture as though she were swatting a fly, "—and says *Ith-AN-sil.*" Kyra frowned slightly. "Or was it '*Ith-an-SIL?*' Anyway, it's one of the two."

Ash's green eyes were riveted to the dirt patch where her flame would appear. He wore an anticipative smile.

Kyra cleared her throat. The healer's conviction in her abilities felt like a weight on her shoulders. It was an added pressure to produce a spell, to do something useful to help her companions. Kyra couldn't let him—or Jyls— down. "Here we go." She raised her hand, drawing up the picture of the blue flames flickering silently in the campfire. Her fingers tingled with the sensation of bubbles popping against her skin. Kyra breathed in deeply. She kept her palm steadily pointed at the ground. "*Ith-AN-sil,*" she sighed.

A small blue flame whisked into existence on the dirt patch. Kyra dropped her hand. She turned to Ash.

"You did it!" Ash exclaimed in amazement.

Kyra tried to look unsurprised. "Of course I did," she replied. Kyra couldn't suppress a pleased smile. She rocked back on her heels and placed her hands in front of the fire. The flames warmed her. Kyra let out a small sigh. "If only I could remember the spell Solarus used when we got out of the river," she commented in a partly apologetic, partly rueful tone. "It's much more effective."

Ash also rubbed his hands before the flames. "This will do," he replied encouragingly. As soon as his hands were dry, the healer turned back to Jyls. Ash picked up a piece of cloth and began sponging the water from Jyls' head. At the same time, he resumed his quiet, steady chanting.

Kyra studied Ash while he worked. He was a different person. All traces of Ash's usual uncertainty had evaporated in the face of the danger to his friend. The contrast was so stark that Kyra wondered if Ash had secretly traded places with a twin while she was at the stream, one who exuded an unassuming confidence built on expertise. Ash placed the cloth to the side and touched Jyls' temple with his fingers. The healer bowed his head and spoke in a low breath.

Minutes later, Ash noticed Kyra's intent expression. He broke off his steady stream of intonations and brushed back his wet, red shocks of hair. "What's wrong?" he asked.

Kyra smiled and shook her head. "Just admiring the work of a healer." Her gaze flickered to Jyls. Her grin faded into a troubled frown. "How is he? How badly was Jyls hurt? He hasn't woken up yet."

"The wound isn't as bad as it looks," Ash reassured her. "The salve will prevent the exposed area from becoming infected, though not having used it before, I'm not sure how quickly it will help the skin close." The healer's brows furrowed. "Normally, a shallow laceration like this wouldn't cause someone to lose consciousness. I'm wondering if Jyls was hit by whatever spell destroyed the wall. Can magic to deflect off stone?"

Kyra leaned back on her palms with a sigh. "I'm not sure what a wizard can and can't do with a spell or how magic moves when it's released. So far, I've witnessed energy as a bolt, flame, cloud, and shield. That doesn't mean much, given I have no memories of life before returning to Ilian. We'll have to ask Solarus."

The thought of their missing companions made Kyra's heart thud painfully. "You were chanting when you treated Raff and now with Jyls," she changed topics, trying to distract herself from her rising anxiety. "I didn't recognize the words. Is that a form of magic? Something only healers are taught?"

"The phrases aren't magic," Ash replied. "They are blessings from a language called Lokorov. It's the oldest language in Ilian. At least, the oldest that's been recorded by scribes. No one speaks it anymore except the healers. Even then, we use only fragments of the language."

"Why do the healers learn Lokorov?"

Ash touched the tattoo on the back of his neck. "There are two reasons. The Lokorovian blessings are supplications to Inishmore to heal the patient. We believe Inishmore is everything that was, is, and will be. The second reason is that if a sound or set of sounds is combined with an action, the action can be remembered more quickly. Every second matters when it comes to binding a wound or treating an illness. The recitation of the phrases helps healers move instinctively to diagnose and then remedy the problem. It takes too long to think through each step. I find the rhythm is the most helpful part." Ash set the cauldron in the middle of the fire and removed the herbs from their packet.

Kyra leaned back on her hands. A yawn escaped her. The blue flames brought a comfortable, if not hypnotic, glow to the underlit forest. Kyra wondered if dusk had set in or if it was evening. She watched as Talis approached the fire.

"Where are we, Talis?" Kyra asked as he crouched beside her.

"We are east of the river that separates Silvias from Farcaren," Talis answered. "These woods—" he indicated the trees with a turn of his head, "—were joined with those of the Realm a millennium ago. At that time, the river was merely a stream narrow and shallow enough to cross by foot. Over the centuries, the banks were eroded by heavy rains. The stream widened, and its currents became swifter, ultimately forming what today is the river. The river serves as Silvias' westernmost boundary. This part of the forest has been cut off and belongs to Farcaren."

Talis reached over Kyra and took the jar of salve. "You should apply a thin layer over the skin that has been burned," he instructed, handing it to her. "Where we go next will require more of your strength. You need to be as whole of body and mind as possible."

The elf didn't elaborate as he rose. Puzzled, Kyra watched Talis resume his patrolling of the glen. What did that mean, "whole of body and mind?" Where were they going? Kyra let go of her questions and unscrewed the lid of the jar. As before, the balm smelled strongly of mint. Kyra scooped the sap onto two fingers and dabbed it over the burns on her neck. A refreshing coolness seeped into her muscles and soothed her blistered skin. She smeared the salve on her shoulder, then on as much of her back as she could reach. The skin that went neglected throbbed. With a slight sigh, Kyra set the jar down anyway. The only way to reach the burns was with help. Kyra felt awkward asking one of her male companions to rub the salve. She stretched her legs out and rolled her aching shoulders.

There was nothing left to do but wait for Hayden and Solarus. Kyra and Ash ate a meager dinner of dried meat, bread, and something akin to the lemongrass Talis had collected. The food stuck like chalk in Kyra's mouth. She fidgeted with every bite, compulsively glancing around the dark campsite. Why hadn't they come yet? Were Hayden and Solarus trapped in the castle? Should she and Talis go back and find them? And what would Callum's fate be? Kyra wasn't convinced that Arkin would let Callum's insubordination go unpunished, no matter how much the king needed his support to rally the people of Farcaren.

Kyra weathered her concerns by asking Ash more questions about healers. Ash gladly indulged her curiosity, more talkative than he had ever been with her. It was easy to see the passion in Ash's sparkling green eyes. Kyra reclined contentedly against a tree. She listened to Ash describe remedies for various ailments.

"There's nothing better than myrrh for a toothache," Ash said as he twisted a blade of grass between his fingers. "It's a resin that comes from thornbushes in Calonia. My father used it for my younger brother Racer when he was a baby."

Kyra looked thoughtful. "What else can myrrh do?"

"Lots of things." Ash grinned mischievously. "If you put it in boiling water, it can cure bad breath."

Kyra laughed richly.

"Is it too much to ask for you to whisper? My head's a bit delicate. Although I'll admit, hearing Ash talk to a woman about bad breath might be worth the pain."

Kyra and Ash spun around. Jyls had propped himself up on an elbow and was tenderly massaging his temple. Color was restored to his face. His bird's nest of hair sagged, covering his ears. The bandage held firm on his forehead.

"Jyls, you're awake!" Ash exclaimed. He and Kyra scrambled to their feet and dropped next to their friend. Jyls squeezed his eyes shut with a grimace.

"That's the opposite of 'whisper,'" the thief muttered.

Ash peered inquisitively at Jyls. "How do you feel?" he asked in a lower tone.

Jyls opened his eyes. The midnight blue was tinged with glassiness, and he touched the bandage on his forehead tenderly. "Like a swarm of hornets mistook my head for a hive."

"Here, take these." Ash picked up another packet and untied it. "I don't have ginger to help with the ringing in your head, but the thraxen berries will dull the pain." Jyls stretched out his hand. Ash sprinkled pea-sized, orange berries into his open palm. "Chew on them until they lose their flavor, then spit them out. Don't swallow any, or you'll have an upset stomach until morning."

"How pleasant." Jyls took a tentative whiff of the berries. "Ugh!" he said, recoiling from the offensive smell. "You weren't conspiring to off me in that discussion of yours?"

"Chew," Ash repeated in a no-nonsense tone.

Holding his breath, Jyls thrust the fruit into his mouth. A look of surprise crossed his face. "This isn't bad," he remarked through a mouth full of a gummy substance. "Tastes like blackberries." Chewing merrily, his gaze circled the dimly lit camp. He turned his head and spat out the remainder of the berries. "I take it our gallant escape was a success if we're here," Jyls said, wiping his mouth on his sleeve. "And *where* are we exactly? How did we get ourselves out of that mess?" Jyls started to lever himself upright. "Are our valiant companions still—ow!" Jyls' mouth twisted painfully. He lifted his shirt and looked down. Black and blue stirrup-shaped bruises tattooed his chest. "What in the name of Jaren and Garen did you do to me?"

Ash filled Jyls in on the events after the explosion while Kyra impulsively looked for Talis. The blue fire illuminated only part of the campsite. She eventually made out Talis' shadowy profile as he kept his post at the perimeter of the glen. He leaned against a tree, leg raised, arms folded.

"You did *what?*" she heard Jyls' shocked tone. Kyra tore her gaze back to him. The thief stared at his stomach in disbelief.

"It was that or you fell off Odin," Ash defended.

Jyls scowled. When Ash finished the story, he laid back on the grass. "I wouldn't fret over our valiant companions," he remarked. "They've faced worse."

Moments later, Kyra heard the snapping of twigs and crushing of forest litter. Talis dropped his leg from the tree. Grayhaven and Willow stepped through the opening to the glen. Solarus' staff shone with a brilliant turquoise light that made the campsite as bright as day. Kyra's anxiety melted away. He and Hayden's features were laced with fatigue, but they were unharmed. Oddly, Kyra noticed they were both dry.

The relief Kyra had at the sight of her friends was short-lived. Hayden and Solarus didn't dismount but instead had the group on their feet and ready to ride again.

"Callum bought us time," Hayden told them without preamble as Ash secured Jyls' bedroll on Odin's saddlebags. "Enough time to get a head start on Arkin and Adakis' retinues. We can maintain a good distance if we ride hard enough."

"Before we go . . ." Solarus stepped toward Kyra. He held his staff to one side. With his free hand, Solarus gripped her wrist. "*Is-ter-AH-ha,*" he uttered.

A pleasant warmth spread across Kyra's skin like a mist, evaporating the water until all that was left was steam. Kyra patted her head. Her hair was soft and fell in waves. "I really need to learn that spell," she said.

Solarus gave her a wry smile, then moved on to Ash.

Hayden was already mounted when Solarus had reached all the companions. Hayden's expression was severe.

"We'll ride east as the crow flies. Adakis has an aversion to common sense but not Galakis and Nymphrys. If we reach the woods, they'll be wise enough not to follow."

Jyls, whose foot was in Odin's stirrup, glanced sideways at Hayden with a grim look. Talis' eyes flashed with uncharacteristic dread. Solarus rubbed his chin but seemed unfazed by the news. Ash seemed to share Kyra's confusion at their companions' reactions. With a puzzled frown, Ash hitched Autumnstar's reins in his hands.

Hayden walked Willow to Raven. He snatched a scabbard from a loop on his saddlebag. Hayden held it out to Kyra with a somber smile. "This belongs to you."

Kyra accepted the sword with a grin. She started to buckle the scabbard onto her belt.

"Don't strap it on yet," Hayden instructed as Talis turned Windchaser toward the opening in the trees. "You aren't used to carrying a weapon at your side, and we're traveling through dense underbrush. If your scabbard catches, you'll be thrown from your saddle. Normally, a sore back or sprained wrist is the result and is bad enough. Losing your seat on this path is unquestionably fatal."

Kyra's smile dissolved. She reluctantly removed the scabbard, turned in her saddle, and stuck the sword at an angle in her saddlebag. The hilt poked through the flap. "I get to experiment with my magic some more?"

"No." Hayden's tone was so sharp Kyra glanced up. "We aren't fighting anything in the forest. If we're attacked, you ride, and you ride hard. Magic isn't a recourse, no matter what."

Kyra could almost hear the dread that crashed in her stomach. Her eyes went to Talis. His face was filled with resolve, but his eyes had a haunted look. She swallowed hard.

What was so terrible it could scare an elf?

***

It became clear to Kyra that something was . . . *wrong* with the forest. They ventured into the trees, with Solarus' staff ringing the group with a halo of light. Even with the staff, though, Kyra couldn't see beyond Jyls' horse, who was directly in front of her. Then she felt a vibration in her bones. It reminded Kyra of the tingling in her hands when her magic heralded its arrival—except it also buzzed in her arms and legs as though they had fallen asleep. The hair on the back of Kyra's neck pricked. She darted looks left and right. Were the dark wizards skulking nearby? The inky blackness pressed against her. Kyra's pulse quickened.

One look at her companions told Kyra she wasn't the only one spooked by the intangible feeling. When Hayden finally announced a break, Ash looked as though he was about to topple from his saddle. His face was colorless, and his hands quaked. He slid off Autumnstar. "Is it safe to stay here?" Ash asked nervously, not leaving the filly's side. "It feels like someone's watching us." Ash turned his head in all directions. "From the ground. Above us, in the trees. Everywhere."

Hayden kneaded a knot in his shoulder. "We're safe," he replied. He let his arm drop. "Adakis and Arkin haven't quested after us." He glanced at Talis for confirmation. The elf nodded once. Hayden patted Willow and walked to a thick elm. He sat heavily, his back against its rough bark. "Get some sleep," he instructed. Hayden leaned his head back and closed his eyes. "We have a long day ahead of us tomorrow."

Kyra lay on the ground, not bothering to remove her bedroll. The subtle tremors continued within her bones. She rested her head on her arm. Ash's description was frighteningly like her own apprehension. Being watched from all over. Despite Kyra's determination to stay awake, frightened of whatever terrible creature awaited her in the darkness, the grueling demands of the day dragged her into a deep sleep.

At daybreak, Hayden woke the group. The whites of his eyes were lined red, and the skin at the corners sagged from lack of sleep. Judging by the sluggishness of her companions, Kyra guessed they hadn't rested much either. She looked for the campfire, hoping a jolt of coffee would help her get through the day's ride.

The forest floor was empty. Puzzled, Kyra's eyes swept over the group. Hayden rummaged through his saddlebag. Solarus stood near Grayhaven, chewing distractedly on the end of his pipe. Talis sat cross-legged. He braided long grasses together, a blank look in his eyes.

"Why isn't there a fire?" Ash came beside Kyra, voicing her same question.

"More important, why isn't there coffee?" Jyls put in with a long yawn.

Overhearing, Solarus glanced at Jyls. Strangely, he didn't respond. His eyes were focused on an invisible point. Hayden removed a leather satchel from the saddlebag.

It was Talis who answered. "It's dangerous to use magic in this part of the forest," he said hollowly. He let the woven grass fall, face taut and pallid. "We are in what was once one of Silvias' sacred ancestral lands. It used to be like the *Y'cartim Allegra*, or the Ancient Forest. This area was ravaged during the War of Calonia. Malus' wizards had reached the river to Silvias. *Veralyn* Clasil was prepared to make his final stand at the border. Then Malus was killed at the Seven Rings Pass. *Veralyn* Clasil crossed the river and drove Malus' surviving factions to the Southern Mountains. In their retreat, Malus' wizards channeled their hatred into the elven land. They set streams ablaze. They poured pestilence into every blade of grass and rot into every plant. They infected the roots of the trees with spirits of wickedness and vengeance. Nowhere else in Ilian suffered as did these woods. That is why it is named the *Wysteria Allegra*. The Forgotten Forest." Talis' voice cracked. He lowered his gaze again to the grass.

Hayden, who carried the leather satchel and waterskins to the group, paused beside the elf. His gray gaze was filled with concern. Talis didn't look up. He lifted the discarded blades of grass and quietly resumed his work. Hayden opened his mouth, then decided against whatever he wanted to say. Hayden joined Ash and removed dried provisions from the satchel.

"And so it remains centuries later," Solarus took up the thread. He puffed on his pipe contemplatively from his spot near Grayhaven. "The blighted earth has never recovered. The purity of magic born by Silvias has been eternally corrupted by the wizards' perverse energy."

Water rimmed Kyra's eyes. The words evoked a deep sense of helplessness and loss within her. Kyra swiped the tears with the back of her hand as Solarus fixed an icy gaze on her.

"You are to refrain from summoning magic until we have reached Silvias' border," he ordered. "I do not care if Diamantas himself arrives with an army of Reapers. For this part of our journey, pretend you are not a wizard."

"Why?" Kyra asked with a sigh. Even hypothetically facing an evil wizard with a vanguard of ghastly creatures was unsettling. "If we're attacked, I need to protect myself. Although I have my sword now . . ." *With no clue how to use it*, Kyra finished silently.

Solarus raised his eyes toward the sky. "Since you cannot simply listen to my instruction without questioning it," he responded curtly, "I will tell you why. The forest is a living being. It harbors centuries of wickedness and houses unsavory beings looking to prey on travelers. The evil that pervades 'everywhere,' as Ash put it, is like a parasite. It feasts on the magic and emotions of those passing through. Your magic, Kyra, is reliably unreliable. It is reactive. One golden spark from your hands, and the woods will gorge on that energy. Wizards and elves with more control and power than you have fallen to madness and hallucinations here."

Kyra's heart pounded against her chest. "Is that why you didn't create a fire? Because it works against you too?"

Solarus somehow looked offended and uneasy at the same time. "It works against any who enter," he answered in an affronted tone. "It would naturally affect me less, as I have experience. I can ward off some of the evil machinations. It behooves us to at least have light in the forest," Solarus added, glancing at his staff. "Have no fear. I shall stop when the forest's magic begins to swallow my own. I see no reason to give the evils here a means with which to manipulate me."

"What about people without magic?" Ash ventured hesitantly. "Is the forest a threat to us?"

"Equally," Hayden responded. He took a portion of food for himself and Ash, then distributed the remainder to Jyls and Kyra. "Remember what Solarus said. The forest feeds on emotion. The creatures here sniff out fear and anxiety, and the forest enhances those negative emotions, creating an unending cycle of terror. It pushes men to madness just the same as those with magic. You keep your mind clear of thoughts, good or bad."

Based on the horror that washed over Ash's face at the mention of an "unending cycle of terror," Kyra assumed Hayden had heightened the healer's frightful thoughts.

"You mentioned there were 'beings' here too?" Kyra addressed Talis. The elf's head stayed bowed. "What kinds of beings? Greeloks?"

When Talis didn't answer, Solarus supplied, "Far worse. They are apparitions, fragmented souls of Malus' followers who did not escape the woods. Some were killed by *Veralyn* Clasil's coalition. Others were too far behind their companions and were caught in the wake of devastation. Their spirits haunt the woods, warped by the magic. They bear no resemblance to their earthly forms. Inishmore willing, we will not encounter any."

The group was silent as they ate a rushed meal. Kyra's appetite was as phantom as the beings Solarus described. She choked down the bread anyway. Kyra couldn't rely on another break any time soon. Not if the woods were so deadly. Kyra's jitteriness took the place of the coffee, her eyes wide and alert.

"We will follow Windchaser," Hayden said when they had finished and were again astride the horses. "You must stay in line and go *exactly* where he treads. The paths are not easily found nor are they easily passable. As you've seen, dangers abound. Avoid speaking unless you spy something unusual. The phantoms are always listening and watching. They won't forgo an opportunity to feed on fresh energy." Hayden's voice had dropped a notch. The need for silence had already begun.

Kyra gave Ash a sidelong look. Horror was splayed across his face as he stroked Autumnstar's neck more forcefully than normal. The filly shook her mane free of Ash's hand with an intensely annoyed look.

"Don't eat or drink anything from the forest," Hayden added. "The taint and poisons of the forest are deadly. There's no cure for the plagues brought on by taste or touch. Windchaser will help us avoid thorns and burrs on the path."

Solarus stroked his trimmed beard. His gaze was on the woods before them. The trees were blotted out by a supernatural darkness. "Today we will pass through the forest's core and the most potent source of evil." He glanced at his staff and muttered, "*Ascera*." A brilliant light cast a sphere of rays around the woods. "We must be as invisible to the wraiths as they are to us. Kyra, remember, you are to—"

"Not use magic," she ended the sentence tensely. "I know."

Solarus raised a brow at Kyra's tone but said nothing. Jyls walked Odin beside Raven. He held a knife and twirled it in his hand. "Peregrinians have their own delightful nickname for this place. 'The Forest of Eternal Nightmares.' Not something I ever wanted to see, and here we are." Jyls caught the knife and slid it into his belt. He regarded Hayden gravely. "Let's get this over with."

The faint tremor in the thief's voice made Kyra wonder if they would make it out alive.

Chapter 18

The procession moved slowly at first. Talis steered Windchaser through the woods and over the stream with long, deliberate strides. Solarus went next, sitting rigidly in his saddle. His staff's light guided them. Ash followed, biting his lip as he intensely stared at Grayhaven's hooves. Kyra fell in line behind him, then Hayden. Jyls brought up the rear, a knife at the ready in his hand.

Kyra's head rotated in all directions. Fear festered as her imagination ran amok with images of the specters awaiting them. So far, Kyra's impression of Ilian was that its lands were an idyllic testament to beauty. She couldn't imagine a forest scarred by black magic and impregnated with evil. Until now.

Solarus tilted his staff toward the first of the deformed trees. Withered branch limbs twisted like rope and stretched at awkward angles. Bark peeled like scabs. Wind raced through the cathedral-like canopy overhead. Combined with the ghastly forms of the trees, the forest itself seemed to be screaming.

Kyra heard beneath the wind the low murmur of Ash's ceaseless chanting. "*Pazhtorana tak skoola. Ya zabludina. Ya patronizka . . .*"

Fortunately, and unfortunately, Kyra didn't have time to dwell on the unearthly sounds. Her attention was riveted on the trees' large, diseased-looking leaves. Kyra could see most of the branches that sought to unseat unsuspecting riders. Yet even with Raven's careful placement of his hooves in Windchaser's path, Kyra was more than once forced to duck at the last second.

The warped landscape was nothing compared to the pervasive, sinister magic that sluiced over her like ice water. Her heart raced. The stench of decay turned her stomach. Out of the corner of her eye, Kyra glimpsed something darting back and forth in the underbrush. Kyra's eyes widened. The ghosts. Were they already closing in? Or was it a trick of Solarus' light, splintered among the trees? *Relax*, Kyra ordered herself even as her anxiety skyrocketed. *You're panicking over shadows.*

The sure-footed Windchaser chose the safest path, nimbly hopping over snakelike vines, foot-long thorns, and gnarled roots. The other horses didn't deviate from his route. Autumnstar tossed her mane restlessly while Odin tread with heavy steps. Raven's ears were flat against his head. Talis reined in the palomino at intervals, scanning the woods for danger.

Without warning, Solarus' light vanished as though with the flick of a switch. The forest was swathed in a blinding blackness. Seized with panic, Kyra sharply pulled on Raven's reins.

"What happened?" Ash's voice came as a tremulous whisper. "Hayden?"

Solarus shushed the healer. "We proceed without magic from here on."

Kyra's heart plummeted. She heard a flint strike. An incandescent light sprang to life, illuminating Talis' face. He held up a lantern. His eyes looked strained with foreboding. The elf used the lantern to light two more, then passed them all back to Solarus. The wizard kept one and handed two to Ash, who in turn gave them to Kyra. Her hands trembled. Unable to trust herself not to drop one, Kyra passed the two lanterns to Hayden. He secured one lantern to his saddle and gave Jyls the last.

Kyra was puzzled as she saw Hayden remove a bow and quiver. He had carried it since Edoin Forest, but she hadn't ever seen him use it. Hayden flipped the bow in his hand. It was obvious he was equally comfortable with the weapon as he was with his sword. As Hayden buckled the quiver to his side, Kyra wondered why he wanted it now. Hadn't Hayden said they weren't going to fight? What good could arrows do against spirits anyway? Kyra noticed the fletching had a faint green glow surrounding it. Hayden slung the bow over his back. Seeing Talis' gaze on him, Hayden nodded.

Talis turned forward and clicked his tongue. Windchaser set off again, though his steps were increasingly reluctant.

Minutes passed. Then the forest's wrathful energy hit Kyra with the force of a tidal wave. Her blood froze. Invisible cords devilishly wound themselves around her legs and arms. Her throat constricted as the magic curled around her neck. An abyss of despair opened in her heart. Feelings of hope and happiness and love crumbled into the cold crevasse, leaving the most terrible emotions teetering on the icy brink. The same shock and powerlessness she felt standing before the fire in Chicago. Loneliness and sorrow at leaving Millie and James. Frustration over a mind devoid of memories.

"Venus," she heard Solarus' anguished whisper in front of her. "Why did you not answer the summons? Did they capture you? Please. Tell me you are safe."

Solarus' head turned to the side. His ocean blue eyes were filled with the desperation of a man drowning.

"I can't do this," Ash croaked. He had ceased his chanting and dropped Autumnstar's reins. His body shook, his chest wracked with sobs. "I'm not good enough. You shouldn't have chosen me. I'll never be good enough. I have to go." Tears running down his cheeks, Ash slid a boot from his stirrup and made to climb down.

Kyra didn't hesitate. She piloted Raven next to Autumnstar. Slipping her feet from her own stirrups, Kyra pushed herself up until her knees were on the saddle. She stretched her right leg out to Autumnstar's back. With a hard push, Kyra launched herself forward with her left hand. She slid behind Ash in the saddle. The healer was too stricken by his thoughts to react. Kyra reached around him and seized Autumnstar's reins. She held Ash in place as Jyls had with her when they crossed the river.

"It's okay, Ash," Kyra cooed softly. "I'm going to ride with you. You can't leave. We need you. Hold on to the saddle, and keep your feet in the stirrups. There you go, just like that. It's going to be okay."

"Kyra, you've got to keep moving," came Jyls' voice urgently. "There's something out here, and it's not some hallucination."

Kyra racked her brain to remember words Ash used from Lokorov. "*Preeyatna, port, prot* . . . Ash, say it with me. *Preeyatna, port* . . . *Preeyatna* . . ."

"*Portentia*," Ash supplied hoarsely. "*Preeyatna roskana. Preeyatna* . . ." The chant slowly anchored the healer to reality. The fear in his green eyes eased.

Talis clapped his heels into Windchaser.

Kyra did the same, awkwardly holding Ash upright between her arms as Autumnstar galloped through the trees. Kyra chanced a look over her shoulder. Raven was right behind them, hooves crushing vines and underbrush.

This time, Kyra was certain phantoms flew among the trees. Their presence suffocated the air. Kyra's breath came shorter and shorter as the forest latched on to her fear and despair.

No.

Kyra centered her attention on Ash. He was her priority. He needed her help.

Suddenly, Autumnstar skidded to a halt. Kyra fell into the healer. Ash instinctively grabbed both sides of the saddle. Kyra straightened carefully. *What was happening?*

She craned her neck around Ash. Ahead, Talis had unslung his bow and had a hand on his quiver. The lantern swung from the strap of the saddlebag. The elf stared at a spot to his left. The terror imprinted on his face shone in the lantern's light. "Merinn!" he shouted. "He has control over the monsters. He's sent them to hunt you. Go to Carina, get to the sanctuary of the Realm. I will slow them." In a blink of an eye, Talis twisted in his saddle, bow raised to his cheek, an arrow nocked. Its sharp tip was aimed directly at Solarus. "Call back your underlings, Diamantas," Talis growled in a frighteningly dark voice. "So long as I draw breath, you won't capture Merinn, and you won't have the talisman."

Solarus made no move to defend himself. He stared at Talis with a look of shock and horror.

"Talis, *Estienen!*" Hayden's words sailed past Kyra. "*Nathanial sal in orria,* Talis. We have a short distance to Silvias' borders. Press on, *Estienen.*"

Hayden's words stalled Talis. The elf's gaze moved past Solarus, eyes glassy. "Don't you see the creatures, Hayden? Diamantas will not call them off. He *knows.* Merinn has been betrayed. There's no escape for him. I must end this."

"There are no monsters, Talis. Diamantas isn't before you. It's Solarus." An urgency belied Hayden's placating tone. "This is an illusion of the forest, *Estienen*. Please, *nathanial sal in oria.* Lower your bow."

Talis' eyes narrowed. For a spine-chilling moment, Kyra thought the elf would release the arrow. Talis shook his head. The glassiness in his amber gaze disappeared. When Talis again looked at Solarus, his pale countenance morphed from anger to horror. The bow and its arrow dropped to Talis' side.

Solarus' jaw relaxed marginally. He expelled a terse breath.

"I'm sorry," Talis whispered. "The forest is at its strongest. They're here." His bow shot up. He swiveled and loosed the nocked arrow into the trees. A banshee-like scream resonated in the darkness.

Kyra's eyes darted to the inky black gaps. These weren't part of Talis' imagination. As Hayden fired a round at the same time as the elf, she saw tall, wispy beings snaking between the trees. They had heads and arms and shapeless bodies, as though the apparitions were wearing sheets for dresses. The phantom that screamed had Talis' arrow buried where a chest would be. Hayden's arrow struck another of the specters. It released the same bloodcurdling shriek.

Elsewhere in the trees moved mastiff-sized, four-legged shadows. One bounded forward. Jyls' knife pinwheeled through the air and smacked the beast.

Windchaser and Willow bolted through the trees as Talis and Hayden continued to deter the spirits. It was all Kyra could do to keep hold of the reins as Autumnstar deftly maneuvered after them. Ash chanted under his breath. More screams followed in their wake.

Kyra felt her hands fizzing with energy. Ash gasped. Kyra saw him look down, green eyes wide. Peering around him, Kyra's heart sank. Crimson magic swirled around her hands. Her fear spiked. She couldn't lose control. But Kyra's apprehension began to ebb as a manic desire flooded her. She was powerful. The crimson magic wasn't something to be tamed. Kyra could destroy the loathsome beings and the wraiths with them. She could rid the forest of them all. Kyra grinned wickedly. She raised her hand. The crimson energy gyrated eagerly around it.

Resist temptation. Quench the flames. Stay true to yourself.

The sensation gusted into her heart. Kyra hesitated, her throat constricting. *Why should I stop?*

Resist temptation. Quench the flames. Stay true to yourself.

Kyra's trancelike state shattered. She fought with every vestige of energy against unbridling the dangerous magic. It strained even more vigorously to be released, like a shark caught on a line. Kyra wrestled the energy back. Finally, the magic coiled and vanished.

Autumnstar burst through the edge of dark woods. Kyra's heart thrummed as she and Ash were bathed in breathtakingly clear daylight. The filly didn't slow. She clambered down a sharp bank and into a wide, rocky stream that rose to Kyra and Ash's knees. The river's frigid waters seeped into Kyra's trousers. Ash stared forward as though unaware they had entered the stream. Autumnstar churned her legs against the current. With a final surge, the filly clomped onto the opposite bank. As soon as Autumnstar's hooves touched the earth, Kyra felt something invisible snap inside her. She gasped. The tentacles of magic had been chopped away.

Wearily, Kyra steered Autumnstar to the side to allow the other horses space on the bank. She cast a last look at the woods. Black smoke billowed at the edge of the tree line, with red and gold flashing and bursting like lightning within it. The phantoms and four-legged creatures crept behind the unnatural cloud. Kyra's eyes widened. The black haze rolled toward the stream. And stopped before the bank. Outraged shrieks rebounded.

"Where in the name of Jaren and Garen did that cloud come from?" Jyls asked, his face drained of color.

"It is the vilest mutation of magic that exists in the forest," Solarus answered stiltedly. The shell-shocked expression lined every plane of his face, and his cloak seemed to hang limply around him. "The black is the manifestation of the evil we described. The shadows that tear at the soul and mind. The ghosts and beasts are inextricably bound by that energy. They can no more cross the stream than the black magic."

Kyra stared speechlessly as the fumes curled back inside the forest. There was one final flash from within the fog. Kyra covered her mouth in horror. The image projected armies of elves, wizards, and men dropping to their knees, faces contorted in agony, as the dark wizards' magical blaze washed over them. Then it vanished.

Kyra shakily slid down Autumnstar's saddle. Her legs wobbled on the soft bank beneath her feet. *We survived,* Kyra told herself. *Everything's fine now.* She glanced up at Ash. He leaned against Autumnstar, one arm draped around her neck, eyes squeezed shut.

"Are you okay?" Kyra asked. Ash nodded weakly but didn't open his eyes.

Unsure of what else to do, Kyra looked over to Talis. The elf pressed a palm against his forehead. Whatever he had seen—and whoever Merinn was—had disturbed him so much it seemed to push him to the brink of insanity. Kyra diverted her attention, his helplessness digging at her heart.

Hayden swung a leg over Willow and dismounted. He moved with an uncharacteristic fatigue. "The water is befouled with magic," he stated, nodding to the stream behind them. "There should be brooks further in if I remember correctly. Right, Talis?"

The elf glanced up. He nodded mutely, amber eyes vacant.

"We have enough water yet," Hayden said in a voice that hoped it could carry the group forward. "We can rest when we find the brooks. This is the Forgotten Forest, and I don't want to risk new creatures."

"We're still in the Forest?" Kyra responded. She couldn't mask the quiver in her tone. "We didn't cross out of it over the stream?"

Solarus regarded her grimly. "We are out of the worst of the forest. The magic stretches almost to Silvias' border. Do you not feel the vibrations?"

Kyra pulled her attention inward. Solarus was right. Her bones rattled, like a pile of logs teetering unsteadily. As Solarus looked forward, Kyra silently prayed for the courage to finish the journey.

***

Hayden decided they would proceed on foot. The group trudged through the woods in subdued silence. The horses trod heavily, infected by their riders' solemnity. Even Windchaser lost his pep. He worriedly flicked his head in Talis' direction. The elf's shoulders were stooped, head down. Daylight continued to stream through the thinning tree canopy.

Though they had ridden for what she assumed were a couple hours, Kyra felt as though she had traveled for days. Fortunately, as Hayden predicted, they came across a brook not far from the tree line. Talis determined the clear waters were uncorrupted. Hayden allowed them a longer rest than usual. Kyra and Ash gathered the groups' waterskins and brought them to the brook. Kyra filled hers, drank it dry, refilled the waterskins, and drank again. The horses gorged themselves on the sweet grass. Solarus said they hadn't put enough distance between themselves and the forest to risk creating a magical flame. The group had to settle on their rations of dried meat and fruit. None of the companions showed any desire to eat. Even Jyls picked at his meal without his normal gusto.

Kyra was grateful when Hayden announced they would ride until evening. There wasn't any point in staying near the horrific woods. No one objected. They silently mounted and continued, lost in their own thoughts.

Night couldn't come soon enough for Kyra. When a crescent moon began to take its shift in the sky, Hayden halted the group for the night. They made camp. Kyra forewent another cold meal. All she wanted was to shut her eyes and put the awful day behind her.

Sleep didn't come easily. Even though the night was pleasantly mild, Kyra shivered as she pulled her bedroll over her. The terrible emotions summoned by the forest gonged inside her heart like Millie's old grandfather clock.

Millie. London. Millie and James. They had been her bedrock. Guilt swelled within her. No matter how she justified her abrupt departure, Kyra knew she had caused Millie agonizing heartbreak. Would Kyra ever have the chance to explain what had happened? Had it only been a little over a week since she entered Ilian? The last time she had truly considered returning to her old home was during her conversation with Raff. Kyra wasn't sure whether it was possible. She was even less certain she *should* return if it were. London had been peaceful until the experience with the Variavryk Reuben. It had also felt predictable and stable. Until James revealed he was a Lyneera. When the dark wizards forced her through the white void connecting London to Ilian, everything changed. Forever. As her eyelids flickered shut, Kyra understood her time in London was over. The sooner she accepted her life was now in Ilian, the sooner she could move on. The knowledge didn't prevent tears from spilling down the sides of Kyra's face as she drifted off to sleep.

***

Kyra woke with a start. Her tunic was drenched with sweat. Long strands of hair stuck to the nape of her neck.

It was a nightmare unlike any Kyra had had. She was back in Thanesgard's dungeon. In one corner, a staff pulsed with a white light that illuminated everything except the wizard holding it. Solarus and Hayden were sprawled unconscious on the floor. Their faces were bloodied and pale. Kyra's legs were frozen in consternation as she stared at the prone figures. She had to reach them. A crushing sense of vulnerability restrained her. Kyra was terrified of the hidden wizard. It was safer to be as far from him and her friends as possible.

The unseen wizard aimed his immaculate black staff toward Solarus and Hayden. Red and blue flames ignited on the ground. They intertwined and became a giant snake. It slithered forward. Kyra's horror overpowered her fear. She screamed at her magic, willed it to defend her friends. The golden energy wisped faintly in the air. *It's not working!* Kyra watched helplessly as the snake lowered its jaw, its fangs dripping venom. It reared over Solarus. Then . . .

Kyra wrenched herself from the dream. Was the wizard a spirit from the forest? A remnant of the dark magic? Pulse racing, Kyra threw a glance around the area, half expecting the trees to rip free from their roots and grab at her with their gnarled branches.

Rubbing an eye, Kyra yawned and shook her head. She unsuccessfully tried to flatten her tousled hair. Gratefully, Talis' salve had soothed the burning in her neck and shoulders. Kyra stretched her arms over her head. She gritted her teeth. The untreated part of her lower back sent shards of pain down her skin. Kyra made a mental note to use more of the ointment before they began the day's ride.

The flavorful aroma of coffee with undertones of charred wood wafted toward her. Kyra took a deep breath, relishing the scent of the drink. Her eyes perused the campsite. They landed on Jyls. His back was turned to her as he stirred a cauldron heated by a small fire. The flames popped and cracked merrily. Beside the fire were mugs, a bag of sugar, spoons, and a loaf of cinnamon bread.

Kyra's brow knitted as Jyls put down the spoon. When did Solarus' fire pop and crack? She did a double take. The flames weren't their familiar blue. Instead, they flared a brilliant orange and yellow. Pieces of wood atop twigs and leaves fed the fire. Jyls picked up a thick stick and poked the kindling.

Where was Solarus? Kyra's gaze coasted over the area. He sat near the horses, legs crossed, a pipe beside him. The black leather book was in his hands. Solarus' square glasses fell down the bridge of his nose as he skimmed a page. It dawned on Kyra that using magic could be dangerous in this part of the woods. *Unless,* she thought as Solarus took up his pipe, s*omething happened to Solarus in the forest? Something that's scaring him from using his abilities?* Kyra wondered for the first time if other wizards experienced the frenetic, red magic if their emotions spun out of control.

Solarus puffed broodingly for a moment. With a shuddering sigh, he returned to his reading with half-hearted interest.

Kyra's gaze journeyed onward to Ash. He robotically chopped apples and pears on a wooden board. His hands quavered. More than once, Ash stopped, wiped his eyes with the back of his hand, and resumed cutting.

Talis paced in an arc around the trees. His hands were folded behind him, eyes staring vacantly into the forest. The elf's bow was conspicuously absent.

Not seeing Hayden, Kyra half-turned and glanced over her shoulder. She found him rubbing his ring, gray eyes pensively watching the actions of the group. His face was drawn. When Hayden saw Kyra, he offered her a soft grin. Kyra weakly forced her lips upward. The somber mood of the camp repressed any happiness. When Talis paced back in his direction, Hayden walked to him.

The elf barely paused as Hayden placed a hand on his shoulder. He spoke in an undertone. Talis' expression was hollow.

Kyra despondently rose and joined Jyls. He glanced up as she sat in front of the fire. To her surprise, Jyls was fully restored to his good spirits. A fresh bandage patched the wound on his forehead.

"Good morning," Jyls greeted with a crooked smile. "Or maybe 'average' morning. It's morning anyway." He picked up a handful of twigs, set them next to the fire, then shoved the bunch below the burning wood with his stick. "Ready for another go at ghastly ghosts and grotesque goblins?"

"There are goblins in the forest?"

Jyls shrugged, poking a loose twig. "Rumors from Peregrine are there used to be goblins in the Mountains. Then again, Peregrinians also claim fairies bewitch sailors and turn them into sea monsters. Whatever the truth is, nasty creatures want to make a meal of us, and they're nearby." He lifted one of the mugs and scooped coffee from the cauldron into it. "We're not out of the woods yet."

Kyra wondered if the phrase was a pun in Ilian too. Jyls' wink gave her the answer. Taking the mug from Jyls, she spooned sugar into the coffee and mixed it. "That's why you made a fire and not Solarus? Because the forest can . . . use our magic?"

Jyls raised his eyes to Solarus. The wizard's glasses were off, his book face down in his lap, as he puffed on his pipe. "Don't know," Jyls replied. His expression was uncharacteristically solemn as he regarded Solarus. "When I woke up and didn't see our delightful blue flame, I made a very boring and very nonmagical fire. Granted, it was a bit of a nuisance collecting the tinder." Jyls flicked a small twig at the flames. "Wicked magic or not, I'm not suffering two days without coffee."

A grin slipped onto Kyra's face. Jyls' easy manner gave her some sense of normalcy. "That's good for me, since I won't have to suffer either." She sipped the warm drink. "Jyls, the others . . . They look as bad today as they did in the other part of the forest. Is that normal? That they would be affected now? Or do you think this might not be temporary . . ."

Jyls understood the unfinished question. He filled another mug with coffee and took it for himself before answering. "I was asking myself that earlier. Say Malus' wizards were hightailing it to the Southern Mountains. They would have to stop the greatest threats along the way, correct? That means they attack wizards first, then elves. Men are expendable. Never thought I'd be happy about that, but I am right now." Jyls' midnight blue eyes shifted to Talis. The elf stood in front of a tree, head bowed, as Hayden continued to talk to him. "Good thing Hayden didn't lose his head," Jyls remarked, tilting back the mug. "I'd rather swim with a dozen daggerfish then face an elf with an arrow pointed at me." Jyls took a swig of coffee and immediately spit it out. "That's hot," he said, touching his tongue.

"Ash is upset," Kyra continued, unnoticing. Her heart swelled with sympathy for the healer as she watched him chop the fruit. By this time, Kyra imagined the bits were too small to eat with anything other than a spoon. "He kept repeating he wasn't good enough. I was afraid he would run toward those creatures."

"Ash probably would have, but you kept your head too." Jyls' casual tone was belied by a curious—or was it suspicious?—glance in Kyra's direction. "Solarus and Talis were pretty shaken in the woods. As far as my paltry knowledge of wizards and elves goes, it seems like anyone with magic should have been affected. But you were fine. I wonder why."

Kyra silently cradled the cup in her hand. She hadn't been fine. The red magic appeared. Kyra was lucky that she didn't lose control. Solarus and Talis had been entranced, trapped in their personal nightmares. The relentless vibrations unsettled Kyra, but they hadn't instilled the same fear as they had her friends. "That makes two of us," she said with a light sigh. "I'm new to magic. Solarus said wizards weren't considered 'of age' until they're sixteen. Maybe I don't have the power or experience?"

"Maybe you're not actually a wizard," Jyls joked. He blew on the coffee and took a tentative drink.

"What about you?" Kyra asked. "You didn't have any reaction to the magic. Not yesterday, and definitely not right now."

Jyls reciprocated Kyra's bewildered expression with a nonchalant shrug. "Thieves are callous, repugnant men and women. We steal coins from a widow and bread from an orphan. Not much of an emotional sort." Jyls returned to the task of maintaining the fire. He couldn't hide the sorrow that skated across his face.

Kyra reflected on this as she returned her attention to Talis. He wasn't near the trees. Instead, the elf was on one knee next to Solarus, speaking in hushed tones. The wizard acknowledged Talis' words with an occasional nod. Talis extended a hand. Solarus accepted the gesture regally. They both rose. Kyra quickly turned back to Jyls, not wanting to look like she had been nosing in on their private matters.

Hayden and Ash walked toward the fire. The forlorn look in the healer's green eyes was gone as he scrutinized Jyls. Ash placed his hands on his hips.

"Hayden told me you were complaining of a headache," the healer said in an accusatory tone. "Why didn't you mention that this morning when I was changing the bandage?"

"I, what?" Jyls stopped prodding the fire, brows arched. He looked suspiciously at Hayden. "When? What headache?"

Hayden gestured toward the thief as though he hadn't spoken. "You see, that's just it," Hayden told Ash. "He's disoriented. I asked Solarus if it was a result of magic. He didn't think so. The explosion might have injured Jyls worse than we thought. You've seen how soldiers act when they have taken a blow to their helmet: dazed, slow to respond to questions, confused, combative . . ."

Ash scratched his chin meditatively. "I didn't notice that before. The symptoms can be delayed. Pressure in the head can be dangerous."

Jyls' mouth had been open with a retort, but Hayden shot him a covert look. The thief's eyes lit with comprehension. He clamped his jaw shut. Kyra looked from one to the other, trying to decipher what had passed between them.

"Oh, right, dizziness," Jyls replied. He put a hand over the bandage with a dramatic flair. "I forgot. Which is part of being whacked in the forehead, isn't it? Forgetting things." Jyls made a show of staring at the flames, then wincing. "Where did that other fire come from? The light's so bright. It's making me dizzy, jumping around like that."

"Lie down and keep your eyes closed," Ash instructed as he crouched beside Jyls. "I'll bring you more thraxen berries for your headache." The healer peeled back the bandage on Jyls' forehead and inspected the wound. Jyls opened an eye, faking a befuddled expression. "This is healing well," Ash commented, resealing the bandage. "I wonder if I missed other lacerations under your hair. It's thick enough to hide an injury. And the rain yesterday might have washed off the blood. I wouldn't have noticed there were other problems." Ash pushed himself onto his feet. "If you have pain and light-headedness, I'll have to cut out some bunches of hair to see your scalp properly." Ash turned to Hayden as Jyls' façade of confusion dropped into disbelief. "Thanks for telling me about this, Hayden." The healer's expression was businesslike as he strode back to Autumnstar.

"'Cut out some bunches?'" Jyls echoed when Ash was out of earshot. With a scandalized look, he patted his bushy tresses as though to reassure himself they were untouched. "Jaren and Garen, if he removes a single strand . . ."

"A patient with severe head pain shouldn't talk too much," Hayden interrupted. He raised a brow unapologetically. "Didn't our healer order you to close your eyes and rest? I could also mention that your behavior is erratic. That's a sign that you have another infected wound. Probably on your scalp. Kyra, do you agree?"

Kyra feigned serious consideration of Hayden's words. "Now that you mention it, Hayden, Jyls looks terrible. Vampire-white skin and spots on his face. He could have chicken pox or some other disease . . ."

"I don't know what 'vampire-white' is or a pox that comes from chickens," Jyls interrupted. "I'm guessing from the sarcasm, it's an insult. I look the same as I always do."

Hayden nodded. "Ash should shave all his hair to be safe."

Grumbling under his breath, Jyls collapsed back-first onto the grass. "Fine," he capitulated. He put his hands behind his head and closed his eyes. "Seeing as how I'm too feeble to move from this spot, someone else is going to have to tend the fire."

Kyra and Hayden exchanged a grin. Hayden knelt beside the fire and used the thick stick to poke the embers and twigs. Kyra glanced toward the horses. Ash held a vial up to the sunlight. He squinted as he swirled the liquid within it. Ash pocketed the vial and fished through his saddlebag again. Kyra edged closer to Hayden so that their shoulders were almost touching. His gray gaze shifted from the fire to her.

"I was concerned Ash wouldn't recover from what happened," Kyra said in a low tone. "This morning, he was so . . . lost. Now he's relaxed. Ash is always happier when he has someone to take care of."

Hayden crossed his arms over his knee and rested the stick on his leg. "A person working in the service of another feels useful. Ash has to be reminded that he has the gift to help in ways others can't. Ash hasn't realized yet that we value him for more than his occupation. He's a friend, an extremely devoted one. I hope Ash one day understands that. He judges his worth by his skill as a healer but doesn't appreciate his character and kindness and generosity. Ash hasn't learned to be comfortable as himself."

Kyra suddenly grasped Hayden's exchange with the thief. "That's why you made up the story about Jyls' condition." She watched as Ash patted Autumnstar while juggling a cloth full of supplies. "You took his mind off the forest. You focused him on Jyls instead. And Jyls knew what you were doing. That's why he played along."

A smile worked its way onto Hayden's lips. "Ash needed a sense of purpose. We all do. Without one, you question whether your existence matters. If you decide the answer is 'no,' life loses its meaning." A peculiar expression filled Hayden's eyes as he spoke. He resumed stoking the fire, even though the flames were tall and bright.

"Hayden," Kyra asked hesitantly. "Did *you* see anything in the forest? Did you hear voices like Solarus and Talis?"

Hayden's back was partially to Kyra, obscuring his face as he answered, "Yes. I did."

"Who were they?"

Hayden's reply was as faint as a dying breath. "Ghosts."

***

The group made quick work of the coffee. Then, having eaten little the night before, they tucked into a large breakfast. Ash's fruit was a juicy mash of food, but Kyra grinned encouragingly at the healer and scooped it up with a spoon. Talis provided Kyra more salve for her burns. His amber eyes were clear and untroubled. Solarus, meanwhile, stared balefully at his clothing. Without magic, he had no way of removing the flecks of dirt and stains obtained during their ride. Solarus sourly primped his vest and tunic as best he could.

Kyra hid her relief as she observed her companions. Things were back to normal. Except that, as Kyra mounted Raven, she felt the ever-present humming of wicked magic and its malicious yearning for fresh energy.

The horses were also revitalized from their evening's rest. Talis rode several paces ahead of the group, his eagle-eyed gaze looking for threats concealed in the woods. The trees' warped branches were adorned with healthy jade- and shamrock-colored leaves. A lone hawk soared high above. Flies assaulted the horses, and a chorus of insects filled the birdsong-absent space.

The path became a switchback of hills and woods. Rocks burgeoned in between patches of grass as the land dipped and rose. At one point, Windchaser swerved abruptly from a line of trees. Puzzled, Kyra stood in her stirrups. Beyond the trees, land dropped as though sliced off with a knife, leaving a free fall to the ground below. Sitting, Kyra silently thanked Windchaser for his keen perception. She also took solace knowing she rode the other elven horse in the group. Kyra trusted Raven could as readily identify a perilous site and avoid it.

The group took one short break and rode into the night. The woods thinned. Talis eventually spotted a knitting of trees that provided some protection. Hayden made a fire using deadwood from nearby trees as the rest of the group spread their bedrolls on the ground. Hayden vetoed Talis' volunteering to take the watch. The elf protested. When Hayden pointed to Talis' slumped posture and pale skin lined with gray, Talis relented. Even elves needed sleep, Hayden reminded him. Ash and Kyra were also excluded from the duty. Like Talis, the pair argued to contribute. Hayden remained firm in his decision.

"We've already sustained one injury on the journey," he responded first to Ash as Solarus laid his staff beside his bedroll. "We're going to do everything we can to prevent others, but I can't promise we won't need a healer's hands. You need to be levelheaded, which means rested. Our lives could depend on it. As for you, Kyra—" Hayden turned to her with a pointed look, "—Solarus and I are of one mind on this. Solarus believes you are using a lot of energy to keep your magic bound. Without sleep, you can lose that tenuous hold. Inishmore knows what the consequence would be. It's not a risk we're willing to take."

After that, Kyra didn't protest. She hadn't mentioned the appearance of the red magic to Hayden or Solarus. Hayden's response would be one of concern; Solarus' would be a tongue-lashing about ignoring his instructions. Kyra laid down on the bedroll and let the warmth of the fire lull her to sleep.

The next day passed without incident. Talis led them onto a wide dirt lane divided by a grassy median. The horses walked two abreast. Kyra was surprised when Ash trotted Autumnstar beside her. The muscles in his face had lost some of their nervous tension. Ash gave her a half-smile. Kyra returned it. They rode together in amiable silence.

Hayden pushed them to a patchwork of trees that fringed a stream and boulders stricken with moss and lichen. When darkness settled in, they settled near the burbling waters.

As he had at every stop, Ash checked Jyls' bandage. The wound had closed. Also, much to Jyls' relief, the healer hadn't clipped any of his precious locks of hair. "These herbs are simply *magical*," Jyls had proclaimed loudly. "You did it, Ash, I'm all fixed up. Look, no wooziness." Jyls leapt to his feet and danced a small jig around the fire. Kyra laughed. Ash wore a dubious expression as though Jyls really had gone mad. Jyls sat back down. "No reason to hack off snarls in this nest." He patted his hair affectionately as though he had almost lost a treasured pet.

Ash shook his head.

Kyra's own burns were also nearly healed. The skin Kyra could see was its usual shade. She expected her untreated back was still speckled with hues of red. The burns had lost some of their sting, though they ached after a long day's ride.

At dawn, the group ate a rushed breakfast and set off along the dirt road. Soon, the hilly forest with its slopes and dips transformed into a flat stretch of meadow with stunted grass and red poppies. Cotton-white clouds lazed in a robin's egg blue sky. Kyra tilted her head back and enjoyed the warm sunlight on her face. Talis spurred the group into a canter across the open land. Kyra's wavy hair flowed in the wind. Her dread whisked away as she relished riding across the bright, open land. After a while, stands of trees sporadically cropped up again, and Talis reduced their pace to a trot. Kyra felt a twinge of disappointment as she reluctantly reined in.

At midday, Hayden allowed them a break to stretch and eat. Then the group continued onward until the sun started its descent. Talis walked them to a series of zigzagging brooks. Dusk's pinks and purples sparkled on the clear waters, under which minnows zipped along in groups. The elf confirmed the water was safe to drink. The horses, whose flanks were patched in sweat, guzzled the water eagerly.

Talis let out a resigned breath. "'Take some, save some' is lost on a thirsty steed," he muttered.

"Barring any obstacles, we'll reach Silvias' border tomorrow," Hayden announced as Jyls hunkered by the stream and splashed water on his face.

"Be vigilant," Solarus advised. The wizard slid his staff free from the straps along the saddlebags. "We may yet encounter greelok packs or the Reapers, if they have made their way through the forest."

"Greeloks?" Ash looked to Jyls, who used his sleeve to dry his face. "I heard stories about them in Hillith. They're the monsters from the Southern Mountains? The doglike ones with tusks?"

"Yep," Jyls answered. He rose and wiped his hands on his pants. "We haven't run into any since I've met you, but there's always a first time." Seeing the horror on Ash's face, he added, "Don't worry. Greeloks do fear some things."

The healer rubbed his tattoo nervously. "Like what?"

"Women."

Kyra, who was untangling a knot in her hair, harrumphed. "If you were smart, you would be afraid of them, too."

Jyls' freckles crinkled as he grinned unabashedly. "Who said I wasn't?"

Chapter 19

Kyra's instincts screamed at her to wake up. Her eyes fluttered open. Kyra pushed herself up on her elbows. Her gaze scanned the trees, sensing, rather than seeing, movement. She heard twigs snapping. Heart jumping to her throat, Kyra threw aside her bedroll, straggled to her feet, and dashed toward the campfire.

Hayden was on watch. He reclined against a tree with his knees raised. His sword and scabbard lay on the ground beside him. Hayden's brows knitted in puzzlement as Kyra dropped breathlessly beside him.

"There's something out there, in the forest," she whispered, her gaze darting from the moss-covered boulders to gaps in the trees. "I heard it. Could it be a bear or a wolf or other animal?" *Or some hideous, bloodthirsty monster?*

"Not likely." Hayden snatched up his scabbard and was on his feet in an instant. His gray gaze roved past the campsite and to the woods beyond where Kyra had been sleeping. Kyra could see his mind whirring as he assessed what danger might lay in wait. Lips pressed together, Hayden buckled the scabbard around his waist. "The magic here might be less of a threat, but it is a threat," he said, eyes fixed on the trees. "Animals can sense this as well as we can. There isn't any reason for them to linger in the forest when they can find food and water elsewhere. I would venture that what you heard is a creature or presence less amenable to intruders." Hayden glanced down at Kyra. She rubbed the goose bumps that sprouted on her arm. "Let's wake the others. I'd rather not be here if whatever you heard gets bolder and decides to greet us."

Kyra's alarm was reflected in her companions' countenances as Hayden relayed what she had seen. They wolfed down bread and refilled their waterskins before packing up the campsite. The group then mounted and, with Hayden in the lead, made their way back into the woods. Kyra's heart scratched with anxiety. She started at every sound, swiveling her head, looking for danger, unable to shake the feeling of being watched. The tree canopy screened the bright morning rays of sunlight and created pockets of shadows that were eerily life-like. Kyra held Raven's reins in a white-knuckled grip. She steered the roan behind Odin. Raven's body was taut, eyes alert, ears pricked and turning back and forth.

The dense forest ended abruptly as though sheared off from the open field that followed. The contrast between the darkness of the woods and the brilliant light was almost blinding as Kyra stepped Raven out from the trees. She shaded her eyes with her hand. Kyra's apprehension gave way to curiosity. She and her companions had entered a large, grassy space hosting a circle of boulders. Exposed to the sun, the rock faces were free from moss and bald as a man's head. The boulders formed peculiar shapes in the field. Each had two columns and was capped by a long, horizontal slab. They reminded Kyra of the pi symbols from her math lessons with Mrs. Lakshmi. The largest of these mysterious boulders towered at least four meters. *Are they decorative or a boundary, a gate to the next town?*

Kyra looked left, then right. The forest arced around both sides of the grassy circle without encroaching upon the space. As Raven clopped through one of the openings between the boulders, Kyra saw no trees grew within the circle either. Her gaze moved beyond the southernmost gates. Boulders cropped up like daisies in a meadow, with sparse stands of trees growing like weeds between them. The boulders seemed to be tinged in a yellow light as the sun beat down on them.

Kyra brought Raven to a halt, marveling at the gates and the boulder-field. In front of her, Ash gazed around the circle in awe. Solarus, who had walked Grayhaven near Odin, stared at the nearest gate. To Kyra's surprise, the wizard's expression was also one of wonder. He ran a finger absently along the Z line in his hair as he silently studied the gate from top to bottom. Jyls drank from his waterskin. Talis guided Windchaser from one gate to another. His amber eyes searched each opening until, at one, he reined in Windchaser unexpectedly. Talis squinted. In a swift motion, he slid his bow from his back. Hayden brought Willow beside Windchaser.

"It would be greatly appreciated if you could spare a quiver," Talis commented without turning to look at Hayden. His face was grave. "I haven't fashioned any arrows to replace the ones I've used."

Hayden swiftly untied a spare from his saddlebag. He tossed it to Talis with a grim look. The elf caught it effortlessly as Hayden questioned, "Do I want to ask why you're in need of so many?"

"Why *we* are in need of so many." Talis quickly strapped the quiver to his side. In an instant, Talis dismounted and had his bow loaded and lifted, the string pulled back to the corner of his mouth. He aimed at an unknown point through the opening of the pi-shaped boulders. "Two bands of greeloks are on their hunt. They are approaching the western and northern gates. I hadn't noticed them in the forest." His amber gaze flickered from his bowstring to the strange boulders and back. "We'll have to fight."

Solarus seized his staff from its strap along the saddlebags. He angled the weapon across his lap. Solarus' gaze roved the gates, waiting for the threat he couldn't yet see.

"Two bands?" Hayden repeated curiously. "That's unusual." He leapt from Willow and moved to his saddlebags. He untied the strap that had secured the bow alongside them and snatched up the weapon in his left hand. "I wonder what forced them together." Hayden took up a place beside Talis, who kept his bow raised at the ready.

"How large is a band?" Kyra asked.

Hayden fit an arrow to the string. "A dozen. It's not uncommon for greeloks to hunt with other packs when prey is plentiful. It's also not uncommon for them to turn on each other to get the best of the catch. They're greedy but opportunistic creatures."

Solarus swung a leg around Grayhaven and dropped to the ground nimbly. He stepped beside Hayden and faced the third gate, gripping his staff tightly in his hand. Jyls hopped from Odin's back, landing softly on his feet. He snatched two knives from his belt. Twirling a blade leisurely in each hand, Jyls positioned himself next to Solarus. He cast the wizard a sly grin. "Don't worry, I'll protect you."

Solarus raised his eyes to the sky and shook his head. "Inishmore save me from the day I need your help."

Jyls' grin widened, but his eyes reflected the gravity of the situation about to unfold. He turned back toward the gate. Jyls, Solarus, Hayden, and Talis formed an arc before the gates, protecting the routes to the north and east.

"How can we fight two packs?" Ash asked with a look of trepidation. He drew Jyls' dagger and held it awkwardly as though it were an animal squirming to get free of his grasp. "You said it takes three men to defend against one of them."

"*Technically*," Jyls corrected, "we are three men, two wizards, and one elf. That improves our odds. Climb down here with us," he added, gesturing with his knife. "Greeloks have a nasty tendency to sink their teeth in a rider's boot and drag him down."

"A horse's stomach is an equally preferred target for a greelok," Solarus put in as Ash hurriedly dismounted. "We must protect our steeds as much as ourselves. Attempting an escape through the woods will not work in our favor." Solarus' gaze fell on Kyra, his tone laden with warning. "The rules that have governed our travel through the forest have not changed. Refrain from calling forth your magic."

Kyra nodded and jumped to the ground. She hurriedly threw open the flap to her front saddlebag, from which the hilt of her sword protruded. Kyra gently pulled out the velvet scabbard. She wasn't convinced she could wield the weapon effectively enough to land even one blow against their four-legged foes. Kyra hoped the blade's sharp edges would at least dissuade a greelok from getting closer.

Kyra slid the sword free of the scabbard. As in the blacksmith's shop, she was somewhat comforted by the familiarity and weight of the blade. Holding her breath, not daring to hope, Kyra experimentally sliced the air. Her movement wasn't graceful; it also wasn't completely novice. Kyra wanted to laugh, despite her fear. Her muscles retained a modicum of her previous training. Kyra decided against fiddling with strapping the scabbard around her waist. She shoved it back into the saddlebag. Kyra then positioned herself between Ash and Hayden. Hayden's sidelong glance was accompanied with a tight grin of encouragement.

Meanwhile, the horses formed their own defensive positions. Raven, Willow, and Grayhaven, seasoned veterans, set themselves squarely against the threat. Odin snorted, his eyes fierce and inviting the challenge. Autumnstar backed up skittishly. Windchaser pawed the ground with the confidence borne of youth and inexperience.

A shrill bark pierced the silence. Talis' bowstring twanged. The arrow cut the eerie cry short. A discordant chorus of snarls and baying resounded beyond the gates. Kyra's mouth went dry. Her gaze sailed from Jyls at one end of the arc, down the line to Talis at the other. Unconsciously, Kyra squeezed the hilt of her sword with a white-knuckled grip.

Then, as though materializing from the air, the greeloks were upon them.

Kyra recoiled. The grotesque, doglike mutations the size of wild boars were as ghastly of those from Hayden's memory. Their long tusks swayed as they ran, milky white eyes staring at nothing. What Kyra hadn't noticed in the wintery scene was the color of their fur. The greeloks' coats had the lime green tint of the grass. Several of the creatures sported patches of brown, providing the perfect camouflage against the landscape. Kyra's heart drummed in fear. The greeloks of Hayden's memory were images, not creatures of flesh and blood like those that charged forward. She was no longer a bystander but a participant in this horrifying battle.

The greelok closest to Kyra snapped viciously at Raven. The roan kicked with his hooves, striking the creature. The greelok shrieked. It dropped on all fours as blood streamed from its shoulder. Without hesitation, the creature attacked again, its claws seeking Raven's neck.

An arrow pierced the greelok's temple. Kyra swiveled to see Hayden's bow trained on the greelok as it fell. Behind him, Kyra spied another creature slinking forward. The greelok went unnoticed by Hayden as he started to reach for another arrow.

"Hayden, behind you!" Kyra cried out. Hayden immediately pivoted on one foot. As the creature leapt, he whipped the bow sideways, carving into the greelok's exposed underside. The beast howled and collapsed. Willow's hooves finished the creature off. Bile rose in the back of Kyra's throat as she saw red pooling around the lifeless beast. Hayden snatched another arrow from his quiver and fired into the fray.

Kyra heard Raven neigh in alarm. She watched a pair of greeloks making a joint onslaught against the roan. They snapped with their razor-like teeth at his legs. Raven reared, desperately trying to avoid their fangs and claws. Blood pounded in Kyra's ears. She sped forward and slashed at the greeloks without any regard for her own safety. Her blade miraculously bit into the first greelok's leg. The creature buckled with a bellow. The second greelok snarled and rounded on Kyra. Kyra managed to sidestep away from the creature as it bounded forward. Its tusks impaled the air, missing her chest by inches.

Yelps, the thwack of arrows, and the slamming of bodies bombarded Kyra's ears. Her gaze flew across her companions. The defensive arc had dissolved as they battled greeloks from all directions.

"Kyra!" Raven's whinny soared over the din.

Kyra ripped her attention back to the pair of greeloks. The one she had stuck limped away from her. Meanwhile, its partner took advantage of Kyra's distraction. It launched itself at her with renewed brutishness, claws extended, milky eyes as blind to her as its ears were keen. Time slowed. Kyra dropped to the ground and instinctively raised her sword. Her hand shook as metal met the greelok's tough skin. The creature didn't have time to shriek before it crashed to the ground a few paces away. Breathing heavily, Kyra remained on one knee. Her hand was on the hilt of her sword as she waited for the greelok's next attack.

An attack that never came. The greeloks lay in a motionless heap on the earth.

Sweat pearled on Kyra's forehead. She swiped it away with her free hand. Kyra's sword arm quivered from the strain of exercising muscles that she couldn't ever remember using. But Kyra couldn't rest. Three greeloks had again converged on Raven. Instead of fighting, the roan turned and galloped through one of the towering gates. The greeloks loped after him, mouths open, saliva slinging from their tongues.

"Raven, wait!" Kyra yelled. She used the point of her sword to lever herself off the ground and onto her feet. Without hesitating, Kyra broke into a sprint after Raven. The gate before her was clear of greeloks. She dashed through it and entered the forest of boulders. The gray slabs formed a giant, uneven labyrinth. Holding the sword close to her body, Kyra ran through the narrow spaces between the boulders. She followed the greeloks' barks and shrieks as the clamor of the fighting faded behind her.

The maze slowly widened, revealing a larger space beyond. Stands of trees appeared near the boulders, making it harder to see either Raven or the greeloks. Kyra paused. Her head swiveled from left to right, looking for the roan. Kyra suddenly spied Raven galloping around a stone slab that loomed like a giant wielding a club. The greeloks loped closely behind him. Panting, Kyra began running again. Raven twisted and turned around the boulders, dropping in and out of Kyra's sight, as the greeloks relentlessly maintained their pursuit. They didn't have to push much further. At the edge of a copse were twin boulders shaped like rams' horns. Raven spun around. Eyes rolling frantically, the roan high-stepped back and forth as the greeloks slowed their pace. Kyra's stomach plummeted. The greeloks knew they had cornered their prey. They crept forward in savage anticipation. Raven stamped the ground in terror.

Kyra readjusted the grip of her sword in her sweaty hand as she looked to close the distance between them. She caught a movement out of the corner of her eye. Heart thudding, Kyra skidded to a stop just in time. Two greeloks dashed out from behind a boulder to her left. Another tore out from a boulder to her right. Kyra backpedaled away from the trio, who effectively prevented her from reaching Raven.

Kyra groaned inwardly. She had been so fixated on saving Raven she hadn't considered other threats. The greeloks had stalked her in the labyrinth without her noticing. Kyra swallowed. How was she supposed to fend off three at once without magic? The largest of the greeloks licked its lips. Its large paw was covered in blood, though Kyra couldn't tell if it came from the greelok itself or someone it attacked. In a fatigued-induced haze, Kyra didn't think to raise her sword to protect herself. She stared at the greeloks with the point facing the ground. The greeloks crouched low, poised to spring.

"AHHHHH!"

Kyra saw the shock of red hair first. She lethargically turned her head to see Ash bolt past her. Dagger in hand, the healer inserted himself between Kyra and the greeloks. Kyra stared at Ash, flabbergasted, as he held the blade out in front of him. The healer had more courage than Kyra realized.

Ash's abrupt yell startled the greeloks. Though its milky white eyes couldn't see its foe, the largest of the greeloks sniffed the air experimentally. It took only a couple seconds before the creature had located Ash. The greelok bellowed and sprang forward.

Ash had courage, but he lacked experience. When the healer awkwardly slashed at the air to protect himself, the greelok caught the blade between its teeth. It clamped down on the flat metal and yanked the dagger from Ash's grasp. The healer's eyes widened. The greelok shook its head, tossing the blade aside. The creature landed deftly on its paws as the dagger embedded itself in the earth. With a snarl, the greelok bared its teeth at the healer. Unarmed and crippled by fear, Ash watched as the greelok again charged.

Kyra finally broke free from her stupor. She leapt next to Ash, shoved him to the side with her sword hand, and threw up her open left palm. "*Zephryn!*" she shouted. Kyra's insides felt like ice as golden magic gusted from her fingertips. The greelok was seized mid-flight by rapid, whirling winds. The creature howled as it spun helplessly in the twister, suspended in a magical, golden grip. Kyra clenched her hand. The twister obediently glided toward her. Then it slammed the greelok to the ground. Kyra's fingers tingled as she flung the golden tornado at the other two greeloks. They, too, were seized by the raging winds and catapulted into the forest.

Red began to lace Kyra's golden winds. Her hair whipped behind her. Kyra's eyes glowed as the wild magic coursed through her, feeding on her delicious energy. Kyra's gaze travelled to Raven, trapped by his attackers. She cast the winds to the three beasts. The twister wrapped up one greelok, then a second. With spine-chilling screams, the beasts were hurled into the trees. Raven trampled the final greelok. The roan tossed his head, fear in his eyes as he observed the angry, red whirlwind.

Now Kyra's greatest enemy was the dark magic. It spread like an infection through her. She shuddered as the tornado sought to free itself. "Go, I don't need you anymore," Kyra commanded the red energy through gritted teeth. She raised a hand toward the winds. Gold shimmered at the tips of her fingers and spiraled around the red. "I brought you here, and I'm taking you back. Leave. *Now.*" With all her effort, Kyra forced the golden light from her hands. It shot out like a streak of lightning and cut through the twister. Pierced by so much light, the red tornado's winds burst in all directions. Then it was gone. Kyra dropped her arms. Her body trembled like dried rushes in the wind. Her eyes stopped glowing and returned to their jade-flecked hue. Her magic whooshed out of existence. Drained yet relieved, Kyra turned to grin at the healer. Her smile was wiped from her face before it had fully formed.

Ash stood, mouth agape, as he stared at the lifeless greelok at his feet. His pale green eyes shifted to the boulder where two others lay crumpled. Ash's gaze finally traveled to Kyra's hands. Kyra was shocked to see the horror in his eyes. "You shouldn't have done that," he whispered. "You could have . . . It wasn't worth my life, risking what you did."

The sudden chill that swept through Kyra had nothing to do with her magic. "I wish there had been another way, Ash," she replied, desperate for him to understand. "I didn't have a choice. You saved my life. The greeloks hesitated. The only way I could rescue you was through magic. It doesn't matter if they died in a whirlwind or by a sword, does it?"

Ash's mortified expression showed he didn't agree. His cheeks reddened, and he averted his eyes. "I'm sorry, Kyra," Ash apologized. "No, it doesn't. You said you didn't have a choice, but you did. You acted without hesitating because you were focused on saving me, not on the consequence of what the magic might do to you. I didn't mean to sound ungrateful. Thank you. I hope you don't need it again."

Raven walked forward. He bobbed his head anxiously. "The battle is not yet over, Kyra. We must aid the others."

Without exchanging a word, Kyra swung astride the roan, then helped Ash up behind her. The healer wrapped his arms around Kyra's waist. Kyra took ahold of the reins with her left hand and adjusted the grip of her sword in her right. She had barely touched Raven's sides with her heels before he galloped back through the maze of boulders. Blood pounded in Kyra's head, and her hair flew in the wind. Ash held onto her tightly. Kyra was silently grateful for the roan's sense of direction. As they neared the epicenter of the battle, Kyra's ears were filled with a rush of cries and barks and the screeching of claws of metal.

Raven charged out of the labyrinth. Kyra's stomach lurched. Greeloks were strewn across the grass at the edge of the gates, dark splotches underneath. Kyra mentally counted the fallen creatures. Hayden had estimated two dozen greeloks; the number on the ground was already that many. Kyra alone had fended off six. More greeloks streamed out of the forest from the north and west and onto the grassy circle. Talis had spotted only two packs. It was clear many more were joining the fight.

Raven stopped and ducked through an opening. Ash released Kyra and slid down the side of the roan. Once Ash was safely to the side, Kyra vaulted from the saddle, her sword in hand. Her gaze quickly scanned the group.

Jyls stood with his right shoulder facing one of the stone gates. He had traded his knives for a short sword. Hayden stood back-to-back with him. Hayden also held a sword, blocking swipes from the greeloks with the flat of his blade. Blood stained the arm of Hayden's jacket. Kyra's heart leapt to her throat. He was fighting with his left hand, though Kyra had noticed he did everything else with his right. How badly hurt was he?

Talis darted among the greeloks, slicing and carving into the creatures with the edge of his bow. He flipped over the back of one greelok, dropped into a crouch, and snapped the weapon in a circle like a whip. Two greeloks howled and fell. Talis jumped and rolled as a greelok landed where he had been a second earlier. The elf rose, breathing hard.

Solarus fended off attackers with his staff as fluidly as Talis with his bow. Solarus punched his staff into the air and caught a greelok beneath its chin. Without pausing, Solarus spun around and walloped the next greelok in the side. Kyra felt a surge of admiration for the wizard as he continued in a flurry of movements. Solarus was clearly capable of defending himself with or without magic.

Even so, Solarus' expression was strained. His boot was ripped down the side. "More come, Hayden!" he yelled at the same time a greelok fastened its jaws on his staff. Solarus' eyes flashed. A blaze of turquoise magic flared through the wood. The greelok yelped and collapsed. "We cannot hope to defeat them!"

"We can't outrun them either," Hayden hollered back. His gray gaze shot to Kyra and Ash. A wall of greeloks blocked them from Hayden. "Kyra," he yelled as Jyls slid around him and threw a knife with his free hand. "We have to split up. You and Ash ride with Talis to the Realm. Once you're in the woods, the rest of us will follow."

Talis didn't respond at first. His back was to one of the columns, with two greeloks in front of him. Kyra's throat was caught with a scream as they launched themselves. When their claws were a hair's breadth from him, the elf ducked and rolled to the side. The creatures smashed headfirst into the boulder. Talis didn't watch them slump to the ground as he called to Hayden, "Let Jyls take them. He knows the way. You need me here."

"Thanks for the vote of confidence," Jyls said. His breath was haggard. "To be fair, I'm out of knives, so I'm not as useful as Talis. You need us here to fight. The greeloks have a teeny advantage on us by numbers." He nodded to the northern gate. A host of greeloks waited outside, hackles raised, tongues lolling.

Kyra looked at Ash in despair. Without magic, what could they do?

Raven's ears perked up. He raised a leg and looked to the east. Had Kyra not seen his movement, she never would have seen them. Helmetless warriors wearing iridescent white uniforms and golden armor surged through the trees and around the boulders. The riders were as lean as the horses they rode. Deep emerald-green capes flapped behind them. As the warriors and steeds whipped past Kyra and into the fray, she saw their pointed ears and shimmering hair.

Elves.

The first wave of warriors cut down the greeloks with sharp blades. Unable to see their attackers, the greeloks whirled around, trying to gain a scent. The elves were too fast. A merciless flurry of arrows found their targets. One by one, the greeloks crumpled to the ground. The elves devastated the greeloks with such ease that Kyra could hardly believe she and her friends were almost defeated moments earlier.

As quickly as it had begun, the fight was over. A heap of dead greeloks lay piled on the ground. The air was still. Kyra heard the sound of the elven horses' deep exhalations, Autumnstar's relieved whicker, and Grayhaven and Odin's stomping. Her stomach turned as the stench of animal flesh and insides reached her. She focused her attention on their elven champions.

The elven leader sat astride a piebald mare. He was larger in build than Talis, with a firm, square jaw. The elf's long, mocha-brown hair was parted so that half was tied back while the rest settled behind his ears and past broad shoulders. His olive-skinned complexion was flawless. Like the other warriors, the leader wore golden armor. His left gauntlet was unique among the group, a dazzling magenta with an etching of a winged horse rearing on its hind legs.

The leader's gaze was fixed on the northern gate. He waved two fingers toward it. "*Erolis il alin*," he said to his warriors. "There may be other packs nearby."

Four elves spurred their horses forward. They passed their leader in pairs, bows in hand. The six remaining warriors positioned their steeds around Kyra and her companions to form a protective guard. The elven leader walked his steed beside Windchaser. His eyes, striking sapphire irises haloed with gold, sparkled. "*Aliori*, Talis," he greeted as he clasped hands with Talis. "It seems good fortune delivered the *Hydranyle* and me to these woods. Timely assistance, isn't it?"

"*Aliori*, Therial," Talis replied as they released hands. "I expect fortune had less a role to play than the direction of *Raenalyn* Carina. But, I agree, it is timely."

Therial laughed, his voice smooth and musical. Kyra immediately liked Therial's friendly, open demeanor. She wondered if they had met before she left Silvias.

"*Raenalyn* Carina divined where you might be when we started our search," Therial replied. He adjusted his magenta-colored gauntlet. "However, I will also assume credit for my warriors. They tracked you to this place. Their efforts are why you're alive and well. Or so I assume you are well," Therial added, expression serious.

Kyra followed Therial's gaze. Ash's face was white-sheeted. He stood beside Autumnstar, speaking to her in a low tone as he stroked the side of her neck.

Solarus inspected his mud-splattered blue vest and white tunic. His sour expression indicated that suffering an injury would have been a more acceptable outcome of the fight.

Jyls squatted beside a greelok. The thief's clothes had dark red splotches on the sides. Kyra's stomach clenched as she saw him bend over. *Was he hurt?* Then Jyls pulled a knife from the greelok's back. With an expression of disgust, the thief used his shirt to wipe blood from the weapon. Kyra let out a small sigh. *He's fine.*

Kyra turned lastly to Hayden, dreading what she would see. Like Jyls, his clothing was blood-stained. Yet also like Jyls, Kyra noticed that the long, dark streak on his sleeve was the same length as a gash in a greelok at the top of the pile. Kyra's shoulders sagged in relief. Why he had used his left hand to fend off the attackers, she couldn't say. The important thing was he was okay.

Hayden walked to Willow and quickly mounted. "*Aliori, Jaelyn* Therial," he welcomed the elven leader. Therial clasped hands with Hayden.

"It's good to see you, Hayden," Therial replied with the same smile. "You also, Solarus," he called over Hayden's shoulder.

Solarus picked his way through the bodies of greeloks. The wizard inclined his head toward the elven leader.

Therial's eyes flickered to the stone gate. The four warriors darted through, their bows at their sides.

"We scouted as far as the Arstad brook and spied no other packs, *Jaelyn*," a female warrior reported.

Therial nodded. "Longer greetings and introductions are better left for when we are in Silvias," he said to the group. "We will lead you to the river. Luckily, we aren't too far."

Kyra opened her saddlebag and returned her sword to its scabbard. Her eyes lit on a waterskin. As Kyra lifted it from the saddlebag and uncorked the top, she couldn't remember being more grateful for a drink. Her throat was parched, both from fighting and from fear. Kyra emptied the waterskin as her companions mounted their steeds, preparing to leave. Returning the waterskin, Kyra swung astride. She took up the reins as Solarus brought Grayhaven beside Raven. Solarus' brows angled sharply. "I need to find you a book of terms when we reach Silvias," he said dryly. "Your interpretation of 'refrain from' was the exact opposite of its definition. To refrain from doing something is to *not* do it."

Kyra tried to assume a guilt-free look. *Does Solarus know about the greeloks and the tornado?* Kyra wondered silently. *He couldn't have. He wasn't anywhere near me when I used my magic.* "A book of terms," she asked out loud. "You mean a dictionary? I *didn't* do anything. If I had, you said there would be some catastrophic result, and look—" she made a sweeping gesture across the field, "—everything's fine."

"Greeloks do not tend to fly through the air of their own volition. Do I need to define the phrase 'didn't do anything' for you as well?"

That's how he knew. But Solarus didn't mention the red magic, which means he didn't see it. Kyra withheld a sigh of relief. "If I didn't, Ash and Raven wouldn't have survived," she replied defensively. "I didn't have a choice. And again, *nothing happened*."

"You always have a choice, and you risked something happening." As Therial and Talis rode to the front of the group, Solarus pointed at her with his staff. "There are worse things than the loss of a man and a horse."

Kyra stared, thunderstruck. How could he say that? Nothing could have been more terrible.

Therial signaled their departure with an upturn of his chin. The elven warriors steered their steeds in perfect synchronization. Four of the elven warriors trotted to the back of the group and formed a disciplined row. Three more elves flanked Kyra and her companions. Satisfied, Therial set his steed into a canter with Talis at his side. Solarus followed. Hayden and Kyra were close behind. Jyls and Ash came last.

In a short time, the copses converged again into thick, healthy woods. Spongy moss carpeted the ground in place of the Forgotten Forest's tattered underbrush. Bushes teemed with flowers instead of thorns. The trees had smooth, unblemished bark and leaves so intensely green that Kyra lacked a word to describe them. Her gaze wandered upward. A vaulted tree canopy formed a spotty roof overhead, with a misty light streaming through gaps in the leaves. The air here was as pure as the air in the Forgotten Forest was poisoned. Kyra let out a soft breath. After four days of the crushing weight of an omnipresent danger, these woods' gentle aura refreshed her like a breeze on a summer's day.

Therial slowed his mare from a canter to a steady trot. He guided the steed so that he paralleled a stream that cut through the trees. The waters began as a whisper in the woods, then grew steadily louder as the stream separated into rivulets. The bank expanded. The water rose. The trees peeled back like curtains on a stage. The rushing waters crowded out the quiet of the woods. Kyra felt a breeze tousle her hair, and resplendent sunlight shone on her face. *Where are we?* she wondered, enjoying the peace of the moment.

Kyra soon had her answer. Therial and Talis filed out of the forest in a single line. The warriors and Kyra's companions followed suit. Raven stepped through the trees, providing Kyra with her first glimpse of what lay beyond the woods. Tears swam in Kyra's eyes but not from sadness. The sight filled her with pure elation.

"Where are we?" Kyra repeated her question aloud.

Raven sighed, his muscles rippling beneath her. "This is the border of Silvias. We're home, Kyra."

Chapter 20

Speechless, Kyra let her eyes travel across the land. The splendor reminded her of one of Millie's pieces of art. Kyra and her companions had emerged from the forest onto the bank of a crystal blue river. As wide as a dozen football fields, the water snaked its way through tall hills textured with woods. Cliffs on both sides of the river looked painted into the hills with long strokes of a brush. Waterfalls cascaded down the rock, forming pools of mist and spray. Leaves in every hue of green were sponged like dots against a backdrop of dazzling blue sky. Brightly plumed birds soared overhead.

Kyra couldn't envision a more beautiful place to call home.

The lone obstacle seemed to be the river. Kyra's gaze returned to the vast stretch of water. The current was swift, the waters flying down as though racing each other. She couldn't see any rocks or branches lying in wait below the crystalline surface. But, Kyra thought, that didn't mean there weren't any.

"This river is a lot faster than the one we crossed," Kyra commented quietly to Raven in what she hoped was a casual tone.

"Right now, it is," the roan agreed. "The river swells after the winter snows and spring rains. By midsummer, it will be tamer."

"How deep is it?"

"Deep enough to trap any who try and cross without the blessing of the elves. This is the river that stalled Malus in his attempt to infiltrate Silvias. The wizards he sent to ford our waters drowned in the endeavor. Malus' only option was to attack from the north. Unfortunately for him, that would have meant traversing the *Y'cartim Allegra*—the Ancient Forest. The forest is not forgiving of interlopers. Thus, Malus never managed to bring the war into the elves' kingdom."

The roan stepped forward to allow Odin and Autumnstar through the woods. The bank was too crowded for the elven warriors to join them.

Kyra stared at the river, her stomach twisting. "If the wizards couldn't swim across, or I'm assuming that's what they did, how will we?"

Raven lifted his head and let out a neigh that reminded Kyra of a chuckle. "We are not swimming across, Kyra. The elves have their own methods to enter the Realm." He jerked his head toward Therial, who had guided his horse to the edge of the riverbank. "Watch."

Therial held out his palm. He murmured a stream of words in elvish. The air over the river scintillated, and a long, planked bridge materialized. It arced over the swiftly moving waters and allowed three horses to comfortably ride side by side. Rails the height of the horses' backs lined both sides of the bridge. The planks were so seamlessly constructed, they seemed to be made from a single, titanic tree. The water kicked up spray, yet the boards remained dry.

Hayden laughed as Kyra leaned forward in astonishment. She glanced over to see him and Talis smiling at her. Kyra cleared her throat and eased herself back into the saddle. "That's convenient, having a bridge to cross," she remarked, trying to sound unimpressed and failing.

Therial clapped his heels into his mare. The steed mounted a series of steps onto the bridge. Windchaser confidently clopped up after them.

A mess of emotions cluttered within Kyra as Raven proceeded forward. *Home.* This is what she had longed for. Home meant safety and comfort, like a warm blanket on a snowy day. Home meant regaining memories. Home meant remembering who she had been, what she had learned, even what she liked and disliked. Home meant being reunited with childhood friends, friends her own age, something she had never had in London. No one could replace James, but he was more sophisticated and knowledgeable than Kyra. James was also a Lyneera. That complicated things.

Even as Kyra breathed in the beauty around her, her excitement and curiosity were curbed by misgivings. She wanted with every fiber of her being to believe retrieving memories would make her happy. Because she hoped the memories themselves were happy. That they would give her a sense of belonging to a community. To a family. Neither Kyra's mind nor her heart accepted this as a given truth. Kyra was a wizard. In an elven kingdom. In a land where wizards were received with suspicion, fear, and hate. What if Kyra's childhood hadn't been the carefree existence she envisioned? What if she had struggled to fit in? What if Kyra had *never* fit in? After all, Talis didn't mention elves sharing in her mishaps during their conversation in Edoin Forest. He had said that *she* had gotten into her fair share of mischief.

Everyone has friends, Kyra fought against her anxiety as they neared the end of the bridge. *Children don't care if you're an elf or a wizard or a gnome with hives. They want to have fun.* Of course, Kyra reasoned as Therial led his horse down steps leading to the base of the hills, being a child was one thing. She hadn't interacted with other teenagers in London outside of making a purchase at a store or saying 'hi' on the Tube. Teenagers all felt and acted the same way she did, in some situations at least, didn't they? How different could elven teenagers be from human ones? Assuming they were similar, and presuming Kyra had had friends, had her relationships with those elves survived her year away? What if they had forgotten about her? Had they moved on?

Raven tramped down the steps after Willow and walked along the bank. When the last elven warrior had left the bridge, Therial again reached out his palm. He whispered a new string of elven phrases, too quiet for Kyra to hear. The bridge glimmered and vanished.

Someone sneezed once, then twice. Talis wrinkled his nose with a piqued expression. His eyes trailed to a group of trees with grape-sized pink flowers. "We're far into the season," he said ruefully to Therial. "The ervills should have shed their spring buds by now."

"The rains came late to Silvias this year." Therial's smile lit his face as he exchanged a knowing look with Hayden. "Many of Silvias' trees haven't developed their full foliage. Apologies, cousin, but we have some days left."

Talis turned to the side and covered another sneeze with a sleeve. Sniffing, the elf turned his head. Talis glowered at Hayden, who placed a hand over his mouth to cover a grin.

Ash looked contemplative. "Are all elves allergic to ervills?"

"Not to ervills specifically. We all have an intolerance for some plant or flower or tree. Mine is to ervill buds." Talis sighed. "I hoped to avoid them this year. Fortunately, their season is of short duration." Talis inclined his head to other trees lining the bank. "The *Jaelyn's* sensitivity is to the beeches. They're far more common in the Realm and bloom for a longer period."

Therial grinned good-naturedly. "Yes, my suffering will soon commence." He urged his horse to begin the ascent up the hill's steep slope. Kyra leaned forward in her saddle as Raven's hooves dug into the soft earth, kicking up clumps of dirt and grass.

"That seems unusual, for elves to have an affliction caused by buds and pollen," Ash picked up the thread of his professional curiosity. "I've treated patients with similar symptoms. They were usually from a city and later moved to an area with more flora. Elves live in harmony with nature though. I'd assume you wouldn't experience adverse effects."

"That's a logical conclusion," Therial replied over his shoulder, "but it isn't our reality. No elven healer has an explanation for this other than it simply is."

"It's obvious why," Jyls put in. Though Kyra couldn't see the thief, she heard a distinct amusement at the elves' predicament. "Inishmore wants to remind elves that they're as flawed and imperfect as us inferior beings. Makes you happy you aren't one, doesn't it, Ash?"

Kyra and Hayden laughed. Even Therial and Talis chuckled at the joke.

The hill's incline eased to reveal a path of compacted grasses and dirt. The trees receded, and rays from the afternoon sun smiled down upon them. Therial piloted his mare onto the summit of the hill. As Raven joined him on the crest, Kyra gasped. Below them, nestled in a valley, was the most stunning lake Kyra had ever seen. Its white waters glittered as though made from millions of opals. A breathtaking, life-sized winged horse perched at the top of the hill. It reared on its hind legs, its large, feathered wings spread ready for flight. Sunlight undulated over its graceful form, transforming its deep emerald green color to shades of lighter green.

Therial, noticing her innocent wonderment, smiled kindly. "This kaemin marks the entry into the Elven Realm," he explained. "Among elves, the kaemin is usually represented as an Iona. That's what the winged horses are called. Accounts tell of Lyneera assuming the form of Iona during the War of Calonia. They brought many of our kind to safety, particularly from dragons and other winged monsters impervious to our arrows and blades."

Therial led the group back down the hill. The blissful, magical aura continued to saturate the air as thickly as the smell of rain before a storm. Kyra breathed deeply, a wave of longing coursing through her. After a while, the trees thinned. The underbrush gave way to a well-trodden path wide enough for the horses to proceed two-abreast. At times, the path forked. Kyra observed that both directions offered avenues with minimal forest litter. At each juncture, Therial steered the group east. The group finally reached the mouth of the forest and rode onto a trail marked by an expanse of lush grasses and elven homes. The homes were fashioned from colorful spun glass that captured the rays of the midday sun.

Therial trotted his steed at an easy pace down the center street of the town. "This is the main route to the palace," he announced. "We will arrive anon." As her companions had already visited Silvias, Kyra knew the captain made the statement for her sake.

Kyra's head swiveled as they rode. The elven realm couldn't be more different from what she had seen in Farcaren. Thanesgard had imposed a strict symmetry and order on its environment. Here, the elven structures flowed into their surroundings. Grasses and flowers weren't confined to gardens. They grew wildly, with reckless abandon, claiming any part of land on which they found themselves. Trees sprouted wherever they chose, and the elves integrated the trees as part of their homes. The glass spiraled up their trunks, bending around and over branches. Bridges with glass planks connected elven homes to their neighbors. More houses were situated on the land. Vines of wisteria hung loosely like tassels over the doors. Flowers sprouted in the grass as plentifully as sand on a beach.

Kyra's gaze migrated to the elves. Their clothing shimmered as though woven from delicate gossamer threads as they walked gracefully down the road. Adults dipped their heads and placed their hands over their hearts in respect when they saw Therial and the warriors. Therial, Talis, and the warriors returned the gesture. As they rode by, Kyra noticed the elves' attention shifted to her. She smiled at them. Kyra glimpsed their fleeting looks of curiosity, wonder, and, her heart sank at the realization, suspicion.

A small girl with copper skin and mahogany hair stopped and stared. She tugged on her mother's hand. "Mother," the girl said eagerly. "That's her, isn't it, Mother? She's the wizard, isn't she? Didn't *Raenalyn* Carina say . . ."

"Hush," the mother scolded. "It's impolite to speak about others. Proper manners are to greet individuals, not to gape like a fish with its mouth open." The mother's rose-colored gown swayed as she held her hand over her heart. "*Aliori, Jaelyn* Therial and *Firth* Talis. And a warm welcome to the rest of your company."

The girl's gaze remained transfixed on Kyra as she and her companions passed by. The girl's fascination made Kyra uneasy. How familiar were the elves with Kyra? It was clear she and the young girl had never met. How did she recognize Kyra then? *Because you don't look like an elf,* Kyra told herself as they continued past the homes. *Obviously, she would have heard about 'the wizard' living in Silvias from . . . someone.*

The land sloped upward, and the homes grew more numerous and tightly packed together. Beyond them, Kyra caught her first glimpse of the elven palace. Her heart skipped a beat. If the homes were as splendid as gems, the palace was the majestic crown. It was comprised of three towers that resembled lighthouses. Like the elven homes, the enormous structures lacked the constraints of rigid lines and rules of architecture. They had wide bases that tapered into twisting spires. The center tower stood several meters taller than the two buildings abutting it. A white-stoned courtyard resembling a square with amorphous edges was the centerpiece.

The two outermost towers were framed by walled-in courtyards. One courtyard with rounded arches adjoined the eastern tower. The west tower's wall was a latticework of tree branches woven together like a straw basket. Outdoor stairwells and bridges linked both outer buildings. Kyra followed the stairwells and bridges with her eyes. They were flat, angled, shot straight upward like escalators, or corkscrewed down to doorframes. She felt an overwhelming impulse to climb them and explore where they led.

The path transformed from grass to a road of flat stones in elaborate geometric patterns. Their surfaces glistened a pristine white like freshly fallen snow. Therial and Talis led the train of horses onto the road. The horses' hooves clacked on the hard surface as they approached the courtyard. A cool breeze tousled Kyra's hair. She absently brushed a stray strand to the side.

Closer to the palace, Kyra could better view the elves bustling in and out of doors and up and down the bridges and stairwells. Many carried baskets with laundry or an assortment of wares. Others strolled serenely through the arches and openings to the courtyards. A group of elven guards rode past the eastern tower to the fields.

The palace's glass bedazzled Kyra. *Is it glass?* she mused as the group rode toward the white-stoned courtyard. It reminded Kyra of the kaemins; the palace was every color and no color at the same time. Flashes of prismatic sunlight refracted through the glass, which twinkled white and silver, then pink and purple, orange and red, and everything in between. It made Thanesgard look like a flavorless slab of rock.

"There's no palace its equal," came Talis as though reading Kyra's thoughts. He had directed Windchaser beside Raven. Talis held the palomino's reins in one hand while his other hand rested on his leg. Talis' eyes sparkled as he gazed upon the palace. "Our first king, *Veralyn* Ellynirith, welcomed our kin to contribute their magic to its foundation. Hundreds of artists and craftsmen volunteered, each pouring part of his or her inner energy into the palace. Ellynirith himself gave the most. He depleted his life force to ensure the structure was worthy of the Realm. It was a palace to last for all time. This bond of elven magic created the form and rhythm you see today."

How did Ellynirith "deplete his life force?" Kyra wondered. An involuntary chill ran down her spine. If pouring energy into something was as straightforward as it sounded, the elven king had made a tremendous sacrifice for his people.

"It's stunning," Kyra said aloud. The breeze again loosed waves of hair, which she brushed from her face. Kyra glanced down as she did so, looked up, then did a double-take. The stones in the courtyard formed asymmetrical, geometric shapes. Like the houses, they were a patchwork. Gaps between each stone allowed wildflowers and free-flowing grasses to grow. "What is the palace made from?" Kyra resumed her conversation with Talis as she raised her gaze. "Is it kaemin? I've never seen glass reflect light this way. It's like watching the ebb and flow of waves on a shore."

"This is a similar element to kaemin called *zylith*—what you would call sea stone," Talis replied. "*Zylith* contains every color. Which shade you see depends on the location from which you view it. The stone was discovered along the shores of the Aurielle Sea in the days of our founders. The chronicles of elven history describe how the stone was harvested and used to build the palace. Stores of *zylith* that were not gathered remained at the Aurielle Sea. *Raenalyn* Carina sent elves to the Sea in search of those stones. So far, we haven't found any. The material is more durable than any gem. Hence how the palace has withstood two thousand years of time's degradations."

"*Zylith* is similar to elves then," Kyra remarked with a grin. "It doesn't age."

"We age. Gracefully."

Talis pulled Windchaser to a halt. They had reached the far end of the courtyard near the entrance to the center tower. The sight of the warriors and the odd company of wizards and men attracted some attention from the elves. Unlike those Kyra had seen earlier, they were discreet and greeted their kin with inscrutable expressions. The breeze carried the rich, earthly aroma of balsam to Kyra. She spied trees with white bark and petite, silver green leaves that ringed the courtyard.

Kyra's eye caught one particular tree. Unlike its slender cousins, this was thick and stout. Its branches were reminiscent of the blacksmith Makral's burly arms. The hand-sized leaves were more silvery than white, and Kyra knew intuitively the bark was as soft as velvet. Warmth filled her. Kyra felt a connection with the tree, as though it were an old friend . . .

> "*She is outside.*"
>
> *Kyra was sure the authoritative voice was talking about her. She poked her head out from behind the squat machi tree, pushing aside its silver green leaves with her hand. Raenalyn Carina stood in the courtyard. The queen's heart-shaped lips were downturned into a frown, her arms crossed under the folds of a golden cloak. Or Kyra assumed they were. Carina always crossed her arms when they were in front of her.*
>
> *A man waited beside her. He stroked a neatly trimmed beard. A line like a cursive Z ran along the side of his hair. Kyra didn't need to see the staff in the figure's hands to know he was the mysterious wizard. She had spied him in Silvias with Hayden. Solarus, Kyra suddenly remembered the wizard's name. Hayden had mentioned Solarus would visit the Realm more often.*

Kyra's question as to why had been left unanswered. Maybe now was when "more often" was starting.

Carina's emerald gaze skimmed the white-stoned courtyard and locked onto Kyra's tree.

Kyra let the leaves drop and spun around. A scowl dropped to Kyra's lips. The queen always pinpointed where she was hiding. Kyra secretly asked Inishmore to keep Carina busy until the hunter game ended. If Kyra had any say in it, that would be soon. Sure, the elven children hadn't yet lost to her. Not even when Kyra was the hunter. The hunter's job was to uncover the others' hiding places and fight them in a mock battle. If the hunter won, he or she would search for the other elves until they were all defeated. If the hunter lost, the victor of the battle became the hunter, and the game continued.

The elves teased Kyra. A human girl couldn't track an elf, they said. Even if she could, how would she beat one? Kyra admitted secretly they were probably right. She never found them. They always *found her*. How many times had an elf sneaked behind, over, or around her and struck her staff? Kyra had proven she could hold her own in a battle. Yes, she had become the hunter before. She just hadn't gone further than that. The elves were too good at hiding.

This time it was going to be different. Kyra begged Firth Montrelin to teach her to identify signs of trails. She knew Firth Montrelin was busy. As the Realm's premier tracker, his responsibilities were to the queen. Kyra pleaded with Firth Montrelin. Eventually, he said 'yes.' Kyra worked hard. She wanted Firth Montrelin to see his dedication to her wasn't wasted. Kyra remembered the first time she noticed broken blades of grass, identified weasel tracks in the forest. She was even able to veil her own prints.

"You would make a fine tracker yourself," Firth Montrelin had told her after their last lesson. He had a fatherly smile. Kyra had never felt so confident.

She sidled up behind the odd-shaped tree near the palace. She hid behind its low branches, staff in hand. All she had to do was wait and watch the hunter. Then Kyra would surprise him. She would finally *win*.

Please keep Raenalyn *Carina away,* Kyra asked Inishmore silently. *Just a few minutes longer.*

Leaves rustled behind her. Kyra turned. Beyond the tree, she saw Yuli leap down from atop one of the stone walls of the Edenia fel Coralyn. Aila, her best friend and the current hunter, walked beside this wall, suspecting one of her peers was nearby. The sounds of the leaves gave Yuli away. Kyra grinned. Aila sprang to the side before Yuli landed. He swung his staff mightily at her. But Aila was strong and met the attack with a block of her own. The small female elf swept her weapon under Yuli's feet. He gave a startled yelp and fell. Kyra laughed at Yuli's petulant expression. She saw Aila glance up.

"Oh Kyyyyyrrrrrrrrrraaa," she called, creeping in the direction of Kyra's tree. Kyra grasped her weapon firmly against her side.

Aila glanced to her right. She froze, then straightened. Kyra's ballooning happiness was punctured as she watched Aila offer a perfected bow.

"*Aliori*, Raenalyn *Carina*," Aila said, eyes downturned.

"At the risk of spoiling your activities," Carina's strict voice came from around the tree, "I must unfortunately request you end this game."

Kyra let out a frustrated sigh. She stepped out from her hiding spot. The elven queen tucked her arms within her cloak, expression severe. The wizard Solarus smiled in amusement. Off to the side, Yuli had gotten to his feet.

Kyra walked beside Aila onto one of the white stones. Aila stood at attention. The two girls exchanged a sidelong look. Aila's golden eyes relayed her sympathy. Her best friend knew today was the closest Kyra had ever come to winning.

"If I understand correctly, Finna Fiora instructed that you use the morning's break for real training." Carina gave the pair a pointed look. "Not for frivolous amusements."

Kyra felt as guilty as a cat caught clawing a palace rug. She, too, bowed as Yuli trod over to them. His shoulders were hunched, and he wore an equally shamed expression.

"Raenalyn *Carina*," Aila spoke up daringly, "the Sirenyle practice tracking and sparring. That's what we're doing."

"You are not a Sirenyle, Aila," Carina replied. Her raised brow prevented another protest. "Your elders determine your duty to the Realm, not you. I believe practice identifying the plants in the forest or spending time reviewing your studies in the library is a better use of your time." The queen's tone made it clear this was not a suggestion but a command.

Aila knew better than to contradict the queen. "Yes, Raenalyn *Carina*."

Carina's eagle-eyed gaze soared across the courtyard. She removed her hands from her cloak and gestured broadly with a slender hand. "That goes for everyone."

The faint patter of feet sounded from around the courtyard. Young elves scaled down the white bark of the machi trees, slipped out from behind the walls of the two nearest gardens, and exited the palace's open doors. The elves hung their heads, staffs and wooden swords in hand. They uniformly avoided Carina's stern gaze.

"Yes, Raenalyn *Carina*," the elven children chorused. They skirted out of the courtyard in the direction of the forest. Kyra, Aila, and Yuli, being closest to the queen, bowed again. Then they pivoted briskly, all too eager to leave.

"Not you, Kyra. I should like to have a word yet."

Kyra's stomach fluttered with butterflies of anxiety. Why was she being singled out? Aila offered Kyra another tacit look of sympathy. Yuli's expression displayed open relief that Carina's ire wasn't focused further on him. He and Aila loped after their classmates.

Kyra tried to look innocently curious as Carina's gaze ran over her. "Kyra, you have met Solarus." She motioned to the wizard.

"Hello, Kyra," Solarus greeted. His ocean blue eyes appraised her.

Kyra self-consciously tucked a lock of hair behind her ear. "Hello," she replied.

"Raenalyn Carina mentioned you have seen something unusual these past few weeks," Solarus continued in a kind tone. "She said you saw a golden glow around your hands. Is that correct?"

Kyra looked to Carina before answering. The queen's expression was grave. "Yes, I've seen it," Kyra answered. "I don't know what it is though. None of the elves have one."

"You possess an energy quite different from the elven children." Solarus' tone remained casual, though Kyra saw something flicker in his eyes. "I am here to help you learn about that glow and what it means. How you can use it."

"You are to begin lessons separate from your peers," Carina added. There was a strained note in her voice.

"What lessons?"

"Lessons in magic."

Kyra's eyes lit with excitement. "Really?"

Solarus seemed pleased with her reaction. "You are nine years old. Do not expect we will go quickly. Your experience with this glow is something we should explore, is it not?"

"I have already spoken with Finna Fiora," Carina continued as Kyra clasped her hands together, barely able to contain her delight. "The training will not interfere with your other studies."

Solarus twisted his staff meditatively. "Shall we go for a walk?" he asked Kyra. "There is much to discuss."

Kyra's smile didn't leave her face as she and Solarus set off together. For the first time, she was happy she was different from her elven friends. She had "talents." Kyra had something they didn't.

Out of habit, Kyra glanced back at Lady Carina. She didn't understand why the queen's gaze seemed clouded or why a tight, worried line formed on her lips . . .

The sound of boots landing on the ground brought Kyra back to the present. Ash had thudded heavily on a stone as he dismounted. He gave Kyra an abashed look before adjusting a tie on his boot that had come undone. In a haze, Kyra looked upon the rest of her companions. Hayden gently teased out leaves from Willow's brown mane. Solarus pulled his staff free from the straps along Grayhaven's saddle. Talis spoke in low tones to Therial. Jyls had his hands on his hips, head swiveling as he took in the courtyard. The thief's eyes raised to a butterfly that landed atop his head. Jyls brushed the butterfly from his hair, watched it drift away, then continued his examination of the area. Meanwhile, the elven warriors had formed two lines in front of their steeds, staring at a point to the right of the palace's center tower. Even in the waning daylight, the warriors' armor shone brightly.

With the tendrils of her memory lingering, Kyra swung her leg over the saddle and dropped to the ground. Her heart pounded with excitement as Raven let out a contented breath. Kyra absently rubbed his muzzle. It was a memory. Kyra's *own* memory, not one she had borrowed from Hayden or Talis. A memory that proved she *did* have friends. Raven butted Kyra with his head.

"I see you," she muttered. Kyra placed her hand again on his nose though her gaze was focused inward.

"It is not *me* who requires your attention," Raven responded. Kyra looked up. Talis and Therial had ceased their conversation and were looking in the same direction as the elven warriors. Hayden walked past Solarus, who now had his staff in hand, and stopped beside Jyls. Their attention was uniformly riveted to a point. Kyra turned as well. She could still visualize the elven queen in her memory. How Carina strode forward with imperial elegance, her flowing silver hair offset by golden-tanned skin. How silent the courtyard became when the elven children saw her.

It's so strange, Kyra thought as the figure strode nearer. *I remember it so clearly. It's like I'm seeing the woman in real life.*

The roan again nudged her, this time more subtly. "One does not gawp at a queen, Kyra," he stated in a low tone.

Kyra's eyes widened in surprise. Carina wasn't a figment of her imagination. She was *there*. Which explained the hush that had descended on the group.

The queen's hands were folded serenely behind her back as she strode forward. She wore a silvery lavender cape, as translucent as the glass of the palace, that fluttered close to the ground. Her steps were noiseless. Carina walked solely on the patches of soft earth and grasses that grew between the stones. Her slender face held dignity and wisdom. As her eyes found Kyra, a sliver of a smile touched the queen's lips.

Joy rushed through Kyra, followed immediately by traces of guilt. She almost laughed. Given the memory Kyra had just experienced, a sense of wrongdoing seemed like a natural response. Four elves with long, gold-trimmed capes waited several paces behind the queen. They watched passively, arms folded beneath their long sleeves like monks.

Therial bowed deeply. "*Aliori, Raenalyn* Carina," the captain greeted. He straightened and inclined his head toward Talis and the rest of the group. "We have returned with your charges, as ordered."

Carina unfolded her hands. Her gaze skimmed the flecks of blood on Talis' shirt, then the larger patches on Hayden and Jyls. "The greeloks were at our border then," she said, a severe look crossing her face. "Are any injured? Or are these marks of their defeat?"

"No injuries, *Raenalyn* Carina," Therial replied. "Your warriors are a determined force with which no creature of Harkimer can reckon." He made a wide gesture to the elves behind him. They wore stoic expressions, one hand gripping the hilts of their swords, the other resting at their sides. The horses displayed the same composure as the warriors. Even the irrepressible Windchaser had forgone his antics. He proudly stood at attention as if in deference to the queen. Kyra wondered if it was a trait of elven horses or of any experienced animal. One glimpse of Willow and Grayhaven's faces, and she guessed it was the latter.

"However," Therial added, turning from the warriors to the queen, "Talis and his companions might not have required our assistance at all. They had disposed of more than half of the beasts before we arrived."

Carina nodded. "Blessings to Inishmore for your safe return," she said widely to the group. Kyra noticed the queen's gaze lingered on Talis, an unreadable expression on her face. Talis' eyes didn't meet Carina's. He bowed, keeping his head low as though there were something of interest on the white stones. The queen's lips tugged into a brief frown before she looked at the elven warriors. "I thank you for your bravery and service to the Realm. You honor the tradition of the *Hydranyle*. Bring the horses to the pastures, and then allow yourselves rest."

The warriors saluted in unison, placing closed fists over their hearts. The elven warrior nearest Therial clicked her tongue. The first row of warriors pivoted and strode toward their horses with synchronized steps. The second row did the same. They moved soundlessly, despite the metal adorning their bodies, the swords at their sides, and their boots touching the stone. Their armor shimmered with dusk's pink and purple hues. The warriors mounted their steeds in unison. Then the female warrior steered her horse toward the eastern tower. Hooves clacked against the stone as the warriors trotted their steeds past the four elves in golden cloaks. The warriors acknowledged the four, this time placing open hands over their hearts. The elves in the golden cloaks reciprocated the gesture. The warriors continued eastward in what Kyra assumed was the direction of the fields. The elves in the golden cloaks again folded their arms within their sleeves and silently observed their queen.

Carina's attention returned to Talis. She motioned to him with a crook of her finger. When Talis stepped closer, the queen leaned forward and murmured something in his ear. Talis shook his head. The queen's lips pinched together.

"What matters is that by the moon and the stars, you have been returned to us," she declared as Talis rejoined Therial. His gaze was troubled as Carina turned to Hayden and Solarus. "Hayden, Solarus, welcome. It is good to see you have been returned to us in good health and spirits. I am also pleased to welcome you back to the Realm, *Firth* Jyls and *Ethernyle* Akheeran," Carina directed her greeting to the two men. "I am pleased to be visited by such respected company."

"It is an honor to return to the Realm," Jyls replied solemnly. He was as poised as a knight. "We are deeply grateful for the hospitality of your venerated kingdom. I hope one day we can share with you the delights of our own homes."

Kyra's jaw dropped. The rough and scruffy thief switched off his carelessly casual speech and flicked on a courtly one. As Carina turned, Jyls winked at Kyra.

"*Aliori*, Kyra," Carina welcomed. Her eyes shimmered like emerald pools. "Or rather, *Finna* Kyra. The seers foretold of your return, though we could only reflect upon when or in what manner." A fond smile broached the queen's stern features. "When I saw you last, you were coming of age. Now you return a beautiful young woman."

"This is Her Majesty, *Raenalyn* Carina," Hayden put in as Kyra mimicked her companions' respectful bows. "She is the queen of the Elven Realm."

Kyra nodded. She mentally reminded herself to tell Hayden about the scene with the hunter game when they were alone.

"Talis wrote that you have few recollections of these lands," the queen went on. "However, do not despair. Your memories are not lost. The seeds of knowledge lie dormant in your mind. They will grow again. Inishmore will determine when the time is right."

"Thank you, Your Majesty," Kyra replied stiltedly. Her cheeks grew hot as she felt all eyes on her. "I do remember a little about Silvias. I'm hoping spending time here will help me rebuild my past."

Carina seemed satisfied with Kyra's response. She motioned with to the four elves standing placidly behind her. "These are the four lords and ladies of the Elven Realm. They each oversee a domain within the Realm and are my most cherished advisors. We were holding council when I learned of your arrival."

If Kyra had blinked, she would have missed the queen's gaze again flicker to Talis. Puzzled, Kyra glanced to the side. Talis had stiffened. Hayden was also watched the elf carefully. His gaze was strangely shadowed, though not on account of the deep blue of the slowly spreading evening sky.

"*Safinnalyn* Marisol oversees the East," Carina introduced one of the female elves. Marisol gave Kyra a gentle smile. Her caramel eyes and dark skin glimmered, and her white dress was embroidered with the same gold as the trim on her cape. "Never in our history has there been a confrontation along our eastern border. Our neighbors there are largely peaceful."

"*Safinnalyn* Hesperia is responsible for our western border, where thornier problems present themselves." Carina acknowledged another female with short, crimped hair the color of a ripe peach.

"*Safirthelyn* Valorian is responsible for the happenings of the North, including those in the Ancient Forest." Valorian's eyes were bright and cheerful. As he inclined his head, a lock of his dark brown mane fell over his shoulder. His maple-brown skin was radiant against the shimmering green and gold of his clothes.

"*Safirthelyn* Orison maintains the security of the southern border," Carina concluded. "The wilderness beyond the Kayanan Eria is inhabited by creatures from darker times. *Safirthelyn* Orison is more than a match for them."

Orison's sky-blue gaze was cold as an arctic night as he scrutinized Kyra. His tunic matched his eyes and white hair that shone like silk. Kyra had noticed Orison's manner had been standoffish as Carina introduced the other lords and ladies. Now, as he removed his arms from his cloak and rubbed his chin, Orison's lips formed a thin line of contempt. More than contempt, Kyra thought as she met his gaze; Orison seemed to *hate* her. Why? Kyra's bewilderment was equal to the sense of foreboding that cloaked her.

"A pleasure to see you all," Hayden said. He stepped next to Kyra and placed a hand on her shoulder. Talis wordlessly walked to Kyra's other side. Kyra checked her companions' expressions again. The elf's placid features were dark. Hayden's eyes were the charcoal gray of storm clouds. Even Solarus tilted his staff subtly toward the southern lord.

Orison angled his head. His hands dropped to his hips. "How generous of you to take time to visit our Realm," the elf said, not bothering to conceal his disdain. Orison's gaze slid from Kyra to Talis. "It must have been difficult for you to extract yourself from your . . . other duties across Ilian. It's a grand gesture to pay respect to our queen."

"My queen always has my respect and service, should she require it." Talis' voice was as unforgiving as Kyra had ever heard him. He clenched a fist at his side.

"Thank you for coming, *Safinnalyn* and *Safirthelyn*," Carina cut in. The queen shot Orison a look of warning. Orison clasped his hands behind his back. "We are adjourned for the day. I need time to meditate on your advice. Be prepared for me to call upon you again."

The *Safinnalyn* and *Safirthelyn* bowed in unison. Orison shot Kyra one last look of loathing as the others strode toward the palace. Hayden's grip on Kyra's shoulder tightened. The elf's golden cloak fanned out as he stormed after his fellow royals.

Carina's gaze lingered on Orison. The queen's hands were clasped together, and she let out a short sigh. "You and your steeds need refreshment," Carina stated in a distracted tone. "A meal awaits you in the dining hall. Talis, please see that our guests have whatever they desire during their stay."

Kyra's stomach rumbled at the mention of food. They hadn't eaten since the morning.

"*Jaelyn* Therial, have the groomsmen tend to the horses," Carina instructed. "Then report to me in my study."

Therial bowed respectfully. "Yes, Your Majesty." The captain clicked his tongue. The mare clopped obediently beside him, reins dangling over the sides of her saddle. Therial swung astride effortlessly. "Don't worry, they will be well cared for," the captain told Kyra and her companions. "You can visit them tomorrow if you would like."

It was self-evident to the companions' horses that they would be departing with Therial. Windchaser pranced forward eagerly. He butted Raven and tossed his mane. The roan let out an irritated breath, then cast a meaningful look at Windchaser. Kyra watched as they both smiled. It was the bond they shared as elven horses, Kyra realized. The bond of returning home. Therial steered his mare in the direction of the fields. He set her off at a trot with the other horses in tow. They deftly navigated around the elves strolling the palace grounds and rode out of sight.

"I remember the dining hall," Jyls commented to Kyra and Ash. He linked each arm around one of theirs. "The elves have lip-smacking food in Ilian that you have to taste to believe. Not to mention the claret."

Kyra rolled her eyes, then grinned despite herself. *Out goes the courteous Jyls. In returns the rough and scruffy version.*

"*Raenalyn* Carina, might we speak in private?" Hayden's tone was urgent. "Talis relayed the contents of the message he sent. Much was omitted, however. We didn't want to risk elaboration in the event the animal scout was intercepted by our adversaries. Our conversations with Farcaren's king and our interactions with the dark wizards have brought to light details of Diamantas' strategy. It concerns Silvias as much as the other kingdoms."

A cloud passed over Carina's face, though her expression wasn't one of surprise. "Yes, it was clear from the generality of the missive that you were wary of interference. You were wise to keep the details secret. I had faith you would deliver them to me in person. Let us confer immediately, if I might be so impolite as to take you from a well-earned meal. There are questions to which I must have answers, and they cannot wait."

Hayden nodded. He began to indicate for Talis and Solarus to follow. Carina shook her head. "Talis, Solarus, you may join your companions. I require only Hayden's report. We will convene after supper. I have my own observations to share. Use this time as a respite. Talis, your companions are under your charge."

Kyra wondered if she imagined the slight frown that came to Hayden's lips as Talis bowed. "*Raenalyn*."

Solarus dipped his head to Carina. His expression was decorated with displeasure at having been excluded from the meeting.

Carina folded her hands behind her. Kyra was certain she saw Hayden offer Talis an apologetic look. The elf gave an imperceptible shake of his head. Hayden fell in step with the queen as she began to walk toward the central tower.

Kyra's brows knitted. Why would the queen want to hear from Hayden? Wouldn't it make more sense to speak with Talis first, as the elf in their ranks?

What if Carina didn't trust Hayden? A confidential meeting would give Carina a chance to determine the truth of Hayden's words. She could compare what Hayden told her to what Talis would report later. Even as Kyra finished the thought, she dismissed it as far-fetched. Carina was sincere in her greeting. Hayden didn't pose any more of a threat to the queen than Talis.

Was it that Carina didn't trust Solarus? Kyra mused over this as Solarus strode toward the palace, stabbing the ground with his staff. He was a wizard after all. Based on the reactions of the people of Thanesgard and the few looks of suspicion from the elves, it was safe to assume wizards—free or from Harkimer—were viewed as Ilian's greatest menace. The queen was astute; an invitation extended to Hayden and Talis would have clued Solarus into her reservations about his intentions. By leaving Talis out of the conversation, Solarus wouldn't be inclined to question Carina's motives.

Kyra again shot down the theory. In her memory, the relationship between Carina and Solarus had been cordial. If the queen was so mistrusting of wizards, Solarus have been barred from entering Silvias. There had to be another explanation.

Which left one other individual. Kyra wanted to dismiss the idea as absurd and found she couldn't. A year of logic and reasoning lessons with Mr. Stevens left her mind bird-dogging the possibility. The queen blocked Talis from the meeting because she had misgivings about *him*. What if Talis had done something that garnered suspicion? Kyra felt guilty and kicked away the theory. That was ridiculous. Unconsciously, her gaze sought Talis out. His steps were uncharacteristically wooden as he trailed behind Solarus, his shoulders slightly stooped. Kyra's heart panged with sympathy. Was he worried about Hayden? Or could there be a grain of truth that there was a conflict with Carina after all?

"It's all settled then," Jyls remarked, oblivious to the tension that filled the air. "Let's get going. My stomach is having choice words with me about my shameful neglect."

Jyls skipped toward the eastern tower. Kyra and Ash, arms linked with the thief, were towed along with him. The evening light was dim. The cloudless sky lost the sun's illumination but hadn't yet donned its glittering visage of the moon and stars. Despite the darkness, Jyls nimbly hopped from stone to stone. The healer wasn't as agile. Ash's boot caught the edge of one of the stones. He tripped over the gap and yelped as he pitched forward. Jyls jerked the healer upright before he tumbled, simultaneously pulling Kyra to a stop beside him. The healer straightened on wobbly legs. With a roll of his eyes, Jyls said dryly, "The sooner we reach the kitchens, the sooner a glass of claret is in my hand. Which means not falling in the process."

Ash offered him an apologetic look. Keeping their arms locked, Jyls took long, deliberate steps toward the palace door.

Kyra started to pull away from Jyls. She was concerned about Talis. She wanted to ask what was worrying him, why he seemed downtrodden despite having returned to his own kingdom. But something in Talis' expression prevented her from approaching him.

Feeling helpless and worried, Kyra quietly matched Jyls' brisk pace, leaving the elf, head bowed, to his troubled thoughts.

Chapter 21

Jyls was right. At a table set with glass chalices and plates, Kyra dined on sumptuous food that excited her taste buds. Fruits burst with sweet juices. Grilled vegetables had hints of rosemary and sage. Cod-like fish flaked from her fork, and roasted game from the forest dissolved in her mouth. A tea, made from the bark of the courtyard's silver green-leaved machi trees, tasted like cream soda. The dessert platter was adorned with tarts, cobblers, and, to Kyra's pure delight, a food she never expected to see in this foreign land.

"They have *chocolate* here?" she exclaimed to Talis.

The elf's mood had cleared upon entering the dining hall. Talis reciprocated Kyra's enthusiasm with a smile of his own. "Why shouldn't we?" he asked, cutting into a warm blueberry tart that made Kyra's mouth water.

"I thought it was something they only had in the other world," Kyra responded. Her eyes greedily took in the triple-decked cakes.

"Who needs chocolate when you have this fine drink?" Jyls put in lazily. He swirled his glass of claret, complete with three coffee beans. "Finest claret in Ilian they have here, the elves. Good thing we're staying awhile in Silvias."

Kyra grinned at him as Ash cut himself a slice of cake. While the food was exquisite, the dining hall was a masterpiece within the art that was the palace. The *zylith* walls were stenciled with images of forests and streams so realistic Kyra thought she could see the leaves rustling and the water flowing. An inky black night sky had spread over the Realm, yet inside the dining hall, the ceiling sparkled every color of the rainbow as it absorbed the bright moon and starlight. In addition to the main entrance were two stairwells that led into the room. One stairwell was yellow-orange and spiraled down from the upper hall. The second stairwell was blue, with a straight rail and stairs. A smaller hall led away from the room. As Kyra watched attendants flow in and around the tables, she assumed the hall was reserved for the kitchen staff.

When the meal was over, Talis rose to lead the group to their chambers. Jyls stretched leisurely as Ash put his serviette on the table. Kyra pushed back her chair to follow. Solarus stalled her with a raise of his hand.

"I would like to talk about tomorrow," he stated. His tone implied it wasn't a request. Puzzled, Kyra sat back and folded her hands in her lap.

Talis seemed to have anticipated Solarus' wish to talk to Kyra in private. "An attendant will take you to your rooms," he said. Solarus nodded his thanks as Talis turned to Jyls and Ash. "This staircase goes to the chambers," he informed them, gesturing to the yellow-orange staircase. The *zylith* shimmered, and the light undulating under the steps made the staircase look like an escalator. "You can also take the outside bridges and walkways. Until you're familiar with the palace and its grounds, I recommend using the simplest route."

Kyra's eyes followed her companions as they crossed the room and marched up the spiral staircase. Their footsteps echoed off the *zylith* as they climbed higher. Kyra's gaze returned to Solarus, then dropped downward. The elven attendants had finished collecting the leftover plates and food. With nothing to distract her from Solarus' grave tone, Kyra took up Ash's serviette and wrung it in her hands. After several moments, when Solarus remained quiet, Kyra glanced up at him.

The wizard's eyes were deeply serious. He laced his hands together on the table and leaned forward. "I want to be clear as to what is expected of you, Kyra. We are no longer fleeing Diamantas' wizards, nor are we distracted with the machinations of the king of Farcaren. Therefore, your task in Silvias is twofold. You need to learn as much as you can about your previous time in the Realm. That includes what led to your disappearance. Without knowing the cause of the first time, we cannot guarantee it will not happen a second."

Kyra's heart plunged into her stomach. She had assumed if she wanted to return to London—if it were possible—it would be her choice. It hadn't occurred to Kyra that she could be taken against her will. Kyra also had lost all her memories when she left Ilian. What was to say that another disappearance wouldn't wipe her mind clear of everything she had gained? Including the year she spent with Millie and James?

Kyra's horror was stamped on her face. Solarus continued in a gentler tone, "I might add it is improbable you will disappear. I merely would like to be convinced we know how to prevent another occurrence. Your other task is to recall what you can, if anything, of your magical instruction; relearn what you cannot; and advance your magic so that you can direct it, not the other way around. Your magic must become an unconscious part of yourself, something as natural as breathing. The dark wizards will attack again. Your confidence in and mastery of the weapons afforded to you will determine the outcome." Solarus separated his hands and ran a finger down the Z line in his hair. "Of course, magic itself does not make one an able warrior, as illustrated by the wondrously inept Adakis. One must also possess sound judgment, sharp instincts, and calm in the face of danger."

Kyra's mind deviated to the uncertainties that surfaced in Thanesgard's dungeon. Did Diamantas need to find her because she and her parents had escaped Harkimer? Was she a dark wizard? What could Solarus tell her? *Would* he tell her anything during their practice?

Kyra opened her mouth to speak, but Solarus interrupted her. "You have undoubtedly saved a deluge of questions for me. I will need hours to answer them to your satisfaction. However, tonight, my sole undertaking is sleeping without interruption. Yours should be the same."

Kyra bristled at Solarus' accusatory tone. She threw the serviette on the table even though she knew the action was childish. "What makes you think I was going to ask you anything?"

Solarus fixed a long-suffering gaze on Kyra. "Your recollections of Ilian and our sessions together have been affected. Mine have not. The expression you displayed before this scowl is the one that forms when you have an inquiry. Inqui*ries*, that is."

Kyra crossed her arms furiously. Solarus calmly reached into his vest pocket. He produced his long pipe and a packet of crushed kolker leaves. "I am not inclined to repeat myself, but it seems necessary to do so. Instruction properly given produces knowledge as a slow, steady flow. Not as a flood. You do not have enough information to produce a cup of water, let alone a brook. Which means you do not even know what questions you *should* be asking."

An elven attendant had arrived. He waited at a respectful distance from the table.

Solarus made no attempt to rise. He tapped the leaves into the end of the pipe. "Your lessons begin tomorrow. If you are half as dedicated to your studies as you are to sating your curiosity, we will make expeditious work of your forgotten magic."

Solarus' patronizing tone grated on Kyra's nerves. Yet she had to admit he was right. It would take weeks for her to sift through the questions heaped in the corners of her brain like leaf piles.

Kyra stood and made to follow the attendant.

"I amend my previous statement," Solarus' words drifted to her, half-muffled by the pipe. "Your first lesson is to remember and heed what I have told you today. Tomorrow we start with your second lesson: to recite this one." Kyra smelled the apple and spices of the kolker as Solarus added dryly, "If you can do at least this much and your impatience has lessened, you will do well in our sessions."

***

Carina and Hayden walked solemnly through an alcove from the palace's interior and onto the balcony of the upper spire. The scent of recent rains, fresh foliage, and the mossy earthen floor hung in the air. Stars blinked over the palace courtyards, trees, hills, and homes below. Hayden paused. The night sky was so clear he could see the square training fields in the distance.

This particular outcropping was the highest in the palace and secret to all but a privileged few. *Veralyn* Ellynirith had desired that kings and queens of Silvias have a place of solitude, a space to ponder issues facing the Realm without interruption. A place where the burden of ruling could be, temporarily, lifted from their shoulders. Ellynirith built the balcony, yet his magic wasn't enough to conceal the area. He beseeched the *Y'cartim Allegra* and its denizens for assistance. The forest consented to the king's request. It threaded ivy over the balcony nearest the palace's apex and imbued the ivy with magic. From that day on, only sitting kings and queens of Silvias and those they granted special permission had the authority to pass onto the balcony. Even after two thousand years, the sanctuary remained a secret among the elven monarchs. Not even Silvias' lords and ladies knew of its existence.

Carina paused in one corner of the balcony. An Iona kaemin was situated on a rail. Unlike the Iona on the hilltop, its hooves were planted on the ground, its wings folded along its body. The kaemin shimmered purple in the bright moonlight. Carina placed a hand on the Iona's back. The planes of her face were bathed in concern as she stared across her kingdom.

Hayden stood silently to the side, one hand under his chin. At Carina's request, he had given an account of their trip since finding Kyra in Edoin Forest. It was thorough—mostly. Hayden glossed over information about their journey through the Forgotten Forest. He mentioned the demons they had seen but not the reactions of his companions. Talis' momentary belief that Solarus was Diamantas and that Merinn was present would have frightened the queen. Carina knew elves could be affected by the magic of the Forest; her worry would be that *Talis* had suffered the hallucination. That Talis was still tormented by Merinn's disappearance. Just like Hayden and Carina were. It served no purpose to stir up feelings of hopelessness.

"Arkin has been blinded by his loss and cannot be trusted to ever recover from it," Carina finally said with a sigh. "I do not worry about Silvias, however. An army of men and a handful of wizards are as much a danger as an army of ants. Malus, the most powerful wizard in a thousand years, tested the impregnability of the Realm. He failed. Arkin will not succeed should he attack my people. What concerns me is that the king's tears of sorrow and rage will barrage the kingdoms of men like hail from a storm." Carina grazed the back of the Iona with her fingers with a meditative look. "Yet, as *Raenalyn* Imineral said, 'News often appears to arrive at an unpropitious time; but in fact, it comes at the exact time in which it is most needed.' Silvias' scouts stand ready to assist you, should you like to send word to the other kingdoms of these events."

"Thank you, *Raenalyn* Carina," Hayden answered. His tone was quiet.

Carina observed him shrewdly. "That is not the matter about which you hoped to speak, though. What has given you such pause?"

Hayden twisted the ring on his finger. The silver shimmered as though forged from one of the stars overhead. "I'd like for Kyra to remain in Silvias," Hayden said at length. "It isn't safe for her elsewhere."

Carina's face was as grave as it was ageless. A breeze swept her long hair to the side. With a sigh, the queen gave a regretful shake of her head. "I cannot grant that request, Caleril. I am sorry."

Hayden took a single step forward, face pained. "Kyra is exposed in a way she has never been. When the dark wizards sought Kyra before, she had some understanding of the threat and was able to survive the attacks. Now she's unfamiliar with Ilian. While I believe Kyra trusts us more than she did, she is still guarded. We don't know what she saw or what happened in the other world."

"Which is evidence enough of the folly of keeping her in here." Carina turned. Her deep, otherworldly gaze met Hayden's gray eyes. "You say she has divulged nothing of her absence? A year apart from us, and Kyra has provided no account from that time. Neither to you nor Talis? Is this silence not unusual to you?"

"She may be more comfortable with friends her age," Hayden replied, though his tone was doubtful. "Kyra may also be more open with a female mentor, someone who could sympathize with her in ways we can't. At least since she returned to Ilian, Kyra hasn't had that chance."

"This all may be true," Carina conceded. "Kyra has changed, though. The Kyra I knew would have confided in you. Not everything, nor most things, I suspect. She has discretion, a trait that I have always admired in her, particularly in one so young."

"The Kyra we remember doesn't remember *us*. Yes, things have changed." Hayden wearily rubbed his eyes. "Talis and I thought that if she spends time with her friends, if she can open up to them . . ."

"That is not all that has changed, Caleril." That Carina used Hayden's honorary elven name underscored the gravity of the situation. "It will not be possible for us to rely on Kyra's childhood peers to be of comfort to her."

"Why not?"

"Kyra was not of age when she departed. She is now. Kyra's magical instruction was harmless without an ability to access the well of power within her. Further, her elven peers are now apprenticed and have assumed their places in this society." Carina's hand pressed against the back of the Iona as though seeking reassurance from it. "Kyra and the elves are like stars. They share the same sky yet occupy different constellations. We knew this. It was preordained."

Hayden placed his palms on the balcony. Silence cocooned the pair, leaving even the chirp of crickets far below. Hayden's heart ached as much as his temple. The more he tried to protect Kyra, the more he sealed her fate to the prophecy. "It came so quickly," he muttered. "Kyra might not have a life here any longer. Nonetheless, she should stay for now. Adakis was willing to kill her in Thanesgard. That means Diamantas sees Kyra as a menace to his hoped-for reign. He has abandoned hopes to persuade her to be his ally. Isn't that reason enough for us to want Kyra to become as strong as she can? Even if Arkin is hindered by Silvias' borders, Diamantas may overcome them. He could be far worse than Malus ever was."

Carina's emerald gaze was as hard as the gem it resembled. "He will never set foot in the Realm. I am sorry, Caleril. I would break my oath to the Realm were I to allow Kyra's unconditional inhabitance. She is a wizard, even if she was raised among my kin. The elves have been generous with her. As we have been with Solarus." The kaemin pulsed a dark purple under Carina's hand. "Need I remind you Kyra was with him on the day she disappeared. Solarus has claimed it necessary to not disclose to where they traveled or for what purpose, merely that it was essential for her to accompany him. This at a time when Diamantas was marshalling support for his cause." The queen's voice grew increasingly louder as her anger impregnated her words. "Then, upon his return, Solarus admitted his responsibility for Kyra's disappearance. He refuses to impart knowledge of where he took her." Carina's fury rang through the balcony. The breeze whipped up around her, her silvery lavender cloak flapping like a banner. Green magic flared around the spire. The trees' leaves shone with a white-green light. "Is Solarus' reticence due to shame for his neglect? Or does his silence hide some immoral action?"

Hayden pushed himself off the balcony. The green magic sent icy waves through him, and he unconsciously pulled his jacket tighter. "Solarus has my complete trust and confidence," he replied in a measured tone. "He has always been a loyal friend. I would place my life as readily in his hands as in Talis'."

"Something that I would not. Who is the fool, I wonder."

"'We all share the duty that, before condemning an individual, we have cultivated his integrity and compassion. We have leached out the poisons infecting his mind. If we have not done these two things, we have failed more fully than the condemned ever could.'"

Carina stared at Hayden. The supernatural glow faded from her eyes, and the wind died out. Carina chuckled darkly. "I forget how well versed you are in our teachings. *Raenalyn* Imineral would be honored." The queen took a deep breath and exhaled. The trees below the spire stilled, returning to their evening slumber as the magic disappeared. "I will grant Kyra the same privilege during her stay as a guest as I did when she was one of our own," Carina decided. Her face betrayed her misgivings. "But be aware, Caleril: her time is limited. If I receive word that Diamantas, his wizards, or the Reapers or other foul beasts are afoot near our border, Kyra must leave. She will not endanger my people. The prophecy is clear. Kyra's fate is inseparable from that of Ilian's. Neither you nor I nor any seer can predict what she will choose to become, in the end."

"We took on this responsibility knowingly," Hayden replied, frustration creeping into his voice. He hesitated, then went on in a softer tone, "*Raenalyn* Carina, I hope you are not punishing Kyra for my mistakes. Please know I never would have asked Talis to be her guardian if I had known what future was expected of him within the Realm. If you would consider his reinstatement . . ."

"I will not mourn the decisions of the past. I cannot change them. Inishmore guided Talis' hand, as it guided yours, as it has guided mine. Inishmore tests our faith with how well we bear the pain and consequences resulting from our actions. Actions within our control and those beyond our control. This applies to Kyra as much as it does to us," the queen added pointedly.

Hayden's eyes searched Carina's imploringly. "Kyra doesn't even know about the prophecy."

"She will, when the time is right." Carina raised her hand in a gesture of friendship. "Be at peace, Caleril. I know what is in your heart. It is the same love as in mine. However, you do Kyra a disservice if you tell her of the prophecy before she is prepared to receive it. Have patience." After a pause, Carina added softly, "Please do not disclose our conversation to Talis. His heart is already burdened."

As is yours, Hayden responded silently. He nodded once, fingers brushing over his ring.

Carina folded her hands behind her back. Green mist swirled around her as she stepped gracefully along the perimeter of the castle. Enfolded in the magical shroud, Hayden trod silently after her.

Chapter 22

Callum had always disapproved of the secret passages' existence. If he could spy on Arkin's enemies through them, what prevented others from spying on him in turn? The irony wasn't lost on Callum as he jogged stealthily along the dry and well-trodden earth. These snaking paths were now the surest means of sparing him and the lives of the Royal Guards.

The corridor was cramped and narrow. Dust choked the air. The rhythmic clapping of dozens of scabbards reassured Callum that the guards were with him. He hoped the echoes weren't as loud beyond the passage walls as they sounded within.

Callum and the guards had already passed by the guest quarters and were steadily working their way around the western side of the palace. Save for the light from a torch carried by Edyn, who followed behind him, the corridor was concealed in darkness. It was a necessary precaution. Arkin had posted sentries in and around the passages. The king knew of most of the hidden entrances. Most, not all.

Callum pulled at the side of his collar. Sweat made his leather uniform uncomfortably itchy. Still, he was grateful for the flexibility and protection the leather offered. Wearing a full uniform of metal was loud and unwieldy, and the guards needed a surreptitious escape. The metal breastplate was the one piece of armor Callum and the guards wore. With the prospect of fighting Royal Guards that hadn't chosen to flee, in addition to soldiers and men-at-arms posted in the rings, Callum decided they needed that extra protection. Wiping his brow, Callum raced forward.

He and the guards continued until a wall obstructed their path. Callum looked left to where the passage arced and disappeared. He knew this part of the corridor looped back to the main kitchens. Callum put his hand on the stone. His fingers probed the wall until he found a nook large enough to grasp. Callum pushed gently on the hidden door. A sliver of light trickled into the corridor, refracting off the dust particles that danced in the air.

Callum peered out of the secret door into the courtyard. Though the moon shone above, black clouds scudded across the sky, and the muggy air was thick with the scents of an impending storm. Callum welcomed the sight. The darkness of a storm worked to the guards' advantage.

He glanced around the courtyard. They were opposite the servants' quarters. The dungeon's entrance was also nearby. As Callum suspected, a handful of Arkin's regular guards and soldiers patrolled this side of the palace. Arkin wouldn't expect someone escaping the castle to enter the dungeon. Especially since the king wasn't aware this exit existed.

Thank goodness for the foresight of the captains centuries ago. They had ensured they could quash a monarch who chose tyranny over loyalty to his people, if it ever came to that. And it had.

Callum glanced over his shoulder. Edyn placed the torch in a sconce on the wall, the last one before the exit. Nodding to himself, Callum turned back to the courtyard. The guards and soldiers strode across the grounds tensely, heads swiveling, spears in hand. He counted under his breath the time that passed before a second pair of guards followed the first. Six seconds between them. Callum's gaze raked the area. No other guards came. He waited, body taut. The first set of guards soon paced back to their original side of the courtyard. The moment they passed, the captain sprinted across the open area and slipped, unnoticed, inside the door to a servant's house.

A man with a bald head, thick frame, and gloved hands was removing a small spit from an open fire. He spun as Callum entered. The man's face lit into a grin. "Ah," Makral said. His tone wasn't surprised but expectant. He set the spit on a table beside the fire and removed his gloves. The room was austere, with scant pieces of furniture and a rug dressing the floor. "Captain. You'll be needing use of the entrance, eh? Was wondering if you'd be on the lam, seeing as Arkin's set a trial for you. The king doesn't waste time, does he? Sticks to the regulations and laws, doesn't complicate things with morals and kinship."

Callum nodded grimly. "If I thought the trial would be fair, I would stay." Sweat trickled down his back, and the leather scratched at his skin. Callum again pulled at his collar. Makral's home was as hot as his smithy. "Arkin has already stripped me of my rank and privileges," Callum continued as his fellow guards ran inside. "He will have an easy time convincing his advisors of my guilt. That's not why I'm leaving, though. I do this for my guards. I won't stand by and watch them arrested and tried. Their association with me makes them equally culpable in Arkin's eyes. And equally deserving of death."

"That's why we've guarded this escape, isn't it?" Makral grinned, the few teeth in his mouth shining like pearls. He moved across the room to the fire. "In case kings and queens do something that doesn't befit the protection of the kingdom." He knelt beside a large chair in the living room. He pushed the chair aside with ease and picked up a hammer. Makral used the flat of the hammer to pry up a board in his floor. It creaked open. He did the same to the boards around the area until it was the width of Callum's chest with the breastplate. Within the hole were stairs descending into a black beyond. "My father and father's father and father's father's father have never doubted their king," Makral commented, sitting back on his heels. "I've the bad luck to put this hideout to use. When you're all through, I'll seal it up. Quite the surprise you'll be giving your uncle, giving him the slip from his own fortress."

The Royal Guards crowded the room, silently waiting for their captain's orders. They donned the leather garments like Callum, appropriate for fighting and stealth. Flame from the fire danced off their metal breastplates and the hilts of their weapons. Makral stood and ushered them forward. Callum wormed his way into the hole first. "There are thirty guards on their way," he called up.

"Wait a few moments more after them if you would. I don't want to leave anyone behind."

"Makral's the man for you," the smith replied, smacking the hammer in his hand. He snatched up a lantern from beside the fire and handed it to Edyn, who queued up next at the hole. "Good luck."

Callum crept down the stairs. He waited for Edyn before taking off. The light from Edyn's lantern stayed close to him as though he was surrounded by a cloud of fireflies. The passages within the palace had been plugged with dust, and they reeked of mildew and decay. When Callum came to the first sconce on the wall, he paused. Edyn placed the lantern on the ground, took up a torch, and lit it. The torch's light carried further than that of the lantern. Callum again sprinted down the tunnel.

As with the palace passages, only the captains and their seconds knew of the underground tunnels that led away from the dungeon. During his training, Callum had spent hours memorizing the route. Now he was grateful for the time he spent. The torchlight illuminated his path enough to see several paces ahead. Callum's memory of the tunnels helped him lead the guards through twists and turns and more twists. He mentally counted the sconces in the walls as they ran.

Callum narrowly avoided running into a wall that appeared abruptly in the tunnel. He raised a hand to signal for Edyn to wait. Callum's brow creased. The wall hadn't existed when he first explored these routes. When did Arkin fill in this part of the tunnel? And for what purpose? Callum retraced his steps to the beginning of the passage, then led his company down parallel corridors. He sent Inishmore a silent plea to help them in their escape.

Callum circled back after two more dead ends before he tallied his fifteenth sconce. The captain stopped. The flicker of torchlight stayed behind him. Callum glanced up at the ceiling. Unlike the others, it was as flat as Makral's anvil and completely even. Not a hint of moisture collected on it. Callum expelled a tense breath. They were standing directly under the outer wall. It was the lone hollow section of the walls surrounding the palace, where the stone had been removed to allow for the hidden door into the outer ring. The tunnel ended a short way ahead. The moat was the last obstruction to the guards, and the secret tunnels didn't go beneath the water. Now success relied on the guard's ability to sneak into the ring and cross the bridge undetected.

Callum moved toward the sconce, with Edyn holding the torch close to the wall. A metal ring glinted in the light. Callum grasped the ring and heaved it toward him. It stuck at first. Callum pulled harder. A hidden door scraped the hard earth, opening to a narrow staircase made of the same stone as the defensive walls surrounding the palace. The opening was barely wide enough for Callum to fit through. He half-turned and took the torch from Edyn. Then he cautiously mounted the stairs. He heard the guards' boots clacking against the stone steps as they ascended behind him. At the top of the stairs was another metal ring.

Scarcely able to twist his shoulders in the cramped space, Callum reached across his body and handed the torch back to Edyn. Light would attract unwanted attention. He knew guards were stationed outside this section of the wall. Not only because Arkin had put the castle guards and soldiers on alert since Callum's demotion as captain; Callum himself always paired one Royal Guards with the regular sentries in the event someone misused the egress. As he were doing.

Callum inched the door back. He heard the murmur of conversation as his eyes adjusted to the outdoors. The black clouds rolling through the sky veiled the moon and stars. Rain fell gently. Torches in sconces appeared intermittently between the tall hedgerows, their light fuzzy. The hedgerows' tall, wavering shadows resembled colossal watchmen looking for trespassers. Through the slit of the door, Callum could see the profile of a guard wearing a stiff breastplate and armor over his arms and thighs. Not a Royal Guard then, Callum assessed. The king's regular guards and soldiers received coarser uniforms and heavier, cheaper metal than that of the Royal Guards. Of course, they weren't the king's personal protectors either. The soldier with the breastplate gestured impatiently toward the top of the wall.

Callum's gaze followed the direction of the guard's finger. Archers paced stiffly, crossbows resting in their arms. Callum hoped the rain obscured their vision of the palace grounds. A second voice spoke. Its owner was beyond the sight of the door. Though the words were muffled by the wood, the firm tone was clear. The soldier who gestured dropped his hand. Scowling, the soldier spun on his heel. Callum quickly moved to the side of the door as the soldier stomped past in agitation. Where the other guard was, Callum didn't know, though he assumed he remained nearby.

The soft sound of metal traveled down the stairs as Callum slid his sword from its scabbard. Holding the naked blade in his hand, he glanced over his shoulder. Edyn's spring green eyes shone like garnets in the light from the torch she held. Callum raised his hands. He clenched his fist and held up five fingers on his free hand. He clenched his fist again and then held up three. Edyn nodded her understanding. She half-turned and tapped the guard behind her. She mimed Callum's motion. The guard nodded and passed the signal down the line.

Callum's jaw tightened with anticipation. He would leave the corridor first. Edyn would wait ten seconds before extinguishing the flame and following. Then eight of his guards would follow. He didn't know if anyone was aware of their movements or if an ambush awaited them. Callum was willing to risk a handful of his men and women. If the situation was secure, Callum would retrieve the others.

Callum pressed the door open and pussyfooted into the ring. The second guard—a Royal Guard, Callum identified by his attire—lingered by the hedgerows, face masked by the darkness between the torches. He scratched the side of his head. Callum stole forward. Hearing Callum's steps, the guard started. Before he could draw his sword, Callum's blade was leveled at his throat.

The captain's head swiveled in the direction where the other guard had stormed off. Torches along the ring lit half of the path. Further down, the wall arced, making it impossible to see anyone beyond. For now, no other guards or soldiers patrolled the area. Callum dropped his sword and shot forward. He grabbed the guard by the side of his chest and slammed him, back-first, against the wall. The guard gasped. Light dimly lit the contours of his pale face.

Callum's brown eyes widened. He released the guard with an astounded look. The guard doubled over, coughing. "Dev?" Callum exclaimed in a loud whisper.

The guard froze. Tentatively, he looked up and regarded his assailant for the first time. "Captain?"

Callum's shoulders sagged with relief. "Thank Inishmore I found you," he said, as Dev straightened. "You didn't respond when I sent word for the guards to gather. I was worried someone had intercepted the message or that you had been imprisoned. Where is the other guard that was here with you?"

Dev stared at Callum with an equally thunderstruck expression. "He went to find Shanta . . . Captain Shanta, I mean . . . and demand she send more guards and soldiers. I told Captain Shanta the king wanted the guards, particularly the remaining Royal Guards, closer to the inner ring. The king was worried about his personal safety. Shanta . . . Captain Shanta . . . she followed the king's order." Dev descended into silence.

Callum wiped his blond hair, matted by rain, from his forehead. "Inishmore is with us. Arkin hasn't discovered our plans yet. The king's wrath is making him careless. 'Anger is a wasted emotion,' Hayden always said. Anger is the cause of our mistakes and worsens an already terrible situation. Arkin neglected the drills and training of the soldiers. That shoddiness grants us the time we need to . . ."

Callum stopped at the sound of the door groaning open. Edyn ghosted out and sprinted across the width of the ring. Seven more Royal Guards moved like spirits behind her, swords gripped firmly in their hands. The eighth and final guard slipped into the outer ring, his weapon sheathed. He set his hands against the heavy door. Grunting as he pushed, the door slid halfway closed. A hand from inside grabbed the metal ring and heaved it inward. The door shut with a thump.

Edyn reached Callum's side. The dagger raised in her hand cast shadows the length of a spear on the wall. The suspicious line on her mouth melted into a smile.

"Dev, you found us!" Edyn said softly as the other guards pressed themselves against the wall. They looked left and right down the outer ring. The path remained eerily vacant. Dev stared mutely at Edyn. The thunderstruck expression was stitched on his face.

"You five." Callum indicated Edyn and four other Royal Guards with his index finger. "Disable the archers on the fourth wall. Edyn, you're the most agile among us. I want you to test the wall, see if there are enough holds for you to climb. If it's possible, the others can follow. You four—" Callum's gaze roamed to the remaining Royal Guards, "—subdue the archers in the crenellations along the outer wall. We can't contend with a shower of arrows if the alarm is raised. Don't kill anyone unless you have no other option. They are still our countrymen."

Edyn's expression was solemn. She faced the fourth wall and scanned the stone. Closer to the sconce, flames illuminated small chips and irregularities in rock from centuries of wear, weather, and war. The stone was slick, making the climb more challenging. Exhaling deeply, Edyn placed a toe onto a small protrusion. She stretched her fingers, groping for another edge of rock. Finding a small shelf, Edyn gripped the stone with both hands and pulled herself up. When her feet were planted on the shelf, Edyn continued upward.

Her four companions spread out along the wall. The second group of guards sprinted across the ring and stayed, backs flat, against the outer wall, waiting for Callum's signal.

The captain's brown eyes tracked Edyn. His heart pounded in fear that she would fall or be seen. Edyn expertly scrambled higher. When she had progressed more than halfway, Callum nodded to the guards beside him. They covertly began to scale the wall. Callum cast a glance to the guards near the outer ring and flicked his finger toward the parapets. The guards began their ascent.

Callum's gaze moved up the wall. The archers' attention scrolled the bridges and roads leading away from the palace. Good. They were unaware of the guards stealthily creeping up the wall. "You have no idea how worried we were, Dev. We got lucky that you were posted outside this exit. I don't know if we could have freed you from the dungeon."

Callum looked back at Dev. The guard hadn't spoken since Edyn had arrived. Now Callum saw a pained expression tightening the corners of his eyes and stretching the muscles in his face. Dev's upper body was tense. He swallowed hard. "Captain," he said quietly, "I didn't answer the summons because I'm not leaving."

Callum eyed Dev incredulously. "What do you mean, you aren't leaving?"

Dev diverted his gaze down the outer ring. Faint chatter trickled from around the bend. "I swore an oath to the king as a member of the Royal Guards. I swore my honorable and loyal service. As did you, Captain. Calling the guards to you and ordering their departure, it breaks that vow."

For a moment, Callum could only stare at Dev, mouth agape. "Dev, you don't understand," he whispered, eyes pleading. "You heard his speech. He declared the Royal Guards were complicit in Hayden and his friends' escape. He accused us of treason. Were Arkin to find me guilty at the trial—and he would—he would have grounds to arrest the entirety of the Royal Guards. He could purge Farcaren of his political opponents by declaring they, too, were part of the plot. As my second, Larisa would be executed without a second thought." Callum saw Dev wince at his words. The voices around the bend were growing steadily louder. Callum put a hand on Dev's shoulder. "You have to come with us. If you don't, it will mean your death."

Dev met Callum's eyes. His expression was haunted. "The trial will be fair. The king is being coerced by the dark wizards. He won't condemn you or the guards. If you do this, Captain, if you refuse his summons, you *will* be wrong. You are leading a revolt."

"We aren't fighting the king, Dev!" Callum's voice shook. "Listen to me, please. This is a flight, not a revolt. The oath we swore was one of fealty to our countrymen. To Farcaren. Not to one man. The king is a steward of his people. My uncle used to embrace this role with honor, Dev. I know this more than anyone else." Callum released Dev's shoulder and peered around the hedge. The way forward, away from the approaching soldiers, was empty. "King Arkin changed, Dev. His values have been corrupted. He traded the safety of his people for a deal with the dark wizards. I more than anyone wish it weren't so. But I can't feign ignorance of the situation. Flight is the one option we—the Royal Guards—have until my uncle extricates himself from their web of evil."

Thuds and grunts sounded from above. Dev and Callum both glanced up as Edyn appeared in an open space of the parapet. She made a circle with her hand. The archers were down.

Callum waved to show his understanding. He motioned with his finger down the parapet. Edyn nodded and soft-shoed along to the next grouping of archers. The other four guards came into view within the open spaces. Callum readjusted the sword in his hand. Raindrops pelted his forehead and streamed down his face. Callum looked back at Dev.

The guard's eyes were swollen with pain. "If what you say is true, Captain, then the king needs the Royal Guards more than ever. We can't abandon him or Farcaren to the wizards. We have to support him and repair the damage that has been done. The guards are meant to protect the king. We can't do that if we're hiding like rabbits in a warren, waiting for the foxes to leave."

"We don't have any more time to debate this, Dev. If you won't come with us, you have to stand aside."

Dev shifted his feet slightly. The guard's hand strayed to the hilt of his weapon. He glanced down the ring, mouth open to shout a warning to the approaching soldiers.

Callum lunged forward. The maneuver was perfectly placed. Dev choked on his words, a strangled sound coming from the back of his throat. Shock slid across Dev's face as he crumpled to the ground. Rain pattered on his face. His eyes were glassy, staring without seeing.

Callum pushed back the platinum blond hair plastered to his face. With a trembling hand, Callum fished a cloth from his pocket. He wiped his sword free of the blood that stained it.

"I'm sorry, Dev," he muttered to the fallen guard. "You are right about the oaths we swore. I must defend Farcaren." Callum sheathed his sword before turning away from the grisly scene. His pulse raced. Callum took two deep breaths. Then he drew a dagger from his belt and sprinted back to the hidden door in the outer wall. He pounded on it with his fist. He stepped back as the door was forced open.

Arkin's soldiers had rounded the bend. A sergeant halted at the sight of Callum. His hand flew forward, grabbing his fellow solider. "It's them!" he shouted. "It's Callum. Arrest him!"

Callum waved to the Royal Guards lined up at the door's entrance. "Let's go, hurry!"

The guards filed out and sprinted down the ring. With Callum leading the way, they cut down the soldiers and guards with silent efficiency. Overhead, Edyn and the eight guards worked through the archers, appearing as black blots behind the shroud of rain.

Callum soon saw the portcullis. He motioned for his contingent of guards to slow down. The guards had made their way so quietly that the soldiers manning the crank were oblivious to their approach. Pulling on his leather collar, soaked through from the rain, Callum looked up the wall. Edyn and the guards descended, spiderlike, into the ring. Callum waited until they leapt the last meter to the ground. Edyn's expression was grimly satisfied. She had performed her work professionally and without killing the archers. Her hands carried scratches from the climb. Callum waved to the rest of the guards in the ring. They swept toward the portcullis. The soldiers had barely glanced up before they were rendered unconscious.

Callum was about to let out a terse sigh of relief when the gonging of a bell resonated through the night air. He grimaced. The alarm had been sounded.

Two of the Royal Guards ran to the crank and wrenched it back. The chain squealed and screeched as the portcullis was raised. Boots stomped and confused shouts rang from within the castle. The Royal Guards' time was running out.

Callum sheathed his sword and rushed to the wall. A lever was embedded within it. Together with another of the guards, Callum strained to pull the latch down. It released the wooden bridge that spanned the moat.

"Go, go, hurry!" Callum commanded even before the bridge was fully lowered across the water. He and the guards bolted across, rain pelting them like blunted arrows. The bell reverberated behind them. Callum didn't slow as he led the guards into the forest beyond the bridge. The foliage provided some cover from the storm. When the guards' stables came into sight, Callum stopped. He clutched a stitch in his side, his gaze flying over the scene.

The grounds were a hive of activity. Royal Guards raced in and out of the stables. Some grabbed satchels with provisions, others secured the straps to saddles and bridles, and still others tossed bows to their companions. A clap of thunder drowned out their calls to each other as they raced back and forth. The horses stomped the ground, infected by their riders' urgency.

Callum spotted Larisa and Nikolas among the crowd. Larisa held the reins to Callum's steed in her hand. Her blond tresses were tangled and knotted, and dirt spattered her clothing. Nikolas' grizzled features were charged and alert as he gazed in the direction of the bells. Callum rushed toward them and tapped Larisa on the shoulder. She turned. Her cinnamon-colored eyes widened.

"Captain!" she said, her voice filled with concern. Callum massaged his side, wincing, his breath ragged. "Are you all right?"

"I'm fine." Callum let his hand drop. "Our time is short. We have to gain as much distance from Arkin's soldiers and the wizards as we can. Were you able to rally the others?"

"Most of them," Larisa reported with a somber look. "We couldn't convince everyone to join us."

"Where's Dev?" Nikolas' gaze ranged the new arrivals, who were receiving their saddled steeds from the guards at the stables. At the sound of the name, Larisa looked around in anticipation. She brushed long, wet strands of hair from her face.

"Dev?" she called, searching the press of bodies around her. "Dev, can you hear me? I'm over here." Frowning, Larissa handed Nikolas the reins to Callum's horse. She forced her way past a pair of guards. "Dev?"

Nikolas' gaze suddenly fell on Callum's arm. "There's blood on your sleeve. Are you injured?"

Callum's heart plummeted. Though the leather was soaked by the rain, it didn't mask the large, dark splotch on his cuff.

Larisa rushed back with a frantic look. "Captain, where is Dev? I don't see him. Please. Where is Dev?"

Callum's expression contorted with pain. Thunder rumbled overhead. "He didn't make it out of the castle. I'm so sorry, Larisa."

Larisa took a step back. Blood drained from her face. "It's not true. He's here somewhere." She turned back to the crowded grounds. "Dev, answer me! Dev!"

Callum stepped forward and gently took Larisa's hand between his. Larisa reluctantly looked back at him. Water rimmed her eyes, lips parted in shock. "Please tell me it isn't true, Captain," she whispered. "You made a mistake. It was someone else."

"I saw him, Larisa, with my own eyes. He lay bleeding in the ring." Callum let out a shuddering breath. "I was with him when he left this world. By the Healer's mercy, Inishmore will have delivered him to eternal peace."

Tears streamed down Larisa's cheeks. Pulling her hands free from Callum's, she half-walked, half-dragged herself to a spot away from the horses. She sank to her knees. Then Larisa buried her face in her hands, body shaking with sobs of grief.

"Inishmore be with him," Nikolas murmured the blessing. "Dev was a good man. Is that his blood then that I see?" The guard's eyes had roved back to Callum's uniform.

Callum unconsciously rubbed the ugly stain. "Yes," he replied hollowly. "The mark of the sword was that of a guard, Nikolas. I didn't linger when I saw Dev couldn't be saved. What unspeakable times we have entered when the loyalties of our fellow guards are cleaved. All due to the arrogance and power of one, corrupted man." He raised his hand. The black liquid coated his fingertips, but the rain quickly washed it away.

The contours of Nikolas' face were menacing. "Whoever dared take Dev's life forfeited his. Dev will have justice."

A guard approached leading Nikolas' and Larissa's horse. Nikolas passed the reins in his hand to Callum and accepted those of his and Larissa's steeds from the guard. Callum removed his scabbard and sword and put them a saddlebag. He glanced back at Larisa.

The guard had lifted her head and stared beyond the woods. Larissa's face was dressed in a dark rage, and tears streaked down her face like war paint. She stood. Her boots cut into the ground as though the earth deserved her vengeance as she joined Callum and Nikolas.

"The man who killed my fiancé will rue this day," Larissa said coldly. "He will feel pain a hundred times worse than Dev. I promise you that."

The rain was cold. Even with the leather, Callum felt goose bumps pricking his skin. But the chill didn't come from the rain at all. "Arkin will answer for his crimes, I promise you."

Larisa stared at him. In a sudden burst of emotion, she hugged Callum tightly. "Thank you, Captain. I've never been more grateful to have you to lead us."

Callum released her and gave her a somber half-smile. He mounted as Nikolas passed the reins of Larisa's horse to her. When all three were astride, Nikolas steered so that he was parallel to Callum. "What are your orders, Captain?"

"We will rally others who will stand at our side. Nikolas, you have currency with men in Plover. The marquis staunchly supports Arkin, yet his disdain for men-at-arms is no secret. How often has he derided them as intellectual inferiors to the members of his court? You need to speak with his guards. Give them my pledge that should they fight alongside us, they will be treated with dignity and received as equals."

Nikolas bent his head in assent. "You will find them willing."

Callum looked at Larisa. "Ride to Adea and speak with your aunt, the duchess. I believe she and her husband would readily throw their lot with ours."

Larissa's eyes blazed. "Yes, Captain."

"The duchess will not likely be receptive, Captain," Nikolas commented. "Her estates lie far to the south. She will not risk her lands and servants for a war conducted from Thanesgard."

"The duchess is a merchant first and foremost. War means disrupted trade. If she can't afford her lands or feed her citizens, she will lose her status among her peers in Ilian, one that would be difficult to regain. The duchess can be swayed. The earl of Cheslynn also resides in the south and has open enmity against Arkin. He is a certain ally." Callum maneuvered his horse so that he was facing Larisa and Nikolas. "Each of you, take a company of guards. We've ridden across the lands before. We won't raise suspicion. At least, not until the king's messengers reach the nobility. I hope that is after we have approached them. We will meet in the town of Dale Thatch in three weeks' time."

Nikolas' forehead creased. "Is it wise to travel through Edoin Forest? If Harkimer's wizards are in Thanesgard? Might they not also seek passage through the woods?"

"We don't have a choice. Arkin will mobilize his forces against us. He wouldn't suspect we would risk a confrontation with the dark wizards, should they indeed be in Edoin." Callum shifted in his saddle. "If anything goes awry, send a messenger immediately."

"We will defeat Arkin." Larisa's knuckles were white as she gripped the reins to her horse. "He can wind up all the soldiers in Farcaren and loose them against us. It won't make a difference. We will win. For Dev."

Callum looked down at the stripes on his sleeve cuff. The stain was untouched by the rain. "May Inishmore watch over us," he replied in a strained voice. "I couldn't bear to lose you as well."

Chapter 23

"It's kind of nice being a guest," Kyra remarked to herself. She stretched her legs under the steaming bathwater, which was discreetly perfumed with rose oil. "I doubt when I lived here before I woke up to rose petals. Or—" Kyra's eyes strayed to the atrium beside the bath, "—had my own private forest."

Unlike her room in Thanesgard, Kyra's elven chamber had not a tub but an open, sea green pool. Kyra found the bath warm when she entered the room the night before, and it had been the same temperature ever since. Lilac trees surrounded the pool. Magnificent morning sunlight streamed through a *zylith* ceiling directly overhead, glittering on the surface of the water and warming Kyra's damp hair. She smiled and closed her eyes.

The pool was one of many unique features of the elven chamber. Like the *zylith* of the palace, every piece of furniture had a gentle luster. Fascinatingly lifelike images of wisteria, identical to the flowers hanging over the elven homes, were painted onto translucent turquoise walls. The feather-light bedsheets and cover shimmered white. The mirror and sink were the purplish-pink of a dawn morning. Candles were conspicuously absent. Instead, the chamber was illuminated by soft lights of various colors that popped to life when Kyra entered the room. Like tiny fairies, the lights bobbed around Kyra wherever she walked. When she lay down, the lights faded, allowing the darkness of night to cradle Kyra to sleep.

Kyra's grin faltered. She picked up the soapstone and scrubbed her arms again. Her skin had long since pruned. "It's going to be a great day," Kyra told herself. "If Hayden and a couple of adults thought I was good enough to be around, my friends are going to be excited. I bet they're waiting outside while I'm dilly-dallying in the water . . ."

The night before, Kyra held imagined conversations with her friends. She pictured her friends as thrilled with her return, eager to show her around Silvias. As wanting to share stories of their childhood together. If it turned out that her experiences were less than pleasant, Kyra wouldn't have wasted her free time fretting. If Kyra's friends *were* ecstatic to see her, then her expectations would be met.

Kyra's self-coaching began the moment she rose. Half an hour later, neither the bath nor her pep talk had completely sloughed off the doubts she wore like a second skin. Instead, butterflies flittered to and fro inside her stomach.

"They're going to say, 'a wizard, hey, that's something!'" Kyra carried on her conversation as she climbed out of the pool. She grabbed a large, fluffy towel. "And I'll say, yep, a wizard. What have I missed since I've been gone?'" Throwing the towel on the bed, Kyra went to the washbasin, scooped up a scentless lotion, and rubbed it over her shoulders and back. "'Nothing, same old, same old,' they'll tell me. 'It's been a bit of a bore without you.'" Kyra's face broke into a grin. She hurriedly combed her hair. "'Want to play a round of hunter?' they'll ask. 'Sure, why not?' I'll answer. 'I've learned a trick or two since the last—' ow!" Kyra scowled as the tines of the comb caught in a large knot. She delicately teased out the strands until her hair fell in loose waves, glossy from the pool and oils.

"'The last go-around,'" Kyra finished. She snatched up elven garments that had been left for her on the side of the bath. Her traveling clothes lay folded on a glass-spun chair. Her new attire consisted of a featherweight silver shirt that dropped just below her knees and a dark blue corded belt; a turquoise vest with, to Kyra's pleasure, laces instead of buttons; robin's-egg trousers; and her leather, calf-high boots. The leather shone from a recent cleaning.

Kyra turned to the last item. Delight lit in her eyes as she gazed upon a shimmering azure cloak. The cloak Kyra had stored in her closet in London. The cloak of a wizard. Kyra carefully lifted the cloak, its material as soft as the finest silk. She turned it over in her hand and noticed how the morning light rippled over the material like waves in the ocean. With reverence, Kyra set the cloak back on the bed. She had the full trappings of her new—or rediscovered—identity.

Someone rapped on the door. Anxiety and anticipation skirmished for dominance inside her heart. *So much for relaxed, positive thinking.* "Coming!" she called.

The elven clothing conformed to her body as Kyra slid the shirt over her head. She would have compared it to the fit of a sock—except she had never felt a sock so comfortable or so unnoticeable as though she were naked. Kyra's cheeks flushed at the thought. She double-checked in the mirror on the washbasin that she was, in fact, fully dressed. Kyra rushed back and draped the cloak over her shoulders. The familiarity brought a sigh to her lips. Putting a large smile on her face, Kyra strode to the door and opened it grandly.

To see Solarus standing behind it. As always, his hornbeam staff was at his side. "Good morning." Solarus arched a brow as he studied her. "Were you expecting someone?"

"Of course not, no," Kyra said hastily, unaware her crestfallen expression conveyed an opposite message. "Who would I be expecting?" Her elven friends weren't aware she had returned. That was okay. She could find them later.

Solarus' gaze probed her, looking unconvinced. Gratefully, he didn't press the matter. Solarus inclined his head toward her attire. "I see you have discovered your cloak."

"Yes, it's gorgeous, thank you," Kyra replied. She walked into the hall, face flushed, and closed the door noiselessly behind her. "What time is it? Did I miss breakfast?"

"No," the wizard responded. He motioned with his staff. "The others are already in the dining hall. Let us walk together. You can recite your first lesson. Assuming you were paying enough attention to have heard it."

Distracted from her disappointment over her friends, Kyra wracked her brain for an answer. "We had a lesson last night? I thought we started today . .

. Oh, that lesson," she remembered as Solarus regarded her with a sternly raised brow. "'Remember and heed what I have told you.'"

Solarus' brow remained raised. "And here I was losing hope."

"I was curious about the cloak," Kyra commented as they descended the spiraling stairs, passing elven attendants along the way. "You wear an azure color. The dark wizards' cloaks are black. Is there a reason for that?"

"An observant question," Solarus replied. He placed a hand on the railing and traced a line in the *zylith* as he reached the end of the stairs. "All wizards wore azure once. The color symbolizes loyalty. Truth. Strength. Faith."

"What about black?"

"Sable," Solarus answered as they proceeded down a carpeted hallway. "It symbolizes wisdom. Or it did. Before the War of Calonia, wizards commonly chose sable to demonstrate their higher stature in society, particularly those in the Wizards' High Council. After the war, wizards who had fought against Malus embraced sable but not for its wisdom. They wished it to represent that which is hidden from the world. It is the color of the shadows, both physically and of the mind. Befitting wizards in exile, I would say. Now to your lessons—" Solarus switched topics as they walked side by side through an arched door and into the sparkling morning sunlight, "—I will meet you at the steps to the palace at the top of the hour. Do not be late."

Talis and Hayden were alone in the dining hall when Kyra rushed in. Her face fell. Where were her elven friends? Kyra chided herself for being impatient as she approached the table. Even if they had heard of her return, Talis mentioned the elves had apprenticeships. Naturally, they couldn't drop their work simply to pop by and say hi. *There's no urgency to see them right now,* she reassured herself. *My friends live here. I can find them later.*

Eager to meet Solarus, Kyra sat beside Talis and Hayden and gulped down the meal as quickly yet politely as possible. Talis and Hayden regarded the azure cloak with contrary expressions. With her mouth full, Kyra smiled proudly at the cloak. The elf reciprocated Kyra's smile. Hayden, on the other hand, shied from Kyra's expectant look. His gray eyes were as dark as charcoal as he silently drank his coffee. Kyra's grin slid from her lips. Knowing something was wrong and unable to place what it was, Kyra scraped her plate clean, put down her serviette, sprang up from the table, and said a rushed goodbye.

Solarus waited on the stairs as promised. Kyra smelled the rich scent of kolker leaves even before she saw Solarus' pipe. He shook the pipe over the ground as he contemplatively watched the goings-on near the palace. Kyra paused in the doorframe as she followed his gaze. Elves bustled over the white stones, their paces brisk and at the same time effortless. A triplet of guards rode their horses in the direction of the woods while two women held laundry baskets. A male and female elf held hands and disappeared into the garden abutting the western tower. Kyra's eyes dropped back to Solarus. His staff was propped up against the wall. Tucked in the crook of his left arm was an object wrapped in a bundle of blankets. "You have already proven you understand the second lesson of the day," Solarus said as Kyra approached. "Always be punctual. This applies to lessons, meetings, or a meal with a friend. Reliability practiced in small ways becomes a habit. That habit becomes important for more critical aspects of life. If you cannot manage promptness, arrive early." Solarus put the pipe back in his mouth and turned. "This is yours." He handed her the mysteriously long object.

Kyra stripped off the first layer of blankets curiously. Her fingers grazed a smooth wooden surface. Kyra unwrapped the rest of the blankets and gasped. It was a cherrywood staff. Kyra lifted it reverently. The staff was surprisingly light. It stood a couple inches above her head, its tip shaped like the scroll of a violin. Kyra's hand trembled as she placed it on the ground. Her sword was comfortable; the staff created a more personal connection, as though she had lost an old friend. Tears of joy sprang to her eyes. Kyra coughed and made a show of flattening rumples in the rumple-free fabric of the cloak. "Thank you," she managed to get out.

"There is no need to thank," Solarus replied. He graciously became interested in his own staff as Kyra sniffed and rubbed her nose inelegantly on her sleeve. "This staff was given to you when you began your training. It is yours to reclaim. Queen Carina took the liberty of holding it and a wizard's cloak for safekeeping when you first disappeared." Solarus hesitated, looking unusually uncomfortable. He cleared his throat. "These were to remain in Silvias if—until—you returned. You have clearly returned."

Kyra's brow knitted. "I thought only the staff's owner can touch a staff safely. Callum said he used a baldric to move yours in Thanesgard. Is that how Carina handled it?"

"A staff belonging to a fully trained wizard poses a threat," Solarus clarified. "However, novice wizards do not have enough magic stored to render it unusable by others. When you disappeared, you had had little practice with the staff. It was quite harmless." Solarus descended the steps and walked onto a lime green light that meandered around the palace. Kyra frowned slightly. Had the light been there before? "Ask questions while we walk, or else you will fritter away time we need for your lessons."

"Frittering away time" was the last thing Kyra wanted. She hopped down after Solarus, continuing to marvel at the staff. It was a weapon of beauty. Kyra wondered how much magic a wizard had to amass in a staff to inflict horrendous pain on those who tried to seize it. Her thoughts enveloped her so fully, she scarcely noticed the elves' furtive glances in her and Solarus' direction as they walked.

Kyra and Solarus traveled beyond the city limits to the surrounding hills of Silvias. The sun was hot, its rays beating down on the pair. Despite her light elven clothing, sweat trickled down the nape of Kyra's neck and along her back. She used her staff as a hiking stick as they threaded their way up the increasingly steep slope. Solarus strode along untiringly. He seemed to know exactly where they were headed. Pausing to swipe sweat from her brow, Kyra stopped suddenly. The lime green path was no longer under their feet.

Solarus paused further up, resting his foot on a tree root. "Beginning your instruction requires arriving at our destination."

"I'm coming," Kyra answered, traipsing up the hill. Solarus turned his back to her and continued. "I wonder if there's a spell to transform into a bird," Kyra grumbled. "Then I could fly to wherever we're going."

She was puzzled when, moments later, Solarus stepped through the tree line and onto the grassy apex. Sunlight lapped at his face. He beckoned to Kyra. "Here is where you will be spending much of your days to come."

Raising a hand to shade her eyes, Kyra stepped up beside Solarus. A welcome breeze cooled her brow. Then Kyra's jaw dropped. They had come out directly above Silvias' valley and looked down upon the lake Kyra had noticed the day prior. The water's surface sparkled in the brilliant light. The lake formed a giant C, tapering at one end into a long, uneven tail that disappeared into the valley. Two tiny islands were situated at the far end of the lake, with trees dotting each one.

"The elves guard their realm and its secrets as a mother does her child," Solarus told Kyra as her eyes fell on a pair of swans flying below them. The birds glided onto the surface, barely stirring the waters. They flapped their wings and shook their slender necks. "Only those in the queen's good graces are permitted to travel so far within Silvias unescorted."

Solarus' supercilious tone relayed his opinion that he was one of those in the queen's good graces. Kyra grinned.

It was an easy descent to the lake. Solarus gestured with his staff for Kyra to sit on the spongy bank. The swans drifted past. Kyra unclasped her cloak and set it delicately next to her staff. Then she settled on the grass with her knees bent and resting to the side.

Solarus assumed a cross-legged position. He laid his hornbeam staff across the ground in front of him. "Now—" Solarus assumed his now familiar, didactic tone, "—we will start with the history and evolution of magic as we know it."

Kyra groaned inwardly. More lecturing. Not magicking.

Solarus reached into his tunic pocket. He removed a hand-sized book with a soft tan leather cover and a stiff spine and presented it to Kyra. As it usually did, Kyra's curiosity overrode her disappointment as she took the book. Its cover was embossed with faded gold, silver, and white designs. "'Magic,'" she read the title out loud. The word was underlined by a slender golden rectangle with a diamond embedded in one end. As Solarus again extracted his pipe, Kyra traced the other strange symbols with her forefinger: a white, egg-shaped image dwarfed by a circle of silver; a short rectangle with something scrawled within it; a large golden loop with squiggly lines overlapping with a silver oval like Venn diagrams from Kyra's math lessons; and finally, at the bottom of the cover, a cross on its side.

As she tried to decode the images, Kyra was reminded strikingly of those on her heptagon coin. "What are these?" she questioned, pointing to the symbols.

"Enticingly intriguing forms lacking purpose or meaning, except, apparently, to provide further distraction to students," Solarus replied dryly. "I did not provide the book for you to judge the cover. It is the content that merits study. Read the first page."

Kyra peeled back the cover. "'As one undertakes the pursuit of magic, one must understand the elemental foundation behind it: Inishmore,'" she dutifully read aloud. "'Inishmore is the essence of being and energy. It encompasses everything in the land. In return, everything in the land is joined to it. Inishmore is energy unseen and felt. Inishmore is energy seen and touched. Inishmore is everything sentient. Every creature of this world is of Inishmore.'"

"We have touched upon the importance of Inishmore briefly since you arrived," Solarus remarked as Kyra lowered the book. "If you remember our discussion in Edoin about intrinsic and learned magic, I mentioned that learned magic is derived from Inishmore. I also told you that every creature has a unique bond to Inishmore. This is because, as the book states, it is the essence of being. It is energy. It is everywhere."

"I remember," Kyra responded with a hint of impatience. "Can we skip to the next chapter?" *On to something less vague and more useful, like casting spells?*

Solarus' amused grin didn't improve her mood. "We have already arrived at your third lesson. Have patience, which I can tell is as contrary to your nature now as it was in the past. You must practice it all the same. If that is too difficult, pretend. Patience is the ability to tolerate the time in which you do not have immediate answers, solutions, or clarity without becoming irritated or angry in the process."

"I know what patience means," Kyra grumbled.

"You were unfamiliar with the term 'refrain from' back in the Forgotten Forest. I will not assume you know words paramount to your instruction." Solarus ignored Kyra's glower and lit his pipe with a tap of his finger. "You may apply this lesson on patience to your study of the book."

Solarus emphasized "you may." Kyra knew to interpret the phrase as an unarguable "you will."

"The introduction is the most daunting section of the book," Solarus continued. "However, you must understand magic's theoretical and historical context before you can extract its uses. Wizards spend years contemplating the meaning of Inishmore to improve their abilities. Read on."

Kyra pushed herself from the ground with her right hand, picked up the book, and leaned on her left hand. "'Inishmore is translated as 'air' or 'breath.' Records from the beginning of Ilian's founding relate that Inishmore is an ever-present force. Inishmore guides us in times of uncertainty, helps us decide what action to take, and warns us of hardships to come.'"

Kyra broke off. She silently reread the last sentence. *Inishmore guides us in times of uncertainty, helps us decide what action to take, and warns us of hardships to come.* James had made that exact statement when he described Inishmore. He must have read the text that was now in her hands. But how? Why would James study magic? Kyra's heart panged at the thought. How much she missed him.

Solarus tapped his pipe on his leg with a vexed look. "We will be here for many hours if you choose to stop at each segment," he commented dryly.

Clearing her throat, Kyra went on. "'Inishmore's energy is as subtle as a whisper in the wind. It touches the heart with the softest of sighs. One must recognize these sensations before one can interpret them. One must also choose whether to heed the guidance received.'"

Kyra's skin pricked with goose bumps. The description could have come from her own lips, remembering the sensations that breezed against her heart. As Kyra opened her mouth to tell Solarus about her experiences, something prevented the words from leaving her lips. The intimacy of those whispers was deeply personal. A bond between her and, according to the passage, Inishmore. Something too personal to share.

A new thought kindled in her mind. Inishmore had provided Kyra comfort when she needed it most. It had also intervened in the Forgotten Forest when she wanted to attack the phantoms with the crimson magic. More than intervened—it had compelled her, broken her free from her manic, dangerous desires.

That didn't guarantee Inishmore *always* directed someone to do something virtuous, did it? What if Inishmore convinced someone to undertake something wicked instead? Was Diamantas imploring Inishmore for help too?

Kyra set the book on the ground and voiced the last of these thoughts, leaving out mention of the Forest.

Solarus studied her with a rare, approving look. "Perceptive questions, to neither of which I have an answer. It is possible, though I am guessing unlikely, that Inishmore has gifted individuals with less than noble intentions with insights. We do not have the records, oral or written, to confirm if this is true. If accounts do exist, at least starting from the days of Malus and beyond, Malus' descendants have locked them away in Harkimer. The underlying matter is how Inishmore judges our intentions. What is deemed honorable and what villainous? You asked about Diamantas. As I have said before, he is a complex and complicated individual. His ambitions, if his claims can be trusted, are to 'liberate' the wizards of Harkimer. His goal to conquer Ilian is to ensure wizards are never again banished to the Mountains. Is Diamantas motivated by his interpretation of loyalty and duty? Does he believe it his divine responsibility to save his kin no matter the bloodshed? Would Inishmore support him in this crusade? Perhaps, perhaps not. We shall see."

Kyra brushed her palm against the grass. The soft blades tickled her skin. "What about Arkin? He said he was a faithful servant to Inishmore. Then his wife and child died. If Inishmore helps those who try and do good for the world, why did he suffer so much?"

Solarus' face fell, his expression uncharacteristically sympathetic. He puffed on his pipe before answering. "Such a tragedy would make the most devout adherents to Inishmore question whether their faith was justified. We do not always know why things happen the way they do."

When it was clear Solarus wasn't going to speak further, Kyra lifted the book again. "'Magic is the harnessing of Inishmore's energy. Wizards define the purpose of magic as to create, manipulate, and eradicate.'" Kyra bit her lip.

Creation sounded innocent. Manipulation and eradication, not so much. "That's not very heartening," she observed.

Solarus released a breath into the air, filling it with the pleasant scent of spiced apples. "It is an archaic definition. Long before the time of Malus, wizards used the terms as the basis for their covenant with men and elves to live in harmony. 'Creation' is self-explanatory. 'Manipulation' was intended to be interpreted as 'the use of' or 'the employing of' magic to *aid* a community or kingdom.

"There is a famous story to this effect," Solarus continued, gazing out to the lake. "There was a severe drought in what is today the kingdom of Hogarth. Farms suffered seasons without rain or snowfall. The earth could not sustain crops. Streambeds dried up, and grass withered. Fish and cattle were also affected. They were unable to obtain water or food. Families were forced to abandon their homesteads and travel west in search of fertile grounds. The journey was perilous. Many were killed by greeloks or perished from famine or disease. Were it not for three wizard sisters traveling through the same lands, the farming communities would have ceased to exist.

"When the wizard sisters learned of the plight of the families, they used their powers to summon water from the Aurielle Sea. The Sea, as you know, lies to the north of Hogarth. The Sea's waters spilled through every crack in the earth and nourished every root that had the barest spark of life left. In short time, the soil was again rich, the streams were full, and the fields flourished. That was the spirit of 'manipulation.'"

Kyra looked at the grass beneath her fingertips, then out at the lake. "How do you summon enough water to restore an entire kingdom? Did it have something to do with their staffs? You talked about storing energy to use later."

"According to the scribes, no. They directed the Sea with their hands."

Kyra's brows raised in surprise. "Can *you* do that?"

Solarus returned her intense curiosity with an aloof hmph. "Ilian has not faced a drought of proportions that merited the removal of a sea since that time," he replied with an upturned chin. "However, I could undoubtably perform such a task were it necessary to do so."

"Okay," Kyra said, plucking a blade of grass. "What about 'eradication'? How can that have any positive aspect to it?"

"Eradication was an honorable ambition, the same as manipulation. Wizards combated pestilence, plagues, and diseases that befell men. Children and the elderly were cured of illnesses that assuredly would have cost them their lives otherwise. Wizards were revered as saviors." Solarus snorted. "You witnessed the attitude of those in Thanesgard. At best, we are mistrusted and avoided. Had I not been in the company of a woman and an elf, I suspect more than one passerby would have shown his contempt by doing more than offering a strongly worded rebuke." Solarus rubbed the Z line on the side of his head. "Of course, one cannot fault men completely for their perceptions of us. Several wizards predating Malus contributed to our present ignominy. They strangled the purity of magic as they became obsessed with power. Manipulation became the exploitation of others for personal gain. Eradication became the annihilation of competition through the infliction of plagues, not the prevention of them. Creation became the wizards' conception of monsters to gain dominance over other wizards.

"We on the Wizards' High Council agreed years ago that these tenets were derelict and required amending," Solarus continued. The water rippled as the petite head of a turtle popped out. It looked around, sniffing the air. "Though it is not reflected in your book, we now refer to magic as a means to 'create, communicate, and unite.' Creation is again as it sounds. Communicate and unite is dialogue within the wizarding community to promote trust and build alliances. It was also an accord demonstrating to our neighbors that we wanted to co-inhabit Ilian, not be its masters. Through these canons, we sought to prevent unnecessary conflicts."

Kyra caught the inflection of Solarus' last phrase. "You believe some conflicts are necessary."

Solarus didn't respond right away. His eyes were on the turtle as it kicked its legs and dove back under the water, the surface barely disturbed by the movements. Silence drifted in the air until a puff from Solarus' pipe disbanded it. "Sometimes. If it will end the savage brutality of whoever imposes it. Some conflicts are unavoidable. For more than a decade, I have seen the polarization of our kin. They either supported Harkimer or defended against its future exploits. It is like a humid summer's day. The air is so thick you are drinking not breathing it in, and relief comes only when the storm breaks. The storm is inevitable even if we cannot predict precisely when it will arrive."

Kyra stretched. She switched the book to her right hand as she shifted her weight from one arm back to the other. "Am I just learning history and theory or is there something . . . practical here?"

"There are enchantments and spells in subsequent chapters. As you are refreshing your magical training, or starting anew, there is no need to visit them yet." Solarus set down his pipe and again reached into his vest pocket. He produced a black leather book. Kyra recognized it as what Solarus had often consulted during their travel. It was identical to her book, save for its weatherworn cover that had been bleached by sunlight. "I, too, refer to these pages," Solarus said as though reading her thoughts. He thumbed through the book. "These volumes were once distributed to all wizards as part of their base knowledge. Following the War of Calonia, men and elves set all books they found ablaze. They foolishly believed that would prevent wizards from ever again attempting to usurp Ilian's monarchs." Solarus set the book aside. "As though books are the sole means by which one learns one's craft. Besides, could they have uncovered all copies? Of course not. Those preserved by wizarding families have been handed down from generation to generation. The Academy of Scribes and Seers also retains copies. I believe Silvias acquired a handful. One can presume the texts were brought to Harkimer by Malus' followers as well. That means the dark wizards are privy to the same knowledge as we are."

Solarus raised a hand to halt another half-formed question on Kyra's tongue. "Read the rest of the introduction tonight. I need a respite from your curiosity. We will resume our discussion tomorrow." Solarus again picked up his pipe. "Now to return to the question of more 'practical' applications of magic as it were." He used it to gesture toward the lake's calm waters, a slim smile on his face. "Let us find out if you remember any."

Chapter 24

Adakis huffed and grumbled to himself. He pulled on his goatee as though trying to strangle it. The goatee, as pointed as an icepick, didn't yield a single hair. The woods around Adakis whirred with a loud, nightly chorus of insects and the flapping of bats among the trees. Moonlight leaked through holes in the inky black clouds overhead. Adakis squinted at the ground as a bush rustled. A fat form lumbered out in front of him. Its long quills swayed. It snorted, then ambled back into the trees. Adakis caught the sounds of rodents foraging, but it was too dark to see them in the forest litter.

Adakis released his goatee. He chanced a look at the wizard standing silently beside a large oak tree. The moonlight dribbled on Diamantas' slicked-back gray hair and trickled over the planes of his face. His bright, almost otherworldly blue eyes shone like gems in a mine. The wizard gazed off at some unknown point, occasionally rapping the obsidian staff on the ground. Diamantas hadn't spoken since Adakis finished with his report.

Adakis brooded as his unease grew. Why was *he*, Adakis, there, having to explain the failure of others? He knew, of course. Adakis had the right to be insulted by the turn of events. Diamantas certainly hadn't applauded his efforts. Why would he? Diamantas didn't understand what Adakis had to put up with. As though any of this had been *his* fault.

There were so many reasons why it hadn't gone right. Reasons beyond his control. Hayden and Solarus accompanied Kyra. She had made use of her magic which, even Diamantas presumed, had been long forgotten. The dark wizards tasked to help Adakis capture the brat were the dregs of Harkimer. Inept. Bungling. Useless. He had been given *Janus* of all wizards! Why Janus? Why any of them?

Galakis coughed. Adakis had forgotten he wasn't alone with Diamantas. Galakis had pointed out Adakis needed a wizard to accompany him when Adakis went to deliver his report. In the event Adakis was ambushed, Galakis had reasoned. Adakis hmphed at the thought. The other wizards' skills paled in comparison to his own. Like he would need *their* help. But Galakis was right about the Forgotten Forest. It was foolhardy to travel near that vile place alone. Not with the ghosts and horrors within. Diamantas himself wouldn't begrudge an ally there.

In the same breath, Galakis noted that Diamantas would be more forgiving of Adakis, as their leader, if another wizard was there to attest to the hardships they had faced. This seemed reasonable to Adakis. Nymphrys came across as, untrue as it was, a more powerful wizard than he. That wouldn't do. Janus was too anxious to be of any use. Orkanis was insufferable. The three would only contribute to their dilemma. The dilemma being the fiasco leading to Kyra's escape. In Adakis' opinion, Galakis was the best choice, if a choice needed to be made.

Adakis acquiesced.

Now he awaited Diamantas' response. Adakis was too busy silently berating his companions to notice that Diamantas' shrewd gaze was on him.

"Where are Janus, Orkanis, and Nymphrys?" Diamantas' tone was deceptively conversational, like an interrogator's friendly offer of a meal to a prisoner before the torturous questioning began.

"I sent Orkanis onward to the next rendezvous point and ordered him to wait for further instructions. Janus and Nymphrys returned to the Southern Mountains. I make the best decisions, Diamantas, you know I do. I decided in this instance you needed someone on the field preparing for the upcoming battle. That was Orkanis' job. There wasn't any reason to send Janus and Nymphrys yet."

The account complete, Diamantas' gaze fluttered over Adakis' shoulder to Galakis. Not for the first time in his meeting with Diamantas, Adakis squirmed. Did the dark wizard suspect it had been Galakis' suggestion, not Adakis', that Orkanis proceed to the camp while Janus and Nymphrys rest before the next encounter? Did Diamantas think less of Adakis for not having come up with the solution himself?

"I would have gone to Tetris myself had it not been an unforgivable error for someone else to report to you," Adakis put in as a gulf of silence extended between them. "It is a known fact that I have one of the best memories in Harkimer. You needed the most reliable account of events which, naturally, meant I was to come to you and not to Tetris."

Diamantas regarded his obsidian staff, twisting it in his hand. Then he tapped it twice on the ground. "I thank you for your consideration and judgment," he said calmly. The thin sarcasm on the word "judgment" was lost on Adakis, who beamed at Diamantas' false praise. "However, I am displeased—" Diamantas rapped the staff on the ground two more times, "—that you were unable to keep Kyra in your custody. Her escorts are made of flesh and blood. If they were a hindrance, you should have removed them."

Adakis opened his mouth to provide a rebuttal. Diamantas bulldozed through his unspoken words. "I also discovered that you, with a rash display of magic, undermined the carefully—" Diamantas struck the ground once, "—crafted—" he struck it again, "—image that is requisite for maintaining allies or, at the very least, neutrality with men in Ilian."

Adakis' cheeks flushed scarlet, though the color was masked in the darkness. "We would have captured Kyra if we had more resources. That captain of Arkin's Royal Guards sided with them, and then . . ."

"You are quick to justify your ignominious failures, Adakis," Diamantas cut in, this time wearing his vexation openly. "I wish your tongue more readily found recommendations for success."

"I was merely explaining the circumstances in which we found ourselves," Adakis protested. He pulled on his beard. "Janus shouldn't have been party to the attack. He was a liability. If I did not have to repeatedly compensate for his mistakes . . ."

"You are entering dangerous waters, Adakis." Diamantas' tone was so cold it would have made a glacier would shiver. "Janus is my nephew. Filial loyalty is everlasting; any other form can be bought given the right incentives. If you speak ill of Janus, your responsibilities in the future will be to replace the straw in your mattress and empty the chamber pot in your cell."

Adakis released his beard and licked his dry lips. "I'm certainly grateful for Janus' company. Your faith in me to teach him as my . . . protégé is well placed."

Galakis coughed again.

"Were we to have more wizards to deal with that waif," Adakis forged on, "we would without question . . ."

"Find yourself in an equally fruitless position as you are now." Diamantas tilted his staff to the front. Beneath the gnarled stone that curved around the staff's tip, a white light began to shimmer and pulse. The staff's energy intensified. Diamantas pointed it toward the clouds and muttered under his breath. The white light shot from the staff's tip and into the night sky. The storm clouds parted. Moonlight spilled into the forest and onto the forms of the three wizards.

"More wizards do not compensate for a poor strategy," Diamantas said, lowering his staff. "Do you remember the tenets of magic, Adakis? First, create." Diamantas touched the staff's glowing white tip to the bark of the oak tree. Silver snakes instantly appeared and spooled around the trunk. "Second, manipulate." He moved the staff. The snakes obediently wriggled to the ground. The forest grew still. The rustling in the underbrush disappeared as rodents fled the presence of the magically spun predators.

Adakis' eyes widened, consternation splaying across his face. He took a tentative step back as the snakes slithered toward him.

"Third, eradicate." Diamantas mercilessly gored the largest snake with the end of his staff. The silver creatures exploded into smoke and drifted into the air. With a flare, the white light of the obsidian staff whooshed out of existence. The troop of clouds again laid siege to the moon and stars, and the woods descended into darkness.

Adakis' maladroit handling of the situation has cost me valuable time, Diamantas thought, a line of revulsion on his lips. He sighed. Arrogant as he was, Adakis would do whatever Diamantas commanded of him. It took years to nurture that kind of unquestioning devotion. Maintaining it now demanded patience.

"Fortunately, this incident is a minor setback." Diamantas assumed the same, unconcerned tone he had at the beginning of their conversation. "We have also learned from it. In sending five wizards for this task, I displayed shortsightedness. Not because my earlier observations were incorrect. Your methods were lacking. However, I should have sent seven wizards for this task. It is the divine number. Inishmore would have granted us its blessings." Diamantas paused and looked down. Rodents again rummaged near the trees, convinced the silver snakes were gone. "I am imparting to you the knowledge I have gained through my own shortcomings, Adakis," he said, lifting his gaze. "I believe you can become more capable. If I did not, would I spend a single breath correcting you? Teaching you?"

Adakis mentally turned over Diamantas' words. Haughtiness flew into his expression. "No. I am your most loyal servant, Diamantas. There is no one on whom better to bestow your wisdom than me . . . and Janus," Adakis inserted. He was smugly convinced he had said the right thing. "Naturally, you would waste your time on anyone else."

An aggrieved breath came from behind Adakis. Adakis stiffened. Until he reminded himself, what did he care what Galakis thought?

As Adakis turned to smirk at his companion, Diamantas forced back his own irritation. "Create, manipulate, eradicate," he repeated. Diamantas put a hand on the tree where the silver had first appeared. "These are the bedrock principles of magic. They are easy to recite, yet only wizards with discernment know which is appropriate for a given situation. It is often neither prudent nor effectual to use more than one at once."

Diamantas' piercing gaze bypassed Adakis' and settled on Galakis. In the darkness, Diamantas could make out the wizard's thin form and the untamed hair beneath his cloak's cowl. Not his expression. Galakis was uncommonly levelheaded and exceedingly competent. He was neither arrogant nor ambitious. Galakis had never voiced regrets about the past or aspirations for the future. He seemed to live entirely in the present. Diamantas, who had long studied the motivations of his fellow wizards, was impressed by Galakis' steadfast mindset. He was also discomfited by it. Galakis remained an enigmatic personality, and Diamantas wasn't keen on wizards he couldn't manipulate.

"Galakis understands these principles," Diamantas stated. "He has this discernment. Come forward, Galakis."

Galakis obeyed, face concealed by his cowl.

"Do you not have this discernment, Galakis?"

"If you say it to be true, then it is true, Diamantas," Galakis responded from under his cowl. "Whatever judgment I possess is attributed to years of observing your leadership. I seek only to liberate our brethren as you do."

Unlike with Adakis, there were no traces of obsequiousness in Galakis' voice. Diamantas nodded. Adakis rubbed his ear, his mouth scrunched like a sulking child.

Diamantas turned so that neither wizard could see his expression. He turned over Adakis' account once more in his mind. Kyra's escape was unfortunate news. That Reapers patrolled the lands was unsettling. *How did they cross into Ilian?* he pondered. Diamantas' countenance was unreadable as Adakis described seeing the creatures in Edoin. *Four Reapers, one over two meters in height, unusually large even by their own standards . . .* Diamantas was certain he knew the existence of every entrance to and egress from the Mountains. Could he have overlooked one? Had the Reapers broken free of the Mountains unbeknownst to him? The latter question was inconceivable. Diamantas had magic strung like spiderwebs at every exit. When someone or something left the Mountains, Diamantas was alerted to its departure through reverberations in the obsidian staff. No wizard could have unleashed the Reapers, save him. The only conclusion was the former. Diamantas frowned. He conceded that everyone, himself included, had a deficiency. At least his imperfections, unlike Adakis', were easily repaired.

Diamantas ran a finger down the smooth stone of the obsidian. *It* was perfection. "Truly a weapon of unequaled power," he declared softly, speaking to the staff and not Adakis and Galakis. "A wooden staff containing spells stored from generations of wizards is to this obsidian as an eaglet to its parent: vulnerable and inferior. This staff represents Harkimer's hope. If the spirit of Malus has, after seven hundred and seventy-seven years, bestowed on us such a powerful gift, we are deserving of Ilian's land." Diamantas had a peculiar smile on his face. "Galakis."

"Yes, Diamantas?"

"You believe Kyra has no memory of these lands?"

"She did not recognize us at Edoin. She wasn't confident in her magic."

Adakis tried to catch Galakis' eye. Galakis stared straight ahead, emphatically ignoring his companion.

"My conversation with Kyra was cut short when we last spoke." Diamantas tapped the ground, counting to seven. "It is time she learns of her importance to wizard kind. A true champion of Harkimer." Diamantas' cloak swept the ground as he faced the forest. "Galakis, you and Adakis ride due north and wait for me at the edge of the Wizards' High Council."

Galakis' brow furrowed in puzzlement. This time, he glanced back at Adakis. Adakis wore an incurious look, scratching an oversized ear and nodding even though Diamantas, with his back turned, couldn't see him.

"When shall we expect you to meet us?" Galakis asked.

Diamantas put his free hand in his pocket and withdrew a silver coin. The etchings on the surface glinted in slivers of moonlight. He rubbed it between his thumb and forefinger. "Not more than two days, I expect. Do not leave the river before I return unless Kyra herself is crossing."

No other questions were asked as the heptagon coin began to glow.

Chapter 25

Kyra waded into the lake until she was waist deep. The water was pleasantly warm, with a mushy silt bottom that squished beneath her feet. She looked down. Minnows darted through clusters of seaweed-like plants. There were no stones or shells, nor did the waters release the stench of fish and plants that Kyra remembered from her runs past the Serpentine in London. She splashed water on her face, hot from the sun. Refreshed, Kyra turned around so she faced the bank.

"We will start with elementary forms of magic," Solarus told Kyra as she swished her arms through the water. "You studied these already. Still, we will reconstruct your magical foundation as though it never existed. Your previous knowledge is of service to us if your memory returns." Solarus scratched his beard, blue eyes bright and cavernous. "Today's second lesson: if you can perform a spell in water, you can perform it out of water. Obviously, you will not have a lake at your disposal when you face the dark wizards. However, water and air are both part of Inishmore. Energy moves in currents through them. The reason we will train in water is because it is easier to see your magic.

"Magic manifests differently in each wizard," he continued. "Mine, in its purest form, is turquoise in color. Yours appears to be gold. If you are performing the spells properly, you will see this same gold within the water. You can also perceive if, during your casting, you inadvertently unloose an uncontrolled and dangerous form of energy."

There was that edge in Solarus' voice again. Uncontrolled and dangerous. Kyra's stomach churned. She felt the rebelliousness in the magic when it went red. Had this always been part of Solarus' lecture? Or did he mention this specifically for her? Kyra's thoughts cartwheeled back to her possible origins in Harkimer. That could easily explain Solarus' comment.

"Is it normal for wizards to accidentally create 'dangerous energy?'" Kyra questioned as casually as she could. She kept her gaze focused on the fish zipping around her.

"Yes and no." Solarus' tone was more vexed than suspicious. "You should pay more attention to my words. You will make half as much progress if we are perpetually reviewing that which I have already explained. In the Forgotten Forest, I elucidated that wizards are susceptible to stronger emotions than others. It is because we channel energy externally *and* amass it internally and through our staffs. This concentration of energy intensifies our emotions. Apprentices experimenting with their abilities can stumble into dark magic because they lack discipline and experience. As we discussed with your magic pulling you to other sources. Remember what I said then: magic attracts magic." Solarus steepled his hands. "We will begin with the simplest summoning. Close your eyes. Focus on any tension in your body. Feel the rigidity in your feet, the tightness in your legs and arms, and the stiffness in your back and neck. Feel how these together lock your body."

Kyra didn't understand how recalling a state of paralysis would be helpful. She complied anyway. Kyra felt the water encompassing her, and she heard the cheeping of birds overhead. She waited for the next instruction. She was met by silence. Kyra forced herself to keep her eyes shut.

"Good," Solarus' voice came finally. "Next, you will rid yourself of this tension. Inhale deeply. When you exhale, let your breath be the freeing force that loosens your feet, your legs, your arms, your back, and your neck. Release the tension. Tightness in the body constricts magic just as shackles constrain the body's movement. Body and mind must be relaxed. Be alert and agile."

Kyra breathed in deeply. She creaked her neck and rolled her shoulders forward and back. Then she exhaled, trying to pull the air through her aching limbs. Her muscles loosened. She repeated her breaths. *Body loose. Mind relaxed.*

"Now we will call upon your energy as you did in the dungeon. Picture the gold in your mind's eye. Picture it as a drop of ink in your heart. That ink spreads as though on wet paper, flowing in every direction and through every limb. Just as your body was eased by the freeing of tension, so is your mind uncaged by the discharge of energy within you. You are in control of the gold, however. It spreads because you direct it to. Bring some of the gold to your core."

On the blank canvas of her mind came a blot of gold. Kyra mentally tried to force the splatter she envisioned into an orb that she could transport. The gold mulishly resisted. It was like trying to pull and push on a door at the same time. Kyra's lips pressed together in frustration. How was she supposed to pin down the energy and let it spider off at the same time?

"The gold trickles into your wrists, then your hands, out your fingertips, and into the water. Your internal energy binds to the energy of the lake."

Giving up trying to find her core, Kyra moved her hands through the water as though she were an orchestra conductor. The magic was her music. Responding to the rhythm, the gold tickled her fingers. It was a pleasant feeling, like bubbles popping against her skin. A welcome change from the prickling and itching Kyra usually experienced when her magic appeared. If the tickling was, in fact, the golden energy. Kyra tentatively opened her eyes. Her face broke into a euphoric grin. The golden glow had streamed into the water. It swayed gently, even as it remained tethered to her hands.

"Pull the energy into arcs," Solarus commanded. As Kyra looked to the bank, she saw him make a wide, sweeping crescent with his hand, palm down. "Hold firmly onto the energy throughout the motions. If you do not, your connection with the gold will break."

Kyra copycatted Solarus' movements. The streams of gold undulated beneath her fingertips without following the arcs she created. Kyra repeated the motion, feeling the weightlessness of her arms as she swung them. The gold energy seized. The abruptness surprised Kyra. She held firm. The gold twisted and bent around itself. Kyra watched, bewildered, as it finally produced a chain of diamond shapes on the lake's floor. Kyra glanced back at Solarus. His eyes gleamed with satisfaction.

"Release the magic and do it again," he ordered. Kyra obeyed. Dispelling the magic was easier than drawing it into the water. Her second attempt at creating the arcs was clumsy; her third flowed more naturally. After a few more attempts, Solarus instructed her to expand the arcs.

Kyra summoned the magic with gusto and snapped her hands to the side. The gesture was so forceful that her hands broke through the lake's surface. The golden magic, tethered to her hands, whipped into the air in a graceful curve. As did the wave of water surrounding it.

The wave doused Solarus with a loud splash. Kyra failed to suppress a giggle as the wizard blinked. Water dripped from his hair and down his goatee and soaked his impeccable clothing. Solarus' sour countenance reminded Kyra of a cat caught in a rainstorm. Maybe like Fifi, she thought.

Solarus' mouth was pressed into a vexed line. "*Is-ter-AH-ha*," he said dryly. Steam rose from his clothes and his hair as the water evaporated. Solarus' eyes narrowed as Kyra collected herself. "Less zeal. More concentration."

Kyra nodded as solemnly as she could. The image of a drenched Fifi capered in her mind. "I'll try to dampen my enthusiasm," she replied. Kyra coughed and looked down at the water with a grin. Solarus glowered at her.

They labored straight through the morning. When Kyra's arms became lethargic and her motions sloppy, Solarus intervened. "That is enough for one day," he announced. "We are fortunate that your skills have not completely diminished. That will save us time."

Kyra pushed through the water with effort and plopped on the bank next to Solarus. Her cheeks and nose stung of sunburn. Blessedly, a gentle breeze alleviated the early afternoon heat. Bending over, Kyra brushed silt from between her toes, listening to the cheerful tweets and chirps of birds flying over the lake.

Solarus handed Kyra a waterskin. "It will take time to regain your strength," Solarus told Kyra as she slaked her thirst. "Developing magic is akin to rehabilitating an atrophied muscle. You will tire easily at first since you are not accustomed to using it. However, a muscle strengthens with work. The more you practice magic, the longer you will be able to perform it."

Kyra's stomach growled crankily. A smile crept onto Solarus' face as Kyra rubbed her side. "You look ready to snatch fish from the lake and eat them raw. You should have a properly cooked meal. You cannot afford to waste days in the healer's hall on the account of a fickle stomach."

Grinning, Kyra scooped up her boots and cloak in one hand and her staff in the other. There was a loud honking behind her as she stood. Kyra glanced over her shoulder to see the swan couple flapping their large white wings and taking to the cloudless sky. She watched as they flew overhead. Kyra's gaze followed the swan's flight over the crest of the hill. Her eyes widened. Standing just beyond the fringe of the woods was a figure.

What is Hayden doing here? Even at a distance, Kyra could tell it was him. Hayden's leg was on a rock, knee bent, gray eyes intent as he twisted his ring. Kyra thought she could make out a disquieted expression.

Hayden hadn't mentioned he would be watching the session. And he hadn't said a word of greeting or acknowledgment. That didn't seem like him.

Kyra turned quizzically to Solarus. He was dispersing remnants of golden magic in the lake and didn't seem to notice Hayden on the hill. Biting her lip, Kyra's gaze wandered upward.

Hayden had disappeared. Troubled, Kyra didn't say anything to Solarus as he stood, gripping his staff and stretching. She hiked up the hill beside him. Her fatigue and hunger shoved aside any further musings over Hayden's secretive observation.

***

Solarus left Kyra at the palace entrance. He had errands to attend to, the wizard explained. As Kyra made her way toward the dining hall, her thoughts strayed to who might be waiting for her. By now, Kyra's childhood friends would have heard she returned. They had to have a midday break for lunch. Were they gathered in the hall at that very moment to surprise her? To tell her how worried they had been about her? How excited they were to see her again? The more Kyra considered the idea, the more her heart danced with elated anticipation. Of course they were! Solarus' "errands" must have been an excuse for Kyra to reunite with them in private. It was oddly considerate of the wizard. Kyra rushed through the doors with a wide grin.

To find an empty hall.

Kyra's face fell, crestfallen. She looked left, then right. The only elves in the room were the attendants perfunctorily going about their day's work. Kyra's heart's merry jig faded into a forlorn dirge. *My first day back at "home," and I'm by myself,* Kyra thought. She miserably plunked into a chair at the table. An elven attendant brought her a plate of fruit, greens, and thinly sliced cheese with bread. Kyra ate mechanically. Her appetite was as absent as the homecoming she had envisioned.

"Talis requested you join him in the *Edenia fel Sirinith*," the elven attendant said as she collected Kyra's half-finished plate. Seeing Kyra's confused expression, the attendant clarified kindly, "The *Edenia fel Sirinith*, My Lady. The Garden of Sight. It is on the east side of the palace."

"Thank you," Kyra replied numbly. The attendant dipped her head in response and glided off. Kyra rose, anxious to be gone from the hall.

Kyra stepped outside, her eyes sweeping the grounds for the garden the attendant mentioned. The palace looked like a sentient being as sunlight played on its surface. The colorful glass curved and pirouetted like a troupe of lissome dancers caught in an endless performance. A breeze rustled the thick waves of grasses and flowers in the courtyard shook the silver green leaves of the machi trees. The leaves chimed melodically as they brushed against each other. The trees' balsam perfumed the air.

Kyra scratched her head. She could see smaller courtyards on both sides of the palace. Which was the Garden of Sight? Had she visited it as a child? Unlike the leaves, the name didn't ring a bell. "Is the Garden of Sight on the other side of the palace?" she mused aloud.

The grass beneath her feet shimmered. Startled, Kyra stepped backward as a lime green light appeared. It rippled and rolled out before her, creating a long green lane. Kyra peered at it curiously. It was the same path that Solarus and she had followed to the hills. "Where did you come from?" Kyra murmured.

Magic tugged gently and insistently at Kyra's hands as though willing her to follow. She darted a look around to confirm it wasn't Solarus or another elf who had created the path. Kyra was alone. She looked down to the green lane. It almost seemed to beckon to her as it undulated under her feet.

"Okaaaaay," Kyra drew out the word. "I guess there's nothing to lose by following you, is there?" She shook her head with a slight laugh as she started walking. "I'm talking to the grass. And I wonder why no one has come to see me yet."

Kyra was soon grateful for her green escort. It ushered her around the courtyard of the eastern tower. There Kyra came upon dozens of courtyards woven together in a labyrinth of trees and flowering bushes. Some were made of wood, others of glass—or, as Kyra supposed, *zylith*. Many courtyards had arches with climbing vines and flowers draped along the sides. Each courtyard also had a distinct architecture. Somewhere in the corner of her mind, Kyra remembered being told the architectures were representative of the time periods in which they were built. She didn't know which courtyards were the oldest. She found them equally stunning.

Kyra paused in front of a courtyard with garnet and gold-colored walls. Its delicate curves and points looked like thousands of autumn leaves had been carved from the glass. "Is it this one?" Kyra asked herself. She stepped off the shimmering ground to look more closely at the openings. The path didn't follow. Instead, it recoiled strongly. Kyra placed her foot back on the green light. The undercurrent of magic loosened. "I get it, that means no," Kyra told the path. "Where else then?"

The path piloted Kyra past two more courtyards. It finally stopped at a wall that had two oval openings like a giant hawk's eyes and a trellis in the center. A rich fragrance of lilies wafted through the opening, and the sound of water trickling gently tickled her ears. Curious, Kyra walked through the trellis and into a square courtyard. She grinned. The courtyard was framed by a waist-high wall of glittering moonstones. Long vines with tiny bell-like red and yellow flowers curtained more trellises within. Three enormous machi trees formed a triangle, with one at each of the three walls.

Kyra's eyes rested on a two-tiered circular fountain. It was carved from the same sparkling, white-blue gems as the wall and the stones that ringed the ground around it. A statue of an elven woman stood atop the highest tier in the center. Water flowed over her tall boots and fell into the larger circle below. She held a sword in her left hand. Her right hand was open and empty, palm raised to the sky. The elven warrior wore a circlet with a single gem and a necklace braided in a Celtic-like pattern. Her supple robes billowed around her as though frozen in a storm. Her timeless gaze was focused on the horizon.

Sitting on the edge of the fountain was Talis. His bow lay across one leg. The elf's amber eyes followed his hand as he ran a rough cloth against the wood, reworking it into a smooth curve.

Its job complete, the magical path released Kyra to the courtyard. She looked down. The green blinked into the sunlight and vanished. When she raised her gaze, Kyra saw that Talis had stopped his work on his bow. He smiled quietly at her. Kyra returned his grin. The white-blue stones crunched under her boots as she walked to the fountain. Its pristine waters burbled merrily. Kyra's gaze roamed up again to the statue of the warrior elf.

Talis glanced over his shoulder. "*Raenalyn* Imineral," he answered Kyra's unspoken question. He moved over as Kyra sat beside him. "She was Silvias' queen a millennium ago and one of the finest elven warriors of our history. *Raenalyn* Imineral led the elven army against wizards who sought to desolate our lands and destroy our people. The wizards quickly learned their wager was a poor one."

"Hayden found a book with her writings in Farcaren," Kyra recalled. She turned and reached out a hand, letting the fountain's cool water stream over her fingers.

"*Raenalyn* Imineral was a dedicated scholar," Talis replied with a nod. "She founded Silvias' library. She sent healers on expeditions to other kingdoms to study other medicines and practices. And she established the network of elven scouts. *Raenalyn* Imineral also negotiated a treaty with the *Al-Ethran*—the animal kingdom's Council of Elders—so that their scouts and ours would support each other. *Raenalyn* Carina is her direct descendant." Talis set the cloth aside. "How was your lesson?"

Kyra lowered her hand and leaned on the edge of the fountain. Her thoughts returned to the bitter disappointment of her lonely meal. "It was . . . very good," she replied feebly. "Solarus seemed happy with it." When Talis nodded, Kyra added in a tone she hoped was offhand, "I, um, didn't see anyone in the dining hall."

"Ash and Jyls went with one of the *Ethernyle*—the elven healers—to examine the Sadyran tree," Talis answered. "Hayden is tending to his own matters. And, as you have already discovered, I am here," he teased.

"Oh, right, Ash and Jyls and Hayden," Kyra answered awkwardly. She tucked a lock of hair behind her ear. "Them too. I meant I haven't run into any other elves yet. The elves my age. My classmates, from before I disappeared." *And friends, if I had any.* A new theory took hold. What if the elves did remember Kyra? What if it was *because* they knew who Kyra was that they steered clear? Was her memory of the hunter game a fantasy born of her desperate desire for friends?

Talis gave her a reassuring grin. "Hayden and I suspected you would want to reunite with your course mates. While he and I are respectful company, we can't replace confidants your own age. That's why I wished to see you."

Kyra tried not to look too eager as she leaned forward. Talis understood after all.

"Your friends haven't finished with their work for the day. I thought we could use the time to reacquaint you with the Realm itself." Talis took the cloth and folded it. "It's difficult to resume a life you cannot remember."

Kyra spirits lifted. "I'd love that."

Talis pocketed the cloth and rose, slinging the bow over his shoulder. He and Kyra exited the courtyard. Oddly, no path materialized to guide their steps. *The path forms when someone doesn't know the way,* Kyra realized. Talis had a destination in mind, so the magical green lane wasn't needed.

"Can you tell me more about the apprenticeships?" Kyra asked as Talis strode away from the palace with long, relaxed steps.

"Elves end their general studies on their sixteenth birthday," Talis explained as they passed a huddle of female elves in glimmering jade-colored dresses. They walked as soundlessly as deer through a meadow.

"Afterward they begin their apprenticeships," Talis continued. "The first apprenticeship they undertake does not always become the one in which they serve. The craftsman must choose the apprentice as much as the apprentice chooses the craftsman and profession. It is a lock that requires a specific key."

"Unless you can open the lock without the key," Kyra said, thinking of Jyls and his abilities in the dungeon. "Then you have something that isn't supposed to fit and does."

Talis laughed appreciatively. "Elves and men differ on that point. Once apprentices and their mentors are matched, the apprentices spend four years in training. What happens afterward depends on one's profession. Apprentices to craftsmen can retain positions with their mentors and continue to work together. Apprentices may also open their own shop. Those who become scouts are assigned to any kingdom the *Raenalyn* or *Veralyn* deems necessary. Others join the service directly supporting the palace, such as the *Equinyle*, or groomsmen. They are charged with caring for the royal horses within Silvias."

As Talis spoke, spun glass shops budded around them. They possessed the same aesthetic elegance as the palace. Laughter rang through an open window of one shop. Kyra peeked inside. Elven craftswomen sat around a long table, meticulously crimping the edges of a thin sheet of gold.

Talis paused beside Kyra. "These are the shops of the *Firth* and *Finna.*" He nodded to the craftswomen. "That shop is owned by *Finna* Ewewil, our *Gelinyle.* The goldsmith. Her apprentice was an elf two years' your senior."

A group of three elves stepped out of the shop and descended the stairs. Unlike the other elves Kyra had seen, these wore short-sleeved tunics. The female elf had an egg-white complexion. Large, golden earrings with feathers dangled from her ears. The male elves both had a beige hue. The arm of the shorter elf was tattooed in a golden pattern that ranged from his shoulder down to his wrist. The elves noticed Talis at the same time Talis saw them. Talis suddenly stiffened. Kyra frowned, puzzled. The female's lips twisted into a derisive look. The tattooed elf had an equally contemptuous expression. The third elf's nose wrinkled. He sneezed loudly and rubbed his nose.

Talis placed his hand over his heart. "*Aliori*, warriors of the South." Talis' tone was respectful, but his amber eyes flashed with disdain. Confused, Kyra copied Talis' gesture. The tattooed elf's eyes skipped over Talis to her. He barely shifted his hand as he replied coldly, "*Aliori*, Talis." The other two elves didn't reciprocate the sign of welcome.

What's going on? Kyra glanced from the group to Talis and back. The elves departed without another word. Talis' face housed uncharacteristic resentment. When the trio was far up the road, he relaxed, marginally. Without speaking, Talis continued forward.

"Who were they?" Kyra asked, falling in step with her friend.

"No one of consequence."

Talis' brusque response deterred Kyra from pressing him further. She switched to what she assumed was a safer topic. "I was meaning to ask you about some of the elven words. *Raenalyn* means queen. I'm guessing *Safirthelyn* is the word for 'lord' and *Safinnalyn* is used for 'lady.'"

Talis affirmed her hunch with a nod.

"What about *Jaelyn*? And *Firth* and *Finna*? Queen Carina used the titles for Jyls and me and not Solarus or Ash."

Talis turned left, steering Kyra between two buildings with mushroom-capped roofs. "*Jaelyn* means 'captain.' As a rule, titles for nobility, whether blooded or bestowed, end in *-lyn*. This is the same for our word for 'king.' You've already heard this when we were discussing *Veralyn* Ellynirith, the first king of Silvias.

"As for *Firth* and *Finna*, there is no direct translation for the language of men," Talis continued as he circumvented a row of shops. "They are honorifics given to elves who have achieved mastery of some craft. They are also generally given to non-elven guests. Without knowing the background of the individuals, it's courteous to presume they are skilled in some occupation. We refer to vocations with the suffix *-nyle*. Hence the scouts are *Sirenyle* and the goldsmiths *Gelinyle*. Ash is a healer and therefore is called by his title, *Ethernyle*."

"Wizards don't own a title?"

Talis shook his head. More sets of open windows and the sounds of conversations within piqued Kyra's curiosity. Were her peers inside? Uncertainty again bloomed in her stomach as she revisited the idea the elves were *choosing* not to visit. Kyra hurried past the windows, not daring to find out. "Where did you apprentice?" she asked Talis, trying to shake her anxiety. "What's your profession in Silvias? Other than having to chaperone clueless teenage wizards," she joked.

The elf brushed his long braid from his face. "I was trained as a *Litthrinyle*. A *Litthrinyle* studies the art of weaving and braiding knots and patterns. For example, a *Litthrinyle* fashions chain mail for the scouts. They can also weave nets and litters, often from whatever materials present themselves in a forest or other environment. The best *Litthrinyle* secure equipment with knots that can't be undone expect through the cut of a blade."

"Did we already pass the shop you worked in? Is your mentor there?"

"No, and no." Talis put a hand on the string of his bow and readjusted it on his back. "I apprenticed in the south, the domain administrated by Lord Orison." Talis' amber eyes darkened, like dusk turning to night. Kyra again was puzzled by her friend's sudden shift in mood. It was the same as when *Raenalyn* Carina had introduced Orison. "My mentor was the most renowned *Litthrinyle* in the Realm. I was humbled by her knowledge and skill. Unfortunately, she passed onto the Healer some years back."

"I'm sorry." Kyra paused, then asked, "Did you apprentice with her because she lived in the South? Rather than here?"

"My family hails from the South. My mother was close friends with my mentor, and I grew up with an appreciation for the craft. Had my mentor been here in the capital, I would have petitioned to join her."

"Have I been to the South?"

"No. You stayed at and around the palace."

A pinkish-purple structure shaped like a vase stretched upward. Smoke curled upward from the top, though Kyra couldn't see a chimney. "How do you know which building is which? I haven't seen any signs."

Talis laughed. "The shops haven't changed location since the founding of Silvias. Craftswomen and craftsmen come and go; the shops don't. Those that are independently established by newly graduated apprentices are easily spotted because they are exceptions. We don't have a need for signs."

"Solarus told me wizards are nomadic," Kyra commented thoughtfully. "I wonder if they specialize in anything. I'm sure they make the azure cloaks themselves. The fabric is different from any other clothes I've worn, like there's magic woven into them. Then there are the books about magic and their staffs obviously. I don't know if wizards have anything culturally or historically unique to them. Like paintings or jewelry. Although," she put in, remembering Hayden and her discussion in Thanesgard's marketplace, "I know there are wizard kaemin mages."

"Wizards do fashion magical items like those you mentioned," Talis answered with an equally contemplative expression. "We don't know if each wizard specializes in an object or whether they have enough general training to create whatever is required. Solarus once told me wizards also have apprentices. It seems reasonable that if they don't have frequent contact with one another, wizards would equip their mentees with the skills to make many things. That is, excluding that which they can buy, such as tack for their steeds."

Kyra turned this over in her mind. What was a wizard's purpose then? In London, life had been straightforward, with a tidy timeline defined by social expectations: finish school at seventeen, attend university at eighteen, graduate, and start working. It was an uncomplicated, prearranged plan. In Ilian, elves and men seemed to have similar paths. Not wizards. Kyra sighed. It would help to have a goal. Fleeing dark wizards in an endless game of cat and mouse wasn't a satisfying life pursuit.

The grass blended into two shimmering white lanes. The lanes brought them to a maze of bushes. Even before they entered, the air was infused with a pleasant aroma of jasmine.

Talis led her through the bushes. Kyra's jaw dropped. She unconsciously slowed her pace, wanting to see everything at once. A rainbow of flowers flowed around glass statues of elves and animals, machi trees, and pools of water with a pink-colored sheen. Butterflies fluttered around the bushes, and fish zipped within the pools. Elves sat on small glass benches, making broad strokes with paint brushes on the easels before them. Their serene expressions brought a smile to Kyra's face.

Noticing Kyra's wonder, Talis shortened his stride. "This is the *Edenian fel Coralyn*. You would call them the Royal Gardens. The gardeners use elven magic to ensure the plants blossom year-round. Even when snow blankets the earth, the *Edenian fel Coralyn*'s petals are untouched and are ever cheerful."

Kyra grinned. She made a note to explore the gardens in more detail. She and Talis exited the maze and gardens and entered a large field. Slender firs divided the open grass into tidy, regular plots like a series of tennis courts. Pink and white azaleas formed a barrier between the fields and passersby. Talis stopped at the first plot. Two elves with daggers dueled against each other. Their classmates circled around the two fighters and cheered them on. The elves clashed vigorously, metal shrilly sliding against metal. The instructor, a female with sheared orange hair and warrior's garb, stood off to the side. Her dark eyes critically appraised the fighters. Kyra put a hand on the azaleas and leaned over for a closer look.

"These are the training grounds," Talis explained. "There are many, and they stretch far beyond what you can see. This one is reserved for closed-fist combat, which incorporates any weapon one utilizes on the ground. Students can use daggers, like you see here, or swords."

Kyra leafed through her mind for a recollection of the place. As usual, she drew up blank sheaves. Kyra and Talis watched the elves a moment longer until the instructor stepped forward to halt the fight. She took the dagger from the taller of the two elves and demonstrated a defensive technique. Talis motioned to Kyra with a nod of his head, indicating for them to move on. They left the field together, Kyra eager to see more.

The next two fields also showcased students training with weapons. The first group had staffs. The second group wielded curved blades the size of short swords. The weapons reminded Kyra of farmer's scythes. The students held one of these weapons in each hand. As they moved to the third field, Kyra's pulse inexplicably quickened. The palpable anxiety built within her as she and Talis came to a wide swath of land with bales of hay spaced evenly apart from each other. Kyra's eyes ran over the line of elves in the field. Some fit arrows to their bowstrings. Others aimed their bows at the bales of hay. Two instructors with jet-black hair, almond-shaped eyes, and porcelain-like features paced the line, hands folded behind their backs.

Kyra groaned inwardly. The archery range. A field where she had spent countless, distressingly fruitless hours trying to mimic the precision of her elven course mates. "I think a little amnesia about my past is a good thing," Kyra remarked sullenly.

Talis' lips parted into a smile. "The archery field is the one part of Silvias I know you have 'seen,' since you viewed it through my thoughts. As vexing as the experience with the bow had been, the memory here will help you recall your—"

"Humiliation? Clumsiness? Complete lack of coordination?"

Talis frowned. "I was going to say perseverance."

"Unless it was persevering in failure, then no," Kyra replied bitterly. The only seed the archery field had planted was self-doubt, that Kyra was inferior to the elves. "I've recalled are my spectacular shortcomings as a wizard."

Talis was silent as Kyra's gaze toured the students. A young elf stood in front of one of the bales. Three arrows were clustered together high in the corner. He stood on his tippy toes as he stretched his fingers toward the fletching of the closest arrow. His hand brushed the back, but he couldn't grasp it. A female elf walked beside him. Grinning down at the boy, who came up to her elbow, the female elf plucked the arrows from the hay and handed them to him.

Kyra pointed at the boy, who gleefully returned the arrows to his quiver. "That child there? He's maybe, what, seven years old, and his grouping of arrows is closer than I've probably ever managed."

The boy skipped back to the line beside a teenage elf who had an arrow nocked. Crimped, wheat-colored hair streaked with strawberry blond strands flowed down her back. The elf held the bow steady. Only the slight narrowing of the elf's eyes betrayed that she was flesh and blood and not a flawless, stone sculpture like *Raenalyn* Imineral. Kyra watched breathlessly as the female elf loosed the arrow. It hit the bullseye with a clean sound.

"She's obviously perfect," Kyra said crossly without looking at Talis. "Any one of the elves here could outshoot me no matter how many times I practiced."

The female elf with the wheat and strawberry blond hair jerked her head toward the azalea bushes. Her gaze traced over Talis, then landed on Kyra. The elf's indigo-colored eyes narrowed. It suddenly occurred to Kyra that the elf's keen ears might have overheard her comment. Kyra's face grew hot.

"You're right," she heard Talis answer ruefully. Kyra glanced sideways. Talis' expression was lined with self-incrimination, his arms folded across his chest. "I shouldn't have brought you here. We are trying to restore memories that grant you confidence, not take it away. It was poor judgment. I didn't consider the pain this could cause. Forgive me."

Talis' tormented visage swept aside Kyra's resentment. Regret and shame took its place as Kyra reprimanded herself for her self-pitying sentiments. "It's okay, Talis, I'm sorry. Really, it wasn't that bad." Kyra underscored the words with a large smile. "I'm being crabby. I'm so desperate to find a memory. It's like I'm digging through cobwebs in an empty attic. No matter how much I look, there's nothing there. It's frustrating." Kyra let out a short breath. "I thought my old friends would be knocking down my door to see me. Honestly, I was as nervous as I was excited at the thought of meeting them. They know so much about me, and I don't have a clue about what our lives were like. I don't know why I worried. None of them has plucked up the courage to say hi." Kyra tucked a lock of hair behind her ear. She listened to the sounds of arrows thwacking against the targets before admitting, "It's hard to accept no one cares or that my friends moved on. Anyway, I'm sorry, Talis. You didn't do anything wrong."

"Things will get easier with time," Talis responded. He unfolded his arms. "Until then, you must be patient."

"I've been hearing that a lot recently," Kyra muttered, rubbing her forehead. Her gaze swung back to the female elf with the streaked hair. The elf's eyes hadn't left her. Kyra's brow knitted. She had noticed the suspicious looks from the other elves. This female's expression was laden with hostility, her lips were downturned into a sneer. Talis had turned and walked away. Kyra hastened to keep pace with him, leaving the range, the elf, and her anxiety behind.

The neighboring fields were empty. Talis explained they were dedicated to students needing remedial training in a particular skill. Kyra couldn't fathom how an elf could be "remedial" in anything. At the border of the training fields was a forest of firs. Sunlight sprinkled into the woods and hung in the air like mist. Kyra and Talis negotiated a path over fallen fir needles and across a cheerful brook. The full-bodied scent of fresh pines imbued the air. Kyra smiled sadly. The fragrance evoked a melancholy nostalgia for Christmas in Millie's house. As she always did when thinking of Millie, Kyra silently hoped her aunt was happy.

In a short time, distant nickers and answering neighs floated into the forest. The woods opened like barn doors to a vast meadow littered with gold and green shoots of grass. Kyra grabbed Talis' arm elatedly. "Are these the equestrian fields?"

Talis' face eased into a smile. "Yes, and where you learned to ride." He laughed as Kyra half-dragged him behind her as she jogged closer.

Ivy, knotted and braided over itself, created a fence between Kyra and the fifteen riders and steeds facing the far end of the field. The riders sat tall, their backs to Kyra. They held spears at their sides. Therial calmly observed the riders astride his piebald mare. At the other end of the field, three tall, green poles were embedded in the ground. Colored pegs stuck out from each pole like twigs in a bird's nest. The pegs on the right side were black. The left pegs were brown.

Unlike the archers, these elves were excited, even jittery, as they jostled the spears in their hands. Two russet-colored male elves swapped cocksure grins. Another elf with eggshell-white skin and a bandaged wrist stole a look at a red-haired female elf to his right. He leaned to the side, his shoulder-length, pencil-straight black hair swaying, as he whispered something to her. The female elf giggled. The boy shifted back into his saddle. He yelped as the rider to his left elbowed him. As the elf with the bandage rubbed his side ruefully, his neighbor shook his head in disapproval. His stature was similar to the boy's, as was his pale complexion. The distinction was his ink-black hair was half-tied up in a ponytail, half draped along the sides of his face. Kyra wondered if the two were related.

Therial cleared his throat loudly. The pair of elves and the female elf immediately sat upright in their saddles. Walking his horse forward, Therial called out, "*Ithnain!*"

The students lowered their spears, holding the weapons horizontally. Therial repeated the command. The elves clapped their heels into the horses' flanks. The steeds galloped down the field. The elves lifted the spears over their heads in unison.

"*Hedranim!*" Therial's voice rang over the thundering of hooves.

Fifteen spears whistled though the air. With a succession of thumps, the spears struck the black and brown pegs. Two spears scored the poles.

"Another volley," Therial hollered. The elves reined in their steeds to a walk, removing the spears from the pegs. The red-haired female elf triumphantly pulled her spear from the center pole. The elf with the bandaged wrist extracted his spear with his good hand, which had found its mark directly above hers. The two grinned at each other. They swiveled their horses and trotted back to the line with their course mates. The boy with the bandaged wrist gave his neighbor an exaggerated smile. The other responded with a scathing look. He pulled his ponytail more tightly and brushed black strands of hair from his face.

"You and Raven gave your peers several lessons in humility," Talis commented. His hand ran over the ivy and one of its many knots. "Therial was your instructor. You had, and have still, an intuitive sense of balance and a light touch of the reins. It was more effective than the forced guidance some elves begin with. Therial always pointed to you as the paragon of a rider."

"I wouldn't consider myself naturally gifted," Kyra corrected with an uncertain look. "Most of the time I'm clinging to the reins as I flee whatever it is I'm fleeing at that moment. That's not competency. It's desperation and survival."

"Two very effective motivators." Talis removed his bow and placed it on the ground. "Aila was as eager a student. You and she competed enthusiastically in all things. In this domain, you progressed more quickly than she did. Aila refused to accept that she couldn't ride as swiftly as you. Aila consented to training at a pace appropriate to her abilities only when her back was black and blue from being unseated so often."

Warmth blanketed Kyra at the name. "You know Aila?" Kyra's gaze skimmed over the elves trotting their horses back from the opposite end of the field. It should be easy to see a magenta-blond elf.

"Of course," Talis replied. He knelt and wrapped part of the ivy vine over itself. "She was your closest friend. And she's Therial's daughter."

Kyra wasn't sure which part of Talis' statement stunned her more. She glanced over at Therial. Was that why his gauntlet was magenta? The same color as Aila's hair?

"Shortly after you disappeared, Therial requested Aila be trained as a *Sirenyle*. He had foreseen her potential in that field and not merely because he was Aila's father. It was evident that Aila was exceptional. She possessed the fortitude and judgment required of the *Sirenyle*. Any other captain would have made the same request. Aila was not yet finished with her general studies at that time. However, Therial made his case for Aila. *Raenalyn* Carina consented to exempt Aila from her remaining courses."

"I don't see her here," Kyra said as the group reformed their line. Therial walked his horse toward the nearest student and took the spear from her hand. "Is Aila on another field? Did we pass her?"

Talis delicately tied the ivy so that it plugged the previously neglected space. "Aila isn't here. She excelled in her education as a *Sirenyle*. She was sent to apprentice under a scout named Jatherin in Calonia. She has been there ever since. It's an anomaly to start as young as she did, which proves Aila's dedication and competence. She is well-deserving of the position."

Kyra's face fell. "I guess I won't see her then." She kicked a stone aside with her boot. Another dead end in the long road to remembering old friends.

Therial's voice called out. This time, his voice was accompanied by a single set of hooves. Kyra looked up. Therial's steed galloped down the field. The captain's spear was raised. Therial heaved the weapon toward the middle pole. The spear head buried itself in the center with pinpoint precision.

Talis stood. "Do you recognize Ellynor?" he asked, rearranging the small leaves so they covered the matrix of vines. "Or Wynorrel?"

"Ellynor and Wynorrel? Who are they?"

Talis inclined his head toward the students. "Wynorrel wears the bandage. Apparently, he broke his wrist when an acrobatic stunt meant to impress the female students ended in him inelegantly falling off his horse. The student to his left is Wynorrel's older brother, Ellynor. Ellynor was in your class."

Kyra curiously regarded the elf with the bandage and his brother. Ellynor was again pulling his ponytail straight. Wynorrel leaned casually in his saddle. Their horses were angled off the line so that Kyra could see their expressions.

She sighed. "No, they don't look familiar."

"I had hoped you would recognize at least one of them." Talis watched Wynorrel point to something down the field. Ellynor's thin, almond-shaped eyes narrowed. He lifted his chin as though to show he was ignoring his brother. "Wynorrel isn't in your year. You knew him through Ellynor. Wynorrel has a gift for masonry and will be under the tutelage of the *Kavrinyle*—that is, the royal architects—next year. It is owing to you that this was possible." Seeing Kyra's quizzical look, Talis elaborated, "He once crafted a statue of an Iona using stone he chipped from the Garden of Truth. As a birthday gift for you. You showed the statue to me, which is when we discovered Wynorrel's talent. His reproduction of Silvias' kaemins was remarkable. He has already contributed to the architects' work. They say he has the aptitude to be among the greatest in several generations."

"Oh." Kyra knew the single word wasn't an adequate response. Unfortunately, it was all she could utter as she stared at the two brothers.

Kyra's temple throbbed. She massaged it with her thumb, suddenly flooded with exhaustion. The Realm was supposedly a fertile ground for helping Kyra regain her past; unfortunately, her mind was as barren as a fallow field, and it might never bear any memories.

Talis untied a waterskin from his belt and handed it to her. "There is one more field I would like to show you before we return to the palace," he said. Kyra uncorked the skin and tipped it to her lips. She tasted an invigorating tang of lemon and cucumber. "It might lift your spirits."

I doubt anything with elves and weapons will lift my spirits, Kyra thought gloomily. It was more likely to push her few scraps of confidence off a cliff. She drank the skin dry as Talis took up his bow again and slung it over his back.

Talis headed back into the fir and pinewood forest. Instead of walking toward the training grounds, he changed course and took Kyra north along a wide path. Before she knew it, they had reached a circular glade. It was wide enough for a dozen people to camp comfortably. The tufted grass was shamrock green, and the soft ground yielded readily to Kyra's steps. Needle-straight pines shot upward, allowing the hot sunlight to beam down on the exposed space.

Kyra let out a breath she didn't realize she had been holding. "Where are we?" she asked Talis.

"A special area for training," Talis answered with an amused expression. "This was your favorite. You don't remember, do you? That's okay. This is where I taught you open-hand combat."

"Open-hand combat?"

"We saw closed-hand combat earlier. As the name suggests, this is the opposite. How to fight if you find yourself weaponless—and without magic, in your case. For example, when you intervened on behalf of the beleaguered Captain Callum in Thanesgard, you used skills learned in this glade. It's sufficiently ingrained in your mind and body."

Kyra nodded as she thought back to Somerset House. Hadn't she disabled Jude and Preet easily? "I was able to handle two boys when I was in the other world too," she told him excitedly.

Talis made a show of glancing around the area. "Do you want to test the extent of what you remember? Or would you rather rest? It's been a long day."

"Not for me. If *you're* too tired, we can go back."

The sly grin on Kyra's face garnered a laugh from Talis. They positioned themselves in the center of the glade. Talis removed his waterskins and set them off to the side. Kyra's eyes locked on the elf. She crouched into a defensive stance.

Talis tilted his head and motioned. "Come on then."

For the next hour, the two traded wrist locks, leg sweeps, and holds. Talis blocked one of Kyra's punches, grabbed her arm, and spun her around so that her back was to him. He used his arm to trap her. Instinctively, Kyra leaned forward, easing his grip, then pushed up with her ankles and legs. Talis was forced to let go as she flipped backward over the elf, landing in a crouch. She swept her leg at Talis' feet. The elf agilely jumped into the air and rolled on the ground. Talis rose without breaking the fluidity of his movement. He and Kyra stood simultaneously, hands in front of them.

Talis' eyes shone with pride. "Not bad for your first practice in Silvias."

Kyra glowed with exhilaration even as her chest heaved from the effort. She dropped her hands. "Why do we bother with archery? I can yank on a man's pinky and take him out of the fight like that." She snapped her fingers.

Talis also relaxed his guard. He retrieved the waterskins, brushing his braid from his sweat-lined brow. "Elves don't choose to practice that at which they are best." He handed Kyra the full waterskin. "There is a priority of skills. First you master those that allow you to inflict harm from afar. Magic and archery fall under that category. If closer combat is unavoidable, you use the next longest extension you have for defense. The staff."

"Except me being a wizard, no one can touch my staff," Kyra observed. "Defending with it isn't something I need to know."

"Maybe so, maybe not," Talis conceded as Kyra gulped down the crisp water. "For elves, that is the succession of knowledge. Equally important is the ability to move quickly with a sword. Then, if all else fails—and it truly is *all else*—one can resort to using one's hands and feet as weapons. Thus, open-hand combat. If you want, we could fit a couple sessions a week in between your time with Solarus."

Kyra grinned. "Talis, that's the best news I've heard all day."

Chapter 26

Kyra woke to a shrill whining in her ears like a dog whistle. She tried to rise. And groaned. Every muscle in her body ached as though she had been thrown from one of Thanesgard's thick walls. A long bath under the lilac trees alleviated some of her fatigue, but the ear-piercing noise remained.

"That is an effect of expending your energy yesterday," Solarus explained when Kyra described the whistling during breakfast.

Kyra poked a finger in her ear. "It shouldn't be," she said crossly. "My head feels like Makral is using it as an anvil to pound his swords on. It's never been this bad before. I didn't feel anything in the dungeon when we were trying to scrape the magic off the bars. That took a lot more effort since I didn't know what I was doing."

"That was also a short-term endeavor," Solarus pointed out. Ash, who sat on Kyra's right, studied her with concern. "Forcing such concentration for hours at one time is as battering as standing in a hailstorm. Remember what I told you. Your magic is no different than an atrophied muscle. You strengthen your body through consistent and laborious training. Your muscles will protest until they adapt to the exercise. The same with magic. The pain will subside. Scowling will not ease your aches," Solarus added dryly, noticing Kyra's expression. "Suffer it and move on."

Solarus' lecturing tone didn't improve Kyra's sourness. She caught the heady scent of hazelnut coffee and looked for a mug. At least caffeine would perk her up before the day's session. Kyra reached for the closest one to her.

Ash stalled her by placing his hand on her arm. Kyra turned to him, surprised. The healer smiled and held out a different mug. The steam curling into the air had the scent of fresh mint wrapped in strong spices.

"Solarus mentioned you wouldn't be feeling well this morning," the healer explained as Kyra curiously took the proffered mug. "This is a tea brewed from ginger and mint. It's used to reduce the effect of dizziness and any ringing in your ears. Ginger also helps with an unsettled stomach. For your headache, I brought the thraxen berries." Ash lifted a plate and set it next to the mug. Kyra recognized the pea-sized, orange berries as the same ones Ash gave to Jyls after their escape from Thanesgard. "If that doesn't work, I had the chef bake xaltrop powder into your bread. It's a sour-tasting spice. The cinnamon in the bread masks the taste." He shoved a final plate with a petite loaf in front of her.

"That's the way we give pets their medicine," Kyra commented, reminded of when Millie gave Albert a pill for his weight. "We grind up their pills and hide it in the food. The difference is I have a warning that there's something extra in my meal." She lifted a couple thraxen berries from the plate. "I chew these until they're bitter, right?"

Ash nodded.

Jyls, who was reclined in his chair across the table, gave Kyra a crooked grin. "Better you than me," he said, spinning a butter knife in his hand.

Kyra dutifully drank Ash's ginger-mint tea and ate his specially prepared bread. The shrill orchestra tapered off into a mild hum, and her muscles slackened. Then Kyra put the herbs in her mouth. Jyls watched her as she ground them between her teeth. The herbs tasted distinctly like blackberries. Kyra raised her serviette to her mouth, trying to look mannerly as she spit out the gummy substance.

After breakfast, Solarus unpityingly took Kyra to the lake. Kyra pushed her unwilling legs forward as they hiked up the hill. She again pondered whether Solarus had a shape-shifting spell so she could turn into a swan and fly to their destination. *He probably wouldn't teach me the spell, even if he could*, Kyra thought with a grimace. Solarus seemed almost amused by her aches. When they finally descended the hill onto the soft bank, Solarus had Kyra recite the axiom he had taught her the day before ("Dig the well before you thirst for a drink."). Then Kyra waded into the lake. She sighed as the cool waters numbed the stiffness in her legs. Kyra spent the next few hours pulling forward the golden links from her fingertips. It wasn't a minute too soon when Solarus released her for the day. Kyra ate a quick meal, returned to her chamber, and collapsed on her bed. She didn't even remove her boots as she dropped into sleep.

The short nap refreshed Kyra in time for her meeting with Talis that afternoon. Kyra was apprehensive about again visiting the training fields. The previous night, Kyra had planned to seek out Yuli, the one friend she remembered. Her sore body sidelined her aspirations to connect with him that day. Kyra wanted to see him when she wasn't shambling along like an uncoordinated ox.

Thankfully, Talis' tour was of the palace. They strolled through the courtyards, full of plants and flowers, statues and fountains. To Kyra's surprise, the courtyards Talis picked were empty of elves. As Talis related the history of each one, Kyra puzzled over their luck. A quick glance at Talis made her suspect luck had nothing to do with his choices; he intentionally avoided other elves on her behalf. Kyra felt a swell of gratitude for her friend. That night, Kyra soaked in her natural bath, eyes closed. The oil in the warm, sea green waters assuaged the aches in her body. Kyra was drowsy when she changed into her nightclothes, and sleep came easily.

Kyra's exhaustion trickled into the next few days. Ash continued to prepare her the ginger-mint tea and had her chew on the thraxen berries. Kyra slogged through her morning sessions with Solarus. She napped after lunch. Some afternoons, Hayden accompanied Kyra and Talis on excursions through the forest or to other areas in Silvias including, to Kyra's delight, the elven library. Kyra didn't realize how much she had missed reading her novels and plays or studying science and history. Kyra's intellectual craving was sated as she spent an afternoon with books recommended by Hayden. That evening, she wolfed down her meal and went straight to her chamber.

As busy as she was during the day, Kyra normally drifted off into a fatigue-induced sleep. Tonight, though, Kyra fidgeted under her soft sheets. The fragrant smell of lilacs laced the air. Kyra let out a tense sigh. When would she be healed enough to look for Yuli? Why hadn't anyone called on her yet? It had been five days. Five days and not a single elf had come by. Kyra twisted and turned in her bed. The bath should have relaxed her, eased her mind. It didn't. Kyra's impatience and frustration had dug themselves too deeply in her conscious to pry loose. She needed a way to shovel out the negative thoughts.

Kyra sat upright. Her eyes trailed to the boots. They waited invitingly beside her door. Orb-like lights blinked into existence as Kyra pushed the sheets off her bed and, with them, her weariness. Kyra slid off and went to a chair near the washbasin. Kyra changed quickly out of her nightgown, grabbed her vest and trousers from the chair, and stuffed her feet in her boots. With her day clothes on, Kyra headed out the door. She was long overdue for a run.

***

"No. No. No. Wait, is that . . . ? Rats. No." Kyra peered around the pine boughs. Gray clouds were strewn across the sky like dust, obscuring the hot noon sun and her sight of the equestrian fields. Her stomach stewed with excitement and anticipation. Kyra's eyes skimmed over the elven students that passed. They carried staffs and spears, with which they trained with while astride their horses. Unlike the willowy elves Kyra usually spied in Silvias, these students had thick frames like maple trees. Their sculpted features reminded her of Therial. The students casually joked and chatted and elbowed each other good-naturedly. Kyra felt a pang of loneliness. What she wouldn't give to have friends. Still, Kyra perked up at the thought that she would have at least one, soon.

Earlier at breakfast, Kyra had begged Solarus to postpone their lesson until the afternoon. Finding Yuli had become an obsession. Solarus refused her request. Then Hayden suggested a childhood friend could trigger the first of a flood of memories. Including those of her magic lessons.

"You could save time if she recalls the basics," Hayden had pointed out to the wizard.

Solarus finally relented with the caveat that Kyra was to meet him at two in the afternoon. Punctually. "And if you cannot manage that . . ."

"'Arrive early,'" Kyra finished promptly. "Got it." Grinning, she had dashed off.

"I know this is the right place," Kyra murmured now. Talis told her Yuli was in an advanced weapons class for the Royal Guards. They broke for lunch at midday. That was why Kyra surreptitiously observed the students as they ambled by her hiding spot. Kyra released a light laugh, trying to loosen her bunched-up nerves. *It's like when we were kids. Hiding and waiting.* Kyra glimpsed an elf who stood a head taller than the others. Her heart skipped a beat. Though Kyra's memory was of a rangy elf with high cheekbones, her instincts confirmed this was Yuli. The elf with the dark, cropped hair and chocolate-brown eyes carried himself confidently as he strode around the trees. He had developed a sturdy jaw, and his face lit with a relaxed smile. In his left hand was a staff.

"Yuli!" Kyra exclaimed. She sprang out from behind the trees. Yuli started. His eyes widened as his gaze met Kyra's. Yuli moved his staff to the side as Kyra pulled him into a joyful embrace. "I can't believe it's really you!"

Yuli's surprise gave way to a grin. As she released him, Kyra saw hesitation in his eyes, an indecipherable expression underlying his smile. He anxiously glanced to his side as his peers streamed past. Some paused, noticing Kyra. They whispered to each other. Kyra flushed, self-conscious and angry at the same time. She glowered at the students until they left, then turned her attention back to Yuli. He seemed oddly uncomfortable.

"Kyra," Yuli replied stiltedly. "It's . . . it's good to see you again. We heard you were in Silvias. I'm sorry I, ah, haven't visited you yet. I've been . . . I'm terribly busy with my training, and . . . um . . ."

"It's okay," Kyra interrupted. Her disappointment from the past few days was replaced by elation. "I'm so happy to see you. I don't remember much about Silvias except playing games like hunter with you and Aila."

Yuli rubbed the back of his neck. He cast a nervous glance over his shoulder. "We did spend time together. I had heard something about your memory being affected by your, um, disappearance."

A peculiar silence punctuated his words. Kyra looked at him, expecting more. Yuli mutely cast a glance around the woods. Her excitement ebbing, Kyra tried again. "Talis said you're training to be one of the Royal Guards?"

The question elicited a genuine smile from Yuli. He pulled his attention back to Kyra. "Yes. Honestly, I was shocked when they asked me. It was always my dream to join the *Hydranyle*. To be a defender of the Realm. No one thought I'd become one." Kyra was taken aback by the bitterness that curled around Yuli's tone. His eyes locked on the staff in his hand. He tightened his grip.

"I don't understand, Yuli," Kyra said gently.

"That's a benefit of forgetting the past." Yuli turned the staff as though boring it into the ground. "You may not remember good memories. But you can't be chased by the bad either. I was shorter than the other elven students in our year, male and female, up until little over a year ago. It was hard to keep up in our drills. I wasn't as powerful as the others. I wasn't as quick. I never won a bout. The single skill I had was with a bow. I didn't need to compete with anyone besides myself. Our classmates, they . . . they had nicknames for me. They thought it was funny that I struggled." Despite his dark complexion, red tinged Yuli's neck and cheeks. "After a while, the instructors stopped pairing me with other male students. You were normally my partner."

Kyra wasn't sure how to respond. Presumably, Yuli was assigned to Kyra because, as the wizard, she was the worst student in the class. Did he view her as a reminder of a tormented past? Or had Yuli been grateful for her company? Kyra never would have teased Yuli because of his height. Her memory of the hunter game led her to believe she appreciated him as a friend.

"That must have lifted your spirits a bit, sparring with me," Kyra said finally with self-deprecating humor. "When you have someone you can beat repeatedly."

To Kyra's surprise, Yuli laughed. The tone was sonorous and pure. "Actually, it was the opposite. Half of my time was spent on my toes, the other half on my back, with you standing over me grinning like a bear with a honeycomb. The way you're grinning right now. That is, when we were paying attention. I told you back then that I wanted to be in the *Hydranyle*. You never laughed about it."

Kyra smiled encouragingly as Yuli's words ran freely. The malice had disappeared.

"We had mock battles, me as the noble Guard, you as the villain. At least until *Finna* Fiora caught us. She always had this sour look on her face that could have curdled milk. Then we trained like we were supposed to. I used to practice for hours alone in the mornings before classes began. I knew one day the next round would be mine." Yuli twirled his staff once with ease. He flashed Kyra an impish smile. "Maybe after a year away, we're evenly matched."

"I'm not sure I want to fight against you until I've some confidence I won't embarrass myself." Kyra noticed the flow of students had slowed. A pair of female elves straggled behind.

"You wouldn't," Yuli said unhesitatingly. "Everyone doubted me and look, I became a guard. I had a mentor before you left who taught me proper form. He believed in me. He told me the elves had their own problems. I trained even harder, and I got better, especially with the staff. That's the weapon I was worst at, back then. Our classmates used to jeer at me and told me the guards would accept a hedgehog sooner than an inept elf. Because the hedgehog has a natural defense with its spikes. Their insults motivated me. Then I grew two heads taller after I came of age. I challenged every student who mocked me to a match. Only a couple bested me. I applied for an apprenticeship with the guards, and they took me in. Now elves respect me. I proved myself, just like I knew I would."

"That's wonderful, Yuli. I'm happy for you."

Strangely, Yuli's assured expression shifted to self-consciousness. He cleared his throat. "I owe a lot to you and Aila. You always supported me. You didn't care about how I looked or how well I could jab at someone with a sword. I . . . I really appreciate what you did."

The admission made Kyra's heart swell with joy. She *had* had friends after all. Even more, Kyra had someone who had relied on her. It was the first time Kyra ever remembered being needed. What an amazing feeling. Kyra had picked up on something else in Yuli's words.

Aila.

Though Kyra knew Aila wasn't in Silvias, her gaze unconsciously roved past Yuli to the two female elves. "Talis said Aila became a scout and is posted to Calonia," Kyra remarked.

One of the female elves nudged her friend, jerked a thumb in Kyra's direction, and said something. The other elf snickered. Kyra looked away and tried to ignore them.

"She is in Calonia as a *Sirenyle*." Yuli's pride brimmed in his tone. He seemed to have completely forgotten any other elves who could be lingering from his lesson. "I'm not sure how much you know about the scouts. The position as a *Sirenyle* is one of the most coveted in Silvias."

"I've been told," Kyra replied, thankful for her fragment of knowledge. "When we were in Thanesgard, Talis needed scouts to send a message to Silvias. He never found them, so I haven't met one myself."

The female elf who had gestured in Kyra's direction left her friend and strolled toward them. She tossed long, crimped wheat-colored tresses striped with strawberry streaks over her shoulder. An ivory-white birch wood staff was slung in a baldric on her back. Closer up, Kyra recognized her. It was the elf Kyra had pointed out to Talis at the archery range. The one she had declared was perfect. What did *she* want?

Yuli's brow furrowed. He glanced over his shoulder to see what Kyra was looking at. His expression turned to one of guilt, like a dog caught digging up a garden. Kyra didn't have time to wonder about his abrupt change in behavior as the female elf came up behind him. Her expression was mocking.

"The *Sirenyle* are 'the fleetest of riders, the finest of orators, and the fiercest of warriors,'" she entered the conversation, tone laced with sarcasm. "'They represent the elven elite and epitomize the virtues of the Realm.' Or so Therial says." She snorted. "You'd think the other elves in Silvias trudge around like slobbering trolls the way he gushes over the scouts. Particularly the *marvelous* Aila." The elf flipped her hair and said with exaggerated praise, "'Oh, you're so clever and gifted, Aila. There's no elf as worthy of joining the *Sirenyle* as *you*!'" The female elf huffed as Yuli looked away uncomfortably. "She's nothing special. Thank Inishmore she was assigned to Calonia, so I don't have to see her every day. Therial's bragging makes me sick."

Kyra's eyes narrowed. She immediately disliked this female elf, whoever she was. Kyra couldn't remember Aila beyond the hunter game. Her heart told her Aila had been a true friend to her in the past. What right did this elf have to say such things? Furthermore, insulting the captain of the queen's Royal Guards was disrespectful. Therial had struck Kyra as kind, compassionate, and competent. He didn't deserve the scorn of this teenager. Kyra looked to Yuli for support. After all, hadn't he moments earlier mentioned how proud he was to train as one of the Guards?

To Kyra's surprise and disappointment, Yuli clammed up. He studiously avoided Kyra's questioning gaze, shifting from one foot to the other.

The female elf didn't seem bothered by Yuli's silence. "It's strange a wizard is allowed to waltz around the Elven Realm. But you're *special*, just like Aila. Everyone in Silvias knows about the famous Kyra." The female elf slipped her arm under Yuli's with an unmistakable possessiveness. Yuli made no move to step away from her. "I'm Loralai. Yuli's *partner*. We've been together almost a year now."

So that was it. Why Yuli hadn't defended Aila or her. Kyra felt a stab of jealousy as a half-affectionate, half-awkward smile came to Yuli's lips. Kyra had confirmed she had a friend in the past. A sincere friend. Now, with this pretentious female elf in the picture, Kyra's hope of reconnecting was scattered like pieces on an upended checkerboard. "Obviously, elves know about me, seeing as how I grew up in Silvias," Kyra countered. "Yuli and I have been friends since childhood. Funny, though, I don't remember *you* at all." *Unless I intentionally scrubbed out memories of you witch of an elf.*

Loralai dismissed her words with a snooty wave. "I had better things to do than play with silly wooden swords. I began training with the *regular* students when I was fifteen. You wouldn't know that, would you? You ran off to wherever you wizards go."

"Loralai was promoted to staff master last year," Yuli put in. It was a clear attempt to tack the conversation in a more positive direction. "She's the best staff fighter in Silvias."

Yuli's words of praise for Loralai stung. Kyra imitated Nymphrys, imposing a disinterested expression on her face. "Is that her specialty then? I thought elves excelled in *all* areas, not just one." Kyra met Loralai's glower. "Does it take you so much effort to be 'the best staff fighter' that you're average in everything else?" Kyra felt some satisfaction to see animosity register in Loralai's eyes.

"A wizard would say such things," the female elf retorted. "You'd never in a lifetime measure up to an elf. Not in staff fighting, not in grace, and certainly not in beauty. Of course, you found that out when Hayden dumped you off in the *elves'* Realm. As an *outsider*."

Kyra's neck burned. Her hands began to prick painfully as though she had dragged them through a briar patch. Anger simmering, Kyra glanced down. Her eyes grew wide. Red energy sparked around her wrists, trying to ignite into flame. Heart pounding, Kyra crossed her hands behind her back. She silently struggled to smother the red energy before it could burst out of control.

The elves hadn't noticed the red glow. Yuli turned to Loralai. "Kyra was the top of our class in open-hand combat before she . . . left," he said, a note of apology in his voice. "You would have been a good match. She knows . . . a lot."

Loralai reciprocated Yuli's words with a withering glare. "Your imagination of what she was like and the reality of what she *is* like aren't the same. I'm sure she told you how wonderful she became in the last year. It's a lie and you know it. Wizards have an elevated view of their importance. And even if that were true—" Loralai bayoneted Yuli's protest as it formed on his lips, "—this wizard *knew* a lot." Contempt danced within Loralai's indigo-colored eyes. "Rumors are her head is as empty as a cloud. She wouldn't be able to compete with an elven child, let alone hold her ground against you. Certainly not against *me*."

The red energy gnashed its teeth in fury. Kyra was half-tempted to release it. Loralai's scorn wouldn't have stabbed her heart if the elf hadn't been right. Hadn't Kyra said herself she couldn't match the skills of the boy in the archery fields? Still, Kyra had magic. Deliciously powerful magic. She could wipe the smirk off Loralai's lips with one bolt of energy. The red feasted on her fury.

No. Kyra gritted her teeth. Loralai wasn't worth it. Kyra wouldn't let anyone provoke her into losing her control. She locked eyes with the female elf. "One thing I've always admired about Yuli is how patient he is with elves who aren't very bright. You know, the insecure, mediocre elves who hide their faults by being conceited, obnoxious, and have—what did you call it? —'elevated views of importance.' Fortunately for me, I'm an inherently imperfect wizard. I don't have to be as good as the elves." Kyra looked Loralai up and down. "That's why you cling to Yuli. He took pity on you. You're 'the best.' Kind of him to make sure your fragile ego isn't shattered with the truth. Of course, I'm not judging you." Kyra smiled with sugary sweetness. "You can't help being born average any more than I can help being born a wizard. So, we all have our challenges."

Loralai's pale cheeks turned a shade of burgundy. She opened her mouth to retort, then closed it. Yuli stood speechlessly. His eyes ranged from Kyra to Loralai and then to the ground, apparently deciding it was the only safe spot for his gaze to be.

Finally, Loralai raised her chin haughtily. "A wizard would use such pathetic insults. If I were Carina, I would have banished you from Silvias. Come on, Yuli." Loralai yanked Yuli's arm as she trekked into the woods. "She can go and do whatever miserable things wizards do."

Kyra ignored the dig as best she could. She kept the red energy tied around her hands. "Yuli, let's meet for dinner and catch up tonight. Seven o'clock. In the small dining room at the palace?"

"Um, sure, I'll see—" Yuli's words were cut off as Loralai dragged him after her. He cast Kyra a guilt-ridden look before matching Loralai's brisk pace.

Kyra's anger receded slowly as the elves disappeared into the woods. Her heart thumped loudly in her chest. She unclasped her hands and brought them in front of her. The red had waned. The golden-orange energy continued to pop. Kyra towed the magic back within her until it had disappeared completely. Expelling a tense breath, Kyra glanced up at the pines. Gray light drizzled into the forest, and the air was thick with the scent of a coming storm. She began to trudge through the forest.

Why had Loralai gotten under her skin so easily? Kyra wondered as thunder rumbled in the distance. The answer was simple. Yuli had mutely accepted Loralai's attack, including the statement that Kyra didn't belong in Silvias. He had also claimed Kyra had offered him comfort when he needed it; but Yuli hadn't reciprocated that support.

But there was more to Kyra's hurt. Loralai's words created a familiar pain. Kyra *wasn't* an elf. She didn't belong there. Where Kyra did belong, that was the question she couldn't answer. *Harkimer?* Kyra's heart thudded. She felt like a dark stain on a white silken gown.

Raindrops began to fall softly on the pines. Kyra didn't notice the water rolling down her neck as she made her way through the forest, lost in her thoughts. Silvias wasn't the fairy-tale kingdom she had hoped for.

***

Kyra's eyes flitted to the open doors to the dining hall. Elves passed by; none entered. Her gaze coasted up the wall to the clock. Twelve blue raindrop-shaped points shimmered fuzzily in a circle. It was the strangest clock Kyra had ever seen. The two glowing green lines joined at the center seemed to slither, rather than tick, from one minute to the next. Kyra watched as the long hand slid upward.

Seven forty-five.

Kyra fidgeted, tucking a strand of hair behind her ear. She glanced down at the untouched chocolate pastries on her plate. *He'll come. The lesson must have run over. He'll be here. Unless he forgot.*

"I think you would have welcomed a compliment, since I am not in the habit of giving them."

"What?" Kyra's glanced at Solarus. The wizard's fingers were steepled as he rested his arms on the table. His lips were buttoned with a peevish expression. "Oh, I'm sorry," Kyra apologized, belatedly realizing he had spoken to her. "I didn't hear you."

"Clearly," Solarus replied flatly. "What I *said* was that you performed admirably this afternoon. It would be helpful to review the first chapter of *Magic* tonight."

It was obvious Solarus' recommendation was really assigned homework.

"Right," Kyra answered in a detached tone. "The first chapter." Her gaze compulsively returned to the door.

Hayden and Jyls sat around the circular table with Kyra and Solarus. Jyls savored a shot of claret, complemented by the coffee beans at the bottom of the glass. Hayden nursed a steaming mug of chamomile tea. Talis and Ash had already finished dinner and left, the healer wanting to examine plants he had collected from the forest.

"Relax," Jyls said. "You're as anxious as an ant in the shadow of a boot heel." He held out his claret. "Drink some of this. It'll help the time pass."

"It will also make you regret any food you ate beforehand," Hayden interjected, giving the thief a disapproving look.

Jyls shrugged. "Just trying to help."

As Solarus shook his head, Kyra picked at her dessert disinterestedly. *Yuli will come*, she repeated as though it were the refrain to a lonely song. *He won't let me down. He'll come.*

After a few more moments, Solarus departed, looking to enjoy his pipe in the temperate night air.

Jyls quaffed the last of the claret. Setting the glass on the table with a loud clink, he pushed his chair back and rose. "I'm off," the thief announced. He stretched his arms behind him. "So much to explore, so little time."

Hayden sat quietly, studying Kyra.

Kyra's eyes flitted to the clock. Quarter past eight. "Yuli's going to be here any minute," Kyra stated, though her voice lacked conviction.

Jyls exchanged a sideways glance with Hayden.

"I'm not quite finished with my tea," Hayden remarked offhandedly. He took a spoon from a jar of honey on the table and stirred it in his mug. "I'll stay a while longer. That is," he addressed Kyra, "if you don't mind some company while you wait?"

"Not at all," Kyra replied. Secretly, she was grateful for a distraction. Kyra's gaze followed Jyls as he ambled out of the room.

Hayden and Kyra sat in silence. Hayden blew on his tea to cool it, then swirled more honey into the drink. Plates and glasses clinked as elven attendants cleared them from the table.

"Are you finished, my Lady?" one attendant asked. Her arms were full as her eyes dropped to the half-eaten pastry on Kyra's plate.

"Yes, thank you," Kyra replied. Her disappointment had robbed her of the pastry's taste. "I'll keep my tea, please."

The attendant nodded and scooped up the plate. As the elf glided away, Kyra drummed her fingers on the table. The minutes moved agonizingly slowly. Suddenly aware that Hayden's gray eyes were on her, Kyra invited him into a conversation. "I didn't think elves needed clocks to tell time."

Hayden stopped his rhythmic stirring and smiled. "They don't. I had the same question when I was first in this room. Carina told me that, centuries ago, elves added the clocks for the sake of foreign dignitaries. The punctuality Solarus prizes is also valued and expected among the elves. Arriving late is viewed as disrespectful. Elves instituted the clocks after misunderstandings led to a brawl or two between elven aristocracy and men perceived as slighting the king."

Kyra's lips spread into a grin. She tried to imagine a "brawl" between the stately, serene elves and royals like Arkin, with their costly and not-too-practical-for-a-brawl attire. Then Loralai sprung to mind. And Yuli. Kyra's happiness was immediately leached away. *New topic.*

"Hayden, I was wondering something else. Talis mentioned that elves apprenticed for their future careers. He said he had been trained as a *Litthrinyle*. We know Ash is a healer, and Jyls was a thief and . . . whatever he is now."

Hayden's eyes held a discerning look. Kyra was certain he was anticipating her next question. "I never asked what you did. That is, I don't know your profession. The bookseller in Thanesgard said you looked like a hunter or a tracker. Is that true? I mean, not your appearance. Were you trained to be one or the other?"

To her surprise, Hayden laughed. "I've served as a hunter and tracker," he answered with an amused grin. "I wouldn't consider myself an expert in either of those areas though. I didn't have any formal instruction, no."

"Then what did you apprentice in? Or is it different with men than it is with elves?"

"It depends," Hayden answered. He set aside his mug and rubbed his chin thoughtfully. "Take the profession of a trader, for example. It often remains within families, as the secrets they protect can be shared solely with those in which they have complete trust. On the other hand, scholars and scribes attend classes at the Academy in Calonia. Then you have merchants, whose qualifications are to produce a product worth buying. The nobility, well, they're involved in managing their estates and workers—and contributing to the unnecessarily complex and often toxic politics of their kingdoms."

It didn't escape Kyra that Hayden hadn't answered her first question. Hayden read Kyra's inquiring expression and grinned wryly. "You're curious if I do something other than riding through forests in the company of wizards and elves."

"Well, yes. If you're not a tracker or a hunter, then did you apprentice as a guard?" Hayden had proven in their encounters with the dark wizards and the greeloks how skilled he was as a warrior.

"I can wield a sword. I never desired to become a guard. It wasn't my calling." Hayden stirred his tea meditatively as Kyra's perplexed look deepened. *What was it then?* "Unlike Ash," Hayden continued, "there isn't a category or single occupation in which to fit myself. Life isn't always so neatly defined as 'healer' or 'hunter' or 'knight.' I am employed for different tasks. Fortunately, I'm adequate enough in those to secure food and provisions for myself and Willow and a room in which to sleep."

The cryptic answer left Kyra more bewildered than before. She shelved her questions as Hayden moved on to a new subject. They talked as the minute hand circled the clock. After a while, Kyra glanced up. It was past nine. She capitulated. "He isn't coming," Kyra murmured. She stood, trying to press the hurt from her expression. "I should do my reading before tomorrow's lesson," Kyra told Hayden. "Thanks for staying with me."

Hayden nodded. His compassionate gray gaze brought tears to Kyra's eyes. Turning so he couldn't see her pain, Kyra scurried from the dining room.

The gloomy night sky greeted Kyra as she fled to the courtyard. Owls hooted loudly, and the balsam essence of the machi trees laced the air. Kyra swiped away the water that brimmed in her eyes. Yuli had been one of her closest friends. It didn't seem like it was that way now. Kyra had seen Yuli's gaze of affection when he looked at Loralai. But was Loralai's disdain enough of a reason to deter Yuli from coming to dinner? What if Yuli stayed away for some other reason? What if he had a problem with Kyra herself? Kyra's hurt was chased away by resentment.

"The only way I'll know what Yuli thinks of me is to ask him," Kyra said aloud. She bent down and retied the laces on her boots. "Of course, if he doesn't show up when we make plans to meet, I can't exactly ask him."

Kyra straightened. Her lips pressed together resolutely. She took the thin scarf from around her neck and tied her hair up in a ponytail. Kyra's eyes scanned the courtyard, then strayed in the direction of the hills. Her gaze dipped to the ground.

"I need a path to the woods, away from elven eyes," she told it. The magical green path shimmered beneath her feet. It unfurled and undulated as though beckoning with a finger for her to follow. Brushing a strand of hair from her face, Kyra loped after it as quickly as her legs would take her.

Chapter 27

A little over an hour later, Kyra stretched her arms over her head. She stood on the lake's bank. Moonlight sprinkled on her head, and the stars glimmered off the lake's rippling waters. The magical lane had led Kyra across a flat, winding path through the hills, rather than over the ridge where she usually walked with Solarus. It was a longer route. Kyra was grateful. She needed the time to stomp out her pent-up frustration. Every strike of her heel on the earth seemed to get rid of a sliver of anger. Now, on the bank, nothing was left except a fatigued peace.

Kyra undid her ponytail. A cool breeze swept through Kyra's honey-brown tresses, bringing welcome relief from the sweat and heat of the run. The hypnotic chirping of crickets and croaking of frogs echoed across the lake.

Calmer now, Kyra was able to focus more clearly on her situation in Silvias. Without contact with her peers, Kyra had as much of a chance of unlocking a memory as she did growing pointed ears. Kyra was tempted to try to drop herself into a student's memory. It was worth it if the image provided her with even an inkling of her identity. Kyra sighed and nixed the idea. If the elves discovered Kyra could enter their thoughts, it would cement their mistrust. And without trust, Kyra would never reconnect with her friends.

The frogs' croaking suddenly ceased. The insects' chirping quieted. The hiccup of silence jolted Kyra from her thoughts. Instinctively, she looked over her shoulder and up the hill. Her heart jumped to her throat.

Tall figures glided soundlessly through the woods and down the hill. Long cloaks fluttered behind them. Kyra watched, stunned. Her magic hadn't reacted to the cloaked individuals. That meant they weren't dark wizards. Their movements were eerily swift and fluid as they made their way closer.

Phantoms. The spine-chilling recognition seized Kyra's muscles. The ghosts from the Forgotten Forest had found their way into the Elven Realm. Her mind whirred with questions; her body was paralyzed by fear. Solarus said they couldn't cross the water. Yet they were here. How?

One of the spirits ducked his head and sneezed. He paused on the hill, rubbing his nose.

Kyra's expression moved to puzzlement. *Phantoms don't sneeze. But . . . elves with allergies do.* As the figures came into bright moonlight, Kyra's suspicions were confirmed. The elves' cloaks shone, a weave of greens that made them appear like blades of grass against the backdrop of forest. Kyra should have been comforted. Elves weren't a threat. Then why were sirens of alarm wailing in her head?

The lead elf stopped a few arm's lengths from Kyra. Like his companions, he wore a short-sleeved tunic beneath the cloak. A golden tattoo that ran from his shoulder down his arm sparkled in the veiled moonlight. Kyra's brow knitted. The tattoo was somehow familiar. Her gaze darted to a female elf. She wore dangling, golden earrings adorned with feathers. *They were at the goldsmith's shop*, Kyra remembered. They were two of the three elves who had shot Talis a dark look. Kyra's eyes toured the group. *Where is the third?*

"It's an odd time to stroll around our lake, wizard," the elf with the golden tattoo opened in an accusatory tone. There was no warmth in his colorless eyes as he regarded her.

The elves' accents differed from those she was used to hearing around the palace. Kyra was certain she had heard them before. "I was going for a run," Kyra answered cautiously. "I prefer being out at night. It's not as hot."

"A run?" the elf who sneezed derided. "From whom are you running? The deer? Or the shame of knowing a wizard is a pestilence on the purity of our lands?"

Blood coursed hotly through Kyra's ears. Her rational self knew the concept of running for the sake of running seemed strange in Ilian; everyday chores and weapons training was arduous enough without wasting extra energy. Kyra's emotional self fought to respond. "I'm not running *from* anyone. I'm exploring the hills. It's easier to cover more ground running than walking."

"A weak lie, wizard," the elf with the golden tattoo sneered. "We know why you're here. You want to experiment with your dark methods away from elven eyes or ears. You seek to warp the magic of our lands. Your kind isn't welcome in Silvias."

"*Raenalyn* Carina would disagree with you," Kyra responded, feeling her anger spike. "Would she appreciate you harassing her guest? Especially since this was my home as much as yours."

Another sneeze interrupted the conversation. The elf with the golden tattoo glared at his companion. "Pallion, control yourself."

"Chop down the beech trees and I will, Kynder," Pallion retorted with a baleful look.

"This was never your home, wizard," the female elf with the earrings came in. Closer, Kyra saw her muscular, lean gazelle-like body complemented by the predatory expression of a hyena. "The *Raenalyn* is making decisions with her heart and not with the clear-headedness required to protect her people. She also hasn't punished those who shirk their responsibilities to watch over wizard spies."

"Lucerne," Kynder snapped. "Watch your tongue."

Lucerne rolled her eyes.

Kyra didn't understand whether it was Lucerne's criticism about the queen or the "punishment of others" that prompted Kynder's warning. Whatever the case, Kyra counted six elves in the group. Six hostile elves with no love for wizards. Kyra gritted her teeth. She had to avoid using magic at all costs. An attack on an elf would guarantee her eviction from Silvias. Her mind reeled.

"Is there something you want help with?" Kyra asked Kynder with as detached an expression as she could muster. "Because if not, I'd like to finish my run."

Kynder grinned mirthlessly. "We don't need a wizard in our midst. Who knows what mischief you're planning." He flexed his hands as the elves closed in on Kyra. "You haven't explained your disappearance or what you learned during that time. The story that you have no memory is a clever one. Feigning ignorance allows you to guard your secrets and whatever they taught you in Harkimer. The *Raenalyn* may not see through the screen of deceit, but we can. No dark wizard has ever infiltrated Silvias' borders. Save you."

Kyra's heart skipped a beat. Was Kynder confirming her suspicions? Or was he guessing? "How do you know I'm a dark wizard?" Kyra asked, shocked to honesty.

"You admit it!" Lucerne spat.

Kynder's colorless eyes glinted in the shavings of moonlight falling through the clouds. He ran his hand along the golden pattern on his arm. "We know because all wizards are aligned with Harkimer, despite some claiming to be 'free wizards.' None of you is innocent. You are a scourge. We elves may not be able to confront Diamantas or the rest of your ilk yet. We *can* deal with a wizard who trespasses into the Realm." He glanced sideways and gave a flick of his head. "Lucerne, Farrow."

Lucerne and a broad-shouldered elf with a purple tattoo ringing his eye stepped forward. The hyena-like grin spread across Lucerne's face. She and Farrow raised their palms over the earth. Kyra's eyes darted left and right. She wouldn't be able to escape into the lake, and there wasn't much room for her to flee the bank and run into the hills. Not with the elves blocking her. She had to stall. "What about *Raenalyn* Carina?" Kyra challenged, keeping Lucerne and Farrow in her peripheral vision. "What happens when she finds out her own people attacked me?"

"Who will tell her?" Kynder let his gaze slowly and deliberately move to the lake. "Silvias has many dangers within its borders for non-elven kind. The land preceded our inhabitation of it, and we are stewards and guests upon it. The Ancient Forest guards some paths so closely that none may tread there." Kynder centered his attention again on Kyra. He reminded her of a bloodthirsty vulture craving fresh meat. "An eager, naïve wizard wouldn't be aware of these prohibited places. Not if she had no memories of Silvias, as she said. We would have to deliver *Raenalyn* Carina the terrible news that you offended the Forest with your transgression. The Forest exacted punishment for it. The *Raenalyn* would understand. It was a tragedy that couldn't be prevented."

Lucerne and Farrow's irises shone neon green. Kyra recognized the color. It was the same as Talis' when he used magic to distract Galakis and Orkanis in Edoin Forest. Green fog poured from Lucerne and Farrow's hands and mushroomed around them. Kyra took a step back. She watched, wide-eyed, as the fog rolled in front of the elves like storm clouds and condensed into two forms. Elven forms. Kyra sucked in a breath, pulse racing. The magical green figures were exact replicas of Lucerne and Farrow. The real Lucerne and Farrow directed their magical doppelgangers to move forward.

Kyra balled her hands into fists. Being exiled from Silvias was preferable to dying. She had to fight. Vague memories told Kyra that any contact with the figures would cause as much pain as grabbing a wizard's staff. That meant avoiding contact with the elves' strange shadow selves. Kyra commanded the fatigue to leave her body, thrust aside her mental exhaustion from the day, and zeroed in on her core. She took a deep breath and exhaled. After so much practice with the golden energy, she could summon it in her defense.

Except that Kyra couldn't. Panic rose within her. *I'm bringing forth streams of gold*, she thought.

The magical Lucerne and Farrow split from each other. Lucerne went to the left, Farrow to the right.

Golden streams flow from my hands into the air like they do in currents of the water. Nothing.

Aghast, Kyra centered her attention outward. The whole process had taken a fraction of a second, and she knew instinctively her magic was failing. Was the elven magic stronger and blocking hers, or did Kyra need time to draw upon her internal strength? She couldn't guess, and it didn't matter. Kyra balled her fists, steeling herself for the pain that was certain to follow.

The magical Farrow attacked first. He shot forward so quickly, Kyra barely had time to react. He threw a punch at her head. Kyra ducked, avoiding the blow. The green figure anticipated her response and swung with an elbow. Kyra slid back. With the speed of a snake, Farrow struck toward her kneecap with his heel. The magical elf's blow came too quickly to evade. Kyra didn't hesitate, couldn't think of the imminent pain. She brought her knee up and blocked his leg to the side.

Kyra's defense had surprising strength against her larger opponent. More shocking, she didn't feel anything except the contact of the magical Farrow's leg. No burning, no pain.

The magical Farrow froze like a marionette whose strings had been cut. The magical Lucerne didn't move either.

Breathless, Kyra raised her hands. Her heart skipped a beat. They shimmered with a blue-green glow. Not just her hands, Kyra discovered as strands of hair loosed from her ponytail and framed her face. The hair glimmered, as did—Kyra saw as she glanced down—her entire body. It looked like she had dipped into a pool of blue-green light. *Where is it coming from?*

Whatever the source of the magic, it armored Kyra against the elves' magic. Her eyes moved behind the magical green forms to the real Lucerne and Farrow. The elves wore identically stunned expressions. Kynder's mouth was agape. Lucerne turned to look at Kynder, as though waiting for a new instruction.

Fresh confidence pumped through Kyra. She squared off against the green forms, hands raised. The elves weren't using weapons, and she couldn't feel the sting of their magic. That left the green copies of Lucerne and Farrow with one option: open-hand combat. Of all her skills, Kyra was the most capable in this field. Capable enough to fend off her opponents and give her a chance of escaping.

Kyra darted to the magical Lucerne. She grabbed the elf's left wrist, slipped inside toward the elf's chest, and threw her arm under the elf's right arm. Out of the corner of her eye, Kyra saw the real Lucerne jerk her hands to the side. Kyra twisted, using her hips to throw the magical form to the side. The magical Lucerne flipped in the air, deftly landing on her feet. Kyra turned. A staff materialized in the magical Lucerne's hand. Kyra's head swiveled toward the green Farrow. He also wielded a staff.

The magical Lucerne leapt into the air and whipped the staff across her body. Kyra sidestepped and kicked the staff away. Lucerne immediately pressed forward with another attack. This time, the weapon struck Kyra hard in the side. Kyra was knocked off her feet, a sharp pain in her ribs. Gasping, Kyra pushed herself onto one knee. She glanced to the side as Farrow lunged forward. Without hesitating, Kyra sprang over the staff and landed firmly on her feet. Kyra spun, hands raised protectively in front of her face. It was almost too late. Farrow brought the staff down with all his might. Kyra crossed her arms into an X over her head, anticipating the crushing blow. The blue-green magic flared around her.

The magical staff crashed into the crescent shield above her arms. Kyra's body quaked from the impact, but the weapon didn't touch her. Reaching with her shield, Kyra grabbed the staff and yanked down as hard as she could. The magical Farrow was thrown off-balance and fell to the ground.

Kyra flipped the staff to the side. She turned to the magical Lucerne. To her surprise, the magical Lucerne dissipated into a cloud. The staff in Kyra's hand wisped away. More green mist that drifted to Kyra told her the form of Farrow had also disappeared. The blue-green glow around Kyra glimmered brightly and faded into the night.

Sweating and winded, Kyra stared up at the elves on the bank. Kynder's shock melted into an expression of hate. Kyra wondered if she imagined a hint of fear behind his belligerent expression.

"Dark magic," Kynder spat. "You can't defeat us all, wizard. You've met your end."

Kynder chanted something indecipherable. The other elves picked up on his words and joined their voices to his. Green poured from their hands. Six bands of energy spread out and coiled around each other. This time, Kyra couldn't see a way out. She was drained and light-headed. The green energy curved and surrounded her like a giant net. Mouth dry, Kyra frantically spun around as the green sparked and hissed.

From the hilltop came a sound like a crack. It was followed by more cracks and then a sizzling. Brilliant neon-green magic burnt a hole through the net encasing her.

"I recommend you release Kyra. Unless you want to see what a real ambush looks like, not one on a teenage girl."

Kyra almost wilted in relief at the sound of Hayden's voice. The green net immediately fizzled out. Kynder and the other elves had turned, startled. Hayden descended the hill, his sword strapped to his side. A wrathful-looking Talis followed. His hand was extended toward the bank. Neon-green smoke crackled around it. His amber eyes were unnaturally bright with green light. Talis closed his hand. The green vanished.

Kynder and the elves faced Hayden as he walked onto the bank. His sword remained sheathed, yet the fury in his bearing was enough to make Kynder unconsciously step back. The elf rubbed the golden tattoo on his arm. Kyra didn't move, watching the standoff.

Hayden glanced at her. "Are you all right?"

Kyra's side smarted from where she had been hit by the magical Lucerne. She forced herself not to rub the muscle. "I'm fine."

"We shouldn't be surprised you're here." Lucerne spoke up with a scathing look at Hayden. The green in his eyes disappeared as it did in Farrow's. "You're the reason the wizard is in Silvias in the first place. Haven't you interfered in elven affairs enough? You won't even let the girl fight her own battles?"

"Wizards display cowardice," Kynder added caustically, having found his voice. "An elf would face the challenge presented to him with honor and courage."

Talis leapt from his place on the hill to the bank. He landed a few arm's lengths from Kynder. "Cowardice is when one comes with five companions to attack an unarmed individual. An individual who has the protection of Silvias' queen."

Kynder's pale face flushed red. "Do not speak to *me* of cowardice, Talis," he sneered. "You're as misguided as you always have been. First, with assuming the guardianship for this wizard and asserting her innocence. Now you bring her back without any account for the last year. Haven't you caused enough problems for 'Silvias' queen?' Or have you forgotten the harm you did to the Realm?"

Hayden caught Talis' arm as he stepped forward. Cold fury swirled in Talis' eyes. "Are those *Safirthelyn* Orison's words or your own?" Hayden asked. "*Raenalyn* Carina will be curious to know from whose lips these accusations and from whose hands the threat to Kyra come."

Orison. The Lord of Silvias' Southern domain. Kyra could now place the accent of the individuals before her. They belonged to Orison's territory.

The question stalled Kynder's words. Lucerne again intervened. "*Raenalyn* Carina is blinded by emotion, as are you. We are not. We are the most able to deal with this situation."

"Does your lack of emotion allow you to shelve your morals and the laws of the Realm?" Hayden answered coolly. He gave Talis a sideways glance before releasing his arm. "There is no 'situation' regarding Kyra."

"There is a situation so long as a wizard's fabrications are believed by the queen." Kynder snapped. A sneeze interrupted his next words. The look Kynder gave Pallion was so full of malice that Pallion held his nose as another sneeze threatened to surface. "You have fallen for the wizard's manipulations. I haven't. Nothing you say will convince me to accept her. She is an outsider." Kynder's disparaging gaze fell on Kyra, who defiantly met his stare. "She was then, she is now, and she always will be."

"Kyra is no more an outsider to Silvias than I am," Talis growled.

Kynder's mouth twisted into a strange smile. "That is one fact upon which we agree."

"Am I also, Kynder of the South, not belonging to this Realm?" a voice came from the woods. Therial guided his horse down the side of the hill. He donned a sword, as did the four warriors flanking him. The warriors' expressions were hard and threatening. Kyra recognized one of the warriors with porcelain-like features and dark hair as the instructor from the closed-hand combat sessions. The instructor and the other warriors reined in their horses as Therial advanced. His golden-haloed eyes flared with anger.

Kynder's expression immediately changed to one of obedience. He bowed stiffly. "*Jaelyn* Therial," he stated as his fellow elves also bowed. "You have my deepest respect. I would never claim . . . I'm surprised to see you here at such a late hour."

"I didn't plan to be. However, Talis kindly informed me that you and your retinue had departed to the hills." Therial's hand brushed the hilt of his sword. His magenta gauntlet gleamed in the starlight. "He was curious to know what would draw your attention at such an hour. When Hayden came from the palace looking for Kyra and couldn't find her, we decided we should ask you as to her whereabouts."

Despite her deference to Therial's rank, Lucerne bristled. "Why did you think *we* knew? What accusations did you have against us?"

"None. I believed if Kyra wasn't in her room nor on the palace grounds—and you were also awake—there was a chance, however slight, that you may have encountered one another." The grin Therial offered had no trace of his affability. Kyra saw for the first time why Therial, who radiated unyielding authority, had been chosen as the queen's captain. "Look at how Inishmore unites us. We found you and, through you, her. What we didn't expect was such wickedness from the Lord of the South's second and your company. Your craven attack on Kyra is enough to banish you from the Realm. It's a pity that I cannot deliver justice. Be sure *Raenalyn* Carina and *Safirthelyn* Orison will know of these acts. They will decide your fate. You will be escorted by my warriors to the palace."

The feathers on Lucerne's golden earrings swayed as she violently shook her head. "You can't blame us for defending ourselves against the wizard."

"Had you not followed Kyra, you wouldn't have engaged her nor needed to 'defend' yourselves."

"We are servants of the Realm," Kynder demurred. "We submit to the wisdom of *Raenalyn* Carina and *Safirthelyn* Orison." His eyes shot to Kyra. "I believe they will see reason."

"They assuredly will. They will see the reason why you broke the treaty of peace within the Realm: you are chained to your arrogance. You disobeyed your superiors. I need not say more than that." Therial nodded curtly to his warriors. The warriors turned their horses so that they faced the Southern elves.

Kynder led the ascent up the hill. Pallion was in tow, sneezing. His steps noticeably lacked the grace of his companions. Lucerne took up the rear of the group. She sent one last contemptuous look over her shoulder. The female elf's glower wasn't directed at Kyra. It fell on Talis. Two of the warriors steered their horses behind the Southern Elves. The remaining two took point. Then they marched the steeds into the woods.

Therial followed the procession with his eyes. When they were out of sight, the captain reached down to pat his mare's neck. "I don't like that you were right about this," Therial remarked to Hayden and Talis with a troubled look. "Orison is hardheaded, but he hasn't ever openly challenged the queen's decisions."

"It may not be him," Hayden pointed out. "Kynder may have acted of his own volition without Orison's awareness of the fact. Orison is one of the Lords of the Realm. He doesn't have the luxury of breaking his vows to *Raenalyn* Carina simply because he doesn't like wizards. Orison is accountable to his people."

"Unlike Kynder, even though he is Orison's second." Therial shook his head. "That role should never have been given to such a self-serving and untrustworthy elf. Carina should encourage Orison to consider a new candidate." The captain's emphasis on the word "encourage" made clear he wanted the queen to order the change. "I will see you in the palace." Therial shifted the magenta gauntlet on his wrist. Then, gripping the reins to his mare, Therial smiled grimly at Kyra. "Take care. Kynder won't bother you again. Also, he doesn't speak for the Realm, nor does he represent the elves. I regard you as one of us."

Kyra was touched by the captain's words. "Thank you, Therial," she replied with a tired smile.

Therial guided his mare up the slope. As they cantered off, Kyra looked back at Talis with concern. Guilt stuck to the roof of her mouth like peanut butter. If she hadn't gone to the lake at night, there wouldn't have been a confrontation between Talis and the Southern elves. She was certain there was history between him and Kynder. Kyra had accidentally resurrected the feud.

"Why did you follow me?" she asked Hayden.

"That should be obvious," Hayden replied with a raised brow. "You were upset when you left the dining hall. Which, given that Yuli didn't make your appointment, would be cause for disappointment. I wanted to check on you. Then, as Therial mentioned, Talis caught sight of Kynder heading to the hills."

Hayden's sincere concern stoked Kyra's guilt. "I'm grateful," she said, her neck hot. "Yuli probably forgot, that's all. Or something came up at the last minute with the Royal Guards, and he didn't have time to tell me. It wasn't personal." Kyra didn't believe in the statement any more than Hayden seemed to.

Hayden's gray gaze moved to Talis. The elf seemed to break out of his trance.

"You shouldn't be here," Talis said in a reprimanding tone. "If Hayden and I had known you planned to run off, neither of us would have allowed it. It was rash and thoughtless. You put yourself in unnecessary jeopardy."

Kyra was too taken aback to answer. Talis had never been so short with her. Kyra's shame at his rebuke prompted her defensive response. "Kynder is as pleasant as a rash. He isn't tough though. I was handling them myself." Kyra's claim sounded ridiculous even to her, but she pressed on. "I'm not a child. I don't need bodyguards. I've gotten out of tough situations before, alone."

"True, you held your own before we arrived," Talis conceded. "Kynder anticipated a weaker opponent. However, the Southern elves are not to be underestimated. You had Inishmore on your side."

"Besides," Hayden put in, "challenging Kynder has consequences beyond the physical fight. You are a wizard in the elven territories. Magic used against Kynder could be seen as a threat to the queen's people. I wore my sword—" he rested a hand on the hilt, "—as a precaution in case other beings lurked in the trees. I never intended on using it."

Kyra jabbed her finger into the air. "For the record, *they* challenged *me*. I didn't *want* or *expect* company. How was I supposed to assume elves would stalk me and try to drown me in their immaculate lake. Honestly!" Kyra threw up her hands in exasperation. "This is Silvias, the one place in Ilian where people live in harmony. There isn't supposed to be bickering neighbors or feuding families or scheming lords and ladies."

"Elves are like any other race," Talis said. He twisted his long braid. "They both have goodness and wickedness within them."

Hayden folded his arms. "I don't suppose this is the first night you've spent at the lake."

"I've been here the last few nights," Kyra confessed, though a fiery expression lit on her face. "I never had any problems before. Running is the only time I get for myself. I can let my mind wander and not obsess over what I should remember or who is supposed to meet me and doesn't show up or . . ." Kyra's face grew hot. She stopped herself. Kyra had been on the cusp of admitting her hurt and frustration. "It doesn't matter. The point is, I'm not going to stop going out because Kynder decided I shouldn't be here."

"I disagree. You can't be out by yourself at night. As Talis said, you're putting your life in jeopardy, and we're doing everything we can to keep you safe." Hayden stalled Kyra's protest with a pacifying raising of his hand. "I said you couldn't run *alone*. It doesn't mean you can't run. One of us will accompany you from now on."

Kyra bit her lip. So much for her independence and solitude. Hayden's tone forbade argument. It was the best arrangement Kyra could hope for given that she knew he and Talis were right. She couldn't let her guard down, not even in

Silvias. She trekked up the hill beside Hayden and Talis, replaying the events of the night in her mind. The willingness of the elves to assault her. The blue-green magic that shielded her. Kynder's accusations.

"Hayden, Kynder told me he knew I was from Harkimer," Kyra said unthinkingly. "Is it true?" Kyra clamped her mouth shut as the fear she had harbored for so long left her lips. It was too late to retract the question.

Hayden's step faltered. Talis stopped short also. Kyra thought she caught the two sharing a look of shock before Hayden turned fully to see her. She must have imagined it though. Hayden laughed lightly.

"Kynder claims all wizards are from Harkimer," he answered with a sigh. "He refuses to believe—as does Orison—that there's a distinction between free wizards, who have fought alongside elves and men for centuries, and Malus' descendants in the Mountains. It's the way he is. I wouldn't worry about it."

Kyra frowned. It bothered her that Hayden had continued to appear on the hill's crest from time to time, watching her practice. Hayden didn't know Kyra had spied him there. And *that* wasn't a subject she wanted to broach. *Although*, Kyra reasoned as she tried to read Talis' cryptic expression, *it would make sense if I were a dark wizard*. "Kynder seemed pretty confident," she responded. "You said you didn't meet my parents when you found me. So, it's possible that I'm a dark wizard, isn't it? And that could be why Diamantas is spending so much time trying to find me?"

"You are *not* a dark wizard," Hayden answered firmly. "Diamantas has his plans, and whatever they are, they involve you. I'm sure there are others he pursues. He isn't that fond of Talis, Solarus, and me either."

"The *Raenalyn* also wouldn't willingly let a dark wizard into the Realm," Talis added. "I don't believe Orison ordered Kynder's actions tonight. However, as Hayden said, you must be cautious. Always."

"Then I'm not from Harkimer." Kyra let out a long sigh of relief. Her fears had been unfounded. Kyra might lack an explanation about why the red energy manifested, but she wasn't a dark wizard. That was all that mattered.

Kyra's thoughts prevented her from seeing the troubled, meaningful look that passed between Hayden and Talis. Or realize that while they had dismissed the notion of her as a dark wizard, they hadn't answered her question. If she was from Harkimer.

Chapter 28

The morning brought a deluge of rain to Silvias. It didn't bring Yuli. Droplets the size of cherry pits pummeled the silver green leaves of the machi trees, and an earthy aroma pervaded the air. Elves in cloaks with raised cowls strode quickly and purposefully as they went about their day.

Kyra's heart pestered her to demand an explanation from Yuli. He could he cite duties relating to the Royal Guards that genuinely excused his absence. If that were the case, Kyra would graciously dismiss Yuli's apology and take him as a friend. *If.* Kyra erected barriers around her heart as solid as Thanesgard's walls to prevent her riotous emotions from spilling out.

Despite the woeful weather, Solarus wouldn't cancel the day's lesson. "The dark wizards will not be so kind as to limit their attacks to sunny days," he pointed out as they trudged up the muddy slope of the hill. "Now is a perfect opportunity to see how well you do in less than favorable conditions."

Thunder pealed through the trees. Kyra glanced up at the turquoise shield of energy Solarus had raised over them. The rain punched the roof as though trying to drill a hole through it.

"Easy to say when you have a cover over your head to stay dry," Kyra replied. "It's going to stay up while you watch me get drenched, isn't it?"

Solarus' lips formed a thin smile. Kyra didn't bother arguing for a reprieve. Solarus wasn't a wizard to be persuaded. Kyra spent a miserable morning in the lake's cold waters. The equally cold rain obscured her vision and dripped down her hair. When the lesson was over, Kyra's toes were numb, and her lips were blue. The drying spell stopped her shivering. Kyra stayed under the protection of Solarus' shield until they were back inside the palace.

Hayden and Talis were more merciful. They postponed the day's weaponry practice. Kyra instead spent the afternoon around a parlor table with Jyls and Ash, learning a Peregrinian card game. The concentration on the game kept Kyra's mind off Yuli and Kynder. Ash, having already been taught by the game by Jyls, had mastered the complex rules and tricks. After several rounds, he had collected all the porry seeds they used as currency for their bets.

"Any healer would do as well," Ash said humbly as he swept the seeds into a pouch. "We're taught to memorize things quickly. Cards aren't any different from the names and properties of plants."

Jyls rolled his eyes. "Peregrinians also normally do well. We're taught that everyone responds to a blade at their side. If you're down, you make sure the other players know they'll lose more than porry seeds if they don't throw a few hands."

Ash frowned. "That's cheating."

"That's Peregrine."

When it was time for dinner, Kyra realized she had laughed more during their game than she had since they arrived.

Another two days passed with unrelenting rain. On the fourth day, the sun returned to Silvias' skies. Kyra yearned to go on another run, having forgone the previous days. Fortunately, the day flew by. In the evening, Kyra changed into a light blouse, tied her hair back, and met Hayden outside the palace entrance. Together, they loped off, with Kyra leading the way. She didn't think her mind could wander. Kyra felt compelled to speak if Hayden was accompanying her. Thankfully, Hayden was quiet, seeming lost in his own thoughts. Kyra smiled as she enjoyed the wind in her face, the feeling of her arms and legs pumping in unison, the sounds of the forest touching her ears. It was a perfect, companionable silence.

Kyra settled into a routine. Mornings were dedicated to her magic studies, rain or shine. Most afternoons were spent on lessons in weaponry with Talis, Hayden, and occasionally even Therial as her instructors. Evenings remained reserved for Kyra's runs. As promised, Hayden, Talis, or both loped alongside her. Those days she had free, Kyra joined Jyls and Ash or took the time to be alone.

During one of her many runs, Kyra had stumbled upon a secluded glade. It was high on the hilltop and had a clear view of the palace and houses below. Talis had been with her. He smiled as Kyra breathlessly looked around. The glade was stunning, peaceful, and oddly familiar. It was also close enough to the palace that Talis deemed it safe for Kyra to return on her own. Talis noted she had been to the glade before in her childhood. That explained the familiarity. Kyra loved the feeling.

When she wanted solitude, Kyra visited the spot. She would lean against one of the ervil trees, with their smooth bark and their bulbous branches, take out her latest novel, and read for hours to the background of birdsong. Sometimes on particularly sunny days, Kyra put down the book and gazed contentedly across the land. The palace's *zylith* waved from one color into another. Elves, mini-figurines in the distance, moved in and out of their glass-spun houses and promenaded down the road to the shops. The courtyards and gardens teemed with life. Kyra let out a sigh. She imagined she had whittled away many hours there as a child.

As for the elven students, Kyra gave up any pretense of trying to reconnect. She might be a carnation among roses in Silvias, but she refused to be treated like one. Kyra adopted Solarus' aloof bearing and expression of royal indifference. When she went to visit Raven or to a training session, she strode with confident, precise steps, chin raised. Elves surreptitiously shot her the curious and suspicious looks she had grown accustomed to seeing; Kyra resolutely ignored them. "You're not worth my time," she muttered when she reached the pine forest. "I have plenty of people happy to see me. And horses," Kyra added when she reached Raven's pasture. She grinned as the horse trotted forward for the day's treats of carrots and apples.

The problem with avoiding the students was Kyra wasn't advancing as quickly as her impatience demanded. Solarus had told Kyra from their first night she had two goals, one of which was to remember her time in Silvias prior to her disappearance. How could she do that without talking to friends who shared those memories? Kyra knew that her learning was painfully stalled, like a kid resisting a visit to the dentist. There wasn't much she could do. Kyra spent two weeks learning how to direct her energy purposefully. She was frustrated by her slow progress; Solarus, on the other hand, seemed pleased.

"The principle of control is the foundation of all other aspects of your training," he told her as they sat on the bank after a rigorous session. "Refining your ability to summon, direct, and restrain your energy is a lifelong exercise. Any wizard who believes he has full mastery of his magic is a fool. If you learn nothing else, it suffices that you can hone your skills with regular repetition. The bearer determines the effectiveness of the staff. Without control, you can as predictably expect to be stung by its magic as if you were attempting to corral a swarm of bees."

Solarus moved on from summoning energy to teaching Kyra simple incantations. She easily recalled the drying spell *"Is-ter-AH-ha."* One humid day, Solarus showed her its opposite, the dampening spell.

"Why would I want to wet something?" Kyra inquired after repeating *"Nis-ter-AH-hil."*

Solarus raised a brow. "Might it be helpful if something were, perhaps, aflame?"

Kyra grinned sheepishly. "Right."

"One more time, please. *Nis-ter-AH-hil.*"

Kyra copied Solarus' tone, emphasizing the "ah" in the word. The spell sucked water from the air and infused it in her clothing until her sleeves hung flaccidly from the weight. *"Is-ter-AH-ha,"* Kyra stated confidently. Her clothes steamed as the water evaporated.

The most complex spell Solarus taught her was the one that formed the magical roof. After multiple tries, Kyra conjured up a golden, saucer-shaped ceiling. It wasn't perfect. Sunlight streamed through pinprick-sized holes. Kyra bit her lip. Solarus' shield had deflected exploding trees during their fight in Edoin Forest and acted as a buffer against rain. That potency was what Kyra wanted. She worked tirelessly to strengthen her golden ceiling.

"Solarus, I have another question," Kyra said when they had finished one morning.

"How unusual."

Kyra grinned at Solarus' dry response. She was acclimatized to his mannerisms. Solarus puffed on his pipe with a relaxed expression. When he exhaled, Kyra breathed in the pleasant aroma of apple and spices. *The kolker must be Solarus' reward to himself,* Kyra thought with a grin. *For getting through another mishap-free session with me.* She linked her fingers together and stretched out her arms. "Every wizard we've met has a name ending in *s*. Why is that?"

"The naming conventions of wizards were established prior to the War of Calonia," Solarus explained. He tapped the end of the pipe on the grass. "Before the War, wizards were venerated among men. They shared an equal status with royalty. I am not in the habit of repeating myself, so I do not need to remind you of our first lesson when I described the magnanimous deeds they performed in the service of non-wizards."

Solarus looked at her expectantly. Kyra knew nothing except agreement was acceptable. She nodded. The wizard took another draw from his pipe.

"It should come as no surprise," Solarus went on as he released the vapors, "that, like royalty, some wizards came to believe their positions within Ilian were divine. Positions bestowed upon them by Inishmore and the Healer. The wizards devised a naming convention to symbolize their superiority to men and elves. Similar to the honorifics of 'Your Majesty' or 'Your Grace.'"

Kyra's mind went to Adakis with his petulant expression and perpetual blustering. "A wizard like Adakis has the ego the size of Thanesgard and the abilities of an ant. He can't be the only arrogant one in the history of wizards. Don't we have standards about who's 'equal to royalty?'"

Solarus looked at her down his nose. "I did not create wizards' social norms. I merely repeat them. Besides, a wizard's potential is not discovered until he comes of age. Adakis, like all wizards, was presumed to be competent. He proved otherwise. Therefore, it is quite rational to apply the naming convention to all wizards when they are born."

"Wizards should be able to revoke the *s* if someone turns out to be a disaster," Kyra said flatly. She unlocked her fingers and plucked a piece of grass. "Talis and Jyls have names that end in *s*. Is that a coincidence?"

"It is a matter of logic. If you are a wizard, your name ends in *s*. The converse is not true. Non-wizards' names can end in s. They have no relation to us."

Kyra felt a pang of melancholy as she thought back to her lessons with Mr. Stevens. He would have enjoyed intellectually sparring with Solarus. "Wait." Kyra looked up suddenly, letting the grass fall. "What about me? My name doesn't end in an *s*, and I'm a wizard."

"'Kyras is not an appealing name. Kyra is a better fit."

"I didn't have to be Kyras. I could have been Alexis or Iris or Wizardess or something else."

"You are not Alexis or Iris or 'something else.' You are Kyra."

He was skirting the question. "Why then?" Kyra pressed. She scooted closer and made eye contact with him. "Why Kyra?"

This time, Solarus didn't answer immediately. His gaze fell on his tunic. Fastidiously smoothing the few wrinkles it had, he answered without glancing up, "You told Hayden your name was Kyra when you first met, so that is what we call you. We assumed you would know that much."

Kyra's brows knitted. "Why wouldn't my parents use the convention if it's so important to wizards?"

Solarus straightened his cuff. "As Hayden and I told you, we did not meet your parents, nor have we ever found them. I can speculate, that is all."

The protracted silence following his words was unbearable. "And? Solarus, tell me! Please," she added more softly.

Solarus finally looked up. He donned a neutral expression, though his eyes held concern. "It is possible you had one parent who was a wizard and one who was not. Hence the variation."

Kyra recoiled in shock. Why hadn't they told her this before? "That's . . . that's not common, is it? That wizards would marry non-wizards?"

"Who is to say what is common. We do not have much information about the habits of Harkimer's wizards. The wizards of Ilian do not maintain close enough contact to provide that knowledge either. However, the fact that you have not met others with similar circumstances does not mean they do not exist. We are finished." Solarus had changed the topic abruptly. He dumped the remains of the kolker leaves on the ground and pocketed the pipe. Then he scooped up his staff and rose. Without another word, Solarus started up the hill.

Kyra hastily gathered her own staff and cloak and jumped to her feet. As she followed Solarus, a peculiar thought entered her mind. If the *s* branded someone as a wizard, what if her parents had given her a name that would hide her identity? And if they did . . . what or who were they hiding her from?

***

Kyra had intended on questioning Solarus about her parents again the next day. Solarus had come armed with a sour expression and brusqueness that deterred her from delving further. She obeyed his instructions and went about her lesson as usual. Kyra was thankful she had the afternoon off. She needed time alone to mull over the thoughts that swarmed in her head like a scourge of mosquitoes. Kyra asked for fruit and nuts from an attendant, retrieved a book on elven folklore from her room, and retreated to the Garden of Sight.

The garden was empty, as Kyra had hoped. The statue of Imineral greeted her. Kyra sat on the edge of the fountain. The steady, burbling water comforted her. Putting the book down beside her, Kyra swung her legs up onto the stone, drew her knees close, and wrapped her arms around them. Kyra's gaze tracked a ruby red hummingbird that zipped to a flower trailing down a trellis. The sweet smell of nectar drifted through the air. Kyra let out a soft breath, ready to deal with the niggling questions zooming through her head.

Solarus had said Kyra potentially had only one wizard parent. If Solarus had insight into Kyra's history, she assumed Hayden and Talis did also. None of the three had offered a theory as to from where the other parent came. Kyra had crossed off the possibility she had elven heritage when she first asked about her childhood in Silvias. That left someone from one of the four kingdoms of men. Why didn't Solarus or the others discuss her heritage sooner? It wasn't as though there weren't ample opportunities on their journey. Kyra had asked several times about her parents and her background. What were Solarus, Hayden, and Talis afraid of? Was that why they worried about her control of her magic? Because Kyra was born with half the powers of a full-blooded wizard and likely, a lack of innate abilities?

With a heavy heart, Kyra rested her chin on her knees. She dully watched an emerald green hummingbird whiz through the courtyard and join the red one at the trellis. Another theory surfaced. Kyra's birth name wasn't necessarily Kyra. It was what she had told Hayden when he found her. Kyra had also believed she was Kate Smith in Chicago. The police *gave* her the identity. Kyra didn't know until she came to Ilian that it wasn't hers. Was this situation the same? What if Kyra's last interaction was with a person who mistook her for someone else? That would mean—Kyra's heart skipped a beat—she had had another identity foisted upon her that wasn't her given name. Kyra's original name could have carried the traditional *s*. She *could* be a wizard through and through. Unless Solarus and Hayden had other reasons to believe her parents weren't both wizards. Reasons Kyra doubted they would share with her.

Kyra rubbed her temples. Any of those explanations was reasonable. Sighing, Kyra followed the hummingbirds with her eyes as they zoomed out of the courtyard. Then she lifted her book and rested it on her knees. Whatever the answer, she wasn't going to figure it out today. Kyra began reading and lost herself in the adventures of Shareefa the Wise.

The sun stretched its arms lethargically in the sky as the time passed. Sweat trickled down Kyra's neck and slid down her back. Setting the book aside, Kyra dipped her hand in the fountain. She wiped her brow and rubbed her neck, relishing the cool water on her skin. She splashed water over her arms also, whose golden-brown color had been baked a shade of red.

"Kyra! I heard you were back!" someone exclaimed from the entrance to the courtyard.

Kyra's head shot up. There, standing under the arch leading to the garden, was an elf with pencil-straight black hair and porcelain skin. Kyra recognized him as the elf with the bandaged wrist from the equestrian fields. The bandage was gone, and a large smile stretched across his delicate features. Talis had identified the elf as Wynorrel. Supposedly an old friend. Kyra's body went taut as Wynorrel almost tripped running forward. What was he now?

Kyra had barely risen when the elf pulled her into an embrace. Kyra's tension melted with relief and happiness.

When he pulled away, water from her arms on his shirt, Wynorrel's dark eyes sparkled with a childlike joy. "It's been ages. I wanted to find you earlier. With the apprenticeship and studies and training, it's been hard to get away. When *Jaelyn* Therial gave us leave this morning, I asked around the palace to find you."

"I'm glad you did, Wynorrel," Kyra replied with a sincere grin.

"Wyn." Wynorrel flashed a smile, showing pearly-white teeth. "Everyone calls me Wyn."

"Oh, right, Wyn." Kyra brushed a strand of hair from her brow before admitting, "You're actually my first friend—" Kyra had a fleeting thought of Yuli except he had proven himself unworthy of the title, "—I've seen since I've been back. Talis mentioned everyone had started their apprenticeships while I was . . . gone. I guess they couldn't spare any time to say hi." Kyra hoped her statement would prompt Wyn to provide an explanation.

Wyn gave her an apologetic smile. "Apprenticeships are demanding," he reassured her. "Especially in the first year. The *Firth* and *Finna* barely let their apprentices out of their sight. They want to see if we're willing to work hard enough to invest more time in us. Ell constantly gripes about how *Finna* Sarika makes him rewrite the same calligraphic phrase until he's used two wells of ink. Sometimes three if she isn't satisfied. Then Ell must do it all over again with the next sentence."

"Ell?" Kyra interrupted with a puzzled look.

"Sorry, Ell is my older brother. His full name is Ellyonar. He's from your year."

"Ah, right. Ellynor."

"His work, I think it's tedious. Still, he wants to be a *Wisternyle*. Ell's got to prove he's a worthy successor." Wyn smiled again and tilted of his head. "The elves in your class are busier than any of the others."

Kyra reciprocated his smile. "Talis said your apprenticeship is unusual because you aren't of age yet. That's fantastic."

Wyn's cheeks flushed. He glanced around the courtyard with an anxious look as though someone was sneaking up behind them. His eyes roved to Imineral's statue atop the fountain. "It is unusual," Wyn replied, scratching the back of his head. "*Firth* Oran discovered I carved stone and glass and karia wood. He asked me to craft a few pieces for him. Then *Firth* Oran offered that I apprentice for him as a *Kavrinyle*. But . . ." Wyn's train of words dropped off a precipice. He avoided Kyra's puzzled gaze, staring instead at the moonstone walls. "You don't remember how he found out about my work, though."

Kyra privately recalled Talis' story of how Wyn had fashioned an Iona figurine for her birthday. Seeing Wyn's uncomfortable look, Kyra lied, "No, I'm sorry."

"It's okay. Anyway, I'm sorry I didn't talk to you sooner. And with the other elves . . ." Wyn's voice dropped a pitch. "It isn't their fault, Kyra, and it isn't your fault either, that they haven't welcomed you. Honestly, I'm not even supposed to be here."

Kyra's brow knitted. "What do you mean, you're not supposed to be here?"

"I'm not allowed." Wyn's face clouded. He threw another look around the courtyard. No elves were nearby. Wyn turned back to Kyra, his dark eyes full of sympathy. "None of us are. Yes, the apprenticeships do fill the day. It isn't that though. We've . . . we've been told we aren't to have any contact with you."

Kyra's anger spiked before splintering into humiliation. *Loralai*. No other elf despised Kyra as much as Loralai did, except for Kynder and his company. Kynder wasn't the king of Silvias, though, and Kyra doubted he had any power outside of the Southern domain. "Is this about Loralai?" Kyra demanded. "Is she scaring everyone off? Because if she is, I've got a few words to say about her . . ."

A confused expression crossed Wyn's face. "It isn't because of Loralai. Before you came, an order was . . ."

"There you are, Wyn."

Wyn and Kyra together turned at the voice. Wyn's brother Ellyonar ducked under the arch. Impatience was pressed into his pale features. "Why are you hiding in here? I've been looking all over—" Ellyonar cut himself off as his gaze wandered to Kyra. His lips formed a tight, choleric line. "What are you doing here?" he demanded.

Kyra cranked back her openness with Wyn until it was securely chained to her heart. She gestured to the book lying on the side of the fountain. "I was reading," she replied evenly. "Wyn was kind enough to stop by and catch up. It's good to see you, Ellyonar," she added, hoping to calm his anger. It was markedly out of place among the sanctity of Lady Imineral's gardens.

Ellyonar ignored her greeting. He turned to his younger brother. "Come on. I want to go to the training grounds before the guards start their drills. The horses are saddled. We can practice the *athlin* technique for tomorrow's test."

Wyn's body went rigid. "Like Kyra said, we're chatting, Ell. Practice can wait an hour."

"No, it can't." Ellynor glowered at Wyn with an intensity that could bore a hole through steel. "I'm doing this more for you than me. You've been sloppy with your form the past few weeks. I saw one of the junior students with better aim than you. Not to mention Vale almost bucked you off again yesterday." Ellyonar snorted derisively. "Or are you hoping another injury will have Sierra cooing over you?"

Wyn's face turned beet red, though whether it was out of anger or embarrassment Kyra couldn't tell. He unconsciously rubbed his once bandaged wrist. "It has nothing to do with Sierra," Wyn retorted. "I fell because I wasn't paying attention. I'm healed. Done. My focus is fine."

"Really. Which is why you'd prefer Kyra's company over mine and risk failing tomorrow?"

Wyn fell silent. He continued to rub his wrist as though the motion soothed him.

The cool hostility in Ellyonar's tone made Kyra's blood burn. Yuli hadn't spoken up when Loralai belittled her. This time, Ellyonar was the bully, and Wyn was the victim.

"That's enough," Kyra cut in sharply. She stepped toward Ellyonar. The older brother stared at her, surprised by her assertiveness. "If you must leave, Ellyonar, then leave. You don't need to harass your brother to get me to go away. I've got other things to do, and none of them involve listening to you." Ignoring a stunned Ellyonar, Kyra turned to Wyn. He seemed equally taken aback by Kyra's outburst of emotion. "Thanks for coming by, Wyn. If you have the time and *permission* to talk more, Talis usually knows where I am."

"Kyra . . ." Wyn protested feebly.

Kyra grabbed her book from the edge of the fountain. She stormed past both brothers and through the arch leading out of the courtyard.

"Why did you do that?" she heard Wyn accuse Ellyonar angrily. "I wasn't violating the order. I wanted to talk to her, that's all."

"Are you so brainless?" Ellyonar snapped. "Talking to her *is* violating the order. You're in an open space for Imineral's sake! Anyone could have seen or overheard your conversation. If I wasn't your brother, I would have reported you myself."

Kyra stopped dead in her tracks. A conversation with her was *forbidden*? By whom? Why? Her heart pounded in her chest as she turned and dashed to the side of the wall. She hunkered low near one of the hawk's-eye-like openings. Kyra peered in covertly.

Wyn wrinkled his nose, then sneezed. "I *know* that, Ell," he replied, sniffing. "I'm not an idiot. This whole thing is ridiculous. They think something 'might' happen. They have no idea if something *has* happened. What right do they have to treat Kyra like a murderer?"

They. Kyra's stomach sloshed with dread. It wasn't Loralai who drove the elves' avoidance of her. Was it Kynder and the Southern elves then? Could they have convinced Carina that Kyra was a scourge in their Realm? Or—the word stole her breath—a "murderer," past or future? Kyra carried the secret of the fire in Chicago like a nail in her heel, a stabbing pain hidden to everyone but herself. Did this confirm that she was the cause?

Wyn hadn't finished. "Can you imagine how *Kyra* feels? She doesn't have a clue why her friends won't talk to her. Then you barge into our conversation as testy as a bear with a toothache." His gaze roamed to the arch as he spoke. Kyra shrank away from the hole where she eavesdropped, hoping Wyn hadn't seen her outside.

"It doesn't matter what she feels," Ellyonar countered unsympathetically. He pulled at the sides of his ponytail to straighten it. "We don't question the seers." With a final tug on his hair, Ellyonar glared at his brother. "What would *Firth* Oran do if he found out you were disobeying the rules? He takes on *trustworthy* apprentices as architects. How confident would he be in your dependability if he caught you speaking with a wizard? Especially *this* wizard?"

"*Firth* Oran doesn't agree with the order either. He's spoken with Kyra before, and he likes her." Wyn's eyes sank to the ground. He crouched down and scooped up a handful of gemlike stones. Turning them over in his hand, Wyn added in a tone so soft Kyra had to strain over the fountain's burbling to hear him, "Talis showed him the figurine I made for Kyra when we were kids. The sapphire Iona. *Firth* Oran told me if it wasn't for that carving, I wouldn't have been selected for an early apprenticeship." Wyn opened his hand, letting all except the two largest stones spill through his fingers.

"I'm eternally grateful Kyra opened the door to *Firth* Oran. That's the past. I'm talking about now." Ellyonar's eyes narrowed. "Kyra's rattled your head worse than when you were thrown from the horse. You're risking your future for a girl you liked. You can't see that that girl—" Ellyonar wagged a finger at the entrance to the courtyard, "—is a full-fledged wizard now. The rules have changed."

Kyra could almost hear the red burning in Wyn's white cheeks. "I'm not rattled, Ell. I owe her my friendship. *Firth* Oran would understand."

"Friendship? Is that what you call a dalliance in the garden?"

"It's not a dalliance! Shouldn't I be overjoyed that one of my friends is alive?" Wyn turned and heatedly threw one of the stones into the fountain. It cut through the waters with a plunk and a splash. "Why are you being such a pompous *haskin*?"

"Because I'm looking out for you, you clod! You're my younger brother. What am I supposed to do? You have no sense when it comes to Kyra." In a swift movement, Ellyonar reached forward and snatched the other rock from Wyn's hand. Ellyonar pitched the stone into the fountain with more force than his brother. He pointed to the spot with his forefinger. "You'll be like that rock. You're willing to sink to the bottom of society when right now you're floating on top like a leaf. You're skilled. Our parents are proud of us. Now. They won't be if you throw away your opportunity with *Firth* Oran. You would disgrace them and yourself. That's not a good enough reason to stay away from Kyra? *Firth* Oran isn't going to disobey explicit orders any more than I am. Inishmore help me, I'll march to his shop right now. Maybe you'll listen to him when he threatens to end your training."

"You wouldn't dare."

"I would, if that's what it takes to keep you from sabotaging your future."

Wyn stared morosely at the rock under the surface of the water. He expelled a resigned breath. "If I could change the past, I would have kept the figurine for myself. I wouldn't be with *Firth* Oran. I wouldn't have the responsibility to Ilia. Neither you nor our parents would be disappointed if I lost my position and moved to something else. And I could give Kyra the explanation she deserves about why everyone either spurns her or is afraid to talk to her."

"You can't provide her that, and you won't." Ellyonar's tone was calmer in response to Wyn's resignation. "Besides, no matter what profession you end up in, you aren't above Silvias' laws, Wyn. It's for the best." He put an arm around his younger brother. "Let's go to the fields. Training will take your mind away from this."

Kyra's last sliver of hope of having an old friend flaked away like dead skin. Wyn nodded mutely. Back pressed flat against the wall, she slid to the ground. Kyra put her head in her hands. Tears pricked her eyes. If Wyn, an elf who had feelings for her, could be persuaded to cut off from her, then no one would give her a chance.

Engrossed in her thoughts, Kyra belatedly heard the brothers walk out of the courtyard. It was too late to hide. She glanced up half-heartedly. What would Wyn say to her? The brothers walked in the opposite direction, unaware of her presence. Wyn's head hung as Ellyonar steered him away. Kyra looked down at the grass, a sick feeling in her heart.

"They're wrong though, Ell." Wyn's voice drifted to her. "Kyra isn't a threat to Ilian. She's the only one who can stop the dark wizards, and she will."

***

Wyn's words had a chilling effect on Kyra. Someone had commanded the elves to keep their distance. If Ell was right and Wyn's mentor would disown him for having an innocent conversation, that someone had authority. Was it Therial? No, Kyra firmly rejected the idea. He had treated her with respect and was truly happy to see her. What about a lord or lady? Like Orison? After all, it was his elves who had cornered Kyra at the lake's shores. Did Orison have enough influence to intimidate the elves? If the southern lord was behind the order, how would Carina respond? Kyra couldn't imagine the queen letting him get away with such a tyrannical move. Kyra dismissed the idea of speaking directly with Carina. Kyra wasn't a child. She would handle the situation on her own.

Apart from Talis and Therial, Kyra stayed close to only her non-elven companions. Jyls always coaxed a laugh from her. Solarus sincerely wanted her to succeed with her magic. Hayden was a patient mentor. Her friends filled her time and, for the most part, Kyra could create her own bubble of normalcy in the otherwise unfriendly Realm.

Kyra continued to feel a unique camaraderie with Ash. It wasn't just because they were closest in age; like Kyra, the healer faced his own personal torment. On one afternoon, as Kyra stood next to Jyls and gazed out into the riding fields, she reflected on Ash's struggles. They started in their first days in Silvias. Hayden had invited Ash, Jyls, and Kyra to visit their horses in the pastures. As usual, Kyra had brought treats for Raven. Autumnstar gazed longingly at the carrots and apples Raven chomped from Kyra's hand. Smiling, Kyra shared the remainder of the snacks with Ash. As the filly happily crunched on an apple, Ash's gaze had trailed to the equestrian fields neighboring the pastures. Therial drilled a set of young, spear-carrying students. Ash bit his lip as the students trotted down the green expanse in unison.

"Therial has kindly granted us the use of his fields," Hayden had informed the healer casually.

Ash had torn his gaze back to Hayden, face pale.

"He will restrict his students to half the area on the days you are here," Hayden had continued. "Talis will coach you on how to develop a finer sense of balance in the saddle. With the space allotted here, you can canter unimpeded."

"Therial's the thoughtful one, isn't he, Ash?" Jyls had commented with a grin.

Ash's grimace showed he would be happier treating pus-filled boils than spending extra time in a saddle. "That isn't necessary," he had put in hastily. "Therial shouldn't change his lessons for me. What if the students need the whole field? I don't want to disturb them . . ."

"Therial wouldn't have offered a suggestion that hampered his lesson," Hayden had answered smoothly. "In Silvias, you don't have wizards, rogue guards, or phantoms on your heels. We can improve your riding abilities at our leisure. You should enjoy the opportunity."

Enjoyment seemed the furthest thing from Ash's mind. "I think trotting would be the most useful practice," he had suggested timidly. "Cantering . . . I don't need that really." Ash glanced to Kyra and Talis for help. Kyra gave him a sympathetic look, unsure how to respond. She rubbed Raven's nose. Talis smiled. Finding no allies among the group, Ash's shoulders drooped.

Hayden's gray gaze was thoughtful. "You've galloped through forests, dodged arrows, and evaded magic all at once. A canter is achievable." Hayden put a finger in his mouth and whistled. Windchaser's ears perked. Talis called out to the horses in elvish. The palomino pranced over to the edge of the fields, a wide horsey grin on his lips. Autumnstar shook her glossy, corral-colored mane with an air of importance.

"The weather's agreeable today," Hayden had commented as Windchaser nosed around Ash and Kyra for a spare carrot. Kyra laughed. She reached into her pocket and pulled out her last carrot. The palomino gobbled up the gift in one bite. Raven rolled his eyes. "A few rounds around the field would be appropriate," Hayden had concluded. "Right, Talis?"

"Agreed," the elf had replied.

Ash had miserably followed Talis into the pasture for his first lesson.

After that initial experience with Ash, Kyra became too preoccupied with her lessons and desperate for her old friends to return to the fields. The day after her encounter with Wyn, Kyra joined Jyls again in watching Ash's lessons. She wanted to show her support for Ash. Kyra empathized with having to master a skill she only somewhat understood. Over the course of the next three weeks, Kyra saw Ash's improvement. The only problem was his newfound abilities were as unpredictable as squirrels zipping and zagging across a road.

Today, Kyra witnessed the best and worst of Ash's riding. One minute he was bouncing up and down in his saddle with professional ease; the next he smacked his thighs against the hard leather, completely out of sync with Autumnstar's gentle pace. Once, Ash pushed himself up from his stirrups to reposition himself in the center of the saddle. His heels slipped. Kyra winced as Ash slid sideways. He dropped to the ground with a yelp. Kyra started forward, worried Ash was injured. The healer rose awkwardly and rubbed his backside. Kyra let out a sigh of relief. She pretended to fuss with her tunic sleeves as Ash sneaked an embarrassed glance in her direction.

Jyls, on the other hand, clapped boisterously. "You almost landed a flip that time, Ash!" he shouted loud enough to draw the attention of two female elves from the neighboring field. "Have another go—let's see those catlike reflexes!"

Kyra shook her head. The two female elves tittered with laughter. Ash's humiliation was visibly sorer than his bruises. His cheeks and neck were as red as his hair as he tromped back to Autumnstar. Wyn, who sat beside the female elves, swiveled in his saddle. A guilt-ridden expression was instantly stamped on his face as he spied Kyra.

Kyra noticed Wyn also. Resolutely ignoring the elf's gaze, Kyra turned to Jyls. "As helpful as those comments are," she said dryly, "Ash might benefit more from something like, 'You're doing great, Ash, keep going! It's looking a lot better! You've got this!'"

Jyls shook his shaggy mane of hair. "That's the difference between men and women. Women would cheerfully tell a street robber he's okay, he's doing great, if he looked pitiful enough. The street robber would love a woman's attention. If a man gave him the same encouragement or, perish the thought, sympathy, it would be demeaning. Men don't need their morale boosted by another man. We need a good ribbing to shake off our humiliation."

Kyra rolled her eyes as Therial's voice rang out. The riders streaked down the field, Wyn and Ell among them. Jyls pushed himself off the azalea bushes marking the border of the field and meandered to Ash. The healer had remounted, his back to them. Disheartenment spread from Ash's head hanging low through his hunched shoulders. Kyra turned to Talis. The elf, who stood at her side, had silently watched her exchange with Jyls.

"I don't understand," Kyra said in an undertone. "When we were in Farcaren and fleeing like rabid greeloks, Ash was fine. He rode so confidently, and he was keeping Jyls upright. He made it to Silvias without falling off once. Now it's like he's never been in a saddle before."

Talis leaned on the bushes and folded his hands. "Ash thinks too much." The elf's eyes tracked Autumnstar. She walked with slow, steady steps, sensing the healer's nervousness. "When Ash was focused on Jyls, his intuition guided him. He didn't have time to question his balance. He didn't puzzle through how to hold the reins. Ash allowed his instincts to follow Autumnstar's rhythm. That's the mark of an experienced rider. Riders don't *control* their steeds. The pairs are like dancers. They're united in their movements, working together with a grace neither could accomplish separately." Talis gestured to Therial's students. They were lined up at the far end of the field, hearkening to Therial's next instructions. "Ash also measures himself unfairly against riders like the elves. Elves are astride a horse the moment they can run. Ash forgets the students here aren't healers. Anyone can learn to ride a horse; not everyone has the gifts to save a person's life." Talis shook his head. "Comparing oneself to another has no advantage."

Ash trotted Autumnstar down the field toward Kyra and Talis. He impulsively darted looks toward the crop of students beside him. They, too, trotted down the field, heads held high, looking every bit proud elven warriors. The two female elves glimpsed Ash riding parallel to them. One smiled and tossed her braided black hair over her shoulder. Ash seemed to shrink in his saddle.

Jyls' head swiveled toward the female elves. A crooked grin spread over his face. As the healer steered Autumnstar to Kyra and Talis, Jyls moseyed back along the bush line.

"I wish they would go somewhere else," Ash muttered dolefully when he was within earshot.

"Who, the female elves?" Jyls asked. "You didn't have any women in Hillith? Besides your mother."

Ash shifted uncomfortably on Autumnstar, though his unease had nothing to do with the horse. "Of course we do. The women in Hillith aren't like, well, *them*." Ash glanced at the female elves. The one with the black braid whispered to her friend, her eyes on the healer. The friend laughed melodically.

"Aren't like them, as in stunningly gorgeous?" Jyls rested an elbow on the bushes. "Alluring members of society? Delightful prospects for courting? What, it's true," the thief defended as Talis flashed him an irritated look.

Ash's countenance was sullen. "I just wish they weren't here."

Jyls laughed. "Why don't we have Talis ask that one over," he suggested, pointing to the female with the long braid. "Request a personal session. On riding. Or on anything really. Talis can teach you how to woo this devastatingly attractive woman before your first lesson with her."

Talis' eyes narrowed. "I don't 'woo.'" The elf returned his attention to the healer, who rubbed the back of his neck with a painfully self-consciousness expression. "Ash, take one more pass down the field, if you would."

The healer navigated Autumnstar away from the bushes.

Talis turned to Jyls. "I agree with Kyra. Jesting might be a remedy for you, but Ash is sensitive to his perceived failures."

"Ash has to get used to the fact that women are a part of life," Jyls replied with a shrug. "As desirable as it would be for our young friend, female kind isn't going to poof! disappear. Unless," he said, addressing Kyra with a roguish grin, "you convince Solarus to magick them away to a deserted island in the Bibi Sea."

Mimicking Jyls, Kyra raised a brow. "Or we can magick away the men. Since they have no worthwhile qualities other than pestering women."

"Touché."

Kyra and Talis watched Ash a while longer before heading back to the palace. Kyra cast a last glance over her shoulder. Jyls waved unabashedly to the female elves who, giggling, waved back. Kyra grinned. *Magick away women indeed.*

Chapter 29

"Your stance should be wider." With his non-sword hand, Hayden reached forward and lightly pushed Kyra. She rocked onto her heels, her arms windmilling. Kyra managed to plant her back foot on the grassy earth before she fell. Looking sheepishly at Hayden, Kyra turned the hilt of her sword in her palm.

Hayden indicated her feet with his wooden blade. "Now you see why I said your stance is the most critical element in our training. If you're off-balance, Ilian's sharpest blade will be as useful to you as an underwater bridge. Your feet should form a triangle."

Kyra nodded. With the back of her hand, she wiped sweat from her brow. The dusk air was cool, but the effort of concentration coupled with the physical rigor of swordplay matted her loose, long-sleeved shirt to her back and hair to her neck. The grass was bathed in a pinkish-golden light. Doves cooed from the trees while the occasional nicker came from the horses' pastures.

Kyra let out a light sigh. Hayden had taken responsibility for her training in swordsmanship upon their arrival in Silvias. As with Ash, their sessions took place in the equestrian fields. They started after the students had gone home for the day.

From their first lesson, Hayden had armed himself with a wooden sword. Kyra used her real one. "You should grow accustomed to the sword you'll draw in battle," he had advised. "There's no point in adapting to the weight of a weapon you will never use. I'd rather spar against you with a practice weapon, at least initially. We want to avoid accidents."

"Like me skewering myself on your sword or stabbing myself in the toe with my own, right?"

Hayden laughed. "You have the foundational knowledge within you. We aren't starting with learning the difference between the blade and the hilt. This is an opportunity to refine your use of the weapon."

Kyra's skeptical expression deepened as she stared at her sword. "I doubt there's anything to 'refine,' but sure. Possibly."

Hayden bent his knees and spread his legs shoulder width apart. "Do what I do," he instructed.

Kyra mirrored Hayden's movements. She slid her front foot forward and kept her back foot set on the ground.

Hayden straightened. He again pushed Kyra's shoulder. This time, her upper body shifted against his touch. Her lower half held steady. Hayden nodded his approval. "Good. When you move, slide to close the distance between us. Don't hop. The last time, you lifted your foot from the ground to get closer. Having two feet down provides greater stability than one." Hayden resumed his stance and hugged his sword tightly against his body, the hilt resting above his hips.

"Swordplay is as much about defending as it is about attacking. Keep your arms bent at the elbow. Have a firm but relaxed grip on the hilt. Most importantly, hold the weapon close to your body. There are three reasons for this. First, stretching your arm can make you lose your footing if you're defending against a strike from a stronger opponent. Second, the more of your arm that's extended, the more it's exposed to your opponent's blade. Third, you can parry a thrust more quickly if your sword is ready at your side."

Kyra looked at her legs and then her arms, checking if everything was in line. She felt as uncoordinated as a toddler on stilts. "There are a lot of parts to remember."

"At first. It will get easier." Hayden angled his sword slightly. "Attack my left side with a jab."

Kyra stepped forward, half-swinging, half-stabbing. She knew as soon as she presented her sword that it was a sloppy move. Hayden tilted the wooden weapon almost imperceptibly and punched the blade toward her. Kyra's sword was knocked back, leaving her chest and right shoulder open to attack. Hayden glided forward and tapped the blunt end of his sword against her heart. Smiling, Hayden spun his weapon so that the blade was pointed downward.

"You swung," Hayden assessed as Kyra grimaced. "Keep your wrist strong. Arms steady against your body. Steady and relaxed. You also raised your front foot. Feet on the ground. This time, I'll swing overhead rather than jab. Block it. Feel the weight and balance of your blade."

Kyra reached her sword upward. With a flick of his wrist, Hayden swept his sword beneath Kyra's blade and tipped it effortlessly to the side. He finished the move by touching the sword to a spot near her armpit. Kyra let out an aggravated breath through her nostrils.

"Wait until the swing is lower before you parry," Hayden instructed. "Your sword met mine too high, which you see exposed you to a fatal blow."

"This is ridiculous," Kyra groused. "Can't I just practice with my staff and hand combat? Do I really need a sword?"

"Yes. Solarus and I agree that you can usually default to using your magic once you have control. You should always have another tool at your disposal. Your magic might fail you, or you might not be in a situation where you're able to call on it."

"Like in the Forbidden Forest," Kyra recalled with a slight frown.

"Like in the Forbidden Forest. Don't get frustrated though." Hayden reset his stance. "You can learn as much from your mistakes as you can from your successes. Remember the elven saying: 'Slow is fast, fast is slow.' Rushing through the fundamentals means you can develop bad habits. Bad habits will lead you to lose every confrontation, which isn't the goal of our lessons. Hence—" Hayden grinned encouragingly, "—let me see it again."

As their lessons progressed over the weeks, Kyra was confident Hayden didn't need to worry about her going 'fast.' Every iota of progress was followed by what she considered an epic failure. Or failures, Kyra thought during one particularly infuriating session. Kyra desperately thrusted her sword from left to right to block Hayden's lightning-fast strikes. When his sword suddenly snaked to the side, Kyra instinctively ducked and lowered her head. She felt a light tap on the nape of her neck. Kyra groaned. She glanced up as Hayden lifted the wooden sword. "Always keep your eyes and head up. If you offer your neck, your opponent will gladly take it."

It was the fourth time that day that Hayden had trapped her in an unwinnable situation. Kyra jabbed the sword in the grass as though it had personally affronted her.

Hayden raised a brow. "You're doing better than you think you are," he said, leaning on his sword. "It takes time to get comfortable with the movements."

Kyra continued to puncture the earth with a sour expression. "I think I'm brilliantly guaranteeing my opponent will kill me."

To her surprise, Hayden laughed. "Callum felt the same way when we first started. He always wanted to rush ahead of his skill." Hayden's gray eyes strayed across the fields. The air was heavy with the scent of oncoming rain. "He only grasped the meaning of 'fast is slow' when he tried a technique he had watched me use and had never had instruction in himself. Instead of throwing me to the ground, Callum ended up with a sprained ankle. The weeks that Callum spent on the mend and not in the field involved written instruction and theory. Not incredibly exciting for a teenager." Hayden winked at Kyra. "The time studying at a desk convinced Callum to heed my words when he returned to the field."

Kyra had perked up at the mention of the captain's name. She paused in her assault on the grass. "Callum was impatient too?"

"Equally, if not more so."

"And he became a captain." Kyra beamed. "That's comforting. At Thanesgard," she added suddenly, as a thought dawned on her. "Did you see him? I never asked how you and Solarus escaped after we rode to the forest."

"You didn't, did you." Hayden walked to the azalea bushes demarcating the edge of the training field. He settled his sword, hilt up, against the nearest one. Kyra followed suit. Hayden slowly rolled his right shoulder. Kyra caught a hint of pain on Hayden's lips as he stretched. Then Hayden bent down and picked up their waterskins. He offered one to Kyra, which she accepted gratefully. After drinking from his own, Hayden wiped his mouth. "No, we didn't come across Callum. What happened was . . ."

Kyra listened attentively as Hayden recounted the story. It went exactly as Callum had described: that Edyn had found Solarus and Hayden as they rode back through the rings; that another guard watched their horses as she surreptitiously led them to the guards' room; that Solarus' staff and Hayden and Kyra's swords were being safeguarded by other guards loyal to Callum; and that after retrieving their belongings, Solarus and Hayden fled to their horses and galloped through the castle, seeking to avoid the wizards and guards hunting them.

The tale diverged from Callum's account once Hayden and Solarus ran into the dark wizards and a troop of Arkin's soldiers. According to Hayden, the fight didn't last long.

"Orkanis was crippled by his contact with my sword," Hayden explained. He took another swig from his waterskin. "Janus tripped over one of the guards, and I was able to knock away his staff. After that, he hid behind Orkanis, who wasn't the best choice for protection. Orkanis cast a few spells without his staff and managed to disable a couple of the soldiers on his side. He didn't land a strike at either Solarus or me. The remaining soldiers were spooked by Solarus' bolts of lightning. Intimidation was likely the purpose of the display, seeing as how the magic was directed toward the sky and not at the men themselves."

Kyra remembered the blue streak that crackled in the air as she rode away from the castle. "You didn't mention Adakis," she observed. "What did he do?"

Hayden grinned wolfishly. "Adakis is more of a spectator than a participant in battles. He blustered as usual. He claimed to be the cleverest wizard of the group, then ordered the other wizards to attack. It didn't turn out too well for Orkanis, Janus, and Arkin's soldiers. I imagine it would have been even worse had Adakis lent a hand. I owe Talis another pair of florins," Hayden remarked as an afterthought. "Adakis never touched the weapons. He was barely close enough to see the fight." A strong wind flattened the grass, and the clouds darkened from a silvery gray to a deep charcoal. Hayden's eyes locked in on the sky. "We have a little while longer to practice if your temperament can handle it."

Kyra's face grew hot from shame at her grouchiness. "I'm sorry," she apologized. Kyra stooped down to lay the waterskin beside the azalea bush. "Consistently losing is a new experience for me. Outside of archery. Thank goodness I don't have to practice that anymore."

Hayden rubbed his chin. "You're overanalyzing the movements. Tell me. In your studies with Solarus, do you review every part of a spell when you summon one? Or are your actions instinctual?"

Kyra guessed Hayden already knew the answer. He continued to appear on the hill's crest, intently watching her instruction. She also suspected Hayden still wasn't aware she knew of his presence. "Instinctual if it's a familiar spell," Kyra responded. "If I'm experimenting with something new, I have to walk through the steps. When I'm comfortable enough, I do what feels right. What fits."

"Exactly. You've run through the motions enough times that thinking is an obstacle." Hayden took up his wooden sword with his left hand and stepped away from the bushes. Kyra grabbed her own sword by the hilt. Thunder pealed distantly.

Hayden raised his sword. "Respond to my moves as though you were channeling magic. Trust your instincts."

Kyra drew upon the meditative techniques from her magic lessons and swept aside her cluttered thoughts. She clutched the sword tightly against her hip. "I'm ready."

Hayden attacked. Kyra anticipated his thrust and sidestepped. She fluidly blocked his blade to the side. Twisting her wrist, Kyra's hand held her sword pointed steadily at Hayden's chest. Her face lit up. As did Hayden's.

"Perfect," he said. A light drizzle began to fall. "We can stop for the day."

"Not before we have another round, though." Kyra moved back, grinning. Her confidence was buoyed by this fresh approach.

A smile ghosted across Hayden's lips. He brushed strands of damp hair from his forehead. "Another round then."

Chapter 30

Diamantas wasn't surprised to see the hooded figure waiting at the stream. No matter when or where he summoned her—or she summoned him—using the heptagon coins' magic, she always arrived at their meeting point first. The gray skies veiled the figure who, like Diamantas, was fully cloaked in black. Her cowl was raised, and her hands were tucked in the folds of her sleeves. A nondescript, silver-brown staff was implanted in the spongy ground. Around her, a morning mist rose like steam, partially shrouding the cattails and tall grasses that lined the streambed. Slowly flowing waters murmured. The scents of plants and mud filled the air.

The cloaked figure inclined her head as Diamantas stepped forward. "I will admit, Diamantas," a pleasant-sounding voice said from under the hood, "I remain impressed by your foresight. Spelling these relics has proved useful in communicating across such distances." The wizard unclasped her hands and held up her heptagon coin. It no longer pulsed red and orange. The silver shimmered in the muted dawn light.

Diamantas' lips curled into a smile at the compliment. He rubbed his thumb against the smooth obsidian staff in his hand. "In battle, those with the swiftest exchanges win the day. I wanted such an advantage for our own. That the coins have seven sides, the divine number, is a favorable sign from Inishmore. Inishmore gives us its blessing in our fight. My only regret is that we do not have more of these relics."

"Your only regret." The cloaked figure sounded amused. Whatever inference she was making she didn't share with Diamantas. Instead, she turned the coin over in her pale hand. "If you acquired other relics, to whom would you entrust them? Adakis? He would betray that advantage through his inability to keep his mouth shut. Janus would reveal our intentions through his incompetence. Lilias would not be able to resist the temptation to use our conversations to pursue her own ends. No, Diamantas, it is best that only two exist and that we are the ones to use them."

Diamantas gave a nod of agreement. He privately knew there had been three coins. Regrettably, the third had disappeared at the same time as Kyra. He suspected it had fallen from his pocket during the skirmish with the dragons. Diamantas personally had never returned to the site to look for the coin. He didn't want to attract more attention to the battle by returning to the area himself. Deploying Syndrominous was the sounder decision. Syndrominous had spent months scouring the site, looking to gather clues to Kyra's whereabouts. If anyone were to turn the relic to his benefit, it would have been Diamantas' ever-conspiring rival. Yet Syndrominous had never intruded upon Diamantas' meetings. Which meant either Syndrominous hadn't found the coin or, if he had, he hadn't discovered how to make use of it. Both possibilities accomplished the same end; no one could eavesdrop when Diamantas sought counsel from his mentor.

"We captured Kyra in Thanesgard," Diamantas said aloud as the hooded figure returned the coin to her cloak pocket. "To be brief, the situation was poorly handled. Kyra, Solarus, and the others escaped. They have claimed refuge within Silvias. My sources within the Realm have told me the elves are not amenable to safeguarding Kyra for long. She will be expelled. We must only wait."

"What do you plan to do should Kyra by chance deliver herself to you?"

Diamantas had anticipated the question. "I plan to offer her another opportunity to be part of our cause. To become a liberator of our people. I am not so naïve as to expect her to accompany me to Harkimer. I do have confidence that I can persuade her to meet with a group of wizards, hand-selected by us. I want women and children among them. Their tales, particularly one coming from a child, will give Kyra pause, if not convince her to have a longer discourse with us. We may sway her to volunteer her loyalty to Harkimer. After all—" Diamantas' eyes glinted as he rapped his staff on the ground "—you advised me once that words well-chosen can turn an enemy into an ally."

The hooded figure laughed humorously. "I did. The greater the effort, the greater the gain. I would caution you to be careful in your overtures, however. Kyra may be swayed by your reasoning. She is young and, I would surmise, more receptive to the argument of a silver-tongued orator. Kyra will not be so suggestible for long. Do not underestimate Solarus and Hayden's influence. They can coax orchards withered by drought to produce sweet fruits. Combine this with the slipshod attempts of Adakis and the other wizards to capture Kyra, and you may find attempts at persuasion futile."

The sharp lines on Diamantas' face hardened with displeasure. He stroked his beard with a dark look. "Has the scribe offered any information?"

The female wizard snorted. "None. He is as mute as a corpse." The hood turned briefly as a bat flapped over her head and disappeared into the woods. A second and third bat flitted by. "The scribe said he will take his secrets to the grave. You should allow him the honor." The hood's attention moved from the bats back to Diamantas. "Syndrominous attempts to sow dissent in your absence. I am handling him. You will have to reiterate to the Council the importance of your efforts when you return. The best work unseen does nothing. Your presence will be enough to silence some detractors. You will have to work hard to reclaim the more ardent supporters of your rival."

Diamantas stabbed his staff into the soft ground like a spear. He didn't speak at first, his expression pensive. The cloaked figure waited. Diamantas suddenly smiled. "I will promote Syndrominous to general upon my return. When the war begins, he will be at the head of the forces and the first to engage our enemies. We will see if he survives the attack."

The figure's laugh was so malicious it sent an involuntary shudder down Diamantas' spine. "It is not a war, Diamantas. It is a conquest." The hooded figure snatched the silver-brown staff from the ground. "You have done well.

May you be gifted with fortitude and fortune. Malus himself would have been victorious had he possessed those traits."

Diamantas bowed respectfully to the hooded figure. He heard the grasses and cattails rustle softly. When he looked up, the female wizard was gone, mist filling the space where she had stood a moment before.

Chapter 31

The late spring days began melting under a sweltering sun impatient for the start of summer. A week of rain stripped the buds from Silvias' ervil trees. They became adorned with brilliant golden leaves while the woods flourished with even brighter greens. Lush grasses carpeted the ground. Their earthy scent surrounded the palace. Occasionally Kyra walked barefoot, enjoying the fresh air tickling her toes.

The warmer weather also teased out a potpourri of scents from the courtyards. The Garden of Joy carried the enticing aroma of crushed nutmeg and cinnamon. The Garden of Wisdom's savory herbs made Kyra's mouth water. Kyra's favorite garden remained the Garden of Sight, where soft floral scents swirled from the bell-like red and yellow flowers climbing along the archways and trellises.

The fresh blooms weren't welcomed by everyone in the Elven Realm. Kyra noticed as she traversed the training fields that many students sneezed and sniffled their way through their lessons—including Loralai. Kyra smiled with satisfaction at the elf's misery. She surreptitiously watched Loralai from behind the azalea bushes as the elf lost her staff-fighting bouts, distracted by fits of sneezing. To Kyra's surprise, the elf didn't once complain about her defeats. Neither did Loralai blame her performance on her invasive allergies. She simply bowed to her opponent and stepped aside to let the next pair spar. Kyra felt a begrudging respect for Loralai. As the bouts continued, Kyra scarpered off to her own afternoon sessions.

While Kyra's routine with Solarus and her companions kept her busy, Kyra still found it hard to endure the scorn and neglect from the elven teenagers. Their staring and gossiping dogged her steps. Kyra ignored them as best she could. She kept her head held high, eyes forward, with an expression indicating the elves were too insignificant to merit the slightest glance. At times, Kyra's curiosity pulled her from her feigned apathy. Times like when she saw Wyn and Ell at the equestrian fields. While Kyra fixed her eyes away from the students, she couldn't shut her ears to Wyn's jesting and the tittering from the female elves. Kyra's heart panged with loneliness and envy. Her hurt was buried deeply within her, and she felt like her body was covered in invisible bruises that ached at the thought of rejection.

Once, Wyn glanced over his shoulder at the same time Kyra hastened along the edge of the enclosure. His laughter died away. Kyra caught Wyn's guilt-ridden expression as he followed her with his dark eyes.

Ell cuffed his brother on the back of the head. "Eyes forward," he scolded Wyn.

As Wyn complied, Kyra trotted away, hoping she could outpace her pain.

The hardest friendship to let go of was with Yuli. Between Loralai's jealousy and the ambiguous command to the elves, Kyra knew any communication was impossible. Yet she hadn't recovered any memories since she arrived in Silvias. Except for the hunter game. Which meant, Kyra accepted sadly, Yuli and Aila had been the only two elves she knew could help her rebuild her past. Kyra was almost glad Aila was in Calonia. She wasn't sure she could handle her dismissal also. If Kyra didn't meet the magenta-haired elf, she could at least dream that they were close friends.

Yuli was usually in the company of the emerald-clad Royal Guards who, inevitably, spent hours near the palace. Kyra skirted under a courtyard entrance or ducked behind a tree when she heard his animated conversation. Like a lion crouched in the savannah, Kyra would watch as Yuli promenaded past. He gestured as he spoke, face beaming with clear delight at being among the guards. When the group was out of sight, Kyra waited for the count of a few, deep breaths, letting enough of the frustration out before leaving.

Fortunately, Kyra's lessons absorbed most of her time. In addition to the morning's magic sessions, Kyra's afternoons were alternately occupied with either sword fighting with Hayden or hand combat with Talis. Kyra never won against Hayden; she often came to a stalemate with Talis. Therial also graciously offered her sessions in staff fighting in his free hours. Kyra's face would become tinged red from the heat, and sweat would stick her clothing to her back. She uncomplainingly plowed forward in her grueling lessons. Shunned by her elven peers, Kyra had renewed gratitude for the few friends she had. Even if they bested her in every bout.

Oftentimes, Kyra visited the lake before dinner. It was a refreshing respite from the heat. The first few days she went alone, contentedly swimming in her full attire through the cooler waters. Then Kyra cajoled Ash and Jyls to join her. They eagerly accepted. After two weeks, the trio had established a routine of taking jaunts to the lake. It lightened Kyra's heart to have company, even if Jyls and Ash preferred to laze on the bank, the only part of their bodies in the water their bare feet.

If Kyra knew what was coming, no sunlight would be warm enough to melt the icy dread awaiting her.

***

The animals darted through the woods with a terror-driven urgency. Menacing charcoal-gray clouds soared overhead. Raindrops the size of walnuts found their way through gaps in the tree canopy and pelted the animals mercilessly. The air stank of slime and rot beneath the blanket of forest debris. Paws muddied, thick fur matted, skin scratched by creeping brambles and thorns, the trio pressed onward.

Raff pivoted sharply. Hazel maneuvered beside him. They hurdled a fallen tree, their steps in sync. More mud splattered on Hazel's coat as she landed in a deep pit. Raff's paws barely touched the surface. His yellow-orbed eyes followed the form of the whippet, Chloe. She loped before them with breakneck speed, water streaming down her back.

"We shouldn't have left her alone," Hazel panted. "Kyra was safe with us."

"She is not alone," Raff replied loudly over the wind. The storm raged against the trees, sending a shower of leaves upon them. The panther shook the leaves free from his head and continued, "Hayden and Talis guarded Kyra long before the *Al-Ethran* became interested in her. And I am grateful for that fact. I would stake that Khron would have made certain a cub of a wizard never reached adulthood. Then the prophecy would never be realized, one way or the other."

"The *Al-Ethran* should have at least consented to provide Kyra asylum," Hazel insisted breathlessly. "With us. In the woods. It is well concealed."

"That is how they would like to keep it. I cannot begrudge the Council their desire to safeguard our secret. The War of Calonia is almost eight hundred years in the past, yet our kin's sacrifices seem recent. The balance that has existed in Ilian is more precarious than ever. I do agree that exceptional circumstances might warrant a change of strategy. The risk of leaving Kyra in the hands of others is greater than the risk of our secret being revealed."

Hazel didn't respond, only ran harder. The panther took in a labored breath. He and Hazel had journeyed for three weeks to reach the *Al-Ethran*. The trip should have taken two. Greeloks forced the duo to take a long, winding route. They even doubled-back at times to throw off any scent that would attract the odious creatures. When Raff and Hazel finally reached the animals' sacred gathering place, they summoned the Council of Elders. Its members listened with grave expressions to Raff's report: the retrieval of Kyra in London; the battle with the dark wizards at Edoin; the rescue by Hayden and his companions. Their successes were overshadowed by the news of Kyra's lost memories of Ilian.

The Council had peppered Raff and Hazel with questions.

"What magic had Kyra performed in this other world, this 'London?'" "You are certain she did not recognize the dark wizards?" "Do you believe her claim of ignorance about Ilian was genuine? Could it have been a ruse?" "Is there any indication she has been turned from friend to foe?"

Khron had thrust the most forceful accusations against Kyra. The bear had snorted derisively after Raff and Hazel bore witness to Kyra's genuine confusion about, and determination to resist, the dark wizards. "You cannot trust a wizard. I do not care what she says. Magic can manipulate feelings and create illusions of conviction and purity. I reject her return."

The debates that ensued stretched out over the course of three days. At the conclusion, the *Al-Ethran* was divided about how Kyra's sudden homecoming was actualizing the prophecy. Then Chloe had arrived.

"More ill and portentous tidings," Blackhunter had stated solemnly after Chloe had recited Talis' message. "Reapers freely traversing the forest. Spies within Thanesgard. Likely wizards." The large black wolf had turned her lavender gaze to Raff and Hazel. "What the elven queen will do with this knowledge, I cannot say. We have come to a point where we need allies beyond the people of Silvias. For good or evil, Kyra's return ushers in a new era. What has been set into motion cannot be delayed, nor should it be. It is Inishmore's plan. How we respond to that plan, however, is our choice." Blackhunter's eyes swept across the group. "We suspected when the elf Merinn disappeared that Diamantas' sources ran deep. You remember the words of our seers. Not six months past, they foretold that the kingdom of the *Y'cartim Allegra* would be rotted from the inside until the entire foundation upon which it stood collapsed. If the premonition is correct, this kingdom is Silvias. I believe the wizard with the obsidian staff has already courted the *Raenalyn*'s kin. The absence of the scouts had been a part of this plan. If elves have been corrupted, Ilian has begun to fall."

There had been murmuring among the group, nervous pawing, ears flattening, and a few snarls from Khron.

"I put forward to the Council that Kyra be accompanied by one of its members," Blackhunter's voice boomed through the glade. "We can no longer rely on wizards, men, and elves. We must observe the happenings ourselves. Our teeth, talons, and claws must be ready to undertake whatever action is required. Whether Kyra remains true to Ilian or becomes an adversary of it, we must be the first to know. It is the only way to save our kind. What does the *Al-Ethran* say to this?"

Without hesitation, the Council unanimously agreed. Raff and Hazel had again volunteered for the task, arguing that with threats from all sides, two members had to be present. Chloe would accompany them until they neared Thanesgard, at which point she would return to her post at the castle. The panther and collie would continue to Silvias.

Thus, with nary a few days' rest behind them, Raff, Hazel, and Chloe abandoned the Council's haven and sprinted eastward.

Now the animals sprinted with grim purpose through the vengeful storm. They reached what had once been a clear stream. Barraged by rain, the waters were brown and dangerous, the current threatening to sweep them under. Hazel stopped beside Raff. Her head turned left and right as they sought a way across.

"We can pass here!" Chloe called. She waited by a tree whose branches had been dragged halfway under the water. Those that managed to stay afloat spanned almost the full length of the stream. Broken slabs of moss-covered rock jutted out like giant sprigs of grass. If the animals could reach the rocks, they could reach the opposite bank.

Chloe stepped up to the first branch. Her tiny paws disappeared beneath the water. For a heart-stopping moment, the whippet was pushed to the side by the might of the waters. Chloe lunged forward. She bounded from one branch to another, paws skimming the surface of the water, until she landed on the first boulder. The whippet didn't count on the slick green moss. Chloe's nails scraped the surface of the rock. Her hind legs peddled as she desperately tried to keep her purchase. Yelping in panic, the whippet slowly slid back toward the stream.

Raff and Hazel loped to the tree. "We're coming, Chloe!" the collie barked as she climbed onto the branches. The whippet's body trembled with effort. Raff sprang onto the tree and vaulted past Hazel. As Chloe's strength gave way, the panther had positioned himself on the rock beneath her. Raff blocked Chloe with his body, preventing her from being swept up by the ferocious waters. Twisting around his spine, Raff placed his paw in the stream and growled. The stream flared a neon blue. Then, like dough being removed from a pie crust, the waters peeled away from the jutting rocks. Chloe chanced a look down. The neon blue water receded, revealing flat, paver-like stones beneath. They formed a straight path to the bank. Righting herself as best she could against Raff, Chloe launched herself onto the flat surface. In a few leaps, Chloe was safely on the opposite side. She quivered, thin fur and skin soaked through.

"Hazel!" Raff called across the tree branch. He kept his paw in the water.

The collie had almost reached him. The waters smashed against the invisible magic that separated them from the flat stones. Hazel effortlessly crossed the rocks and joined Chloe on the bank.

Seeing the dogs safe, Raff lifted his paw, swiveled, and hurtled over the rocks in one motion. The neon blue flashed and was gone. Freed from the magical obstruction, the brown waters surged upward. As Raff jumped off the last of the slabs, the stream furiously surged upward and crashed over the rocks.

Chloe again assumed the lead. "There is a den nearby," the whippet told them as they ran. Chloe panted, her pace hampered by her flagging energy. "We can wait out the storm if the entrance has not been blocked by debris."

The forest's landscape of leaves, mud, and underbrush began to host worn chunks of rock. Stone ledges formed between the trees. Fewer leaves carpeted the ground, with pebbles appearing among them. Chloe determinedly led Raff and Hazel through the new section of woods. Then she let out a bark of relief. They had arrived at a mishmash of rocks that partially hid a large overhang. Rain cascaded over the lip as though being poured from a bottomless pitcher. Ears down, Chloe sprinted through the water and into the den. Raff and Hazel jetted in after her. The rain noisily smacked the ground outside the entrance, echoing off the den's walls.

The animals splashed through puddles as they entered. Chloe immediately lapped up the cold water. Hazel and Raff joined her, their throats as dry as their fur was wet. When they were finished, Hazel and Raff shook water from their thick coats, spraying the walls. Chloe wearily stepped toward one of beds of pine needles scattered across the hard earth. She half-toppled onto it. Chloe trembled.

Hazel's gaze was riddled with concern. She trotted to Chloe and settled down, pressing her dense, damp fur against the whippet's skinny body. "We will get you warm," Hazel told the whippet soothingly as though speaking to a pup. As Chloe looked at her with a wretched expression, Hazel realized how young the whippet actually was. Barely a year old and already a scout. Hazel rubbed her nose against Chloe's ear. The whippet laid her head on the collie's paws in exhaustion and closed her eyes.

Hazel glanced sideways at Raff. He stood near the den's entrance. The thundering of water reverberated around them. "We have not eaten properly since the rains started three days past," Hazel raised her voice over it. "Can we find anything in the midst of this storm for Chloe?"

"We will have to try." Raff's whiskers twitched. He looked piqued as he stared at the downpour. "I abhor being wet. Cats are not meant for the rain." Raff took a step forward. Hazel noticed he moved more sluggishly than usual.

"Are you all right?"

Raff nodded. "Using as much magic as I did has robbed me of energy. I had hoped we could cross without it. Do not worry, though. I will recover fast enough."

"Be careful," Hazel warned. "My nose is so full with the stench of worms and plants that it is impossible to pick up other scents. I am afraid creatures may have followed us, and I cannot sense them. And you are not wholly well."

"Then let us hope that what disguises our predators to us similarly disguises us to them, should they be in the woods." The water spilling over the lip of the stone thick. Raff pushed through it as though it were a heavy velvet curtain.

The drumming drowned out all other sounds as Raff jogged between the trees. His ears flickered, seeking unusual sounds. He found a hole under a tangle of roots and sniffed it. As Hazel noted, the rain plugged any smells of possible prey. Raff raised his head and soldiered on.

Continue through Edoin Forest, Raff mentally rehearsed their route to Silvias. *Head north to circuit the Forgotten Forest. Cross at the confluence of the rivers, then south through the Ancient Forest.* By then they would either happen upon elven guards or would have an unimpeded path to the palace.

Raff spied a glen. He slowed his pace to a prowl, whiskers twitching in the rain. A cluster of plump birds disguised by nondescript brown and white feathers pecked at the ground. One yanked a long worm from the earth and shook it. Raff padded out silently. He crouched low, poised to spring. The bird suddenly looked up. Eyes bugging out of his head at the sight of the panther, the bird's mouth opened. The worm fell out unnoticed. Squawking loudly, the bird half-waddled, half-bounced away. Raff shot forward. The birds escaped to the refuge of the trees.

Raff's whiskers downturned in vexation. How had they noticed him?

His answer came quickly. Magic pervaded the air. Beneath his mottled paws, Raff felt the earth vibrate from the pounding of hooves. The panther spun around. His golden orbed eyes spotted the cloaked riders even through the rain.

The wizards had found them.

Raising his head stoically, water streaming down his face, Raff roared into the storm. Thunder boomed, amplifying his challenge. His claws extended as the riders burst into the glen. Raff's eyes widened in surprise. They weren't who he expected.

Chapter 32

Am I asking for much? Kyra grumbled to herself. She brushed a wave of honey-brown hair from her eyes as she stared down from the hill's crest. *Elves have avoided me like I'm a leper for weeks, and the one elf I wouldn't mind giving a disease to is this one. Can't I have* one *spot in Silvias that's mine?*

The question grated on Kyra as she gave Solarus a sideways glance. He leaned against his hornbeam staff, one hand raised over his eyes to shield the bright morning light. He squinted at the lake. Like Kyra, he had noticed the figure. Her arms were folded, her back to them, as she stood on the shore. Solarus' eyes held a reflective expression.

Kyra and Solarus had set out before dawn for a rigorous day of training. The scent of fresh dew perfumed the air as they meandered up the hill. When they reached the apex, Kyra spotted the elf. At first, the glare obscured the elf's features. Then light glimmered on the figure's crimped, wheat-colored, strawberry blond mane, as glossy as if it had been treated with fine oils. The cloudless, blue morning sky didn't alter Kyra's dour expression when she recognized the elf as Loralai.

"Do you intend to remain on this hill, or shall we proceed to our lesson?" Solarus turned to Kyra, lowering his hand. His tone implied the latter was the only acceptable answer.

"A delay would be nice. I don't make it a *habit*—" she deliberately used Solarus' trademarked phrase, to which he smiled slightly, "—of talking to pampered elves with puffed-up egos. Nothing good is going to come out of me seeing her."

"And yet, I was roused from my delightful slumber to extend today's lesson because of its importance." Solarus took up his staff and began to descend hill. "You can make an exception for one day."

"Since when do you make exceptions?" Kyra muttered. She adjusted her cherrywood staff and stomped down after him.

They approached Loralai from the side as they neared the shore. Loralai's profile was clearer now. Her expression lacked its usual haughtiness. The corners of Loralai's eyes were crinkled with troubled contemplation, and her eyes held a faraway look. Water softly lapped the bank. Loralai absently scraped the spongy soil with the tip of her boot.

Part of Kyra felt a mothlike twinge of pity as she stepped onto the bank behind Loralai. The other part sorely tempted her to push the elf into the cool waters.

Solarus coughed deliberately. Loralai spun around like a startled deer, dropping her arms to the side. Her eyes found Solarus first. Loralai collected herself as he gave her a slight incline of his head. Her gaze sailed past Solarus to Kyra. Eyes narrowing, Loralai's lips curled scornfully.

I should have pushed her in, Kyra thought.

"Good morning, Your Highness," Solarus said courteously. "You chose a fine day to visit the lake."

Kyra gawked at Solarus. *Your Highness? Loralai is royalty?* She couldn't have been more shocked if Solarus had announced his mother was a dolphin and his father was a crab. As if the elf could have a larger ego. When Solarus' gaze tacitly flitted to Kyra, she clamped her mouth shut.

Loralai planted her hands on her hips. "It's always enjoyable visiting the lake," she answered frostily without returning the greeting, "I don't have to deal with others." The elf's glower made clear she meant Kyra was ruining her peaceful freedom. "I didn't expect company, and I don't desire it."

"We will not provide any, if you so choose." Solarus' demeanor held its usual air of superiority even in the face of the elven royal. "However, I must request that you continue your ruminations elsewhere. *Raenalyn* Carina has granted us leave to use this lake in the morning hours."

"You 'must request?'" Loralai stared at Solarus in disbelief. Kyra guessed she wasn't used to being addressed so bluntly. "This is *my* lake. I don't have to go anywhere just because *she*—" Loralai tossed Kyra another scathing look, "—has the *Raenalyn*'s permission to sit on the bank."

Solarus' tone was polite. "Our purposes are more than to lounge in tranquil solitude."

Loralai's eyes narrowed in suspicion. "What purposes?"

"None with which you need to concern yourself. You seem to have enough occupying your thoughts to complicate them with the trifling affairs of wizards."

Loralai's affronted expression freed Kyra's grin. Watching the elf face off against Solarus reminded her of two peacocks fanning their feathers. The difference was the young Loralai was a peachick compared to the mature and unflappable Solarus who, Kyra was convinced, had never lost an argument.

A honking followed by two splashes drew Kyra's attention. Loralai also glanced over her shoulder. A pair of swans shook water from their wings as they settled comfortably atop the lake's waters.

"Everything concerns me," Loralai finally shot back. She returned her gaze to Solarus. "Silvias is the realm of the *elves*, and *I* am the future *Raenalyn*. If you won't share your reasons for intruding on my privacy, I'll ask *Raenalyn* Carina."

"Please do." Solarus ran a finger along the cursive Z line in his hair. "If *Raenalyn* Carina withdraws her consent, then we will leave. Until that time, Kyra and I will continue as we have since we arrived. However—," Solarus again smiled like a cat in a nest of mice, "—I welcome you to join us. Kyra has had instruction in the lake. She has lacked opponents against which to see if her lessons have borne fruit. Kyra would benefit from testing her mettle against a worthy partner. A future *Raenalyn* would be quite a challenge, would you not agree?"

Loralai was conspicuously unnerved by the invitation. The lake's breeze teased strands of hair along her face. Loralai brushed them to the side with a scowl. "I wouldn't dare impose on your sessions and your 'purposes,' the ones that don't concern me," she replied imperiously. "Only an ungracious host would humiliate a guest by accidentally dredging her in the lake."

"I agree," Kyra spoke for the first time. She locked eyes with Loralai. "It would be equally impolite to embarrass my 'gracious host' in a mock battle. I mean, if you lost your footing and splashed into the lake, you'd have to spend hours brushing your hair to make it pretty and perfect again."

Kyra's dig found its mark. Loralai's pale face flushed a strawberry-red. She flung a look at Solarus. "Enjoy your time. Make sure she cleans up the messes she makes."

Solarus again dipped his head. "We shall miss your company."

Kyra stepped aside as Loralai stormed past. It took all of Kyra's self-control to stop the desire to cast the wetting spell on the elf. Kyra watched her tromp up the hill, then turned to Solarus. "Loralai's a princess?"

Solarus' eyes were also on Loralai. She peevishly shoved a tree bough aside, ducked beneath the foliage, and disappeared into the woods. "She is."

"Unbelievable." Kyra kicked the bank's soft earth with the toe of her boot, sending chunks of dirt flying. "What an irritating, narcissistic, royal pain in the . . ."

"Leave it be," Solarus reprimanded though not without a trace of amusement. "Loralai is rude and self-important, traits that are not uncommon in those in positions of power. If you believe one has undesirable qualities, you do not want to adopt those qualities yourself. Be well-mannered and humble instead. Besides," he added, twisting the staff in his hands, "we will not endear ourselves to our elven hosts by insulting their future queen. I need use of this lake."

Kyra gave him a rankled look. "*You* insulted her."

"I did not insult her," Solarus replied calmly. "I presented facts and invited her to participate at her pleasure." Solarus moved up to the line of grass behind the bank and sat cross-legged.

"I thought, apparently falsely, that kings and queens and princesses were taught the same values as us *commoners*," Kyra said snappily. "Like, I don't know, courtesy and kindness and *manners* . . ."

"Loralai was schooled in all these and chooses to behave contrary to them," Solarus interrupted. He set his staff lengthwise before him on the grass and rested his palms on his knees. "Being born with royal blood does not mean much. The lineage merely determines an individual's status, not her character. You do not have to like Loralai. You must tolerate her." Solarus underscored his words with a look that brooked no argument.

"Fine." Kyra raked a hand through her hair in frustration. "I can 'tolerate' her."

"I am pleased to hear it." Solarus craned his neck and cast an exaggerated look over Kyra's shoulder. "How inviting the water looks."

Kyra took the not-so-subtle hint. As she unlaced her boots, Kyra remarked, "Between Arkin and Loralai, my faith in Ilian's leaders isn't very high. She acts as though she's so put out whenever I see her, and here she's a princess. What a terrible burden." Kyra furiously yanked off a boot and dropped it beside her.

From the corner of her eye, Kyra saw a grin slide across Solarus' face. "My mother had a saying," Solarus said as Kyra shook off the other boot with equal irreverence. "'Suffering is a matter of perception; happiness is a matter of choice.' I take it you believe the elven princess has a life preferable to your own. Or that Loralai does not endure tribulations beyond bathing in tepid waters or having insufficient down in her pillows."

Kyra imagined an irate Loralai sitting on her bed and throwing her pillows to the floor like a child. "I'm sure being a member of elven royalty is extremely taxing." Kyra put her hand on her chin, pretending to be lost in thought. "What dress shall I wear to the ball? Should it be satin or velvet? Will the hem have frills, or should the cuffs have lace? And the color, oh the color of the gown, that's the toughest choice." Kyra clapped her hands together with such embellished dismay that Solarus rolled his eyes. "Gold matches my gorgeous, flowing tresses. On the other hand, a sky blue would make my eyes shine like sapphires." Shaking her head, Kyra dropped the act and unfastened her cloak. "Decisions, decisions. What a life."

Solarus rubbed his temple as though massaging a headache. "While I am sure a princess in Ilian has had to deal with such precarious situations as choices of attire, most have other matters that fill their time. You assume Loralai has no concerns because of your petty squabble." Solarus raised a hand to forestall Kyra's retort. "It is not an insult. It is a fact. Teenagers behave thus. What I want you to understand is that a royal's gilded room can be as much a prison as a comfort."

Skepticism creased Kyra's face. She folded her cloak and set it aside. "Really. A prison."

Solarus leaned back, resting his palms again on his knees. "Monarchs do not possess personal freedoms like you and I. Monarchs fill roles, as much as any actor. These roles come with expectations and obligations. 'Loralai,' as the individual, disappears the moment the coronation ends. She becomes to all, including her kin, 'Her Majesty the Queen.' Loralai will assume the responsibilities to the kingdom as a mother to her children, expected to attend to every need, desire, and grievance of her people. She will be pushed some days to exhaustion. She will work through illness since the duties of the Realm must be fulfilled. She will make decisions that will be praised by one half of the citizens and reviled by the other.

"Furthermore," Solarus continued as Kyra broodingly picked blades of glass, "because of these many duties, Loralai will have no privacy as queen. She will not roam the kingdom or, as you put it, 'go for a run' on a whim. A monarch is the cornerstone of the Realm; she will never be without protection, not even within her own borders. Loralai will often be accompanied by escorts when she travels from the palace. Therefore, if you value your moments of solitude and cherish your anonymity, it is better to be a rock in the ravine: unmarkable, forgettable, and plain. Loralai will be a gem, dazzling and attracting all to her."

"That's debatable," Kyra muttered with a peevish expression. She rubbed the grass between her fingers.

Solarus gave her a pointed look. "It is not debatable. It is true. *That* is the world in which Loralai will find herself. And this is to mention nothing about her own wishes and desires. Now, I ask you. Will Loralai suffer? Will she be happy?"

"The position doesn't sound very appealing," Kyra admitted. Her eyes moved to a dragonfly hovering over the lake's tranquil waters. It zoomed toward the bank and fluttered over her head. "You aren't mentioning what things a queen *can* do. She has the power to help her people. The elves rely on her. Unlike me. Nothing I do impacts anyone else or makes a difference. No one needs me."

The honest statement slipped out from Kyra before she could stop it. She cleared her throat and focused intently on the grass, hoping Solarus hadn't heard the heartache in her voice. Was Kyra *jealous* of Loralai? Because the elves would depend on the snooty princess? Maybe a hint jealous, Kyra confessed to herself. Kyra didn't have a purpose. She would never be a queen. She was a burden, even on her friends. It was all Kyra could do to blink back her tears. "*Raenalyn* Carina doesn't seem to be overwhelmed or unable to do all those things you're describing. How do we know if she's happy or unhappy? She wouldn't share her feelings with a stranger." Kyra swiped tears away with the back of her hand.

Kyra saw a rare expression of sympathy from Solarus. "I believe *Raenalyn* Carina is content, if not happy, with her position. This is because Carina chooses to be content, just as one chooses to be happy." He took out his pipe from his vest pocket. Without looking up, Solarus went on, "The queen has made many sacrifices to be the leader her people require. We all make sacrifices. Every individual upon whom you look has something in her life she wishes to change. The difference is in how one wakes up every morning. Do you decide to carry misery into your day or good humor? It is astonishing to me how many prefer to complain rather than act." Solarus snorted derisively as though to underscore he wasn't a member of the group. "What you should take from this conversation is that unless you know one's background, it is better not to assume anything about them." A piqued look replaced Solarus' sympathetic one. "There was obviously no point to my waking early to extend our lesson. The time I intended for us has been squandered by correcting your conjecture."

Kyra's cheeks burned. She tried to decide which emotion plagued her more: her shame, her envy, or her frustration with herself. Solarus was right; if Kyra hadn't been so fixated on Loralai, she would have had more practice directing her magic. That was Kyra's priority.

Kyra stood and waded into the lake until the waters were chest-high. She remained facing away from Solarus. During their past few lessons, Solarus wanted Kyra's attention to be on her magic, rather than, as was her tendency, looking at him to confirm her motions were correct. Even the smallest bit of distraction caused Kyra's energy to waver.

"You are familiar with the routine of our lessons," Solarus said from behind her. His words were followed by the sound of him tapping his finger and the rustling of what Kyra knew was a bag of kolker leaves.

Kyra breathed in deeply. As she exhaled, she swished her arms under the surface and visualized gold flowing from her hands. Light twinkled in the water. It ballooned slowly, obscuring the lake's bottom like silt churned up from a storm.

"Today's goal is to replace the haphazard energy you bring into the water with contained and recognizable shapes," Solarus instructed. "This will be similar to what you accomplished in Thanesgard's dungeon when you formed columns with your magic." There was a pause. Kyra's nose was tickled by the sweet, spiced-apple aroma of kolker smoke. "Collect the energy in the water. Feel its will serving your own. Bunch the magic in your hands as though you are carrying handfuls of scarves."

Kyra bit her lip and studied the nebulous gold energy. Collecting the magic was the easier of the two parts. She wrapped the "scarves" around her hands and pressed the gold against itself. The light magnified as the magic shrank.

"That suffices. Now you will condense the energy into bars of gold. Focus on its size and direction. See the magic as straight as needles and as uniform as if thread were woven through them."

Kyra silently squeezed the strands of magic together. The silty bottom of the lake came into focus as the remnants of the golden cloud were sucked into thick, albeit misshapen, bars. Kyra grinned. She tugged on the bars experimentally. They danced forward toward her, water sloshing on the surface. Kyra pushed. The bars pirouetted backward. "Ha!" she exclaimed. Kyra's face lit with triumph. "Not bad, right? That's what you wanted?"

"Exactly right."

Still smiling, Kyra set a tempo for her movements. The golden bars passed over her bare feet, back and forth, back and forth, shimmering merrily. The light glinted off something zipping in the water. Kyra glanced over. They were the scales of a school of fish. Most were a brilliant yellow or red with silver stripes. A few, smaller fish were brown and plain in comparison. The striped fish aggressively chased the panicked unstriped fish past Kyra's golden bars. Kyra stared. Her thoughts were torn back to Loralai. Royal, vain, bossy Loralai.

Kyra raised her gaze to the hills across the waters, feeling the magic roped securely to her hands. Loralai was exactly like those fish: a bully. Yuli might have risked the ire of the other elves and shown up for dinner, but Loralai scared him off. Kyra might have had other friends, like Wyn. Except Loralai had made her contempt for Kyra public. A thought sprang to mind. Could the directive Wyn mentioned, the one warning elves to keep their distance . . . could it have come from Loralai? Did an elven princess have the power to make an order? Anger bubbled up within Kyra. Its heat washed over her like lava over a volcano.

Kyra felt a sharp, splitting sensation in her hands. She glanced down. Kyra's eyes flashed with dismay. The bars had flattened and were disintegrating within the water. Panicked, Kyra tried to bring them back. *Stay!* she commanded. It was no use. The bars dissolved completely. Incensed, Kyra slapped the water with her palm.

"She's done it again!" Kyra's heart pounded with rage as though ready to burst from her chest. "Loralai's ruined something again, and she isn't even here! I *hate* that elf!"

In her fury, Kyra hadn't noticed the lake's waters heaving in agitation. Her skin itched as though hives had broken out over her entire body. Crimson light burning through the lake's surface finally attracted Kyra's gaze. Her anger vaporized as horror set in. The wicked energy was bolder and denser than the golden cloud, staining the clear blue waters an ugly red.

With equal shock, Kyra realized the magic was the cause of the blistering pain on her skin. Before, the red energy festered around her hands or drifted into the air; in the water, Kyra was steeped in it. The dangerous magic bore through every pore, moving through her veins like her own blood. She was infused with a manic desire to destroy. Destroy everything.

"Kyra, stop!" Solarus bellowed from the shore. His voice was filled with alarm. "Break the connection! Break free of it, Kyra, set your will against it. You must fight, Kyra, fight back!"

Solarus' voice reached Kyra distantly, as though her head were under water. In her mind's eye, Kyra saw gold and red in her core, tangled together like a hundred balled-up necklace chains. The gold sparked. The red flared. Kyra latched on to the gold. She was desperate to extricate herself from the impulse to annihilate everything. The gold unraveled. It began to force the red from her heart. Sweat poured down Kyra's face. She thrust her hands in front of her and propelled the red into the air. The evil magic flew upward. The red light pulsed, its glow growing fainter and fainter, as Kyra sent streamers of gold after it. The gold wrapped around the red. Then, to Kyra's relief, the red disappeared.

Kyra almost sank into the water as the gold also vanished. She stepped back, catching herself. Her feet scraped something rough. Bewildered, Kyra looked down. The mushy silt was hard and fractured, like barren earth baked by the sun. A breeze tossed Kyra's hair. There was a cracking sound. Kyra stared, aghast, at the reeds and plants girdling the lake. The once healthy plants were as desiccated as the ground, their leaves brown and stalks brittle. As another breeze shook them, bits of the dead plants broke off and whisked over the lake's surface.

A striped fish bobbed through the water. Its belly was upturned toward the sky. More fish popped up, their eyes open, seeing nothing. Kyra's head turned wildly as fish dotted the waters like drops of rain. Desperate to stop the death, and conscious she was powerless to do so, Kyra's horror morphed to disbelief. *This isn't happening. This didn't happen.* Kyra cast a look across the lake to its opposite shores. Bile rose in her throat. The swan pair that had landed moments earlier drifted lifelessly on the water's surface. Their heads were entwined on each other's backs. Small waves moved them up and down like empty vessels.

Kyra was unable to look away from the grisly scene. *I did this. I killed them.* She needed to flee. Run away. No. Solarus was there. He would know what to do.

Kyra whipped around, facing the bank for the first time. And froze.

Solarus was on his feet, hornbeam staff in hand. Turquoise flame ran the length of it. The same fire orbited his free hand. The alarm that registered in Solarus' eyes was the same Kyra felt at the sight. Because Solarus' staff was aimed directly at her.

Chapter 33

Kyra hardly dared to breathe. For a fraction of a second, she expected her mentor would attack. Solarus dropped his hand. The flames whooshed out of existence, as did those on his staff. His expression was horror-struck.

"Get out of the water," Solarus ordered in a strained tone. He half-sat, half-fell to the ground and laid his staff vertically beside him. Kyra noticed his hand rested over the wood.

Kyra swallowed hard. She pushed through the water and scampered up the bank. The heat of the red energy had dried her clothes even before she was out of the water. The skin on Kyra's hands itched painfully. She saw they were cracked and bleeding in spots. The stench of dead fish filled her nostrils. Waves of nausea rippled through her, her terror roiling her stomach as much as the putrid smells.

Solarus studied Kyra silently as she collapsed on the grass. She trembled as she used both hands to rake her hair from her face. Never in Kyra's experiences with the wild red magic had she done something so terrible. "Solarus, what . . . what happened?" she stammered. "The red energy, I didn't try and create it, it was like it had its own life. The lake . . . it burned. The ground is dry. And the fish and plants and . . . the swans. How, Solarus?" Chills ran uncontrollably down Kyra's spine as she spoke. "Where did it come from?"

Solarus' eyes were replete with sorrow. He ran a finger down the cursive Z in his hair, seeming unsure—or unwilling—to answer. Solarus' hesitation magnified Kyra's apprehension. "Do you remember when I told you magic draws energy from the natural world?" he answered finally. His voice had a peculiarly hollow note to it. "You can amass energy from the sun, the water, and the earth. You can also harvest the life force of insects and animals. And larger beings."

"Larger? Like greeloks? Or Reapers?"

"Those. And men. Elves. Wizards." Solarus lingered on each word, as though they were unspeakable curses he was forced to articulate. "Energy inhabits all of Ilian. This is why wizards are powerful. This is why they have come to be feared." He gestured broadly to the lake. "The consequences of unbridled magic can be fatal. Draining the life force from another being is the worst form of death. No weapon of man can cause such devastation."

Kyra's mouth was dry. She lifted her cloak from the ground and wrapped it around her shoulders. The supple material embraced her with the comfort of an old friend. "Why didn't you want to tell me before? If I had known that I could, that it was possible to . . . to do this . . . couldn't I have stopped it?"

"It would have made no difference had I mentioned this point or not," Solarus responded sharply. Kyra shrank under his tone. She lowered her eyes to the very green, very much living grass. "It would have only served to scare you. Fear limits one's ability to think. To act. To maintain self-control. If you had governed your emotions as I have said countless times during our sessions, you never would have witnessed the red energy. However, this lesson is better learned with minnows and birds than with men."

The tension that filled the air was so thick, not even one of Solarus' lightning bolts could slice through it. Kyra's insides turned to ice. She reached for her waterskin, uncorked it, and drank slowly. Her eyes flew up the hill to the apex. If Hayden had seen her . . .

Hayden wasn't there.

Kyra couldn't help defending herself as she recorked the skin. "I'd rather have all the information about my abilities. Good and . . . terrible. Maybe I would have been more alert when the magic appeared and prevented it from escaping. Or maybe I could have . . ."

"Worked harder on the aforementioned self-discipline and mindfulness?"

Kyra's cheeks burned with shame. She silently pulled on her boots as Solarus took up his staff and cloak. He stood.

"We are finished for today." Solarus' gaze scanned the periphery of the lake. "I will see you this evening."

Kyra glanced up as she tied her laces. "You aren't coming with me?"

Solarus walked to the edge of the bank. "I must see what damage I can repair. The plants may at least be regenerated. The fish and swans must be removed."

Kyra wasn't sure what Solarus meant by "removed," but the words sent new shivers down her spine. "Solarus, what's going to happen when the elves find out about this? What will they do?" *To me* was Kyra's complete statement. She didn't dare voice the final two words.

"They will not do anything, because they will not find out. I will not tell them. You will not tell them."

"What if Loralai comes back? She saw us this morning."

"We will deal with Loralai if and when we must. And Kyra," Solarus added without turning to look at her. "When I mean that you will not share what occurred here, that includes any mention to our companions."

Kyra's eyes reflected her confusion. "Why not?"

"Because that is my instruction. We will not yet burden Hayden and Talis with this knowledge. Is that understood?"

Kyra lacked the energy to mull over Solarus' cryptic request. Collecting her staff, Kyra rose. Solarus raised a hand toward the water, murmuring an incantation under his breath. Kyra lumbered up the hill. The sick feeling formed a leaden pit in her stomach.

She was too weary to notice that Solarus' hand was trembling.

***

The fire crackled cheerfully, filling the den with a welcome warmth. Chloe sighed. The whippet contentedly rested her head on her paws and closed her eyes. A bowl of water and the orange, gummy remains of half-chewed thraxen berries lay to her left. To Chloe's right, the female *Sirenyle* sat cross-legged. The elf stroked Chloe's back rhythmically. Hazel gobbled up her share of meat on the thin bones of the francolins the elves had brought with them. Raff leisurely licked his paws.

The female elf gently ran a finger along Chloe's cheek bone. The whippet shuddered and twitched in her deep slumber. The female elf's brow furrowed with concern. "Emmeth, Chloe's skin is cold, and her lips are tinged blue," she addressed the male *Sirenyle* seated on the other side of the bright yellow and orange flames. "The thraxen berries should have reduced her fever. I don't have any other plants that can counteract an infection if that's what she has."

"The effects of the berries aren't immediate on animals, Muireann," her companion assured her. "She drank some water, and her chills aren't nearly as bad as when we first arrived. The thraxen berries will restore her strength. I'll add some lyole to the fire though." Emmeth glanced around the cramped, dry, stone walls of the den. He reached into a small leather bag on the ground. "We're lucky the lyole absorbs the smoke," Emmeth commented as he pulled out a mosslike plant. "With the rain as heavy as it is and the space this cramped, we wouldn't be able to risk a flame."

As Muireann ran her hand over Chloe's fur, Emmeth picked off a marble-sized portion of the plant. He tossed it into the fire. The flames flared as they consumed the lyole. With a satisfied nod, Emmeth brushed back his almost dry, mousy brown hair. Then he placed a hand over the ground, palm down. The words he muttered were too quiet to be heard over the fire and the roar of water spilling over the eaves of the den's entrance. A glittering green mist appeared beneath his open palm and formed a long ribbon. The magic hovered over the ground before slipping out the den's entrance and disappearing into the storm.

Emmeth glanced over at Hazel, continuing to hold his hand over the earth. The collie had finished her meal. Grease from the meat added a sheen to her wet nose. Hazel rubbed away the grease with her paw. Emmeth's mahogany-colored eyes moved along to Raff. The panther stretched his legs and folded his paws over each other before lying down. His long black tail curled around his body. The *Sirenyle* returned his attention to the green magic pulsing around his hand.

Raff gave a quiet thanks to Inishmore for sending the elven scouts and not dark wizards as he had feared. The panther had wasted no time in guiding them to the den. He had hoped they carried lyole. It was a rare and coveted plant found in patches hidden deep within the Ancient Forest. Lyole was imbued with powerful magic; a pebble's worth created a fire that could last for hours. That same magic repelled water. It was an invaluable item among a satchel of invaluable items bestowed upon the *Sirenyle*. Like the animal scouts, the *Sirenyle* could be called upon for a mission with little notice and would travel in the harshest conditions. Neither white-out blizzards nor torrential rains nor scorching summer days would deter a *Sirenyle* from his mission. Raff reflected on this as he watched Muireann scratch Chloe behind the ear. Yes, they had been lucky.

"I regret leaving Thanesgard when we did," Muireann said now. Her pallid features were lined with concern. "The elven messenger pressed us to depart for the coastal villages immediately. He said it was at the *Raenalyn*'s command. Dark wizards were rumored to be lurking near the Sea, and there hadn't been any indication of wizards in Thanesgard. According to the messenger, wizards were harassing fishermen to get information on a weapon. The messenger claimed no further information on the weapon, nor could his network describe it. We assumed it was magical in nature. We didn't have time to find Chloe before we left." A remorseful note filled Muireann's voice. She glanced at the den's entrance, deep brown eyes fastened on the sheet of rain that beat against the ground. "Thank Inishmore for the falcons outside Thanesgard. They brought us news of the dark wizards' attack and Kyra's escape. That's how we learned Diamantas had established a foothold in Farcaren." Muireann's jaw clenched. "The wizards' influence is poison. It originates within the city limits and will spread with insidious speed to the neighboring villages and beyond. If the wizards' corruption hasn't already infected the rest of the kingdom, we may be able to contain it."

"Elven arrows are the best antidote for rogue wizards' contagion," Emmeth put in with a glint in his eyes. He raised his free hand toward the fire, the green still undulating under his other.

"Indeed." Raff's ears flickered. "What did you find in the coastal villages? Were there dark wizards present?"

"If there were, neither we nor the fishermen were aware of any," Emmeth took up the story. "We met with an elder in the village of Tarrant, a man named Henrik. The fishermen are a proud and private folk. The *Sirenyle* rarely visit the coast. When we do, the tidings are usually as welcome as a headful of lice."

Muireann nodded in agreement. "When we told Henrik about what we had heard, he seemed more bewildered than suspicious. He told us dark wizards hadn't invaded Tarrant. He also hadn't received any communications from the northern villages suggesting something had happened there. The one change Henrik had noticed was that the Sea's waters were rougher this year than in previous seasons. Henrik explained that it wasn't unusual."

Muireann broke off as Emmeth tilted his head. "I don't sense anything beyond the den," he announced. "That doesn't tell us much though. The rain is diluting my magic. We may have wizards or other creatures skulking around the forest."

"Or, little brother, Harkimer's creatures prefer to skulk in drier conditions," Muireann said with a teasing smile.

"I'll go with that explanation." Emmeth turned his hand and tugged on the green as though he were reeling in a boat to its dock. The green wave switched directions. It tapered until the tail end spiraled around Emmeth's hand. As Emmeth clenched his fist, the green vanished.

Hazel's tail beat on the ground. "What did you do after you were in Tarrant?"

Muireann rubbed her hands together before the fire. The light from the flames highlighted the disquiet in her eyes. "We spent two fruitless weeks searching for dark wizards. Henrik accompanied us to each of the villages. He was worried dark wizards might have overrun them and were preventing dispatches for help. All we confirmed was that the report from the messenger was false. Which, for a *Sirenyle*, is unusual." Muireann exchanged a meaningful look with Emmeth.

"That is why the Council sent us," Raff said somberly. "There is concern that Diamantas has bribed elves to be his spies in Silvias. You should be prudent in choosing those in whom to confide."

Emmeth leaned back and adjusted the cloak that pooled around his body. "Muireann and I don't believe the messenger from the coast deceived us. It's more likely that whoever first conveyed the information did. Either way, it makes me angry and a bit frightened to think Diamantas has infiltrated the Realm. Still. Were we in Thanesgard while the king harbored the dark wizards, we could have forewarned Talis and prevented the attack." Emmeth again took up his satchel and removed a piece of dried fruit. He chewed on it, eyes burning with anger. "The cowards."

"Inishmore may have guided you to take exactly those actions," Raff pointed out. "Had you not left Thanesgard, we may never have discovered Arkin's involvement with the dark wizards. Your meetings with the fishermen may also have made them more conscious of the need for vigilance. And…" Raff added with a raise of his paw for emphasis, "the queen will be alerted to possible enemies within her circle."

Muireann's expression cleared. "You may be right. Inishmore may have intended this to happen. Emmeth and I also wouldn't have been granted the chance to see Kyra again." Muireann spoke these last words with a mixture of wonder and delight. "I can't believe she's back. We never gave up hope. To know that she has returned to Silvias is like a dream. I've thought of her so often. Aila and I were convinced that if she hadn't been a wizard, she would have been a scout like us." Muireann sat back with a slight sigh. "I've missed her."

"Me too," Emmeth agreed. His eyes trailed to the entrance of the den. The rain's musical forte had quieted. "The weather is clearing." Emmeth turned to Raff and Hazel. "You should rest. As soon as the storm ends, we can set off. That is, if Chloe is able to?"

The question was directed to Muireann. The *Sirenyle* gazed down at the sleeping whippet and put a hand on her fur. Chloe's skin was pleasantly warm to the touch. "She should be ready."

Hazel crossed her front legs and laid her head over them. Raff, too, rested his head on his giant paws. The scouts sat in companionable silence, listening as the rain concluded its long concerto.

Muireann woke the animals midmorning. Gray lingered in the sky, with stray shafts of light punching through the clouds. Chloe rose from her slumber alert, refreshed, and ravenous. As the animals lapped up water from a large puddle outside the cave, Emmeth disappeared into the woods with his bow and quiver. He returned with five large fish under his arm. He and Muireann scaled and cooked the fish on the lyole-fed fire, which had burned faithfully through the night. The *Sirenyle* each took one fish for themselves and gave the rest to Raff, Hazel, and Chloe. Sated, Muireann and Emmeth collected their satchels and led the group out of the cave. Their steeds had sheltered under a dense cropping of trees. The *Sirenyle* quickly mounted. Then with Raff, Hazel, and Chloe at their side, Muireann and Emmeth plunged into the woods.

The elven horses galloped through the slick foliage, their hooves barely digging into the saturated earth. When the night sky encased the woods in black, the group stopped. Starlight gleamed on wet leaves. Muireann and Emmeth replenished their waterskins at a nearby stream, bloated from the rain, while the horses and animals drank their fill. The *Sirenyle* distributed rations of dried meat and bread. When they had finished their meagre meal, the *Sirenyle* remounted. The group sprinted into the darkness.

Raff, Hazel, and Chloe maintained the pace set by the *Sirenyle* until morning. The air beneath the tree canopy was muggy and rife with the scents of fresh rains to come. At midday, they briefly rested. Despite their lack of sleep and countless hours of riding, Muireann and Emmeth moved with the same vigor as they had the night prior. Emmeth again foraged for food. He returned with nuts, large-capped mushrooms, and crunchy dandelion roots that sprouted among the underbrush. Emmeth kept the these for himself and his sister while Muireann apportioned more of the dried meat. Provisions were low, and the groups' stomachs vocally demanded more food after the meal. There was no time. They raced through the forest, the *Sirenyle* in the lead.

By evening, the grueling pace was taking its toll on the animals. Hazel's paw caught more than once on a corded tree branch hidden under the thick debris. Chloe trotted with shallow breaths, tail drooped. Even the indefatigable Raff had stopped leaping over forest litter. Instead, he carefully climbed over branches with leaden steps. The weariness of their companions wasn't lost on the *Sirenyle*. Muireann halted the group. They had covered enough ground to merit a few hours' rest, she told the animals. Raff, Hazel, and Chloe plopped on the ground and were instantly asleep.

Emmeth and Muireann remained astride their horses, quietly listening to the chirruping and buzzing of insects. Emmeth's gaze trailed up to a gap in the tree canopy. A translucent gray haze muted the moonlight. "We are less than a day's journey to the river," he said to his sister. "I hope for the sake of the animals that we reach Silvias soon. The rains will come by tomorrow's eve."

"If they come at all," Muireann replied, also tilting her head toward the night sky. "It may pass us by. Either way, we'll cross into Silvias well before we are hit with another storm. Inishmore is with us."

Emmeth's smooth features spread into a grin. "Thank the Healer for that."

The hours passed peacefully. The *Sirenyle* roused the animals just before dawn. Hazel awoke, wincing in pain. Her front paw was inflamed, the skin an ugly shade of red. Emmeth examined it tenderly as the others wolfed down the last of Muireann's provisions. He touched a spot between two toes. "You scraped your paw on one of the brambles," Emmeth determined. "The scratch is infected, though mildly."

Hazel's blue eyes shone with dismay as Emmeth gently released her paw. "I will slow our pace. You must ride ahead without me."

Emmeth rummaged through his satchel. He removed a jar and unscrewed the top. "The salve will reduce the swelling and assuage the pain," Emmeth reassured her. He scooped out a gel on his finger and dabbed it on Hazel's paw. "You'll be fine. If we must, you can ride with me until we enter the Realm."

The collie tilted her head with what could have passed as a raising of a brow. "I have been a passenger astride a horse before. I prefer to travel on my own legs."

Emmeth laughed as he returned the jar to his satchel. "If traveling by your own means is preferable, then our steeds will accommodate the pace. 'Slow is fast, fast is slow,' as the elves say. If trouble comes, my saddle is comfortable enough to fit two."

Overnight, the haze had condensed into a soot-gray veil that now blocked the sun's warm light. A strange sense of foreboding hung in the air. Excepting a chip and chirp from a stray bird, the woods were hauntingly silent.

The group pressed on with spirited determination. The elven horses strained against their reins, sensing they were approaching their home. Muireann held her mare's gait at a trot. She glanced down at Hazel, mindful of the collie's injury. For her part, Hazel trotted beside Emmeth's horse cheerfully. The salve had soothed the ache in her paw, though she carried an almost imperceptible limp. Craning her neck over her shoulder, Muireann saw Chloe and Raff jogging behind the horses with ease. Satisfied, the *Sirenyle* returned her attention to the front. She secured the reins more firmly in her hands.

"Do you remember when you tried to steal Kyra's figurine?" Muireann said abruptly to Emmeth. "The one of the Iona Wyn made for her?"

Emmeth gave Muireann a sidelong look. A nostalgic smile lent a softness to his sister's face. "It's hard to forget being fried by a bolt of magic," he replied. Emmeth grinned and rubbed his upper chest with his palm. "Even if I did, I'd always have the scar as a memento. It wasn't my idea," he added. "Sneaking into Kyra's room. Aila taunted me. She told me if I didn't have the stealth to pocket a figurine, I shouldn't vie for a position as a scout."

Muireann let out a hmph. "I remember. It isn't Aila's fault you accepted the dare, little brother."

"If Kyra had been exploring somewhere like she normally did, it would have been simple," Emmeth defended in a teasing tone. He adjusted his position in the saddle as the path through the forest narrowed. "We all knew Kyra's habits. The instant we were dismissed for lunch, Kyra stole off."

Muireann laughed. She kept her horse in step with Emmeth's. "You said she was always late to class."

"She was." Emmeth's dark eyes shone as he reminisced. "Yuli usually stole a snack for her. I watched Kyra sprint away after class the day Aila challenged me about the Iona. I even checked the dining hall to make sure she'd left. In hindsight, I should have reconnoitered the corridors and staircases before breaking into her room."

"Because it didn't occur to you that startling a wizard might have undesirable consequences," Muireann pointed out slyly. The trees rustled as a gust of wind whipped through the air, tousling Muireann's black trusses.

"I was so focused on proving myself to Aila I didn't hear Kyra's footsteps inside the room. I completely missed that Kyra's door was unlocked." Emmeth pulled his cloak more tightly around his shoulders more wind sped through the woods. "I opened the door so confidently. Like a king strutting into his treasure room, with the figurine soon to be my treasure. Except Kyra was standing right there. She shrieked so loudly I jumped. That's when she whomped me with that golden light." He patted his chest with a good-natured grin. "It was humiliating. I'm not sure how I ended up being chosen as a *Sirenyle* after the experience."

"You're lucky the worst that happened to you was the burn on your chest. Imagine if Kyra had thought you were a real threat. She would have done more than knocked you down." A peculiar, pained expression crossed Muireann's face. "I remember when Kyra came to the dining hall to find me. Her face was so pale. I sprang off the bench and held her hands she was shaking so badly. When Kyra mentioned your name, I thought you must be near death for her to be so stunned. We raced to the Healer's Hall, and there you were. You looked as miserable and guilty as a puppy caught thieving bones from a chef's plate. Of course, the burn on your chest and incriminating story washed away any worry or sympathy I had for you."

"It was painful," Emmeth countered. His steed flicked his head as the trees quaked in the riotous wind. The *Sirenyle* patted the horse's neck soothingly. "Kyra's of age now. If she could cause so much damage at fourteen, I wonder what she's capable of now." He paused. "I wonder if *she* knows what she's capable of. No one told her about the prophecy, at least not when she was in Silvias."

"*Raenalyn* Carina was so careful to hide it from her. You and I were only briefed on the seers' foretelling when we became *Sirenyle*, in the event Kyra was ever found and returned to Ilian. The dark wizards' aggression has increased in the last year. Is there a connection to her disappearance?"

Emmeth shrugged. "I'm not sure. I never agreed with the *Raenalyn*'s decision to hide the truth. Things might be different now. The *Raenalyn* might have mentioned it to her since . . ." Emmeth broke off suddenly. Loud shrieks and screeching swept through the wind, shattering the quiet. "What in Inishmore's name is that?"

Muireann's gaze soared upward. She gasped as the tree's foliage was ripped asunder by hundreds of frenzied birds. "*RELITH!*" Muireann screamed, reining in her mare. The power in Muireann's voice briefly drowned out the sounds of branches snapping. The ground trembled under heavy footfall.

Emmeth's horse also reacted to Muireann's command, hooves cutting into the earth. Chloe yelped. She skidded to a stop to avoid a collision with the steeds. Raff leapt nimbly to the side. His yellow orbed eyes narrowed. Hazel's ears pricked.

Muireann seized the bow strapped beside her saddle. In a blink of an eye, she raised and readied an arrow, then fired it into the trees as the frenetic crashing grew louder. An unseen foe bellowed in pain. The wind whipped up Muireann's hair as she drew another arrow. "Reapers!" she yelled to her brother. "Four, I count four of them!"

Emmeth unblinkingly grasped a throwing knife from his belt. "Only four?"

Muireann readied two more arrows and held the string against her cheek. "I'm sorry, four aren't enough?"

The grisly monsters were unmistakable. The Reapers pounded the ground as they zigzagged through the trees. Their wings hung loosely at their sides, mouths gaping with savage grins. Their tails snapped behind them.

"No, four seem to be plenty." Emmeth hurled the knife at the closest Reaper. The blade sliced through the wind, scoring a mark on the Reaper's foot. The creature shrieked irately. Emmeth glanced over at his sister. "Who would have thought we would be the first *Sirenyle* since Malus' days to see one?"

"I don't consider it an honor to be those *Sirenyle*, Emmeth!" Muireann loosed her pair of arrows in the direction of another Reaper. The weapons harmlessly deflected off the Reaper's chest, unable to penetrate its slate gray, armor-like skin. "Pay attention!"

Emmeth's eyes shot back to his opponent. The Reaper yanked the blade from its foot and tossed it aside as carelessly as though it had been pricked by a needle. The creature darted forward with alarming speed. Emmeth's horse reared in panic. A blur of black fur sprang past the horse. With a ferocious roar, Raff put himself between the Reaper and Emmeth. The monster swiped at the panther with a hand the size of a plate. Raff nimbly evaded the blow. The panther swiped at the Reaper's already injured foot. The Reaper let out a shriek of pain as Raff's claws dug into its skin. The panther leapt back, teeth bared, as the monster charged again.

The other Reapers had reached the group. They stood and stretched their massive wings. At their full height, two of the Reapers were eye-level with the scouts astride their horses. The third was a head taller, a goliath even among his kin. His eyes were calculating and as black as though light were afraid to exist within them. The Reaper licked his jagged teeth with his blood-red tongue. Muireann slung the bow over her back. She and Emmeth unsheathed their swords in unison and wore matching expressions of stoic resolve.

"Run, Chloe!" Hazel barked to the whippet. Chloe stared, petrified, at the raging battle. Unlike her companions, the whippet had no defenses against the raging creatures. "You must go to Silvias." Hazel bounded to Chloe and butted the whippet's side. "You cannot do more here. You are a scout, Chloe. This mission is now your responsibility. Warn the queen that the Reapers are on her border. Protect Kyra. Fulfill the promise of the *Al-Ethran*. Go!"

The collie pushed Chloe one last time with her head. Without waiting another moment, Hazel turned, teeth bared, and bound over to Raff, who continued to parry the Reaper's attacks. She snapped at the Reaper's tail with her long canines. Catching the tip, Hazel clamped her mouth closed. The force wasn't enough to hurt the Reaper, but it distracted the creature. Raff raked the Reaper's unprotected face. The Reaper howled. Covering an eye, he lashed out erratically. The Reaper's fist grazed Hazel's head. Stunned, the collie was sent tumbling down the hill. Thorns and brambles tore at Hazel's fur until she slid to a stop. Hazel lay on her side, panting.

"Hazel!" Raff called out.

Chloe hadn't moved. Her distress wafted through the air, drawing another of the Reapers toward her. The Reaper crashed against the ground. The whippet backed up tremulously. She watched her companions locked in a battle for survival against the savage monsters of Harkimer. The sight gave Chloe new resolve despite her terror.

"I am a scout," she said. The whippet pulled her gaze back to the Reaper. He had spread its wings to their full span. "I was chosen by the *Al-Ethran*." Chloe sprinted through the trees away from the fighting. The Reaper roared and dropped again on all fours. Branches snapped and underbrush quaked as the monster broke away from his company in pursuit of his prey.

Meanwhile, Hazel struggled to stand. Her hind leg buckled as pain seared through her. "I'm okay!" she barked to Raff despite the injury. She shook her leg and forced it straight. Teeth clenched, the collie bounded back into the fight.

Emmeth had exchanged his sword for two shorter blades. His grotesque opponent leapt into the air. The wind caught the Reaper under his wings and carried him high. The Reaper poised his heel downward for a fatal strike. Emmeth spurred his horse to the side as the Reaper hurtled toward the ground. Sliding both feet so he was crouched in the saddle, the *Sirenyle* flipped from his horse's back and into the air, thrusting his left sword up in one fluid motion. The blade found the soft spot on the Reaper's breastbone. The creature plummeted to the earth and fell on one knee. The wound in its chest bled profusely. Rage pounded out the Reaper's pain. He jetted forward with an uncoordinated but savage set of slashes.

From the ground, Emmeth blocked the Reaper's first swing, then a second and third. The monsters relentlessly attacked. The *Sirenyle* backflipped and struck the creatures' claws back with his swords. One Reaper lowered himself on all fours. He spun on his legs like a lizard and hissed at Emmeth's steed. The horse crow-hopped in terror. Emmeth's eyes flashed with surprise as he watched his steed gallop off into the woods.

"Kithlin, where are you going?" he shouted into the gusting wind. Sweat streamed down Emmeth's face. "You're an *elven* horse, Kithlin! You're a *Sirenyle*'s steed, the boldest, most noble . . ." As the Reaper turned and stood, Emmeth trailed off. He had to tilt his head to view the head of the Reaper. ". .

. most noble and completely useless horse," he finished. Emmeth shifted the swords in his hands and steeled himself for the next attack.

Behind him, Muireann circled her steed around the Reaper with the torn wing. The Reaper, in turn, tracked the elf with a predatory look. He walked counterclockwise around the *Sirenyle*. Muireann let out a fierce cry. She spurred her steed forward and swung at the already damaged wing. The Reaper dodged the attack and spun. His whip-like tail snapped through the air. It wrapped around the hilt of Muireann's sword and ripped the weapon free. The *Sirenyle* quickly unslung her bow. She held it against her side like a staff, taking short, labored breaths.

The Reaper unexpectedly pivoted—and bolted around Muireann's horse. The *Sirenyle* realized too late that her brother was behind her.

Emmeth didn't see the Reaper. Pain exploded in his upper back, and light burst like suns in his eyes. Emmeth collapsed, facedown. His legs went numb. A dark wetness spread around him, but his vision was too blurred to see what it was. Emmeth's ears caught a distant scream. Muireann's scream. He tried to call back to his sister. A gurgling sound left his lips. He was cold, as though frozen in ice. *Why was it so cold?* The wind quieted, the sounds of battle slipped away. Emmeth felt a tender breeze, a whisper in his heart, and warmth embraced him. The *Sirenyle*'s last breath was a peaceful sigh.

The Reapers shrieked in victory.

"Emmeth!" Muireann screamed again in anguish. Tears streamed down her cheeks as her eyes landed on her brother's prone figure. A pair of Reapers stood over him. Muireann's green gaze migrated to Raff and Hazel. The panther and collie were locked in a brutal stalemate with the largest Reaper. Muireann jerked on the reins of her horse and barreled headfirst at the Reaper. The sudden onslaught surprised the creature. He stumbled back as Muireann inserted herself and her steed between him and the animals. Her face was awash with wrath, sorrow, and resignation. "Flee, Raff and Hazel!" she shouted. "I'll buy you as much time as I can."

"Chloe is on the way to Silvias!" Hazel barked in response. Her long snout had a cut across the top, and her blue eyes were glassy. "We're staying!"

"No," Raff intervened abruptly. His yellow-orbed gaze had flashed to Emmeth. The sight of fallen *Sirenyle* encompassed the entirety of their plight. "Chloe may have escaped, yet the Reapers are swift. There is no choice to be made, Hazel. We are of the *Al-Ethran*. Our duty is to Ilian." The Reapers had regrouped and stomped toward them. Raff half-bowed to the elf. "May Inishmore protect you, *Sirenyle*."

Tears painted Muireann's face. She raised her head resolutely. "Tell Kyra we love her."

Raff loped away. Hazel's heart welled with grief as she sprinted after the panther.

The wounded Reaper lunged first. Muireann nocked an arrow, aiming squarely at his chest, hand steady. The arrow buried itself in the Reaper's heart. The creature crumpled noiselessly to the ground. At the same time, the second

Reaper leapt into the air. He seized the bow from her grasp and snapped the karia wood in two. Muireann's steed buckled underneath her as the largest Reaper grabbed the horse's hindquarters. The *Sirenyle* was already standing in her stirrups and leaping for a tree branch as her steed was brought down.

Muireann scaled the tree as nimbly as a trapeze artist. Her cloak flapped wildly in the raging wind. She heard the Reapers scream in fury at their escaping prey. The branches suddenly quaked. Muireann had to cover her head with her arm as leaves and loose twigs showered down on her. She chanced a look below. The behemoth Reaper clung to the tree. His claws dug into the bark like spikes as he climbed after her. Muireann's head turned toward the sky. She scrambled and swung up the branches until she had reached the tree canopy. A bellow was the only warning Muireann had before the Reaper sprang clear of the tree and flapped above her in the open skies. Balanced on a branch, Muireann unsheathed her dagger. It was her only remaining weapon. She sent a silent prayer to Inishmore.

There was no fear in Muireann's deep brown eyes as the Reaper folded its wings and came crashing down. Muireann lithely jumped to the side and slashed at the Reaper's neck. The monster's shriek echoed over the treetops. Muireann watched as the Reaper careened from the air. She let out a shuddering sight of relief. Until the Reaper snatched her ankle. Lurching forward, Muireann smashed against a branch as she was dragged down by the monster.

May Inishmore protect you, Kyra, Muireann said silently as the branches battered her. Her final thought was of Emmeth.

Then it was over.

From the ground, the Reaper stretched his wings. He bellowed into the wind. His fellow Reaper took up the cry. They thundered past the bodies of the *Sirenyle* in pursuit of Raff and Hazel, leaving a mournful silence in their wake.

***

Kyra thought summoning magic was challenging; summoning magic when she secretly wanted it to stay put was a thousand times worse.

The first morning after the incident with the red energy, Kyra had waded into the lake. The ground was as rough as sandpaper. Kyra had to tread carefully not to scrape the bottom of her feet. Without the mushy silt between her toes, the lake didn't feel like a lake at all; it was like Kyra walked on flooded pavement.

Solarus had managed to regenerate much of the plant life and reeds that bordered the waters. Some brown, withered husks remained though. As was her habit, Kyra's eyes wandered to the opposite shore. The swan pair was conspicuously absent. It took Kyra a second to remember they had died. By her hands. They weren't drifting like empty shells anymore. Kyra suspected Solarus had done something to take them away. *How* he had done that . . .

Kyra shuddered, feeling queasy. She swallowed down her apprehension and focused on the water. The morning light danced on the surface as it always did.

As there wasn't any mud to stir, the lake was clearer than usual. Too clear. Too still. Not a single fish zoomed by her, striped or otherwise.

Solarus had Kyra face him for the lesson. His normally stern gaze was softened with concern. Kyra was relieved to look at the bank and not at the remainders of destruction around her. When Kyra first tried to pull out the golden rings, she couldn't produce even a spark of gold. She halfheartedly repeated her efforts. It was as though the gold sensed the tug-of-war within her—Kyra' desire to develop her energy on the one side and Kyra's fear of bringing out the red magic on the other. Solarus patiently took Kyra back to the basics. In a soothing and surprisingly gentle tone, he coaxed her to draw out her gold energy. The red was gone, Solarus told her. Only the gold. The gold was an intrinsic part of her. The red had been a flash in the pan, a match that was lit and had burned out. By the end of the lesson, Kyra brought gold to her fingertips. Her abilities plateaued there. Solarus had nothing but praise for her perseverance. It would take time, he reassured her as they started back toward the palace together. Kyra's confidence would return. It would take time and, Solarus reminded her, patience.

"Govern your feelings, and the red will never come again," Solarus had repeated. "'Anger is a wasted emotion,' Hayden is fond of saying. Be mindful of your self-control. Trust your will. It will be all right."

Kyra labored through the next day's lesson, then the next. Each time, Kyra unloosed the chains she had used to arrest the gold, ready at a moment's notice to yank back any sign of red energy. Fortunately, the red was tamed. After a week, Kyra's muscle memory and instincts had overtaken her fear. Solarus had her again face away from him as they practiced. When Solarus' tone took on its customary tartness, Kyra knew everything was back to normal.

***

Every breath was hard-earned. Possibly their last. The skin over Raff and Hazel's ribs stretched agonizingly tight as they gasped. Their legs cramped. Their muscles threatened to seize. Blood pounded so forcefully in their ears it almost deafened them to the Reapers' roars and frenetic crashing through the forest.

"I see the river!" Raff shouted to Hazel. His black fur was matted with long strokes of blood, dirt, and sweat.

Hazel wheezed as she struggled to keep pace with the panther. The wound on her leg had split into a wider gash. Pain wracked her body. Hazel tried to keep her weight on her uninjured leg. On the uneven ground, it was impossible.

Raff did everything he could to steady her. When they encountered fallen trees, the panther flattened himself, enabling Hazel to limp onto his back. Raff rose and pushed the collie up onto the trunk. Then he sprang over himself and again crouched low. "You will make it, Hazel," Raff encouraged in his deep voice. Hazel stepped from his back onto the ground. "We cannot waver. Even if Chloe escaped, we have our duty to the *Al-Ethran*. One of us must reach Kyra.

Inishmore will give us strength." Raff's ears perked up. "The Reapers are almost upon us. Stay the course. No matter what."

The forest began to dip, the slope a hazard of slick leaves, moss, and mud. Despite Hazel picking her way down as carefully as she could, her paws slipped often. Raff padded forward confidently. Water crashed and thundered below them as the spaces between the trees widened. Hope supplanted Hazel's raw fear. They had reached the river.

Raff had passed the collie and was halfway down the hill when a Reaper screamed. The panther stopped, paw raised. He swiveled deftly. His yellow-orbed gaze pierced the muted twilight of the woods. Hazel's eyes were wide with consternation. She paused, leaning on her healthy leg.

Unhesitatingly, Raff bounded back up the hill, his claws digging into the earth. "Go, Hazel, get to the bank!" he shouted as he passed her.

The collie glanced back in dismay as the first Reaper burst through the trees. His tail flayed the air, and his wings were folded on his back. Raff was a streak of black lightning that struck with electric fury. The Reaper reeled in surprise as Raff slashed at its neck and face. The second Reaper charged Raff. The panther launched himself at the newcomer with equal vengeance.

Helpless and terrified, Hazel turned and quick-stepped down the hill at an angle. Her leg dragged behind her. The collie knew at such a hindered pace, she would never make it to the river. Throwing caution to the wind, Hazel tried to run. Her slender paws immediately skidded over a patch of mud. Hazel yelped as she slid uncontrollably. She frantically pushed off the ground with her three good paws and scrambled for purchase. To Hazel's relief, the mud ended at a mossy mound formed between the trees. Hazel gasped for air. Behind her came the sound of groaning, the snapping of tree branches, the violent shaking of leaves, and the sound of roots being ripped from earth. Hazel cast her gaze to Raff.

The larger of the Reapers bore the massive trunk of an oak tree in his hands. Raff's back was turned as he relentlessly assailed the other Reaper. Hazel watched in horror as the mammoth Reaper shot forward and swung its makeshift weapon. The trunk smashed into the panther's side with a sickening crack. Raff flew into the air before tumbling onto a dense grouping of ferns. He didn't make any motion to rise.

"Raff!" Hazel cried out. The panther didn't answer.

The collie's shout alerted the Reapers to her presence. The larger Reaper, bleeding from his cuts, snaked his head in her direction. The creature howled and sprinted down the bank.

Hazel desperately leapt from the mound onto the leaves. She allowed herself to be propelled down the hillside as though she were riding a sled. Hazel hit the bottom of the hill with full force. For a moment, all the collie could see were black spots from the excruciating pain in her leg. Hazel shook her head. *Deliver the message. Find Kyra. Protect her.*

Hazel hobbled forward. She could almost hear the Reaper's breath, so close was he. Unhesitatingly, Hazel sprang into the river. The cold current dragged

Hazel down. She bobbed up, paddling furiously to keep her head above the surface. Hazel barely heard the incensed shrieks of the Reapers as water thundered in her ears.

From the corner of her eye, Hazel caught sight of the two Reapers at the edge of the river. One had slung Raff over his shoulder like a limp rag doll. As they started up the hill, Hazel clung to her singular purpose: *Find Kyra and protect her.* The collie battled the river's waters and her grief as the current carried her away from Harkimer's monsters.

***

"Come on in!" Kyra called to Jyls and Ash. She was treading water in the lake. A grin spread across her face. During Kyra's morning session with Solarus, the air was muggy and uncomfortable. The sky seemed to threaten rain, but a wind had shoved the gray clouds over the hills. Now sunlight showered down on Kyra's hair and face. "It's too hot to be out there."

Ash sat upright. His trouser cuffs were rolled up to his knees. Moisture beaded on his forehead. Ash's pale skin was uniformly sunburnt, though after applying generous amounts of Talis' miracle salve, the stinging red had been tempered to a milder pink. Jyls inclined, shirtless, on the hill beside him. Unlike Ash, the thief had tanned. His freckles formed a prominent line across his cheeks and the bridge of his nose. The silver bird pendant glittered in the sunlight as Jyls folded his hands behind his head. He looked as content as a frog on a lily pad.

"The fish don't bite," Kyra called again. It was amazing to Kyra that there *were* fish again in the lake after the harrowing day with the red magic. As destructive as it had been, Kyra's dark magic couldn't contend with Solarus' magic and the elven magic that permeated the lake. Combined, they had healed and restored the waters and the bank in a few days. Kyra wondered if Loralai had come to the lake's shore in the time between the incident and the lake's resurrection. She doubted it. If Loralai had seen any damage, she would have reported it to the queen. What consequences Kyra would have faced as a result . . . Kyra shook the thoughts free. Nothing had happened. All she could do was put the incident behind her and fight so that it would never happen again.

Kyra swam forward with a breaststroke, then stopped when she was nearer to the bank. "Ash, wade in a bit. You'll love it, I promise."

Ash stood. He wiped the sweat from under his bushy red hair. "I wouldn't mind cooling off," he said. Ash stepped into the lake until the water was up to his knees. His spring green eyes lit up with delight. The healer returned Kyra's smile as he wiggled his toes under the mushy silt. "That's wonderful," Ash sighed. He bent down and scooped up a handful of water, washing his face, before glancing over his shoulder at Jyls. The thief hadn't moved from his spot. "What's wrong?"

Jyls wrinkled his nose. "Where I come from, you don't stroll into open water," he replied, eying the lake suspiciously. "Lots of unpleasant things lurk under the surface. Sure, the fish don't bite. Joxers and daggerfish do. You've also got snapping turtles who, as you might have guessed by their name, snap. Then you include waterborne diseases, poisonous floor-plants, and slimy insects worming their way through the mud." He stretched his arms and shook his head. "Nope, I'll stay safe on shore, thanks kindly."

Kyra rolled her eyes. She continued to swish her arms. "This isn't a swamp, Jyls. It's a lake. An *elven* lake. You won't find more pristine, disease- and disgusting-creature-free waters." *I'm assuming,* Kyra added silently as the thief raised a brow. Having limited experience in Ilian, Kyra relied on what she had seen so far: fish, turtles, and birds. Kyra certainly didn't suffer any health problems, and she had stood in the lake's waters for weeks.

Jyls' response was interrupted by the sound of hoofbeats. The thief pushed himself upward and spun around. Kyra and Ash glanced at the hill. A black horse with an elven rider appeared on the crest. He wore the uniform of the queen's Royal Guard. A grim expression tainted his porcelain white features. The elf held the reins to three steeds he had in tow.

"Lady Kyra," the elf's solemn voice echoed across the water. "*Raenalyn* Carina summons you and your friends to the Healer's Hall. One of your companions is gravely wounded. I am to escort you there."

Kyra swam forward as a white-faced Ash raced onto the bank. Jyls threw his shirt over his head. Ash jammed his silt-covered feet into his socks and boots. Kyra slogged out of the water and quickly stuffed her feet into her own boots. Jyls handed her the azure cloak. The trio sprinted up the hill to the elf. He handed each of them the reins to a horse.

Dread writhed in Kyra's stomach as she mounted. Who was injured? How grave was 'grave?' She exchanged a look with Jyls. His midnight blue eyes mirrored her dread.

"Follow me." The elven rider set off without further explanation.

Therial waited outside the palace when they arrived. His face was drawn. The gold that haloed his sapphire eyes was shadowed, like the sun drowned in stormy skies. Therial greeted the elven guard, placing a hand on his heart.

Kyra and Jyls vaulted from their steeds. "Who was hurt?" Jyls demanded as Ash slid out of his saddle. The elven guard took the reins to the steeds and strode away.

Therial turned to the group. "It's better for us to speak inside," he said in a hollow tone.

Kyra, Jyls, and Ash were at Therial's elbow. He took long, torpid steps, as though he were pushing through a bog. The queasy feeling in Kyra's stomach expanded. Therial led them to the western tower. During her time in Silvias, Kyra had never entered this section of the palace. Two guards bowed to Therial and opened the main doors. The captain unhesitatingly navigated a meandering series of halls, *zylith* twinkling around them. The cheerful colors were a jarring juxtaposition against the bleakness in Kyra's heart.

Therial finally stopped at a set of white doors. They had translucent etchings of elves in long robes with sashes and slippers. One carried a handful of plants, another a scale, and a third a bowl.

It was the Healer's Hall.

Kyra grimaced. She remembered her visit to the doctor in London for a check-up. The waiting room had the pervasive smell of sickness while the office had pungent fumes of bleach cleaners. Kyra braced herself for a similar stench of illness. Therial pushed open the doors and proceeded inside.

The delicate fragrance of mint and citrus coasted into the hallway. Brows arched in surprise, Kyra followed the captain. She entered a spacious room filled with beds and adorned with beige trees bearing unfamiliar fruits. Like the rest of the elven architecture, the Healer's Hall was shapeless, with bends and rounded corners. Beds for the patients were arranged around the trees and along the walls. Windows curved around the room, their sills speckled with potted plants and herbs. Sunlight sprinkled onto Kyra as her gaze flickered to an occupied bed.

An elf dressed in a white robe tied at the waist with a blue sash wrapped a bandage around a young girl's fingers. The girl burbled with energy, her lively chatter filling the air. Further down, another white-robed elf sponged the head of an elderly man, who moaned faintly. More elves measured powders and leaves on a scale like the one Kyra saw in the etching. Others pulped the fruits from the beige trees. Around one corner of the room, Kyra heard a worried murmuring.

Therial steered the group toward the bodiless voices. Kyra spotted Hayden and Solarus first. Their backs were to her as they watched a male elf with dark, corded hair hovering over the bed before them. Hayden twisted his ring. Solarus' arms were crossed. He and Hayden blocked the view of the patient on the bed.

On a table next to the elf—who Kyra guessed was the elven healer—was a pile of bandages, a large bowl with colored water, a small knife, and a roll of shimmering thread as fine as gossamer. Hayden's expression was layered with pain.

"Carina has suffered loss before," Hayden was saying in a soft tone. "Still, this will be particularly hard."

"It also may change our course," Solarus replied in an equally quiet voice.

As Kyra came closer, she saw the healer remove a white cloth stained with red. He dipped the cloth in the water and squeezed it free of blood.

Suddenly, Kyra looked wildly around the room.

Talis wasn't there.

Oh, god. Talis.

Heart bursting with terror, Kyra broke into a sprint. Hayden turned as she tried to shove past him to the bed. He caught her arm.

"She's alive and very weak," Hayden told Kyra as she stared at him. "The *Ethernyle*—the elven healer—has tended to her most serious wounds. He can't identify what is causing the tremors in her paws. We need Ash's expertise."

"She? Her paws?"

Hayden released Kyra's arm. Solarus stepped to the side to allow Kyra to squeeze in between them. Her gaze dipped down to the bed, terrified of what she would see. It wasn't what she was expecting.

Kyra's hand flew to her mouth. "Hazel!"

The blue merle collie lay motionless on her side. Her eyes were shut, and she seemed to fight for every shuddering, irregular breath. The fur on Hazel's hind leg had been shaved. Long, golden stiches made from the shimmering thread extended from her hock to her knee. Hazel's bone was set with a long splint. Blood was caked onto her other back leg.

The *Ethernyle* took the clean, damp cloth and began to dab away the remainder of the blood.

Ash immediately hastened to the bed as Jyls and Therial somberly joined the group. The healer placed a hand gently on top of Hazel's head and closed his eyes. "*Rashtatorov*," Ash chanted under his breath. "*Porto zovutt rashtatorov . . .*"

The *Ethernyle*'s mouth formed a puzzled line. He began to reach toward Ash as though to stop him. "I must ask you—"

"This is Ash, the healer from Calonia we mentioned," Hayden supplied.

The elven healer's chocolate gaze moved to the tattoo on Ash's neck. His eyes lit up in recognition. The *Ethernyle* nodded respectfully and continued blotting Hazel's leg.

Kyra looking imploringly at Hayden. Her stomach twisted in knots. "What happened? How did she get here?"

Hayden didn't answer. His eyes flickered expectantly to Therial. The captain's gaze was fixed on his magenta gauntlet, which he rubbed robotically. "My guards found Hazel half-drowned on the shores this side of Silvias' river," he spoke finally. "The collie is a friend of the elves. Scouts have met with her as a representative of the *Al-Ethran*, though this is the first time I have seen her personally. One of the scouts recognized Hazel and brought her to the Healer's Hall. A guard then informed me of her precarious state. I, in turn, sent for the rest of you." He paused. Kyra waited for him to elaborate. Therial silently ran his hand over his gauntlet.

"Did Hazel say anything?" Kyra asked, returning her attention to Hayden. "Did she tell you why she crossed the river or how she was hurt?"

"Hazel revived long enough to describe her journey, yes," Hayden answered. He and Solarus wore matching grim countenances. "When we were in Farcaren, you might remember that Talis wanted to send a dispatch to Silvias. Normally, the *Sirenyle* stationed at the castle are responsible for delivering messages. Given that the scouts weren't present, Talis asked for help from an animal scout posted to Thanesgard. The scout was a dog named Chloe. Chloe delivered the message to *Raenalyn* Carina. Then she traveled to the *Al-Ethran*. Hazel and Raff volunteered to return to Silvias. Hazel's mind is too clouded by the fever for her to remember for what purpose. The only other information she could share was about the two *Sirenyle* they met on their way here. They were the missing *Sirenyle* from Thanesgard."

Kyra's brows shot up in surprise. Before she could ask about the scouts, Ash interrupted, "What other injuries does Hazel have besides her leg?"

The *Ethernyle* frowned. "She suffered several shallow abrasions that I treated with the sap of the Sadyran plant. I found no signs of parasites beneath the skin. Based on her symptoms, I also do not believe she was poisoned."

Ash put a finger to his lip, green eyes contemplative. "Fatigue and a damaged leg wouldn't account for the fever," he muttered more to himself than the *Ethernyle*. "The heat is centered mostly in her back and behind her ears. We're missing something."

As Ash resumed his examination, Jyls spoke for the first time since entering the Hall. "Where are these scouts? The elves and the dog? Or Raff? Shouldn't they be the ones we're asking about what happened?"

Water rimmed Therial's eyes. "They encountered Reapers in the forest, and they fought. The panther was captured. Hazel couldn't tell us if he survived. The animal scout Chloe fled into the woods. The guards are searching for her now. If Chloe sought to enter Silvias, she, like Hazel, would have had to cross the river."

"And the *Sirenyle*?" Jyls responded in an unusually sober tone.

"Their names were Muireann and Emmeth. They were siblings. I trained them both. Muireann was two years' older than Emmeth. Kyra and he were course mates and friends. Muireann and Emmeth fought the Reapers, even though they should have run." Therial bowed his head and covered it with one hand. Tears slid between his fingers. "They died." Hayden put a hand on Therial's shoulder.

Kyra stared at the captain. His raw sorrow washed over her as though she had been thrown into melted ice. Another of Kyra's course mates. Friends. The names didn't conjure up any memories. Therial saw something behind his closed eyes. In her own mind, Kyra felt herself suddenly entangled in his feelings and thoughts. Her toes and fingers went numb. Kyra plummeted fully into Therial's memory.

Numb. Kyra had heard the word associated with grief. The desperation to escape from such all-consuming pain. Kyra couldn't tear herself away from the scenes springing to life in front of her. This time, though, the memories blinked from one image to the next as quickly as a camera reel.

> *Emmeth scaling a machi tree, glancing down with a wide grin, as Kyra scampered up below him. Muireann and Therial watching from the ground, Muireann with a worried frown, the captain with an amused smile.*
>
> *The scent of fresh pine logs burning in a large hearth, Emmeth and Muireann sitting cross-legged in a circle, playing cards with Aila and Kyra. Therial passing by, glancing in their direction, smiling. Snow falling outside the palace window.*
>
> *Muireann touching the edge of a track in the mud, lips scrunched together, with Therial standing over her, waiting to hear what animal she determined had made the mark.*

Therial holding a magenta-haired toddler on his lap, speaking to her in a soothing tone as a healer patched up her scraped knees.

Kyra spiraled into the final scene and found herself standing next to Therial under a large arch. Therial's arms were folded. A soft smile drifted over his lips. Kyra was overwhelmed by boisterous chatter, laughter, quick footsteps, and the clinking of hundreds of pieces of silverware. Flavorful scents of cooked meats filled the air. Kyra looked out from the arch into a large dining room crammed with students. She glanced sideways at Therial, wondering what was special about this moment. Kyra followed the captain's gaze across the room.

She gasped. Kyra saw a younger version of herself at a table, heartily tucking into her meal. Muireann was beside her, drinking from a tall glass. Emmeth and Aila sat across the table, pretending to duel with their spoons.

"Emmeth, seriously," Muireann reprimanded as she put down the glass. "This is the dining hall, not the training field. You'll have a sword in the afternoon's lesson, won't you?"

"Sure, but spoons are more fun to use," Emmeth replied, fending off Aila's swipes. The spoons "tinged" as they struck each other. "And why are you telling me to stop? Aila's doing it, too."

"Aila isn't my younger brother."

Kyra stopped eating, fork raised. "Aila, this is the dining hall, not the training field," she repeated in an exact likeness of Muireann's voice.

Aila grinned. Emmeth laughed. Muireann rolled her eyes.

"Fine," Muireann said, poking a piece of potato. "When you get into trouble, don't blame me."

"Future scouts are supposed to get into trouble," Aila responded casually. She knocked aside Emmeth's spoon. It flew down the table and onto another student's plate. "Ooops, sorry, Felicity!" Aila apologized as the elf lifted the spoon from her plate and wiped off gravy stuck to the bottom.

"You're eleven, you don't know you'll be a scout," Muireann said pointedly to Aila. "Unless you're relying on your father to do everything."

"I'll be a scout, because I'm good enough to be a scout," Aila replied. "I can ride. I'm a fearless warrior." She held her hand out as Felicity slid the spoon down the table.

"Thanks," Aila called. She picked up the spoon and returned it to Emmeth, who unabashedly began ladling soup into his mouth. "And I'm good at convincing elves to do things."

Muireann let out an aggrieved sigh. "The expression is Sirenyle are 'the fleetest of riders, the finest of orators, and the fiercest of warriors.'"

"That's what I said."

Kyra grinned at her friend. "You'd be a great scout."

Aila beamed at Kyra. "Thank you."

"Then I'll be a scout, too," Emmeth came in between sips. "I mean, if Aila's a scout, we can all be scouts."

> *Aila tried to hit Emmeth with her spoon. He deftly deflected it with a flick of his own.*
>
> *Muireann sighed again. Aila and Kyra traded wide smiles.*
>
> *"I bet you will be, too."*

Therial's statement startled Kyra. She had forgotten he stood beside her. His golden-haloed eyes twinkled as he regarded the group. *I bet you will be, too.* Was Therial speaking about Aila or all three elves?

> *Therial radiated an intense pride and love as he turned and strode away from the dining hall. The voices dimmed...*

"Are there red jury bushes in Silvias?" Ash's voice came distantly.

As quickly as she was pulled into the abyss of Therial's sorrow, Kyra was thrust back into the present. Her eyes burned, and her cheeks were wet. Kyra brushed the tears away. Her gaze traveled to the Therial of the present. His head was buried in his hands. Therial wasn't only grieving Emmeth and Muireann, Kyra understood now. He was terrified for Aila, his daughter. She was another scout far away in a kingdom and away from his protection. Possibly defending against monsters like the Reapers. Therial let out a shuddering sigh. He finally raised his gaze to Hayden. Hayden squeezed his shoulder. Therial nodded in thanks.

Kyra's heart skipped a beat as Hayden lowered his hand. Had he or Solarus noticed her accidental intrusion on the captain's thoughts? A furtive glance in their direction, though, and Kyra guessed they hadn't.

"Red jury bushes?" the *Ethernyle* repeated, bewildered. "They do not grow in Silvias. You may find them hidden among the underbrush in Edoin Forest."

Comprehension dawned in Ash's eyes. "Hazel's infection comes from that bush, or rather, a thorn from the bush. The rash here—" Ash placed his finger above a spot behind the collie's ear, "—is unique to the red juries. The poison bubbles beneath the skin and causes the area to become hot. Do you have any goran plants?" The elven healer nodded. "I need juice from its leaves. They must be freshly picked, or the liquid won't be strong enough to counter the infection. It's already starting to spread. We don't have much time."

"I will bring some at once, Master Healer," the *Ethernyle* said deferentially. He glided away noiselessly on white slippers.

Kyra choked back a sob. She felt as though acid had been poured over her heart, dissolving it bit by bit, so deep was her shared anguish with Therial.

"Kyra." Hazel's eyes fluttered open. Her crystal blue gaze was glassy, and her words were barely more than a breath. The collie tried to raise her head and failed.

Kyra crouched so that she was eye level with the collie. "I'm here, Hazel." She put a hand on Hazel's front paw. "I'm right here."

The collie inhaled, then winced with pain as she exhaled. Hazel again tried to turn her head. "Muireann and Emmeth. They died, Kyra. I'm sorry. I'm so sorry."

"I know." Kyra's voice cracked. "You're going to be okay, Hazel. Ash is getting something to heal you. You need to rest. It's all going to be fine."

"No, that's not it. Muireann said to tell you . . . she said they loved you." The collie's voice grew faint. Kyra leaned in, searching the collie's face. "They were so happy, Kyra." Hazel sighed, closing her eyes. "They loved you dearly. I'm sorry."

Kyra couldn't catch the rogue tears that escaped the corners of her eyes. Sniffing, she stood. The Healer's Hall was suddenly confining. She needed to escape. "I'm going for a walk," Kyra mumbled to no one in particular. The words sounded as though they came from someone else. Keeping her head down and eyes averted, Kyra turned and hurried away from the bed. Talis, who had just then entered the room, watched her with a troubled look as she sped by wordlessly.

"Kyra, where are you going?" she heard him ask.

"She needs time alone," Hayden's voice responded softly. "Kyra was told about the *Sirenyle*. Give her time. She'll be all right."

All right. Kyra shivered despite the sunlight that showered down on her through the windows. Not even the prismatic colors could spark light in the black void of her heart. She mourned the deaths of possibly her only remaining childhood friends. Kyra wondered if she would ever be "all right" again.

Chapter 34

Kyra wandered the palace without a destination. Crying had purged some of her pain. But it left her feeling empty and hollow. Her legs brought her to the Garden of Sight. The bright ruby and emerald hummingbirds drank nectar from the flowers, and sparrows bathed in the fountain. Kyra looked up listlessly at the statue of Lady Imineral. As always, the elven warrior's stone gaze was fixed on a point in the distance. Water trickled over the sides of the fountain. It created a harmonious rhythm to the birds' melody. With heavy steps, Kyra walked forward and sat on the edge. She held one knee close to her body and rested her head on it. Her body ached as though her tears waterlogged every muscle.

For hours, Kyra stared blankly at the glittering moonstone walls. She tried to gather the thoughts that her emotions had shredded like confetti in her mind. Since Kyra returned to Ilian, she and her companions had met the dark wizards and Arkin's soldiers head-on in battle; escaped the wicked Forgotten Forest and its phantoms; and fought against the grotesque greeloks. In all that time, the injuries they suffered were cuts, bruises, magical burns, and a concussion. Now two of Kyra's childhood friends were dead. Ones that, through Therial's memory, Kyra cherished and grieved for as though she had seen them the day before.

Kyra pressed the heels of her hands against her eyes. *It's my fault*, the thought played through her mind. *If Diamantas weren't looking for me, the dark wizards wouldn't have been in Thanesgard. Talis wouldn't have sent the message with the animal scout, Raff and Hazel wouldn't have been in Edoin Forest, and Muireann and Emmeth . . .* Kyra looked up. She didn't know why the *Sirenyle* had left Thanesgard. What if it didn't have anything to do with her? What if there was a reason besides the dark wizards? Kyra didn't have the answer. Hazel might, but the collie wouldn't be able to tell her until she had recovered. Kyra also didn't have an explanation for why the Reapers had ventured into Edoin. Did Diamantas send Harkimer's monsters to catch her? Or was it a coincidence? Kyra tried to take some comfort in that the blame, at least for Muireann and Emmeth's deaths, might not rest with her at all. It was an artificial comfort. Her friends were gone.

Kyra reached into her vest pocket. Her fingers touched the heptagon coin. Removing it, Kyra slowly traced the etchings with her forefinger. Her grief was crowded out by a different guilt. After weeks of lessons with Solarus, what had Kyra accomplished? A rudimentary control of her magic. Mastery of trivial spells. Drying and wetting things. Incantations that were as helpful against the dark wizards as giving them a stern talking-to. Kyra gripped the coin tightly in her fist.

"I haven't been training hard enough," she said out loud. "I should have spent more time reading the book on magic. I should have spent more hours in the lake and less time trying to get better with a sword I'll never use. I should have asked Solarus to teach me spells to attack the dark wizards."

The train of admonishment steamed along the tracks in her mind. There were so many things she should have done. Kyra knew Diamantas was out there, in Ilian. Why hadn't she ridden out to meet him before he did more harm? A shiver went down Kyra's spine. Solarus had told her how dangerous Diamantas was, how powerful the obsidian staff made him. If her mentor couldn't fight him, how could Kyra be expected to face him and survive? Besides, she wasn't as brave as Hayden. She wasn't as nimble as Talis. She couldn't throw a knife like Jyls. If she were injured, she couldn't dress her wounds like Ash.

A reserve of tears spilled onto Kyra's cheeks. She let out a shuddering breath. Whether it was cowardice or her true lack of skills that prevented her from setting out of Silvias, Kyra wasn't sure. She wrapped her arms around her legs and rested her chin on her knees. Kyra closed her eyes and listened to the water dribbling from the fountain.

When the sky's golden light began sinking behind the walls of the garden, Kyra rose. She returned the coin to her pocket. Salt was encrusted on her cheeks. Kyra scooped up the fountain's waters and splashed her face. Wiping it clean with her sleeve, Kyra trudged to her room. Her stomach was too stuffed with pain to eat dinner. She collapsed on her bed without removing her clothes. Kyra's sleep was haunted by Emmeth and Muireann's faces and laughter, lost to her forever.

***

The next day, Kyra struggled to concentrate. Her commitment to improve her magic had cemented itself in her heart. Unfortunately, it made bungling the simplest magic outstandingly frustrating. Kyra wondered if she imagined it or if Solarus was also more impatient and aggravated with her poor performance than usual. The wizard barked at her every time she made a mistake. When Kyra's golden bars refused to meld together, Solarus' lips formed a thin, angry line.

"If you choose not to focus, you are wasting my time," he berated.

"I'm *trying*," Kyra snapped in her exhaustion.

"Try harder."

After her disastrous morning, Kyra was looking forward to a sword fighting lesson with Hayden that afternoon. He greeted her with a weary smile. The skin under his eyes was gray and shadowed. They trained for only an hour before Hayden ended their session, citing a meeting with Talis. With nothing left to do, Kyra debated whether she should retreat to the Garden of Sight or if she should redouble her efforts at the lake. She had to practice. But Solarus' irritation had lowered her spirits. The temptation to sequester herself in the garden was hard to resist.

In the end, Kyra ended up doing neither. Jyls and Ash found her before she had made a decision. Reluctantly, Kyra joined them for an afternoon swim. Jyls' good-natured humor had her laughing by the end of their time. Kyra's heart was lighter as she went with Jyls and Ash to the dining hall. Hayden, Solarus, and Talis were absent. Kyra was too sapped to puzzle over where they might be. As she did the previous day, Kyra retired to her room early. Her dreams were plagued with images of Emmeth and Muireann, lying prone, Therial standing over them, body wracked with sobs.

The next day Kyra had recovered some of her stolen sleep. Her manipulation of the golden magic was more graceful though far from perfect. While Kyra's abilities had improved, Solarus' mood hadn't. He pounced on the smallest mistake like a cat on a cricket. Kyra held back her retorts and focused on following his commands. After lunch, she practically ran to meet Talis. A bit of open-hand sparring would help Kyra vent her anger and pent-up sorrow. Uncharacteristically, Talis postponed their session. He offered his apologies but no explanation as to why. As he strode to the eastern wing of the palace, Kyra saw Hayden waiting for him. Hayden's expression was fatigued and severe. He wordlessly fell into step with Talis. As Kyra watched the pair walk into the palace, her apprehension climbed. Whatever was keeping Hayden, Talis, and Solarus away at night seemed to be taking its toll. Her only respite came from the increased time in Jyls and Ash's company. She swam in the lake, with Ash wading in up to his knees. Kyra's worries drifted into the warm air as she laughed and verbally jousted with Jyls. When dusk set in, Kyra hiked up the hill with a bounce in her step.

Except Solarus, Hayden, and Talis were again nowhere to be found. Kyra's brow furrowed as she, Jyls, and Ash had dinner. When she laid her head on her pillow that evening, Kyra again wondered where they had gone. More importantly, what conversations were they having? And why were Kyra and her other companions excluded?

***

Kyra woke hours later, thrashing beneath a tangle of sheets. She finally freed herself, almost falling off the bed in the process. Kyra shot upright. Her shirt was wet and clung to her back. Her breaths came as small gasps. Another nightmare.

Kyra's gaze skated across the room. Outside, the moon and stars were stitched into a navy-blue sky like sequins on a dress. The machi trees' balsam fragrance wisped in. The twitter and chirps of birds heralded the approach of dawn.

Kyra lay back down and squeezed her eyes closed. She dreamt she had lost Raff in a blizzard. Reapers had cornered Talis, and Kyra's legs refused to move. She screamed to him. The flash of blinding white light jolted her out of the dream.

Kyra pulled the sheets to her chin. She listened to the birds' chipper chorus, trying to lasso their happiness as she drove the images of the blizzard from her mind. The nightmare stuck like gum on a shoe. Kyra changed positions and dragged the blanket over her head. She needed to concentrate on something boring.

One sheep, Kyra counted silently. *Two sheep. Three sheep. Why are they called sheep and not sheeps?* The mental tangent pulled her from the steady rhythm. *Four sheep. Five sheep. You have goose and geese but not shoop and sheep. Six sheep.*

Letting out a small, aggrieved breath, Kyra again threw back the sheets. She sat upright and raked a hand through her mussed hair. "Farm animals clearly aren't working," she muttered to herself. "I guess sleep isn't on my to-do list right now. Really wish it were."

Kyra's eyes trailed back to the window. There was enough sunlight to go for a short run before breakfast. Kyra slid her legs over the bed and stood. Her legs wobbled as the soft, fairy-like lights in the room blinked to life. It wouldn't be one of her more enjoyable excursions. But it didn't matter. Running was her release. Her legs would have to manage.

As Kyra removed her nightgown, she voiced her thoughts. "Someone is going to tell me what's going on. Hayden and Solarus aren't going to dodge my questions or give me some vague answer." The fuzzy lights flitted around Kyra as she gathered her trousers, tunic, and braided belt. "If Hayden and Solarus think the dark wizards are annoying, they've never had to deal with a stubborn teenager." Rubbing an eye, Kyra took up her feather-light leather boots. "I'll be on them like a cockroach on a trash heap." Kyra sat on her bed and eased her foot into the boot. "I shouldn't compare myself to a germ-infested insect. Unfortunately, the idea's right."

Knowledge both frees and constrains the mind. The answer you desire will be given—if you ask.

Kyra froze as the sensation struck her. It had been weeks since she had such an experience. Her pulse quickened. Usually, the feeling was a whisper, soft and subtle. This time, the message was as clear as though someone had stamped her heart with the words.

"Ask who?" Kyra asked the room. "Where?"

What has been spoken cannot be unspoken. What has been heard cannot be unheard.

Goose bumps pricked Kyra's skin. The feeling came as a warning. What did it mean?

She awaits you in the archery fields.

"*Who* is waiting?"

Kyra let a minute pass to see if there was an answer. The sensations had finished. As curious as she was unsettled, Kyra rose. She automatically went to her bow. Kyra's fingers slid down the smooth bend in the karia wood. Kyra never subscribed to the idea that ignorance was bliss. Particularly now, since her purpose in coming to Ilian was to gather information about her past and her magic. Kyra's words moments earlier now were her mantra. Kyra was going to blast through Solarus and Hayden's silence and get the truth. Had she interpreted the impression correctly though? Was her destination the archery fields? Kyra doubted she would find enlightenment in a place where she had almost no confidence. Kyra swore she felt the bow whir under her fingertips. Her eyes lit up. A golden glow shimmered around the karia like a fine mist. Kyra covered her mouth as she yawned deeply. She shook her head. As soon as she lifted the bow from its peg, the gold disappeared.

"I guess you're it then," Kyra said to the bow. "The bane of my weapon mastery, and you're the weapon chosen for me. I have nothing to lose by figuring out why, right?"

Kyra snatched a quiver of arrows from the floor and strapped it to her side. Slinging the bow over her shoulder, Kyra stole out of her room and headed for the fields.

***

Kyra's lips pursed quizzically. Dark purple and orange rays bathed the dew-covered grass on the archery fields. The air was pleasantly cool. Standing in the middle of the fields was a young elven girl. Strawberry blond ringlets twined with silver hung past her shoulders and glimmered in the light. The girl held a bow pointed toward the ground, its wood as slender as her wrists. A quiver girdled her waist. Bales of hay sat several meters down the field. Her expression was one of extreme concentration, as though the targets were the sole objects that existed in her world. As Kyra approached slowly, she estimated the girl was eleven or twelve years' old.

The girl readied her bow with an arrow and raised it. She drew the string back. Kyra noticed her arm twitched right before she released. The errant arrow arced briefly before plowing into a point in front of the bales. The girl's face fell. She glanced up at a dove flapping out from the trees as tears slid down her cheeks.

Kyra's heart went out to the girl. She was certain this young elf was the "she." The breeze that touched Kyra's heart confirmed her suspicion. She proceeded toward the girl, who swiped away the tears with one hand.

"Hi, there," Kyra called out with deliberate cheerfulness.

The girl started at the sound. Her teal-colored eyes widened in consternation when she saw Kyra.

Kyra immediately felt guilty. It hadn't occurred to her that she was intruding on the girl's privacy. Kyra fixed a reassuring smile on her lips. "I didn't realize someone else would be on the fields so early. Do you mind if I join you?"

The girl's embarrassed expression remained. She looked down mutely and nodded.

Kyra casually unslung her bow. "I'm horrible at archery," she continued in the same, sunny tone. "I was hoping to practice without the other students around. I always get nervous when they watch me. The harder I try to get it right, the worse I end up doing."

Kyra's words brought a shy smile to the girl's face. "Me, too." The girl lifted her eyes and studied Kyra. She added hesitantly, "Couldn't you make the arrow go where you want? I mean, because you're a . . . I mean, if you have magic, you could put a spell on your bow . . . ?" The girl's words trailed off as the pink of her cheeks turned cranberry red. She anxiously wound a silver curl around her forefinger.

Kyra laughed sincerely. "I wish I could control my arrows with magic. Maybe some wizards can but not me." Owls concealed within the trees hooted softly. Kyra looked down at her bow. "Since you're here," she said, running her hand over the soft wood, "would you mind looking at my form and tell me what I'm doing wrong?"

The girl looked baffled. "You . . . you want *me* to help you?"

"Absolutely. I saw you shoot earlier. You're much better at this than I am."

The girl glanced tentatively in the direction of the arrow embedded in the ground. "You don't want me to teach you," she mumbled.

"Why not?"

"I'm not as good as everyone else." The girl's lower lip trembled. "The instructors tell me I should be better than my classmates. I come out here some mornings and practice and practice and practice. It never works. I'm probably the worst archer in Silvias. The worst archer in the *history* of Silvias."

The girl's crestfallen expression made Kyra's heart pang with sympathy. All Kyra wanted to do was console the girl. "The arrow hit the hay bale, didn't it?" Kyra said in an encouraging tone. "Mine usually go over the top, fly to the side, or plop in front of it. Which makes *me* the worst archer in Silvias. *And* I'm a wizard. That's a terrible combination, isn't it? If you can teach me to at least hit the target, I wouldn't feel so embarrassed."

The girl's mouth twitched into a smile. "Okay. I'll watch you."

Kyra's jade-flecked eyes traveled down the field. The dawn sun now cast long pink and yellow lines across the sky, fishing out the night's stars. In the pale light, Kyra made out concentric circles painted in earthy greens and browns. The silver ring in the center glimmered.

"Most armies wear armor of steel," Kyra recalled Talis telling her during their early lessons together. *"That is the purpose of the silver center. Your eye must habituate itself to the color you will see in battle."* A smile tugged on Kyra's lips. "What's your name?" she asked the girl.

"Evangeline. Everyone calls me Eva though."

"Pleased to meet you, Eva. I'm Kyra."

"I know," Eva responded before she could stop herself. "Everyone knows you." The girl's cheeks turned a darker shade of red. She again dropped her gaze to her feet.

Kyra pretended not to notice Eva's discomfort. Kyra set herself into the stance she recalled from Talis' memory. She led with her left foot and spread her right behind it. Without loading an arrow, Kyra held the bow as straight as a board in front of her and drew back the string. "How does this look?" she asked without turning her head. From her peripheral vision, Kyra saw Eva scrutinizing her form.

"Your feet are in the right places," the girl replied, face scrunched together in thought. "You need to pull the string back more. Your forefinger is supposed to be at the corner of your mouth. Then you put your middle finger and ring finger below it."

"Can you show me?"

Eva nodded. The bow brushed against her curls as she raised it to her cheek. This time, Eva drew back the string with ease, her forefinger hooked on the edge of her lips as she had described. Her posture relaxed. "Don't let go too quickly. You have to be gentle, like snow falling off a leaf."

Kyra suppressed a grin. Those were Talis' exact words. Kyra wondered if elves used the phrase to teach beginners the art of archery.

"Like this." Eva's release was so subtle Kyra barely saw her fingers drop. The string snapped. Lowering the bow, the girl turned to Kyra. "Now you try."

Kyra mimicked her motion. Eva gave her an encouraging grin, then drew an arrow from her quiver. Her movements had a natural finesse as she notched the arrow and raised the bow. Before Kyra could see the whole motion, Eva had fired at the target. The arrow burrowed into the corner of the silver center. Eva let out a small squeal of excitement. When she turned to Kyra, the girl's eyes were alight with joy. Eva quickly donned an instructor-like pose. "That's how it looks," she told Kyra solemnly.

Kyra hid a grin and fit an arrow to her bow. "I don't think I can do as well as you did, but let's see where my arrow ends up." She raised the bow and released the string. There was a satisfying thud as the arrow found its mark in an outer ring. Kyra grinned widely, delighted with the unexpectedly good shot. She glanced over at Eva.

Eva's eyes sparkled even as she continued to impose calm into her demeanor. "Your technique was very good," she praised.

Kyra and Eva emptied their quivers, collected their arrows from the target, and continued to practice. Kyra's grin was infectious and stripped Eva of her feigned composure. The girl jumped with joy as her shots came closer to the center. When Kyra's arrow skimmed the top of the silver, Eva clapped enthusiastically. Kyra laughed. She was, for the first time, having *fun* in the archery fields. *Was that what the impression wanted for me? To enjoy something I feel so inadequate about? Or to give me hope? Hope that even if I don't feel confident in magic, or in any other skill, I can achieve anything with practice?*

When the sun's bright yellow rays flooded the horizon, Kyra and Eva stopped. The crickets' soft tune gave way to the birds' mélange of morning melodies. Kyra restored her arrows to her quiver as Eva's gaze roved the grounds. The girl's expression betrayed her anxiousness of being spotted by her peers. When Kyra recommended they leave for the day, relief spilled over Eva's face. They slung their bows over their backs and headed toward the azalea bushes bordering the field.

The concern about her course mates didn't stop Eva from skipping beside Kyra. "No one would ever believe that *I* was helping *you*," the girl remarked breathlessly. Her cheeks were still a rosy red, this time from exhilaration. "I mean, I was teaching a powerful wizard, and I was shooting well too! My sister, she would be so upset with me if she knew I was talking to you . . ." An ashamed look spread across Eva's face. "You were so nice to me. I don't care if you're a wizard, even if the others do. You're not a dark wizard."

The serenity in Kyra's heart was abruptly squeezed out by Eva's words. "Not all wizards are bad," Kyra replied with effort. "Solarus is kind too, and he's my mentor." Kyra paused for a moment. "Thank you for agreeing to stay, Eva. I couldn't have hit those circles without you."

Eva nodded, but the spring was gone from the girl's step. "They shouldn't say we can't be friends." Eva's tone was laced with frustration. "If they knew you, they would like you. They're just afraid of the dumb prophecy."

Eva's hand flew to her mouth. Her eyes were wide, clearly horrified at what she had revealed.

Kyra stopped midstride. A shiver went down her spine at the word "prophecy." The mere mention of it had transformed Eva's elation moments earlier into a cold fear. "What prophecy?"

The color drained from Eva's face. She twisted a strand of hair around her finger, avoiding Kyra's probing gaze. "I mean, the one about you," she murmured. "I didn't mean to say that. Please don't tell anyone. My sister would be so angry if she knew I talked to you and practiced with you and then mentioned the prophecy, because it's forbidden, and if my aunt found out . . ."

Kyra knelt so that she was eye level with Eva. She gently placed one hand on the girl's shoulder and raised the other to shield her eyes from the bright morning light. Eva winced as though Kyra's touch had burned her. "Eva, it's okay," Kyra said soothingly. "This stays between us like our practice this morning. I promise."

The girl reluctantly raised her gaze. She was on the edge of tears.

"I need you to tell me about the prophecy."

"You . . . you haven't heard it?"

"Sure, I have," Kyra lied. "When I left Silvias, I forgot everything about my time here and what I learned, including the prophecy." Eva's nod confirmed that she, like the other elves, was aware of Kyra's lost memories. "It had something to do with wizards," Kyra ventured in a tone inviting Eva to speak. "You wouldn't be telling me anything *new*, Eva. You're helping jog my memory. That's all. Will you do that for me?"

Eva darted a glance around the fields as though expecting students to descend upon them. "I shouldn't," she replied timidly.

Kyra stood and hugged her bowstring against her chest. "Let's go over here." Kyra steered Eva out of the fields and toward the woods. When they were tucked behind a screen of trees, Kyra turned to the girl. "Now no one can see us. So, Eva, can you share the words with me? You've already been such a big help. It would make me feel better to remember more about my life."

Eva pulled at a long strawberry blond curl, expression conflicted. "The seers made a prophecy a hundred years ago," she finally answered in a small voice. "My aunt told me mystics in the other kingdoms had the same visions as ours. The elven seers I mean. She told me prophecies were rare. That's why this one was so special. This one about you. If it's you. It might not be you. The seers have been wrong."

A sense of foreboding scratched at Kyra's heart. She waited for Eva to continue, but the girl was silent. "It sounds familiar," Kyra prompted. "Could you recite the prophecy for me?"

Eva swallowed hard. "The seers . . . they said this:
'In a century's time, Ilian's peace is imperiled
By a wizard wielding an obsidian staff.
Harkimer's son inspires and heralds
An era of war that swallows all in his path.
Shadows long hidden creep like mist
Across the Sea into Ilian's lands.
Kings who are and who will yet be
Will fight and fall when the time is at hand.
Yet hope remains in the darkest of hours
When a girl is born from a village of ash.
Known to none, but with dangerous powers
The girl with an enigmatic past
Will be born to this world yet come from another,
A girl some believe to be Harkimer's salvation.
A wizard she is part but is like no other:
She either brings Ilian's deliverance or causes its devastation.
Thus, it is presaged.'"

Kyra stared at Eva, thunderstruck. The girl's recitation was imbued with an intensity and fluidity as though she had been one of the seers who made the prophecy. Eva bit her lip.

"Deliverance or devastation," Kyra repeated bleakly. That was it. The explanation behind everything. Her friends. The dark wizards. Solarus' urgency to teach her mastery over the golden energy, over her emotions. Hayden's secret spying from the hilltop. Kyra wasn't treated like a pariah in Silvias because she was a wizard; it was because she could be a greater threat to Ilian than even Diamantas. It was like she was walking on a tightrope between the palace towers, and the elves and her friends were holding their breath below her, wondering if—or when—she would fall.

Kyra's thoughts blew through her mind like tumbleweed in a desert. Why did Hayden and the others believe that Kyra was the girl in the prophecy? Kyra had considered the possibility she had harmed someone with her magic. As she returned to the theory, Kyra added the fact that her magic could have targeted a fellow student. After all, fear and anger unleashed the terrible red energy inside her. Kyra's emotional reaction to Loralai had been strong enough to devastate life in an entire lake. What was more, Kyra struggled to control her magic now at sixteen; Kyra imagined it would have been infinitely harder to restrain her magic when she was younger and unaware of her powers.

Kyra suddenly remembered Eva standing beside her. The girl's shoulders were hunched, her expression miserable.

Kyra plastered what she hoped was a reassuring smile on her face. "Of course, now I remember the prophecy. It's . . . poetic. Thanks for the help, Eva." Kyra gripped her quiver. She hoped Eva didn't see her hand trembling. "We should go back before the morning lessons start. I'll wait here in case the elves come. That way they won't see us together."

Needles were scattered as rodents forged, and birds trilled overhead. Oddly, Kyra didn't hear any laughter or chatter. She checked Eva's expression. The girl also hearkened to the sounds of the forest, but her expression indicated her keen ears hadn't detected any students either. Eva shrugged her bow higher on her shoulders. "Maybe we can practice together again," she offered quietly.

"I'd love that."

Eva's boots were almost noiseless as she hiked back toward the palace. Kyra watched until the girl had disappeared between the trees. Kyra's hands quaked. Her chest was so tight it was hard to breathe. Kyra looked down.

"I need a path to the hills, please," she told the ground. "Without being seen."

The familiar, shimmering green lane materialized. Kyra sprinted down it, leaving the fields behind her.

Chapter 35

Kyra's emotions were like live wires. They jolted the fatigue from her muscles as she sprinted through the forest. Kyra had no direction or destination. Her instincts guided her nimbly over logs, around brambles, and over flattened leaves. Kyra didn't notice.

Deliverance or devastation. The phrase was lodged in her mind like a piece of shrapnel.

Kyra's teeth clenched in hurt and frustration. Hayden, Solarus, and Talis had known all along what potential wickedness lurked in her core, what possibilities the future held for her. Refusing her the critical knowledge about the prophecy was as unforgivable as sending her into a battle without a weapon.

Then there was James. He had insisted Kyra leave London to find a mentor and explore her powers. The unease—no, fear—in his green eyes the night Kyra rescued him from the Variavryk meant James had guessed that Kyra was the subject of the prophecy. If he was acquainted with the prophecy. Kyra admitted that, as a Lyneera, James might have lived—and died—long before the prophecy had been made. Or her best friend simply decided Kyra shouldn't be told about it.

The magical path threaded through the forest where the trees began to thin. The thick underbrush slowly receded to a wide route speckled with pine needles. Kyra mindlessly sprinted along the emerald lane, unaware as her surroundings shifted.

Kyra's frustration was pressed down by her rising anger. Her companions treated her like a child. Well, she wasn't a child anymore. Kyra had proven she could handle the dark wizards, Arkin's soldiers, and even the savage greeloks. Still, Kyra couldn't deny that she had seen the red magic flare through her hands. That she had been responsible for the deaths at the lake. Something within her *was* capable of terrible acts. Even worse . . .

Kyra's blood went cold. What had happened at the lake was dwarfed by a greater evil. An evil that Kyra had grappled with for the past two years.

Chicago. The blue and red flames. The firefighters. Kyra's fear and despair. The sights and smells and sounds were seared into her mind. Kyra may have killed an innocent family. It could have been an uncontrolled surge of anger or accidental release of energy. But didn't Hayden and Talis reassure her she wasn't a dark wizard? They didn't trust her fully. The question was, would Hayden and Talis lie to her outright? The thought drove painful stakes into her heart.

Kyra pounded after the magical lane. Her lungs burned from the exertion of the run, but she pressed onward. The path had widened and was now flat and devoid of leaf litter. She swatted a tree branch away from her face, causing needles to rain down on her head. Sweat poured down her back. Kyra swiped her brow with the back of her hand. Her mind locked onto a different, equally important piece of the puzzle.

What was the role of the seers? Who were they exactly? Where did they come from? Kyra recalled her conversation with Hayden in Thanesgard's marketplace. He had mentioned in passing that seers made divinations for the kingdoms. It wasn't any more information than Eva had provided. Kyra rued not having asked Hayden for more of an explanation of the seers' profession: where they lived, how many existed, and what other predictions they had made in the past that later came true. Of course, there hadn't been a need at the time to delve into the topic.

Kyra stopped. She bent over, hands on her knees, sucking in shallow breaths. The magical green path seemed to take it as a sign Kyra didn't need its services. It shimmered and vanished under her feet.

After a moment, Kyra straightened. She locked her hands and rested them atop her head. Pine needles stuck in Kyra's hair pricked her scalp. Kyra shook her head, flinging the needles to the ground. The movement made her dizzy. Kyra inhaled and exhaled as deeply as she could. As she focused on her breath, Kyra's gaze circuited her surroundings.

Though it had been a bright morning when Kyra started her run, the light within this part of the woods was muted. A smattering of sunlight sprinkled down through gaps in the largest firs Kyra had ever seen. The tree trunks were bare at the base, and the first branches began to sprout a couple meters above the ground. White mist drifted lazily in the air like a long stream of smoke. The mist wound around the wide spaces in between the trees. Fascinated, Kyra's eyes dipped to the ground. The mist hovered just above her feet, obscuring the dirt beneath. The forest was as quiet as a library, save for Kyra's ragged breath.

Kyra unclasped her hands and dropped her arms to her side. As far as she could remember, she had never visited this part of the forest before. Kyra certainly hadn't explored these pines with Talis in their outings. Kyra creaked her neck from left to right, hearing a bone crack. As her breathing steadied, Kyra's thoughts spun like pinwheels in the wind.

If she did confront Hayden, Solarus, and Talis, how would they react? That was easy to predict. Kyra envisioned Solarus' severe torrent of questions. Hayden's alarmed expression. Talis' silent distress that she had uncovered the mystery guiding their actions. Kyra might obliterate the kingdoms. They would insist Kyra stay in Silvias to prevent that from occurring. Kyra would be as much in exile in the Elven Realm as the dark wizards were in the Southern Mountains. That banishment could last months. Years. Hayden and the others wouldn't risk her being captured by the dark wizards. For the first time, Kyra empathized with the wizards of Harkimer. Were they like her? Forced behind stone because others felt they *might* harm others in Ilian?

Kyra sighed. She couldn't do anything about Hayden, Talis, and Solarus. Would Jyls or Ash be an ally? Kyra chewed on her lip. Possibly. Nothing escaped the thief's observations. Even if the others hadn't mentioned the prophecy outright, Jyls would have noticed the nuanced grimaces and uneasy side glances. He might have eavesdropped on a conversation and heard the evasive answers to Kyra's straightforward questions. Jyls would have wondered why their companions acted as they did. He also would have sniffed out the reason. That was if Jyls hadn't independently heard about the prophecy. Kyra assumed thieves always had their ears and eyes open to identify hapless victims while avoiding authorities.

Kyra pushed aside pine needles with her toe. Did that affect Jyls' view of Kyra? He hadn't ever looked at her with mistrust or filtered what he told her. At least, that was Kyra's impression. Jyls had the emotional dexterity of a stage actor. He could fasten any expression on his face if he needed to, no matter how he really felt.

A gentle breeze swept wavy strands of hair across Kyra's face. She brushed them aside. There was still Ash. The healer was the only one who had witnessed her use of red magic. Twice. Once in the Forgotten Forest, then again during the battle against the greeloks. His expression of shock and horror wasn't unlike James'. Kyra had begged Ash not to tell the others about what he saw. As far as she knew, the healer had kept her secret. It showed Ash trusted her, even in the smallest way. Ash had also never mentioned the prophecy during the times he witnessed the red magic. He was shy, but as a healer, Ash had strong values. His purpose was to protect the innocent. Had Ash secretly decided to shield Kyra from the information to try and protect her? Or was Ash as clueless of the divination as she had been? As with Jyls, Kyra couldn't land on a definite answer. This time, when the wind unloosed waves of hair, Kyra didn't bother sweeping them from her face. Kyra could ask Ash. He might confirm her friends knew about the prophecy. And then what? How could Ash help her? The distressing truth was, he couldn't.

Kyra stretched out her arms and exhaled forcefully. There wasn't much she could do. Confronting Solarus, Hayden, and Talis would result in her being held prisoner in Silvias. Kyra refused to be penned up in a kingdom where she had no prospects of making friends. In a kingdom where she had to run with an escort to ensure her safety. In a place where the peace of Kyra's childhood was absent in Kyra's adulthood. It was better to keep her newfound knowledge a secret. *And*, Kyra reminded herself, *I promised Eva I wouldn't tell anyone.* Kyra's friends would try and pry loose the source of her information. It wouldn't take a lot of investigative work on Talis' part to find out that Eva was that source.

Kyra was embarrassed by how weak and vulnerable she felt. Had it really been a few hours earlier that she experienced the impression on her heart? It had guided her to the fields because she wanted answers. The sensation had also warned Kyra of the consequence of obtaining that knowledge.

What has been spoken cannot be unspoken. What has been heard cannot be unheard.

Was it better that Kyra was aware of her unique circumstance? Would she have been happier ignorant of the prophecy? Whatever the answer, it didn't matter. Kyra's world had changed in a matter of minutes. She now carried the inescapable responsibility to prevent a catastrophe from happening, one that she herself could cause. Like the fire in Chicago. Like the lake.

Kyra rubbed her arm as goose bumps pricked her flesh. Her gaze again journeyed around the woods. Kyra's eyes widened in surprise. The white mist, which previously had been a thin trail in the woods, was everywhere. Like pollen in the spring, the mist formed a glittering film on the firs and pines down to the ferns and earth beneath her feet. Kyra raised an arm. The white mist stuck to her clothing. Kyra pushed rogue strands of hair from her face and saw white mist there too. Kyra took in a sharp breath.

And gasped.

Kyra put a hand on her neck. The mist slid down her throat and filled her lungs like water. Coughing violently, Kyra covered her mouth with her sleeve.

It was then that Kyra noticed the whispers. She glanced around wildly. How could she have been so careless? She had bolted from the fields without telling Hayden or Talis. Alone in the woods, Kyra was as exposed to ill-intentioned elves as she had been to Lord Orison's company at the lake. Who had followed her this time? What elves had unleashed the magic around her? The whispering was ubiquitous and grew steadily louder. Kyra's heart was squeezed with every breath. The mist swallowed the sun's rays trickling through the trees, encasing the forest in an eerie twilight. Kyra felt a force strike her in the chest. She staggered back, her hand dropping from her mouth. The pines and firs rustled. The whispering turned into a gale of anger. Kyra stared, thunderstruck, at the trees.

The source of the magic was the forest. The white mist emanated from every bit of dirt, every discarded pine needle, every patch of moss. The energy of Silvias, raw and omniscient, was *rejecting* her. Kyra continued to hold her sleeve over her mouth as her eyes desperately searched the ground.

"The palace, please take me back to the palace," she pleaded hoarsely through her sleeve.

To her overwhelming relief, the neon green path rolled out immediately. Kyra turned, tripping over her own feet, and ran.

***

It took Kyra almost twice the amount of time to return to the palace. The magical lane guided her out of the eerie, pine-studded forest and into the more familiar hills where trees were dressed in lush, green leaves. The white mist fell away from Kyra's hair, skin, and clothing like pollen blown into the wind. Her lungs also expelled the white magic. Kyra drank in sweet, pure air. It was as though Kyra had never before known what breathing felt like.

Kyra evaded the elves with the help of the magical green path. She dashed toward the back of the palace and raced up an outdoor staircase to her room. As soon as she had closed her door, Kyra slid down to the floor, back against the door, panting. She raised her knees and tilted her head back. The soft scents of lilac from Kyra's small arboretum assuaged the fear pumping through her veins. The natural pool glimmered in the bright light streaming through the *zylith* ceiling. Kyra closed her eyes. What she wouldn't give for a nap. It was long past the time for Kyra to start the day's lesson. Solarus would undoubtably have choice words for her about her late arrival. Fortunately, Kyra didn't have the physical or emotional energy to worry about him.

When her breathing had slowed, Kyra opened her eyes again and looked at the pool. She rose on shaky legs, undressed, and lowered herself in. The rose-infused waters seeped into Kyra's skin. She gently massaged out the stiffness in her muscles, sighing contentedly. What a difference the simple comfort of a bath made.

When her fingers began to prune, Kyra climbed out. Her body was reinvigorated. Her mind was overtired. Kyra changed into a new set of clothing, gathered her azure cloak in her hand, and departed for the dining hall. She didn't expect to find Solarus waiting for her. And he wasn't, Kyra discovered as she plodded down the yellow-orange staircase to the room. She plopped into a chair at one of the circular tables and watched, bleary-eyed, as an elven attendant served her water, coffee, and a light meal. Kyra learned from the attendant that "*Firth* Jyls and *Ethernyle* Ash" had breakfasted earlier that morning. Talis hadn't yet appeared. Hayden and Solarus also hadn't eaten in the hall. Perplexed, Kyra sipped her coffee and nibbled on a piece of bread with honey. It was the only food her stomach was amenable to after her early morning.

After a while, Kyra glanced up at the clock on the wall. The serpentine hands pointed to the fuzzy dots at eleven and five. She covered her mouth with the back of her hand as a yawn fought to escape. Normally at this point, Kyra was finishing her lesson at the lake and preparing for a midday break. Kyra pushed her chair back and stood wearily. There wasn't any point in putting off Solarus' tongue-lashing. Better to find him and get it over with. Rubbing an eye, Kyra trod back to the bottom of the yellow-orange staircase. Light flickered off the *zylith*, giving it the striking appearance of a summer sunset.

"... might have shown more restraint in the manner in which you answered, Solarus. Carina solicited our advice. Her intent is to understand what the news means for Silvias. She wasn't ordering us to leave. Not yet."

Kyra froze. Her hand was still on one eye, the other wide in shock. Hayden's voice traveled down into the dining area. Dropping her hand, Kyra spun around. The sound came from the light blue staircase on the opposite side of the room.

"First, the manner in which I replied was no different from that in which I always reply. Second, no one 'orders' me to do anything. Third, *Raenalyn* Carina would do well to heed my words. She forgets that I am the resident wizard among us." Solarus' irascible voice echoed down the same staircase. His words were accompanied by heavy footsteps and the clacking of what Kyra assumed was a staff on the steps.

"I believe *Raenalyn* Carina is quite cognizant of that fact."

Heart racing, Kyra stepped away from the yellow-orange staircase and crossed the room. She sidled beside the banister to the blue staircase, scarcely daring to breathe. *What does Hayden mean, Carina isn't "ordering us to leave?"*

"What I do *not* appreciate," Solarus continued in the same clipped tone, "are my observations being dismissed as though I were a pupil reciting an answer to a teacher's question. If Carina held me in the esteem in which you claim, she would demonstrate due respect. Instead, she patronizes me with warnings about the speed with which Diamantas can strike."

"Be mindful of your words, Solarus. That is your host and *my* queen you're insulting." Talis' voice was as cold and sharp as frostbite on a finger.

Solarus responded with an indignant huff. "Your queen, Talis, has a low opinion of wizards. All wizards. She barely trusted me at the best of times when I tutored Kyra. At *her* request. Must I also remind you why Carina tolerated those visits? It was because the repercussions of Kyra's magic left unchecked were greater than her dislike for me."

"What reason do you give her to trust when you act like a sulking child who hasn't gotten his way?"

The footsteps came to an abrupt halt. Kyra fought the temptation to glance up the staircase. She had never heard Talis and Solarus argue. Kyra's pulse quickened with her mounting anxiety.

"It isn't a matter of trust, Solarus." Hayden's placating tone slipped between Talis and Solarus as though separating two boxers in a ring. "Two *Sirenyle* were killed. For the elves, that's unprecedented, which makes it more terrifying. Scouts are hand-picked for their judgment, their prowess in combat, and their ability to survive. Losing one scout, let alone two, is to Silvias like losing a limb. Not for a hundred years have scouts fallen in battle, and not to monsters like Reapers. And *Estienen*, Solarus holds the deepest respect for the *Raenalyn*. More than some of your kin at times."

Kyra couldn't hear a response. The drawn-out pause led her to believe that Talis had said something low enough for only Hayden and Solarus to hear.

"I don't disagree, Talis," came Hayden again. "What happened in Edoin Forest speaks to the larger problem in the Southern Mountains."

"Precisely." Kyra visualized the puckering of Solarus' lips, so sourly was the word pronounced. "I said it yesterday. I said it last night. I am not in the habit of repeating myself, but this is too important to allow my words to go unnoticed. I will say it again." Solarus drew out each syllable with deliberate slowness. "Wizards, dark or otherwise, *do not control the actions of Reapers*. If Reapers want to kill, they kill. Indiscriminately. Diamantas cannot influence their behavior one way or the other— 'the other' being what the queen fears."

"You don't believe the attack was an attempt to draw us out of Silvias."

"No. It was not." A swishing of a cloak was followed by a new sharp clack of boots on the steps. "However, even if Diamantas' assault does not begin with Silvias, the conflict will spread across the river. It will assail the elves here, in their own home. It is asinine for the queen to ignore this truth. Glare if it suits you, Talis. I refuse to pretend that the queen's dismissal of my advice will benefit anyone. Kyra must stay in Silvias. She is not safe outside the Realm. My stance will not change even if the queen opposes it."

Kyra's blood turned to ice. *Raenalyn* Carina didn't want her in Silvias. The queen thought the scouts were killed because the Reapers were searching for Kyra. Because Diamantas wouldn't quit until he had captured Kyra, no matter the consequences. Kyra's stomach sank to her boots. It was Carina. The queen had issued the directive to the elves. Carina prevented them from talking to her. To a wizard.

Almost too late, Kyra heard two sets of footsteps and the swishing of cloaks. A third should have belonged to Talis though, like all elves, he moved soundlessly. The angry clack of Solarus' staff rang out in the dining room. Kyra turned and quick-stepped to the table. She slid into her seat, grabbed her mug, and held it to her lips.

Hayden descended the last stair. "I don't think—" he was saying as he entered the dining hall. His gray eyes immediately lit upon Kyra at the table. Brows arching in surprise, Hayden abruptly ended his sentence. He glanced over his shoulder as Talis stepped down. The elf also noticed Kyra. The planes of his face were as grave as Kyra had ever seen them. He and Hayden exchanged a meaningful look. Solarus came last. Unlike Hayden and Talis, Solarus' mouth formed a line, aggravated line. He adjusted and readjusted his grip on his staff.

"Good morning, Kyra," Hayden greeted in a measured tone.

Kyra had wiped her expression free of shock. "Good morning."

As Hayden, Solarus, and Talis took up places at the table, Kyra bit her lip. These were her friends. Friends who had spent a year searching for her. Friends who had put themselves in harm's way, more than once, to protect her since she returned to Ilian. Friends who didn't trust her enough to share the one truth that made sense of her place in Ilian. The prophecy clarified why Diamantas, a wizard with a staff of unparalleled powers, devoted so much energy and resources to hunting down a teenage girl.

Kyra studied Talis as he folded his hands on the table. She felt a spike of anger. He had known the reason behind her peers' deliberate shunning. He had seen the torment it caused her. Yet Talis had stayed silent. Was it because of a vow to his queen? Would Talis have kept Kyra in the dark even without Carina's order?

What about Solarus? Kyra watched him slide back a chair. What purpose did it serve to train her without giving her context? Maybe Kyra's dedication would have been greater had she known about the prophecy. Maybe the prophecy would have scared her off. Kyra's gut asserted the former statement would have been true. Another thought came to Kyra. Solarus had explained at the lake that Loralai was important because of her role among the elves as a princess. He had never actually voiced if he, personally, thought Loralai as an individual merited respect.

How did that reasoning transfer to Kyra? If she had been any other wizard, one without a prophecy, would Solarus have invested the same amount of time in her? Did Solarus care about *her* as Kyra? Or was Solarus' commitment to helping her quash her impulses and control her emotions solely because he feared the prophecy? Kyra unconsciously put a hand to her pounding temple.

Hayden's gaze traveled up the wall. The clock's points of light flitted in their circle as the minute-hand slithered forward. He lowered his gaze to Kyra. "You're having a late breakfast this morning," Hayden observed. A trace of a question underlay his statement.

"Indeed," Solarus put in testily before Kyra could answer. He half-leaned, half-thrust his hornbeam staff against an empty chair to his left. "Why are you not at the lake practicing our spells or reviewing the theories in your book?"

Kyra cleared her throat as her mind raced to form a convincing answer. "I waited for you outside this morning, after breakfast. When you didn't come, I thought maybe you had gone to the lake before me. You weren't in the hills or on the bank either. I got worried. You've never been late." Kyra paused as the elven attendant from earlier swept into the room. Two more elves in flowing gowns accompanied her. They carried trays laden with mugs and colorful plates. "I came back to the palace to ask if anyone had seen you." The truth Kyra injected into the last part of her statement made the lie more credible. As the elves set down the trays and distributed the mugs, Kyra added, "I was told you hadn't eaten yet. I decided to have a snack."

"Well, I am here," Solarus replied brusquely. He took a steaming roll from one of the plates and tore it in half as though the dough had wronged him. "Where is your staff?"

Kyra groaned inwardly. If she had come directly from the lake as she claimed, Kyra would naturally have her weapon in hand. "I went to my room when I came back to the palace and left the staff there. There wasn't any reason to carry it while I was looking for you. I can go get it."

Solarus bit into the roll, expression piqued. "While I am loath to postpone our instruction," he said after he swallowed, "others require my immediate presence. Even if they choose to ignore what I say. One might as well invite a rock to a conversation if silence is desired."

Talis hadn't taken any of the proffered food. His amber eyes flashed with disdain as he watched Solarus chew the roll noisily.

Hayden let out a small sigh. His gray eyes were tired. He sipped slowly from his mug. "Where are Jyls and Ash?" he asked offhandedly to Kyra.

"I'm not sure," Kyra responded truthfully. "They might be in the Healer's Hall." She hadn't seen the duo, but she knew Ash made regular visits to Hazel throughout the day.

Hayden gave a slight indication of his head and cradled the mug between his hands. No one spoke. Kyra's heart thrummed. The tension occupying the space between Solarus and Talis was as thick as the honey on her bread. Kyra lowered her eyes and made a pretense of taking a long drink of water.

"What are your plans for the rest of the day?" Hayden ventured suddenly.

To take a nap, the answer popped into Kyra's mind. Her gaze strayed to Solarus, waiting for his instruction.

Solarus clutched his serviette as though he were squeezing juice from an orange. "You have squandered the morning; make better use of your time this afternoon," he said through tight lips. "Go to the lake and review the basics we have covered these past few weeks. Start with bonding your energy. Form links and then compress the links into bars. I want no inconsistencies among them. You should be able to stack each bar on top of the other like cards in a deck. You have practiced this drill often enough. It should be outstandingly simple."

Solarus placed a blunt emphasis on "outstandingly simple," indicating anything less than perfect was unacceptable.

Kyra put down her cup, grateful for an excuse to leave. "I'm sure it will be. I'll get my staff."

"Good." Solarus released his death grip on the serviette. Lifting it by a corner, he snapped it in the air so that it fanned out and then placed it in his lap. "At least *one* person in this room listens to my counsel."

Talis' eyes narrowed. Hayden rubbed his temple with his forefinger.

Kyra shoved her chair back and rose. Her insides twisted like braids of wet rope. Kyra wanted to sprint out of the dining room and leave her companions' secrecy behind her. But she strode calmly and deliberately to the yellow-orange stairwell. Kyra trod up, her steps echoing on the *zylith*. When she was out of sight of the dining room, Kyra paused, her hand on the banister. She hearkened for more conversation, which she assumed would start after she had left. All that reached her ears was silence.

Of course, they wouldn't say anything, Kyra thought. *Talis can hear I haven't gotten to the top yet.*

There were more pressing matters in Kyra's mind. She tromped up the rest of the stairs as though her legs had turned to clay. Kyra had no intention of practicing at the lake any more than she had of taking the tantalizing nap. Kyra reached the top of the staircase. She glanced down a hallway to her left. It led to an outdoor bridge to the eastern tower. Kyra had used it several times after discovering it was a shortcut to her destination: the training fields. Kyra turned and strode outside. She had a long afternoon ahead.

If her resolve to do what was necessary didn't falter before then.

Chapter 36

Time always raced by like a wild horse when Kyra needed every second; it plodded like a lazy mule when she spurred it to run. Today, Kyra rode both animals. She sat on her bedroom floor, knees tucked beneath her, hands resting on her thighs. Dusk's deep pink, purple, and orange rays refracted through the *zylith* ceiling. Kyra's wide pool reflected the colors. The atrium's lilac trees perfumed the air, and small, fairylike lights danced around Kyra's head. Yet even among the soothing sights and smells, anxiety corroded Kyra's heart. She stared at the three neatly arranged piles on the ground.

Before she had begun packing, Kyra had scoured her map of Ilian. Initially, she decided to take a route west toward Farcaren. Kyra had one goal: find Diamantas. If Diamantas was so bent on catching her, Kyra could draw him out by presenting herself as an easy target. She would return to the last location she had encountered dark wizards. Hence, Farcaren. How Kyra would get word to the dark wizards that she was alone and in the kingdom was an unresolved and important part of her plan. Important, ambitious, nebulous, and, in many senses, ludicrous. Voluntarily pitting herself, an amateur wizard, against the ruthlessly capable Diamantas and his allies wasn't an equation for victory. *That's how it's going to be*, Kyra had silently reinforced her decision. The prophecy hadn't left her with a choice. If Kyra wanted to save her friends from Harkimer—and, possibly, from herself—it was the logical solution.

The more Kyra thought about her mission, though, the more she recognized finding Diamantas wasn't enough. Kyra had to be skilled enough to defeat him. It wouldn't help anyone if she died in their first duel. Kyra had a few weeks' magical instruction that she remembered; Diamantas had a lifetime. Kyra's finger had traveled along her map further west. She needed to train. Her finger poised over a kingdom marked "Hogarth." Kyra nodded to herself. Hogarth was the key. She could take refuge and practice until she was ready to challenge Diamantas. If she traveled north through Edoin Forest first, Kyra could avoid Farcaren. That part of her plan was as important and less ambitious, nebulous, and ludicrous.

What remained was the matter of logistics in getting to Hogarth. Kyra decided to take two sets of saddlebags and only partly fill each. Once Kyra was through Edoin, she would travel on foot. She wouldn't endanger Raven on her quest. The unconscious Hazel was a sobering reminder that not even the animals were safe from Harkimer's evil. Kyra would transfer whatever food remained from the saddlebags to a rucksack, one of the many items on the ground. The rucksack was large but even fully packed, light. Kyra would keep her speed and agility while preventing aching muscles and blistered feet. She wanted to escape any trouble she ran into on the way. Kyra's mind flew to the Reapers and greeloks.

Kyra delicately folded the map and placed it beside her rucksack. She mentally inventoried what she had chosen for the journey. The first pile was of outfits Kyra had selected from her wealth of elven garments. She was grateful summer was on the cusp. Kyra didn't have to lug around heavy clothing. She could buy a thicker cloak as the weather cooled. If she hadn't found Diamantas before then. The second pile consisted of her sword, bolas, and staff. Her bow and a quiver of arrows were also among the mix. Kyra had surreptitiously dashed to the archery field. After waiting for a break in the students' lessons, she went to the hay target where she had hidden her bow. To Kyra's relief—or her chagrin, she couldn't decide which—her weapon had remained untouched since the morning. Kyra debated for the hundredth time the wisdom of adding another item to her already crowded collection. It wasn't as though she had practiced archery in Silvias save for her time with Eva. What were the odds that Kyra would hit a target? Yet a nagging instinct told her to bring the bow anyway. Kyra left it in the pile.

Kyra shifted on her knees to regard the last and largest mound on the floor, her potpourri of essentials. In her satchel, Kyra had packed her leather-covered book of magic, a jar of the Sadyran tree salve she had obtained from Ash, a purse with gold and silver florins left over from shopping in Thanesgard, and two of her small pouches. The third pouch was attached securely to Kyra's belt loop, her bolas stashed inside. Her heptagon coin she had left on the floor. Kyra would place it in whatever vest she wore when she left. The silver shimmered in the light shining through the *zylith* ceiling. Kyra traced the grooves of the coin with her finger. As always, it provided her with welcome comfort as a piece from her past.

Kyra brushed a wavy strand of hair from her face. The only items missing were the provisions for the journey. These were crammed into a burlap sack that she had put in a stall in the stables.

Kyra bit her lip. Her visit to the kitchens had proved to be more than a simple task of getting foodstuffs. The experience had churned up new questions and mysteries, neither of which Kyra wanted. She had enough questions and mysteries already to keep her busy.

With the help of her magical green guide, Kyra had located the main kitchens. The room was as large as the dining hall. Attendants moved synchronously around each other, carrying plates, silverware, and food for the chefs, who stood around oblong tables as they prepared the day's meals. The mouthwatering aroma of doughy bread and cinnamon spices filled the air. Kyra's stomach gurgled. A tall elf with a craggy face, sagging jowls, and flour-dappled apron left one of several giant ovens to greet her. He introduced himself as Lyner. He was the head chef who presided over the kitchens' activities. Kyra had caught herself staring at the elf as he smiled kindly. No elf she had encountered had exhibited signs of age. Except this Lyner. How old did an elf have to be to look like he had lived in Silvias since the beginning of time?

Kyra's face grew hot with embarrassment. She cleared her throat and asked if she might have a few meals that she could pack in a saddlebag. She also inquired after grain, apples, and carrots for Raven. Kyra anticipated a litany of questions about the reason for needing so many provisions and had prepared in advance a plausible story. Kyra would describe her plan to spend a few days exploring areas beyond the palace. Technically, Kyra had rationalized, she wouldn't be fibbing to Lyner. Kyra *would* journey to places further afield.

To Kyra's relief, Lyner hadn't sought an explanation. Instead, he cheerfully called for his assistant to help him gather what Kyra had requested. A girl with silver-blond hair and strawberry stripes glanced over her shoulder. She was sliding a long, wooden slab dotted with rolls into an oven. Kyra's eyes widened. It was Eva. She froze when she saw Kyra. A female elf took the slab from Eva's hands and gestured toward Lyner. Eva's cheeks turned pink. She wiped her hands on an apron like Lyner's and approached the pair timidly. Kyra guessed the girl's fear was that Kyra would reveal they had spoken together, despite the queen's order. And that Eva had disclosed the prophecy. As Lyner presented Eva, Kyra simply smiled and greeted the girl as though for the first time. Relief splashed across Eva's features. She darted a quick glance at Lyner, who seemed oblivious to Eva's reaction. The head chef left to retrieve a burlap sack for carrying the provisions. Kyra winked at the girl, eliciting a broad grin from Eva in return. The girl hurried off to help Lyner.

When they returned, Kyra's burlap sack was stuffed as full as a turkey at Thanksgiving. In addition to the grain and snacks for Raven, the head chef had included fresh cuts of meat, vegetables, bread, and fruit for Kyra. He also handed her three full waterskins. There was no sense in searching for a brook or stream if they could fill the skins in the kitchens, Lyner noted astutely.

Kyra thanked the chef, silently thrilled with her success. She turned to escape back to her room.

That was when a glimmering orange light above her caught her eye. Kyra tilted her head up toward one of the many translucent shelves in the kitchen. It was a glass-like statue the size and shape of a rodent. The vibrant orange glow that swirled through the animal like smoke marked it unmistakably as a kaemin. Though the creature was too distant to see clearly, Kyra felt a strange connection to the creature. She had seen it before. Kyra rubbed her lips as she riffled through her memories, trying to place where.

Lyner had observed Kyra's nonplussed look. A grin added another fold to his wrinkled features. "You have an interest in our kaemin, I see," the chef had commented.

Kyra had nodded. "I've seen the Ionas here in Silvias and the wolves in Thanesgard but not that kaemin. It's familiar though. Maybe I came across it when I lived in Silvias as a child. What is it?"

Lyner reached up, lifted the kaemin from the shelf, and set it on the nearest table. Eva stood beside him. Her bright teal eyes were reverently on the statue. Lyner placed a weathered hand on the figurine's back. Orange light eddied under his fingertips like wind trapped beneath its glassy surface. "This kaemin is called a rock creature. They are ancient, sagacious beings that have inhabited the Southern Mountains for more than a millennium. The collective knowledge of all Ilian's scholars and scribes pales in comparison to the wisdom these beings possess. They are reclusive, however. Rock creatures are seen when they choose to be seen."

Kyra leaned closer to the rodent-like figurine. She could now see the creature's tiny paws, clipped tail, and small ears, which were flattened against the side of its head. Its eyes harbored an endless gaze so intense it was unnerving. Kyra's jaw dropped. She *had* seen this rodent before. It was identical to Millie's pika. How many times had Kyra stared at the blue-and-white figurine sitting atop her bedroom mantle? The glass had always seemed so lifelike, soaking up sunlight streaming through her windows.

Questions scrolled rapidly through Kyra's mind. Did kaemins exist outside of Ilian? Was Millie's pika a kaemin itself, as Kyra now suspected it might be? What had Millie told her about the figurine? It was a gift from a friend of Millie's father. A man named Martin Viscarl. He had carved it for Millie personally. Millie recalled Viscarl telling her every statue was unique. Millie had also mentioned the warning she had received from the artisan: no one could touch the pika save for Millie. Millie hadn't asked why. Those bits of information matched exactly what Kyra knew about kaemins. Which meant Millie was the owner of a magic-infused statue from another world, even if she didn't know it. Mesmerized, Kyra stretched out her fingers.

Lyner's hand closed over hers. Kyra glanced into the old elf's face and was puzzled by his concerned expression. "It would be unwise to handle the material," Lyner said softly. Kyra gave him a sheepish look. He gently released Kyra's hand, which she put on the table. Eva silently watched the exchange, winding a strand of hair around her finger.

"Are there more rock creature kaemins in Ilian?" Kyra asked.

Lyner's weathered face twitched into a melancholy smile. "Unfortunately, there are not. You see, Kyra, Ionas and wolves are majestic beasts, as are the lions of Hogarth and the dragons of the coastal villages. They project grace, nobility, and the ability to protect their respective peoples. Rock creatures are not often viewed with the same esteem. They have neither the sharp hooves of the Ionas nor the fangs of the wolves. They lack the claws of the lions of Hogarth and the armor of the dragons of the coastal villages. Yet the underestimation of the rock creatures is one of their greatest strengths. Few hunt them because few are aware of their existence and their importance." Lyner had lifted the kaemin and had placed it back on the shelf. "I believe they are the true Lyneera."

That had been the end of the conversation. Lyner summoned a barrel-chested elf named Ceron to carry the bulging burlap sack to the stables. Kyra said her goodbyes to Eva as Ceron hoisted the bag effortlessly. As Kyra made to follow him, Lyner suddenly snapped his fingers. "I almost forgot." He leaned forward. Lyner was so close that his forehead almost touched hers. Lowering his voice so only she could hear, Lyner murmured, "The forest that lies across the river contains rich wildlife and flora. Should you decide to study these, you will need to call forth the bridge to reach them."

Kyra coughed back her surprise. When she had crossed into Silvias, Talis had told her the words that invoked the bridge were entrusted only to the elves to prevent trespassers. Why was Lyner offering them to her?

In the same, hushed tone, Lyner chanted,
"'We seek the blessed woods and trees
If crossing does Inishmore please.
Enter we with virtuous hearts.
No greed or evil will we impart.
Into sacred lands of old,
We elves Inishmore's creeds uphold.
We pass inside at dawn's first light,
And part with moon and stars' delight.'"

Goose bumps pricked Kyra's arms as Lyner finished. He had straightened with an artless smile as though he had given her a recipe for soup. "Safe travels." Lyner had placed a hand over his heart. Kyra returned the gesture. Then she had followed Ceron, committing the elven spell to memory.

Now Kyra's preparations were complete. Her legs cramped beneath her. Easing them out on her bedroom floor, Kyra raked a shaky hand through her hair. She had miraculously avoided running into Hayden or the others in all that time. *Or maybe not miraculously*, she thought with a pang in her heart. Kyra couldn't deny that part of her secretly hoped her companions *would* chance on her. They could have seen her at the stables. They would have questioned her about why she had a burlap sack half her weight jammed with supplies. Kyra would resist their interrogation at first. Then she would give in. Kyra would tell them she had discovered the prophecy. Hayden and Solarus would have squashed her plans to leave.

Remaining in the cocoon of Hayden and her friends' protection was painfully tempting. The idea of discharging the acid of secrecy eating away at Kyra's heart to Hayden would have been a relief. Kyra felt ashamed at the thought. It was a selfish desire. Kyra had made the decision to seek out Diamantas so her friends weren't caught in the crosshairs of her battle anymore. They had jeopardized their own safety. Kyra couldn't—wouldn't—ask them to do more. As daunting as it was, Kyra had to leave.

With a heavy heart, Kyra stood. The brilliant colors of dusk sank into twilight. Kyra stumped to the door to join her companions for dinner. As she turned the knob, Kyra knew it might be for the last time.

***

Kyra ate quickly and retired early. "Ate" was an exaggeration. Pushed her salad and fish around the plate and nibbled on bread was more accurate. Her body had mutinied against food, her stomach sloshing like a ship tossed in an anxiety-induced storm. Kyra cultivated what she hoped was a convincing look of happiness. She smiled and laughed at all the right times and feigned interest at others. Kyra wondered how much of her apprehension slipped through her façade of contentment. Hayden observed her with a shadow of a frown. He perceived something wrong and couldn't determine what.

Kyra's resolve increasingly waffled as she sat in the comfort of her friends. But her queasiness provided her an authentic excuse to leave the meal. The sooner she departed Silvias, the better. Kyra declined Ash's offer to make her a tea to help her stomach. She did accept a packet of mint brought by an elven attendant. It wouldn't be the last time apprehension would wreak havoc on her stomach. Chewing a pinch of the leaves and pocketing the rest, Kyra said goodnight to her companions. Hayden's gaze followed her as she climbed up the yellow-orange staircase.

When she was back in her chambers, Kyra changed into her traveling clothes. She left her belt and boots at the foot of the bed. Then Kyra forced herself to lie down, despite the jitteriness that shook her deep in her bones. Kyra rested her head on her pillow and stared at the *zylith* ceiling. Sparkling white lights poked holes in the black night sky.

Kyra breathed in the delicate lilac perfume as her mind cartwheeled from one concern to another. *Will anyone see me on the way to the pastures? Will Raven agree to take me out of Silvias? How will I find Diamantas? What if he learns I'm in Hogarth while I'm developing my magic?* At that moment, Kyra had underwhelming odds of success against her nemesis and overwhelming odds of failure. She lacked the magical abilities. Would that ever change? *How long do I need to train to be confident that I can beat Diamantas? Can I ever beat him? Or is this a suicide mission?*

"Get a grip, Kyra," she reprimanded herself out loud. Kyra flipped over on her side with a huff. "You can do this."

Kyra wasn't sure how much time had passed before she heard voices and bootsteps in the stairwell. She stiffened and sat upright. The first belonged to Jyls. His words were muted beyond the door, his mischievous tone traveling into the hallway. It was followed by Ash's laughter, then Solarus' cross and equally indistinguishable response to whatever Jyls had said. Their steps, then conversation, again grew distant. Kyra made to lie back down.

Until someone knocked softly on her door. Kyra kept still. She hoped whoever it was would assume she was sleeping and leave. The person rapped on the door again, this time more forcefully. Kyra glanced at the gap between the door and the floor. The dim light showed two sets of boots outside. She waited on tenterhooks, trying to quiet her breath. Kyra heard Hayden. His words were muffled, but his tone was saturated with concern. Talis replied. *What did they want so late at night?* Kyra wondered. When the boots moved away from her door, Kyra released the breath she had been holding. She let a few minutes pass, hearkening for any new sounds. When she was convinced her companions weren't in the hallway any longer, Kyra dangled her legs over her bed.

It was time to go.

Heart pounding, Kyra hopped down noiselessly. A rainbow of fairy lights blinked into existence around her and cast a hazy glow from Kyra's bed to the pool and trees. Kyra pulled on her boots and strapped the belt around her trousers. Kyra went to her pile of weapons. She lifted the scabbard and girdled it around her waist. Next, Kyra grabbed her azure cloak, fitting it around her shoulders, and clasping it together. The supple material shimmered.

Kyra threw the rucksack and satchel over her right shoulder and hung her bow and quiver awkwardly over her left. She swayed as she stood, unused to the extra weight. Kyra shifted the items on both shoulders. Her legs wobbled. With the bobbing lights traveling around her head, Kyra teetered unsteadily toward the door. She grabbed her staff last. Using it as a crutch for balance, Kyra put her hand on the doorknob and slowly creaked the door ajar. She poked her head out. Kyra glanced left, then right. No one. Kyra's cloak swished along the floor as she stepped into the hall.

Kyra made her way to the stairwell, juggling her items. New lights flitted around her. They were dimmer than the ones in her room as though understanding her unspoken plea to go unseen. When Kyra reached the first step, her bow slipped and clacked against the glass banister. Kyra winced at the sound. She cast a glance over her shoulder. The noise hadn't attracted anyone. Pulse racing, Kyra carefully made her way down the spiraling staircase. She paused at the bottom. Her eyes combed the foyer and the door to the guest quarters. Finally, Kyra's gaze sank to the ground. "Please take me on a path to the stables," she whispered. "One that will keep me hidden from the elves and my friends."

The magical green lane unfurled under her feet faster than she had ever seen it appear. Kyra crept along the center as it fluttered toward the large, closed doors that led to the palace courtyard. The lane passed straight through the *zylith*. Kyra pushed the doors open. The night sky was clear, with millions of white stars sprinkled across it like sugar crystals on a tablecloth. A cool breeze kissed Kyra's cheek, and the machis' balsam fragrance tickled her nose. Insects droned lazily. Letting out a deep breath, Kyra fled the palace.

It wasn't an easy task, jogging with the rucksack. Kyra constantly shrugged the straps that slipped down her arm back over her shoulder, all the while keeping pace with the green lane that glided like mist over the dewy grass. *How on earth am I supposed to carry these without Raven?* At least Kyra wouldn't have the same need for speed and stealth when she left Silvias. The chances she would happen upon anyone, at least as she crossed the river and was back in Edoin, were small.

Kyra was breathless when she arrived at the stables. The doors were open. Owls hooted to the crickets' chorus. The magical path, having completed its duty, twinkled and evaporated. Wiping sweat from her brow, Kyra entered the stables.

Like the other structures in Silvias, the stables weren't built in a shape confined to strict rules of geometry. The wooden building was vaguely rectangular, with a clear, dome-shaped ceiling that allowed in every drop of starlight. Kyra's boots noiselessly sank into the plush grass that carpeted the ground. Small, fuzzy balls of light lined a long corridor dividing the two sides of the stables and provided a milky glow around the stalls. Kyra smiled. The elves didn't scrimp on space for their steeds. There were at least twenty stalls per side, each of which was large enough to fit three horses. The absence of the usual smells of musk, hay, and dust led Kyra to believe the stables hadn't been used often this season. Elven steeds were hardy. Likely they were housed in the stables during the harshest of conditions and were otherwise in the meadow.

Kyra opened the latch to the second stall and pulled open the gate. Small patches of flowers speckled the ground. A stunted tree was half ingrown in the wall. The bulging burlap bag Ceron had deposited for her rested against the thick tree roots. Her two saddlebags were banked up against the wall.

Kyra leaned her staff against the tree trunk. She shook her bow from her shoulders, then removed her satchel. Kyra laid them gently on the ground. She then pulled one of the rucksack's straps free and lifted it from her shoulders. With effort, Kyra set the rucksack beside the satchel. Kyra kneaded her shoulder muscle, feeling a knot forming. She picked up her staff before exiting the stall. Even if someone discovered the other items, Kyra couldn't risk an elf happening upon the weapon.

Kyra closed the latch to the gate. A loud squeaking caused her to start. She hopped back as a mouse skirted under one of the gates and dashed across the corridor to the opposite stall. The rodent squeezed through a slit in the side and disappeared. Kyra's heart pounded. She almost shrieked as a marmalade-colored cat streaked past in pursuit of his prey. The tabby leapt from the ground to the top of the stall gate and jumped down out of sight.

"Okay, I'm a little jumpy," Kyra said with an attempt at a laugh. "Who wouldn't be if they were charging off to face Diamantas?"

Heart still pounding, Kyra walked to the front of the room. Tack and saddles were stored in large cubbies. Saddle pads and blankets were grouped together in heaps beside the shelves.

"Everything's here," Kyra murmured. She put hand on Raven's saddle, which was in a center cubby. "Now I need a horse."

Kyra walked out the stable doors, feeling the breeze tousle her hair. "Please take me to the pastures," she addressed the ground again. "I have to stay hidden from anyone who's out tonight."

The magical lane reappeared under her feet and shot forward like a bullet. Kyra watched, astonished. It was as though the path sensed her haste. Kyra sprinted after it.

The path forked from the stables and glided parallel to the palace. Kyra hadn't spent much time exploring the back of the palace, where the path wanted to keep her. It cut sharply right and dashed through a diamond-shaped opening to a marble-walled garden. Plants with leaves the size of sofa cushions grew freely. Kyra's hands brushed against their fuzzy surface as she pumped her arms, eyes fixed on the glimmering green wave. Even with the starlight, Kyra's sight was hampered by the night's darkness. Several times, Kyra narrowly avoided ramming her staff into the marble wall. She slipped out the egress.

The magic didn't wait for her. Outside the palace grounds, it veered to the left and led Kyra on a wayward course behind the training fields. Unlike the front of the fields, the back end was splattered with trees. The path seemed to loyally circumvent the elves, just as she had entreated. At least, she believed it did. Kyra's human eyes couldn't spy an elf, but an elf's keen eyes would pick her out from a distance, darkness or no darkness. Kyra placed her trust fully in the green lane.

She approached the end of the fields. Rows of firs merged with the woods leading to the pastures. The path zigzagged between the trees, over fallen needles, and traversed the brook. Kyra splashed through the brook heedlessly, cool water spraying her pants. The trees thinned. Then the green magic slowed like a marathoner who crossed a finish line. Kyra stopped. Her lungs burned. She took deep breaths as she looked beyond the fringe of pines. Kyra saw large silhouettes of horses, heads bowed, in an open pasture. A horse sighed. Another horse affectionately nudged its neighbor. Several of the horses lay on the luxurious grass while others stood in a peaceful slumber.

Kyra's gaze dipped to the lane. "Thank you," she said. The green rippled in farewell before disappearing.

Kyra crept up to the pastures, holding her staff close to her side. She didn't want to wake Willow or the other horses if she could help it. Kyra suspected that if they overheard her conversation, they would share her plans with their riders. Now that Kyra was committed to her goal, the last thing she needed was an intervention by Hayden.

Kyra paused at the edge of the pastures. "Raven," she called out softly. "Raven, are you there?"

The roan was nearby. Raven's ears rotated at the sound of her voice, and he raised his head. Kyra waved as the roan turned toward her. Raven flicked his chin upward in greeting. He trotted to the edge of the pasture. His luminous brown eyes shone with concern. "Kyra, it is quite late for a visit. Is something wrong?"

"What? No, nothing's wrong," Kyra fibbed. "Solarus gave me an assignment today. It's about . . . navigation. A navigation spell. The goal is that I use my magic to find my way through the woods to a . . . to a place he designated earlier. Solarus told me to do the assignment at night, so I'm using magic to guide me. He said that during the day, I can cheat and use the paths in the trees. It's too dark at night. I have to rely on the spell."

Raven eyed her with an uncannily humanlike look of suspicion.

I should have come up with a more realistic excuse, Kyra berated herself. She plowed on. "The reason I'm here is that the point Solarus marked is to the north of the river. I was supposed to start a couple hours ago, except I, um, I forgot. Reading. Reading the navigation spell. I memorized the words to make sure I get it right. I lost track of time. That's why I came here. I was hoping you could take me to the river."

"Does that not defeat the purpose of your task if I take you most of the way?"

"Well, no." Kyra's mind worked furiously. "I would use the spell from the river. It would be shorter than if I had to start from the palace. I want to find the spot. Solarus is going to meet me there tomorrow at midday."

"Hmph." Raven angled his head as he studied Kyra. Kyra could tell the roan wasn't convinced. "You do not seem suitably prepared for the journey. I have neither a bridle nor a saddle. Unless you choose to ride without these, which, if you are carrying your staff—" he indicated the weapon in Kyra's hand with a nod of his long nose, "—is not recommended. Falling will not aid your cause. Solarus will be less than pleased if he discovers you attempted to shorten your assignment by riding rather than trekking through the hills."

"The tack and saddle are ready at the stables. They were too heavy to carry here." Kyra darted a look around the pasture. The crickets' chirping did nothing to ease the tension in her muscles. "Please, Raven? I promise, just to the river."

Raven exhaled. He shook his mane in resignation. "Climb up then. I will take you that far."

Suppressing a relieved sigh, Kyra opened the latch to the pastures. Raven trod through and knelt in the soft grass. Kyra slid her leg over his back, looking for something in lieu of reins to hold on to. She seized a handful of his mane with her right hand, the left firmly gripping her staff. "Does that hurt?"

"No, hold tight." Raven carefully stood.

"Oh, and can we use the route behind the palace?"

"For what purpose?"

"I'd rather not wake the elves."

Raven shifted on his hooves. Kyra swore it was the horse's equivalent to a shrug. The roan set off at a canter into the woods. Kyra clutched Raven's long hair. Even though the pace was swift, Raven's motions were smooth. Kyra's one worry was dropping her staff. Kyra clenched the weapon firmly in her fist.

Astride Raven, the trip back to the stables was short. Kyra slid from Raven's back at the entrance and jogged inside. Her eyes roved to the saddle pads. The marmalade-colored tabby Kyra had seen earlier lazed at the apex of the pile. Her eyes were closed and her tail dangled over the edge. Kyra found herself smiling at the creature.

Leaning her staff against the wall, Kyra dashed to the stall with her stash of provisions. She opened the latch to the gate and opened it. Raven clopped into the stables behind her. Kyra knelt beside the burlap sack, untied it, and fished out an apple. Kyra darted out of the stall to Raven. "Here." Kyra held out her palm with the apple. "I brought you a snack."

"Not a snack. A bribe." Raven wasted no time in chomping it from her hand.

"As long as it works."

Kyra lifted Raven's tack from its shelf and placed it on the ground. Then she grabbed the saddle. One of the straps was tangled up in Ash's saddle next to it. Arms straining, Kyra pulled hard on the saddle. She almost fell backward as both came free. She dropped them unceremoniously on the ground. The grassy earth dampened the sound as Kyra rubbed her sore arm.

Kyra glanced at the saddle pads next. The marmalade-colored tabby was still there.

"Um, excuse me, sorry," Kyra said to the cat. The tabby opened a single eye. Kyra had a sneaking suspicion he hadn't been asleep at all. "I have to get one of the saddle pads. Do you mind moving for a moment?"

The cat glowered at her, clearly minding. The tabby rose and stretched his arms with a long yawn. He hopped agilely to the ground and stalked across the room. The tabby plumped down beside a plot of daisies. He folded his paws with a dignified look as though to show he had chosen to leave the saddle pads and was not shooed off.

Kyra took the topmost pad and draped it over the roan's back. She took the saddle and placed it atop the pad. Raven was silent as she adjusted it. Kyra deftly put the tack in place and primed the reins over Raven's neck. She returned to the stall.

Kyra took out the burlap sack first. She tightly retied the top of the sack before crouching down. With a swift motion, Kyra heaved the bag into her hands. She discovered trying to hold the awkwardly shaped bag was like embracing a child throwing a tantrum. Kyra eased the sack back on the ground and instead rolled it out of the gate. She gathered the smaller satchel from the corner of the stall. This Kyra slung over her shoulders. She then bent over and again rolled the burlap sack toward Raven.

The roan watched her with an amused expression as she gave it a final push. "Do you plan to feed the entirety of the river's creatures?"

Kyra swept her hair from her brow, breathing heavily. "I asked the chef to pack a couple meals for me and Solarus and some extra carrots and apples for you. I guess he decided to give us a few options."

She didn't meet Raven's eyes as she hurried back to retrieve her bow, quiver, and sword. She laid these at Raven's side. Next, she returned for the saddlebags. Kyra shouldered one on her arm and gracelessly walked out of the gate. She dumped it on the ground behind Raven. Kyra did the same with the second set of bags. Rubbing her increasingly aching neck muscle, Kyra began balancing the first saddlebag behind Raven's saddle.

The roan turned his head to look at Kyra. "If you would be so kind, please clarify why you are placing your life in jeopardy after our companions and I spent the better part of a year to recover you?"

Kyra stopped fitting the bag. She quickly fixed a calm expression on her face before resuming her work. "What do you mean?" Kyra asked. She injected as much guilelessness as she could into her voice. "I'm only going to the river."

Raven snorted. "You forget, quite literally, that I have watched over you since you were a child, Kyra. Your tone carries the same feigned innocence that it did when you sought to do something impulsive or reckless. Furthermore, for one so inventive, your feeble story poorly disguises your intention. Four saddlebags? A sack of provisions? That is substantial effort for an overnight excursion. It does signify that your plans may involve a longer journey. A journey that could involve, possibly, leaving the borders of Silvias. That would make it difficult to keep you whole and unscathed from dark wizards and Harkimer's beasts."

Kyra released a slight sigh. She pulled the leather straps of the bags tight. There was no use keeping up the pretense. "I wasn't being completely honest," she confessed, tugging experimentally on the sides of the bags. They didn't move. "I do need to reach the river, and I'm not running away from Silvias. That would have been easier than what I'm actually doing."

"Which is?"

"I'm traveling *toward* something. Someone. Specifically, Diamantas."

Raven's nostrils flared. "I think something has clogged my ears. You propose to do *what*?"

"I'm leaving to go after Diamantas. I'm going to confront him when my magic is strong enough before he has another chance to set up an ambush. There's no other way to prevent more attacks from the dark wizards."

"I was hoping I had misheard you. What made you suppose this course of action was reasonable when it demonstrates the contrary?"

"Diamantas wants *me*. Not anyone else. Me." The words spilled from Kyra's lips. She crouched next to the burlap bag and unpacked the dried meats and fruits. Kyra's emotions boiled, and she hoped concentrating on the task at hand would keep her from bursting. "He's dedicated himself to hunting me. In London first, then when I arrived in Ilian. We've been scrambling ever since to avoid him and the dark wizards. We've been attacked more than once. I'm not going to hide behind Hayden like a frightened rabbit or be stuck in Silvias like a prisoner. Diamantas is going to learn that I'm hard to kill."

"I would rather not test that assumption."

"I'd rather not either. It isn't my choice, though. I have to do this." Kyra rose, arms full of vegetables, fruits, and dried meat. She stuffed these into the rearmost saddlebag. "Do you remember the day we met? How you and Raff and Hazel persuaded me to go with you? And James, the Lyneera who led you to me," she added with a slice of pain in her heart. "James had told me a little about Ilian and Inishmore. It was difficult to understand." Kyra again knelt beside the burlap sack and methodically gathered more of her provisions. "What finally encouraged me to leave was this feeling. More than a feeling. It was like a breeze against my heart, a whisper without words. It was a message. That trusting you was the right thing to do. If it weren't for that push, I would have dismissed this whole thing as a bizarre dream or hallucination. I would have gone back inside the pub and locked the door. That's why I came." Kyra stood and carried the remaining foodstuffs to the empty saddlebag on the opposite side of Raven. She shoved the provisions inside unceremoniously. "Then we were chased by wizards who had the power to punch holes in a thick stone bridge as easily as if they were kicking down a leaf pile. It didn't make sense that they were going through so much trouble to get a defenseless teenage girl. A girl who had never seen a wizard before that moment."

"A girl who did not *remember* wizards," Raven amended. "And not a 'defenseless girl' either. A young wizard who had forgotten her abilities."

"Being clueless about magic and wizards and whatever I had been able to do in the past wasn't helpful," Kyra argued. She examined the saddlebags. One was askew. She reached forward and adjusted it so it sat evenly on Raven's back. "Raff said Diamantas was chasing me because I was a free wizard, and all free wizards were a threat. That explanation isn't logical. Unless Diamantas sent swarms of dark wizards all over Ilian—which you probably would have mentioned—then I'm an exception. Why then? I came up with another answer. My parents were dark wizards who fled Harkimer, and Diamantas was desperate to get them, and me, back. It wouldn't have given his followers confidence in his leadership if wizards were willing to abandon the Mountains. Later, Hayden and Talis told me I wasn't a dark wizard. That took me back to square one. Why send four wizards after me and not just one? Any of them individually could have killed me on the spot."

"You give yourself short shrift," the roan responded. "They did attack, and you did not die. In fact, you fended them off with skill for which they were unprepared."

"You, Raff, and Hazel defended me," Kyra countered. "I had no idea what I was doing other than desperately hoping I could dodge the wizards' fireballs until I had a chance to escape. The magic that miraculously shielded me was a result of fear. My only thought was I liked living and wanted to keep doing it. Then Hayden and the others came to my rescue. There wasn't an iota of skill from me. I was lucky."

"Things are also different now," Kyra added before Raven had a chance to interject. "Solarus has drilled the basics of magic into me these past few weeks. I can fight back."

"You are so confident that you would depart the Realm without more time?"

"It's not about confidence. Staying puts everyone around me or that has any connection to me at risk. In Edoin, you all risked your lives to keep me safe and have every step since. With the Reapers. In Thanesgard. Against the greeloks." Kyra lifted the quiver and placed it in one of the front saddlebags. She was careful to keep the flap of the bag half open so as not to bend the arrows' delicate fletching. Kyra placed the sword beside it. Kyra tied the bow to the side of the saddle. "What bothered me most was the way Hayden and the others sometimes treated me even as they fought for me. A lot of times, something seemed . . . off. I couldn't place a finger on it. Hayden and Talis exchanged looks when I brought up my past and my parents. Solarus parried most of the same questions. They were always cautious and maybe suspicious. I caught Hayden spying on me during my lessons with Solarus. I never confronted him about it, though it crossed my mind. It didn't seem like a conversation about him watching me would help anything. Hayden thinks his presence is a secret." Kyra raked a hand through her wavy hair with a frustrated expression. "I asked myself a hundred times why there was this disconnect. That Solarus and Hayden and Talis acted normally around me most times and were mistrustful at others.

And then I found out. They were grooming me to be a hero and not a villain. They're guarded because they can't decide which one I am or which one I'll become. It's the same reason why *Raenalyn* Carina ordered the elves to keep their distance. My friends should have helped me regain my memories. They didn't. Carina considers me a threat. How am I supposed to move forward if I'm being held on a leash like a rabid animal?"

The marmalade tabby suddenly hissed. Kyra glanced over at the small mound of grass. The cat glared at her, tail swishing in agitation. Kyra realized her voice had risen steadily in her anger and passion.

"Kyra." Raven's voice held a note of urgency. "Why do you think you are a 'hero' or 'villain?' Where is this coming from?"

With a half-sigh, Kyra bent down and scooped up her scabbard and sword. "When Hayden found me, I was a harmless orphan. If what he said was true, Hayden adopted me out of pity and brought me here, to Silvias. Then I got older. The elves recognized I was a wizard, and Solarus became my mentor. I get why. Solarus was there to see what damage I was capable of. He was trying to teach me and contain my magic at the same time. Clearly, it didn't work. It wasn't Solarus' fault that he could only help me so much. A falcon doesn't know what nourishes a dragon."

The phrase left Kyra's mouth unbidden. A chill ran down her spine. A memory, a fraction of a second, flashed in front of her. Diamantas was enclosed in a white sphere, obsidian staff in hand, standing against the backdrop of a slate gray mountain. In her mind's eye, Kyra saw his lips moving.

"Diamantas told me that." A pit sank in Kyra's stomach. "He said, 'The dragon eventually outgrows the falcon. It becomes stronger, faster, and deadlier. The falcon must recognize the threat its adopted kit poses before that kit is too powerful.' Diamantas was right. I'm not a falcon, and I'm not a dragon either. That's why everyone is so scared. I'm unpredictable. I'm something *else*."

"What is that something else?"

"The girl in the prophecy." The emotions bottled inside Kyra exploded like gas popping a cork. She moved forward so that she could look Raven in the eye. "Yes, I found out. Why didn't you tell me?" The question came as a harsh accusation.

Raven lifted a hoof and shifted to the other. "It was not my place," he said softly.

Kyra crossed her arms. "That's not good enough for me."

The roan was quiet. "Okay," he agreed finally. "You have hit upon the truth, and you will take this gambit no matter what I tell you. I will offer what I can. The *Al-Ethran* was aware of the prophecy. When we believed you might still be alive, they were uncertain about what would happen should the dark wizards find you."

"Because of the whole 'devastation' part, right?"

The roan nodded. "Raff contended that you were not *destined* to ravage our lands. He believed if we were on the cusp of a new war with Harkimer, you could be the symbol around which Ilian's kingdoms rallied. You would bring them hope and remind them to have faith in Inishmore. You could lead them to victory over the darkness. Yet the *Al-Ethran* has long abstained from involving itself in the affairs of men, wizards, and elves. Animal kind suffered greatly in the War of Calonia. After Malus' defeat, the *Al-Ethran* vowed it would leave the matters of the other kingdoms to providence. The prophecy, however, is an exception. Your fate affects all of us. You can ensure Ilian's survival."

"I 'can' doesn't mean I will." Kyra unfolded her arms and tucked strands of hair behind her ear. "You didn't say the entire Council thought I was some sort of savior. I doubt they all agreed with you. It was important to keep me in check. You needed someone to watch me and make sure I wouldn't turn against you. I bet the Council also wanted someone who could stop me if that happened." Kyra remembered the incident at the lake. Solarus' horrified expression as he pointed his staff at her. At the time, Kyra was genuinely convinced he might attack. She now knew she was right.

Raven spoke again, his voice low and somber. "We fear what we cannot predict, what we cannot control, and what we do not understand. The Council believes you to be all three."

"They may not be wrong, Raven." Kyra hesitated, then continued, "When I was in the other world, a Variavryk was close to killing James. I was too far away to help. I was terrified and desperate. Without having met another wizard, I didn't know what magic was. My energy took a life of its own. It was as wild and powerful and as evil as anything I've seen from the dark wizards. The more fear and rage I felt, the more I wanted to hurt the Variavryk, not save my friend. It was like someone else controlled my body and mind, and I was a bystander. James begged me to stop. That's why I didn't do anything worse. Doesn't that mean I *am* uncontrollable?"

"Is that not why Solarus has been training you? To gain mastery over your emotions? Would that not help stop the red magic, if, as I understand it, the emotions are the stimulus?"

"He's tried. It hasn't worked. I've felt that chaotic energy inside of me here too. In Ilian. I used it. Not intentionally," she inserted hastily. "It did happen more than once though. In the Forgotten Forest, the energy was a spark. Then I used it against the greeloks to save Ash. And the last time . . ." Horror drenched Kyra like a cold sweat. The vivid images of fish bobbing on the lake's surface and the lifeless swans surfaced in her mind. "I saw the consequences. I saw what I was capable of."

Kyra's gaze drifted to her staff that leaned against the wall. She went to it and ran a hand down the smooth cherrywood. "My mind keeps running through what might happen if I lose control again? What if the magic had hurt Ash instead of the greeloks? Or Solarus at the lake? What if it harms you? The fact I exist puts people I care about in jeopardy. I can't risk that. Besides, even if I can eventually control the red magic, I'll always question whether my closest friends fear me."

"They do not fear you," Raven responded. "As you said, their apprehension concerns what you might *become* without proper instruction. Not who you are."

Kyra turned. Leaving the staff, she walked beside Raven and stroked the side of his neck. "Are you afraid of what I 'could become?'"

To her surprise, the roan let out a horsey laugh. "What sense does it make for a steed to fear his rider? As I told you once, rider and steed choose each other. They are bound by love and are bonded in life. To lack faith in your purity would be to believe I am also doomed to inflict harm upon these lands." Raven turned his head upward toward the glass ceiling. Light cascaded through the glass and glimmered on his auburn mane. "When night falls, the sky becomes a black void. It devours any colors left by dusk's descent. One would assume that nothing could survive in such a place. Observe the stars." He paused as Kyra also lifted her gaze. The stars were like pinpricks in the fabric of the sky. "They subsist despite the darkness. Sometimes their light is obscured by a storm, yet the clouds always pass. The stars remain. You are like one of those stars, Kyra. Harkimer's bleakest shadows cannot snuff out the light you carry within. I believe your destiny is deliverance, not devastation."

Staring at the celestial orbs above her, Kyra felt a faint ripple of comfort. Raven's words gave her hope that Hayden and the others might one day share Raven's conviction. They wouldn't view her simply as a subject of a prophecy.

"However, I will not be a party to your death."

Kyra stared at Raven. "I thought you just said I was destined to do good in Ilian."

"*If* you live long enough to develop the skills you require." The roan's expression was burdened as though he carried the weight of Kyra's guilt. "The last time I erred. I allowed myself to be persuaded by your pleas to find some threat. That mistake might have cost you more than your memories. Furthermore, your companions and I suffered a year of penance. I will not lead you toward danger as I did before."

"Wait." Kyra's heart plummeted, the modicum of relief vanishing. "What do you mean, you took me to danger? Is that when I disappeared?"

Raven's ears drooped. He shook his mane dolefully.

Kyra continued to stroke his neck in a calm rhythm. "Raven, please tell me. What happened?"

"I am not exactly sure," the roan answered sadly. "You were with Solarus at a meeting of the Wizards' High Council. You told me you sensed something. Whatever it was alarmed you such that you entreated me to take you to it. You did not mention the peril to any of the wizards at the Council, who were undoubtably better equipped to handle the threat. Against my good judgement, I did not question you. We rode off to discover the source of your apprehension. I do not remember more than that." Raven pawed the ground in frustration. "Whatever magic we encountered was great enough to leave my mind as empty as a grain bag after winter. What I knew was you had disappeared, and I had been involved." Raven turned his head away from Kyra. "What happens if the recklessness of your previous actions leads to a folly anew?"

"Such as disappearing from Ilian again?" Kyra shrugged. "That might be better. Diamantas will be distracted. He will be forced to send his wizards on another goose chase until they find me. You would all be safe. I don't think that's going to happen. Not this time."

The roan abandoned the argument with a chuff of air. "What in the name of the Healer do you intend to do if you are successful in your search?"

Kyra scratched her forehead. "Diamantas isn't immortal, right? He isn't perfect. I don't have to be perfect either, just better than he is. I'll study and practice my magic and face him when I'm ready. I'll find out his weaknesses. Maybe he's allergic to daisies or fears bees or has a bad toe and can't move well. Who knows. I haven't worked it all out yet. Every time we meet, I'll learn something new about him. Then I'll train and improve and confront Diamantas again. For as long as it takes until I've beaten him."

Loud squeaks like the sounds of dogs with chew toys interrupted Kyra's words. She glanced over her shoulder. More mice scurried across the stable floor. The tabby watched his prey without moving from his spot. He blinked and returned his gaze to Kyra as though he was listening intently to the conversation.

"Do you have an idea on Diamantas' whereabouts?" Raven's voice drew Kyra's attention back to him. "Beyond that he may well be in Harkimer. Something more specific?"

"No, but I won't wait until I do." Kyra moved around Raven to her satchel. Bending over and scooping it up, Kyra went on, "Diamantas isn't in Silvias, and the last time we saw the dark wizards was in Farcaren. My plan was to travel west. Any time I enter a town, I'll stay overnight in a tavern and listen for rumors about dark wizards. It's not much of a plan," she admitted.

"It is better than none. I would recommend we travel along the border to the Realm to the outskirts of the Ancient Forest," Raven rumbled contemplatively. "Then we can ford the river and pass into Farcaren from the north. I assume that is what you had in mind?"

Kyra was in the middle of putting the satchel in her saddlebag. Her head jerked to the side. "We?"

"Unfortunately, yes."

"What changed your mind?"

"You have never mentioned not surviving as one of your options when battling the wizards."

Kyra finished putting the satchel in the bag and closed the flap. "That's all it took? Mentioning I'm a fan of self-preservation and will run like the wind if I'm losing?"

Raven let out an amused chuckle. "You haven't formulated a more substantive strategy for dealing with the impending threat than to flee. Nonetheless, you have a strategy. That is an improvement over the Kyra of old. *That* Kyra wanted to indulge her curiosity without any thought to consequences. This is the first time you have expressed caution in an engagement. You acknowledge your limitations."

"You're saying I've learned I'm less gifted than I thought I was."

"What I am saying is your words demonstrate your maturity. Maturity increases your chances for survival. I find survival to be an admirable goal." Raven's tongue-in-cheek statement brought a smile to Kyra's face.

Her heart lighter, Kyra double-checked the weights of the saddlebags. Satisfied, Kyra rolled up the burlap sack and stuffed it in the cubby where Raven's saddle had been.

A sigh breezed from the roan's lips. "I am not keen on contending with the river's waters again."

"We won't have to." Kyra grinned at the roan before striding to the wall. She snatched her staff and spun lightly on her heel. "This time, we'll have a bridge."

Kyra placed the staff through the two loops in the saddlebag on her right. Her eyes swept the stables one last time. The marmalade tabby observed Kyra sedately.

"Life would have been easier as a cat," Kyra said with a slight laugh. Placing a boot in the stirrups, Kyra swung astride Raven. The leather reins rested easily in her hands. Kyra's heart pounded as she steered Raven toward the entrance of the stables. The cool breeze swirled around her, fanning out her hair. The pale fairylike lights flickered out.

As Kyra's eyes adjusted to the darkness, her thoughts flitted to her slumbering companions. When they went to breakfast the next morning, she wouldn't be there. Solarus would wait for her outside, puffing on his kolker pipe, impatience growing with each passing minute. He might seek out their other companions. Solarus' anger would dissolve into concern as they realized Kyra hadn't been seen. He and Hayden would check her room and find it vacant. By that time, Kyra would have put enough distance between herself and the palace that they wouldn't be able to track her before she reached her destination. Kyra's heart ached as her resolve hardened. She was fighting for them in the same way they had fought for her.

"Once we leave, it will be difficult to return," Raven muttered softly.

Kyra sat straighter in her saddle. "I don't plan on returning until this is over."

She clapped her heels into Raven's side. The roan cantered out of the stables and over the open pastures, leaving the palace's sleeping inhabitants behind.

Except for one. In his chamber, Hayden lay awake. He twisted his silver ring as foreboding bore down on him. Hayden reaffirmed his decision. It was time to tell Kyra about the prophecy. It was time to warn her of the dangers she would yet face. It was time to intensify Kyra's trainings so she could defeat her nemesis. Diamantas.

Hayden didn't realize it was already too late. Because the person he had vowed to protect rode swiftly toward the only danger he feared.

The prophecy was in motion. And there was nothing anyone could do to stop it.

**To Be Continued in Book 2 of The Lost Legacy Series:
The First Conquest**

Acknowledgments

When I first told friends and family members that I was leaving my salaried job to become the full-time author for *The Obsidian Staff*, I received one of two responses: "Neat! What's it about? Young Adult (YA) fantasy fiction? What's YA fantasy fiction?"

The second and more common response was, "Write a novel? Live off your savings, give up Starbucks coffee and cable, and have a cat as your coworker? That's too risky. Actually, it's a bit crazy." Yes, it seemed crazy. But I wanted readers to be able to curl up with a novel on a rainy day that has the fantasy of Harry Potter; the twists, turns, and scheming of Game of Thrones; and the intrigue and suspense of a mystery novel. And talking animals, naturally.

Two and a half years later, I offer this exciting novel to you.

There is a saying that it takes a village; I would contend it takes a kingdom. A global kingdom whose citizens, my knights-in-shining-armor, lent their support, encouragement, laughter, insights, and dedication. They inspired me when I hit mental blocks, when the process seemed, as all authors know so well, the literal never-ending story. Because of this, I have many notes of appreciation and thanks to share here.

First, I want to say thank you to my mom, dad, and extended family. Not all parents would be supportive of their daughter or son pursuing their creative passion. I am extremely grateful they were as enthusiastic as I was.

I also want to thank Deborah E. Gordon, Executive Editor with First Design Publishing who has been a steadfast partner in the publishing process. With novels, people do often judge the book by the cover. If my writing is half as good as Debi's artistic creations, you are in for a treat. Debi took my myriad thoughts about potential cover images for *The Obsidian Staff* and crafted the striking book cover you see today. Debi also took my first novel, *The Noble Rogues*, and fashioned a breathtaking cover of a phoenix. She is resourceful, responsive, and cheerful, and I'm excited for our next project, *The First Conquest*.

Next, a hearty thanks to Ted Andrews and Megan Brown for reviewing snippets of the novel. Their suggestions were invaluable; their attention to detail is unparalleled. I also want to thank Jana Kolpen, a dear friend and fellow author. Jana was the first to reach out and send me words of encouragement when I announced this would be my project for the next year.

I also want to share my deepest gratitude to the following individuals who provided me the adrenaline and endurance to keep going when the seventh cup of coffee wasn't enough:

Welcome Wanderers: Eli Boeck, Sharon Daugharty, Frank Mashuda

Bewitching Benefactors: Sean Bath, Rachel Miller, Charlie Raymond, Scott Sklar

Charitable Companions: Melika Behrooz, Sarah, Bryon, Braydon, and Oscar Billings, Elizabeth Brancato, Tucker Brown, Joe Clough and Elizabeth Marina and Berdeen Fabrica Lott Clough, the Daugharty-Parisi family, Sam Gannon, Max and Ursula Gannon-Long and Vicky Long, Kia Henry, Dave Hogan, Craig Kennedy, Christin, YoungJae, and Romi Kjelland, Jana Kolpen, Siobhan Leonard and family, David, Bonnie and Alley Li-MacDonald, Bree Moore, Bill Rhodes, Brianna Robinson, Brian Roller, DeMark Schulze, Matthew Standard, Matt Vossoughian, Anthony Yuen

Elves with Endowments: Megan Brown, Wybe Bruinsma, Codi Cain, Juan, Tom Kalzuny, Melanie, Christopher Rivers, Christopher Schroeder, David S. Stier, Simon, Shelly, and Cameron van Steÿn

Donating Dukes and Duchesses: Dean Arnold, Henri Bore, Andrea Clancy, Gary Clements, Kristin Collins, Heath Hartsock, Les Kayanan, Jack Kolpen, Bob Polk, Mark Sun

Guardians of Ilian: Dave, Emily, and Nora Azari, Marty Hansen, Sarah Rose Jamshidpoor, Nat Schaefle, John Szlenker

Legacy Leavers: Alyksandrei, Olga, Alisa, and Artem Artish, Jonathan Blitt, Rena Edwards, Richard Rachad, Tim and Tracy Waters, Dmitryi and Nicholas Yeremin

I'm equally grateful to my heroes who have wished to remain anonymous. You have given me the gift of friendship and support. Thank you!

Finally, I couldn't have finished without Tp and Carla. Tp always had an uplifting word or note, keeping me focused on my goal. He never let me be too hard on myself when the going seemed to be slower than the slugs that inched their way along my paver stones after a rain. Carla gave me hope on days when I wondered if the novel would ever meet my personal standards. Carla taught me to be patient and helped me charge forward. I am extremely grateful to have them in my life.

I hope this crazy adventure encourages you to pursue whatever dreams you have. It may be a long road with more than a few speed bumps, but it's worth it.

Jaz Azari is a young adult fantasy fiction author currently working on the second novel in *The Lost Legacy Series*, *The First Conquest*. She is also the author of the stand-alone novel, The Noble Rogues. Jaz has been a visiting author with Page After Page at the Maryland Renaissance Festival and hopes to continue the tradition, complete with period attire. She lives with her cat Blitz, who provides input in between hourly requests for a refilled food bowl.

Learn more about the author at
www.thelostlegacyseries.com

Made in the USA
Middletown, DE
20 July 2023